ALEXANDRE DUMAS was born July 24, 1802, at Villers-Cotterets, France, the son of Napoleon's famous mulatto general, Dumas. Alexandre Dumas began writing at an early age and saw his first success in a play he wrote entitled *Henri III et sa Cour* (1829). A prolific author, Dumas was also an adventurer and took part in the Revolution of 1830. Dumas is most famous for his brilliant historical novels, which he wrote with collaborators, mainly Auguste Maquet, and which were serialized in the popular press of the day. His most popular works are *The Three Musketeers* (1844), *The Count of Monte Cristo* (1844–45), and *The Man in the Iron Mask* (1848–1850). Dumas made and lost several fortunes, and died penniless on December 5, 1870.

THE
THREE
MUSKETEERS

Alexandre Dumas

Revised and Updated Translation
by Eleanor Hochman

Introduction by Thomas Flanagan

A SIGNET CLASSIC

SIGNET CLASSIC
Published by the Penguin Group
Penguin Books USA Inc., 375 Hudson Street,
New York, New York 10014, U.S.A.
Penguin Books Ltd, 27 Wrights Lane,
London W8 5TZ, England
Penguin Books Australia Ltd, Ringwood,
Victoria, Australia
Penguin Books Canada Ltd, 10 Alcorn Avenue,
Toronto, Ontario, Canada M4V 3B2
Penguin Books (N.Z.) Ltd, 182–190 Wairau Road,
Auckland 10, New Zealand

Penguin Books Ltd, Registered Offices:
Harmondsworth, Middlesex, England

Published by Signet Classic,
an imprint of Dutton Signet,
a division of Penguin Books USA Inc.

First Signet Classic Printing, October, 1991
10 9 8 7 6 5 4 3 2

 REGISTERED TRADEMARK—MARCA REGISTRADA

Library of Congress Catalog Card Number: 91-061016

Printed in the United States of America

Contents

Introduction

IN THE SULTRY, airless late July of 1830, the future historical novelist of *The Three Musketeers* and *The Count of Monte Cristo* encountered history itself.

The year before, at the age of twenty-seven, Alexandre Dumas had made his name with *Henri III et sa cour*, one of the first triumphs of the French romantic theater. Now romantic history was taking place all around him. Paris had risen up against the Bourbon monarchy of Charles X. Its citizens, its students in particular, were building barricades and searching for weapons. By the account in his memoirs, Dumas was everywhere at once: at the barricades, marching with fifty men toward the Hôtel de Ville, with a mob pouring into the Musée de l'Artillerie. At the Tuileries, he recovered from the bedroom of the Duchesse de Berry the copy of his play *Christine*, bound in violet leather, which he had presented to her. And from Lafayette, the ancient liberal patriot who had assumed command, he received a commission to ride to Soissons, sixty miles away, to requisition gunpowder.

He returned to discover that Lafayette had handed over the throne vacated by Charles X to the Duc d'Orleans, who as Louis-Philippe was to govern for the next eighteen years on behalf of a vulgar and acquisitive bourgeoisie. At times in later years, Dumas affected to despise the virtues and limitations of this triumphant social class, but in fact he embodied them. He was a manifestation in the literary world of its energy, copiousness, and boundless self-confidence. With the help of a stable of secretaries, collaborators and assorted hacks, he was able to put his name to more than three hundred books, some of them immensely long. He had brought to literary production the factory method of his century. But he also added two extraordinary works to the storehouse of the world's imagination.

During the revolution, he tells us, he saved from looters the helmet, shield, and sword of François I, and an arquebus which had belonged to Charles IX. This is somehow emblematic of his relationship to history, which he regarded as decorative, richly colored, and manipulable—"the nail on which I hang my novels."

His father, though, had been molded by history and was at last destroyed by it. Thomas-Alexandre Dumas was born on the Caribbean island of Santo Domingo, one of the bastard children of a dissolute plantation owner named Alexandre-Antoine Davy and a black slave called Marie-Cessette Dumas, perhaps the surname of a former owner. His father brought him to France, where he enlisted in the army. When the great revolution broke out in 1789, his abilities carried him upward so swiftly that by 1793, he was a general in command of the army of the western Pyrenees. He joined Bonaparte for the Italian campaign, distinguished himself by his energy and audacity, and then sailed with him for the campaign in Egypt. Here too he proved himself a decisive commander, putting down a local revolt, but for reasons which are not known he incurred Bonaparte's deep and lasting hostility. He applied for permission to return to France, but fell into Neapolitan hands and spent the next two years in one of their wretched fortress-prisons on the Mediterranean coast. He returned at last to his wife's town of Villers-Cotterêts, outside Paris, and a son, Alexandre, was born. But his spirit and health were broken; the vengefulness of Bonaparte saw him stricken from the active list, and even his petitions for arrears of pay were left unanswered. When he died, in 1806, his family was left in poverty and Bonaparte had become the Emperor Napoleon.

It was all like a Dumas novel.

Dumas speaks of this dimly remembered father with understandable respect and sympathy; but another figure seems also to have kindled his imagination, as he had the imagination of all Europe. In March 1815, the exiled emperor returned from Elba, and three months later passed through Villers-Cotterêts on his way to meet the English and Prussian armies. He passed through a second time, on the retreat from Waterloo, and as fresh horses were harnessed for him at the inn, he sat waxen-faced and immobile as young Dumas peered at him.

Napoleon had destroyed Dumas's father, but in a sense which defied chronology, he had also created him. To the European imagination, it was Napoleon, more vividly than revolution, who had flung open careers to talent, placing the baton of a general in the knapsack of a slave's son. And it was Napoleon who gave to the youth of Europe the fairytale of the young man from the provinces who conquers the world. After Waterloo, it was to be a conquest won not upon the battlefield, but in the glittering and complex world of the great modern city—in London on occasion, but more often in Paris, which Walter Benjamin was to call "the capital of the nineteenth century." This is the great subject of Stendhal's *The Red and the Black*, of Dickens's *Great Expectations*, of Balzac's *Père Goriot* and *Lost Illusions*.

In his introduction to the Signet Classic edition of *The Count of Monte Cristo*, Robert Wilson reminds us that it is also the subject of that novel, together with its complementary theme of revenge. And he suggests persuasively that the career of Edmond Dantès is the reverse of the career of Dumas's father—Dantès rising from prison to limitless wealth and power as the Count of Monte Cristo, whereas the father was "a victim of a society so fluid that one could be a hero of the Revolution and a goat of the Empire."

He might perhaps have added that both Thomas-Alexandre Dumas and Edmond Dantès were imprisoned in a Mediterranean fortress, but where Dumas was released to spend final years humiliated by a mean but powerful foe—an emperor, no less—Dantès escapes by a nearly mythic rebirth in water, sewn into the burial-cloth from which he cuts himself free, his own midwife.

To be sure, when we turn from a *Great Expectations* or a Balzac novel to a novel by Dumas, we move from one order of imaginative experience to another and a lesser one. All three may have been written to be published in installments for popular audiences and written with responsiveness to the tastes of such audiences. But in Dickens and in Balzac we experience a thickness of social and literary textures, imaginations working at white heat, formidable and probing intelligences. Dumas could seize upon themes of magnificent resonance, but he brought to them gifts which are primarily those of the fabulist and entertainer. It is useless to go to *The Count of Monte Cristo* to inform oneself as to the manners, politics, and way of life of the European nineteenth century, or even to learn how it thought about itself. But one can learn about its life of dream, of fantasy, impulse, about its cravings for limitless wealth, coffers of diamonds and rubies, absolute power over enemies. "After that," says Jay Gatsby, the spiritual son of both d'Artagnan and the Count of Monte Cristo, "I lived like a young rajah in all the capitals of Europe—Paris, Venice, Rome—collecting jewels, chiefly rubies, hunting big game, painting a little, things for myself only, and trying to forget something very sad that had happened to me long ago." The very phrases were worn threadbare, thinks Nick Carraway, Sancho Panza to his Don Quixote.

And on the first page of *The Three Musketeers*, where we meet d'Artagnan, a young man from Gascony, most provincial of provinces, we are asked to imagine a Don Quixote of eighteen, but without a coat of mail, and armed for his assault upon Paris with nothing save three paternal gifts—a horse as ludicrous as Rosinante, a purse of fifteen écu and a letter from his father to his old friend M. de Tréville, now captain of the king's musketeers. The year is 1625 and the king is Louis XIII. But behind Louis stands the real power, the Duc de Richelieu, as brilliant, devious, and cruel as a Bonaparte. Much as, in 1823, young Dumas set off for Paris, with letters written long before to his father by three of Napoleon's marshals, now powerful in the monarchy of Charles X.

The Three Musketeers is one of those books—like *Treasure Island* and *Tom Sawyer* and *Oliver Twist* and *Robinson Crusoe*—which we seem always to have known, even if we have never read them. Partly, this is because we first read or hear about them in childhood or adolescence, and partly because they contain scenes of such iconic power that they have passed into the general memory—Tom Sawyer in the cave with Becky and Injun Joe, Oliver in the workhouse asking for more gruel, Robinson Crusoe finding a set of footprints, d'Artagnan and his friends joining swords. But when we come back to these books, they are likely to prove strange and unexpected, disturbing our recollections.

Money, one discovers with surprise upon a fresh reading of *The Three Musketeers*, is as staple an ingredient as swordplay or comradeship or romantic love or devotion to the king. Near the outset, the king gives d'Artagnan a purse of exactly forty pistoles, which he divides with his friends. Thereafter, he and the musketeers are forever putting pistoles in their pockets or else spending them upon lodgings or lackeys or meals or wine, and always in precise amounts. We learn the exact cost of the diamond studs upon which part of the plot turns. The words for various coins, and especially the word *pistole*, clink and jingle throughout the text. And yet these pistoles have a curious weightlessness, lacking the specific gravity with which Balzac would have endowed them, or the gleams and thumbprints of guineas and shillings in a novel by Dickens. In part, this is because the text is obsessed by money and yet embarrassed by its obsession. In nothing is the book more thoroughly and revealingly bourgeois than in its aristocratic airs and its affected disdain for bourgeois values and for the bourgeoisie.

Dumas and his collaborator, Auguste Maquet, believed that they were building, although very loosely, upon fact. As he was to write, his habit was to devise a story, and then to "search through the annals of the past to find a frame in which to set it." Charles de Baatz d'Artagnan had indeed lived, although not at quite the time required for the story. He was rather improbably an ancestor of the modern nobleman upon whom Proust was to base his Baron Charlus. From his memoirs, Dumas took the character and name, some episodes, the outlines if not the characters of the musketeers, Athos, Porthos, and Aramis, and assorted details. He may not have known that these memoirs were not by d'Artagnan himself but were written, decades after his death, by Gatien de Courtilz de Sandras. If he did not, it is pleasant to think of Courtilz de Sandras as a third collaborator, leaning over the shoulders of his successors. It was Dumas's custom, although not an unvaried one, to describe to one of his collaborators the scene he wanted, have the collaborator write it in draft, and then himself rework it. Some notes which Dumas sent to Maquet during composition of this

novel have survived, but they are brief and hurried, because he was also at work on two other books. "In our
next chapter," one reads, "we have to learn from Aramis
who has promised to inquire for d'Artagnan in which
convent is Madame Bonacieux and what protection of
the queen surrounds her." And again: "It is strange, I
had written you this morning to introduce the executioner in this scene; then I threw the letter in the fire,
thinking that I will introduce him myself."

Literature in the Paris of Louis-Philippe was becoming
an industry. Balzac was of course both fascinated by this
as an artist and obsessed by it as a would-be industrialist.
His novels, *Lost Illusions* in particular, are thick with
accounts of the manufacture of paper, the mechanics of
printing and folding, the mechanics of producing novels,
and journalism as fodder for these machines. Dumas,
apparently, was less interested than Balzac in the tech-
nology by which both writers were being made rich. It
was more gentlemanly to write of pistoles in the pockets
of musketeers and diamond rings discreetly passed from
queens to young adventurers.

The extent of Dumas's collaboration became an open
scandal as early as 1845, the year after *The Three Musketeers*, when Eugène de Mirecourt published his devastating
but extravagant *Fabrique de Romans, Maison Alexandre
Dumas et Compagnie*. This lampoon, with its vicious
description of the collaborators as "black slaves working
under the whip of a half-caste overseer," deservedly earned
its author a brief spell in prison. Nevertheless, scholars
and admirers of Dumas have ever since been at work
rescuing him from his "novel factory," and with considerable success. He had a vivid, nervous literary personality
which stamps itself with equal clarity upon both the pages
he wrote and those he rewrote.

The defense is beside the point, though. He may have
written about other centuries, but he was a child of his
own, and in nothing so much as in his conjunction of
immense literary productivity with the transformations of
publication and dissemination made possible by technol-
ogy and the expansion of a literate audience. The question of collaborators, of factories of writers, is dwarfed
by this. Scott and Balzac never employed collaborators;
but all three of these children of their century grew rich

upon an enormous output of fiction; all three built vulgar mansions in celebration of their wealth; all three went bankrupt; and all three spent long years writing themselves back into solvency.

A fashionable methodology of our own time argues that works of literature are produced by society itself, with the individual writer serving at best as a kind of amanuensis, to which the society dictates its fantasies. Some support for this argument can be found, as I have suggested, not merely in Dumas's methods of production but also in those movements of the novel beneath the skin of its prose. No moment in *The Three Musketeers* rests so securely within our cultural memory as that in which the four musketeers unsheathe their rapiers and join them with the cry: "One for all and all for one!" It has been made famous in dramatizations of the novel, in the once-famous musical based upon it, in illustrated editions of the novel, and in comic-book versions of the novel. A similar moment occurs when D'Artagnan, alone in his room, ponders the fact that he has been eating his meals recently at the expense of his three friends, and resolves that the four of them will band together, "devoted to one another with their lives as well as their purses." And his thoughts, as he elaborates upon his ambition, mingle the language of a stock company with that of a chivalric brotherhood.

It is possible to read *The Three Musketeers* as often it is read, as "a rousing good yarn," which carries us back to an age of swordplay, gallantry, and romance. So it does, but it may gain in interest perhaps to see it also as a novel written in the nineteenth century, in the Paris of Louis-Philippe, a novel which may well escape into a more colorful age, as many of its admirers claim, but which does so not by eluding the energies of its own time. Rather, it transforms some of those energies, poeticizes some of them, denies some of them. Whether this transformation is worked by the genius of society or the genius of Dumas or by a collaboration between the two is a question which awaits its answer.

NOTE

There is a good abridged translation, by Jules Eckert Goodman, of Dumas's memoirs: *The Road to Monte Cristo* (New York, Scribner's, 1956). *The Titans* (New York, Harper and Row, 1957) is a translation by Gerald Hopkins of the generational study by André Maurois of the novelist, his father, and his son, the author of *Camille*. By far the most poised and alert biography in English is *Alexandre Dumas: The King of Romance* by F. W. J. Hemmings (New York, Scribner's, 1979). Claude Schopp's *Alexandre Dumas, Genius of Life*, translated by A. J. Koch (Franklin Watts, New York, 1988), is concerned with both Dumas's work and his flamboyant personality. Schopps is currently editor of the Pléiade edition of Dumas's works.

—Thomas Flanagan

Author's Preface

In which it is proved that there is nothing mythological—despite their names ending in *os* and *is*—about the heroes of the story I am going to have the honor of telling my readers.

A SHORT TIME AGO, while I was doing research in the Royal Library for my history of Louis XIV, I stumbled by chance on the *Memoirs of M. d'Artagnan,* printed—as were most of the works of that period, in which authors could not tell the truth without risking a long residence in the Bastille—in Amsterdam, by Pierre Rouge. The title attracted me; I took it home with me, with the librarian's permission, of course, and devoured it.

It is not my intention here to analyze that curious work; I will merely refer such of my readers as appreciate the period to its pages. There they will find portraits sketched by a master's hand, and although most of them may be drawn on barracks doors and tavern walls, they will be found to be as faithful to the originals—Louis XIII, Anne of Austria, Richelieu, Mazarin, and the courtiers of the period—as those described in M. Anquetil's history.

But, as is well known, what strikes the poet's capricious mind is not always what affects most readers. For example, while I admired, as others doubtless will also admire, the details I have mentioned, I was most interested in a matter to which no one else had ever given a thought.

D'Artagnan writes that on his first visit to M. de Tréville, captain of the king's Musketeers, he met in the anteroom three young men serving in the illustrious corps into which he was soliciting the honor of being received, and that those young men were called Athos, Porthos, and Aramis.

I must confess that I was struck by those three strange names; and it immediately occurred to me that they were only pseudonyms, either used by d'Artagnan to disguise names that were perhaps illustrious, or chosen by the bearers themselves when they had donned the simple uniform of a Musketeer—whether from caprice, discontent, or lack of money.

From then on I had no rest until I found some trace in contemporary works of those extraordinary names which had so strongly awakened my curiosity.

The list of the books I read with this object in mind would alone fill a whole chapter, which might be very instructive but would certainly not be very amusing for my readers. Let it suffice, then, to say that just as I had become discouraged by so many fruitless investigations and was about to abandon my search, I finally found, guided by the advice of my illustrious friend Paulin Pâris, a folio manuscript numbered 4772 or 4773, I have forgotten which, entitled, *Memoirs of the Comte de la Fère, About Some Events That Occurred In France Toward the End of the Reign of King Louis XIII and the Beginning of the Reign of King Louis XIV.*

Imagine how great was my joy when, in examining this manuscript, my last hope, I found on the twentieth page the name of Athos, on the twenty-seventh the name of Porthos, and on the thirty-first the name of Aramis.

The discovery of a completely unknown manuscript, at a time when historical science is at such a high level, seemed almost miraculous. I therefore immediately asked for permission to print it, intending some day to present myself with someone else's writing to the Académie des Inscriptions et Belles Lettres, if—as was very likely—I should not gain admission to the Académie Française with my own. This permission, I am happy to say, was graciously granted, so I must here publicly contradict the malicious slanderers who claim that we live under a government that does not do much for men of letters.

What follows is the first part of that precious manuscript. Having restored its proper title, I am offering it to my readers, promising that if it achieves the success it deserves—as I am sure it will—I will publish the second part immediately thereafter.

　　Meanwhile, since the godfather is like a second father, I ask the reader to hold me, and not the Comte de la Fère, responsible for his pleasure or his boredom.

　　This being understood, let us proceed with our story.

1

The Three Presents
of M. d'Artagnan the Elder

ON THE FIRST Monday of April, 1625, the market town
of Meung, in which the author of the *Romance of the
Rose* was born, seemed to be in as much of a state of
revolution as if the Huguenots had just turned it into a
second La Rochelle. Many of the men, seeing the women
rushing toward the main street and hearing the children
crying at their doorways, hurriedly put on their breast-
plates, added further support to their uncertain courage
by picking up a musket or a partisan, and headed for the
Franc Meunier inn, in front of which was gathering an
ever-growing, noisy, and curious crowd.

In those times panics were common, and few days
passed without some city or other recording such an
event in its archives. Noblemen made war against each
other; the king made war against the cardinal; Spain
made war against the king. Then, in addition to these
concealed or public wars, there were robbers, beggars,
Huguenots, wolves, and scoundrels, who made war on
everybody. The citizens always took up arms against robbers, wolves, or scoundrels; often against noblemen or
Huguenots; sometimes against the king—but never against
the cardinal or Spain. And that was why the townsmen,
on that first Monday of April, 1625, hearing the clamor
and seeing neither the red and yellow Spanish flag nor
the livery of the Duc de Richelieu, made their way to
the Franc Meunier inn.

When they arrived, the cause of the tumult was apparent to everyone.

A young man—let us sketch his portrait quickly. Imagine to yourself a Don Quixote of eighteen: a Don Quixote with neither breastplate nor thigh armor, but
wearing a woolen doublet whose original blue color had
faded into a nameless shade between burgundy and
azure. His face was long and brown, with high cheekbones—a mark of intelligence; his jaw muscles were very

pronounced—an infallible sign by which a Gascon may always be recognized, even without his beret, and our young man was wearing one set off with a sort of feather; his eyes were open and intelligent; his nose was hooked, but finely chiseled. Too big for a youth, too small for a grown man, he might have been taken by an inexperienced eye for a farmer's son on a journey had it not been for the long sword that dangled from a leather baldric, or shoulder belt, striking his calves when he walked, and the shaggy side of his horse when he rode.

For our young man had a horse, one so remarkable that it was the observed of all the observers. It was a yellowish Béarnese pony, twelve to fourteen years old, without a hair in his tail but with windgalls on his legs. Though he went about with his head lower than his knees, making a martingale quite unnecessary, he nevertheless managed to do his eight leagues a day. Unfortunately, his good qualities were so well concealed under his strange-colored hide and his peculiar gait that at a time when everybody was a connoisseur of horseflesh, his appearance at Meung—which he had entered about a quarter of an hour before through the Beaugency gate—elicited a ridicule that extended to his rider.

This reaction had been the more painfully perceived by young d'Artagnan—for so was the Don Quixote of this second Rosinante named—because he was quite aware of the ridiculous appearance that such a steed gave him, excellent rider though he was. That was why he had sighed so deeply when accepting the horse as a gift from M. d'Artagnan the elder: he was well aware that the beast was worth at least twenty écus, and the words that had accompanied the present were beyond price.

"My son," the old Gascon gentleman had said, in that pure Béarnese *patois* that King Henry IV could never lose, "this horse was born in my stables about thirteen years ago and has remained in it ever since, which ought to make you love him. Never sell him, but let him die peacefully and honorably of old age, and if you go into battle with him, take as much care of him as you would of an old servant. At court, provided you ever have the honor to go there—an honor to which your old and noble lineage gives you the right—be worthy of your name, which has been worthily borne by your ancestors for five hundred years. For your own sake and the sake of those who belong to you—I mean your relatives and friends—tolerate no slights from anyone except Monsieur le Cardinal and the king. Understand that it is by his courage and by his courage alone that a gentleman can make his way nowadays. Whoever hesitates for even one second may lose the chance offered him by fortune during that very second. You are young, and you should be brave for two reasons: the first is that you are a Gascon, and the second is that you are my son. Never fear quarrels, and seek out adventures. I have taught you how to handle a sword. You have legs of iron and a wrist of steel. Fight duels on all occasions, the more so because duels are forbidden and consequently it takes twice as much courage to fight them.

"I have nothing to give you, my son, except fifteen écus, my horse, and the advice you have just heard. Your mother will add a recipe for a certain ointment, which she got from a Bohemian and which has the miraculous virtue of curing all wounds that do not reach the heart. Take advantage of everything, and live happily and long.

"I have only one word to add, and that is to propose a model for you—not myself, because I have never appeared at court, and have taken part only in the wars of religion as a volunteer. I speak of Monsieur de Tréville, who was formerly my neighbor and who as a child had the honor to be the playfellow of our king, Louis the Thirteenth, whom God preserve! Sometimes their playing degenerated into fighting, and in those fights the king was not always the stronger. The blows that he received from M. de Tréville greatly increased his esteem and friendship for that gentleman. Later, Monsieur de Tréville fought with others: five times on his first journey to Paris, seven times from the death of the late king till the young one came of age, without counting wars and sieges, and from then to the present day, perhaps a hundred times! So in spite of edicts, ordinances, and decrees, there he is, captain of the Musketeers—head of a legion of Cæsars, whom the king admires and whom the cardinal dreads—he who dreads nothing, it is said. Furthermore, Monsieur de Tréville earns ten thousand écus a year and is therefore a great lord. . . . He began as

you begin. Go to him with this letter, and make him
your model in order that you may do as he has done."

Upon which M. d'Artagnan the elder girded his own
sword around his son, kissed him tenderly on both
cheeks, and gave him his blessing.

On leaving his father's room, the young man found his
mother waiting for him with the previously mentioned
ointment—an ointment that might have to be used quite
frequently if he were to follow the advice we have just
repeated. The farewells on this side were longer and
more tender than they had been on the other—not that
M. d'Artagnan did not love his son, who was his only
offspring, but M. d'Artagnan was a man and would have
considered it unworthy of a man to give way to his feelings; whereas Mme. d'Artagnan was not only a woman
but a mother. She wept abundantly; and—let it be said
to the credit of M. d'Artagnan the younger—despite his
efforts to remain as firm as he thought a future Musketeer should be, nature prevailed, and he too shed many
tears, succeeding with great difficulty in concealing about
half of them.

That same day the young man set forth on his journey,
taking the three paternal gifts consisting of fifteen écus,
the horse, and the letter for M. de Tréville—the advice
having been thrown into the bargain.

With such provisions d'Artagnan was morally and
physically an exact copy of Cervantes's hero, to whom
we so justly compared him when our duty as a historian
made it necessary to sketch his portrait. Don Quixote
took windmills for giants and sheep for armies; d'Artagnan took every smile for an insult and every look as
a provocation—with the result that from Tarbes to
Meung his fist was constantly clenched, or his hand on
the pommel of his sword. And yet the fist did not connect
with any jaw, and the sword did not emerge from its
scabbard. It was not that the sight of the wretched pony
did not elicit numerous smiles from the passersby; but
since against the side of the pony rattled a sword of
respectable length, and since over the sword gleamed an
eye more ferocious than haughty, those passersby
repressed their hilarity—or if hilarity prevailed over
prudence, they at least tried to laugh only on one side,
like the masks of the ancients. D'Artagnan therefore

remained majestic and untouched in his sensitivity till he came to the unlucky city of Meung.

But there, as he was getting off his mount at the gate of the Franc Meunier inn—without anyone, host, waiter, or hostler, coming to hold his stirrup or take his horse—d'Artagnan noticed, through an open window on the ground floor, a well-built, self-assured, rather stern-looking nobleman talking with two persons who seemed to be listening to him with respect. As usual, d'Artagnan of course thought that he must be the subject of their conversation, and he listened. This time he was only partly mistaken; he himself was not in question, but his horse was. The nobleman appeared to be enumerating all the horse's qualities to his auditors; and because the auditors seemed, as we have mentioned, to have great respect for the narrator, they were constantly bursting into laughter. Since even a half-smile was sufficient to awaken the young man's irascibility, the effect produced on him by such boisterous mirth may easily be imagined.

Nevertheless, he first wanted to get a closer look at the impertinent personage who was ridiculing him. He fixed his haughty eyes on the stranger and saw a man about forty or forty-five years old, with black, piercing eyes, a pale complexion, a prominent nose, and a black, well-shaped mustache. He was dressed in a purple doublet and hose, with laces of the same color and without any ornament other than the usual slashes through which his shirt appeared. The doublet and hose, though new, were creased, like traveling clothes that had been packed in a trunk for a long time. D'Artagnan noticed all this with the rapidity of a most attentive observer—and doubtless also from an instinctive feeling that the stranger was destined to have a great influence over his future life.

At the very moment in which d'Artagnan was examining the gentleman in the purple doublet, that gentleman made one of his most pointed remarks about the Béarnese pony, his two listeners laughed ever louder than before, and he himself, though it was contrary to his custom, allowed a pale smile (if I may be permitted to use such an expression) to stray over his face. This time there could be no doubt: d'Artagnan had truly been insulted. Fully convinced of this, he pulled his beret

down over his eyes and, trying to copy some of the court
manners he had picked up from young noblemen traveling in Gascony, advanced with one hand on the hilt of
his sword and the other resting on his hip. Unfortunately,
his anger increased with every step; and instead of the
proper and lordly speech he had prepared as a prelude
to his challenge, he found nothing at the tip of his tongue
but some crude words accompanied by a furious gesture.

"I say, sir, you, sir, who are hiding behind that shutter—yes, you, sir, tell me what you are laughing at, and
we will laugh together!"

The gentleman raised his eyes slowly from the nag to
its cavalier, as if he needed some time to determine if
those strange remarks were being addressed to him;
then, when there could be no possible doubt about it, he
frowned slightly and said, in a tone of irony and insolence
impossible to describe, "I was not speaking to you, sir."

"But *I* am speaking to *you!*" replied the young man,
additionally exasperated by that mixture of insolence and
good manners, politeness and scorn.

The stranger looked at him for a few moments with
his slight smile, then left the window, slowly came out
of the inn, and stopped in front of the horse, within two
paces of d'Artagnan. His quiet manner and the ironical
expression had redoubled the mirth of the persons with
whom he had been talking and who still remained at the
window.

Seeing him approach, d'Artagnan had drawn his sword
a foot out of the scabbard.

"This horse is surely—or rather was in his youth—a
buttercup," resumed the stranger, addressing himself to
his auditors at the window and continuing the remarks
he had begun, without paying the least attention to d'Artagnan's exasperation even though the young man had
placed himself between him and them. "It is a color very
well known in botany, but very rare among horses."

"There are people who laugh at the horse who would
not dare laugh at its master!" exclaimed the furious
young emulator of Tréville.

"I do not often laugh, sir," replied the stranger, "as
you may see by the expression of my face, but I retain
the privilege to laugh when I please."

"And I," cried d'Artagnan, "will allow no man to laugh when it displeases me!"

"Indeed, sir," continued the stranger, more imperturbable than ever, "that is as it should be!"

He turned on his heel and was about to reenter the inn by the front gate, near which d'Artagnan on arriving had observed a saddled horse.

But d'Artagnan was not the person to allow a man who had had the insolence to ridicule him to thus escape him. He drew his sword entirely from the scabbard and followed him, shouting, "Turn, turn, Master Mocker, lest I pierce you from behind!"

"Pierce me!" said the other, turning on his heels and surveying the young man with as much astonishment as contempt. "Why, my good fellow, you must be mad!"

Then, in a low voice, as if speaking to himself, he continued, "What a godsend he would be for his Majesty, who is always looking everywhere for brave men to join his Musketeers!"

He had scarcely finished when d'Artagnan made such a furious lunge at him that if he had not sprung nimbly backward, it is probable that he would have mocked for the last time. The stranger then realized that the matter had gone beyond raillery, drew his sword, saluted his adversary, and seriously placed himself on guard. But at that same moment his two auditors, accompanied by the innkeeper, fell upon d'Artagnan with sticks, shovels, and tongs. This caused so sudden and complete a diversion that while d'Artagnan turned around to face the rain of blows, his adversary sheathed his sword with the same precision with which he had drawn it and became, instead of an actor, which he had nearly been, a spectator of the fight—a role he played with his usual impassiveness.

"A plague on these Gascons! Put him back on his carroty horse, and send him off," he muttered.

"Not before I have killed you, you coward!" cried d'Artagnan, fighting as well as possible and never retreating one step before his three assailants, who continued to shower blows upon him.

"Another gasconade!" murmured the gentleman. "By my honor, these Gascons are incorrigible! Keep up the dance, then, since he will have it so. When he is tired of it, he will say so."

But the stranger did not yet know how headstrong d'Artagnan was: he was not the man ever to cry for quarter. The fight therefore continued for some seconds more, but finally an exhausted d'Artagnan had to drop his sword, which was broken in two by the blow of a stick. Another blow full upon his forehead at the same time brought him to the ground, covered with blood and almost unconscious.

That was when people came flocking to the scene from all sides. The host, afraid of what might happen, with the help of his servants carried the wounded man into the kitchen, where they made some half-hearted efforts to treat him.

As for the stranger, he had returned to his place at the window and was watching the crowd with a certain impatience, evidently annoyed by their continued presence.

"Well, how is the madman?" he asked, turning around as the noise of the door announced the entrance of the host.

"Your Excellency is safe and sound?" the innkeeper asked.

"Oh, yes, perfectly safe and sound, my good host, and I wish to know what has become of our young man."

"He is better," said the host. "He has fainted quite away."

"Indeed!"

"But before he fainted, he summoned all his strength to defy you and challenge you."

"Why, he must be the devil in person!"

"Oh, no, your Excellency, he is not the devil," replied the host with a contemptuous sneer. "After he fainted, we rummaged through his bag and found nothing but a clean shirt and eleven écus—which did not keep him from saying, while he was still conscious, that if such a thing had happened in Paris you would have repented of it instantly, but since it happened here, you will have to repent of it later."

"Then he must be some prince in disguise," said the stranger coolly.

"I am telling you this, good sir, so that you may be on your guard."

"Did he name anyone in his excitement?"

"Yes. He struck his pocket and said, 'We'll see what Monsieur de Tréville will think about this insult to his protégé.' "

"Monsieur de Tréville?" said the stranger, becoming attentive. "He put his hand on his pocket while pronouncing the name of Monsieur de Tréville? Well, my dear host, while your young man was unconscious, I am quite sure you did not fail to discover what that pocket contained. What did you find there?"

"A letter addressed to Monsieur de Tréville, captain of the Musketeers."

"Indeed!"

"Exactly as I have the honor to tell your Excellency."

The host, who was not very observant, did not notice the reaction of the stranger to his words. The latter left the window, upon the sill of which he had been leaning, and frowned.

"The devil!" he muttered between his teeth. "Can Tréville have set this Gascon on me? He is very young—but a sword thrust is a sword thrust, whatever the age of the one who gives it, and I would be less likely to suspect a youth than an older man."

He fell into a reverie that lasted several minutes. "Even a small obstacle is sometimes sufficient to destroy a great plan."

He turned to the host. "Could you not manage to get rid of this frantic boy for me? In conscience, I cannot kill him, and yet," he added with a coldly menacing expression, "he annoys me. Where is he?"

"In my wife's room on the first floor. They are dressing his wounds."

"His things and his bag are with him? Has he taken off his doublet?"

"No, everything is in the kitchen. But if he annoys you . . ."

"To be sure he does, and he is causing a disturbance in your inn, which respectable people cannot put up with. Go. Make out my bill, and notify my servant that we are leaving."

"What, monsieur, you are leaving us so soon?"

"You must know that I am, because I gave the order to saddle my horse. Have they not obeyed me?"

"Yes, of course they have. As your Excellency may

have observed, your horse is at the main gateway, all ready for your departure."

"Very well. Do as I have ordered you, then."

"What the devil," the host thought, "can he be afraid of that boy?"

But an imperious glance from the stranger put an end to his questioning; he bowed humbly and left.

"Milady should not be seen by this fellow," the stranger said to himself. "She will be here soon—she is already late. I had better ride out to meet her. . . . If only I knew what that letter to Tréville contains."

And still muttering to himself, he directed his steps to the kitchen.

Meanwhile the host, who had no doubt that it was the presence of the young man that was driving the stranger from his hostelry, went back up to his wife's room and found d'Artagnan just regaining consciousness. Telling him that the police would deal with him very severely for having sought a quarrel with a great lord—for in his opinion the stranger could be nothing less than a great lord—he insisted that despite his weakness d'Artagnan should get up and leave as quickly as possible. Half dazed, without his doublet and with his head bound up with a linen bandage, d'Artagnan stood up and, urged by the host, began to go down the stairs. When he arrived at the kitchen, however, the first thing he saw was his antagonist talking calmly at the step of a heavy carriage drawn by two large Norman horses.

The person he was talking to, whose head was framed by the carriage window, was a woman about twenty or twenty-two years old. We have already observed the rapidity with which d'Artagnan grasped every element of a face, and he saw at a glance that she was young and beautiful; and her style of beauty struck him the more forcibly because it was totally different from that of the southern regions in which d'Artagnan had always lived. She was pale and fair, with long curls falling in profusion over her shoulders; she also had large, blue, languid eyes, rosy lips, and hands as white as alabaster. She was talking with great animation to the stranger.

"His Eminence, then, orders me . . ." said the lady.

"To return to England immediately and to inform him as soon as the duke leaves London."

"And my other instructions?" asked the fair traveler.

"They are in this box, which you will not open until you are on the other side of the Channel."

"Very well. And you—what will you do?"

"I return to Paris."

"What, without chastising that insolent boy?"

The stranger was about to reply, but just as he opened his mouth, d'Artagnan, who had heard everything, rushed out the door.

"This insolent boy chastises others!" he cried. "And I hope that this time the one he must chastise will not escape him as before."

"Will not escape him?" replied the stranger, frowning.

"No, because I assume you would not dare to run away in front of a lady."

"Remember," said Milady, seeing the stranger lay his hand on his sword, "the least delay may ruin everything."

"You are right," said the gentleman. "Go your way, then, and I will go mine as quickly."

Bowing to the lady, he sprang into his saddle while her coachman applied his whip vigorously to his horses. They thus separated, galloping off in opposite directions.

"Your bill!" cried the host, whose esteem for the traveler was changed into profound contempt on seeing him depart without settling his account.

"Pay him, idiot!" cried the stranger to his servant, without slowing down, and the man threw two or three silver coins at the host's feet and galloped after his master.

"Base coward! False gentleman!" cried d'Artagnan, rushing after the servant.

But his wound had made him too weak for such exertion. After scarcely ten steps his ears began to ring, a cloud of blood passed over his eyes, and he fell in the middle of the street, still shouting, "Coward! coward! coward!"

"Indeed he is a coward," grumbled the host, approaching d'Artagnan and trying by this little flattery to make matters up with the young man.

"Yes, a base coward," murmured d'Artagnan. "But she . . . she was very beautiful."

"What *she?*" asked the host

"Milady," d'Artagnan answered weakly, and fainted a second time.

"I have lost two customers," thought the host, "but this one remains, and I'm pretty certain of him for some days to come. That will be eleven écus gained!"

Eleven écus was just the sum that remained in d'Artagnan's purse.

The host had counted on eleven days of confinement at one écu a day, but he had not counted on his guest. On the following morning at five o'clock d'Artagnan arose; went down to the kitchen without help; asked for—among other ingredients the list of which has not come down to us—some oil, wine, and rosemary; and with his mother's recipe in his hand compounded an ointment that he put on his numerous wounds, replacing his bandages himself and positively refusing the assistance of any doctor. Thanks, no doubt, to the efficacy of the Gypsy recipe, and perhaps also thanks to the absence of any doctor, d'Artagnan was walking about that same evening and was almost cured by the next day.

But when the time came to pay for the rosemary, oil, and wine—the only expense the master had incurred, because he had preserved a strict abstinence, while, on the contrary, the yellow horse, at least according to the account of the hostler, had eaten three times as much as a horse of his size could reasonably be supposed to have done—d'Artagnan found nothing in his pocket but his old velvet purse with the eleven écus it contained: the letter addressed to M. de Tréville had disappeared.

The young man began to search for it with the greatest patience, turning out all his pockets over and over and again, rummaging and rerummaging in his bag and opening and reopening his purse; but when he was convinced that the letter was not to be found, he flew, for the third time, into such a rage as nearly cost him a fresh consumption of wine, oil, and rosemary—for the host, seeing the hot-headed youth become enraged and hearing him threaten to destroy everything in the establishment if his letter were not found, had picked up a pike while his wife reached for a broom handle and the servants for the same sticks they had used the day before.

"My letter of introduction!" d'Artagnan roared. "Give

me my letter of introduction or by God, I will spit you all like little birds."

Unfortunately, there was a powerful obstacle to the accomplishment of this threat. As we have seen, his sword had been broken in two during his first conflict, a circumstance that he had entirely forgotten. So when he proceeded to draw in earnest, he was surprised to find himself armed only with a stump of a sword eight or nine inches long, which the host had carefully replaced in the scabbard; the cook had slyly put the rest of the blade to one side in order to make himself a larding pin.

But this would probably not have stopped our fiery young man if the host had not decided that his guest's demand was perfectly just.

"But after all, where is this letter?" he asked, lowering his pike.

"Yes, where *is* it?" cried d'Artagnan. "In the first place, I warn you that that letter is for Monsieur de Tréville, and it must be found. If it is not found, he will surely know how to find it."

This threat completely intimidated the host. After the king and the cardinal, M. de Tréville was the man whose name was perhaps most frequently spoken by both soldiers and ordinary citizens. There was, to be sure, Father Joseph, but such was the terror inspired by the Gray Eminence, as the cardinal's familiar was called, that his name was only pronounced in a whisper.

Throwing down his pike and ordering his wife to do the same with her broom handle and the servants with their sticks, he set the example of beginning an earnest search for the lost letter.

"Does it contain anything valuable?" he asked after a few minutes of useless investigation.

"It does indeed!" cried the Gascon, who was counting on the letter for making his way at court. "It contained my fortune!"

"Bills on Spain?" asked the disturbed host.

"Bills on his Majesty's private treasury," answered d'Artagnan, who hoped to enter the king's service by means of the letter of introduction and believed he could hazard this reply without telling a falsehood.

"The devil!" cried the host, at his wit's end.

"But that's not important," continued d'Artagnan,

with his usual assurance. "The money is nothing—that letter was everything. I would rather have lost a thousand pistoles than have lost that letter."

He would not have risked more if he had said twenty thousand, but a certain youthful modesty restrained him.

A ray of light all at once broke upon the mind of the host as he was cursing himself for not finding it.

"That letter is not lost!" he cried.

"What do you mean?" asked d'Artagnan.

"It has been stolen!"

"Stolen! By whom?"

"By the gentleman who was here yesterday. He came down into the kitchen, where your doublet was, and he remained there for some time alone. I would bet he stole it."

"Do you think so?" said d'Artagnan dubiously.

He knew better than anyone else how entirely personal was the value of that letter, so could see no reason for it to tempt anyone's cupidity. None of the servants, none of the other travelers, could possibly gain anything by having that piece of paper.

"So you say," he resumed, "that you suspect that impertinent gentleman?"

"I tell you I am sure of it. When I told him that you were a protégé of Monsieur de Tréville and that you even had a letter for that illustrious gentleman, he seemed very disturbed, asked me where the letter was, and immediately went down to the kitchen, knowing your doublet was there."

"Then that's my thief! I will complain to Monsieur de Tréville, and Monsieur de Tréville will complain to the king."

He then majestically took two écus from his purse and gave them to the host—who accompanied him, cap in hand, to the gate—and remounted his yellow horse, which bore him without further incident to the Porte St. Antoine in Paris. There his owner sold him for three écus, which was a very good price considering that he had ridden him hard during the last stage of his journey. The dealer to whom d'Artagnan sold the horse did not conceal from the young man that he had paid such an enormous sum for him only because of the originality of his color.

Thus d'Artagnan entered Paris on foot, carrying his little packet under his arm, and walked about till he found a room to rent for an amount suited to his meager means. The room was a sort of garret on the Rue des Fossoyeurs, near the Luxembourg.

As soon as the deposit was paid, d'Artagnan took possession of his lodging and spent most of the rest of the day sewing onto his doublet and hose some ornamental braiding that his mother had taken off his father's almost-new doublet and secretly given her son. He then went to the Quai de la Ferraille to have a new blade put on his sword, after which he turned toward the Louvre and asked the first Musketeer he met for the location of M. de Tréville's house, which proved to be on the Rue du Vieux-Colombier—very close to the room he had rented. It seemed to him a good omen for his success.

Finally, satisfied with the way in which he had conducted himself at Meung, without remorse for the past, confident in the present, and full of hope for the future, he went to bed and slept the sleep of the brave.

That sleep, still a provincial one, brought him to nine o'clock in the morning, when he rose in order to present himself at the residence of M. de Tréville, who in his father's estimation was the third most important man in the kingdom.

2

M. de Tréville's Anteroom

M. DE TROISVILLE, as his family was still called in Gascony—or M. de Tréville, as he had styled himself in Paris—had indeed begun life as d'Artagnan now did: without a sou in his pocket but with that fund of audacity, shrewdness, and intelligence which makes the poorest Gascon gentleman often benefit more from his expectations of a paternal inheritance than the richest gentleman from Perigord or Berry benefits in reality from his. His insolent bravery, his still more insolent success at a time when the buffets of misfortune were commonplace, had made it possible for him to vault to the top of that difficult ladder called Court Favor.

He was the friend of the king, who greatly honored, as everyone knows, the memory of his father, Henry IV. The father of M. de Tréville had served the latter so faithfully in his wars against the League that in default of money—a lack the Béarnais endured all his life, so that he had to constantly pay his debts with the only thing he never had to borrow, that is, his ready wit—in default of money, we repeat, the king authorized him, after the surrender of Paris, to take for his coat of arms a golden lion passant upon gules, with the motto *Fidelis et fortis*. This was a great matter in the way of honor, but very little in the way of wealth, so when this illustrious companion of the great Henry died, the only inheritance he could leave his son was his sword and his motto. Thanks to this double gift and the spotless name that accompanied it, M. de Tréville was admitted into the young prince's household, where he made such good use of his sword and was so faithful to his motto that Louis XIII, one of the best swordsmen of his kingdom, often said that if he had a friend who was about to fight a duel, he would advise him to choose as a second, himself first, and Tréville next—or perhaps even Tréville first.

So Louis XIII had a real liking for Tréville—a royal liking, a self-interested liking, but still a liking. At that unhappy period it was important to be surrounded by such men as Tréville. Many noblemen might claim the epithet *strong*, which formed the second part of his motto, but very few could lay claim to the *faithful*, which constituted the first. Tréville was one of those few. He was one of those rare beings endowed with the obedient intelligence of the dog together with a reckless courage, a quick eye, and a prompt hand—one of those to whom sight appeared to have been given only to see if the king were displeased with anyone, and hands only to strike that displeasing personage, were he a Besme, a Maurevers, a Poltiot de Méré, or a Vitry. At first Tréville had lacked nothing but opportunity; but he was ever on the watch for it, and he faithfully promised himself that he would not fail to seize it whenever it came within reach. Finally Louis XIII made Tréville the captain of his Musketeers, who were to Louis XIII in their devotion, or rather in their fanaticism, what his Ordinaries had been to Henry III and his Scottish Guard to Louis XI.

On this point, the cardinal was not outdone by the king. When he saw the formidable and elite corps with which Louis XIII surrounded himself, this second—or rather this first—king of France also wished for a guard. He thus had *his* Musketeers just as Louis XIII had his, and the two powerful rivals vied with each other to procure the most celebrated swordsmen from all the provinces of France and even from other countries. It was not uncommon for Richelieu and Louis XIII to argue over their evening game of chess about the merits of their respective people. Each boasted the bearing and the courage of his own and while exclaiming loudly against duels and brawls, each secretly pushed his men to quarrel, deriving enormous satisfaction or genuine regret from every victory or defeat of their own combatants. At least so it is said in the memoirs of a man who took part in some of those defeats and many of those victories.

Tréville had understood his master's weak side, and it was to this observation that he owed the long and constant favor of a king who does not have the reputation of being very faithful in his friendships. He paraded his Musketeers before the Cardinal Armand Duplessis with a mocking air that made his Eminence's gray mustache curl with anger. Tréville had an admirable grasp of the methods of war of that period—he who could not live at the expense of the enemy must live at the expense of his compatriots—and his soldiers formed a legion of devil-may-care fellows whose behavior was completely undisciplined.

Loose-living, hard-drinking, battle-scarred, the king's Musketeers, or rather M. de Tréville's Musketeers, were everywhere—in the taverns, along the promenades, and at the public games—shouting, twirling their mustaches, clanking their swords, taking great pleasure in annoying the cardinal's Guards whenever they met them, and fighting boisterously in the streets, as if nothing could be more fun. Sometimes they were killed, but they were sure in that case to be both mourned and avenged; often they killed others, but they were sure of not rotting in prison because M. de Tréville was there to claim them. They all worshipped M. de Tréville and praised him to the highest degree; ruffians though they were, they trembled before him like schoolboys before their master, obedient to his least word and ready to sacrifice themselves to erase his smallest reproach.

M. de Tréville employed this powerful weapon primarily for the king and the king's friends, and then for himself and his own friends. And nowhere in the memoirs of that period, which has left so many memoirs, does one find this worthy gentleman accused even by his enemies—and he had many such, among men of the pen as well as among men of the sword—of deriving personal advantage from selling the services of his minions. Endowed with a rare genius for intrigue, which made him the equal of the most skillful schemers, he remained an honest man. In addition, despite sword thrusts that weaken and painful exercises that fatigue, he had become one of the most gallant frequenters of fetes, one of the most seductive of ladies' men, one of the softest whisperers of interesting nothings of his day; his success with women was as talked about as that of M. de Bassompierre had been twenty years earlier, and that was saying a great deal. The captain of the Musketeers was therefore admired, feared, and loved: the zenith of human fortune.

Louis XIV was to absorb all the smaller stars of his court in his own vast radiance; but his father, a sun *pluribus impar,* left each of his favorites his personal splendor, each of his courtiers his individual worth. In addition to the levees of the king and cardinal, there were in Paris at that time more than two hundred smaller but still noteworthy levees, and among those two hundred levees, Tréville's was one of the most popular.

By six o'clock in the morning in summer and eight o'clock in winter the courtyard of his house on the Rue du Vieux-Colombier resembled a camp. From fifty to sixty Musketeers, who seemed to replace one another in relays so as to always be present in imposing numbers, were constantly parading about, armed to the teeth and ready for anything. On one of those immense staircases, upon whose space modern civilization would build a whole house, ascended and descended Parisians seeking favors, gentlemen from the provinces eager to be enrolled in the Musketeers, and servants in all sorts of liveries, carrying messages between their masters and M. de Tréville. In the anteroom, on long circular benches, sat the elect: those who had been summoned. There was a continuous buzz of conversation from morning till night, while M. de Tréville, in the study next to this room, received visits, listened to complaints, gave orders, and like the king at his balcony at the Louvre, had only to look out the window to review his soldiers.

The day on which d'Artagnan presented himself, the assemblage was imposing, especially for a provincial just arriving from his province. (It is true that this provincial was a Gascon, and that in those days, d'Artagnan's compatriots had the reputation of not being easily intimidated.) When he had passed through the massive gate studded with long square-headed nails, he found himself among a troop of shouting, quarreling, boisterous swordsmen; in order to force a passage through those turbulent waves, it was best to be an officer, a great nobleman, or a pretty woman.

It was into the midst of that tumultuous and disorderly crowd that our young man advanced with a beating heart, his long rapier dangling against his lanky leg, one hand on the brim of his hat, and smiling with that half-smile of the embarrassed provincial who wishes to put up a good front. Every time he passed a group he breathed more freely; but he could not help observing that the men turned around to look at him, and for the first time in his life d'Artagnan—who had till that day entertained a very good opinion of himself—felt ridiculous.

It was even worse when he got to the staircase. There were four Musketeers on the bottom steps, amusing themselves with the following sport, while ten or twelve of their comrades waited on the landing to take their turn.

One of them, stationed on the top step, naked sword in hand, was preventing, or at least trying to prevent, the three others from climbing up.

Those three others were fencing against him with what d'Artagnan at first took for capped foils; but he soon noticed some bleeding scratches and realized every weapon was pointed and sharpened. At each scratch not only the spectators but the actors themselves laughed like madmen.

The man who was occupying the upper step was skillfully holding his adversaries in check. A circle had formed around them. The rule was that at every hit the man who was touched would yield his turn on the waiting list for an audience with M. de Tréville to the man who had touched him. In five minutes all three were slightly wounded, one on the hand, another on the chin, and the third on the ear, by the defender of the step, who himself remained intact—a level of skill worth three turns according to the rules.

However difficult it was, or rather however difficult he pretended it was, to astonish our young traveler, this pastime really did astonish him. He had seen in his province—a region in which tempers flare easily—much swordplay, but the daring of those four fencers was greater than anything he had ever seen even in Gascony. He felt himself transported into that famous country of giants, where Gulliver was so frightened, and yet he had not even gained the goal, for there were still the landing place and the anteroom.

On the landing they were no longer fighting, but telling stories about women, and in the anteroom, stories about the court. On the landing d'Artagnan blushed; in the anteroom he trembled. His warm and errant imagination, which in Gascony had made him dangerous to young chambermaids and sometimes even to their mistresses, had never even in moments of delirium dreamed of half the amorous wonders or a quarter of the feats of gallantry that were here detailed in connection with the best-known names. But if his morals were shocked on the landing, his respect for the cardinal was scandalized in the anteroom. There, to his great astonishment, d'Artagnan heard criticized, aloud and openly, both the cardinal's public policy, which made all Europe tremble, and his private life, which so many powerful noblemen had been punished for trying to pry into. That great man so revered by d'Artagnan the elder served as an object of ridicule to Tréville's Musketeers, who joked about his bandy legs and his stooped shoulders. Some were singing ballads about Mme. d'Aiguillon, his mistress, and Mme. Cambalet, his niece; while others were making plans to annoy his pages and guards—all of which appeared to d'Artagnan as monstrous impossibilities.

Nevertheless, when the name of the king was occasionally mentioned in the midst of all those jests against the cardinal, a sort of gag would seem to close for a moment all the jeering mouths. They would look around cautiously and appear to doubt the thickness of the partition between them and M. de Tréville's study; but a fresh allusion would soon bring the conversation back to his Eminence, and the laughter would recover its heartiness as all his actions were held up to the most searching scrutiny.

"These fellows will surely all be either imprisoned or hanged," thought the terrified d'Artagnan, "and I with them, because from the moment I have listened to them, I can be taken as their accomplice. What would my good father say—he who so strongly recommended me to respect the cardinal—if he knew I was with such pagans?"

We have no need, therefore, to say that d'Artagnan did not dare join in the conversation, but merely looked with all his eyes and listened with all his ears, stretching his five senses so as to lose nothing; and despite his confidence in those paternal recommendations, he felt himself urged by his tastes and led by his instincts to praise rather than to blame the unheard-of things that were taking place.

Because he was a perfect stranger in the crowd of M. de Tréville's courtiers, and this his first appearance in that place, he was soon noticed, and somebody came to ask him what he wanted. D'Artagnan gave his name very modestly, emphasized the fact that he was a compatriot of M. de Tréville, and asked the servant to request a moment's audience with his master—a request that the other promised to transmit in due time.

A little recovered from his first surprise, d'Artagnan now had the leisure to study the clothes and the faces around him.

The center of the most animated group was a Musketeer of great height and haughty air, dressed so peculiarly as to attract general attention. He was not wearing the uniform cloak—which was not obligatory during that time of less liberty but more independence—but a faded and worn sky-blue doublet, and over this a magnificent gold-embroidered baldric that shone like ripples of water in the sun. A long cloak of crimson velvet fell in graceful folds from his shoulders, disclosing the splendid baldric, from which was suspended a gigantic rapier.

This Musketeer had just come off guard duty and was complaining of having a cold, coughing affectedly from time to time. It was because of his cough, he said to those around him, that he had put on his cloak; and while he was speaking so loftily and twisting his mustache so disdainfully, everyone admired his embroidered baldric, d'Artagnan more than anyone.

"What would you?" said the Musketeer. "It is the latest fashion—a folly, I admit, but still it is the fashion. Besides, one must spend one's inheritance somehow."

"Ah, Porthos," said one of his companions, "don't try to make us believe that baldric comes from paternal generosity. It was given to you by that veiled lady I saw you with the other Sunday, near the Porte St. Honoré."

"No, on my honor and by the faith of a gentleman, I bought it with the contents of my own purse," replied the Musketeer they had called Porthos.

"Yes, in about the same way that I bought this new purse with what my mistress put into the old one," said another Musketeer.

"It's true, though," said Porthos, "and the proof is that I paid twelve pistoles for it."

The wonder increased, though the doubt continued to exist.

"Isn't that so, Aramis?" said Porthos, turning to another Musketeer.

This one formed a perfect contrast to his interrogator, who had just called him Aramis. He was about twenty-two or -three, with an open, ingenuous face, black, mild eyes, and cheeks as rosy and downy as an autumn peach. His thin mustache marked a perfectly straight line across his upper lip; he seemed reluctant to lower his hands lest their veins should swell, and he would pinch the tips of his ears from time to time to preserve their delicate pink transparency. He spoke little and slowly, bowed frequently, and laughed silently, showing his fine teeth, which he appeared to take as much care of as the rest of his person. He answered his friend's appeal by an affirmative nod.

This affirmation evidently dispelled all doubts about the baldric. Everyone continued to admire it but said no more about it, and the conversation turned suddenly to another subject.

"What do you think of the story Chalais's equerry is telling?" asked another Musketeer, not addressing anyone in particular but speaking to everybody.

"What does he say?" Porthos asked self-importantly.

"He says that in Brussels he met Rochefort, the cardinal's tool, disguised as a Capuchin, and that thanks to this disguise, Rochefort was able to trick Monsieur de Laigues like the idiot he is."

"An idiot, indeed," said Porthos, "but is the story true?"

"I heard it from Aramis," replied the Musketeer.

"Really?"

"Why, you knew it, Porthos," said Aramis. "I told you about it yesterday. Let us say no more about it."

"Say no more about it? That's *your* opinion!" replied Porthos. "Say no more about it! *Peste*, but you make these decisions quickly! The cardinal sets a spy on a gentleman, has his letters stolen from him by means of a traitor, a brigand, a rascal—then, with the help of that spy and thanks to those letters, has Chalais's throat cut under the stupid pretext that he wanted to kill the king and marry the queen to the king's brother! Nobody knew anything about all that until you unraveled it yesterday, to our great satisfaction, and now, while we are still gasping at the news, you come and tell us today, 'Let us say no more about it.' "

"Very well, then, let us talk about it, since you wish to," replied Aramis patiently.

"If I were poor Chalais's equerry, this Rochefort would spend a very uncomfortable minute or two with me!" Porthos exclaimed.

"And you would spend a rather unhappy quarter-hour with the Red Duke," replied Aramis.

"Oh, the Red Duke! Bravo!" cried Porthos, clapping his hands and nodding his head. "The 'Red Duke' is a capital name for the cardinal! I'll circulate that saying, be assured, my friend. I've always said Aramis was witty! What a pity that you couldn't follow your first vocation— what a delightful priest you would have made!"

"Oh, it's only a temporary postponement," replied Aramis; "I will be one someday. You know perfectly well, Porthos, that I am continuing to study theology for just that purpose."

"He will be one, as he says," cried Porthos. "He will be one, sooner or later."

"Sooner," said Aramis.

"He is waiting for only one thing before resuming his cassock, which hangs behind his uniform," said one of the Musketeers.

"What is he waiting for?" asked another.

"For the queen to give an heir to the crown of France."

"No jesting on that subject, gentlemen," said Porthos. "Thank God, the queen is still of an age to do so!"

"They say that the Duke of Buckingham is in France," replied Aramis, with a significant smile that gave this seemingly simple sentence a tolerably scandalous meaning.

"Aramis, my friend, this time you are wrong," interrupted Porthos. "Your wit is always leading you beyond bounds. If Monsieur de Tréville heard you, you would regret having spoken like that."

"Are you going to lecture me, Porthos?" cried Aramis, his usually mild eyes flashing.

"My dear fellow, be a Musketeer or a priest. Be one or the other, but not both," replied Porthos. "You know what Athos told you the other day—you eat at everybody's table; let's not quarrel, I beg of you. It would be pointless—you know what you, Athos, and I have agreed on. . . . You go to Madame d'Aiguillon and pay your court to her, you go to Madame de Bois-Tracy, the cousin of Madame de Chevreuse, and you are said to be very high in her favor. Oh, you don't have to talk about your good luck! No one is asking for your secret—the whole world knows your discretion. But since you have that virtue, why the devil don't you make use of it with respect to her Majesty? Let whoever likes talk of the king and the cardinal, and however he likes—but the queen is sacred, and if anyone speaks of her, let it be respectfully."

"Porthos, you are as vain as Narcissus," replied Aramis. "You know I hate moralizing, except when it is done by Athos. And as for you, you are wearing too magnificent a baldric to pretend to such piety. I will be a priest, if it suits me, but meanwhile I am a Musketeer.

As such I say what I please, and at this moment it pleases me to say that you are annoying me."

"Aramis!"

"Porthos!"

"Gentlemen! Gentlemen!" cried the surrounding group.

"Monsieur de Tréville awaits Monsieur d'Artagnan," cried a servant, throwing open the study door.

At those words, during which the door remained open, everyone became silent, and amid that general silence the young man crossed part of the length of the anteroom and entered the study of the captain of the Musketeers, congratulating himself with all his heart at having so narrowly escaped the end of that strange quarrel.

3

The Audience

THOUGH M. DE TRÉVILLE was at the moment in a bad mood, he nevertheless greeted the young man politely and smiled when he heard d'Artagnan's response, the Béarnese accent of which reminded him both of his youth and his native province—a double memory that makes a man smile at any age. He walked over to the door leading to the anteroom, looked at d'Artagnan as if to ask his permission to finish with the others before he began with him, and called out three times, his voice becoming louder at each name and becoming progressively more irritated.

"Athos! Porthos! Aramis!"

The two Musketeers whom we have already met, and who answered to the last two of the three names, immediately left their group and advanced toward the study, the door of which closed behind them as soon as they had entered. Their manner was not precisely casual, but it demonstrated such an easy combination of dignity and deference that it evoked d'Artagnan's strong admiration; he saw in the two men demigods, and in their leader an Olympian Jupiter armed with all his thunderbolts.

After the two Musketeers had come in and closed the

door behind them; after the buzzing murmur of the ante-room, to which their summons had doubtless furnished fresh food, had begun again; after M. de Tréville, with a slight frown, had three or four times silently paced the whole length of his study, passing each time in front of Porthos and Aramis, who were as stiff and silent as if on parade—after all that he stopped suddenly and swept them from head to foot with an angry look.

"Do you know what the king said to me last night? Do you know, gentlemen?"

"No, sir, we do not," replied the two Musketeers after a moment's silence.

"But I hope that you will do us the honor to tell us," Aramis added in his politest tone and with the most graceful bow.

"He told me that he would henceforth recruit his Mus-keteers from among the cardinal's Guards!"

"The cardinal's Guards! Why?" asked Porthos, heatedly.

"Obviously he feels that his wine has been watered down too much and must be improved by adding some stronger vintage to it."

The two Musketeers reddened to the whites of their eyes. D'Artagnan did not know what he was doing there and wished himself a hundred feet underground.

"Yes," continued M. de Tréville, becoming angrier as he spoke, "and his Majesty was right, because it is true that the Musketeers cut a miserable figure at court. Last night, while playing cards with the king, the cardinal, with a condescending air of condolence that was very displeasing to me, told a story. He described how, the day before yesterday, those *hell-raising Musketeers*, those *daredevils*—and he dwelt on those words with a sarcasm still more displeasing to me—those *braggarts*, he added, glancing at me with his tiger-cat's eye, had caused a riot in a tavern on the Rue Férou, and how a party of his Guards—I thought he was going to laugh in my face—had been forced to arrest them. *Morbleu!* You must know something about it! Arrest Musketeers! You were among them—yes, you were! Don't deny it—you were recognized, and the cardinal mentioned you. But it's all my fault—yes, it's my fault because I myself choose my men. You, Aramis, why the devil did you ask me for a uniform when a cassock would have suited you so much better? And you, Porthos, do you wear such a fine golden baldric only to suspend a sword of straw from it? And Athos—I don't see Athos. Where is he?"

"Sir," Aramis replied in a sorrowful tone, "he is ill, very ill."

"Ill—very ill? And what is his illness?"

"They are afraid it may be smallpox, sir," replied Porthos, wishing to take his turn in the conversation, "and if it is, it will be a pity because it will certainly spoil his face."

"Smallpox! that's a fine story to tell me, Porthos! Sick of smallpox at his age! Never! But probably wounded and possibly killed. Ah, if I only knew! Gentlemen, I will not have you congregating in low taverns, quarreling in the streets, fencing at the crossways. Above all, I will not have you give the cardinal's Guards—who are brave, quiet, skillful men who never put themselves in a position to be arrested, and who, besides, would never allow themselves to be arrested—any occasion to laugh at you! I am sure they would prefer dying on the spot to being arrested or to retreating even one step. To save yourselves, to run away, to flee—what splendid behavior for the king's Musketeers!"

Porthos and Aramis were trembling with rage. They would cheerfully have strangled M. de Tréville if they had not been sure that it was only his great love for them that made him speak this way. They stamped their feet on the carpeted floor; they bit their lips till the blood came; they grasped the hilts of their swords with all their might. Everyone outside had heard Athos, Porthos, and Aramis called, and had guessed, from M. de Tréville's tone of voice that he was very angry about something. Ten curious faces were now pressed to the door, turned white with fury, for the Musketeers could hear every syllable; and even as Tréville spoke, they repeated his insulting comments to all the others in the anteroom. In an instant, from the study door to the street gate, the whole house was boiling over.

"So the king's Musketeers allow themselves to be arrested by the cardinal's Guards, do they?" M. de Tréville continued, as furious at heart as his soldiers, but keeping his voice steady and deliberately plunging his words, one by one, like so many dagger thrusts, into his auditors' hearts. "What? Six of his Eminence's Guards arrest six of his Majesty's Musketeers? Well, I know what I am going to do. I am going straight to the Louvre, as captain of the king's Musketeers, and ask for a lieutenancy in the cardinal's Guards—and if he refuses me, *morbleu*, I will become a priest!"

At those words, the murmur from outside became an explosion; nothing could be heard but cries and blasphemies. The *morbleus*, the *sang Dieus*, the *morts de touts les diables*, filled the air. D'Artagnan looked for some tapestry behind which he might hide himself, and felt an enormous desire to crawl under the table.

"Well, my Captain," said Porthos, quite beside himself, "it's truth that we were six against six, but we were not captured by fair means. Before we had time to draw our swords, two of our party were dead and Athos, seriously wounded, was very little better than dead. You know Athos—well, Captain, he tried twice to get up, and fell again twice. And we did not surrender—no! They dragged us away by force. On the way we escaped. As for Athos, they thought he was dead, and left him on the field of battle, not thinking it worth the trouble to carry him away. That's the whole story. What the devil, Captain, one cannot win every battle! The great Pompey lost the Battle of Pharsalus, and Francis the First, who was, from what I have heard, as good a man as ever lived, nevertheless lost the Battle of Pavia."

"And I have the honor of assuring you that I killed one of them with his own sword, because mine was broken at the first parry," said Aramis. "Killed him or stabbed him, sir, as you please."

"I did not know that," replied M. de Tréville, in a somewhat softer tone. "The cardinal has exaggerated, I see."

"But please, sir," continued Aramis, who, seeing his captain calmer, ventured to risk a request, "do not say that Athos is wounded. He would be in despair if that should come to the ears of the king, and as the wound is very serious, since the blade went through his shoulder and penetrates the chest, I am afraid . . ."

At that instant the tapestry at the door was pushed

aside, and a noble, handsome, but terribly pale face appeared.

"Athos!" cried the two Musketeers.

"Athos!" repeated M. de Tréville.

"My comrades informed me that you have sent for me, sir, and I have come to receive your orders. What do you want me to do?" Athos asked M. de Tréville in a feeble yet perfectly steady voice.

With these words the Musketeer, irreproachably dressed as usual, entered the study with a tolerably firm step.

M. de Tréville, deeply moved by this proof of courage, sprang toward him.

"I was about to say to these gentlemen," he said, "that I forbid my Musketeers to risk their lives needlessly— brave men are very dear to the king, and he knows that his Musketeers are the bravest fellows on earth. Your hand, Athos!"

And without waiting for the newcomer's answer to this proof of affection, M. de Tréville grasped his right hand and gripped it with all his might, not noticing that Athos, despite his self-command, allowed a slight murmur of pain to escape him and turned more pale, if possible, than before.

So strong was the excitement produced by the arrival of Athos, whose wound, though kept a secret, was known to all, that the door had remained open. A roar of satisfaction hailed the captain's last words, and two or three of the listeners were so carried away by the enthusiasm of the moment, that they showed their faces through the openings of the tapestry. M. de Tréville was about to reprimand such a lack of manners when he felt Athos's hand stiffen within his and saw that he was about to faint. At the same instant Athos, who had rallied all his strength to contend against the pain, was finally overcome by it and fell to the floor as if he were dead.

"A doctor!" cried M. de Tréville. "Mine! The king's! The best! A doctor or my brave Athos will die!"

At those words, everyone in the anteroom rushed into the study—M. de Tréville not thinking to shut the door against them—and crowded around the wounded man. But all this eager attention would have been useless if the doctor had not happened to be in the house. He pushed through the crowd, approached the still unconscious Athos, and, as all the noise and commotion greatly inconvenienced him, insisted that the first and most urgent thing to be done was to carry the Musketeer into an adjoining room. M. de Tréville immediately opened the door and pointed the way to Porthos and Aramis, who carried their comrade. Behind them walked the doctor, and behind the doctor the door was closed.

M. de Tréville's study, generally held so sacred, became in an instant an annex of the anteroom. Everyone was talking, haranguing, shouting, swearing, cursing, and consigning the cardinal and his Guards to all the devils.

After a moment, Porthos and Aramis returned, the doctor and M. de Tréville remaining with the wounded man.

Finally M. de Tréville himself returned. Athos had regained consciousness and the doctor had said that the Musketeer's condition need not alarm his friends; he had fainted only from loss of blood.

M. de Tréville then motioned everyone to withdraw, and all retired except d'Artagnan, who had not forgotten that he had an audience and who, with the tenacity of a Gascon, had remained in his place.

When all had gone out and the door was closed, M. de Tréville turned around and found himself alone with the young man. The event that had just occurred had somewhat broken the thread of his ideas, so he asked what his persevering visitor wanted. D'Artagnan repeated his name, and M. de Tréville immediately recovered his memory and grasped the situation.

"Excuse me," he said, smiling, "excuse me, my compatriot, but I had wholly forgotten you. I cannot help it, because a captain is like a father of a family, but with an even greater responsibility than the father of an ordinary family. Soldiers are big children, but since I must see that the king's orders, and especially the cardinal's orders, are executed . . ."

D'Artagnan could not restrain a smile, and by this smile M. de Tréville understood that he was not dealing with a fool. Changing the subject, he came straight to the point.

"I respected your father very much," he said. "What

can I do for his son? Tell me quickly, because my time is not my own."

"Monsieur, when I left Tarbes and came here, it was my intention to ask you, in memory of the friendship that you have not forgotten, for the uniform of a Musketeer. But after what I have seen during the last two hours, I realize that such a favor would be enormous, and I'm afraid I may not deserve it."

"It is indeed a favor, young man, but it may not be so far beyond your hopes as you fear, or rather as you seem to fear. But his Majesty's ruling is firm, and I regret to inform you that no one can become a Musketeer without fighting in several campaigns, performing feats of extraordinary bravery, or serving two years in some other regiment less favored than ours."

D'Artagnan bowed without replying, feeling his desire to wear the Musketeer's uniform vastly increased by the great difficulties that he would have to overcome to earn it.

"But," continued M. de Tréville, fixing on his compatriot a look so piercing that it seemed as if he wanted to penetrate the depths of his heart, "because of my old companion, your father, I will do something for you, young man. Our recruits from Béarn are not usually very rich, and I have no reason to think matters have much changed in this respect since I left the province. I imagine you have not brought too much money with you?"

D'Artagnan drew himself erect with a proud air that plainly said, "I ask no one for charity."

"Oh, that's all very fine, young man," continued M. de Tréville. "I know that look well. I myself came to Paris with four écus in my purse and would have fought with anyone who dared to tell me I was not able to purchase the Louvre."

D'Artagnan's bearing became still more imposing. Thanks to the sale of his horse, he was beginning his career with four écus more than M. de Tréville had possessed at the beginning of his.

"As I was about to say, you should save the money you have, however large the sum may be, but you should also try to perfect yourself in the skills becoming a gentleman. I will write a letter today to the Director of the Royal Academy, and tomorrow he will admit you without any expense to yourself. Do not refuse this little favor. Our best-born and richest gentlemen sometimes ask for it without being able to obtain it. You will learn horsemanship, swordsmanship in all its branches, and dancing. You will make some desirable acquaintances, and from time to time you can call on me to report how you are getting on and to tell me if I can be of further service to you."

D'Artagnan, stranger as he was to court manners, could not but recognize a little coldness in this reception.

"Alas, sir, I see how sadly I miss the letter of introduction that my father gave me to present to you," he said.

"I certainly am surprised that you would undertake so long a journey without such a letter. It is usually the only resource for us poor Béarnese."

"I had one, sir, and, thank God, such a one as I could wish," cried d'Artagnan, "but it was stolen from me."

He then related his adventure in Meung, describing the unknown gentleman in great detail and with a warmth and sincerity that delighted M. de Tréville.

"This is all very strange," M. de Tréville said thoughtfully. "You had mentioned my name?"

"Yes, sir, I certainly did, but why shouldn't I have? A name like yours should be a shield to me on my travels. Why should I not put myself under its protection?"

Flattery was very current at that time, and M. de Tréville loved incense as well as a king or even a cardinal. He could not refrain from a smile of visible satisfaction; but the smile soon disappeared, and he returned to the adventure of Meung.

"Tell me, did this gentleman have a slight scar on his temple?"

"Yes, one that might have been made by the grazing of a bullet."

"Was he a good-looking man?"

"Yes."

"Tall?"

"Yes."

"Pale complexion and brown hair?"

"Yes, yes, that is he! How is it, sir, that you are acquainted with him? If ever I find him again . . . and I will find him, I swear, even if I have to follow him to hell!"

"He was waiting for a woman?" continued Tréville.

"He left immediately after he had spoken to her for a minute."

"You do not know the subject of their conversation?"

"He gave her a box, told her that it contained her instructions, and said she was not to open it until she arrived in London."

"Was the woman English?"

"He called her Milady."

"It is he—it must be he," murmured Tréville. "I thought he was still in Brussels!"

"Oh, sir, if you know this man," cried d'Artagnan, "tell me who he is and where he is, and I will then release you from all your promises—even that of arranging my admission into the Musketeers, because more than anything else, I want my revenge!"

"Beware, young man!" exclaimed Tréville. "If you see him coming on one side of the street, cross to the other. Do not cast yourself against such a rock—he will break you like glass."

"That will not stop me. If I ever find him . . ."

"In the meantime, take my advice and do not look for him."

All at once the captain stopped, as if struck by a sudden suspicion. The great hatred that the young traveler professed for this man who, rather improbably, had stolen his father's letter from him—was there not some treachery concealed under this hatred? Might not this young man have been sent by his Eminence? Might he not have come for the purpose of laying a trap for him? This man who called himself d'Artagnan—could he not be an emissary of the cardinal, whom the cardinal sought to introduce into Tréville's house, to place near him in order to win his confidence and afterward to ruin him, as had been done in a thousand other cases? He examined d'Artagnan even more earnestly than before and was only moderately reassured by the astute intelligence and affected humility he saw. "I know he is a Gascon," he thought, "but he may as easily be for the cardinal as for me. Let me test him."

"My friend," he said slowly, "Since you are the son of an old comrade—for I think your story of the lost letter is perfectly true—I wish to make up for the cold-

ness you may have noticed in me by explaining the
secrets of our policy. The king and the cardinal are the
best of friends, their apparent bickering is only meant to
deceive fools. I do not want a fellow Gascon, a handsome
cavalier, a brave youth who is quite fit to make his way,
to be the dupe of all these pretenses, like so many others
who have been ruined by falling into that trap. Be
assured that I am devoted to both these all-powerful masters, and that my serious desire is nothing other than to
serve the king and the cardinal—one of the greatest
geniuses France has ever produced.

"Now that you understand this, young man, act
accordingly. If you have—because of your family, your
friends, or even your own instincts—any animosity such
as we see constantly breaking out against the cardinal,
bid me adieu and let us separate. I will help you in many
ways, but without admitting you to my household. I hope
that my frankness will at least make you my friend, for
you are the only young man to whom I have ever spoken
in this way."

Tréville said to himself, "If the cardinal, who knows
how bitterly I hate him, has set this young fox on me,
he will certainly have told his spy that the best way to
court me is to rail at him. Therefore, in spite of all my
protestations, if my suspicions are correct, my cunning
friend will assure me that he detests his Eminence."

It proved otherwise.

D'Artagnan answered, with the greatest simplicity, "I
came to Paris with exactly those intentions. My father
advised me to tolerate no slights from anyone but the
king, the cardinal, and yourself—whom he considered
the three most important men in France."

D'Artagnan added M. de Tréville to the two others,
as we can see, but he thought the addition would do no
harm.

"I have the greatest esteem for the cardinal," he continued, "and the most profound respect for his actions.
So much the better for me, sir, if you have spoken
frankly to me, as you said you were, because then you
will do me the honor to appreciate the resemblance of
our opinions. But if you entertained any doubts about
me, as you certainly might, then I have ruined myself by
speaking the truth. Still, I hope you will not respect me

the less for it, and that is what I wish more than anything."

M. de Tréville was astonished. So much acuteness, so much frankness, aroused his admiration but did not entirely remove his suspicions. The more this young man was superior to others, the more he was to be dreaded if he meant to deceive him.

Nevertheless, he clasped d'Artagnan's hand, and said, "You are an honest youth; but at the present moment I can do for you only what I have already offered. My house will always be open to you, and since you will be able to ask for me at all hours and thus take advantage of every opportunity, you will probably eventually get what you wish."

"That means," replied d'Artagnan, "that you will wait till I have proved myself worthy of it. Well, be assured," he added with the familiarity of a Gascon, "you will not wait long."

And he bowed in farewell, as if he considered the future to be in his own hands from then on.

"Wait a minute," said M. de Tréville, stopping him. "I promised you a letter for the director of the Academy. Are you too proud to accept it, young man?"

"No, sir," said d'Artagnan; "and I assure you that this one will not suffer the same fate as the other. I will guard it so carefully that I swear it will arrive at its address, and woe be to anyone who attempts to take it from me!"

M. de Tréville smiled at this flourish, and leaving his young compatriot in the window recess, where they had been talking, he sat down to write the promised letter of recommendation. Meanwhile d'Artagnan, having no better employment, amused himself with tapping out a march on the windowpane and with watching the Musketeers leave one after another, following them with his eyes till they disappeared.

After having written the letter, M. de Tréville sealed it, rose from the desk, and approached the young man in order to give it to him. But at the very moment when d'Artagnan extended his hand to receive it, M. de Tréville was astonished to see his protégé start, become crimson with passion, and rush from the study, crying, "S'blood, he will not escape me this time!"

"Who?" asked M. de Tréville.

"My thief!" replied d'Artagnan.

And he ran out.

"The devil take the madman," murmured M. de Tré-ville. "Unless," he added, "that was just a cunning way to escape after realizing that he had failed in his purpose!"

4

Athos, Porthos, and Aramis

IN A STATE OF FURY, d'Artagnan had crossed the ante-room in three bounds and was darting toward the stairs, when he carelessly ran headfirst into a Musketeer coming out of another door and struck his shoulder violently, making him howl with pain.

"Excuse me," said d'Artagnan, trying to continue on his way, "but I am in a hurry."

He had scarcely gone down the first step when a hand of iron seized him by the belt and stopped him.

"You are in a hurry?" asked the Musketeer, as pale as a sheet. "For that reason you run into me? You say 'Excuse me,' and you believe that that is sufficient? Not at all, young man. Do you think that because you have heard Monsieur de Tréville speak to us a little rudely today that other people may treat us the way he speaks to us? You are mistaken, my friend—you are not Monsieur de Tréville."

D'Artagnan recognized Athos, who was returning home after having his dressing changed by the doctor, and replied, "I did not do it intentionally, and not doing it intentionally, I said 'Excuse me.' It seems to me that is quite enough. I repeat to you, however—and by heavens I think I repeat it too often—that I am in a great hurry. Loosen your hold, please, and allow me to go where my business calls me."

"Monsieur," said Athos, releasing him, "you are not polite. It is easy to see that you come from far away."

D'Artagnan had already gone down three or four steps, but at Athos's last remark he stopped short.

"*Morbleu*, monsieur!" he said. "From however far I

may have come, you are not the one to give me a lesson in good manners, I warn you!"

"We shall see!" said Athos.

"Ah! if I were not in such a hurry, and if I were not running after someone . . ."

"Monsieur Man-in-a-hurry, you can find me without running—*me,* you understand?"

"Yes. Where?"

"Near the Carmes-Deschaux."

"When?"

"About noon."

"About noon? Good. I will be there."

"Try not to make me wait, because at a quarter past twelve, I will go after *you* and cut off your ears as you run!"

"I will be there ten minutes before twelve."

And he again began to run down the stairs as if possessed by the devil, hoping that he might yet catch up with the stranger, who had been walking slowly.

But at the street gate Porthos was talking with the soldier on guard. Between the two, there was just room for a man to pass. D'Artagnan thought it would suffice for him, and he darted forward. But he had reckoned without the wind; as he was about to pass through, it blew out Porthos's long cloak, and d'Artagnan ran right into the middle of it. Porthos must have had reasons for not abandoning that part of his clothing, because instead of letting go of the piece he held in his hand, he pulled it toward him, so that d'Artagnan became rolled up in the velvet and was rotated toward Porthos.

Hearing the Musketeer swear, d'Artagnan tried to escape from the cloak, which was blinding him, and searched for a way out of its folds. He especially wanted to avoid damaging the magnificent baldric we are acquainted with, but when he timidly opened his eyes, he found himself with his nose resting between Porthos's shoulders—that is to say, exactly on the baldric.

Alas, like most things in the world that have nothing in their favor but appearances, the baldric was glittering with gold only in the front and was nothing but simple leather in the back. Vain as he was, and not being able to afford a baldric wholly of gold, he at least had the half of one. It was now easy to understand why he had needed to have a cold and wear a cloak.

Porthos, making strong efforts to disentangle himself from d'Artagnan, who was still wriggling around behind his back, exclaimed, "You must be mad to run into people like that!"

"Excuse me," said d'Artagnan, reappearing under the giant's shoulder, "but I am in a hurry—I was running after someone, and . . ."

"And you always forget your eyes when you run?"

"No," replied d'Artagnan, irritated, "and thanks to my eyes, I can see what other people cannot see."

Whether Porthos did or did not understand him, he said, giving way to his anger, "Monsieur, you run the risk of being trounced if you keep on crashing into Musketeers!"

"Trounced, monsieur! That is a strong word!"

"It is one that a man accustomed to look his enemies in the face may use."

"Ah, *pardieu!* I know very well that you don't turn your back to *yours*."

And the young man, delighted with his joke, hurried away laughing loudly.

Porthos foamed with rage and began to rush after d'Artagnan.

"Later, later," cried the latter, "when you're not wearing your cloak."

"At one o'clock, then, behind the Luxembourg."

"Very well, at one o'clock," replied d'Artagnan, turning the corner.

But neither in the street he had passed through nor in the one he now glanced down eagerly could he see anyone; however slowly the stranger had walked, he had been fast enough to disappear—unless he had perhaps entered some house. D'Artagnan asked everyone he met, went down to the ferry, and came up again by the Rue de Seine and the Croix-Rouge, but nothing, absolutely nothing! This chase was, however, advantageous to him in one way, because the more he perspired, the cooler he became.

He began to think about the events that had occurred; they were numerous and inauspicious. It was scarcely eleven o'clock in the morning, and he was already in disgrace with M. de Tréville, who would certainly think the way in which d'Artagnan had left him a little too abrupt; and moreover, he had drawn upon himself duels with two men, each one capable of killing three d'Artagnans—with two Musketeers, in short, two of those beings whom he admired so much that he thought of them as superior to all other men.

The future seemed bleak. Sure of being killed by Athos, the young man was not even very uneasy about Porthos. But since hope is the last thing extinguished in the human heart, he finished by hoping that he might survive both duels, even though with terrible wounds; and in case he did, he made the following reflections on his own conduct:

"How impetuous and stupid I am! That brave, unfortunate Athos was wounded on the very shoulder against which I rammed into. It's only surprising that he didn't strike me dead at once. He had every reason to do so—the pain must have been atrocious. As for Porthos . . . oh, as for Porthos, faith, that's funny!"

And in spite of himself the young man began to laugh aloud—looking around carefully, however, to see if his laugh, seemingly without reason in the eyes of passersby, offended anyone.

"As for Porthos, yes, it's certainly amusing, but I was a giddy fool with him too. Are people to be run into without warning? No! And have I any right to peep under their cloaks to see what is not there? He would certainly have forgiven me if I hadn't said anything to him about that cursed baldric—in ambiguous words, it is true, but rather wittily ambiguous. Ah, cursed Gascon that I am, I must make jokes no matter what! Friend d'Artagnan," he continued speaking to himself with all the courtesy he thought his due, "if you escape with your life, of which there is not much chance, I would advise you to practice perfect politeness for the future. From now on you must be admired for it and quoted as a model of it. To be obliging and polite does not necessarily make a man a coward. Look at Aramis—he is mildness and courtesy personified, and has anybody ever dreamed of calling him a coward? No, certainly not, and from now on I will try to model myself after him. Oh, how strange—here he is!"

D'Artagnan, walking and soliloquizing, had arrived within a few steps of the d'Aiguillon house, in front of which he saw Aramis chatting gaily with three gentlemen of the king's Guards. Aramis saw d'Artagnan too; but since he had not forgotten that it was in the presence of this young man that M. de Tréville had been so angry in the morning, and since he did not think a witness of the rebuke the Musketeers had received was likely to be at all agreeable, he pretended not to see him. D'Artagnan, however, full of his resolve to be conciliatory and courteous, approached the young men and bowed deeply, smiling graciously at the same time. Aramis nodded, but did not smile, and all four of them immediately broke off their conversation.

D'Artagnan was clever enough to see that he was one too many; but he was not sufficiently worldly to know how to extricate himself easily from the false position of a man who begins to mingle with people he is scarcely acquainted with and interrupts a conversation that does not concern him. He was trying to think of the least awkward way to retreat when he noticed that Aramis had dropped his handkerchief and, by mistake, no doubt, placed his foot on it. This seemed a good opportunity to make up for his intrusion. He bent down, and as gracefully as he could, pulled the handkerchief from under Aramis's foot, despite the latter's resistance.

Holding it out to him, he said, "I believe, monsieur, that this is a handkerchief you would be sorry to lose?"

The handkerchief was indeed richly embroidered, with a coronet and a coat of arms at one of its corners. Aramis blushed, and snatched rather than took the handkerchief from the Gascon's hands.

One of the Guards exclaimed, "Will you persist in saying, most discreet Aramis, that you are not on good terms with Madame de Bois-Tracy when that gracious lady has the kindness to lend you one of her handkerchiefs?"

Aramis gave d'Artagnan one of those looks which inform a man that he has acquired a mortal enemy.

Then, resuming his mild air, he said, "You are mistaken, gentlemen. This handkerchief is not mine, and I cannot imagine why Monsieur has taken it into his head to offer it to me rather than to one of you. As proof of what I say, here is mine in my pocket."

So saying, he pulled out his own handkerchief, also a very elegant one of fine batiste—though batiste was expensive at that time. But it had no embroidery or coat of arms and was ornamented only with the monogram of its owner.

This time d'Artagnan was not impetuous; he perceived his mistake, but Aramis's friends were not at all convinced by his denial, and one of them spoke to the young Musketeer with affected seriousness.

"If what you say is so," he said, "I would be forced, my dear Aramis, to reclaim it, because as you know, Bois-Tracy is an intimate friend of mine and I cannot allow his wife's property to be bandied about as a trophy."

"You make the demand badly," replied Aramis. "Though I acknowledge the justice of what you say, I refuse to give you the handkerchief because of the way you have asked for it."

"The fact is," d'Artagnan hazarded timidly, "I did not see the handkerchief fall from Monsieur Aramis's pocket. His foot was on it, and I thought from his having his foot on it that the handkerchief was his."

"And you were wrong, my dear sir," Aramis replied coldly, unappreciative of his effort to make reparation.

Turning toward the guard who had declared himself the friend of Bois-Tracy, he continued, "Besides, I have reflected, my dear intimate of Bois-Tracy, that I am no less his friend than you can possibly be, so the handkerchief is as likely to have fallen from your pocket as mine."

"No, on my honor!" cried his Majesty's Guardsman.

"You are about to swear on your honor and I on mine, and then it will be obvious that one of us will have lied. Now, Montaran, we will do better than that—let each of us take half."

"Of the handkerchief?"

"Yes."

"Perfectly just!" cried the other two Guardsmen. "The judgment of King Solomon! Aramis, you are full of wisdom!"

The young men all laughed, and as may be supposed, the affair went no further. A moment or two later the conversation ended, and the three Guardsmen and the Musketeer, after having cordially shaken hands, separated, the Guardsmen going one way and Aramis another.

"Now is my time to make my peace with this gallant man," said d'Artagnan to himself, having stood off on one side during the whole of the latter part of the conversation.

With that good intention he drew closer to Aramis, who was departing without paying any attention to him, and said, "Monsieur, you will excuse me, I hope."

"Ah, monsieur," Aramis interrupted, "permit me to observe that you have not acted as a gallant man should."

"What, monsieur!" cried d'Artagnan. "Do you suppose . . ."

"I suppose, monsieur, that you are not a fool and that you know very well, despite coming from Gascony, that people do not stand on handkerchiefs without a reason. Paris is not paved with batiste!"

"Monsieur, you do wrong to try to humiliate me," said d'Artagnan, whose naturally quarrelsome spirit began to speak more loudly than his peaceful resolutions. "I am from Gascony, it is true, and since you know it, there is no need to tell you that Gascons are not very patient. When they have begged to be excused once, even for a folly, they are convinced that they have already done as much as they ought to have done."

"Monsieur, what I say to you," said Aramis, "is not for the sake of seeking a quarrel. Thank God, I am not a bravo! And being a Musketeer only temporarily, I fight only when I am forced to do so and always with great repugnance. But this time the affair is serious, for a lady has been compromised by you."

"By *us*, you mean!" cried d'Artagnan.

"Why were you so tactless about giving me the handkerchief?"

"Why were you so awkward about letting it drop?"

"I have said, monsieur, and I repeat, that the handkerchief did not come from my pocket."

"And thereby you have lied twice, monsieur, because I saw it fall."

"Ah, if you take it that way, Master Gascon, I will have to teach you how to behave yourself."

"And I will send you back to your Mass book, Master Priest. Draw, if you please, and instantly!"

"No, not here, if you please, my good friend. Do you not see that we are opposite the d'Aiguillon house, which is full of the cardinal's men? How do I know that it is not his Eminence who has ordered you to bring him my head? Now, ridiculous as it may seem, I am partial to my head because it seems to suit my shoulders so well. I wish to kill you, certainly, but to kill you quietly in a remote place, where you will not be able to boast of your death to anybody."

"I agree, monsieur. But do not be too confident— bring your handkerchief with you. Whether it belongs to you or another, you may need it."

"Monsieur is a Gascon?" asked Aramis.

"Yes. Monsieur does not postpone our meeting through prudence?"

"Prudence, monsieur, is a virtue quite useless to Musketeers, I know, but indispensable to churchmen, and since I am a Musketeer only provisionally, I think it good to be prudent. At two o'clock I will have the honor of expecting you at Monsieur de Tréville's house. There I will indicate to you the best place and time."

The two young men bowed and separated, Aramis going up the street that led to the Luxembourg, while d'Artagnan, seeing it was nearly noon, took the road to the Carmes-Deschaux, saying to himself, "I certainly can't withdraw, but if I am killed, at least I will be killed by a Musketeer."

5

The King's Musketeers and the Cardinal's Guards

D'ARTAGNAN knew nobody in Paris and therefore went to his appointment with Athos without a second, determined to be satisfied with those his adversary had chosen. Besides, he intended to apologize once again to the brave Musketeer, not humbly or fearfully, but with an understanding of the usual result of a duel in which a strong young man fights with an adversary who is wounded and weak—if conquered, he doubles the triumph of his opponent; if a conqueror, he is accused of foul play and lack of courage.

Unless we have badly described the character of our adventure-seeker, our readers must have already perceived that d'Artagnan was not an ordinary man; therefore, while telling himself that his death was inevitable, he did not resign himself to die quietly, as one less courageous and self-possessed might have done, but began to think about the different characters of the men he was going to fight and to see his situation more clearly. He hoped, by means of his generous excuses, to make a friend of Athos, whose lordly air and austere bearing pleased him. He was sure he would be able to frighten Porthos with the story of the baldric, which he might, if not killed on the spot, tell the world—which would make Porthos look ridiculous. As to Aramis, he did not much fear him; and if he should survive to that point, he determined to finish him off in good style or, at the very least, to disfigure his face, as Cesar had advised his soldiers to do to Pompey's men.

D'Artagnan's resolve was further strengthened by his father's advice, which had taken root in his heart: "Tolerate no slights from anyone except Monsieur le Cardinal and the king. He therefore flew rather than walked toward the Carmes Déchaussés monastery, or rather Carmes-Deschaux, as it was called at that time—a windowless building surrounded by barren fields, a kind of annex to the Pré aux-Clercs that was often used as a dueling place for men who had no time to lose.

When d'Artagnan arrived in sight of the bare spot of ground beside the monastery, Athos had been waiting about five minutes and twelve o'clock was striking. He was exactly on time, and the most rigorous observer of the rules of dueling would have been satisfied.

Athos, who was still suffering from his wound even though it had just been redressed by M. de Tréville's doctor, was seated on a post and waiting for his adversary with that serene expression and noble air that never forsook him. At sight of d'Artagnan, he stood up and politely walked a few steps to meet him. The latter approached him with hat in hand, bowing so low that the feather actually touched the ground.

"Monsieur," said Athos, "I have asked two of my friends to serve as seconds, but they have not yet come—which astonishes me, as it is not at all like them."

"I have no seconds, monsieur," said d'Artagnan. "Having arrived only yesterday in Paris, I as yet know no one but Monsieur de Tréville, to whom I was recommended by my father, who has the honor to be one of his friends."

Athos thought for an instant.

"You know no one but Monsieur de Tréville?" he asked.

"Yes, monsieur, I know only him."

"Then if I kill you, I will seem to be a child-killer," Athos said, speaking half to himself and half to d'Artagnan.

"Not too much so," replied d'Artagnan, with a bow that was not lacking in dignity, "since you do me the honor to draw a sword with me while suffering from a very inconvenient wound."

"Very inconvenient, it is true, and I can tell you that you hurt me like the devil. But I will use my left hand, as I always do in such circumstances. Do not think that I do you a favor, because I use either hand equally well. It will even be a disadvantage to you, since a left-handed man is very troublesome to people who are not prepared for it. I regret I did not inform you about this sooner."

"You are truly courteous, monsieur," said d'Artagnan, bowing again, "and I assure you, I am very grateful."

"You embarrass me," replied Athos, with his gentlemanly air. "Let us talk of something else, if you please. Oh, how you have hurt me—my shoulder is on fire!"

"If you would permit me . . ." d'Artagnan said timidly.

"What, monsieur?"

"I have a miraculous ointment for wounds—one given to me by my mother and which I have tried on myself."

"Well?"

"Well, I am sure that this ointment would cure you in less than three days, and at the end of three days, when you would be cured—well, sir, it would still be a great honor to give you satisfaction."

D'Artagnan said this with a simplicity that gave proof of his courtesy without throwing the least doubt on his courage.

"*Pardieu*, monsieur, there is a proposition that pleases me! Not that I accept it, but it is most gentlemanly. That is how the gallant knights of the time of Charlemagne spoke and acted, and every cavalier ought to model himself on them. Unfortunately, we do not live in the time of the great emperor but in the time of the cardinal, and three days from now, however well the secret might be guarded, it would be known that we were to fight, and our duel would be prevented. . . . Will those fellows never come?"

"If you are in a hurry, monsieur," said d'Artagnan with the same simplicity with which a moment before he had proposed to put off the duel for three days, "and if you wish to dispatch me at once, do not inconvenience yourself, I beg you."

"There is another statement that pleases me," Athos said with a gracious nod to d'Artagnan. "That did not come from a man without brains, and certainly not from a man without a heart. Monsieur, I like men of your stamp, and I foresee that if we don't kill each other, I will have much pleasure in your conversation. We will wait for my seconds, if you please. I have plenty of time, and it will be more correct. Ah, here is one of them now."

In fact, the gigantic Porthos had just appeared at the end of the Rue Vaugirard.

"What!" cried d'Artagnan, "Is one of your seconds Monsieur Porthos?"

"Yes. That disturbs you?"

"By no means."

"And here is the other one."

D'Artagnan turned in the direction Athos pointed to and saw Aramis.

"What!" he cried again, with even greater astonishment than before. "Your other second is Monsieur Aramis?"

"Certainly! Are you not aware that we are never seen one without the others, and that we are called among the Musketeers and the Guards, at court and in the city,

Athos, Porthos, and Aramis, or the Three Inseparables? But since you come from Dax or Pau . . ."

"From Tarbes," said d'Artagnan.

". . . you are probably unaware of this little fact," said Athos.

"You are well named the Inseparables, gentlemen; and my adventure, if it should be talked about, will at least prove that the name is founded on truth."

Meanwhile Porthos had come up and waved to Athos. Then, turning around, he saw d'Artagnan and stood looking at him in amazement.

Let us say in passing that he had changed his baldric and removed his cloak.

"What does this mean?" he asked.

"This is the gentleman I am going to fight with," said Athos, pointing to d'Artagnan and saluting him with the same gesture.

"Why, he is the one I am going to fight with too," said Porthos.

"But not before one o'clock," replied d'Artagnan.

"And I also am to fight with this gentleman," said Aramis, coming up to them.

"But not till two o'clock," d'Artagnan said tranquilly.

"What are you going to fight about, Athos?" Aramis asked.

"I don't really know. He hurt my shoulder. And you, Porthos?"

"Why, I am going to fight—because I am going to fight," answered Porthos, blushing.

Athos, whose keen eye saw everything, noticed a slight sly smile pass over the young Gascon's lips.

"We had a short discussion about clothes," d'Artagnan added.

"And you, Aramis?" asked Athos.

"Oh, ours is a theological quarrel," Aramis replied, signaling d'Artagnan to keep secret the cause of their duel.

Athos saw d'Artagnan smile again.

"Indeed?" Athos asked.

"Yes—a passage of St. Augustine about which we could not agree," said the Gascon.

"Decidedly, this is a clever fellow," Athos said to himself.

"And now that you are all assembled, gentlemen," said d'Artagnan, "permit me to offer you my apologies."

At the word *apologies*, Athos's face clouded over, Porthos's lips curled in a haughty smile, and Aramis shook his head in refusal.

"You do not understand me, gentlemen," said d'Artagnan as he raised his head, the sharp, bold lines of which were just then gilded by a bright ray of the sun. "I asked to be excused in case I should not be able to discharge my debt to all three of you, because Monsieur Athos has the right to kill me first, which must lessen your valor in your own estimation, Monsieur Porthos, and must render yours almost worthless, Monsieur Aramis. So, gentlemen, I repeat, excuse me, but on that account only, and now—on guard!"

At these words, with the most gallant air possible, d'Artagnan drew his sword.

The blood had mounted to his head, and at that moment he would have drawn his sword against every Musketeer in the kingdom as willingly as he now did against Athos, Porthos, and Aramis.

It was a quarter past noon. The sun was at its zenith, and the spot chosen for the scene of the duel was completely exposed to its full glare.

"It is very hot," said Athos, also drawing his sword, "and yet I cannot take off my doublet because I just now felt my wound begin to bleed again and I would not like to annoy Monsieur with the sight of blood that he has not drawn from me himself."

"That is true, monsieur," replied d'Artagnan, "and whether drawn by myself or another, I assure you that I will always regret seeing the blood of so brave a gentleman. I will therefore also fight in my doublet."

"Come, come, enough of such courtesies!" said Porthos. "Remember that we are waiting for our turns."

"Speak for yourself when you are inclined to utter such inanities," Aramis interrupted. "For my part, I think what they say is very well said, and quite worthy of two gentlemen."

"When you please, monsieur," said Athos, putting himself on guard.

"I was awaiting your orders," said d'Artagnan, crossing swords with him.

But scarcely had the two rapiers clashed, when a company of the cardinal's Guards, commanded by M. de Jussac, turned the corner of the monastery.

"The cardinal's Guards!" cried Aramis and Porthos at the same time. "Sheathe your swords, gentlemen!"

But it was too late. The two combatants had been seen in a position that left no doubt of their intentions.

"Halloo!" cried Jussac, advancing toward them and signaling his men to do likewise. "Fighting a duel here, are you? And the edicts? Do you ignore them?"

"You are very generous, gentlemen of the Guards," said Athos, full of rancor, for Jussac was one of the aggressors of the previous day. "If we were to see you fighting, I can assure you that we would make no effort to prevent you. Leave us alone, and you will enjoy a little amusement without cost to yourselves."

"Gentlemen," said Jussac, "it is with great regret that I pronounce the thing impossible. Duty before everything. Sheathe, if you please, and follow us."

"Monsieur," said Aramis, parodying Jussac, "it would give us great pleasure to obey your polite invitation if it were up to us, but unfortunately it is impossible—Monsieur de Tréville has forbidden it. On your way, then; it will be best."

This mockery exasperated Jussac.

"We will charge you if you disobey," he said.

"There are five of them," said Athos, half aloud, "and we are only three. We will be beaten again and must die on the spot, because I swear I will never again face the captain as a conquered man."

Athos, Porthos, and Aramis instantly closed ranks while Jussac drew up his soldiers.

This short interval was sufficient to decide d'Artagnan on the part he was to take. It was one of those events that determine the course of a man's life; it was a choice between the king and the cardinal, a choice which once made, must be persisted in. To fight was to disobey the law, risk his head, make an enemy of a minister more powerful than the king himself. All this the young man understood, and yet—to his praise be it said—he did not hesitate a second.

Turning to Athos and his friends, he said, "Gentlemen, allow me to correct your words, if you please.

You said you were but three, but it seems to me we are four."

"But you are not one of us," said Porthos.

"That's true," replied d'Artagnan; "I do not have the uniform of a Musketeer, but I have the spirit of one. My heart is a Musketeer's heart, and this is what it tells me to do."

"Withdraw, young man," cried Jussac, who had undoubtedly guessed d'Artagnan's plans by his gestures and expression. "You may leave. We consent to that, so save your skin and go quickly."

D'Artagnan did not budge.

"You are assuredly a brave fellow," said Athos, grasping the young man's hand.

"Come on, make up your mind," said Jussac.

"Well, we must do something," Porthos and Aramis said together.

"Monsieur is generous," said Athos.

But all three thought about d'Artagnan's youth and dreaded his inexperience.

"We will be only three men, one of whom is wounded, plus a boy," resumed Athos, "yet it will be said that we were four men."

"Yes, but to yield!" said Porthos.

"That *is* difficult," replied Athos.

D'Artagnan understood their hesitation.

"Test me, gentlemen," he said, "and I swear to you by my honor that I will not leave here alive if we are conquered."

"What is your name, my brave fellow?" asked Athos.

"D'Artagnan, monsieur."

"Well, then, Athos, Porthos, Aramis, and d'Artagnan, forward!" cried Athos.

"Come, gentlemen, have you decided to decide?" cried Jussac for the third time.

"We have, gentlemen," said Athos.

"And what is your choice?" asked Jussac.

"We are about to have the honor of charging you," replied Aramis, lifting his hat with one hand and drawing his sword with the other.

"So you resist, do you?"

"Does that surprise you?"

And the nine combatants rushed upon one another

with a fury that did not, however, exclude a certain degree of method.

Athos fixed upon a certain Cahusac, one of the cardinal's favorites. Porthos had Bicarat, and Aramis found himself with two opponents.

As for d'Artagnan, he went for Jussac himself.

The young Gascon's heart was pounding as if it would burst—not from fear, God be thanked, because he had not the least bit of it, but with the desire to emulate his companions. He fought like a raging tiger, turning ten times around his adversary and changing his ground and his guard twenty times. Jussac was what was then called a fine blade and had had much practice; nevertheless it required all his ability to defend himself against a skillful and energetic adversary who kept departing every instant from the usual rules and attacked him on all sides at once—but who parried like a man who had the greatest respect for his own skin.

The contest finally exhausted Jussac's patience. Furious at being held in check by one he had considered a boy, he became excited and began to make mistakes. D'Artagnan, who lacked practice but had sound theories, redoubled his agility. Jussac was eager to put an end to this and sprang forward, aiming a terrible thrust at his adversary; but the latter parried it, and while Jussac was recovering, d'Artagnan glided like a serpent beneath his blade and ran his sword through his body. Jussac fell like a dead weight.

D'Artagnan then looked quickly over the field of battle.

Aramis had killed one of his adversaries, but the other was pressing him hard. However, Aramis was in a good position and still able to defend himself.

Bicarat and Porthos had just made counterhits: Porthos had received a thrust through his arm and Bicarat one through his thigh. But since neither wound was serious, the two men only fought the more earnestly.

Athos, wounded anew by Cahusac, grew more ashen by the minute but did not give way by even a foot. He had merely changed his sword hand and was fighting with his left hand.

According to the laws of dueling at that time, d'Artagnan was free to assist whom he pleased. While he was trying to find out which of his companions stood in greatest need, he caught a glance from Athos. This glance was sublimely eloquent. Athos would have died rather than ask for help, but he could look, and with the look ask assistance. D'Artagnan understood, and with a bound he approached Cahusac on the side, crying, "To me, Monsieur Guardsman, so I may slay you!"

Cahusac turned. D'Artagnan's intention was timely, for Athos, who had been supported only by his great courage, fell to one knee.

He cried to d'Artagnan, "Do not kill him, young man, I beg you: I have an old affair to settle with him when I am well again. Just disarm him—make sure of his sword. . . . That's it! Very well done!"

Athos had seen Cahusac's sword fly twenty paces away. D'Artagnan and Cahusac sprang forward at the same instant, the one to obtain, the other to recover, the sword; but d'Artagnan, being the more active, reached it first and placed his foot on it.

Cahusac immediately ran to the Guardsman whom Aramis had killed, seized his rapier, and turned back toward d'Artagnan; but on his way he was blocked by Athos, who had recovered his breath during this brief pause that d'Artagnan had procured him and who, fearing that d'Artagnan would kill his enemy, now wanted to resume the fight himself.

D'Artagnan understood that it would be offending Athos not to leave him alone, and in a few minutes Cahusac fell, with a sword thrust through his throat.

At the same instant Aramis was placing his sword point on the chest of his fallen enemy and forcing him to ask for mercy.

Only Porthos and Bicarat remained. Porthos made a thousand foolish jests, asking Bicarat what time it could be, and congratulating him on his brother's having just obtained a company in the Navarre regiment, but, jest as he might, he gained nothing. Bicarat was one of those iron men who fall only with death.

Nevertheless, it was necessary to finish. The watch might come and arrest all the combatants, wounded or not, royalists or cardinalists. Athos, Aramis, and d'Artagnan surrounded Bicarat, and asked him to surrender. Though alone against all of them and with a wound in his thigh, Bicarat wanted to hold out, but Jussac, who had risen upon his elbow, called out to him to yield. Bicarat was a Gascon, like d'Artagnan; he turned a deaf ear, and contented himself with laughing, finding time between two parries to point to a spot of earth with his sword and say, parodying a verse of the Bible, "Here will Bicarat die; for I only am left, and they seek my life."

"But there are four against you! I command you to give up," Jussac said.

"Ah, if you command me, that's another thing," said Bicarat. "Since you are my commander, it is my duty to obey."

Springing backward, he broke his sword across his knee to avoid having to surrender it, threw the pieces over the monastery wall, and crossed his arms, whistling a cardinalist tune.

Bravery is always respected, even in an enemy. The Musketeers saluted Bicarat with their swords and returned them to their sheaths. D'Artagnan did the same. Then, assisted by Bicarat, the only one left standing, he carried Jussac, Cahusac, and the one of Aramis's adversaries who was only wounded, to the monastery porch. The fourth man was dead, as we have said. They then rang the bell and, carrying away four swords out of five, intoxicated with joy, headed for M. de Tréville's house.

They walked arm in arm, occupying the whole width of the street and adding to their number every Musketeer they met, so that in the end it became a triumphal procession. D'Artagnan marched between Athos and Porthos, and was deliriously happy.

"If I am not yet a Musketeer," he said to his new friends as he passed through the gateway of M. de Tréville's house, "I am at least an apprentice, am I not?"

6

His Majesty King Louis XIII

THIS AFFAIR MADE a great stir. M. de Tréville scolded his Musketeers in public and congratulated them in private; but since there was no time to be lost in telling the king, he hurried to report to the Louvre. It was already too late: the king was closeted with the cardinal and too busy to receive him.

In the evening M. de Tréville attended the king's gaming table. The king was winning, and as he was very avaricious, he was in a wonderful mood.

Perceiving M. de Tréville at a distance, he said, "Come here, Monsieur le Capitain, so that I may scold you. Do you know that his Eminence has again been complaining about your Musketeers, and so vehemently that he is indisposed this evening? Ah, those Musketeers of yours are ruffians—fellows who should be hanged!"

"No, sire," replied Tréville, who saw immediately how things stood, "on the contrary, they are good fellows, as meek as lambs, and I swear they have but one desire—that their swords may never leave their scabbards except in your Majesty's service. But what can they do? The Guards of Monsieur le Cardinal are forever seeking quarrels with them, and for the very honor of the corps, the poor young men are obliged to defend themselves."

"Listen to Monsieur de Tréville!" said the king. "It sounds as if he were speaking of a religious community! In truth, my dear Captain, I have a great mind to take away your commission and give it to Mademoiselle de Chemerault, to whom I promised a convent! But don't think that I am going to take you at your word. I am called Louis the Just, Monsieur de Tréville, and by and by, we will see the truth."

"Sire, it is because I trust in that justice that I will wait patiently and quietly to know your pleasure."

"Wait, then, monsieur," said the king. "You will not have to wait long."

In fact, the king's luck turned, and since he was beginning to lose what he had won, he was not sorry to find an excuse for stopping while he was ahead. He therefore stood up and put the money that lay in front of him, the major part of which arose from his winnings, into his pocket.

"La Vieuville," he said, "take my place. I must speak to Monsieur de Tréville about some affair of importance. Oh—I had eighty louis in front of me. Put down the same sum so that those who have lost may have nothing to complain about. Justice above all."

He then turned to M. de Tréville and walked with him to a window recess.

"Well, monsieur," he continued, "you say it is his Eminence's Guards who sought a quarrel with your Musketeers?"

"Yes, sire, as they always do."

"How did it happen? You know, my dear Captain, a judge must hear both sides."

"Sire, in the most simple and natural manner possible. Three of my best soldiers—whom your Majesty knows by name, whose devotion you have more than once appreciated, and who have the king's service much at heart—Athos, Porthos, and Aramis, had arranged some amusement with a young fellow from Gascony, whom I had introduced to them that same morning. It was supposed to take place at St. Germain, I believe, and they had an appointment to meet at the Carmes-Deschaux. There they were disturbed by Jussac, Cahusac, Bicarat, and two other Guardsmen, who had certainly not gone there in such numbers without intending something against the edicts."

"Ah, you may be right," said the king. "They doubtless went there to fight among themselves."

"I do not accuse them, sire, but I leave your Majesty to judge what five armed men could possibly be going to do in such a deserted place as that neighborhood."

"Yes, you are right, Tréville, you are right!"

"Then, seeing my Musketeers, they changed their minds and forgot their private quarrel for their factional quarrel. Your Majesty must know that the Musketeers, who belong to the king and to nobody but the king, are the natural enemies of the Guardsmen, who belong to the cardinal."

"Yes, Tréville," said the king in a melancholy tone, "and it is very sad to see two parties in France, two heads of the kingdom. But all this will end, Tréville. . . . You say that the Guardsmen sought a quarrel with the Musketeers?"

"I say it is likely that things happened that way, but I will not swear to it, sire. You know how difficult it is to discover the truth, and unless a man has that admirable instinct which causes Louis the Thirteenth to be named Louis the Just . . ."

"Quite right, Tréville. But your Musketeers were not alone. They had a youth with them?"

"Yes, sire, and one wounded man, so three of the king's Musketeers—one of whom was wounded—and a youth not only stood their ground against five of the cardinal's fiercest Guardsmen, but absolutely brought down four of them."

"But that is a victory!" cried the king, radiant. "A complete victory!"

"Yes, sire, a complete victory."

"Four men, one of them wounded and one of them a youth, you say?"

"One of them barely a youth, but who handled himself so admirably that I will take the liberty of recommending him to your Majesty."

"What is his name?"

"D'Artagnan, sire. He is the son of one of my oldest friends—the son of a man who served under the king your father, of glorious memory, in the religious war."

"And you say the young man fought well? Tell me how, Tréville—you know how I delight in stories of war and fighting."

And Louis XIII twirled his mustache proudly and put his hand on his hip.

"Sire, as I told you, Monsieur d'Artagnan is little more than a boy, and since he does not have the honor of being a Musketeer, he was dressed as an ordinary citizen. The cardinal's Guards, observing his youth and the fact that he did not belong to the corps, offered to let him withdraw before they attacked."

"So you see, Tréville," the king interrupted, "it was they who attacked."

"That is true, sire—there can be no more doubt about that. When they called on him to withdraw, he answered that he was a Musketeer at heart, entirely devoted to your Majesty, and that he would therefore remain with the Musketeers."

"Brave young man!" murmured the king.

"Well, he did remain with them, and your Majesty has in him so firm a champion that it was he who gave Jussac the terrible sword thrust that has made the cardinal so angry."

"He is the one who wounded Jussac. He, a boy? Tréville, that's impossible!"

"It is as I have the honor to relate it to your Majesty."

"Jussac, one of the best swordsmen in the kingdom?"

"Well, sire, he found his master."

"I will see that young man, Tréville, and if anything can be done for him—well, we will make it our business."

"When will your Majesty deign to receive him?"

"Tomorrow at noon, Tréville."

"Shall I bring him alone?"

"No, bring me all four together. I wish to thank them all at once. Devoted men are so rare, Tréville, that one must reward their devotion."

"At twelve o'clock, sire, we will be at the Louvre."

"Use the private staircase, Tréville. There is no reason to let the cardinal know . . ."

"Yes, sire."

"You understand, Tréville—an edict is still an edict. After all, it is still forbidden to duel."

"But this encounter, sire, was not at all like an ordinary duel. It was a brawl, and the proof is that there were five of the cardinal's Guardsmen against my three Musketeers and Monsieur d'Artagnan."

"That is true," said the king, "but even so, Tréville, use the back staircase."

Tréville smiled; but as it was already something to have prevailed upon this child to rebel against his master, he bowed respectfully to the king and with his permission took leave of him.

That same evening the three Musketeers were informed of the honor that had been accorded them. They had long been acquainted with the king, so they were not very excited; but d'Artagnan, with his Gascon imagination, saw in it his future fortune and spent the night in golden dreams. By eight o'clock in the morning he was at Athos's apartment.

D'Artagnan found him dressed and ready to go out. As their appointment with the king was not till noon, he had arranged with Porthos and Aramis to play a game of tennis in a court near the Luxembourg stables. Athos invited d'Artagnan to join them, and although ignorant of the game, which he had never played, he accepted, not knowing what to do with his time till noon.

The two Musketeers were already there and playing together. Athos, who was expert in all sports, passed with d'Artagnan to the opposite side and challenged them; but even though he was playing with his left hand, he found at his first movement that his wound was still too recent to allow such exertion. D'Artagnan therefore was left alone; and since he declared he was too ignorant of the game to play it properly they merely tossed the balls to one another without keeping score. But one of those balls, launched by Porthos's herculean hand, passed so close to d'Artagnan's face that if it had hit him, he would probably not have been able to have his audience with the king. Now, in his Gascon imagination his future life depended on that audience, so he politely bowed to Aramis and Porthos and declared that he would not resume the game until he should be prepared to play with them on more equal terms. He then left them and took his place in the gallery.

Unfortunately for him, among the spectators was one of his Eminence's Guardsmen, who was still irritated by his companions' defeat the day before and had promised himself to avenge it at the first opportunity. He believed this opportunity had now come.

Addressing his neighbor, he said, "It is not surprising that that young man should be afraid of a ball—he is probably a Musketeer apprentice."

D'Artagnan turned around as if stung by a serpent and he fixed his eyes on the Guardsman who had just made that insolent comment.

"*Pardieu,*" resumed the guard, twirling his mustache,

"look at me as long as you like, little man! I have said what I have said."

"And since that which you have said is too clear to require any explanation," replied d'Artagnan in a low voice, "I beg you to follow me."

"When?" the Guardsman asked with the same jeering tone.

"At once, if you please."

"And you know who I am, without doubt?"

"I have no idea, nor do I much care."

"You are wrong there, for if you knew my name, perhaps you would not be so insistent."

"What is your name?"

"Bernajoux, at your service."

"Very well, Monsieur Bernajoux," said d'Artagnan tranquilly, "I will wait for you at the gate."

"Go, monsieur, I will follow you."

"Do not hurry, monsieur, lest it be observed that we are leaving together. You must be aware that company would be in the way for our undertaking."

"True," said the Guardsman, astonished that his name had produced no effect on the young man.

Indeed, the name of Bernajoux was known to all the world, except perhaps d'Artagnan, for it was one that figured very frequently in the daily brawls which all the cardinal's edicts could not repress.

Porthos and Aramis were so involved with their game, and Athos was watching them so attentively, that they did not even notice their young companion leave to wait outside the gate as he had told the Guardsman he would. A moment later, the Guardsman was also outside. D'Artagnan had no time to lose because of his audience with the king at noon, so he looked around, and saw that the street was empty.

"It is fortunate for you," he said to his adversary, "that even though your name is Bernajoux, you have to deal only with an apprentice Musketeer. But never mind, I will do my best. On guard!"

"But this place is badly chosen, and we would be better behind the St. Germain abbey or in the Pré-aux-Clercs," said he whom d'Artagnan had provoked.

"You are right," replied d'Artagnan, "but unfortunately

I have very little time to spare because I have an appointment at precisely twelve. On guard, then, monsieur!"

Bernajoux was not a man who had to be spoken to in that way twice. In an instant his sword glittered in his hand, and he attacked his adversary, whom he hoped to intimidate because of his great youthfulness.

But d'Artagnan had served his apprenticeship the day before. Sharpened by his victory, full of hopes of future favor, he was resolved not to recoil by even one step. The two swords were crossed close to the hilts, and since d'Artagnan stood firm, it was his adversary who retreated; d'Artagnan seized the opportunity given him by this movement to free his weapon, lunge, and touch his adversary on the shoulder. D'Artagnan immediately stepped back and raised his sword; but Bernajoux cried out that it was nothing and, rushing forward, spitted himself on d'Artagnan's sword. Because he did not fall or declare himself conquered but only broke away toward M. de la Trémouille's residence, where one of his relatives was a member of the household, d'Artagnan did not know how seriously wounded his adversary was: he continued to press him, and would undoubtedly have soon completed his work with a third thrust. However, two of the Guardsman's friends, who had seen him leave after exchanging some words with d'Artagnan, rushed out of the court, swords in hand, and fell upon the victor. But Athos, Porthos, and Aramis quickly appeared in their turn and drove the two Guardsmen back just as they were attacking their young companion. Bernajoux finally fell, and since the Guardsmen were only two against four, they began to call out, "To the rescue!" At these cries, all who were in the La Trémouille house rushed out and fell upon the four companions, who were themselves now shouting, "Musketeers to the rescue!"

Such a cry was generally heeded, for the Musketeers were known to be the cardinal's enemies and were liked because of their hatred for him. Thus soldiers from companies other than those which belonged to the Red Duke, as Aramis had called him, often took the side of the king's Musketeers in these quarrels. Of three Guardsmen of M. Des Essarts's company who were passing, two came to the assistance of the four companions while the other ran toward M. de Tréville's house, crying, "To the rescue, Musketeers! To the rescue!"

As usual, Tréville's house was full of Musketeers, and they hurried to help their comrades. The melee became general, but the numbers favored the Musketeers. The cardinal's Guards and M. de la Trémouille's people retreated into the house and closed the doors just in time to prevent their enemies from entering with them. As for the wounded man, he had been taken in at once, in a very serious condition.

Excitement was high among the Musketeers and their allies, and they were even considering whether they should set fire to the house to punish the insolence of M. de la Trémouille's domestics for daring to attack the king's Musketeers. The proposal had been made, and received with enthusiasm, when fortunately the clock struck eleven. D'Artagnan and his companions remembered their audience, and since they would have regretted that such an act should take place without their presence, they succeeded in calming their friends, who contented themselves with hurling some paving stones against the doors. The doors were too strong, however, so they soon tired of the sport—especially since those who had been the leaders of the enterprise had already left and were making their way toward M. de Tréville's house. He was already informed of this fresh disturbance and was waiting for them.

"Quick, to the Louvre," he said. "We must not lose a minute, and we must try to see the king before he is prejudiced by the cardinal. We will describe this to him as a consequence of yesterday's affair, and the two will pass off together."

M. de Tréville, accompanied by the four young men, directed his course toward the Louvre; but there, to the great astonishment of the captain of the Musketeers, he was informed that the king had gone stag hunting in the St. Germain forest. M. de Tréville asked for this information to be repeated to him twice, and each time his companions saw his face darken.

"Had his Majesty already decided on this hunting party yesterday?" he asked.

"No, your Excellency," replied the servant. "The Master of the Hounds came this morning to inform him that

he had marked down a stag. At first the king answered
that he would not go, but then he could not resist his
love of sport and set out after breakfast.''

"And the king has seen the cardinal?''

"Probably, because I saw the horses harnessed to his
Eminence's carriage this morning, and when I asked
where he was going, they told me, 'To St. Germain.' ''

"We are forestalled," said M. de Tréville. "Gentlemen, I will see the king this evening, but I do not advise
you to risk doing so."

This advice was too reasonable, and moreover came
from a man who knew the king too well, to allow the
four young men to dispute it. M. de Tréville told them
all to go home and wait for news.

On entering his house, M. de Tréville thought it best
to be first in making a complaint. He sent one of his
servants to M. de la Trémouille with a letter asking him
to eject the cardinal's Guardsmen from his house and to
reprimand his people for their audacity in having
attacked the king's Musketeers. But M. de la Trémouille—already prejudiced by his equerry, whose relative, as we know, Bernajoux was—replied that it was not
for either M. de Tréville or his Musketeers to complain,
but, on the contrary, for him, whose people the Musketeers had assaulted and whose home they had tried to
burn down. Since the debate between the two noblemen
might go on indefinitely, each naturally becoming more
firm in his own opinion, M. de Tréville thought he might
end it by going himself to see M. de la Trémouille.

He therefore went immediately to the latter's house
and had himself announced.

The two men greeted each other politely, for if there
was no friendship between them, there was at least
respect. Both were men of courage and honor; and since
M. de la Trémouille—a Protestant who seldom saw the
king—belonged to no party, he did not usually carry any
bias into his social relations. This time, however, his
greeting, though polite, was cooler than usual.

"Monsieur," said M. de Tréville, "we fancy that we
each have cause to complain of the other, and I have
come to try to clear up this affair together."

"I have no objection," replied M. de la Trémouille,

"but I warn you that I am well informed, and the fault is all with your Musketeers."

"You are too just and reasonable a man, monsieur," said Tréville, "not to accept the proposal I am about to make to you."

"Make it, monsieur, I am listening."

"How is Monsieur Bernajoux, your equerry's relative?"

"Very ill indeed, monsieur! In addition to the sword thrust in his arm, which is not dangerous, he received another right through his lungs, which the doctor finds quite alarming."

"But has he remained conscious?"

"Yes."

"Does he talk?"

"With difficulty, but yes."

"Well, monsieur, let us ask him, in the name of the God before whom he must perhaps soon appear, to speak the truth. I will let him be the judge of his own cause and will believe what he says."

M. de la Trémouille thought for a moment, then decided it was a reasonable suggestion and agreed to it.

They went down to the room in which the wounded man was lying. The latter, seeing the two noble lords coming to visit him, tried to raise himself up in his bed; but he was too weak, and exhausted by the effort, he fell back again almost senseless.

M. de la Trémouille approached him and made him inhale some salts, which revived him. Then M. de Tréville, unwilling to be accused of having influenced the wounded man, asked M. de la Trémouille to question him himself.

What happened was what M. de Tréville had foreseen: Bernajoux, between life and death, had no thought of concealing the truth, and he described the affair to the two noblemen exactly as it had happened.

That was all M. de Tréville wanted. He wished Bernajoux a speedy convalescence, took leave of M. de la Trémouille, returned home, and immediately sent word to the four friends that he was inviting them for dinner.

M. de Tréville entertained distinguished but solely anticardinalist company, so all the conversation during dinner was about the two defeats suffered by his Eminence's Guardsmen. Because d'Artagnan had been the hero of those two fights, all the glory fell to him—a situation that Athos, Porthos, and Aramis generously accepted not only as good comrades but as men who had so often had their turn that they could very easily allow him his.

Toward six o'clock M. de Tréville announced that it was time to go to the Louvre; but since the original time set by his Majesty was past, he did not use the entrance reached by the private stairs but waited with the four young men in the anteroom. The king had not yet returned from the hunt, and they had been waiting about half an hour among a crowd of courtiers when all the doors were thrown open, and his Majesty was announced.

D'Artagnan was quivering in every fiber of his being. The next few minutes would in all probability decide the rest of his life, so his eyes were fixed anxiously on the door through which the king must enter.

Louis XIII appeared, walking fast. He was in his dust-covered hunting costume, wearing high boots and holding a whip in his hand. At a glance d'Artagnan could see that the king's mood was stormy.

Visible as this was in his Majesty's bearing, it did not prevent the courtiers from ranging themselves along his path: in royal anterooms it is better to be seen with an angry eye than not to be seen at all. The three Musketeers therefore did not hesitate to step forward, while d'Artagnan remained concealed behind them; but although the king knew Athos, Porthos, and Aramis personally, he passed in front of them without speaking to them, without looking at them—indeed, as if he had never seen them before. As for M. de Tréville, when the king's eyes met his, he sustained the look so firmly that it was the king who turned away first—after which his Majesty, grumbling, entered his apartments.

"Things are going badly," said Athos, smiling, "and we will not be made Chevaliers this time."

"Wait here ten minutes," said M. de Tréville, "and if at the end of that time you do not see me come out, return to my house because it will be useless to wait for me any longer."

The four young men waited ten minutes, a quarter of an hour, twenty minutes; then, seeing that M. de Tréville did not return, they left, very uneasy about what was going to happen.

M. de Tréville had entered the king's study boldly, and found his Majesty in a very bad temper, seated on an armchair and tapping his boot with the handle of his whip. This did not prevent Tréville from coolly asking about his Majesty's health.

"It's bad, monsieur!" replied the king. "I am bored."

In fact this was the worst complaint of Louis XIII, who would sometimes take one of his courtiers to a window and say, "Monsieur So-and-so, let us be bored together."

"Your Majesty is bored? Did you not enjoy the pleasures of the hunt today?"

"A fine pleasure, indeed, monsieur! Upon my soul, everything is in a state of decline, and I don't know if the animals have stopped leaving any scent or if the dogs no longer have a sense of smell. We started a ten-branch stag and chased him for six hours. When he was near being taken—just as St.-Simon was already putting his horn to his mouth to blow the *hallali*—crack, the whole pack of dogs took the wrong scent and set off after a little two-year-old deer! I will be forced to give up stag-hunting, just as I have already given up hawking. Ah, I am an unfortunate king, Monsieur de Tréville! I had but one gyrfalcon left, and he died day before yesterday."

"Indeed, sire, I understand your disappointment. It is a great misfortune, but I think you still have quite a few falcons, sparrow hawks, and tiercelets left."

"And not a man to train them! There are fewer and fewer falconers. I know no one but myself who is acquainted with the noble art of venery. After me it will all be over, and people will hunt only with gins, snares, and traps. If I at least had the time to train pupils! But the cardinal does not leave me a moment's rest—he is always talking to me about Spain or Austria or England! Ah! Apropos of the cardinal, Monsieur de Tréville, I am vexed with you."

This was the chance M. de Tréville had been waiting for. He knew the king of old, and he knew that all those complaints were only a preface—a way to give himself courage—and that he had at last come to his point.

"How have I been so unfortunate as to displease your Majesty?" asked M. de Tréville, pretending the most profound astonishment.

"Is this how you perform your duty, monsieur?" continued the king, without directly replying to Tréville's question. "Have I named you captain of my Musketeers so they could assassinate a man, disturb a whole neighborhood, and try to set fire to Paris without your saying a word? But perhaps I am being too hasty in accusing you. Undoubtedly the rioters are in prison, and you have come to tell me justice has been done."

"Sire," replied M. de Tréville calmly, "on the contrary, I come to demand it of you."

"Against whom?"

"Against calumniators."

"Ah, this is something new! Are you going to tell me that your three damned Musketeers, Athos, Porthos, and Aramis, and your youngster from Béarn, have not attacked, like so many furies, poor Bernajoux, wounding him so seriously that by this time he is probably dead? Are you going to tell me that they did not lay siege to the Duc de la Trémouille's house and try to burn it? That would not perhaps be a great misfortune in time of war, since the house is nothing but a nest of Huguenots, but in time of peace it is a bad example. Tell me, can you deny all this?"

"And who told you this fine story, sire?" asked Tréville quietly.

"Who told me, monsieur? Who should it be but the one who watches while I sleep, who labors while I amuse myself, who controls everything at home and abroad, in France as in Europe?"

"Your Majesty is probably referring to God, because I know no one except God who can be so far above your Majesty."

"No, monsieur, I am speaking of the prop of the state, of my only servant, of my only friend—I am speaking of the cardinal."

"His Eminence is not his Holiness, sire."

"What do you mean, monsieur?"

"That only the Pope is infallible, and that this infallibility does not extend to cardinals."

"You mean to say that he deceives me? You mean to say that he betrays me? You are accusing him? Come, speak up—admit that you are accusing him!"

"No, sire, but I do say that he deceives himself. I say that he is ill-informed. I say that he has hastily accused your Majesty's Musketeers, toward whom he is unjust, and that he has not obtained his information from good sources."

"The accusation comes from Monsieur de la Trémouille, from the duke himself. What do you say to that?"

"I might answer, sire, that he is too deeply concerned in the question to be a very impartial witness. But I know the duke to be an honorable gentleman, so on the contrary I will accept his statement—but on one condition, sire."

"What condition?"

"That your Majesty will make him come here, will question him yourself, alone and without witnesses, and that your Majesty will see me as soon as you have seen the duke and before you see anyone else."

"You will agree to accept what Monsieur de la Trémouille says?"

"Yes, sire."

"You will not dispute his judgment?"

"I will not."

"And you will submit to whatever reparation he may demand?"

"Certainly."

"La Chesnaye!" exclaimed the king. "La Chesnaye!"

Louis XIII's confidential servant, who was always at the door, entered in reply to the summons.

"La Chesnaye," said the king, "let someone go instantly and find Monsieur de la Trémouille. I wish to speak with him this evening."

"Your Majesty gives me your word that you will not see anyone between Monsieur de la Trémouille and myself?"

"No one, by the word of a gentleman."

"Till tomorrow, then, sire."

"Till tomorrow, monsieur."

"At what time, your Majesty?"

"Any time you wish."

"But if I come too early I would be afraid of awakening your Majesty."

"Awaken me! Do you think I ever sleep? I sleep no longer, monsieur. I sometimes dream, but that is all.

Come as early as you like—at seven o'clock. But beware if you and your Musketeers are guilty!"

"If my Musketeers are guilty, sire, the guilty shall be placed in the hands of your Majesty, who will dispose of them as you will. Does your Majesty require anything further? Speak, I am ready to obey."

"No, monsieur, no. I am not called Louis the Just without reason. Till tomorrow, then, monsieur."

"Till then, God preserve your Majesty!"

However badly the king slept, M. de Tréville slept still worse. He had ordered his three Musketeers and their companion to be with him at half past six in the morning. He took them with him, without encouraging them or promising them anything, and without concealing from them that their luck, and even his own, depended on a cast of the dice.

When they reached the foot of the private staircase, he asked them to wait. If the king was still irritated with them, they would leave without being seen; if the king consented to see them, they would only have to be called.

On arriving at the king's private anteroom, M. de Tréville found La Chesnaye, who told him that they had not been able to find M. de la Trémouille at home on the preceding evening, that he had returned there too late to then present himself at the Louvre, that he had just arrived and was at that very moment with the king.

This pleased M. de Tréville very much, because it meant that no outside influence could insinuate itself between M. de la Trémouille's testimony and his own audience with the king.

In fact, ten minutes had barely elapsed when the door of the king's study opened, and M. de Tréville saw M. de la Trémouille come out.

The duke came straight up to him, and said, "Monsieur de Tréville, his Majesty has just sent for me in order to inquire about what took place yesterday at my house. I have told him the truth, which is that the fault lay with my people and that I was ready to offer you my apologies. Since I have the good fortune to meet you here, I beg you to receive that apology and to consider me always as one of your friends."

"Monsieur de la Trémouille," M. de Tréville replied,

"I was so confident of your integrity that I asked for no defender other than yourself before his Majesty. I find that I was not mistaken, and I thank you for being one man in France of whom may be said, without disappointment, what I have said of you."

"Good! Good!" cried the king, who had heard their mutual compliments through the open door. "But tell him, Tréville, since he wishes to be considered your friend, that I would also wish to be one of his, but he neglects me—that it is nearly three years since I last saw him and that I never do see him unless I send for him. Tell him this for me, for these are things a king cannot say for himself."

"Thank you, sire," said the duke, "but your Majesty may be assured that it is not those—I do not speak of Monsieur de Tréville—whom your Majesty sees at all hours of the day that are the most devoted to you."

"Ah, you heard what I said? So much the better, Duke, so much the better," said the king, advancing toward the door. "Tréville, where are your Musketeers? I told you the day before yesterday to bring them with you—why have you not done so?"

"They are below, sire, and with your permission La Chesnaye will tell them to come up."

"Yes, let them come up immediately. It is nearly eight o'clock, and at nine I expect a visit. Go, Duke, and be sure to return often. Come in, Tréville."

The duke bowed and left. Just as he opened the door, the three Musketeers and d'Artagnan, conducted by La Chesnaye, appeared at the top of the staircase.

"Come in, my brave young men," said the king, "because I am going to scold you."

The Musketeers advanced, bowing; d'Artagnan followed closely behind them.

"What the devil!" continued the king. "Seven of his Eminence's Guards killed or wounded by you four men in two days! That's too many, gentlemen! If you go on like that, his Eminence will have to renew his company in three weeks, and I will have to enforce the edicts in all their severity. One now and then, well, I don't say too much about it—but seven in two days is too many, far too many!"

"For that reason, sire, your Majesty can see that they

have come, quite contrite and repentant, to offer you their excuses."

"Quite contrite and repentant! Humph!" said the king. "I place no confidence in their hypocritical faces, especially since one of them has the look of a Gascon. Come here, monsieur."

D'Artagnan, who understood that this compliment was addressed to him, approached, assuming a most woebegone air.

"Why, you told me he was a young man. This is a boy, Tréville, a mere boy! Do you mean to say that it was he who gave Jussac that severe thrust?"

"And those two equally fine ones to Bernajoux."

"Unbelievable!"

"Without considering," said Athos, "that if he had not rescued me from the hands of Cahusac, I would certainly not now have the honor of paying my very humble respects to your Majesty."

"Why, he is a very devil, this Béarnais! *Ventre-saint-gris*, Monsieur de Tréville, as the king my father would have said. But many doublets are probably slashed and many swords broken at this sort of work, and Gascons are always poor, are they not?"

"Sire, I can assure you that they have so far discovered no gold mines in their mountains; though the Lord owes them such a miracle as a reward for the way in which they supported the king your father."

"Which is to say, since I am my father's son, that the Gascons made a king of me, too, is that not so, Tréville? Well, happily, I don't disagree. La Chesnaye, go see if by rummaging through all my pockets you can find forty pistoles, and if you can, bring them to me. And now, young man, with your hand on your conscience, how did it all happen?"

D'Artagnan related the adventure of the previous day in all its details: how, not having been able to sleep because of his joy at the prospect of seeing his Majesty, he had gone to his friends three hours before the time of audience; how they had gone together to the tennis court; and how, because he had been afraid of being struck in the face by a tennis ball, he had left the game and been jeered at by Bernajoux, who had nearly paid for his jeer with his life, and M. de la Trémouille, who had nothing to do with the matter, had almost lost his house.

"This is all true," murmured the king. "It is exactly the same account the duke gave me of the affair. Poor cardinal! Seven men in two days, and those his very best! But that is quite enough, gentlemen—please understand, that is enough! You have taken your revenge for the Rue Férou, and even exceeded it. Be satisfied."

"If your Majesty is," said Tréville, "we are."

"Oh, yes, I am," replied the king, taking some gold coins from La Chesnaye and putting them into d'Artagnan's hand. "Here is a proof of my satisfaction."

At that time, the ideas of pride which are in fashion in our own day did not prevail. A gentleman could receive money from the king, from hand to hand, and not be at all humiliated, so d'Artagnan put his forty pistoles into his pocket without any scruples—on the contrary, thanking his Majesty profusely.

"It is half past eight," said the king, looking at a clock. "You may retire—as I told you, I expect someone at nine. Thank you for your devotion, gentlemen. I may continue to rely upon it, may I not?"

"Oh, sire," cried the four companions with one voice, "we would allow ourselves to be cut to pieces in your Majesty's service!"

"Good, good. But keep whole—that will be better, and you will be more useful to me. Tréville," added the king in a low voice as the others were withdrawing, "since you have no room in the Musketeers, and since we have decided that an apprenticeship is necessary before entering that corps, place this young man in the company of the Guards of Monsieur Des Essarts, your brother-in-law. Oh, Tréville, I am enjoying in advance the face the cardinal will make! He will be furious, but I don't care. I am doing what is right."

The king waved his hand to Tréville, who left him and rejoined the Musketeers, whom he found dividing the forty pistoles with d'Artagnan.

The cardinal, as his Majesty had predicted, was indeed furious, so furious that he stayed away from the king's gaming table for a week, which did not prevent the king from being as polite to him as possible whenever he met him, or from asking in the kindest tone, "Well, Monsieur Cardinal, how are your poor Jussac and your poor Bernajoux doing?"

7

The Musketeers at Home

WHEN LEAVING THE LOUVRE d'Artagnan had consulted his friends about how best to use his share of the forty pistoles. Athos advised him to order a good meal at the Pomme-de-Pin, Porthos to hire a lackey, and Aramis to provide himself with a suitable mistress.

The meal was enjoyed that very day, and the lackey waited at table. The meal had been ordered by Athos, and the lackey furnished by Porthos. He was a Picard, whom the glorious Musketeer had found on the Tournelle Bridge, making rings by spitting into the water. Porthos had decided that this occupation was proof of a reflective and contemplative nature, and he had hired him immediately, without any other recommendation.

Planchet—that was the Picard's name—had been impressed by the noble bearing of the gentlemen he believed would be his master, and was therefore disappointed to learn that Porthos already had a servant named Mousqueton, that the household could not support two servants, and that he would have to enter d'Artagnan's service. Nevertheless, when he waited at d'Artagnan's dinner and saw him take out a handful of gold to pay for it, he believed his fortune made, and thanked heaven for having brought him into the service of such a Crœsus. He preserved this opinion even after the feast, the remains of which enabled him to make up for his own long fast; but when he made his master's bed in the evening, Planchet's illusions faded away. The bed was the only one in the apartment, which consisted of an anteroom and a bedroom. Planchet slept in the anteroom, on a blanket taken from d'Artagnan's bed; d'Artagnan, from that time on, did without.

Athos, on his part, had a servant whom he had trained in a thoroughly peculiar fashion and who was named Grimaud. This worthy gentleman—we mean Athos, of course—was very taciturn: during the five or six years that he had lived in the closest intimacy with Porthos and Aramis, they could remember having often seen him smile, but had never heard him laugh. His words were few and expressive, conveying all that was meant and no more: no embellishments, no frills, no flourishes. His conversation was factual, without any commentary or speculation.

Although he was not quite thirty years old and extremely handsome and intelligent, no one knew if he had ever had a mistress. He never spoke about women. He certainly did not prevent others from speaking about them in his presence, but it was easy to see that this kind of conversation—to which he added only bitter and misanthropic remarks—was very disagreeable to him. His reserve, his lack of sociability, and his silence made almost an old man of him. In order not to disturb his habits, he had accustomed Grimaud to obey him at a simple gesture or movement of his lips, never speaking to him except under the most extraordinary circumstances.

Sometimes Grimaud, who feared his master as he did fire—though he was completely devoted to him and felt a great respect for his talents—would think he had perfectly understood an order, fly to execute it and do precisely the opposite of what Athos had meant. Athos would then shrug his shoulders and, without anger, thrash Grimaud. On those days he spoke a little.

Porthos, as we have seen, was his exact opposite. He not only talked a lot, but he talked loudly—little caring, we must admit, if anybody listened to him or not. He talked for the pleasure of talking and the pleasure of hearing himself talk. He talked about all subjects except scholarly ones, claiming an inveterate hatred of scholars since childhood. He was not so noble-looking as Athos, and the consciousness of his inferiority in this respect had at the beginning of their intimacy often made him treat that gentleman unjustly, trying, for example, to eclipse him by his splendid dress. But with only his simple Musketeer's uniform and the way in which he threw back his head and advanced his foot, Athos would instantly take

the place that was his due and consign the ostentatious
Porthos to a secondary rank. Porthos consoled himself
by filling the anteroom of M. de Tréville and the guard-
room of the Louvre with accounts of his love affairs,
and at the present moment, after having progressed from
professional ladies to military ladies, from the lawyer's
wife to the baroness, there was talk of nothing less than
a foreign princess who was enormously fond of him.

An old proverb says, "Like master like man." Let us
turn, then, from Athos's lackey to Porthos's—from Grimaud to Mousqueton.

Mousqueton was a Norman, whose real but unthreat-
ening name of Boniface his master had changed into the
infinitely more warlike one of Mousqueton. On entering
Porthos's service, he had asked only to be clothed and
lodged, though in a magnificent manner; but he also
claimed two hours a day to himself, which he would
employ in such a way that they would provide for his
other wants. Porthos had agreed to the bargain; the
arrangement suited him perfectly. He had Mousqueton's
doublets cut out of his own old clothes, and thanks to a
very skillful tailor, who made his clothes look as good as
new by turning them and whose wife was suspected of
wishing to make Porthos descend from his aristocratic
amours, Mousqueton made a fine figure when attending
his master.

As for Aramis—whose character we believe we have
already sufficiently explained and which, like that of
his companions, we will be able to follow in its develop-
ment—his lackey was called Bazin. Because of his master's hopes of someday taking orders, Bazin was always
dressed in black, as befits the servant of a churchman.
He was from Berry, about thirty-five or forty years old,
mild, peaceable, sleek, employing his leisure time in the
perusal of pious works, providing intimate dinners for
two consisting of few but excellent dishes. For the rest,
he was blind, deaf, and mute, and of unswerving loyalty.

And now that we are at least superficially acquainted
with the masters and their servants, let us turn to the
dwellings occupied by each of them.

Athos lived on the Rue Férou, very close to the Luxembourg. His apartment consisted of two small rooms,
very nicely arranged, in a house owned by a still young

and quite attractive woman who cast—in vain—tender
glances at him. Some fragments of past splendor appeared
here and there on the walls of this modest lodging: a
sword, for example, richly embossed, which clearly had
been made during the time of Francis I and the hilt of
which alone, set with precious stones, was probably
worth two hundred pistoles—and which nevertheless
Athos had never pawned or sold even in his moments of
greatest distress.

That sword had long been an object of ambition for
Porthos, who would have given ten years of his life to
own it. One day, when he had an appointment with a
duchess, he asked to borrow it. Athos, without saying a
word, emptied his pockets, got together all his jewels,
purses, aiguillettes, and gold chains, and offered them all
to Porthos; but as to the sword, he said it was secured
to its place and would never leave it until its master himself left his lodgings.

In addition to the sword, there was a portrait representing a nobleman in the time of Henry III, dressed
very elegantly and wearing the Order of the Holy Ghost;
this portrait had a certain resemblance to Athos, a certain family likeness which indicated that this great lord
was his ancestor.

Besides these, a chest with magnificent goldwork,
bearing the same arms as the sword and the portrait,
formed a middle ornament of the mantelpiece and
clashed badly with the rest of the furniture. Athos always
carried the key of this chest with him; but one day he
had opened it in front of Porthos, who was then convinced that it contained nothing but letters and papers—
love letters and family papers, no doubt.

Porthos lived in a large and very sumptuous-looking
apartment on the Rue de Vieux-Colombier. Every time
he passed with a friend in front of his windows, at one of
which Mousqueton was sure to be standing in full livery,
Porthos would raise his head and his hand and say, "That
is my residence!" But he was never to be found at home;
he never invited anybody to go up with him; and no one
had any idea of what that sumptuous-seeming apartment
contained in the way of real riches.

Aramis lived in a little ground-floor lodging composed
of a sitting room, a dining room, and a bedroom, which

latter looked out on a small, shady, green garden that was impenetrable to the eyes of his neighbors.

We already know how d'Artagnan was lodged, and we have already met his lackey, Master Planchet.

D'Artagnan, who was by nature very curious—as people who possess a genius for intrigue generally are—did all he could to discover who Athos, Porthos, and Aramis really were, for under those pseudonyms each of the young men concealed an aristocratic family name—especially Athos, who was unmistakably a member of the highest nobility. He asked Porthos about Athos and Aramis, and Aramis about Porthos.

Unfortunately Porthos knew nothing more about the life of his silent companion than what everyone knew. It was said that Athos had met with great disappointments in love and that some terrible treachery had poisoned his life forever. What could that treachery have been? No one knew.

As for Porthos, except for his real name, which only M. de Tréville knew (as was also the case with those of his two comrades), his life was no mystery. Vain and indiscreet, he was as easily seen through as a crystal. The only thing that might have misled an investigator would have been to believe all the good things he said about himself.

With respect to Aramis, despite his air of having no secrets, he was a young fellow made up of mysteries, answering little when questioned about others and eluding those about himself. One day d'Artagnan, having for a long time examined him about Porthos and having heard from him about his supposed success with a princess, wished to learn a little about Aramis's own amorous adventures.

"And what about you, my friend," he said, "you who speak of the baronesses, countesses, and princesses of others?"

"*Pardieu!* I spoke about them because Porthos spoke about them himself, because he has paraded all those fine stories in front of me. But be assured, my dear Monsieur d'Artagnan, that if I had learned about them from any other source, or if they had been confided to me, there would be no confessor more discreet than myself."

"Oh, I don't doubt that," replied d'Artagnan. "But it seems to me that you also are quite familiar with coats of arms—a certain embroidered handkerchief, for instance, to which I owe the honor of your acquaintance . . ."

This time Aramis was not angry but assumed a modest air and replied in a friendly tone, "My friend, do not forget that I wish to belong to the Church and that I avoid all worldly occasions. The handkerchief you saw had not been given to me, but it had been forgotten and left at my house by one of my friends. I was obliged to pick it up in order not to compromise him and the lady he loves. As for myself, I neither have, nor desire to have, a mistress, following in that respect the very judicious example of Athos, who has none any more than I have."

"But what the devil—you are not a priest, you are a Musketeer!"

"A Musketeer only for a time, as the cardinal says. I am a Musketeer against my will and a churchman at heart, believe me. Athos and Porthos brought me into the Musketeers to occupy me. Just before I was to be ordained, I had a little difficulty with . . . But that would not interest you, and I am taking up your valuable time."

"Not at all—it interests me very much," said d'Artagnan. "And at this moment I have absolutely nothing to do."

"But *I* have my breviary to repeat," answered Aramis, "and then I must compose some verses for Madame d'Aiguillon. After that, I must go to the Rue St. Honoré to buy some rouge for Madame de Chevreuse. So you see, my friend, that even if you are not in a hurry, I am." And Aramis cordially held out his hand to his young companion and took leave of him.

Despite all his efforts, d'Artagnan was unable to learn any more about his three new friends. He therefore resolved to believe for the present all that was said of their past and hope for more reliable and extensive revelations in the future. Meanwhile he looked upon Athos as an Achilles, Porthos as an Ajax, and Aramis as a Joseph.

As to the rest, the life of the four young friends was joyous enough. Athos gambled, and as a rule, without much luck. Nevertheless, he never borrowed a sou from his companions, although his purse was always at *their* service, and when he had played on credit, he always awakened his creditor by six o'clock the next morning to pay the debt of the preceding evening.

Porthos also had intervals when he gambled. If he won he was insolent and ostentatious; if he lost, he disappeared completely for several days, then reappeared, thinner and paler, but with money in his purse.

Aramis never gambled. He was the most unusual Musketeer and the most unconvivial companion imaginable. He always had something or other to do. In the middle of dinner, when everyone was enjoying the wine and the lively conversation and believed they still had two or three hours more of such pleasure to come, Aramis would sometimes look at his watch, rise with a bland smile, and take leave of the company—to consult a theologian with whom he had an appointment, he said. At other times he would return home to write a treatise and ask his friends not to disturb him.

At this Athos would smile that charming, melancholy smile so becoming to his noble face, and Porthos would drink some more, swearing that Aramis would never be anything but a village priest.

Planchet, d'Artagnan's servant, behaved very well during the period of good fortune. He received thirty sous a day, and for a month he would return to his lodgings gay as a chaffinch and quite affable toward his master. When the wind of adversity began to blow on the household of the Rue des Fossoyeurs—that is, when the forty pistoles of the king were spent or nearly so—he began to complain in a way that Athos thought sickening, Porthos indecent, and Aramis ridiculous. Athos advised d'Artagnan to dismiss the fellow; Porthos believed that he should give him a good thrashing first; and Aramis contended that a master should never pay attention to anything but a servant's compliments.

"That is very easy for all of you to say," replied d'Artagnan. "You, Athos, live like a dumb man with Grimaud and forbid him to speak, so of course you never have to exchange any words with him at all. You, Porthos, have such a magnificent style that you are a god to Mousqueton. And you, Aramis, are always abstracted by your theological studies and inspire Bazin, who is a mild, religious man, with profound respect. But I am without any income, without any resources, and I am neither a Musketeer nor even a Guardsman—what can I do to inspire either affection, terror, or respect in Planchet?"

"This is a serious problem," answered the three friends. "It is a domestic affair, and it is with servants as with wives—they must be placed at once on the footing in which you wish them to remain. Think about it."

D'Artagnan did think about it and decided to thrash Planchet as a warning, which he did with the conscientious attention that he brought to everything. Then, after having given him a thorough beating, he forbade him to leave his service without his permission, adding, "The future cannot fail to mend. Better times will certainly come and that means your fortune is made if you remain with me. I am too good a master to allow you to miss such a chance by allowing you to leave."

This solution aroused much respect for d'Artagnan's policy among the Musketeers. Planchet was equally filled with admiration and said no more about going away.

The life of the four young men had become communal. D'Artagnan had no settled habits of his own, and since he came from his province into a world quite new to him, he fell easily into those of his friends.

They rose about eight o'clock in winter, about six in summer, and went to M. de Tréville's to get the password and see how things were going. Although d'Artagnan was not a Musketeer, he performed the duty of one with touching fidelity. He was always on guard duty because he always accompanied whichever of his friends was on duty. He was well known to all the Musketeers, and everyone considered him a good comrade. M. de Tréville, who had appreciated him at the first glance and who now felt a real affection for him, never stopped recommending him to the king.

The three Musketeers were also much attached to their young comrade. The friendship that united the four men, and the desire they had to see one another three or four times a day, whether for dueling, business, or pleasure, caused them to be continually running after one another like shadows; and the Inseparables were constantly to be seen seeking one another between the Luxembourg and the Place St. Sulpice or the Rue du Vieux-Colombier.

Meanwhile M. de Tréville's promises were being kept. One fine morning the king commanded M. le Chevalier

Des Essarts to admit d'Artagnan as a cadet in his company of Guards. D'Artagnan sighed as he put on his uniform, which he would have given ten years of his life to exchange for that of a Musketeer. But M. de Tréville promised him this favor after a two-year apprenticeship that might even be shortened if an opportunity should present itself for d'Artagnan to render the king any notable service or to distinguish himself by some brilliant action. With that promise d'Artagnan had to be content, and the next day he began his service.

Then it became the turn of Athos, Porthos, and Aramis to mount guard with d'Artagnan when he was on duty, so M. le Chevalier Des Essarts's company acquired four men instead of one when it admitted d'Artagnan.

8

A Court Intrigue

IN THE MEANTIME, the forty pistoles of King Louis XIII, like all other things of this world, after having had a beginning had an end, and after that end our four companions began to be somewhat financially embarrassed. At first, Athos supported the group for a time with his own means. Then Porthos succeeded him, and thanks to one of his customary disappearances, he was able to provide for them for two weeks. After that it fell to Aramis, who took his turn with good grace and who succeeded in procuring a few pistoles by selling some theological books.

Finally, as was their custom, they had recourse to M. de Tréville, who gave them an advance on their pay; but such an advance could not go far with three Musketeers who were already much in debt and a Guardsman who as yet had no pay at all.

When they found they were about to be really in need, they managed to get together nine or ten pistoles, with which Porthos went to the gaming table. Unfortunately he had a run of bad luck; he lost everything, as well as twenty-five pistoles he had given his word to repay.

The inconvenience became distress. The hungry friends,

followed by their lackeys, were seen haunting the quays and guardrooms, accepting from their acquaintances all the dinner invitations that came their way, for they had followed Aramis's advice and had prudently sown meals right and left in their prosperity so as to reap a few in their time of need.

Athos was invited four times and each time took his friends and their lackeys with him. Porthos had six invitations and also contrived that his friends should partake of them. Aramis had eight: he was a man, as we have already seen, who said little but did much.

Since d'Artagnan still knew nobody in Paris, he was able to garner only one chocolate breakfast at the house of a priest from his own province, and one dinner at the house of an ensign of the Guards. He took his army to the priest's, where they devoured as much food as would have lasted the cleric for two months, and to the ensign's, who performed wonders; but as Planchet said, "People do not eat at once for all time, even when they eat a good deal."

D'Artagnan felt humiliated by having provided only one meal and a half for his companions—the breakfast at the priest's could be counted only as half a meal—in return for the feasts that Athos, Porthos, and Aramis had provided. He imagined himself a burden to the group, forgetting in his youthful generosity that he had fed them all for a month, and he set his mind to work. He felt that such a coalition of four young, brave, enterprising, and active men ought to have some better object than swaggering walks, fencing lessons, and more or less witty practical jokes.

In fact, four such men, devoted to one another with their lives as well as their purses; four men always supporting one another, never yielding, executing singly or together the plans they made together; four arms ready to attack at the four cardinal points or to join together in a single attack—four such men must inevitably, surreptitiously or openly, by cunning or by force, clear a way toward the goal they wished to reach, however well it might be defended or however distant it might seem. The only thing that surprised d'Artagnan was that his friends had not yet thought of this.

He was thinking of it, seriously racking his brain to

find a direction for this single force four times multiplied—with which he did not doubt that they should succeed in moving the world—when someone tapped gently at his door. D'Artagnan awakened Planchet and ordered him to open it.

From the phrase "D'Artagnan awakened Planchet," the reader must not suppose it was night or that day was hardly come. No, it had just struck four o'clock in the afternoon. Two hours earlier, Planchet had asked his master for some dinner, and d'Artagnan had answered him with the proverb, "He who sleeps, dines." So Planchet was dining by sleeping.

Planchet introduced a simply dressed man who looked like a tradesman; by way of dessert, Planchet would have liked to hear the conversation, but the caller told d'Artagnan that what he had to say was important and confidential, and he wished to be left alone with him.

D'Artagnan dismissed Planchet and invited his visitor to be seated.

There was a moment of silence during which the two men looked at each other as if to make a preliminary acquaintance, and then d'Artagnan nodded, as a sign that he was listening.

"I have heard Monsieur d'Artagnan spoken of as a very brave young man," said the visitor, "and this reputation, which he justly enjoys, has decided me to confide a secret to him."

"Speak, monsieur," said d'Artagnan, who instinctively sensed something advantageous in this.

The man paused again and continued.

"I have a wife who is the queen's linen maid, monsieur, and who is not lacking either virtue or beauty. I was persuaded to marry her about three years ago, although she had a very small dowry, because Monsieur de la Porte, the queen's gentleman-in-waiting, is her godfather and befriends her. . . ."

"Go on, monsieur," said d'Artagnan.

"Well, monsieur, my wife was abducted yesterday morning as she was coming out of her workroom."

"And by whom was your wife abducted?"

"I know nothing for sure, monsieur, but I suspect someone."

"And who is the person you suspect?"

"A man who has pursued her for a long time."

"Well!"

"But allow me to tell you, monsieur, that I am convinced there is less love than politics in all this."

"Less love than politics," d'Artagnan said reflectively. "What do you suspect?"

"I do not know if I ought to tell you what I suspect."

"Monsieur, I beg you to observe that I ask you absolutely nothing. It is you who have come to me. It is you who have told me that you had a secret to confide to me. Do what you wish—there is still time to withdraw."

"No, monsieur—you seem to be an honest young man, and I will trust you. I think that it was not because of any affair of her own that my wife has been abducted, but because of that of a lady much greater than herself."

"Ah! Can it be because of Madame de Bois-Tracy?" said d'Artagnan, wishing to give the impression of being aware of court affairs.

"Higher, monsieur, higher."

"Of Madame d'Aiguillon?"

"Still higher."

"Of Madame de Chevreuse?"

"Much higher."

"Of the——" d'Artagnan checked himself.

"Yes, monsieur," the terrified man replied in a tone so low that he was scarcely audible.

"With whom?"

"With whom can it be, if not with the Duke of . . ."

"The Duke of . . ."

"Yes, monsieur," the man said, his voice even fainter.

"But how do you know that?"

"How do I know it?"

"Yes, how do you know it? No half-confidences, or . . . you understand!"

"I know it from my wife herself."

"Who knows it from whom?"

"From Monsieur de la Porte. Didn't I tell you that she was the goddaughter of Monsieur de la Porte, the queen's confidential agent? Well, he found my wife employment near her Majesty in order that our poor queen might have someone on whom she could rely, since she is abandoned by the king, watched by the cardinal, and betrayed by everybody."

"I begin to understand . . ." said d'Artagnan.

"My wife came home on a visit four days ago, monsieur—it was agreed that she could come see me twice a week because, as I have said, she loves me dearly—and confided to me that the queen was very frightened."

"Really?"

"Yes. The cardinal is apparently pursuing and persecuting her more than ever. He cannot forgive her for the incident of the Saraband. You know about the Saraband?"

"Know it!" replied d'Artagnan, who knew nothing about it but who wished to appear to know everything that was going on.

"So he no longer just feels hatred, but he wants vengeance as well."

"Really?"

"And the queen believes . . ."

"Well, what does the queen believe?"

"She believes that someone has written to the Duke of Buckingham in her name."

"In the queen's name?"

"Yes, to make him come to Paris and, when he is here, to draw him into a trap."

"But what does your wife have to do with all this?"

"Her devotion to the queen is known, and those who abducted her must want to separate her from her mistress, or to intimidate her in order to obtain her Majesty's secrets, or to seduce her and make use of her as a spy."

"That is all very possible," said d'Artagnan. "But the man who has abducted her—do you know him?"

"I told you that I think I know him."

"What is his name?"

"I do not know. What I do know is that he is the cardinal's man, his evil genius."

"But you have seen him?"

"Yes, my wife pointed him out to me one day."

"Does he have any special characteristics by which one may recognize him?"

"Oh, yes, he is a noble of very lofty carriage, black hair, swarthy complexion, piercing eyes, white teeth, and a scar on his temple."

"A scar on his temple!" d'Artagnan exclaimed. "And with that, white teeth, piercing eyes, dark complexion, black hair, and haughty bearing—why, that's my man of Meung."

"What do you mean, your 'man of Meung'?"

"Never mind, that has nothing to do with it. No, I am wrong—on the contrary, it simplifies the matter greatly because if your man is mine, then with one blow I will obtain two revenges. Where can I find this man?"

"I do not know."

"Have you no idea about where he lives?"

"None. One day, as I was escorting my wife back to the Louvre, he was coming out as she was going in, and she pointed him out to me."

"All this is very vague," murmured d'Artagnan. "From whom have you learned about your wife's abduction?"

"From Monsieur de la Porte."

"Did he give you any details?"

"He knew none himself."

"And you have learned nothing from anyone else?"

"Yes, I have received . . ."

"What?"

"I am afraid I am being very imprudent."

"You always come back to that, but I must make you see that this time it is too late to retreat."

"I do not retreat, by God!" cried the man, swearing in order to rouse his courage. " Besides, by the word of Bonacieux——"

"You call yourself Bonacieux?" d'Artagnan interrupted.

"Yes, that is my name."

"You said, 'by the word of Bonacieux.' Excuse me for interrupting you, but I think the name is familiar to me."

"Possibly, monsieur. I am your landlord."

"Ah," said d'Artagnan, half rising and bowing, "you are my landlord?"

"Yes, monsieur. And since you have been here for three months and—distracted as you must be by your important occupations—have forgotten to pay me my rent—and since I have not tormented you about it even once, I thought you might appreciate my tact."

"How can it be otherwise, my dear Bonacieux?" replied d'Artagnan. "Believe me, I am grateful for such unusual conduct, and if, as I have told you, I can be of any service to you . . ."

"I believe you, monsieur, and as I was about to say, by the word of Bonacieux, I have confidence in you."

"Then finish what you were about to say."

M. Bonacieux took a sheet of paper from his pocket and gave it to d'Artagnan.

"A letter?" said the young man.

"I received it this morning."

D'Artagnan opened it, and since the daylight was fading, he approached the window to read it. Bonacieux followed him.

" 'Do not seek your wife,' " read d'Artagnan. " 'She will be restored to you when there is no longer any need for her. If you make a single step to find her, you are lost.'

"That's pretty definite," continued d'Artagnan, "but after all, it is only a threat."

"Yes, but that threat terrifies me. I am not a fighting man, monsieur, and I am afraid of the Bastille."

"I have no greater liking for the Bastille than you," said d'Artagnan. "I wouldn't mind if it were only a question of fighting . . ."

"But I have counted on you, monsieur."

"Oh?"

"Seeing you constantly surrounded by superb-looking Musketeers, and knowing that those Musketeers belong to Monsieur de Tréville and are consequently enemies of the cardinal, I thought that you and your friends would be pleased to play his Eminence an ill turn and help our poor queen at the same time."

"Certainly."

"And then I thought that since you owe me three months' rent, about which I have said nothing . . ."

"Yes, yes, you have already given me that reason, and I find it excellent."

"Furthermore, as long as you do me the honor to remain in my house I will *never* speak to you about rent . . ."

"Very kind of you!"

"And finally, if more be needed, I mean to offer you fifty pistoles if you should be short at the present moment—unlikely though that may be."

"Admirable! You are rich then, my dear Monsieur Bonacieux?"

"I am comfortably off, monsieur, that's all. I have an

income of two or three thousand écus a year from money I accumulated in the haberdashery business, and also from investing in the last voyage of the famous navigator Jean Moquet, so that—look!"

"What!" demanded d'Artagnan.

"Look there!"

"Where?"

"In the street, facing your window, in that doorway—a man wrapped in a cloak."

"It is he!" cried d'Artagnan and M. Bonacieux at the same time, each having recognized his man.

"This time he will not escape me!" d'Artagnan exclaimed, reaching for his sword."

Drawing it from its scabbard, he rushed out of the apartment.

On the staircase he met Athos and Porthos, who were coming to see him. They separated, and d'Artagnan darted between them like an arrow.

"Where are you going?" the two Musketeers asked at the same time.

"The man of Meung!" d'Artagnan replied, and disappeared.

He had more than once told his friends about his adventure with the stranger, as well as about the apparition of the beautiful traveler to whom the stranger had confided some important message.

Athos thought that d'Artagnan had lost his letter in the skirmish: a gentleman—and according to d'Artagnan's description, he had to be a gentleman—would be incapable of the baseness of stealing a letter.

Porthos saw nothing in it but a rendezvous given by a lady to a cavalier or by a cavalier to a lady, which had been disturbed by the presence of d'Artagnan and his yellow horse.

Aramis said that affairs of this sort were mysterious, and it was better not to try to get to the bottom of them.

Athos and Porthos therefore understood from d'Artagnan's few words what was happening, and since they thought that he would return to his rooms after either overtaking his man or losing sight of him, they continued upstairs.

When they entered d'Artagnan's apartment, it was empty; the landlord, dreading the consequences of the encounter that was doubtless about to take place between the young man and the stranger, had—consistent with the description of his character that he himself had given—judged it prudent to decamp.

9

D'Artagnan's Merits Become Clear

As Athos and Porthos had foreseen, d'Artagnan returned in a half hour. He had again missed his man, who had disappeared as if by magic. D'Artagnan had run, sword in hand, through all the neighboring streets, but had found nobody resembling the one he was looking for. Then he came back to the point where he ought perhaps to have begun, which was to knock on the door the stranger had been leaning against. This proved useless, however, for though he knocked ten or twelve times, no one answered; and some of the neighbors, who had put their heads out of their windows or had been brought to their doors by the noise, assured him that the house, whose doors and windows were all tightly closed, had been empty for six months.

While d'Artagnan was running through the streets and knocking on doors, Aramis had joined his companions, so when the former returned home, he found the reunion complete.

"Well?" asked the three Musketeers together, seeing d'Artagnan come in with his face covered with perspiration and distorted by anger.

"Well," he said, throwing his sword on the bed, "that man must be the devil himself. He has disappeared like a phantom, like a ghost."

"Do you believe in apparitions?" Athos asked Porthos.

"I never believe in anything I have not seen, and since I have never seen apparitions, I don't believe in them."

"The Bible," said Aramis, "makes our belief in them a law. The ghost of Samuel appeared to Saul, and it is an article of faith that I would be very sorry to see you cast any doubt on Porthos."

"At all events, man or devil, body or shadow, illusion or reality, that man was born to plague me! His disappearance has made us miss a glorious affair, gentlemen— one by which there were a hundred pistoles or maybe more, to be gained."

"How is that?" Porthos and Aramis asked with one voice.

Athos, faithful to his customary reticence, contented himself with interrogating d'Artagnan by a look.

"Planchet," d'Artagnan said to his domestic, who had just then put his head through the half-open door in order to catch some fragments of the conversation, "go down to my landlord, Monsieur Bonacieux, and ask him to send me half a dozen bottles of Beaugency wine."

"Do you have credit with your landlord?" asked Porthos.

"Yes," d'Artagnan replied, "from this very day. And if the wine is bad, we will send him to find better."

"We must use, and not abuse," Aramis said sententiously.

"I always said that d'Artagnan had the best head of us all," said Athos, who having uttered his opinion, which d'Artagnan acknowledged with a bow, immediately resumed his usual silence.

"But what is all this about?" asked Porthos.

"Yes," said Aramis, "tell us, my friend, unless the honor of any lady be threatened by such a confidence, in which case you would do better to keep it to yourself."

"Don't worry," said d'Artagnan. "No one's honor will be at risk because of what I have to tell."

He then related to his friends, word for word, all that had happened between him and his landlord, and explained that the man who had abducted the landlord's wife was the same man with whom he had had the quarrel at the Franc Meunier inn in Meung.

"Your bargain is not a bad one," said Athos, after having tasted the wine like a connoisseur and indicated by a nod that he thought it good, "and we might get fifty or sixty pistoles from Monsieur Bonacieux. But we must decide if those fifty or sixty pistoles are worth risking our four heads."

"But remember," said d'Artagnan, "that there is a woman in the affair—a woman who has been carried off, a woman who is being threatened, perhaps tortured, because she is faithful to her mistress, the queen!"

"Beware, d'Artagnan," said Aramis. "I think you are a little too excited about the fate of Madame Bonacieux. Woman was created for our destruction, and all our miseries come from her."

Hearing this, Athos's face darkened, and he bit his lips.

"It's not Madame Bonacieux about whom I am anxious," said d'Artagnan, "but the queen, whom the king abandons, whom the cardinal persecutes, and who sees the heads of all her friends fall, one after the other."

"Why does she love what we hate most in the world, the Spaniards and the English?"

"Spain is her country," d'Artagnan replied, "and it is very natural that she should love the Spanish, who are the children of the same soil as herself. As for your second reproach, I have heard that she does not love the English, but one Englishman."

"Well, and by my faith," said Athos, "it must be acknowledged that this Englishman is worthy of being loved. I have never seen a man with a nobler air."

"Not to mention that he dresses better than anyone else," said Porthos. "I was at the Louvre on the day when he scattered his pearls, and, *pardieu*, I picked up two that I sold for ten pistoles each. Do you know him, Aramis?"

"As well as you do, gentlemen, because I was among those who seized him in the garden at Amiens, into which Monsieur Putange, the queen's equerry, had taken me. I was in the seminary at the time, and it seemed a cruel trial for the king."

"Which would not prevent me," said d'Artagnan, "if I knew where the Duke of Buckingham was, from taking him by the hand and conducting him to the queen, if only to enrage the cardinal. Because our true, our only, our eternal enemy, gentlemen, is the cardinal, and if we could find a way to frustrate his plans, I would gladly risk my head in doing it."

"And did the haberdasher tell you, d'Artagnan, that the queen thought that Buckingham had been brought over by a forged letter?" Athos asked.

"Yes, he told me that is what she fears."

"Wait a minute," said Aramis.

"What for?" asked Porthos.

"No, go on, while I try to remember something."

"And I am convinced," said d'Artagnan, "that the abduction of the queen's woman is connected with the events we are talking about, and perhaps even with Buckingham's presence in Paris."

"The Gascon is full of ideas," Porthos said admiringly.

"I like to hear him talk," said Athos. "His Gascon accent amuses me."

"Gentlemen," cried Aramis, "listen to this!"

"Let's listen to Aramis," said his three friends.

"Yesterday I was at the house of a doctor of theology, whom I sometimes consult about my studies . . ."

Athos smiled.

"He lives in a quiet neighborhood," Aramis continued. "His tastes and his profession require it. Now, just as I was leaving his house . . ."

Here Aramis paused.

"Well," cried his auditors, "just as you were leaving his house . . ."

Aramis seemed to be having an inner struggle, like a man who finds himself stopped by some unforeseen obstacle while telling a lie; but the eyes of his three friends were fixed on him, their ears were waiting to hear, and there was no way to retreat.

"The doctor has a niece," continued Aramis.

"Ah, he has a niece!" said Porthos, breaking in.

"A very respectable lady," said Aramis.

The three friends burst into laughter.

"Ah, if you laugh at me or don't believe me," replied Aramis, "I will tell you no more."

"We are as believing as Mohammedans and as silent as tombstones," said Athos.

"Then I will continue." Aramis resumed. "This niece sometimes comes to see her uncle and, by chance, was there yesterday at the same time that I was. It was my duty, of course, to offer to conduct her to her carriage."

"Oh, so she has a carriage, this niece of the doctor?" interrupted Porthos, one of whose faults was a great looseness of tongue. "A nice acquaintance, my friend!"

"Porthos," replied Aramis, "I have had the occasion

to observe to you more than once that you are very indiscreet, and that it does you injury among the women."

"Gentlemen, gentlemen," cried d'Artagnan, who was beginning to get a glimpse of the meaning of Aramis's story, "this is serious. Let us try not to jest about it. Go on, Aramis."

"All at once, a tall, dark gentleman . . . Come to think of it, just like yours, d'Artagnan. . . ."

"The same one, perhaps," he said.

"It's possible," continued Aramis. "In any event, he came toward me, accompanied by five or six men who followed about ten paces behind him, and said in the politest tone, 'Duke, and you, madame,' he continued, addressing the lady on my arm—"

"The doctor's niece?"

"Hold your tongue, Porthos," said Athos. "You are insupportable!"

" '—will you please enter this carriage, and that without offering the least resistance or making the least noise?' "

"He took you for Buckingham!" cried d'Artagnan.

"I believe so," replied Aramis.

"But the lady?" asked Porthos.

"He took her for the queen!" said d'Artagnan.

"Exactly," replied Aramis.

"The Gascon is the very devil!" said Athos. "Nothing escapes him!"

"The fact is," said Porthos, "Aramis is the same height and has a similar shape as the duke, but it seems to me that the Musketeer's uniform . . ."

"I was wearing an enormous cloak," said Aramis.

"In July?" exclaimed Porthos. "Is the doctor afraid you might be recognized?"

"I can understand that the spy might have been deceived by your figure, but your face . . ."

"I had a large hat," said Aramis.

"Oh, good Lord, what precautions for the study of theology!" exclaimed Porthos.

"Gentlemen," said d'Artagnan, "let us not lose our time in jesting. Let us separate and try to find the haberdasher's wife—she is the key to the intrigue."

"A woman of such inferior condition! Do you really think so?" said Porthos, curling his lips contemptuously.

"Remember that she is the goddaughter of La Porte, the queen's confidential agent. Besides, her Majesty has probably deliberately chosen her support from the lowly—high heads can be seen from far away, and the cardinal is longsighted."

"Well, first let us make a bargain with the haberdasher, and a good bargain," said Porthos.

"That's useless," d'Artagnan said, "because if he does not pay us, I think we will be well enough paid by another party."

At that moment there was a sudden sound of footsteps on the stairs; the door was thrown violently open, and the unfortunate haberdasher rushed into the room.

"For the love of heaven, save me, gentlemen," he cried. "There are four men come to arrest me. Save me! save me!"

Porthos and Aramis stood up.

"Wait!" cried d'Artagnan, signaling them to replace their half-drawn swords in their scabbards. "It is not courage that is needed, but prudence."

"But we cannot let—" cried Porthos.

"You will let d'Artagnan act as he thinks best," said Athos. "He has, I repeat, the wisest head of any of us, and for my part I declare that I will obey him. Do as you think best, d'Artagnan."

Just then the four men appeared at the door of the anteroom, but seeing four Musketeers standing, their swords at their sides, they hesitated to enter.

"Come in, gentlemen," called d'Artagnan. "You are here in my apartment, and we are all faithful servants of the king and the cardinal."

"Then you will not oppose our executing our orders?" asked one who seemed to be the leader of the party.

"On the contrary, gentlemen, we will help you if necessary."

"Why is he saying that?" grumbled Porthos.

"You are a simpleton," said Athos. "Silence!"

"But you promised me . . ." whispered the poor haberdasher.

"We can only save you by being free ourselves," replied d'Artagnan, speaking softly and quickly, "and if we tried to defend you, they would arrest us with you."

"Nevertheless, it seems . . ."

"Come, gentlemen," d'Artagnan said aloud, "I have no reason to defend this man. I saw him today for the first time, and he can tell you that the occasion was to demand my rent. Isn't that true, Monsieur Bonacieux? Answer!"

"That is the very truth," the haberdasher said, "but Monsieur does not tell you . . ."

"Silence with respect to me, silence with respect to my friends, silence about the queen above all—or you will ruin everybody without saving yourself!" d'Artagnan whispered to M. Bonacieux. "Come, gentlemen," he then said to the Guards, "remove the fellow."

And d'Artagnan pushed the half-stunned man into the agents' hands, saying to him, "You are a shabby old fellow, my man. You came to demand money from me—from a Musketeer! To prison with him! Gentlemen, take him to prison and keep him under key as long as possible—that will give me time to pay him."

The agents were full of thanks as they took away their prey.

As they were leaving, d'Artagnan put his hand on their leader's shoulder.

"May I not drink to your health and you to mine?" said d'Artagnan, filling two glasses with the Beaugency wine he owed to M. Bonacieux's generosity.

"That will do me great honor," replied the leader of the group, "and I accept thankfully."

"Then to your health, monsieur—what is your name?"

"Boisrenard."

"To your health, Monsieur Boisrenard!"

"And to yours, sir! What is your name, if you please?"

"D'Artagnan."

"To your health, Monsieur d'Artagnan."

"And above all others," cried d'Artagnan, as if carried away by his enthusiasm, "to that of the king and the cardinal!"

Boisrenard might have doubted d'Artagnan's sincerity if the wine had been bad, but it was good, and he was convinced.

"What diabolical villainy have you performed here?" Porthos complained when the officer had rejoined his companions and the four friends found themselves alone. "It is a shame for four Musketeers to allow an unfortunate fellow who cried for help to be arrested while they look on! And for a gentleman to drink with a policeman!"

"Porthos," said Aramis, "Athos has already told you that you are a simpleton, and I quite agree. D'Artagnan, you are a great man, and when you occupy Monsieur de Tréville's place, I will ask you to use your influence to secure me an abbey."

"Well, I am amazed," said Porthos. "Do *you* approve of what d'Artagnan has done?"

"Indeed I do," said Athos. "I not only approve of what he has done, but I congratulate him on it."

"And now, gentlemen," said d'Artagnan, without stopping to explain his conduct to Porthos, "all for one, one for all—that is our motto, is it not?"

"And yet . . ." said Porthos.

"Hold out your hand and swear!" cried Athos and Aramis at the same time.

Overruled by their example and grumbling to himself, Porthos nevertheless extended his hand, and the four friends repeated with one voice the motto formulated by d'Artagnan:

"All for one, one for all."

"Good! Now let everyone return to his own home," said d'Artagnan, as if he had done nothing but command all his life. "And be careful—from this moment on, we are at war with the cardinal."

10

A Seventeenth-Century Mousetrap

THE INVENTION of the mousetrap does not date from our day; as soon as societies had formed and invented any kind of police, that police invented mousetraps.

Because the reader may not be familiar with police slang, and because this is the first time since I began writing fifteen years ago that I have used the word in this way, let me explain what a mousetrap is.

When an individual suspected of any crime is arrested in a particular house, the arrest is kept secret and four or five men are stationed in the first room of the house. The door is opened to all who knock, then closed behind them and they are arrested; that way, at the end of two or three days the police have in their hands almost everyone who regularly goes there. And that is a mousetrap.

M. Bonacieux's apartment thus became a mousetrap, and whoever appeared there was taken and questioned by the cardinal's men. Since a separate passage led to the first floor, where d'Artagnan lodged, those who called on him were of course exempt from such detention.

Besides, nobody came there but the three Musketeers, who had all been busy making inquiries, but had discovered nothing. Athos had even questioned M. de Tréville—which, considering the worthy Musketeer's customary reticence, had greatly astonished his captain. But M. de Tréville knew nothing, except that the last time he had seen the cardinal, the king, and the queen, the cardinal had looked very thoughtful, the king uneasy, and the queen's eyes had been red, either from lack of sleep or from tears. But that last circumstance had not seemed unusual, because the queen had slept badly and wept much ever since her marriage.

M. de Tréville asked Athos to remember his duty to the king, and especially to the queen, no matter what happened, and asked him to convey this reminder to his comrades.

D'Artagnan did not leave his apartment. He had converted his room into an observatory, and from his windows he could see all the visitors who were about to be caught. He had also removed the planks from a portion of his floor so that nothing remained but a simple ceiling between him and the room beneath, in which the interrogations were carried out, and he could therefore hear everything that was said between the inquisitors and the accused.

The interrogations were preceded by a careful search of the persons arrested and were almost always worded like this: "Has Madame Bonacieux sent anything to you for her husband or any other person? Has Monsieur Bonacieux sent anything to you for his wife or for any other person? Has either of them confided anything to you by word of mouth?"

"If they knew anything, they would not question people that way," d'Artagnan thought. "Now, what is it they want to know? Why, they want to know if the Duke of Buckingham is in Paris, and if he has had, or is likely to have, an interview with the queen."

From what he heard, this idea seemed quite probable.

In the meantime, the mousetrap continued, and so did d'Artagnan's vigilance.

On the evening of the day after the arrest of poor Bonacieux—just as Athos had left d'Artagnan to report at M. de Tréville's, just as nine o'clock had struck, and just as Planchet, who had not yet made the bed, was beginning his task, there was a knock at the street door, which was instantly opened and shut; someone else had been caught in the mousetrap.

D'Artagnan flew to his hole, laid himself down on the floor at full length, and listened.

He soon heard cries, and then some moans, which someone was trying to stifle. There was no questioning.

"It seems to be a woman," d'Artagnan thought. "They are searching her, she is resisting—they are using force! The scoundrels!"

In spite of his prudence, d'Artagnan could restrain himself only with great difficulty from taking a part in the scene that was going on below.

"But I tell you that I am the mistress of the house, gentlemen! I tell you I am Madame Bonacieux! I tell you I am in the queen's service!" cried the unfortunate woman.

"Madame Bonacieux!" d'Artagnan said softly. "Can I be so lucky as to find what everybody is looking for?"

"You are exactly the one we have been waiting for," declared one of the men.

The voice became more and more indistinct, and the partition shook. The victim was resisting as much as a woman resist four men.

"Please, gentlemen, please," murmured the voice, which now could only be heard making inarticulate sounds.

"They are gagging her—they are going to drag her away!" cried d'Artagnan, springing up from the floor. "My sword! Good, it is right here! Planchet!"

"Monsieur."

"Run and look for Athos, Porthos, and Aramis. One

of them will certainly be at home, and perhaps all three. Tell them to take arms and to come here immediately! Oh—I remember now, Athos is at Monsieur de Tréville's."

"But where are you going, monsieur?"

"I am going down by the window in order to be there the sooner," cried d'Artagnan. "You put back the boards, sweep the floor, leave by the door, then run and do as I told you."

"Oh, monsieur, you will be killed!" cried Planchet.

"Hold your tongue, stupid fellow," said d'Artagnan.

He hung from the edge of the window, then he let himself fall from the first floor, which fortunately was not very high, without doing himself the slightest injury.

He then went straight to the door and knocked, thinking, "I will now be caught in the mousetrap myself, but woe be to the cats that pounce on such a mouse!"

The knocker had scarcely sounded before the tumult ceased, steps approached, the door was opened, and d'Artagnan, sword in hand, rushed into M. Bonacieux's rooms. Activated by a spring, the door slammed shut behind him.

All the residents of Bonacieux's unfortunate house, as well as his closest neighbors, then heard loud cries, stamping feet, clashing swords, and smashing furniture. A moment later, those who had gone to their windows to learn the cause of the noise saw the door open and four men dressed in black not so much *come* out of it, but *fly* out, like so many frightened crows, leaving on the ground and on the corners of the furniture feathers from their wings—that is, patches of their clothes and fragments of their cloaks.

D'Artagnan was the victor—without much effort, it must be confessed, because only one of the men was armed, and even he had defended himself mostly for form's sake. The three others had tried to knock the young man down with chairs, stools, and crockery, but two or three scratches from the Gascon's blade had terrified them. Ten minutes had sufficed for their defeat, and d'Artagnan was master of the battle field.

The neighbors who had opened their windows, with the usual insouciance of Parisians in those times of perpetual riots and disturbances, closed them again as soon as they saw the four men in black flee—their instinct telling them that for the time being the fighting was over. Besides, it was growing late, and then as now, people went to bed early in the Luxembourg neighborhood.

D'Artagnan turned to Mme. Bonacieux: the poor woman sat in the armchair into which she had sunk, more than half unconscious. He examined her with a rapid glance.

She was a charming woman of twenty-five or twenty-six, with dark hair, blue eyes, a slightly turned-up nose, admirable teeth, and a rose-petal complexion. But there ended the signs that might have allowed her to be taken for a lady of rank: her hands were white, but without delicacy; her feet were not those of a woman of quality. Fortunately, d'Artagnan had not yet begun to concern himself with such niceties.

While he was examining Mme. Bonacieux and was, as we have said, looking at her feet, he saw on the ground a fine batiste handkerchief, which he picked up; in the corner was the same monogram he had seen on the handkerchief that had nearly caused him and Aramis to cut each other's throats.

Since then, he had been cautious about monogrammed handkerchiefs, so he therefore placed in the pocket of Mme. Bonacieux the one he had just picked up.

At that moment she regained consciousness. She opened her eyes, looked around her with terror, saw that the apartment was empty and that she was alone with her liberator. She extended her hands to him with a smile. Mme. Bonacieux had the sweetest smile in the world.

"Ah, monsieur," she said, "you have saved me! Allow me to thank you."

"Madame," said d'Artagnan, "I have only done what every gentleman would have done in my place. You owe me no thanks."

"Oh, yes, I do, monsieur, and I hope to prove to you that you have not helped an ingrate. But what could those men, whom I at first took for robbers, have wanted with me, and why is Monsieur Bonacieux not here?"

"Madame, those men were much more dangerous than any robbers could have been, for they are the cardinal's agents, and as for your husband, Monsieur Bonacieux, he is not here because he was taken to the Bastille last night."

"My husband in the Bastille! Oh, my God! What has he done? Poor dear man, he is innocence itself!"

And something like a slight smile passed quickly over her still-terrified features.

"What has he done, madame? I think that his only crime is to be at the same time fortunate and unfortunate enough to be your husband."

"Then you know . . ."

"I know that you have been abducted, madame."

"By whom? Do you know him? Oh, if you know him, tell me!"

"By a man forty or forty-five years old, with black hair, a dark complexion, and a scar on his left temple."

"That is the man, but what is his name?"

"His name? I do not know."

"Did my husband know I had been carried off?"

"He was informed of it by a letter written to him by the abductor himself."

"And does he suspect the reason for it?" Mme. Bonacieux asked with some embarrassment.

"He attributed it to political reasons, I think."

"I doubted that at first, but now I think exactly as he does. So my dear Monsieur Bonacieux has not suspected me for a single instant?"

"Far from it, madame. He was certain of your prudence, and above all, of your love."

A second smile, almost imperceptible, stole over the pretty young woman's rosy lips.

"But how did you escape?" asked d'Artagnan.

"I took advantage of a moment when they left me alone; and because I had known since morning the reason for my abduction, I let myself down from the window with the help of my sheets. Then, since I believed my husband would be at home, I ran here."

"To place yourself under his protection?"

"Oh, no! Poor dear man—I knew very well that he was incapable of defending me! But he might be able to serve us in other ways, so I wanted to talk to him."

"About what?"

"Oh, that is not my secret, so I must not tell you."

"Madame, though I am a Guardsman, I must advise you to be cautious. I do not think this is a good place for imparting confidences. The men I have run off will return with reinforcements, and if they find us here, we are lost. I have sent for three of my friends, but who knows if they were at home?"

"Oh, yes, you are right! Let us fly! Let us save ourselves!" cried the frightened Mme. Bonacieux.

She clutched d'Artagnan's arm and urged him forward eagerly.

"But where should we fly to? Where can we go?"

"First let us leave this house, then we will decide."

Without taking the trouble to shut the door behind them, they quickly walked down the Rue des Fossoyeurs, turned into the Rue des Fossés-Monsieur-le-Prince, and did not stop till they came to the Place St. Sulpice.

"And now what are we going to do? Where do you want me to take you?" asked d'Artagnan.

"I have no idea how to answer you," she replied. "I intended to have my husband speak to Monsieur de La Porte so that he might tell us exactly what has taken place at the Louvre in the last three days and if there is any danger in my returning there."

"I can speak to Monsieur de La Porte."

"No doubt you could, but there is one problem—Monsieur Bonacieux is known at the Louvre and would be allowed to pass, whereas you are not known there, so the gate would be closed against you."

"Bah! You must surely know some gatekeeper who is devoted to you, and who, thanks to a password, would . . ."

Mme. Bonacieux looked at him earnestly.

"And if I gave you this password, would you forget it as soon as you had used it?"

"On my honor and by the faith of a gentleman!" said d'Artagnan, with so sincere a tone that no one could doubt it.

"Then I believe you. You seem to be a brave young man—and besides, your devotion may help your fortunes."

"I will do, willingly and without any such promise, all that I can do to serve the king and be agreeable to the queen. Dispose of me as a friend."

"But I—where can I go meanwhile?"

"Is there nobody from whose house Monsieur de La Porte can come and fetch you?"

"No, I can trust nobody."

"Wait," said d'Artagnan, "we are not far from Athos's house. Yes, here it is. . . ."

"Who is Athos?"

"One of my friends."

"But if he should be at home and see me?"

"He is not at home, and I will carry away the key after having locked you in his apartment."

"But if he should return?"

"Oh, he won't return. And if he does he will be told that I brought a woman with me and that the woman is still in his apartment."

"But that will compromise me, you know."

"No, because nobody knows you. Besides, we are in a situation in which we must ignore such conventions."

"Then let us go to your friend's house. Where does he live?"

"Rue Férou, a few steps from here."

"Let us go!"

They started to walk again.

As d'Artagnan had foreseen, Athos was not home, so he took the key, which was always given him as one of the family, climbed the stairs, and brought Mme. Bonacieux into the little apartment that we have already described.

"You are at home here," he said. "Fasten the door from the inside, and open it to nobody unless you hear three knocks, like this."

He knocked three times—two knocks close together and loud, the other after an interval, and softer.

"Good," said Mme. Bonacieux. "Now let me give you my instructions."

"I am listening."

"Present yourself at the Louvre gate on the side of the Rue de l'Echelle and ask for Germain."

"And then?"

"He will ask you what you want, and you will answer with these words—'Tours' and 'Brussels.' He will then immediately put himself under your orders."

"And what shall I order him to do?"

"To fetch Monsieur de La Porte, the queen's gentleman-in-waiting."

"And when Germain has informed him, and Monsieur de La Porte has come?"

"You will send him to me."

"Very well. But where and how will I see you again?"

"Do you wish to see me again?"

"Certainly."

"Well, leave that to me, and do not worry."

"I depend on your word."

"You may."

D'Artagnan bowed to Mme. Bonacieux, bestowing on her charming person the most loving glance that he possibly could. As he was going down the stairs, he heard her close and double-lock the door. In two bounds he was at the Louvre, arriving at the Echelle gate as ten o'clock was striking. All the events we have just described had taken place within a half hour.

Everything happened as Mme. Bonacieux had prophesied. On hearing the password, Germain bowed; ten minutes later La Porte was at the gate; in a few words d'Artagnan informed him where Mme. Bonacieux was. La Porte assured himself of the address by having it twice repeated, and set off at a run. He had hardly taken ten steps, however, before he returned.

"Young man," he said to d'Artagnan, "a suggestion."

"What?"

"You may get into trouble because of what has taken place."

"You think so?"

"Yes. Have you any friend whose clock is too slow?"

"And if I do?"

"Go call on him so that he may give evidence of your having been with him at half past nine. In a court of justice that is called an alibi."

D'Artagnan found this advice prudent. He took to his heels and was soon at M. de Tréville's, but instead of going into the drawing room with the rest of the crowd, he asked to be shown into M. de Tréville's study. Because d'Artagnan was at the house so often, there was no difficulty about his request, and a servant went to inform M. de Tréville that his young compatriot, having something important to communicate, would like a private audience. Five minutes later, M. de Tréville was asking d'Artagnan what he could do to serve him and what caused his visit at so late an hour.

"Excuse me, monsieur," said d'Artagnan, who had profited by the moment he had been left alone to set

back M. de Tréville's clock three-quarters of an hour,
"but I thought that since it was only twenty-five minutes
past nine, it was not too late to see you."

"Twenty-five minutes past nine!" exclaimed M. de
Tréville, looking at the clock. "Why, that's impossible!"

"Look at the clock, monsieur," said d'Artagnan.

"You are right," said M. de Tréville. "I thought it was
later. But what can I do for you?"

Then d'Artagnan told M. de Tréville a long story about
the queen. He described his fears for her Majesty, and
he told him what he had heard of the cardinal's projects
with regard to Buckingham. He spoke so easily and
openly about all this that M. de Tréville was easily convinced, especially since he himself had, as we have
already said, observed something going on among the
cardinal, the king, and the queen.

As ten o'clock was striking, d'Artagnan left M. de Tréville, who thanked him for his information, again urged
him to have the service of the king and queen always at
heart, and returned to the drawing room. At the foot of
the stairs, however, d'Artagnan remembered that he had
forgotten his cane and hurried back upstairs. He reentered the study, set the clock right again so no one would
see the next day that it had been put wrong, and sure
now that he had a witness to prove his alibi, he ran
downstairs and soon found himself in the street.

11

The Plot Thickens

His visit to M. de Tréville being paid, a pensive d'Artagnan took the longest way home.

About what was d'Artagnan thinking that made him
stray from his path, gaze at the stars, and sometimes
sigh, sometimes smile?

He was thinking of Mme. Bonacieux. For an apprentice Musketeer the young woman was almost an amorous
ideal. Pretty, mysterious, familiar with almost all the
secrets of the court—which gave her pleasing features

such a charming gravity—it also seemed that she was not wholly unmoved by him, an irresistible charm for novices in love. Moreover, d'Artagnan had delivered her from the hands of the fiends who had wanted to search and ill-treat her, and that important service had established between them one of those sentiments of gratitude which so easily assume a more tender character.

So rapid is the flight of our dreams on the wings of imagination that d'Artagnan already fancied himself getting a message from the young woman that would appoint a rendezvous or include a gold chain or a diamond. We have observed that young cavaliers received presents from their king without shame; let us add that in those times of lax morality they were no more delicate with respect to their mistresses, and that the latter almost always gave them valuable and durable mementos of this love—as if they tried to compensate for the fragility of their sentiments by the solidity of their gifts.

Without a blush, men then made their way in the world by means of women. Those who were only beautiful gave their beauty, from which doubtless comes the proverb, "The most beautiful girl in the world can only give what she has." Those who were rich gave in addition a part of their money; and there was many a hero in that gallant period who would neither have won his spurs in the first place nor his battles afterward without the more or less full purse that his mistress fastened to the saddle bow.

D'Artagnan owned nothing. His provincial diffidence— as thin as a layer of varnish, as ephemeral as a flower, as fragile as peach down—had totally disappeared thanks to the unorthodox advice given him by the three Musketeers. D'Artagnan, following the strange custom of the times, considered himself in Paris as if on a campaign, neither more nor less than if he had been in Flanders— with Spain to strive against yonder, and woman to strive against here; in each case there was a conquest to be made, and contributions to be levied.

But at the present moment d'Artagnan was ruled by a much more noble and disinterested feeling. The haberdasher had said that he was rich; the young man might easily guess that with so weak a man as M. Bonacieux it must be the wife who held the purse strings. But that had nothing to do with the feeling produced by the first sight of Mme. Bonacieux; and there was almost no self-interest in the beginning of the love that had been the consequence of that sight. We say *almost*, because the idea that a young, beautiful, kind, and witty woman is at the same time rich takes nothing from the beginning of love, but on the contrary strengthens it.

Affluence allows for many aristocratic indulgences and caprices that are highly becoming to beauty. A fine white stocking, a silk dress, a lace chemisette, a pretty slipper on the foot, a tasteful ribbon on the head, do not make an ugly woman pretty, but they make a pretty woman beautiful—and the hands, too, gain by all this because hands, among women particularly, must be idle to be beautiful.

D'Artagnan, as the reader very well knows—was not wealthy; he hoped to be so someday, but the time that in his own mind he had fixed on for that happy change was still far distant. Meanwhile, how disheartening to see the woman one loves long for those thousands of nothings which constitute a woman's happiness and to be unable to give her those thousands of nothings. At least when the woman is rich and the lover is not, that which he cannot offer her she offers to herself, and although it is generally with her husband's money that she indulges herself, her gratitude seldom benefits that husband.

Prepared to become the most tender of lovers, he was at the same time a very devoted friend. In the midst of his amorous projects for the haberdasher's wife, he did not forget his companions. The pretty Mme. Bonacieux would be just the woman to walk with in the Plaine St. Denis or at the Foire St. Germain, together with Athos, Porthos, and Aramis; he would be proud to display such a conquest to them. Then, when people walk for any length of time d'Artagnan had often noticed that they become hungry: they would all be able to enjoy one of those charming little dinners during which one touches a friend's hand on one side, and a mistress's foot on the other. And during times of extreme difficulty, d'Artagnan would become the preserver of his friends.

And M. Bonacieux, whom d'Artagnan had pushed into the hands of the officers, denying him aloud although he had promised in a whisper to save him? We are compelled to admit to our readers that d'Artagnan thought nothing about him at all; or that if he did think about him, it was only to say to himself that he was very well where he was, wherever that might be. Love is the most selfish of all the passions.

Let our readers be reassured, however. If d'Artagnan forgets his host, or seems to forget him, under the pretense of not knowing where he has been brought, we do not forget him and we know where he is. But for the moment, let us do as did the amorous Gascon; we will return to the worthy haberdasher later.

While d'Artagnan was thinking about his future amours, addressing himself to the beautiful night, and smiling at the stars, he was walking along the Rue Cherche-Midi— or Chasse-Midi as it was then called. Finding himself near Aramis's house, he took it into his head to pay his friend a visit in order to explain why he had sent Planchet for him with a request that he immediately come to the mousetrap. If Aramis had been at home when Planchet came to his apartment, he had certainly hurried to the Rue des Fossoyeurs, and finding nobody there except perhaps his other two companions, all of them would be wondering about what had happened. The mystery required an explanation, or at least, so d'Artagnan told himself.

He also thought it would be an opportunity to talk about pretty little Mme. Bonacieux, of whom his head, if not his heart, was already full. We must never expect discretion in first love: it is accompanied by such excessive joy that unless the joy is allowed to overflow, it will choke you.

For the past two hours Paris had been dark and was now practically empty. All the clocks of the Faubourg St. Germain were now striking eleven. It was delightful weather. D'Artagnan was walking along a lane on the spot where the Rue d'Assas is now situated, breathing the balmy emanations carried by the breeze from the Rue de Vaugirard and its gardens freshened by evening dews. In the distance resounded the songs of merrymakers—muffled however, by sturdy shutters—enjoying themselves in the taverns scattered along the plain. At the end of the lane, d'Artagnan turned left. Aramis's house was between the Rue Cassette and the Rue Servandoni.

D'Artagnan had just passed the Rue Cassette and

could already see the door of his friend's house, shaded by a mass of sycamores and clematis that formed a vast arch in front of it, when he noticed a shadow emerging from the Rue Servandoni. This shadow was enveloped in a cloak, and d'Artagnan at first believed it was a man; but by its small shape, hesitating walk, and indecisive step, he soon realized that it was a woman. Furthermore, as if uncertain of the house she was looking for, she lifted her eyes to look around, stopped, turned around, and then went forward again. D'Artagnan was intrigued.

"Shall I offer her my services?" he thought. "By her step she must be young, and perhaps she is pretty. . . . But a woman who is wandering the streets at this hour can only be out to meet her lover. Disturbing a rendezvous would not be the best way to make her acquaintance."

Meantime the young woman was still advancing, counting the houses and windows. This was neither time-consuming nor difficult. There were only three houses on that part of the street, and only two windows facing front, one of which was in a house next to Aramis's, the other belonging to Aramis himself.

"Pardieu!" d'Artagnan thought, remembering the theologian's niece. "It would be droll if that belated little dove is searching for our friend's house. But it does look as if that is what she is doing. Ah, my dear Aramis, this time I will learn your secret."

And making himself as small as he could, d'Artagnan concealed himself in the darkest spot on the street, near a stone bench at the back of a recess.

The young woman continued to advance; and in addition to the lightness of her step, which had betrayed her, she had just coughed gently, which d'Artagnan thought was a signal.

Nevertheless, either because the cough had been answered by a similar signal that had ended the nocturnal seeker's uncertainty, or because even without this aid she saw that she had arrived at the end of her journey, she resolutely approached Aramis's shutter and tapped on it at three equal intervals.

"It certainly is Aramis's lodging," murmured d'Artagnan. "Ah, Monsieur Hypocrite, I see how you study theology."

The three raps were scarcely struck when the window

was opened and a light appeared through the slats of the outside shutter.

"Ah, not through doors, but through windows! This visit was expected. Now we will see the windows open, and the lady climb inside. Very pretty!"

But to d'Artagnan's great astonishment, the shutter remained closed, and what is more, the light that had been shining disappeared and all was again in obscurity.

He thought this could not last long, and he continued to look and listen very attentively.

He was right; at the end of a few seconds he heard two sharp taps from inside.

The young woman in the street replied by a single tap, and the shutter was partly opened.

The reader may imagine how avidly d'Artagnan looked and listened. Unfortunately the light had been removed into another room; but his eyes were accustomed to the night, and besides, it is said that the eyes of Gascons, like the eyes of cats, have the faculty of seeing in the dark.

D'Artagnan then noticed that the young woman took from her pocket a white object that she unfolded quickly and that took the form of a handkerchief. She made the person in front of her observe one of its corners.

This immediately reminded d'Artagnan about the handkerchief he had found at Mme. Bonacieux's feet, which had in turn reminded him of the one he had found under Aramis's feet.

"What the devil could that handkerchief mean?"

Placed where he was, D'Artagnan could not see Aramis's face. We say Aramis's face because the young man had no doubt that it was his friend who was holding this dialogue from the inside with the lady on the outside. Curiosity prevailed over prudence. Profiting by the preoccupation into which the sight of the handkerchief seemed to have plunged the two personages now on the scene, he stole from his hiding place and, quick as lightning but with the utmost caution, ran over to a corner of the wall, from where he could see into Aramis's room.

Doing so, d'Artagnan almost cried out in surprise; it was not Aramis who was talking to the nocturnal visitor, but another woman! But he could see only enough to recognize the shape of her clothes, not enough to distinguish her features.

Just then the woman inside took a second handkerchief out of her pocket and exchanged it for the one that had just been shown to her. Then the two women spoke some more, and the shutter was again closed. The woman outside the window turned around and passed within four steps of d'Artagnan; she pulled down the hood of her cloak, but the precaution was too late—d'Artagnan had already recognized Mme. Bonacieux.

Mme. Bonacieux! The suspicion that it was she had crossed d'Artagnan's mind when she had taken the handkerchief out of her pocket; but how likely was it that Mme. Bonacieux, who had sent for M. de La Porte in order to be escorted back to the Louvre, would be running about the streets of Paris at half past eleven at night at the risk of being abducted a second time?

It must mean that this was a very important matter— and what is the most important matter to a woman of twenty-five? Love.

But was it on her own account or for someone else that she had exposed herself to such danger? This was the question the young man asked himself as the demon of jealousy gnawed at him as if he were already an accepted lover.

There was a very simple way to satisfy himself about where Mme. Bonacieux was going, and that was to follow her. It was so simple that d'Artagnan did it quite naturally and instinctively.

But at the sight of the young man who detached himself from the wall like a statue leaving its niche, and at the noise of the steps she heard behind her, Mme. Bonacieux uttered a little cry and fled.

D'Artagnan ran after her. It was not difficult for him to overtake a woman burdened by her cloak, and he caught up with her before she had gone a third of the street. She was exhausted, not by fatigue but by terror, and when d'Artagnan put his hand on her shoulder, she fell to one knee and said in a choked voice, "Kill me if you wish, but you will learn nothing!"

D'Artagnan raised her by putting his arm around her waist, but since he could feel by her weight that she was on the point of fainting, he hurried to reassure her by declarations of devotion. The declarations meant nothing to her because such declarations may be made with the worst intentions in the world; but she thought she recognized the voice. She opened her eyes, glanced at the man who had terrified her, recognized at once that it was d'Artagnan, and exclaimed joyfully, "Oh, it is you, it is you! Thank God!"

"Yes, it is I," he said. "God has sent me to watch over you."

"Was that why you followed me?" asked the young woman with a coquettish smile.

Her bantering tone was again apparent; all fear had disappeared from the moment in which she had recognized a friend in one she had taken for an enemy.

"No," he answered. "I admit that it was chance that threw me in your way. I saw a woman tapping on my friend's window."

"Your friend?" interrupted Mme. Bonacieux.

"Yes, Aramis is one of my best friends."

"Aramis? Who is he?"

"Are you going to tell me you don't know Aramis?"

"This is the first time I have ever heard his name."

"Is it the first time that you ever went to that house?"

"Of course."

"And you did not know that a young man lives there?"

"No."

"A Musketeer?"

"No, indeed!"

"Then it was not Aramis you came to see?"

"Not at all. Besides, you must have seen that the person to whom I spoke was a woman."

"That is true, but she is one of Aramis's friends . . ."

"I know nothing about that."

". . . since she is living in his apartment."

"That does not concern me."

"But who is she?"

"Oh, that is not my secret."

"My dear Madame Bonacieux, you are charming, but at the same time you are one of the most mysterious women I have ever met."

"Do I lose by that?"

"No. On the contrary, you are adorable."

"Then give me your arm."

"Most willingly. And now?"

"Now escort me."

"Where?"

"Where I am going."

"But where are you going?"

"You will see, because you will leave me at the door."

"Shall I wait for you?"

"That will not be necessary."

"You will return alone?"

"Perhaps yes, perhaps not."

"But will the person who accompanies you be a man or a woman?"

"I do not know that yet."

"But *I* will know it!"

"How?"

"I will wait till you come out."

"In that case, good-bye."

"Why?"

"I do not need you."

"But you have asked . . ."

". . . the help of a gentleman, not the watchfulness of a spy."

"The word is rather harsh."

"What is the word for those who follow others in spite of their wishes?"

"Indiscreet."

"The word is too mild."

"Well, madame, I see I must do as you wish."

"Why did you deprive yourself of the merit of doing so at once?"

"Is there no merit in repentance?"

"Do you really repent?"

"I do not know. But what I do know is that I promise to do whatever you wish if you will allow me to accompany you where you are going."

"And you will leave me then?"

"Yes."

"Without waiting for my coming out again?"

"Yes."

"On your word of honor?"

"By the faith of a gentleman! Take my arm, and let us go."

D'Artagnan offered his arm to Mme. Bonacieux, who

willingly took it, half laughing, half trembling, and they soon arrived at the end of Rue de la Harpe. Once there, the young woman seemed to hesitate, as she had done before on the Rue Vaugirard, but then she seemed by certain signs to recognize a door and approached it.

"And now, monsieur," she said, "here is where I have business. A thousand thanks for your honorable company, which has saved me from all the dangers to which, alone, I was exposed. But the moment has come to keep your word. I have reached my destination."

"And you will have nothing to fear on your return?"

"Nothing but robbers."

"And is that nothing?"

"What could they take from me? I have not even a sou with me."

"You forget that beautiful monogrammed handkerchief."

"Which handkerchief?"

"The one I found at your feet and put back in your pocket."

"Hold your tongue, you reckless man! Do you wish to destroy me?"

"You see very plainly that you are still in danger, since a single word makes you tremble, and you confess that if that word were heard you would be ruined. Ah, madame," he said, taking her hand and looking at her ardently, "be more generous. Confide in me. Have you not read in my eyes that there is nothing but devotion and sympathy in my heart?"

"Yes, I have, so ask me for my own secrets, and I will reveal them to you. But those of others—that is quite another thing."

"Very well, I shall discover them myself. Since those secrets may have an influence over your life, they must become mine."

"Beware of what you do," the young woman said, so seriously as to impress d'Artagnan in spite of himself. "Oh, please, do not meddle in anything that concerns me. Do not try to help me in what I am doing. I ask this of you in the name of the devotion with which I inspire you and in the name of the service you have rendered me and that I will never forget as long as I live. Believe what I tell you. Do not concern yourself about me. I no longer exist for you, any more than if you had never seen me."

"Must Aramis do the same, madame?" asked d'Artagnan, stung.

"This is the second or third time, monsieur, that you have repeated that name, and yet I have told you that I do not know him."

"You do not know the man at whose shutter you have just knocked? Indeed, madame, you think me too gullible!"

"Confess that it is for the sake of making me talk that you have invented this story and created this man."

"I invent nothing, madame, and I create nothing. I am only speaking the exact truth."

"And you say that one of your friends lives in that house?"

"I say so, and I will repeat it for the third time—that house is lived in by my friend, and that friend is Aramis."

"All this will be cleared up later," she murmured. "No, monsieur, be silent now."

"If you could see my heart," said d'Artagnan, "you would read there so much curiosity that you would instantly pity me, and so much love that you would instantly satisfy my curiosity. You have nothing to fear from one who loves you."

"You speak very suddenly of love, monsieur," said the young woman, shaking her head.

"That is because love has come to me very suddenly, and for the first time, and because I am not even twenty."

The young woman looked at him stealthily.

"Listen. I am already on the trail of something," he resumed. "About three months ago I nearly fought a duel with Aramis about a handkerchief like the one you showed to the woman in his house—a handkerchief that I am sure was marked in the same way."

"Monsieur, you weary me very much, I assure you, with your questions."

"But you, madame, who are so prudent—just think! if you were to be arrested with that handkerchief, would you not be compromised?"

"In what way? The initials are mine—C. B., Constance Bonacieux."

"Or Camille de Bois-Tracy."

"Silence, monsieur! Once again, silence! Oh, since the dangers I incur on my own account cannot stop you, think of those you yourself may run!"

"Me?"

"Yes. You risk imprisonment and even your life by knowing me."

"Then I will not leave you."

"Monsieur," she said, clasping her hands and begging him, "in the name of heaven, by the honor of a soldier and the courtesy of a gentleman, leave me! There, it is midnight, and that is when I am expected."

"Madame," said d'Artagnan, bowing, "I can refuse nothing asked of me in that way. Be content, I will leave."

"You will not follow me? You will not watch me?"

"I will return home instantly."

"Ah, I was sure you were a good and brave young man," she said, holding out one hand to him and placing the other on the knocker of a little door almost hidden in the wall.

D'Artagnan took the hand held out to him and kissed it fervently.

"Oh, I wish I had never seen you!" he cried, with that ingenuous roughness which women often prefer to superficial politeness because it reveals the very depths of a man's heart and proves that feeling prevails over reason.

Pressing the hand that had not relinquished hers, Mme. Bonacieux replied in a voice that was almost caressing, "Well, I will not say the same. What is lost for today may not be lost forever. Who knows if I will not satisfy your curiosity when I shall be free to do so?"

"And will you make the same promise about my love?" cried d'Artagnan, beside himself with joy.

"Oh, as to that, I do not promise. That depends on the sentiments you are able to inspire in me."

"Then today, madame . . ."

"Today I go no further than gratitude."

"Ah, you are too charming," d'Artagnan said sorrowfully, "and you abuse my love."

"No, I use your generosity, that is all. But be of good cheer—all things come to certain people."

"Oh, you make me the happiest of men! Do not forget this evening—do not forget that promise!"

"Be content. In the proper time and place I will remember everything. Now go, in the name of heaven! I was expected at midnight sharp, and I am late."

"Only by five minutes."

"Yes, but in certain circumstances five minutes are five ages."

"When one loves."

"Well, and who told you that my business was not with a lover?"

"Then it is a man who expects you? A man!"

"The discussion is not going to begin again!" said Mme. Bonacieux, with a half-smile that held a tinge of impatience.

"No, I am going. I believe in you, and I want all the merit of my devotion even if that devotion is stupidity. Adieu, madame."

And as if he could detach himself only by a violent effort from the hand he still held, he abruptly sprang away as Mme. Bonacieux knocked on the door as she had knocked on the shutter: three light and regularly spaced taps. When he reached the corner, he turned around. The door had been opened, and shut again; the haberdasher's lovely wife had disappeared.

D'Artagnan went his way. He had given his word not to watch Mme. Bonacieux, and if his life had depended on knowing where she was going or who would be accompanying her, he would have returned home because that was what he had promised. Five minutes later he was on the Rue des Fossoyeurs.

"Poor Athos," he said to himself. "He will never guess what any of this means. He will have fallen asleep waiting for me, or else he will have returned home, where he will have learned that a woman had been there. A woman with Athos! Though after all, there was certainly one with Aramis! This is all very strange, and I am curious to know how it will end."

"Badly, monsieur, badly," replied a voice the young man recognized as that of Planchet; while soliloquizing aloud, as preoccupied people do, he had entered the alley at the end of which were the stairs that led to his room.

"What do you mean 'badly,' you idiot? What has happened?" asked d'Artagnan.

"All sorts of misfortunes."

"What?"

"In the first place, Monsieur Athos was arrested."

"Arrested! Athos arrested! What for?"

"He was found in your lodging, and they took him for you."

"And who arrested him?"

"Guards brought by the men in black whom you put to flight."

"Why did he not tell them his name? Why did he not tell them he knew nothing about this affair?"

"He deliberately did not do so, monsieur. On the contrary, he came up to me and said, 'It is your master that needs his liberty at this moment and not I, since he knows everything and I know nothing. They will believe he is arrested, and that will give him time. In three days I will tell them who I am, and they cannot fail to let me go.'"

"Bravo, Athos! Noble heart!" murmured d'Artagnan. "I recognize him in that act! And what did the Guards do?"

"Four of them took him away, I don't know where—to the Bastille or to For-l'Evêque. Two of them remained with the men in black, who rummaged through everything and took all the papers. The last two stood guard at the door during this examination, then, when it was over, they went away, leaving the house empty and open."

"And Porthos and Aramis?"

"I could not find them, so they did not come."

"But they may come at any moment because you left word that I was waiting for them?"

"Yes, monsieur."

"Well, don't move from here. If they come, tell them what has happened. Let them wait for me at the Pomme-de-Pin. It would be too dangerous here—the house may be watched. I will go to Monsieur de Tréville to tell him about all this, and I will meet them there after that."

"Very well, monsieur."

"But you *will* remain? You are not afraid?" said d'Artagnan, coming back to encourage his lackey.

"Don't worry, monsieur," said Planchet. "You do not know me yet. I am brave when I decide to be, so it is all a question of deciding. Besides, I am a Picard."

"Then it is understood that you would rather let yourself be killed than desert your post?"

"Yes, monsieur, and there is nothing I would not do to prove to Monsieur how loyal I am to him."

"Good," d'Artagnan thought. "It seems as if the method I have adopted with this boy is definitely the best. I will use it again if I have to."

And though his legs were a little tired from the day's activities, he went swiftly to M. de Tréville's.

M. de Tréville was not home. His company was on guard duty at the Louvre and he was there with his company.

He had to reach M. de Tréville; it was important to inform him about what was happening. He resolved to try to get into the Louvre: his uniform of Guardsman in the company of M. Des Essarts ought to be his passport.

He went down the Rue des Petits Augustins and came up to the quay in order to cross at the Pont Neuf. He had thought of crossing by ferry, but on arriving at the riverside, he had mechanically put his hand into his pocket and realized that he did not have the money for his passage.

As he was approaching the end of Rue Guénegaud, he saw two people coming out of the Rue Dauphine and was struck by their appearance. Of the two, one was a man and the other a woman. The woman had the shape of Mme. Bonacieux, and the man so closely resembled Aramis as to be mistaken for him.

Besides, the woman wore that black cloak which d'Artagnan could still see outlined against the shutter of the house on Rue de Vaugirard and on the door of the house on Rue de la Harpe. In addition, the man wore the uniform of a Musketeer.

The woman's hood was pulled down, and the man held a handkerchief to his face. Both, as that double precaution indicated, did not want to be recognized.

They took the bridge, which was also d'Artagnan's road since he was going to the Louvre; he followed them.

He had not gone twenty steps before he was convinced

that the woman really was Mme. Bonacieux and that the man was Aramis.

He felt his heart churning with jealous suspicion and thought himself doubly betrayed, by his friend and by the woman he loved as if she were already his mistress. Mme. Bonacieux had sworn to him that she did not know Aramis, and a quarter of an hour after having sworn it, he found her hanging on Aramis's arm.

D'Artagnan did not consider that he had known the haberdasher's pretty wife for only three hours; that she owed him nothing but a little gratitude for having delivered her from the men in black, who wished to carry her off; and that she had promised him nothing. He considered himself an outraged, betrayed, and ridiculed lover: blood and anger mounted to his face, and he resolved to unravel the mystery.

The young man and young woman had realized they were followed, and redoubled their speed. D'Artagnan made his plans. He ran past them, then turned back so as to meet them exactly in front of the Samaritaine, which was illuminated by a lamp that lit the whole part of the bridge.

D'Artagnan faced them, and they faced him.

"What do you want, monsieur?" demanded the Musketeer, recoiling a step and speaking with a foreign accent, which proved to d'Artagnan that he had been wrong about one of his conjectures.

"It is not Aramis!" he cried.

"No, monsieur, it is not Aramis. And by your exclamation I understand that you have mistaken me for another, and I forgive you."

"You forgive me?"

"Yes. Allow me to pass on, since I am not the man you want."

"You are right, monsieur, I have nothing to do with you, but I wish to talk with madame."

"With madame! You do not know her," replied the stranger.

"You are wrong, monsieur, I know her very well."

"Ah, monsieur, I had your promise as a soldier and your word as a gentleman. I hoped to be able to rely on that," said Mme. Bonacieux, in a tone of reproach.

"And you, madame," said d'Artagnan, embarrassed, "you promised me . . ."

"Take my arm, madame," said the stranger, "and let us continue on our way."

But d'Artagnan, stunned, cast down, overwhelmed by all that happened to him, stood with crossed arms in front of the Musketeer and Mme. Bonacieux.

The Musketeer advanced two steps and pushed d'Artagnan aside. D'Artagnan sprang back and drew his sword. At the same time, and with the rapidity of lightning, the stranger drew his.

"In the name of heaven, my Lord!" cried Mme. Bonacieux, throwing herself between the combatants and seizing a sword in each hand.

"My Lord!" cried d'Artagnan, enlightened by a sudden idea. "Pardon me, monsieur, but are you . . ."

"My Lord the Duke of Buckingham," said Mme. Bonacieux, in a low voice, "and now you may ruin us all."

"My Lord, madame, I ask a hundred pardons! But I love her, my Lord, and was jealous. You know what it is to love, my Lord. Pardon me, and then tell me how I can risk my life to serve your Grace?"

"You are a brave young man," said Buckingham, holding out his hand to d'Artagnan, who took it respectfully. "You offer me your services, and with the same frankness I accept them. Follow us at a distance of twenty paces as far as the Louvre, and if anyone watches us, kill him!"

D'Artagnan placed his naked sword under his arm, allowed the duke and Mme. Bonacieux to get twenty steps ahead of him and then followed them, ready to execute the instructions of the noble and elegant minister of Charles I.

Fortunately, he had no opportunity to give the duke this proof of his devotion, and the young woman and the handsome Musketeer entered the Louvre through the Echelle gate without any interference.

D'Artagnan then immediately went to the Pomme-de-Pin, where he found Porthos and Aramis waiting for him. Without giving them any explanation of the alarm and inconvenience he had caused them, he told them that he had by himself terminated the affair in which he had for a moment believed he should need their assistance.

Meanwhile, carried away as we are by our narrative, we must leave our three friends to themselves and follow the Duke of Buckingham and his guide through the labyrinths of the Louvre.

12

George Villiers, Duke of Buckingham

MME. BONACIEUX and the duke entered the Louvre without difficulty. Mme. Bonacieux was known to be in the queen's service, and the duke wore the uniform of M. de Tréville's Musketeers, who, as we have said, were on guard duty that evening. Besides, Germain served the interests of the queen, and if anything should happen, Mme. Bonacieux would only be accused of having introduced her lover into the Louvre. She took the risk. Her reputation would be lost, but of what value to those in high places was the reputation of a haberdasher's little wife?

Once within the courtyard, the duke and the young woman followed the wall for about twenty-five paces, then Mme. Bonacieux pushed a small servants' door that was open by day but generally locked at night. The door yielded. They entered, and found themselves in darkness; but Mme. Bonacieux knew all the turnings and windings of this part of the Louvre, which was set apart for the people of the household. She closed the door behind them, took the duke by the hand, and after a few experimental steps, grasped a balustrade, put her foot on the bottom step, and began to climb the stairs. The duke counted two flights. She then turned to the right, walked along a corridor, went down a flight of stairs, took a few more steps, introduced a key into a lock, opened a door, and led the duke into a room lighted only by a night lamp, saying, "Remain here, your Grace. Someone will come."

She then went out by the same door, which she locked, so that the duke found himself literally a prisoner.

Even under these circumstances, the Duke of Buckingham did not experience a single instant of fear. One of the major components of his character was a love for the dangerous and the romanesque. He was brave, rash, and enterprising, and this was not the first time he had risked his life in such attempts. He had learned that the message from Anne of Austria, which was his reason for coming to Paris, was a trap; but instead of returning to England, he had taken advantage of the position in which he had been placed and declared to the queen that he would not leave without having seen her. She had at first firmly refused, but then she had become afraid that the duke, if exasperated, would commit some folly. She had already decided to see him and urge his immediate departure when Mme. Bonacieux, whose responsibility it was to fetch the duke and conduct him to the Louvre, had been abducted. For two days no one knew what had become of her, and everything remained in suspense; but once she was free and in touch with La Porte, matters resumed their course, and she had just accomplished the perilous enterprise that would have been concluded three days earlier except for her abduction.

Buckingham, left alone, walked toward a mirror. His Musketeer's uniform was very becoming.

At thirty-five, which was then his age, he justly passed for the handsomest and most elegant nobleman in France or England.

The favorite of two kings, immensely rich, all-powerful in a kingdom that he threw into chaos at his fancy and calmed again at his caprice, George Villiers, Duke of Buckingham, had chosen to live one of those fabulous existences that survive through the centuries as a source of astonishment for posterity.

Sure of himself, convinced of his own power, certain that the laws which rule other men could not reach him, he went straight to the object he aimed at, even if that object was so lofty and so dazzling that it would have been madness for anyone else even to have considered it. That was how he had succeeded in approaching the beautiful and proud Anne of Austria several times, and in making himself loved by dazzling her.

As he stood in front of the mirror, restored the waves in his beautiful hair, which the weight of his hat had flattened, and curled his mustache, his heart swelled with joy and he was happy and proud at the approach of the moment he had so long sighed for; he smiled at himself with pride and hope.

At that moment a door concealed in the tapestry opened, and a woman appeared. Buckingham saw the apparition in the mirror and cried out. It was the queen!

Anne of Austria was then twenty-six or twenty-seven years old and in the full splendor of her beauty.

Her bearing was that of a queen or a goddess. Her eyes, which shone with the brilliancy of emeralds, were perfectly beautiful and at the same time full of both sweetness and majesty. Her mouth was small and rosy; and although her lower lip, like that of all members of the Austrian Royal family, protruded slightly beyond the other, it was superlatively lovely in its smile and profoundly disdainful in its contempt. Her skin was admired for its velvety softness, and her hands and arms were of surpassing beauty, all the poets of the time praising them as incomparable. Her hair, which from being blonde in her youth had become chestnut and which she wore curled and heavily powdered, admirably framed her face, in which the most severe critic could only have wished for a little less rouge, and the most fastidious sculptor a little more finely modeled nose.

Buckingham stood there for a moment, dazzled. At no ball, festival, or military review had Anne of Austria ever seemed as beautiful to him as she seemed at the moment, wearing a simple white satin dress and accompanied by Doña Estefania—the only one of her Spanish women who had not been driven from her by the jealousy of the king or the persecutions of Richelieu.

The queen took two steps forward. Buckingham threw himself at her feet and, before she could prevent him, kissed the hem of her dress.

"Duke, you already know that it was not I who sent you that message."

"Yes, your Majesty," said the duke, "I know that I must have been mad, senseless, to hope that the snow would melt or the marble warm! But what would you? When one loves, one always believes in love. Besides, I have lost nothing by this journey because I see you."

"Yes, but you know why I am seeing you—it is

because, despite the suffering it causes me, you have persisted in remaining in a city where, by remaining, you
risk your life and make me risk my honor. I am seeing
you to tell you that everything separates us—the depths
of the sea, the enmity of kingdoms, the sanctity of vows.
It is sacrilege to struggle against so many things, my
Lord. In short, I am seeing you to tell you that we must
never see each other again."

"Speak on, my Queen. The sweetness of your voice
covers the harshness of your words. You talk of sacrilege—why, the sacrilege is the separation of two hearts
formed by God for each other!"

"My Lord, you forget that I have never said that I
loved you."

"But you have also never told me that you did not
love me, and truly, to speak such words to me would be,
on the part of your Majesty, too great an ingratitude.
For tell me, where could you find a love like mine—a
love that neither time nor absence nor despair can extinguish, a love that contents itself with a lost ribbon, a
stray look, or a chance word?

"It is now three years, madame, since I saw you for
the first time, and during those three years that is the
way I have loved you.

"Shall I tell you how you were dressed the first time
I saw you? Shall I describe each ornament of your clothing? Listen! I can still see you now. You were seated on
cushions in the Spanish fashion. You wore a green-satin
gown embroidered with gold and silver, with full, loose
sleeves gathered with diamonds on your beautiful arms—
those lovely arms! You wore a tight ruff, a small cap the
same color as your gown, and in that cap was a heron's
feather. Oh, wait, wait! When I shut my eyes, I can see
you as you were then. When I open them again, I see
what you are now—a hundred times more beautiful!"

"What folly to feed a useless passion with such memories!" murmured Anne of Austria, who did not have the
courage to find fault with the duke for having so well
preserved her portrait in his heart.

"Then what must I live on? I have nothing but my
memories. They are my happiness, my treasure, my
hope. Every sight of you is a fresh diamond that I keep
embedded in my heart. This is the fourth that you have

let fall and I have picked up, for in three years, madame, I have seen you only four times—the first, which I have just described to you, the second, at Madame de Chevreuse's house, the third, in the garden at Amiens."

"Duke," said the queen, blushing, "never speak about that evening."

"Oh, yes, let us speak about it! That is the happiest and most radiant evening of my life! Do you remember what a beautiful night it was? How soft and perfumed was the air? How lovely the blue star-enameled sky? Ah, then, madame, I was able to be alone with you for a few minutes. You were about to confide in me—to tell me about the isolation of your life, the griefs in your heart. You leaned on my arm—on this arm, madame! I felt your beautiful hair touch my cheek whenever I bent my head toward you, and every time that it touched me I trembled from head to foot. Oh, my queen, you do not know what felicity from heaven, what joys from paradise, are contained in a moment like that! Take my wealth, my fortune, my glory, all the days I have left to live, for another such night, because that night, madame, that night you loved me, I will swear it!"

"Yes my Lord, it is possible that the influence of the place, the charm of the lovely evening, the look in your eyes—in short, the thousand circumstances that sometimes unite to destroy a woman—were grouped around me on that fatal evening. But, my Lord, you saw the queen come to the aid of the woman who weakened. At the first rash word you dared utter, at the first liberty to which I had to respond, I called for help."

"Yes, that is true. And any other love but mine would have been destroyed by that ordeal, but my love only became more ardent and more eternal. You thought you would escape me by returning to Paris—you thought I would not dare to leave the treasure my master had ordered me to guard. But what to me were all the treasures in the world or all the kings of the earth! A week later, I was back again, madame. That time you had nothing to reproach me with. I had risked my position, my life, to see you for only a second, and I did not even touch your hand. You pardoned me when you saw how submissive and repentant I was."

"Yes, but slander seized on all those follies in which, as you well know, my Lord, I had taken no part. The king, driven by the cardinal, made a terrible outcry. Madame de Vernet was sent away from me, Putange was exiled, Madame de Chevreuse fell into disgrace, and when you wished to come back as ambassador to France, the king himself—remember that, my Lord—the king himself opposed it."

"Yes, and France is about to pay for her king's refusal with a war. I am not allowed to see you, madame, but you will at least hear about me every day. What do you think is the object of this expedition to Ré and this alliance with the Protestants of La Rochelle, which I am arranging? The pleasure of seeing you! I have no hope of penetrating, sword in hand, to Paris—I know that quite well. But the war will bring about a peace, and the peace will require a negotiator, and that negotiator will be me. They will not dare to refuse me then, and I will return to Paris, see you again, and be happy for a few moments. Thousands of men, it is true, will have paid for my happiness with their lives, but what is that to me provided I see you again! All this is perhaps folly—perhaps insanity—but tell me, what woman has a lover more truly in love, what queen a more ardent servant?"

"My Lord, you invoke in your defense arguments that only accuse you more strongly. All those proofs of love which you present me with are almost crimes."

"Because you do not love me, madame! If you loved me, you would see it differently. If you loved me—oh, that would be too great a happiness and I would go mad. Ah, Madame de Chevreuse, of whom you just spoke, was less cruel than you. The Earl of Holland loved her, and she responded to his love."

"Madame de Chevreuse was not queen," murmured Anne of Austria, overcome in spite of herself by the expression of so profound a passion.

"Then you would love me if you were not queen? Madame, say that you would love me then! Can I believe that it is only the dignity of your rank that makes you cruel to me? Can I believe that if you had been Madame de Chevreuse, poor Buckingham might have hoped? Thank you for those sweet words! Oh, my beautiful sovereign, a hundred times thank you!"

"My Lord, you have misunderstood, you have wrongly interpreted me. . . . I did not mean to say . . ."

"Silence! If I am happy in an error, do not have the cruelty to correct it. You have told me yourself, madame, that I have been drawn into a trap. I may perhaps leave my life in it—because though it may seem strange, I have for some time had a presentiment that I will soon die."

And the duke smiled, with a smile at once sad and charming.

"Oh, my God!" cried Anne of Austria in a terrified tone that proved how much stronger were her feelings for the duke than she dared admit.

"I do not tell you this to frighten you. No, it is even ridiculous for me to speak of it, and believe me, I pay no attention to such dreams. But the words you have just spoken, the hope you have almost given me, will have been worth everything—even my life."

"Oh, but I also, duke, have had presentiments. I also have had dreams. I dreamed that I saw you lying on the ground, bleeding from a wound."

"On the left side, and from a knife?" interrupted Buckingham.

"Yes, that was it, my Lord! A knife wound on the left side! Who can possibly have told you I had that dream? I have confided it to no one but my God, and that in my prayers."

"I ask for nothing more. You love me, madame, and that is enough."

"I love you? I?"

"Yes. Would God send the same dreams to you as to me if you did not love me? Should we have the same presentiments if our lives were not joined at the heart? You love me, my beautiful queen, and will you weep for me?"

"My God! This is more than I can bear. In the name of heaven, Duke, leave me, go! I do not know if I love you or not, but what I do know is that I will not be faithless to my vows. Take pity on me, and go! Oh, if you were to be wounded in France, if you were to die in France, and if I thought that your love for me was the cause of your death, I could never forgive myself—I would go mad! Leave then, I beg you!"

"Oh, how beautiful you are like this! And how I love you!"

"Go, I beg you, and come back later! Come back as ambassador, come back as minister, come back surrounded with guards who will defend you and servants who will watch over you, and then I will no longer fear for your life, and will be happy in seeing you."

"Is that really true?"

"Yes."

"Then give me some pledge of your indulgence, some object that comes from you and will remind me that I have not been dreaming—something you have worn and that I may wear too, a ring, a necklace, a chain."

"Will you leave if I give you what you want?"

"Yes."

"This very instant?"

"Yes."

"You will leave France and return to England?"

"I will, I swear it."

"Then wait."

She went back to her apartments and came out again almost immediately, holding a monogrammed, gold-inlaid, rosewood jewel box.

"Here, my Lord," she said, "keep this in memory of me."

Buckingham took the jewel box and again fell to his knees.

"You promised to go," said the queen.

"And I keep my word. Your hand, madame, and I leave!"

Closing her eyes, Anne of Austria held out one hand and leaned with the other on Estefania, for she felt that her strength was about to fail her.

Buckingham pressed his lips passionately to that beautiful hand, and then stood up.

"Within six months, if I am not dead, I will have seen you again, madame—even if I have to overturn the world."

And faithful to his promise, he rushed out of the room.

In the corridor he met Mme. Bonacieux, who was waiting for him, and who led him out of the Louvre with the same precautions and the same good luck with which she had led him into it.

13

Monsieur Bonacieux

IN ALL OF THIS, as may have been observed, there is one person with whom, despite his precarious position, we seem to have been very little concerned. That person was M. Bonacieux, the respectable martyr of the political and amorous intrigues so inextricably entangled during that licentious and chivalrous period.

Fortunately, as the reader may or may not remember—we have promised not to lose sight of him.

The policemen who arrested him took him straight to the Bastille and led him, trembling, past a group of soldiers loading their muskets. Then, introduced into a half-subterranean room, he was grossly insulted and harshly treated by those who had brought him: they saw that they were not dealing with a gentleman, and they treated him as if he were a peasant.

At the end of about half an hour, a clerk came to put an end to his torture—but not to his anxiety—by giving the order to conduct M. Bonacieux to the Interrogation Room. Ordinarily, prisoners were questioned in their cells, but they did not think M. Bonacieux important enough for such consideration.

Two guards took charge of him and led him across a courtyard and into a corridor in which there were three sentries; they opened a door and pushed him unceremoniously into a low-ceilinged room that contained only a table, a chair, and a magistrate. The magistrate was seated in the chair and writing at the table.

The guards led the prisoner to the table and, at a signal from the magistrate, withdrew far enough to be out of hearing.

The magistrate, who had till then kept his head down over his papers, looked up to see what sort of person he had to do with; he was a surly-looking man, with a pointed nose, a sallow complexion, prominent cheekbones, and small but keen and penetrating eyes. The total effect was a face that resembled, at one and the same time, a ferret and a fox. His head, supported by a long flexible neck, issued from his large black robe and swayed with a motion very much like that of a turtle thrusting his head out of his shell.

He began by asking M. Bonacieux his name, age, employment, and address.

The accused replied that his name was Jacques Michel Bonacieux, that he was fifty-one years old, a retired haberdasher, and lived at 11, Rue des Fossoyeurs.

Instead of continuing to question him, the magistrate made a long speech about how dangerous it was for an obscure citizen to meddle with public matters. He further complicated this discourse by adding a lecture about the great deeds and the enormous power of the cardinal— that incomparable minister, that superior of all past ministers, that example for all ministers to come—deeds and power that none could thwart with impunity.

After this second part of his oration, he fixed his hawk's eye on poor Bonacieux and told him to reflect on the gravity of his situation.

The haberdasher had already reflected: he cursed the moment when M. de La Porte had had the idea of marrying him to his goddaughter, and especially the moment when that goddaughter had been received as her Majesty's linen maid.

At bottom M. Bonacieux's character was one of profound selfishness mixed with sordid avarice and seasoned with extreme cowardice. The love that his young wife had inspired in him was a secondary sentiment, not strong enough to contend with those primary feelings. Bonacieux indeed thought about what he had just been told.

"But, Monsieur le Commissaire," he said timidly, "believe me when I say that I know and appreciate, more than anybody, the merit of the incomparable eminence by whom we have the honor to be governed."

"Indeed?" the magistrate asked doubtfully. "If that is really so, how do you come to be in the Bastille?"

"How I come here, or rather why I am here," replied Bonacieux, "is entirely impossible for me to tell you, because I don't know myself. But it is certainly not for having, knowingly at least, disobliged Monsieur le Cardinal."

"But you must have committed a crime, since you are here and are accused of high treason."

"Of high treason!" cried Bonacieux, terrified. "How is it possible for a poor haberdasher who detests Huguenots and hates Spaniards to be accused of high treason? Monsieur, the thing is absolutely impossible."

"Monsieur Bonacieux, do you have a wife?" asked the magistrate, looking at the accused as if his little eyes could read into the very depths of a man's heart.

"Yes, monsieur," replied the trembling haberdasher, feeling that this was where the affair was likely to become complicated. "That is, I *had* one."

"What do you mean, you *'had* one'? What have you done with her, if you have her no longer?"

"She has been abducted, monsieur."

"She has been abducted? Ah!"

Bonacieux inferred from this "Ah" that the affair was growing even more complicated.

"She has been abducted," repeated the magistrate. "Do you know the man who has committed this deed?"

"I think I know him."

"Who is he?"

"Remember that I swear to nothing, Monsieur le Commissaire, and that I only suspect."

"Whom do you suspect? Come, answer freely."

M. Bonacieux was in the greatest possible perplexity. Should he deny everything or tell everything? If he denied everything, they might suspect that he knew too much to dare confess everything; if he confessed everything, he might prove his good will. He decided to tell everything.

"I suspect," he said, "a tall, dark man, of lofty bearing, who has the air of a great lord. He followed us several times, I think, when I waited for my wife at the gate of the Louvre to escort her home."

The magistrate seemed a little uneasy.

"And his name?" he asked.

"Oh, as to his name, I have no idea. But if I were ever to meet him, I swear I would recognize him in an instant, even among a thousand people."

The magistrate's face grew still darker.

"You would recognize him among a thousand, you say?"

"That is . . ." Bonacieux stammered, seeing he had taken a false step.

"You said that you would recognize him. Good, that is enough for today. Before we proceed further, I must inform someone that you know your wife's ravisher."

"But I have not said that I know him!" Bonacieux cried in despair. "On the contrary . . ."

"Take the prisoner away," said the magistrate to the two guards.

"Where should we take him?" asked the clerk.

"To a cell."

"Which one?"

"The first one that is handy, provided it is safe," the magistrate replied with an indifference that horrified poor Bonacieux.

"Alas," he thought, "misfortune is hanging over me. My wife must have committed some frightful crime. They think I am her accomplice and will punish me as well as her. She must have confessed everything—a woman is so weak! A cell! The first one that is handy! That's it—a night is soon passed, and tomorrow they will take me to the wheel, to the gallows! Oh, my God, have pity on me!"

Without paying the slightest attention to M. Bonacieux's lamentations—lamentations to which, besides, they must have been pretty well accustomed— each of the two guards took the prisoner by an arm and led him away, while the magistrate hastily wrote a letter and dispatched it by his clerk, who had been waiting for it.

Bonacieux could not sleep, not because his cell was so disagreeable but because his uneasiness was so great. He spent the whole night sitting on his stool and shuddering at the slightest sound, and when the first rays of the sun penetrated into his cell, the dawn itself seemed to have taken on a funereal tint.

Suddenly he heard his bolts drawn, and leaped up in terror. He was sure they were coming to conduct him to the scaffold, so when he only saw the magistrate and his clerk instead of the executioner he had been expecting he was ready to embrace them both.

"Your case has become more complicated since last night, my good man, and I advise you to tell the whole truth. Only your confession can pacify the cardinal's anger," said the magistrate.

"Why, I am ready to tell you everything—at least, everything that I know. I beg you to just ask me questions."

"In the first place where is your wife?"

"But I told you she had been abducted."

"Yes, but at five o'clock yesterday afternoon, thanks to you, she escaped."

"My wife escaped! Oh, the untrustworthy creature! Monsieur, if she has escaped, it is not my fault, I swear!"

"What business did you have in the apartment of Monsieur d'Artagnan, your neighbor, with whom you had a long conversation during the day?"

"Yes, Monsieur le Commissaire, that is true, and I admit that I was wrong. I did go to Monsieur d'Artagnan's."

"What was the purpose of that visit?"

"To beg him to help me find my wife. I thought I had a right to try to find her. I was wrong, it seems, and I beg your pardon."

"What did Monsieur d'Artagnan say?"

"Monsieur d'Artagnan promised to help me, but I soon found out that he was betraying me."

"You are making a mockery of justice! Monsieur d'Artagnan made an agreement with you, and in virtue of that agreement, he put to flight the policemen who had come to arrest your wife and has hidden her away."

"Monsieur d'Artagnan has carried off my wife! What are you saying?"

"Fortunately, Monsieur d'Artagnan is in our hands, and you will be confronted with him."

"By my faith, I ask no better! I will not be sorry to see a familiar face."

"Bring in Monsieur d'Artagnan," the magistrate ordered the guards.

They brought in Athos.

"Monsieur d'Artagnan," said the magistrate, addressing Athos, "describe everything that happened yesterday between you and Monsieur Bonacieux."

"But that man is not Monsieur d'Artagnan!" Bonacieux exclaimed.

"Not Monsieur d'Artagnan?"

"Not the least in the world."

"Then what is this gentleman's name?"

"I cannot tell you. I don't know him."

"You don't know him?"

"No."

"You have never seen him before?"

"Yes, I have seen him, but I don't know his name."

"What is your name?" asked the magistrate.

"Athos," replied the Musketeer.

"But that is not a man's name—it's the name of a mountain!" cried the poor questioner, who was beginning to feel very confused.

"That is my name," said Athos quietly.

"But you said that your name was d'Artagnan."

"Who, I?"

"Yes, you."

"Somebody said to me, 'You are Monsieur d'Artagnan?' I answered, 'You think so?' The guards said they were sure of it, and I did not wish to contradict them. Besides, I might be wrong."

"Monsieur, you are insulting the majesty of the law."

"Not at all," Athos replied imperturbably.

"You are Monsieur d'Artagnan."

"You see, monsieur, you are saying it again."

"But I tell you, Monsieur le Commissaire," Bonacieux interrupted, "there is not the least doubt about the matter. Monsieur d'Artagnan is my tenant, even though he doesn't pay his rent, so I surely know him—especially because he *doesn't* pay his rent! He is a young man, nineteen or twenty, and this gentleman is at least thirty. Monsieur d'Artagnan is in Monsieur Des Essarts's Guards, and this gentleman is one of Monsieur de Tréville's Musketeers. Look at his uniform, Monsieur le Commissaire, look at his uniform!"

"*Pardieu,* that's true," murmured the magistrate.

At that moment the door was thrown open and a messenger, introduced by one of the gatekeepers of the Bastille, gave the magistrate a letter.

"Devil take that woman!" cried the magistrate.

"What are you saying? I hope you are not talking about my wife!"

"On the contrary, I *am* talking about her. Your situation is worse than ever."

"But please, monsieur, tell me how my own situation can become worse by what my wife does while I am in prison?" asked the agitated haberdasher.

"Because what she does is part of a plan arranged between you—an infernal plan."

"I swear to you, Monsieur le Commissaire, that you are making a serious mistake—that I know nothing at all about what my wife was planning to do, that I have no idea about what she has done, and that if she has done anything foolish, I renounce her, I abjure her, I curse her!"

"Bah," said Athos to the magistrate, "if you have no more need of me, send me somewhere else. Your Monsieur Bonacieux is very tiresome."

"Return the prisoners to their cells," said the magistrate, designating by the same gesture Athos and Bonacieux. "Let them be guarded more strictly than ever."

"And yet," said Athos, with his habitual calm, "if it is Monsieur d'Artagnan who is concerned in this matter, I do not quite see how I can take his place."

"Do as I said," cried the magistrate, "and preserve absolute secrecy!"

Athos shrugged his shoulders and followed his guards silently, while M. Bonacieux wailed loudly enough to break the heart of a tiger.

They locked the haberdasher in the same cell in which he had spent the night and left him to himself for the rest of the day. Not being at all a military man, as he himself had informed us, he wept all day like a true haberdasher.

About nine o'clock in the evening, when he had made up his mind to go to bed, he heard steps in the corridor. These steps approached his cell, the door was flung open, and the guards appeared.

"Follow me," said an officer, who had come in behind the guards.

"Follow you?" cried Bonacieux. "At this hour? My God, where?"

"Where we have orders to take you."

"But that is not an answer."

"Nevertheless, it is the only one we can give you."

"My God," murmured the poor haberdasher, "this time I am truly lost!"

And he mechanically and passively followed the guards who had come for him.

He passed along the same corridor as before, crossed a courtyard, then went through a second part of the building; finally, at the gate of the entrance courtyard he found a carriage surrounded by four guards on horseback. They made him get in; the officer sat beside him, the door was locked, and both of them were now in a rolling prison.

The carriage moved as slowly as a hearse. Through the barred windows the prisoner could see only the houses and the pavement, but true Parisian that he was, he could recognize every street by the milestones, the shop signs, and the street lamps. When they reached St. Paul—where those who were condemned at the Bastille were executed—he almost fainted, and crossed himself twice. He thought the carriage was about to stop there, but it kept going.

Farther on, he was again terrified on passing the St. Jean cemetery, where state criminals were buried. One thing, however, reassured him: he remembered that before they were buried, their heads were generally cut off, and he knew that his head was still on his shoulders. But when he saw the carriage take the route to La Grève, when he observed the pointed roof of the Hôtel de Ville and the carriage passed under the arcade, he thought all was over with him. He wished to make his confession to the officer, and on the latter's refusal, cried so piteously that the officer threatened to gag him.

This threat somewhat reassured Bonacieux: if they meant to execute him at La Grève, it would scarcely be worthwhile to gag him because they were nearly there. Indeed, the carriage crossed the fatal spot without stopping, and there remained no other place to fear but the Croix-du-Trahoir: the carriage was taking the direct road to it.

This time there could no longer be any doubt; it was at the Croix-du-Trahoir that lesser criminals were executed. Bonacieux had flattered himself in believing himself worthy of St. Paul or the Place de Grève; it was at the Croix-du-Trahoir that his journey and his life were about to end! He could not yet see that dreadful cross, but he somehow felt as if it were coming to meet him.

When he was within twenty paces of it, he heard the sounds of people and the carriage stopped. This was more than poor Bonacieux, depressed by the successive emotions he had experienced, could endure; he groaned feebly, a sound that might have been taken for the last sigh of a dying man, and fainted.

14

The Man of Meung

THE CROWD was not there to wait for a man about to be hanged, but to look at a man who had already been hanged.

The carriage, which had had to stop for a few minutes, continued on its way, passed through the crowd, moved along the Rue St. Honoré, turned into the Rue des Bons Enfants, and stopped in front of a low door.

The door opened; the officer supporting Bonacieux let him fall into the arms of the two guards waiting to receive him. They half-carried him through a passage and up a flight of stairs, then deposited him in an anteroom.

He had endured all this movement passively: he had walked as though in a dream; he had seen things as through a fog; he had heard sounds without understanding them. If he had been about to be executed, he wouldn't have been able to make a single gesture in his own defense or utter a single cry to implore mercy.

He remained on the bench, his back against the wall and his hands hanging limply, exactly where the guards had placed him.

On looking around him, however—since he could see no threatening object, since nothing indicated that he was in any real danger, since the bench was comfortably padded, since the wall was covered with a beautiful Cordova leather, and since large red damask curtains, fastened back by gold clasps, floated before the window—he began to realize that his fear was exaggerated, and then to turn his head to the right and the left, up and down.

When nobody opposed that movement, he gathered a little courage and ventured to move one leg and then the other; finally, with the help of his two hands he lifted himself from the bench and found himself on his feet.

Just then, a pleasant-looking officer opened a door, continued to talk to someone in the next room, then came up to the prisoner.

"Is your name Bonacieux?" he asked.

"Yes, Monsieur l'Officier," stammered the haberdasher, more dead than alive. "At your service."

"Come in," said the officer.

And he moved out of the way to let Bonacieux pass, which he did without a word. He went into the room, where he seemed to be expected.

It was a large study, enclosed and stuffy, with arms both offensive and defensive on the walls. There was already a fire, although it was not even the end of September. A square table covered with books and papers, on which was spread an enormous map of the city of La Rochelle, occupied the center of the room.

Standing before the fireplace was a man of middle height, with a haughty look, piercing eyes, a broad forehead, and a long, thin face made even longer by a pointed beard surmounted by a mustache. Although he was barely thirty-six or thirty-seven years old, his hair, mustache, and beard were all graying. Except for the fact that he wore no sword, he looked like a soldier, and his buff boots, still lightly covered with dust, indicated that he had been on horseback during the course of the day.

This man was Armand-Jean Du Plessis, Cardinal Richelieu; not as he is often represented—broken down, in pain, his body bent, his voice failing, buried in a large armchair as though in an anticipated tomb, living only by the strength of his genius and maintaining his struggle with Europe only by constant mental application—but as he really was at that time: an active and gallant cavalier, already weak of body but sustained by that intellectual power which made him one of the most extraordinary men who ever lived. After having supported the Duc de Nevers in his duchy of Mantua and taken Nîmes, Castres, and Uzes, he was now preparing to drive the English from the Ile de Ré and lay siege to La Rochelle.

At first sight, nothing indicated that he was the cardinal, and it was impossible for those who did not know his face to guess in whose presence they were.

Bonacieux remained standing at the door while the eyes of the person we have just described were fixed upon him, as if he wished to penetrate into his very depths.

"Is this Bonacieux?" he asked, after a moment of silence.

"Yes, monseigneur," replied the officer.

"Very well. Give me those papers and leave us."

The officer took the designated papers from the table, gave them to the one who asked for them, bowed to the ground, and left.

Bonacieux recognized those papers as the record of his interrogations at the Bastille. From time to time the man at the fireplace raised his eyes from the writing and plunged them like daggers into the poor haberdasher's heart.

At the end of ten minutes of reading and ten seconds of examining Bonacieux, the cardinal was satisfied.

"That head has never conspired," he thought, "but it doesn't matter. We will see. . . ."

"You are accused of high treason," the cardinal said slowly.

"So I have been told, monseigneur," said Bonacieux, giving his interrogator the title he had heard the officer give him, "but I swear that I know nothing about it."

The cardinal repressed a smile.

"You have conspired with your wife, with Madame de Chevreuse, and with the Duke of Buckingham."

"Indeed, monseigneur, I have heard her mention all those names."

"On what occasion?"

"She said that Cardinal Richelieu had lured the Duke of Buckingham to Paris to ruin him and the queen with him."

"She said that?" exclaimed the cardinal.

"Yes, monseigneur, but I told her she was wrong to talk about such things, and that his Eminence was incapable . . ."

"Hold your tongue! You are a fool."

"That's exactly what my wife said, monseigneur."

"Do you know who carried her off?"

"No, monseigneur."

"But you have suspicions?"

"Yes, monseigneur, but those suspicions seemed to be disagreeable to Monsieur le Commissaire, and I no longer have them."

"Your wife has escaped. Did you know that?"

"No, monseigneur. I learned it after I was taken to prison, from the conversation of Monsieur le Commissaire—an amiable man."

The cardinal repressed another smile.

"Then you do not know what has become of your wife since her flight."

"Absolutely not, monseigneur, but she has most likely returned to the Louvre."

"At one o'clock this morning she had not yet returned."

"My God, what can have become of her?"

"We will find out, be assured. Nothing is hidden from the cardinal—he knows everything."

"In that case, monseigneur, do you think the cardinal will be so kind as to tell me what has become of my wife?"

"Perhaps. But first you must tell me all you know about your wife's relations with Madame de Chevreuse."

"But, monseigneur, I know nothing about them. I have never seen Madame de Chevreuse."

"When you went to fetch your wife from the Louvre, did you always return directly home?"

"Almost never. She usually had business to transact with cloth merchants, and I would conduct her to their houses."

"How many cloth merchants were there?"

"Two, monseigneur."

"Where do they live?"

"One on Rue de Vaugirard, the other on Rue de la Harpe."

"Did you go into those houses with her?"

"Never, monseigneur. I waited at the door."

"And what excuse did she give you for entering alone?"

"None. She told me to wait, and I waited."

"You are a very obliging husband, my dear Monsieur Bonacieux!" said the cardinal.

"He calls me his dear Monsieur," the haberdasher thought. "Things are going well."

"Would you recognize those doors again?"

"Yes."

"Do you know the numbers of the houses?"

"Yes."

"What are they?"

"Twenty-five on the Rue de Vaugirard, and seventy-five on the Rue de la Harpe."

"Good," said the cardinal.

He took up a silver bell and rang it; the officer came in.

"Go find Rochefort," he said softly. "If he has returned, tell him to come to me immediately."

"The count is here," said the officer, "and requests to speak with your Eminence at once."

" 'With your Eminence,' " murmured Bonacieux, who knew that this was the title usually given to the cardinal.

"Let him come in!" said the cardinal briskly.

The officer hurried out of the room with that alacrity which all the cardinal's servants displayed in obeying him.

" 'Your Eminence!' " Bonacieux repeated, still astonished by what he had heard.

Barely five seconds had elapsed before the door opened, and someone else came in.

"It is he!" cried Bonacieux.

"He! What he?" asked the cardinal.

"The man who abducted my wife!"

The cardinal rang the bell a second time. The officer reappeared.

"Place this man in the care of his Guards again, and let him wait till I send for him."

"No, monseigneur, it is not the man!" cried Bonacieux. "I was mistaken. This is quite another man and does not resemble him at all. I am sure this gentleman is an honest man."

"Take that fool away!" said the cardinal.

The officer took Bonacieux by the arm and led him back to the anteroom, where he found his two guards.

The newcomer followed Bonacieux impatiently with

his eyes till he had gone out, and the moment the door had closed, he approached the cardinal with urgency and said, "They have seen each other."

"Who?" asked his Eminence.

"She and he."

"The queen and the duke?"

"Yes."

"Where?"

"In the Louvre."

"Are you sure?"

"Perfectly sure."

"Who told you?"

"Madame de Lannoy, who is devoted to your Eminence, as you know."

"Why did she not tell me sooner?"

"Either by chance or because the queen mistrusts her, the queen had Madame de Surgis sleep in her room and detained her there all day."

"Well, we have been beaten! Now let us try to take our revenge."

"I will help you with all my heart, monseigneur. Be assured of that."

"How did it happen?"

"At half past twelve the queen was with her ladies-in-waiting—"

"Where?"

"In her bedroom . . ."

"Go on."

" . . . when someone brought her a handkerchief from her linen maid."

"And then?"

"The queen immediately exhibited strong emotion and evidently turned pale, despite the rouge with which her face was covered."

"And then?"

"Then she stood up and said with a strange voice, 'Ladies, wait for me. I will return in ten minutes.' And she opened the door of her alcove and went out."

"Why did not Madame de Lannoy inform you instantly?"

"Nothing was certain yet. Besides, her Majesty had said, 'Ladies, wait for me,' and she did not dare to disobey the queen."

"How long was the queen out of the room?"

"Three-quarters of an hour."

"None of her women accompanied her?"

"Only Doña Estefania."

"Did she return?"

"Yes, but only to get a little monogrammed rosewood box. She went out again immediately."

"And when she returned again, did she bring that box with her?"

"No."

"Does Madame de Lannoy know what was in the box?"

"Yes. The diamond studs his Majesty gave the queen."

"And she came back without that box?"

"Yes."

"Does Madame de Lannoy think that she gave them to Buckingham?"

"She is sure of it."

"How can she be so sure?"

"In the course of the day Madame de Lannoy, in her capacity as mistress of the robes, looked for the box, appeared uneasy at not finding it, and finally asked the queen about it."

"And the queen . . .?"

"The queen blushed, and replied that she had broken one of the studs the night before and had sent it to her goldsmith to be repaired."

"You must call on him to see if that is true or not."

"I have just been with him."

"And . . . ?"

"The goldsmith has heard nothing about it."

"Well, well! Rochefort, all is not lost! And perhaps— perhaps everything is for the best."

"I do not doubt that your Eminence's genius—"

" . . . will repair the blunders of his agent—is that it?"

"That is exactly what I was going to say, if your Eminence had let me finish my sentence."

"Meanwhile, do you know where Madame de Chevreuse and the Duke of Buckingham are now hiding?"

"No, monseigneur. My people could tell me nothing about that."

"But I know."

"You, monseigneur?"

"Yes; or at least I think I do. One was at 25 Rue de Vaugirard, the other at 75 Rue de la Harpe."

"Does your Eminence command that they both be instantly arrested?"

"It is too late—they will be gone."

"But still, we can at least make sure of that."

"Take ten of my Guardsmen and search the two houses thoroughly."

"Instantly, monseigneur."

And Rochefort dashed out.

The cardinal, now alone, thought for a moment, then rang the bell a third time.

The same officer appeared.

"Bring the prisoner in again," said the cardinal.

M. Bonacieux was again brought in, and at a signal from the cardinal, the officer withdrew.

"You have deceived me!" the cardinal said sternly.

"I?" cried Bonacieux. "I deceive your Eminence?"

"When your wife went to Rue de Vaugirard and Rue de la Harpe, she did not go to see cloth merchants."

"Then why did she go?"

"She went to meet the Duchesse de Chevreuse and the Duke of Buckingham."

Remembering all the circumstances, Bonacieux cried, "Yes, that's it! Your Eminence is right. I told my wife several times that it was surprising that cloth merchants should live in such houses, houses that had no signs outside, but she always laughed at me. Ah, monseigneur," he continued, throwing himself at his Eminence's feet, "you really are the cardinal, the great cardinal, the man of genius whom all the world reveres!"

No matter how contemptible the triumph over such a vulgar person as Bonacieux might be, the cardinal did not the less enjoy it for an instant; then, almost immediately, as if a fresh thought had just occurred to him, he smiled and said, offering his hand to the haberdasher, "Rise, my friend, you are a worthy man."

"The cardinal has touched me with his hand! I have touched the great man's hand! The great man has called me his friend!"

"Yes, my friend, yes," said the cardinal, with that paternal tone he sometimes knew how to assume, but which deceived none who knew him. "And since you have been unjustly suspected, you must be indemnified. Here, take this purse with a hundred pistoles, and forgive me."

"*I* forgive *you*, monseigneur!" said Bonacieux, hesitating to take the purse because he was afraid that the gift might only be a pleasantry. "But you could have me arrested or tortured or hanged because you are the undisputed master, and I would not be able to do anything about it! Pardon you, monseigneur? You cannot mean that!"

"Ah, my dear Monsieur Bonacieux, I see you are a generous man, and I thank you for it. So you will take this purse and leave without being too unhappy?"

"I go away enchanted, Monseigneur.

"Then, farewell, or rather au revoir, for I hope we shall meet again."

"Whenever Monseigneur wishes. I am always at his Eminence's orders."

"And that will be frequently, I assure you, because I have found something extremely agreeable in your conversation."

"Oh, monseigneur!"

"Au revoir, Monsieur Bonacieux."

And the cardinal waved his hand and Bonacieux replied by bowing to the ground and walking out backward. When he was in the anteroom the cardinal heard him shouting enthusiastically, "Long life to Monseigneur! Long life to his Eminence! Long life to the great cardinal!" The cardinal smiled at this vociferous manifestation of M. Bonacieux's feelings, and when Bonacieux's shouts were no longer audible, he thought, "Good! That man would now lay down his life for me."

And the cardinal began to examine with the greatest attention the map of La Rochelle that was spread out on the desk, tracing with a pencil a line representing the famous dike that was to close off the port of the besieged city eighteen months later. While he was absorbed in his strategic meditations, the door opened, and Rochefort came back into the room.

"Well?" asked the cardinal eagerly, rising with a promptitude that proved the importance he attached to the commission he had given the count.

"Well," said the latter, "a young woman between

twenty-six and twenty-eight years old, and a man between thirty-five and forty, have indeed lodged at the two houses pointed out by your Eminence. But the woman left last night, and the man this morning."

"It was they!" cried the cardinal. He looked at the clock. "And now it is too late to have them pursued. The duchess is at Tours, and the duke at Boulogne. It is in London that they must be found."

"What are your Eminence's orders?"

"Not a word about what has happened. Let the queen remain in perfect security, unaware that we know her secret. Let her believe that we are on the trail of some conspiracy or other. Send me Séguier, the keeper of the seals."

"And that man—what has your Eminence done with him?"

"What man?"

"That Bonacieux."

"I have done with him all that could be done—I have made him a man who will spy on his wife."

The Comte de Rochefort bowed like a man who acknowledges the great superiority of his master and withdrew.

Alone again, the cardinal seated himself again and wrote a letter, which he secured with his special seal. Then he rang his bell, and the officer came in for the fourth time.

"Tell Vitray to come to me," the cardinal said, "and tell him to get ready for a journey."

A few minutes later, the man he had asked for was there, booted and spurred.

"Vitray," he said, "you will go with all speed to London. You must not stop an instant on the way. You will deliver this letter to Milady. Here is an order for two hundred pistoles—take it to my treasurer and get the money. You will have as much again if you are back within six days and have executed your commission well."

The messenger, without replying a single word, bowed, took the letter and the order for the two hundred pistoles, and left.

Here is what the letter said:

MILADY,

Be at the first ball the Duke of Buckingham will attend. He will be wearing on his doublet twelve diamond studs. Get as close to him as you can, and cut off two of them.

As soon as those studs are in your possession, inform me.

15

Men of the Robe and Men of the Sword

ON THE DAY after these events had taken place, since Athos had not reappeared, d'Artagnan and Porthos informed M. de Tréville about his arrest. Aramis had asked for five days' leave of absence, and had gone to Rouen on family business—or so he had said.

M. de Tréville was like the father of his soldiers. The lowest or the least known of them, as soon as he put on the Musketeer's uniform, was as sure of his captain's support as if he had been his own brother.

He therefore immediately went to the office of the magistrate for criminal affairs, who sent for the officer who commanded the Croix-Rouge post, and by successive inquiries they learned that Athos was being held in the For-l'Evêque prison.

Athos had been subjected to all the examinations we have seen Bonacieux undergo.

We were present at the scene in which the two captives were confronted with each other. Athos, who had originally said nothing lest d'Artagnan be arrested and not have sufficient time to do what he thought necessary, now firmly declared that his name was Athos and not d'Artagnan. He added that he did not know either M. or Mme. Bonacieux; that he had never spoken to the one or the other; that he had come, at about ten o'clock in the evening, to pay a visit to his friend M. d'Artagnan but that until that time he had been at M. de Tréville's, where he had dined, and that twenty witnesses could ver-

ify the fact, including such a distinguished gentleman as
M. le Duc de la Trémouille.

The second magistrate was as bewildered as the first
had been by the Musketeer's simple and unswerving declaration; he had hoped he would be able to take the
revenge that magistrates—men of the robe—always like
to take on men of the sword, but the names of M. de
Tréville and M. de la Trémouille called for a little
reflection.

Athos was also sent to the cardinal, but unfortunately
the cardinal was at the Louvre with the king.

That was precisely when M. de Tréville, having left
the magistrate for criminal affairs and the governor of
the For-l'Evêque prison without having been able to find
Athos, arrived at the palace.

As captain of the Musketeers, M. de Tréville had the
right of entry at all times.

It is well known how violent the king's prejudices were
against the queen and how carefully those prejudices
were encouraged by the cardinal, who mistrusted women
infinitely more than men in matters of intrigue. One of
the main reasons for his Majesty's prejudice was the
friendship of Anne of Austria for Mme. de Chevreuse:
those two women gave him more uneasiness than the
wars with Spain, the conflicts with England, and the state
of the country's finances. He was convinced that Mme.
de Chevreuse served the queen not only in her political
intrigues but—what tormented him even more—in her
amorous intrigues.

As soon as the cardinal mentioned Mme. de Chevreuse—who, though exiled to Tours and believed to be
in that city, had come to Paris, remained there five days,
and outwitted the police—the king flew into a furious
passion. Capricious and unfaithful, he wished to be called
Louis the Just and Louis the Chaste; posterity will find
it difficult to understand his character because history
explains only by facts and never by the reasons behind
them.

But when the cardinal added that not only had Mme.
de Chevreuse been in Paris but that the queen had
renewed contact with her by means of one of those mysterious networks which at that time was called a *cabal;*
when he claimed that he, the cardinal, had been about

to unravel the closely twisted threads of this intrigue; when he described how at the moment the queen's emissary was to have been arrested with all the evidence against her still on her person, a Musketeer had dared to obstruct the course of justice by attacking the honest men of the law who were charged with investigating the whole affair impartially in order to present it to the king—at that moment Louis XIII could not contain himself any longer and took a step toward the queen's apartments, his face pale with that repressed hunger which led him to acts of the most pitiless cruelty when it broke out.

And in all this, the cardinal had not yet said a word about the Duke of Buckingham.

At that very moment M. de Tréville entered, coolly polite, controlled, and impeccably dressed.

Alerted to what must be happening by the cardinal's presence and the alteration in the king's face, M. de Tréville felt as strong as Samson before the Philistines.

Louis XIII had already placed his hand on the doorknob when he heard M. de Tréville enter; he turned around.

"You arrive in good time, monsieur," said the king, who could not hide his feelings once his passions had been roused to a certain point. "I have learned some fine things about your Musketeers."

"And I," said Tréville coldly, "have some interesting things to tell your Majesty about all these gownsmen, these . . . functionaries."

"What?" the king asked haughtily.

"I have the honor to inform your Majesty," continued M. de Tréville, in the same tone, "that a group of procurators, magistrates and policemen—undoubtedly very estimable people, but very hostile to soldiers—have taken upon themselves to arrest in a house, to lead away through the streets, and to throw into For-l'Evêque, one of my, or rather *your* Musketeers, sire, a man of irreproachable conduct, of an almost illustrious reputation, and whom your Majesty knows favorably—Monsieur Athos. And they have done all this on the basis of an order they have refused to show me!"

"Athos," said the king, repeating the name mechanically. "Yes, certainly I know that name."

"Let your Majesty remember," said Tréville, "that

Monsieur Athos is the Musketeer who had the misfortune to wound Monsieur de Cahusac so seriously in that annoying duel which you are familiar with. Apropos, monseigneur," Tréville continued, addressing the cardinal, "Monsieur de Cahusac is quite recovered, is he not?"

"Yes, thank you," said the cardinal, biting his lips in anger.

Tréville continued. "Athos had gone to pay a visit to one of his friends, a young Béarnais who is a cadet in Des Essarts's company of his Majesty's guards, but who was out at the time. Scarcely had he taken up a book while waiting for him to return when a crowd of bailiffs and soldiers came and laid siege to the house, broke open several doors—"

The cardinal made the king a sign, which signified, "That was because of the affair about which I spoke to you."

"We know all that," interrupted the king. "It was done in our service."

"Then was it also in your Majesty's service that one of my innocent Musketeers was seized and placed between two guards like a criminal—that this gallant man, who has ten times shed his blood in your Majesty's service and is ready to shed it again, was paraded through an insolent mob?"

"Is that how it was managed?" asked the king, shaken.

"Monsieur de Tréville," said the cardinal impassively, "does not tell your Majesty that this innocent Musketeer, this gallant man, had only an hour before attacked, sword in hand, four examining magistrates who had been delegated by me to investigate an affair of the highest importance."

"I defy your Eminence to prove it," Tréville replied with his Gascon outspokenness and military directness. "An hour before his arrest Monsieur Athos—who is, as I can assure your Majesty, a nobleman of the highest rank—was doing me the honor, after having dined with me, to be in my drawing room, talking to the Duc de la Trémouille and the Comte de Châlus, who were also there."

The king looked at the cardinal.

"A written, official statement is proof of it," said the

cardinal, replying aloud to his Majesty's silent question, "and the injured parties have drawn up the following, which I have the honor to present to your Majesty."

"And is a written report of these men of the robe, these gownsmen, compared to the word of honor of a swordsman?" Tréville asked scornfully.

"Come, come, Tréville, hold your tongue," said the king.

"If his Eminence has any suspicions about one of my Musketeers," said Tréville, "the justice of Monsieur le Cardinal is so well known that I myself will demand an inquiry."

"In the house in which the judicial inquiry was made," continued the phlegmatic cardinal, "there lives, I believe, a young Béarnais, a friend of the Musketeer in question."

"Your Eminence means Monsieur d'Artagnan."

"I mean a young man who is your protégé, Monsieur de Tréville."

"Yes, your Eminence, it is the same man."

"Do you not suspect this young man of having given bad advice . . . ?"

"To Athos, a man nearly double his age?" interrupted Tréville. "No, monseigneur. Besides, d'Artagnan spent that evening with me."

"Well," said the cardinal, "everybody seems to have spent the evening with you."

"Does your Eminence doubt my word?" said Tréville, his face flushed with anger.

"No, God forbid!" said the cardinal. "But at what time was he with you?"

"Oh, as to that I can speak positively, your Eminence, because when he came in, I noticed that it was only half past nine although I had thought it was later."

"And what time did he leave your house?"

"At half past ten—an hour after the event."

"But Athos *was* taken in the house on the Rue des Fossoyeurs," replied the cardinal, who did not for an instant suspect Tréville's integrity and who felt victory escaping him.

"Is one friend forbidden to visit another, or a Musketeer of my company to fraternize with a Guard of Des Essarts's company?"

"Yes, when the house where he fraternizes is under suspicion."

"That house is under suspicion, Tréville," said the king. "Perhaps you did not know that?"

"Indeed, sire, I did not. The house may be under suspicion, but I deny that it can be so in the part of it inhabited by Monsieur d'Artagnan, because I can assure you, sire, that from what he says, there does not exist a more devoted servant of your Majesty or a more profound admirer of Monsieur le Cardinal."

"Was it not this d'Artagnan who wounded Jussac in that unfortunate encounter which took place near the Carmes Déchaussés monastery?" asked the king, looking at the cardinal, who colored with vexation.

"Yes, and the next day, Bernajoux. Yes, sire, it is the same man, and your Majesty has a good memory."

"How shall we decide this?" asked the king.

"That concerns your Majesty more than me," replied the cardinal. "I would say he was guilty."

"And I would deny it," said Tréville. "But his Majesty has judges, and those judges will decide."

"Yes, that is best," said the king. "Send the case to the judges. It is their business to judge, and they will judge."

"But," Tréville added, "it is sad that in the unfortunate times in which we live, even the purest life and the most incontestable virtue cannot exempt a man from defamation and persecution. I am sure the army will not be pleased at being subjected to harsh treatment because of police affairs."

The expression was imprudent; but M. de Tréville was fully aware of that when he used it. He wanted an explosion, because that throws forth fire and fire illuminates.

"Police affairs!" cried the king, taking up Tréville's words. "And what do you know about police affairs, Monsieur? Concern yourself with your Musketeers, and do not annoy me like this. According to you, if a Musketeer is mistakenly arrested, France is in danger. What a fuss about one Musketeer! I could have ten of them arrested, a hundred of them, even the whole company, and I would not tolerate a word of complaint about it!"

"From the moment they are suspected by your Majesty," said Tréville, "the Musketeers are guilty. You therefore see me prepared to surrender my sword, for after having accused my soldiers, there can be no doubt that Monsieur le Cardinal will end by accusing me. It is best to make myself a prisoner at once and join Athos, who has already been arrested, and d'Artagnan, who most probably will be."

"Gascon-headed man, have done with this!" said the king.

"Sire," replied Tréville, without changing his tone in the least, "either order my Musketeer to be restored to me or let him be tried."

"He will be tried," said the cardinal.

"So much the better, for in that case I will ask his Majesty for permission to plead his case."

The king feared an outbreak between the two men.

"If his Eminence," he said, "did not have personal motives—"

The cardinal saw what the king was about to say, and interrupted him.

"Pardon me, sire," he said, "but since your Majesty considers me a prejudiced judge, I must withdraw."

"Will you swear, by the memory of my father, that Athos was at your house during these events and that he took no part in them?" the king asked Tréville.

"By the memory of your glorious father, and by yourself, whom I love and respect above all the world, I swear it."

"Be so kind as to reflect, sire," said the cardinal. "If we release the prisoner, we will never know the truth."

"Athos may always be found," replied Tréville, "ready to answer the magistrates whenever it pleases them to question him. He will not desert, Monsieur le Cardinal, be assured of that. I will answer for him."

"No, he will not desert," said the king, "and he can always be found, as Tréville says. Besides," he added, lowering his voice and looking with a suppliant air at the cardinal, "let us give them a sense of security—that is politic."

Richelieu smiled at the king's idea of "politic."

"Give the order, sire. You have the right to pardon."

"Only the guilty can be pardoned," said Tréville, determined to have the last word, "and my Musketeer is innocent. It is not mercy that you are about to accord, sire, it is justice."

"He is in the For-l'Evêque prison?" the king asked.

"Yes, sire, in solitary confinement, in a cell, like the lowest criminal."

"The devil," murmured the king, "what should be done?"

"Sign an order for his release, and that will be sufficient," replied the cardinal. "I believe with your Majesty that Monsieur de Tréville's assurance is more than sufficient."

Tréville bowed very respectfully, with a joy that was not unmixed with fear; he would have preferred an obstinate resistance on the part of the cardinal to this sudden yielding.

The king signed the order for Athos's release, and Tréville took it.

As he was about to leave, the cardinal gave him a friendly smile and said to the king, "A perfect harmony reigns, sire, between the leader of your Musketeers and his soldiers, which must be beneficial to you and honorable to all."

"He will play me some scurvy trick or other, and that immediately," Tréville thought. "One can never have the last word with such a man. But I must be quick—the king may change his mind in an hour, and it is more difficult to put a man back into For-l'Evêque or the Bastille once he is out, than to keep one in who is already there."

M. de Tréville triumphantly entered For-l'Evêque and freed the Musketeer, whose unshakable lack of concern had not abandoned him for a moment.

The first time he saw d'Artagnan, he said to him, "You have come off well. Your Jussac thrust is now paid for, but there is still Bernajoux's, and you must not be too confident."

As for the rest, M. de Tréville had good reason to mistrust the cardinal and to think that all was not over, for scarcely had the captain of the Musketeers closed the door behind him than his Eminence said to the king, "Now that we are finally by ourselves, we will, if your Majesty pleases, talk seriously. Sire, Buckingham has been in Paris for five days, and left only this morning."

16

M. Séguier, Keeper of the Seals,
Again Looks for the Bell
He Rang in His Youth

IT IS IMPOSSIBLE to imagine the impression these few words made on Louis XIII. He turned first ashen and then red, and the cardinal saw at once that he had recovered at a single stroke all the ground he had lost.

"Buckingham in Paris!" cried the king. "Why is he here?"

"To conspire, no doubt, with your enemies, the Huguenots and the Spaniards."

"No, *pardieu*, no! To conspire against my honor with Madame de Chevreuse, Madame de Longueville, and the Condés."

"Oh, sire, what an idea! The queen is too virtuous, and besides, she loves your Majesty too well."

"Woman is weak, Monsieur le Cardinal," said the king. "And as to loving me much, I have my own opinion about that love."

"I nevertheless maintain that the Duke of Buckingham came to Paris for entirely political purposes."

"And I am sure that he came for quite another purpose, Monsieur le Cardinal! But if the queen is guilty, let her tremble!"

"Though even the idea of such treason is repugnant, your Majesty compels me to think of it. Madame de Lannoy, whom according to your Majesty's command I have frequently questioned, told me this morning that the night before last her Majesty was up very late, that today she cried all morning, and that she was writing most of the afternoon."

"To *him*, no doubt! Cardinal, I must have the queen's papers."

"But how are we to get them, sire? It seems to me that neither your Majesty nor I can assume such a mission."

"What did they do with regard to the Maréchale

d'Ancre?" cried the king, in the highest state of fury. "First they thoroughly searched her house, and then she herself was searched."

"The Maréchale d'Ancre was only the Maréchale d'Ancre, nothing but a Florentine adventuress, sire. But your Majesty's wife is Anne of Austria, Queen of France—one of the greatest princesses in the world."

"She is only the more guilty, Monsieur le Duc! The higher her position, the more degrading her fall. Besides, I long ago determined to put an end to all her petty political intrigues and love affairs. She has a certain La Porte close to her . . ."

"Who is, I believe, behind all this," said the cardinal.

"Then you agree that she is deceiving me?" asked the king.

"I believe, and I repeat it to your Majesty, that the queen conspires against the power of the king, but I have not said against his honor."

"And I say she is conspiring against both. I say the queen does not love me. I say she loves another. I say she loves that infamous Buckingham! Why did you not have him arrested while he was in Paris?"

"Arrest the duke! Arrest the prime minister of King Charles I! Just think of the talk it would have caused, sire! And if your Majesty's suspicions had proven justified, what a terrible disclosure! What a fearful scandal!"

"But since he behaved like a vagabond or a thief, he should have been . . ."

Louis XIII stopped, terrified at what he had been about to say, while Richelieu leaned forward expectantly and waited in vain for the word that had died on the king's lips.

"He should have been . . .?"

"Nothing, nothing. But you did not lose sight of him during the time he was in Paris, did you?"

"No, sire."

"Where did he stay?"

"Seventy-five Rue de la Harpe."

"Where is that?"

"Near the Luxembourg."

"And you are certain that the queen and he did not see each other?"

"I believe the queen to have too strong a sense of her duty, sire."

"But they have corresponded. The queen has been writing to him all afternoon. Duke, I must have those letters!"

"But sire . . ."

"At whatever price, Duke, I will have them!"

"I would beg your Majesty to observe . . ."

"Do you also betray me, Monsieur le Cardinal, by thus opposing my will? Are you also in league with Spain and England, with Madame de Chevreuse and the queen?"

"Sire," replied the cardinal, sighing, "I believed myself secure from such a suspicion."

"Monsieur le Cardinal, you have heard me. I will have those letters."

"There is only one way."

"What is that?"

"That would be to charge Monsieur de Séguier, the keeper of the seals, with this mission. The matter is completely within his official responsibilities."

"Let him be sent for instantly."

"He is most likely at my house. I asked him to call on me, but he had not come before I came to the Louvre, so I left orders for him to wait."

"Let him be sent for instantly."

"Your Majesty's orders will be carried out, but . . ."

"But what?"

"But the queen may refuse to obey."

"Refuse to obey my orders?"

"Yes, if she does not know that those orders come from the king."

"Well, I will go and inform her myself, so she will have no doubts about that."

"Your Majesty will not forget that I have done everything in my power to prevent a rupture between you and the queen."

"Yes, Duke, I know you are very indulgent toward the queen, too indulgent perhaps, and I warn you that we shall have occasion at some future time to speak of that."

"Whenever it pleases your Majesty, but I will always be happy and proud, sire, to sacrifice myself to the harmony that I wish to see between you and the Queen of France."

"Very well, Cardinal, very well, but meanwhile send for the Keeper of the Seals. I will go to the queen."

And opening a door, Louis XIII walked down the corridor that led from his apartments to those of Anne of Austria.

The queen was with her ladies-in-waiting—Mme. de Guitaut, Mme. de Sablé, Mme. de Montbazon, and Mme. de Guéménée. In a corner was her Spanish companion, Doña Estefania, who had followed her from Madrid. Mme. Guéménée was reading aloud, and everybody was listening to her attentively except the queen, who had only asked for the reading in order to pursue her own thoughts while pretending to listen.

Those thoughts, gilded though they were by a last reflection of love, were nevertheless sad. Anne of Austria was deprived of the confidence of her husband and pursued by the hatred of the cardinal, who could not forgive her for having repulsed his more tender sentiments. She always remembered the example of the queen-mother, whom that hatred had tormented all her life—although if the memoirs of the time are to be believed, Marie de Medicis had begun by granting the cardinal the favors that Anne of Austria had always refused him. The queen had seen the downfall of her most devoted servants, her most intimate confidants, her dearest friends. Like someone under a fatal curse, she brought misfortune to everyone she knew; her friendship called down persecution: Mme. de Chevreuse and Mme. de Vernet had been exiled, and La Porte did not conceal from his mistress that he expected to be arrested at any moment.

While she was in the midst of these deep and dark reflections the door opened, and the king came in.

The reader stopped instantly. All the ladies rose, and there was a profound silence.

The king made no pretense of politeness; he stopped in front of the queen and said, 'Madame, you are about to receive a visit from Chancellor Séguier, who will at my command speak to you about certain matters."

The unfortunate queen, who was constantly being threatened with divorce, exile, and even being brought to trial, turned pale under her rouge and could not refrain from asking, "But why such a visit, sire? What can the chancellor have to say to me that your Majesty could not say yourself?"

The king turned on his heels, without replying, and almost at the same instant the captain of the Guards, M. de Guitant, announced the chancellor.

When the chancellor appeared, the king had already gone out by another door.

Chancellor Séguier entered, half smiling, half blushing, and as we will probably meet him again in the course of our story, it may be well for our readers to become acquainted with him.

This chancellor had a droll history. He had been introduced to his Eminence as a truly devout man by Des Roches le Masle, canon of Notre Dame and formerly the valet of a bishop. The cardinal trusted him, and it was to his advantage.

Many stories were told about him, and among them this:

After a wild youth, he had retired to a monastery to expiate, at least for a while, his adolescent follies. But when he entered that holy place, the poor penitent was unable to shut the door behind him quickly enough to prevent the passions he was fleeing from entering with him. He was obssessed by them, and the superior, to whom he had confided his misfortune and who wished to help him as much as he could, advised him to conjure away the tempting demon of the flesh by ringing the bell with all his might; at that self-denouncing sound, the monks would become aware that a brother was being besieged by temptation and the whole community would begin to pray.

This seemed like good advice to the future chancellor, and he exorcised the evil spirit with the help of the abundant prayers offered up by the monks. But the devil does not allow himself to be so easily dispossessed; in proportion as the monks redoubled the exorcisms he redoubled the temptations, so that the bell was ringing day and night, announcing the penitent's extreme desire for mortification.

The monks did not have an instant's rest. By day they did nothing but go up and down the steps that led to the chapel; at night, in addition to complines and matins, they also had to leap out of their beds many times and prostrate themselves on the floor of their cells.

It is not known whether it was the devil who gave way or the monks who grew tired, but at the end of three months the penitent reappeared in the world with the reputation of having the most terrible case of possession that ever existed.

On leaving the monastery he entered the magistracy; succeeded his uncle as presiding officer of the High Court; embraced the cardinal's party, which gave proof of considerable wisdom; became chancellor; zealously served his Eminence in his hatred of the queen-mother and his vengeance against Anne of Austria; stimulated the judges in the Chalais affair; and encouraged the efforts of M. de Laffemas. Finally, invested with the full confidence of the cardinal—a confidence he had well earned—he was given the unusual commission that was responsible for him now presenting himself in the queen's apartments.

The queen was still standing when he entered, but as soon as she saw him she sat down again and signaled her women to do the same. With an air of supreme disdain, she said, "What do you wish, monsieur, and why do you present yourself here?"

"Madame, in the name of the king and notwithstanding the respect I owe to your Majesty, I am here to examine all your papers."

"What, monsieur? Examine my papers . . .? *My* papers? Truly, this is an indignity!"

"Be kind enough to pardon me, madame, but in this matter I am only the instrument that the king employs. Has his Majesty not just left you, and has he not himself asked you to prepare for my visit?"

"Search, then, monsieur, since it seems I am a criminal! Estefania, give him the keys to my tables and desks."

For form's sake the chancellor paid a visit to those pieces of furniture named, but he knew very well that the queen would not have put the important letter she had written that day into a piece of furniture.

When the chancellor had opened and shut the desk drawers twenty times, it became necessary, however hesitant he might be, to come to the conclusion of the affair—that is, to search the queen herself. He therefore advanced toward Anne of Austria and said, with great perplexity and embarrassment, "And now I must make the principal examination."

"What do you mean?" asked the queen, who did not understand—or rather was not willing to understand.

"His Majesty is certain that you have written a letter today and that it has not yet been sent to its address. The letter is not in your tables or your desks, yet it must be somewhere."

"Would you dare lay your hand on your queen?" said Anne of Austria, drawing herself up to her full height and looking at him with an almost threatening expression.

"I am a faithful subject of the king, madame, and all that his Majesty commands I shall do."

"The cardinal's spies have served him well! It is true that I wrote a letter today and that it has not yet gone. The letter is here."

The queen put her beautiful hand on her bosom.

"Then give me that letter, madame," said the chancellor.

"I will give it to none but the king, monsieur."

"If the king had wished the letter to be given to him, madame, he would have asked you for it himself. But I repeat—it is I who am ordered to obtain it, and if you do not give it up . . ."

"Well?"

"He has ordered me to take it from you."

"What do you mean?"

"That my orders go far, madame, and that I am authorized to search for that letter even on your Majesty's person."

"How horrible!" cried the queen.

"Be kind enough, then, madame, to be more cooperative."

"This conduct is infamous! Do you know that, monsieur?"

"The king commands it, madame, so forgive me."

"I will not allow it! No, I would rather die!" cried the queen, whose imperious Spanish and Austrian blood began to rebel.

The chancellor made a deep bow; then, clearly resolved not to be stopped from accomplishing his mission, he approached the queen with the determination of an executioner's assistant in a torture chamber. Tears of rage filled her eyes.

As we have said, the queen was very beautiful. The chancellor's mission was a delicate one, but the king's jealousy of Buckingham was so great that he was not jealous of anyone else.

At that moment Chancellor Séguier must have looked around for the rope of the monastery bell, but not finding it, he summoned his resolution and extended his hand toward the place where the queen had acknowledged the paper was to be found.

She stepped back, became so pale that it seemed as if she might be dying, and leaning with her left hand on a table behind her to keep herself from falling, she took the paper from her bosom with her right hand and held it out to the keeper of the seals.

"There is the letter, monsieur!" she said, her voice tremulous. "Take it and relieve me of your odious presence."

The chancellor, who was himself understandably trembling with emotion, took the letter, bowed to the ground, and left.

The door had scarcely closed behind him when the queen sank, half fainting, into the arms of her women.

The chancellor carried the letter to the king without having read a single word of it. The king took it with an unsteady hand, looked for the address, which it did not have, became very pale, opened it slowly, and then, seeing by the first words that it was addressed to the King of Spain, read it rapidly.

It was a complete plan of attack against the cardinal. The queen urged her brother and the Emperor of Austria, who felt themselves injured by Richelieu's policies— the eternal object of which was the abasement of the house of Austria—to pretend to declare war against France and to insist, as a condition of peace, on the dismissal of the cardinal. As to love, there was not a single word about it in the entire letter.

The king, quite delighted, asked if the cardinal was still in the Louvre; he was told that his Eminence was awaiting his Majesty's orders in the study.

The king went straight to him.

"Well, Duke," he said, "you were right, and I was wrong. The whole intrigue is political, and there is not the least mention of love in this letter. On the other hand, there is much mention of you."

The cardinal took the letter and read it very attentively; then, when he had finished it, he read it a second time.

"You see, your Majesty, how far my enemies go," he said. "They threaten you with two wars if you do not dismiss me. In your place, sire, I would yield to such powerful pressure, and for my part, I would be happy to withdraw from public affairs."

"What are you saying, Duke?"

"I say, sire, that my health is failing under these endless struggles and my constant labors. I say that I will probably not be able to withstand the fatigues of the siege of La Rochelle and that it would be far better for you to appoint there Monsieur de Condé, Monsieur de Bassompierre, or some other capable gentleman whose business is war. I am a churchman, yet I am constantly being turned aside from my real vocation to look after matters for which I have no aptitude. Without me, you would have fewer problems in France, sire, and I do not doubt you would be more powerful abroad."

"Monsieur le Cardinal," said the king, "I understand you. Rest assured—all who are named in that letter will be punished as they deserve, even the queen herself."

"What do you say, sire? God forbid that the queen should suffer the least inconvenience on my account! She has always believed me to be her enemy, sire, although your Majesty can bear witness that I have always taken her part warmly, even against you. Oh, if she was betraying your Majesty's honor, it would be quite another thing, and I would be the first to say, 'No mercy, sire—no mercy for the guilty!' But happily there is nothing of the kind, and your Majesty has just had a new proof of it."

"That is true, Monsieur le Cardinal, and you were right, as you always are. But nevertheless the queen deserves my anger."

"It is you, sire, who have now incurred hers. And I could well understand it if she were to be seriously offended. Your Majesty has treated her with a severity . . ."

"It is how I will always treat my enemies and yours,

Duke, however high they may be placed, and whatever danger I may risk in acting severely toward them."

"The queen is my enemy, but not yours, sire. On the contrary, she is a devoted, submissive, and irreproachable wife. Allow me to intercede for her with your Majesty."

"Let her humble herself, then, and come to me first."

"On the contrary, sire, you must set the example. You committed the first wrong, since it was you who suspected her."

"What! I make the first advances? Never!"

"Sire, I entreat you to do so."

"Besides, in what way could I possibly make the first advances even if I wanted to?"

"By doing something that would give her pleasure."

"What?"

"Give a ball. You know how much the queen loves dancing, and I assure you that her resentment will not hold out against such a gesture."

"Monsieur le Cardinal, you know that I do not like worldly pleasures."

"The queen will be all the more grateful to you, since she knows that. Besides, it will be an opportunity for her to wear those beautiful diamond studs you gave her recently for her birthday, and which she has had no occasion to wear."

"We shall see, Monsieur le Cardinal," said the king, who was so overjoyed at finding the queen guilty of a crime he cared little about, and innocent of a fault he had greatly dreaded, that he was ready to be reconciled with her. "We shall see, but you are too indulgent toward her."

"Sire, leave severity to your ministers. Clemency is a royal virtue—use it now, and you will find that it will be to your advantage."

Thereupon the cardinal, hearing the clock strike eleven, bowed low, asked permission to withdraw, and again begged the king to reconcile himself with the queen.

Anne of Austria, who as a consequence of the seizure of her letter had expected reproaches, was astonished the next day to see the king make some overtures to her. Her first response was to reject them. Her womanly pride and queenly dignity had both been so cruelly offended that she could not come around at the first advance, but persuaded by the advice of her women, she at last seemed to begin to forget. The king took advantage of this favorable moment to tell her that he intended to soon give a ball.

A ball was so rare an event for the poor queen that at this announcement, as the cardinal had predicted, the last trace of her resentment disappeared—if not from her heart at least from her face. She asked when the ball would take place, but the king replied that he had to consult the cardinal about that.

Indeed, every day the king asked the cardinal when this event should take place, and every day the cardinal, under some pretext, delayed setting a date.

Ten days went by in this manner.

A week after the scene we have described, the cardinal received a letter from London that contained these lines:

> I have them, but I am unable to leave London for lack of money. Send me five hundred pistoles, and four or five days after I have received them I will be in Paris.

On the same day the cardinal received this letter the king asked his usual question.

Richelieu counted on his fingers and thought, "She will arrive, she says, four or five days after having received the money. It will take four or five days for the money to reach her, four or five days for her to return—that makes ten days. Now, allowing for contrary winds, accidents, and a woman's weakness, that makes twelve days."

"Well, Duke, have you made your calculations?" asked the king.

"Yes, sire. Today is the twentieth of September. The city magistrates are giving a ball on the third of October. That is very convenient because you will not appear to have gone out of your way to please the queen."

Then the cardinal added, "Apropos, sire, do not forget to tell her Majesty the evening before the ball that you would like to see how her diamond studs look on her."

17

Monsieur and Madame Bonacieux
at Home

THAT WAS THE second time the cardinal had mentioned those diamond studs to the king, who was struck by this insistence and began to think that it concealed some mystery.

The king had more than once been humiliated by the cardinal, whose police, without being as efficient as our own, were nevertheless excellent and much better informed about what was going on in his own household than he himself was. He therefore hoped that by talking to the queen he would be able to obtain some secret information and report it to his Eminence—who might or might not already know it, but which in either case would make the cardinal think more highly of the king's abilities.

He therefore went to the queen and, according to his custom, made fresh threats against those who surrounded her. She bowed her head and allowed the torrent to flow on without replying, hoping it would soon stop; but that was not what Louis XIII wanted. He wanted a discussion that would throw some light on the mystery, because he was convinced that the cardinal had something in mind—one of those terrible surprises that his Eminence was so skillful at creating.

The king finally succeeded by dint of his persistent accusations.

"But, sire," cried Anne of Austria, tired of his vague attacks, "you do not tell me all that you have in your heart. I do not know what you are thinking about. What have I done? Let me know what crime I have committed. It is impossible that your Majesty can make all this ado about a letter written to my brother!"

The king, attacked so directly, did not know what to answer, so he decided that this was the moment for expressing the request he was not supposed to have made until the evening before the ball.

"Madame," he said pompously, "there will soon be a

ball at the Hôtel de Ville. In order to do honor to our worthy city magistrates, I wish you to appear in ceremonial dress, and, above all, wearing the diamond studs I gave you on your birthday. That is what I am thinking about."

The answer to the queen's question was a terrible shock. She believed that Louis XIII knew everything and that the cardinal had persuaded him to pretend otherwise for seven or eight days, which was characteristic of his methods. She turned very pale, supported herself by leaning on a console table—her hand seeming to be made of wax—and looked at the king with terror in her eyes; she was unable to speak a single syllable.

"You hear, madame?" the king asked, enjoying her embarrassment to its full extent without guessing its cause.

"Yes, sire, I hear," stammered the queen.

"You will appear at this ball?"

"Yes."

"With those studs?"

"Yes."

The queen's pallor increased; the king noticed it with pleasure, enjoying it with that cold cruelty which was one of the worst sides of his character.

"Then that is understood," he said, "and that is all I had to say to you."

"On what day will this ball take place?"

The queen having put the question in an almost inaudible voice, the king felt instinctively that he ought not to answer it.

"Oh, very shortly, madame, but I do not remember the precise date. I will ask the cardinal."

"Then, it was the cardinal who informed you about the ball?"

"Yes, madame, but why do you ask?"

"It was he who told you to invite me to appear there with my diamond studs?"

"That is to say, madame . . ."

"It was he, sire, it was he!"

"Well, and what does it matter whether it was he or I? Is there any crime in such a request?"

"No, sire."

"Then you will appear at the ball?"

"Yes, sire."

"With your studs?"

"Yes, sire."

"Very well," said the king, withdrawing. "I will count on it."

The queen curtsied, less from etiquette than because her knees could hardly support her.

The king went away enchanted.

"I am lost," murmured the queen. "The cardinal knows everything, and it is he who urges on the king, who knows nothing yet but will soon also know everything. I am lost! My God, my God!"

She knelt on a cushion and prayed, her head buried between her trembling arms.

Her situation was indeed terrible. Buckingham had returned to London; Mme. de Chevreuse was at Tours. More closely watched than ever, the queen felt certain that one of her women was betraying her, although she didn't know which one it was. La Porte could not leave the Louvre, and she had not a soul in the world in whom she could confide.

Thinking about the misfortune that threatened her and the abandonment in which she was left, she burst into tearful sobs.

"Can I be of no service to your Majesty?" asked a voice full of sweetness and pity.

The queen turned around quickly, for there was no mistaking the friendship in that voice.

In fact, the pretty Mme. Bonacieux was standing at one of the doors which opened into the queen's apartment. She had been arranging the dresses and linen in an adjoining closet when the king had entered; she had not been able to get out, and had heard everything.

The queen uttered a startled cry because at first she did not recognize the young woman who had been placed with her by La Porte.

"Oh, fear nothing, madame!" said the young woman, clasping her hands and weeping herself at the queen's anguish. "I am your Majesty's, body and soul, and however inferior my position, I believe I have discovered a way to extricate you from your trouble."

"Look me in the eyes," exclaimed the queen. "I am betrayed on all sides—can I trust you?"

"Oh, madame," cried the young woman, falling to her knees; "I swear I am ready to die for your Majesty!"

This was said from the very bottom of her heart, and there was no mistaking its sincerity.

"Yes, there are traitors here," Mme. Bonacieux continued, "but by the holy name of the Virgin, I swear that no one is more devoted to your Majesty than I am. Those studs the king speaks of—you gave them to the Duke of Buckingham, did you not? They were in a little rosewood box that he held under his arm? Am I wrong? Is it not so, madame?"

"Oh, my God," murmured the queen, her teeth chattering with fright.

"We must get those studs back again," said Mme. Bonacieux.

"Yes, of course we must, but how? How can it be done?"

"Someone must be sent to the duke."

"But who? Whom can I trust?"

"Trust me, madame. Do me that honor, my queen, and I will find a messenger."

"But I will have to write a note."

"Oh, yes, that is indispensable. A few words from your Majesty's hand, and your private seal."

"But those few words could bring about my ruin—could mean divorce, exile!"

"Yes, if they fell into the wrong hands. But I will answer for those few words being delivered to their address."

"Then I must place my life, my honor, my reputation, in your hands?"

"Yes, madame, you must, and I will save them all."

"But how? At least tell me how."

"My husband has been free these last two or three days, and I have not yet had time to see him again. He is a man who feels neither love nor hate for anybody, but will simply do whatever I ask because I ask it. At my request he will set out without knowing what he is carrying, and will take your Majesty's letter, without even knowing it is from your Majesty, to the address that is on it."

With a burst of emotion, the queen took the young woman's two hands, gazed at her as if to read her very heart, and seeing nothing but sincerity in her beautiful eyes, embraced her tenderly.

"Do that," she said, "and you will have saved my life and my honor!"

"Do not exaggerate the service I have the happiness to render your Majesty. Your Majesty does not need to have her honor saved—she is only the victim of treacherous plots."

"That is true, my child. You are right."

"Then give me that letter, madame. We must hurry."

The queen ran to a little table on which were ink, paper, and pens. She wrote two lines, sealed the letter with her private seal, and gave it to Mme. Bonacieux.

"And now," said the queen, "we are forgetting one very necessary thing."

"What is that, madame?"

"Money."

Mme. Bonacieux blushed.

"Yes, that is true," she said, "and I must confess to your Majesty that my husband . . ."

"Your husband has none. Is that what you were about to say?"

"No, he has some, but he is very miserly—that is his failing. But do not worry, your Majesty, we will find a way."

"And I have no money, either," said the queen. (Those who have read Mme. de Motteville's *Memoirs* will not be astonished by this reply.) "But wait. . . ."

The queen ran to her jewel case.

"Here is a very valuable ring, or so I have been told. It came from my brother, the King of Spain, so it is mine, and I am free to dispose of it as I wish. Take this ring and raise money with it, then let your husband set out."

"You will be obeyed within the hour."

"You see the address," said the queen, speaking so softly that Mme. Bonacieux could hardly hear what she said. "To the Duke of Buckingham, London."

"The letter will be given to him personally."

"Generous girl!" cried Anne of Austria.

Mme. Bonacieux kissed the queen's hands, concealed the paper in the bodice of her dress, and disappeared with the lightness of a bird.

Ten minutes later she was at home. As she had told the queen, she had not seen her husband since his release and was therefore unaware of the change that had taken place in him with respect to the cardinal—a change that had since been strengthened by two or three visits from the Comte de Rochefort, who had become Bonacieux's best friend and had persuaded him, without too much trouble, that the abduction of his wife had only been a political precaution.

She found Bonacieux alone. The poor man was trying to restore, with much difficulty, order in his house; he had found the furniture mostly broken and his closets nearly empty—the forces of justice not being one of the three things King Solomon names as leaving no trace of their passage. As to the servant, she had run away at the moment of her master's arrest: terror had had such an effect upon the poor girl that she had walked all the way from Paris to her native province of Burgundy.

The worthy haberdasher had immediately sent his wife word of his happy return, and she had replied by congratulating him, and telling him that the first moment she could steal from her duties would be devoted to paying him a visit.

This first moment had been delayed for five days, which under any other circumstances might have appeared rather long to M. Bonacieux; but the visit he had made to the cardinal and the visits Rochefort had made to him had given him much to think about, and as everybody knows, nothing makes time pass more quickly than thinking.

This was especially so because Bonacieux's thoughts were all rose-colored. Rochefort called him his friend, his dear Bonacieux, and never stopped telling him that the cardinal had a great respect for him. The haberdasher fancied himself already on the high road to honors and fortune.

Mme. Bonacieux had also been thinking, but about something very different from ambition. In spite of herself, her thoughts had constantly returned to that handsome young man who was so brave and who seemed to be so much in love with her. Married at eighteen to M. Bonacieux, having always lived among her husband's friends—people not very capable of inspiring any tender sentiments in a young woman whose ideals were above her station—she had remained indifferent to ordinary attempts to seduce her; but in those days the title of gentleman had a great impact on middle-class women, and d'Artagnan was a gentleman. Besides, he wore the uniform of the Guards, which next to that of the Musketeers was the one most admired by the ladies. He was, we repeat, handsome, young, and bold; he spoke of love like a man who did love and was eager to be loved in return. There was certainly more than enough in all this to turn a head only twenty-three years old, and Mme. Bonacieux had just arrived at that happy period of life.

Although husband and wife had not seen each other for a week, and during that time serious events had taken place in both their lives, they greeted each other with a certain air of preoccupation. Nevertheless, Bonacieux showed real joy at the sight of his wife and advanced toward her with open arms.

Madame Bonacieux presented her cheek to him.

"We must talk," she said.

"What?" said Bonacieux, astonished.

"Yes, I have something very important to tell you."

"And I have some serious questions to put to you. Please tell me about your abduction."

"Oh, that's of no importance now."

"And what is important—my imprisonment?"

"I heard about that the day it happened, but since you were not guilty of any crime or involved in any intrigue, and since you knew nothing that could compromise yourself or anybody else, I did not take it more seriously than it deserved."

"You speak very easily about it, madame," said Bonacieux, hurt by his wife's lack of interest in him. "Do you know that I was buried in a cell of the Bastille for a day and night?"

"Oh, a day and a night soon pass. Let us forget your captivity and return to the reason that brings me here."

"The reason that brings you home to me? Is it not the desire to see a husband from whom you have been separated for a week?" he asked, wounded to the quick.

"Yes, of course, but something else too."

"What?"

"It is something very important, on which our future fortune may depend."

"The state of our fortune has changed very much since I last saw you, Madame Bonacieux, and I would not be surprised if it were to excite the envy of many people in the course of the next few months."

"Yes, particularly if you follow the instructions I am about to give you."

"Me?"

"Yes, you. There is a good and holy action to be performed, monsieur, and much money to be gained at the same time."

Mme. Bonacieux knew that by talking to her husband about money, she was appealing to his most vulnerable side. But a man, even a haberdasher, is no longer the same man after he has talked for ten minutes with Cardinal Richelieu.

"Much money to be gained?" Bonacieux asked.

"Yes."

"How much?"

"A thousand pistoles, perhaps."

"What you are going to ask me to do is serious, then?"

"It is indeed."

"What must be done?"

"You must go somewhere immediately. I will give you a piece of paper that you must not part with on any account, and you will deliver it to the proper hands."

"And where must I go?"

"To London."

"To London? You jest! I have no business in London!"

"But others wish you to go there."

"Who are those others? I warn you that I will never again work in the dark, and that I want to know not only to what I expose myself, but for whom I expose myself."

"An important person is sending you, an important person is awaiting you. The compensation will exceed your expectations, and that is all I can tell you."

"More intrigues! Nothing but intrigues! Thank you, madame, but I am aware of them now—Monsieur le Cardinal has enlightened me."

"The cardinal? You have seen the cardinal?"

"He sent for me," the haberdasher answered proudly.

"And you responded to his bidding, you imprudent man?"

"Well, I did not have much choice of going or not going, because I was taken to him between two Guards. It is also true that since I did not then know his Eminence, I would have been delighted to dispense with the visit."

"Did he mistreat you? Threaten you?"

"He gave me his hand and called me his friend. His friend! Do you hear that, madame? I am the friend of the great cardinal!"

"Of the great cardinal!"

"Would you argue his right to that title, madame?"

"I would argue nothing. But I tell you that a minister's patronage is ephemeral, and a man must be mad to attach himself to a minister. There are powers above his, which do not depend on the whims of a man or the result of an event, and it is to those powers that we should rally."

"I am sorry, madame, but I acknowledge no power other than that of the great man I have the honor to serve."

"You serve the cardinal?"

"Yes, madame, and as his servant, I will not allow you to be involved in plots against the safety of the state or to serve the intrigues of a woman who is not French and who has a Spanish heart. Fortunately the great cardinal is there—his vigilant eyes watch over everything and penetrate to the very bottom of a person's heart."

Bonacieux was repeating word for word a sentence he had heard from the Comte de Rochefort; but the poor wife, who had counted on her husband, and who had, because of that confidence, answered for him to the queen, shuddered—both at the danger she had barely escaped and at the helpless state to which she was reduced. Nevertheless, knowing her husband's weakness, and especially his cupidity, she did not despair of bringing him around to her purpose.

"So you are a cardinalist, monsieur, are you?" she cried. "You serve the party of those who mistreat your wife and insult your queen?"

"Private interests are nothing compared to common

interests. I am for those who save the state," Bonacieux said emphatically.

This was another of the Comte de Rochefort's phrases that he had retained, and now had occasion to use.

"What do you know about the state?" Mme. Bonacieux asked, shrugging her shoulders. "Be satisfied with being a plain, straightforward citizen and turn to the side that offers the most advantages."

"And what do you think about this, Madame Preacher?" said Bonacieux, slapping a plump, round bag that returned a sound of money.

"Where does that money come from?"

"You cannot guess?"

"From the cardinal?"

"From him, and from my friend the Comte de Rochefort."

"The Comte de Rochefort! Why, it was he who abducted me!"

"That may be, madame."

"And you take money from that man!"

"Did you not say that the abduction was entirely political?"

"Yes, but its object was the betrayal of my mistress—to torture me until I said things that might compromise the honor and perhaps the life of my royal mistress."

"Madame, your royal mistress is a treacherous Spaniard, and what the cardinal does is well done."

"Monsieur, I knew you were cowardly, miserly, and foolish, but I did not know you were treacherous!"

"Madame, what are you saying?" said Bonacieux, who had never seen his wife in a passion and who recoiled from this conjugal anger.

"I am saying you are a miserable creature!" continued Mme. Bonacieux, who saw she was regaining some influence over her husband. "You meddle with politics, do you—and even worse, with cardinalist politics? Why, you are selling yourself, body and soul, to the devil—for money!"

"No, to the cardinal."

"It's the same thing! Who names Richelieu names Satan."

"Hold your tongue, madame! You may be overheard."

"Yes, you are right, and I would be ashamed for any-one to know of your baseness."

"But what do you want of me? Tell me."

"I have already told you. You must leave instantly, and accomplish loyally the mission I have deigned to charge you with, and on that condition I pardon every-thing, I forget everything; and what is more"—she held out her hand to him—"I restore my love to you."

Bonacieux was cowardly and miserly, but he loved his wife. He softened; a man of fifty cannot be angry with a wife of twenty-three for very long.

Mme. Bonacieux saw that he was hesitating.

"Well, have you decided?" she asked.

"But my dear love, think about what you are asking me to do. London is far from Paris, very far, and the mission with which you charge me may be dangerous."

"What does it matter, if you avoid the dangers?"

"Madame Bonacieux, I positively refuse. Intrigues ter-rify me now that I have seen the Bastille. My God, that's a frightful place, that Bastille! Only to think about it makes my flesh crawl. They threatened me with torture. Do you know what the torture is? Wooden wedges that they stick between your legs and then apply pressure to until the bones crack! No, I will not go. Why do you not go yourself? For, in truth, I begin to think I have been deceived in you—I believe you must be a man, and a warlike one, too."

"And you, you are a woman—a miserable, stupid woman! You are afraid, are you? Well, if you do not leave for London this very instant, I will have you arrested by the queen's orders and imprisoned in that Bastille which you dread so much!"

Bonacieux thought deeply, weighing the two angers—that of the cardinal and that of the queen: the cardinal's seemed unquestionably heavier.

"Have me arrested by order of the queen," he said, "and I—I will appeal to his Eminence."

Mme. Bonacieux saw at once that she had gone too far, and she was terrified at having told him so much. For a moment she looked fearfully at that stupid face and saw nothing but the unswerving obstinacy of a fright-ened fool.

"Well, so be it!" she said. "You may be right after all.

In the long run, a man knows more about politics than a woman, particularly you, Monsieur Bonacieux, who have spoken with the cardinal. And yet it is very hard," she added, "that the man whose affection I thought I might depend on should treat me so unkindly and not indulge any of my whims."

"That is because your whims go too far," replied the triumphant Bonacieux, "and I mistrust them."

"Well, I will give it all up, then," she said, sighing. "Let us say no more about it."

"If you would at least tell me what I would have to do in London . . ." said Bonacieux, who had just remembered, a little too late, that Rochefort had wanted him to discover his wife's secrets.

"It is no use for you to know anything about it," said the young woman, her instinctive mistrust making her draw back. "It was just about one of those purchases that interest women—a purchase by which much might have been gained."

But the more discreet the young woman was, the more important Bonacieux thought the secret that she refused to confide to him must be. He resolved to go immediately to the Comte de Rochefort and tell him that the queen was looking for a messenger to send to London.

"Excuse me for leaving you, my dear Madame Bonacieux," he said, "but not knowing you would come to see me, I had made an appointment with a friend. If you will wait just a short while for me, I will return as soon as I have finished my business with that friend. Since it is growing late, I will come back and escort you to the Louvre."

"Thank you, monsieur, but you are not brave enough to be of any use to me whatever. I will return very safely to the Louvre all alone."

"As you please. Will I see you again soon?"

"Next week I hope my duties will leave me some time, and I will take advantage of it to come and put things back in order here."

"Very well, I will expect you. You are not angry with me?"

"Not the least in the world."

"I will see you soon."

"I will see you soon."

Bonacieux kissed his wife's hand and left immediately.

"Well," said Mme. Bonacieux, when her husband had shut the street door and she found herself alone, "the only thing that imbecile had not done was to become a cardinalist. And I, who have answered for him to the queen—I, who have promised my poor mistress . . . oh, my God, she will take me for one of those wretches who swarm around the palace, brought there to spy on her! Ah, Monsieur Bonacieux, I never did love you very much, but now it is worse than ever—I hate you, and I swear you will pay for this!"

At the moment she spoke those words a rap on the ceiling made her raise her head, and a voice that reached her through the ceiling called out, "Dear Madame Bonacieux, open the little door on the alley, and I will come down to you."

18

The Lover and the Husband

"Ah, MADAME, allow me to tell you that you have a bad sort of a husband," said d'Artagnan, entering by the door the young woman had opened for him.

"You overheard our conversation?" asked Mme. Bonacieux, looking at him uneasily.

"All of it."

"But how?"

"By means known only to myself, and which I also used when I overheard the livelier conversation you had with the cardinal's police."

"What did you understand from what my husband and I said?"

"A thousand things. In the first place, that your husband is a simpleton and a fool. In the next place, that you are in trouble, which pleases me because it gives me an opportunity to put myself at your service, and God knows I am ready to throw myself into the fire for you. Finally, that the queen wants a brave, intelligent, and loyal man to make a journey to London for her. I have at least two of the three qualities you need, and here I am."

Mme. Bonacieux did not reply, but her heartbeat quickened with joy and secret hope shone in her eyes.

"And what guarantee can you offer me," she asked, "if I consent to give you this mission?"

"My love for you. Speak! Command! What has to be done?"

"My God," murmured the young woman, "should I confide such a secret to you, monsieur? You are little more than a boy."

"I see that you need someone to vouch for me."

"I admit that would reassure me greatly."

"Do you know Athos?"

"No."

"Porthos?"

"No."

"Aramis?"

"No. Who are those gentlemen?"

"Three of the king's Musketeers. Do you know Monsieur de Tréville, their captain?"

"Oh, yes, I know him. Not personally, but from having heard him speak to the queen more than once as a brave and loyal gentleman."

"You are not afraid that he would betray you to the cardinal?"

"Oh, no, certainly not!"

"Well, tell him your secret and ask him whether—however important, valuable, or dangerous it may be—you cannot confide it to me."

"But the secret is not mine, and I have no right to reveal it to anyone."

"You were about to confide it to Monsieur Bonacieux," said d'Artagnan, vexed.

"As one confides a letter to the hollow of a tree, the wing of a pigeon, or the collar of a dog."

"And yet you can plainly see that I love you."

"So you say."

"I am an honorable man."

"So you say."

"I am a gallant man."

"I believe it."

"I am brave."

"Oh, I am sure of that!"

"Then put me to the proof."

Mme. Bonacieux looked at the young man, restrained for a minute by a last hesitation; but there was such ardor in his eyes, such persuasion in his voice, that she felt drawn to confide in him. Besides, she found herself in circumstances where everything must be risked for the sake of everything. The queen might be as injured by too much caution as by too much confidence, and—let us admit it—the involuntary feelings that she felt for her young protector decided her to speak.

"Listen," she said, "I yield to your protestations, I submit to your assurances. But I swear to you, before God who hears us, that if you betray me, and my enemies do not destroy me, I will kill myself and accuse you of my death."

"And I—I swear to you before God, madame, that if I am taken while carrying out the orders you give me, I will die sooner than do or say anything that may compromise anyone."

So she told him the terrible secret, part of which he had already learned by chance in front of the Samaritaine. This was their mutual declaration of love.

D'Artagnan was radiant with joy and pride. This secret that he now knew, this woman whom he loved and who showed such confidence in him, made him feel like a giant.

"I will go at once," he said.

"What do you mean, you will go at once? What about your regiment, your captain?"

"By my soul, you had made me forget all that, dear Constance! Yes, you are right. I must have a leave of absence."

"Still another obstacle," murmured Mme. Bonacieux sorrowfully.

"I will overcome it, be assured," said d'Artagnan, after a moment's thought.

"How?"

"I will go this very evening to Monsieur de Tréville, whom I will request to request this favor for me from his brother-in-law, Monsieur Des Essarts."

"But there is something else . . ."

"What?" he asked, seeing her hesitate.

"Perhaps you have no money?"

"*Perhaps* is a word too much," he said, smiling.

"Then take this bag," replied Mme. Bonacieux, opening a cupboard and taking from it the very bag her husband had caressed so affectionately a half hour earlier."

"The cardinal's?" cried d'Artagnan, breaking into a loud laugh, for remember, he had heard every syllable of the conversation between the haberdasher and his wife.

"The cardinal's. You see it looks very respectable."

"*Pardieu*, it will be doubly amusing to save the queen with the cardinal's money!"

"You are a kind and charming young man," said Mme. Bonacieux. "Believe me, you will not find her Majesty ungrateful."

"Oh, I am already grandly compensated! I love you, and you permit me to tell you that I do—that is already more happiness than I dared to hope for."

"Silence!" Mme. Bonacieux said suddenly.

"What is it?"

"Someone is talking in the street."

"It is . . ."

"My husband! Yes, I recognize his voice!"

D'Artagnan ran to the door and pushed the bolt.

"He cannot come in before I have gone, and when I have, you can open to him."

"But I ought to go, too. How can I explain the disappearance of his money if I am here?"

"You are right. We must both leave."

"How? He will see us if we leave."

"Then you must come up to my room."

"Ah, you say that in a way that frightens me!"

She spoke those words with tears in her eyes and when d'Artagnan saw those tears, he knelt tenderly at her feet.

"You will be as safe with me as in a church. I give you my word as a gentleman."

"Then let us go. I will trust you, my friend!"

D'Artagnan carefully drew back the bolt, and light as shadows, they both glided through the interior door into the passage, climbed the stairs as quietly as possible, and entered d'Artagnan's rooms.

Once there, the young man barricaded the door for greater security. They approached the window, and through a slit in the shutter they saw Bonacieux talking with a man in a cloak.

At the sight of this man d'Artagnan started; half drawing his sword, he rushed to the door.

It was the man of Meung.

"What are you going?" cried Mme. Bonacieux. "You will ruin us all!"

"But I have sworn to kill that man!" said d'Artagnan.

"Your life no longer belongs to you. In the name of the queen I forbid you to throw yourself into any danger not connected with your journey."

"And do you give me no orders in your own name?"

"In my name, I beg you! But listen—they are speaking about me."

D'Artagnan went back to the window and listened.

M. Bonacieux had opened his door and, seeing the apartment empty, had returned to the man in the cloak, whom he had left alone for an instant.

"She is gone," he said. "She must have returned to the Louvre."

"You are sure that she did not suspect your intentions when you went out?" asked the stranger.

"No," replied Bonacieux smugly, "she is not clever enough."

"Is the young Guardsman at home?"

"I do not think so. As you can see, his shutter is closed, and there is no light shining through the slats."

"All the same, it would be best to make sure."

"How?"

"By knocking on his door."

"I will ask his servant."

Bonacieux reentered the house, passed through the same door that had just been used by the two fugitives, went up to d'Artagnan's door, and knocked.

No one answered. Porthos, in order to make an even more splendid impression than usual, had borrowed Planchet that evening, and d'Artagnan was of course careful not to give the least sign of existence.

At the sound of Bonacieux's hand on the door, the two young people felt their hearts beat faster.

"There is nobody there," said Bonacieux.

"Even so, let us return to your apartment. We will be safer there than in a doorway."

"We will hear no more," whispered Mme. Bonacieux.

"On the contrary, we will hear better," d'Artagnan answered.

He raised the three or four boards that made his room another ear of Dionysius, spread a carpet on the floor, went down on his knees, and motioned Mme. Bonacieux to do as he did.

"You are sure there is nobody there?" the stranger asked.

"I am certain," Bonacieux replied.

"And you think that your wife . . ."

"Has returned to the Louvre."

"Without speaking to anyone but you?"

"I am sure of it."

"That is important, do you understand?"

"Then the news I brought you is of interest?"

"The greatest interest, my dear Bonacieux, and I don't conceal it from you."

"And the cardinal will be pleased with me?"

"I have no doubt of it."

"The great cardinal!"

"Are you sure that your wife mentioned no names in her conversation with you?"

"I think not."

"She did not name Madame de Chevreuse, the Duke of Buckingham, or Madame de Vernet?"

"No. She only told me she wished to send me to London to serve the interests of an important person."

"The traitor!" murmured Mme. Bonacieux.

"Silence!" said d'Artagnan, taking her hand, which she unthinkingly abandoned to him.

"Never mind," continued the man in the cloak. "You were a fool not to have pretended to accept the mission. You would then have had the letter. The state, which is now threatened, would be safe, and you . . ."

"And I?"

"Well, you—the cardinal would have made you a nobleman."

"Did he tell you so?"

"Yes, I know that he meant to give you that agreeable surprise."

"Don't worry," said Bonacieux. "My wife adores me, and there is still time."

"The idiot!" murmured Mme. Bonacieux.

"Silence!" said d'Artagnan, holding her hand more tightly.

"How is there still time?" asked the man in the cloak.

"I go to the Louvre, I ask for Madame Bonacieux, I say that I have thought about it, I reopen the discussion, I obtain the letter, and I run directly to the cardinal."

"Well, go quickly! I will return soon to learn the result of your efforts."

The stranger left.

"Silly fool!" said Mme. Bonacieux, addressing this epithet to her husband.

"Silence!" d'Artagnan repeated, holding her hand still more tightly.

A terrible howl interrupted them. Bonacieux had discovered the disappearance of his money bag and was screaming, "Thieves!"

"Oh, my God," cried Mme. Bonacieux, "he will rouse the whole neighborhood."

Bonacieux shouted for a long time; but because such cries were so frequent on the Rue des Fossoyeurs, and also because the haberdasher's house had recently acquired a bad reputation, no one came, and he went out continuing to call, his voice becoming fainter and fainter as he went in the direction of the Rue du Bac.

"And now that he is gone, it is your turn to go," said Mme. Bonacieux. "Courage, my friend—but above all, prudence, and remember that your life is the queen's."

"Hers and yours!" cried d'Artagnan. "Be satisfied, beautiful Constance. I will return worthy of her gratitude—but will I also return worthy of your love?"

The young woman replied only by the beautiful flush that mounted to her cheeks.

A few seconds later d'Artagnan went out enveloped in a large cloak that ill-concealed the sheath of his long sword.

Mme. Bonacieux followed him with her eyes, with that long, fond look with which a woman accompanies the man she loves; but when he had turned the corner, she knelt, clasped her hands, and prayed. "Oh, my God, protect the queen, and protect me!"

19

The Campaign Plan

D'ARTAGNAN went straight to M. de Tréville's. He had reflected that the cardinal would soon be warned by that cursed stranger who appeared to be his agent, and he decided, with reason, that he did not have a moment to lose.

His heart was overflowing with joy. Here was an opportunity to acquire both glory and money, and in addition—a far greater inducement—it brought him into close intimacy with a woman he adored; this chance did more for him at one time than he would have dared ask of Providence.

M. de Tréville was in his drawing room with his usual circle of gentlemen. D'Artagnan, who was known as an intimate of the house, went straight to Tréville's study and sent word that he wished to see him about something important.

D'Artagnan had been there scarcely five minutes when M. de Tréville entered. Seeing d'Artagnan's joy, the estimable captain plainly immediately realized that something new was afoot.

In his way, d'Artagnan had been debating with himself about whether he should confide in M. de Tréville or only ask him to give him carte blanche for some secret affair. But M. de Tréville had always been so thoroughly his friend, was so devoted to the king and queen, and hated the cardinal so wholeheartedly, that the young man resolved to tell him everything.

"Did you ask for me, my friend?" said M. de Tréville.

"Yes, monsieur," said d'Artagnan. "And I hope that when you know the importance of my business you will forgive me for having disturbed you."

"I am listening."

"It concerns nothing less," said d'Artagnan, lowering his voice, "than the honor and perhaps the life of the queen."

"What are you saying?" asked M. de Tréville, glancing around to be sure they were truly alone and then fixing d'Artagnan with his questioning look.

"I am saying, monsieur, that chance has rendered me master of a secret . . ."

"Which I hope you will guard, young man, as you would your life."

"But which I must impart to you, monsieur, for you alone can help me with her Majesty's mission."

"Is this secret your own?"

"No, monsieur, it is her Majesty's."

"Are you authorized by her Majesty to communicate it to me?"

"No, monsieur. On the contrary, I am required to preserve the most complete secrecy."

"Then why are you about to betray it to me?"

"Because, as I said, without you I can do nothing, and I am afraid you will refuse me the favor I have come to ask if you do not know why I ask it."

"Keep your secret, young man, and tell me what you wish."

"I wish you to obtain for me, from Monsieur Des Essarts, a two-week leave of absence."

"Starting when?"

"This very night."

"You are leaving Paris?"

"I am going on a mission."

"May you tell me where?"

"To London."

"Has anyone an interest in preventing your arrival there?"

"The cardinal, I believe, would give the world to stop me."

"And you are going alone?"

"I am going alone."

"In that case I can assure you that you will not get beyond Bondy."

"What do you mean?"

"You will be assassinated."

"Then I will die performing my duty."

"But your mission will not be accomplished."

"That is true."

"Believe me," continued Tréville, "in this kind of enterprise four must set out in order that one may arrive."

"You are right, monsieur. . . . You know Athos, Porthos, and Aramis—can I use them in this matter?"

"Without confiding to them the secret I have not wanted to know?"

"We have sworn, once and for all, to have complete confidence and blind trust in one another. Besides, you can tell them that you have trusted me fully, and they will not question me more than you have."

"I can send to each of them permission for a two-week leave of absence—to Athos, whose wound still pains him, to take the waters at Forges, and to Porthos and Aramis so they can accompany their friend, whom they are not willing to abandon in his suffering. Sending them their leaves will be proof enough that I authorize their journey."

"Thank you, monsieur. You are very good."

"Go find them immediately, and leave tonight! Wait—first write out your request to Des Essarts. You might have had a spy at your heels, and if so, your visit is already known to the cardinal. This will make it seem legitimate."

D'Artagnan wrote out his request, and M. de Tréville, on receiving it, assured him that by two o'clock in the morning the four leaves of absence would be at the respective homes of the travelers.

"Have the goodness to send mine to Athos's. I am afraid of some disagreeable encounter if I go home."

"Very well. Adieu, and a prosperous voyage. . . . Apropros," said M. de Tréville, calling out.

D'Artagnan turned around and walked back to him.

"Do you have any money?"

D'Artagnan tapped the bag he had in his pocket.

"Enough?"

"Three hundred pistoles."

"Good! That can carry you to the end of the world. On your way, then!"

D'Artagnan bowed, and M. de Tréville held out his hand to him; d'Artagnan shook it with a respect mixed with gratitude. Ever since his arrival in Paris, he had had many occasions to honor this excellent man, whom he had always found upright, loyal, and warmhearted.

His first visit was to Aramis, at whose apartment he had not been since the evening on which he had followed Mme. Bonacieux. Furthermore, he had seldom seen the young Musketeer since then, and every time he had, Aramis had seemed very sad.

This evening, too, Aramis was melancholy and thoughtful. D'Artagnan asked him the reason for this prolonged period of gloom, and Aramis pleaded as his excuse a commentary on the eighteenth chapter of St. Augustine, which he had to write, in Latin, for the following week, and which was greatly preoccupying him.

After the two friends had been chatting a few moments, one of M. de Tréville's servants came in, bringing a sealed packet.

"What is that?" asked Aramis.

"The leave of absence Monsieur has asked for," replied the lackey.

"I have not asked for a leave of absence!"

"Hold your tongue and take it!" said d'Artagnan. "And you, my friend, here is a demipistole for your trouble. You will tell Monsieur de Tréville that Monsieur Aramis is very much obliged to him. Go."

The lackey bowed to the ground and departed.

"What does this mean?" asked Aramis.

"Pack what you need for a two-week journey, and follow me."

"But I cannot leave Paris just now, not without knowing . . ."

Aramis stopped in mid-sentence.

" . . . what has become of her? Is that what you mean?" continued d'Artagnan.

"Become of whom?" replied Aramis.

"The woman who was here—the woman with the embroidered handkerchief."

"Who told you there was a woman here?" replied Aramis, turning deathly pale.

"I saw her."

"Do you know who she is?"

"I believe I can at least guess."

"Since you seem to know so many things can you tell me what has happened to that woman?"

"I presume that she has returned to Tours."

"To Tours? Yes, you evidently do know her. But why did she return to Tours without telling me anything?"

"Because she was afraid of being arrested."

"Why has she not written to me?"

"Because she was afraid of compromising you."

"D'Artagnan, you restore me to life!" cried Aramis. "I imagined myself despised, betrayed. I was so delighted to see her again! I could not believe she had risked her liberty for me, and yet for what other reason would she have returned to Paris?"

"For the same reason that is taking us to England today."

"And what is that reason?"

"You will know it someday, Aramis, but for now I must imitate your discretion about the 'doctor's niece.' "

Aramis smiled as he remembered the tale he had told his friends on a certain evening.

"Well, since you are sure she has left Paris, d'Artagnan, nothing prevents me from doing the same, and I am ready to follow you. You say we are going . . ."

"To see Athos now, and if you want to come, please hurry, because we have already lost much time. And by the way, tell Bazin."

"Will Bazin be going with us?" asked Aramis.

"Perhaps. At all events, it would be best for him to follow us to Athos's."

Aramis called Bazin and ordered him to join them at Athos's apartment.

"Let us go!" he said, at the same time taking his cloak, sword, and three pistols and opening in vain two or three drawers to see if he could not find some stray coin. When he was quite sure that his search was useless, he followed d'Artagnan, wondering to himself how the young Guardsman knew so well the identity of the lady to whom he had given hospitality, and how he knew better than himself what had become of her.

As they went out, Aramis put his hand on d'Artagnan's arm and, looking at him earnestly, said, "You have not spoken to anyone about that lady?"

"To no one in the world."

"Not even to Athos or Porthos?"

"I have not breathed a syllable to them."

"Good!"

Reassured about that important point, Aramis continued on his way with d'Artagnan, and both soon arrrived at Athos's dwelling.

They found him holding his leave of absence in one hand and M. de Tréville's note in the other.

"Can you explain the meaning of this leave of absence and this letter, which I have just received?" asked the puzzled Athos.

> MY DEAR ATHOS,
> Since your health absolutely requires it, I wish you to rest for a fortnight. Go take the waters at Forges, or any that may be more agreeable to you, and recuperate as quickly as possible.
> Your affectionate
> TRÉVILLE

"The leave of absence and the letter mean that you must follow me, Athos."

"To the waters at Forges?"

"There or elsewhere."

"In the king's service?"

"Either the king's or the queen's. Are we not their Majesties' servants?"

At that moment Porthos entered.

"*Pardieu*," he exclaimed, "here is a strange thing! Since when have they granted men in the Musketeers leave of absence without their asking for it?"

"Since they have had friends who ask it for them," d'Artagnan responded.

"Ah," said Porthos, "it seems something new has happened."

"Yes, we are leaving," said Aramis.

"Where are we going?" asked Porthos.

"My faith, I do not know," Athos replied. "Ask d'Artagnan."

"To London, gentlemen," said d'Artagnan.

"To London!" cried Porthos. "And what the devil are we going to do in London?"

"That is what I am not at liberty to tell you, gentlemen. You must trust me."

"But in order to go to London," added Porthos, "money is needed, and I have none."

"Nor I," said Aramis.

"Nor I," said Athos.

"I have," said d'Artagnan, pulling out his treasure from his pocket and placing it on the table. "There are three hundred pistoles in this bag. Let each of us take seventy-five—that is enough to take us to London and back. Besides, I do not think we will all arrive in London."

"Why?"

"Because some of us will most likely fall by the wayside."

"Are we embarking on a campaign?"

"A most dangerous one, I warn you."

"Bah! But if we do risk being killed," said Porthos, "at least I would like to know why."

"You would not be much the wiser," said Athos.

"I agree with Porthos," said Aramis.

"Does the king give you such reasons? No. He says to you jauntily, 'Gentlemen, there is fighting in Gascony or in Flanders—go there and fight,' and you go there. Why? You do not concern yourself about it."

"D'Artagnan is right," said Athos. "Here are our three leaves of absence from Monsieur de Tréville, and here are three hundred pistoles from I know not where. So let us go and get killed wherever we are told to go. Is life worth the trouble of so many questions? D'Artagnan, I am ready to follow you."

"And so am I," said Porthos.

"And so am I," said Aramis. "Indeed, I am not sorry to leave Paris—I need a change to distract me."

"Well, you will have distractions enough, gentlemen, I assure you," said d'Artagnan.

"When do we leave?" asked Athos.

"Immediately," replied d'Artagnan. "We have not a minute to lose."

"Grimaud! Planchet! Mousqueton! Bazin!" cried the four young men, calling their lackeys. "Clean my boots, and fetch the horses from Monsieur de Tréville's house."

Each Musketeer was accustomed to use that house as a barrack, leaving there his own horse and that of his lackey.

Planchet, Grimaud, Mousqueton, and Bazin rushed off.

"Now let us plan our campaign," said Porthos. "Where do we go first?"

"To Calais," said d'Artagnan. "That is the most direct route to London."

"Well," said Porthos, "here is my advice . . ."

"Go on."

"Four men traveling together would be suspected. D'Artagnan will give each of us his instructions, then I will go by way of Boulogne to clear the way, Athos will set out two hours later by way of Amiens, and Aramis will follow us by the Noyon road. As to d'Artagnan, he will go by whatever road he thinks best, in Planchet's clothes, while Planchet will follow us wearing d'Artagnan's uniform."

"Gentlemen," said Athos, "my opinion is that it is not proper to allow lackeys to have anything to do in such an affair. A secret may, by chance, be betrayed by gentlemen, but it is almost always sold by lackeys."

"Porthos's plan is impractical," said d'Artagnan, "since I myself am ignorant of what instructions I can give you. I am the bearer of a letter, that is all. I have not made, and I cannot make, three copies of that letter because it is sealed. It seems to me that we must travel together. The letter is here, in this pocket"—and he pointed to the pocket that contained the letter—"and if I should be killed, one of you must take it, and continue. If he is killed, it will be another's turn, and so on. Only one of us need arrive."

"Bravo, d'Artagnan, I agree with you!" cried Athos. "Besides, we must be consistent with the reason for our leaves. I am going to take the waters, and you are accompanying me. Instead of taking the waters at Forges, I have decided to take sea waters, which I am free to do. If anyone tries to stop us, I will show Monsieur de Tréville's letter, and you will show your leaves of absence. If we are attacked, we will defend ourselves, and if we are arrested and tried, we will insist that we were only anxious to dip ourselves in the sea. They would have an easy time of it with four isolated men, but four men together make a troop. We will arm our four lackeys with pistols and muskets—if they send an army out against us, we will give battle, and the survivor, as d'Artagnan says, will carry the letter."

"Well said!" cried Aramis. "You don't often speak, Athos, but when you do, it is like St. John of the Golden Mouth. I agree to Athos's plan. And you, Porthos?"

"I agree to it too," said Porthos, "if d'Artagnan approves of it. He, being the bearer of the letter, is naturally the head of the enterprise. Let him decide, and we will execute."

"Well," said d'Artagnan, "I decide that we should adopt Athos's plan and set off in half an hour."

"Agreed!" shouted the three Musketeers in chorus.

Each one reached into the bag, took his seventy-five pistoles, and made his preparations to set out at the appointed time.

20

The Journey

AT TWO O'CLOCK in the morning, our four adventurers left Paris by the Porte St. Denis. As long as it was dark they remained silent; in spite of themselves they felt the influence of the obscurity and suspected ambushes on every side.

With the first rays of day their tongues were loosened; their gaiety revived with the sun. It was like the eve of a battle: their hearts beat quickly, their eyes laughed, and they felt that the life they were perhaps going to lose, was after all a good thing.

The appearance of their caravan was formidable: the martial bearing and regimental step of the Musketeers' black horses, those noble companions of the soldier, would have betrayed any effort to travel incognito.

The lackeys followed, armed to the teeth.

All went well till they arrived at Chantilly about eight o'clock in the morning. They needed breakfast and stopped at the door of an inn advertised by a sign representing St. Martin giving half his cloak to a poor man.

They ordered the lackeys not to unsaddle the horses and to be ready to set off again immediately.

They entered the dining room and sat down at a table. A gentleman who had just arrived by the Dammartin road was seated at the same table and having breakfast. He began to talk about the weather; the travelers replied. He drank to their good health; the travelers returned his politeness.

But when Mousqueton came to announce that the horses were ready, and they were rising from the table, the stranger proposed to Porthos that they drink a toast to the cardinal. Porthos replied that he asked no better if the stranger, in his turn, would drink the health of the king. The stranger exclaimed that he acknowledged no other king but his Eminence. Porthos called him a drunkard, and the stranger drew his sword.

"You have done something foolish," said Athos, "but it can't be helped—there is no drawing back. Kill the fellow, and rejoin us as soon as you can."

The three of them remounted their horses and set out at a good pace, while Porthos was promising his adversary to perforate him with every thrust known in the fencing schools.

"Well, there is one down," said Athos when they had gone some five hundred paces.

"But why did that man attack Porthos rather than one of us three?" asked Aramis.

"Because Porthos was talking louder than the rest of us, so he took him for the leader," d'Artagnan replied.

"I always said that this Gascon cadet was a well of wisdom," murmured Athos.

The travelers continued on their way.

At Beauvais they stopped for two hours, as much to rest their horses as to wait for Porthos. At the end of the two hours, since Porthos had not come and there was no news of him, they resumed their journey.

A league beyond Beauvais, where the road was unpaved and confined between two high banks, they fell in with eight or nine men who seemed to be repairing the road by digging holes and creating muddy ruts.

Not liking to soil his boots in that artificial bog, Aramis spoke to them rather sharply. Athos tried to restrain him, but it was too late. The laborers began to jeer at the travelers, and their insolence disturbed even Athos's equanimity; he spurred his horse toward one of them.

At that point each of the laborers retreated as far as the ditch and retrieved a concealed musket, which resulted in our seven travelers being outnumbered in weapons. Aramis received a bullet that passed through his shoulder, and Mousqueton another that lodged in the fleshy part of a thigh. Only Mousqueton fell from his horse—not because he was severely wounded, but because he was not able to see the wound and judged it to be more serious than it really was.

"It is an ambush!" d'Artagnan shouted. "Don't waste a charge! Leave!"

Wounded though he was, Aramis clung to his horse's mane and rode along beside the others. Mousqueton's horse rejoined them, riderless, and galloped beside them.

"That will give us a horse for a relay," said Athos.

"I would rather have had a hat," said d'Artagnan. "Mine was carried away by a bullet. By God, it is very fortunate that the letter was not in it."

"Yes, indeed! But they will kill poor Porthos when he gets to that place," said Aramis.

"If Porthos were on his feet, he would have rejoined us by this time," said Athos. "My opinion is that the drunken man became a sober one as soon as they began to fight."

They continued at their best speed for two hours, although the horses were so tired that it was to be feared they would soon refuse to move.

The travelers had chosen a side rode, hoping to meet with less interference; but at Crèvecoeur, Aramis declared that he could proceed no farther. In fact, it had required all the courage underlying his elegant appearance and polished manners to carry him that far. He became more ashen every minute, and his two friends were obliged to support him on his horse. They lifted him off at the door of an inn, left him with Bazin, who, was in any case more embarrassing than useful in a skirmish, and set forth again in the hope of sleeping at Amiens.

As soon as they were again in motion, Athos said, "We are reduced to two masters and Grimaud and Planchet! *Morbleu*, I swear I will not be their dupe again! I will neither open my mouth nor draw my sword between here and Calais. I swear by . . ."

"Don't waste time swearing," said d'Artagnan. "Let us keep riding, if our horses will agree."

And the travelers spurred their horses pitilessly, thus stimulating them to recover their strength. They reached Amiens at midnight, and alighted at the Lis d'Or inn.

The host looked like as honest a man as any on earth. He received the travelers with his candlestick in one hand and his cotton nightcap in the other, and he wished to lodge each of the two travelers in a charming room; but unfortunately those charming rooms were at opposite ends of the inn, and d'Artagnan and Athos refused them. The innkeeper said that he had no other rooms worthy of their Excellencies, but the travelers declared they would sleep in the common room, each on a mattress that could be thrown on the floor. The host insisted, but the travelers were firm; he was obliged to do as they wished.

They had just prepared their beds and barricaded their door from the inside, when someone knocked at the shutter; they asked who was there, recognized the voices of their lackeys, and opened the shutter.

It was indeed Planchet and Grimaud.

"Grimaud can take care of the horses himself," said Planchet. "If you are willing, gentlemen, I will sleep across your doorway, and you will then be sure that nobody can reach you."

"What will you sleep on?" d'Artagnan asked.

"Here is my bed," replied Planchet, producing a bundle of straw.

"You are right," said d'Artagnan. "Mine host's face does not please me at all—it is too gracious."

"I agree," said Athos.

Planchet climbed in through the window and installed himself across the doorway while Grimaud went to shut himself up in the stable, promising that he and the four horses would be ready by five o'clock in the morning.

The night was quiet enough. About two o'clock in the morning somebody tried to open the door, but since Planchet awoke instantly and cried, "Who goes there?" that somebody replied that he had made a mistake and went away.

At four o'clock in the morning they heard a terrible noise in the stables. Grimaud had tried to awaken the stable boys, and they were beating him. When Athos and d'Artagnan opened the window, they saw the poor lad lying senseless, his head split by a blow with a pitchfork.

Planchet went into the courtyard to saddle the horses, but they were all worn out. Mousqueton's horse, which had traveled for five or six hours without a rider the day before, might have been able to continue, but by an inexplicable error the veterinary surgeon, who had apparently been sent for to bleed one of the host's horses, had bled Mousqueton's instead.

The situation began to be worrisome: all those successive accidents might have happened by chance, but they might also be the result of a plot. Athos and d'Artagnan went out, while Planchet was sent to inquire if there were three horses for sale in the nieghborhood. At the door of the inn stood two horses, fresh, strong, and fully equipped. They would be fine. He asked where their masters were, and was informed that they had spent the night in the inn and were just settling their bill with the host.

Athos went to pay the reckoning while d'Artagnan and Planchet stood at the street door. The host was in a low-ceilinged back room, and Athos was asked to go there.

He entered without the least mistrust and took out two pistoles to pay the bill. The host was alone and seated at his desk, one of the drawers of which was partly open. He took the money Athos offered him, turned it over and over in his hands, and suddenly cried out that it was counterfeit and that he was going to have him and his companions arrested as forgers.

"You scoundrel!" shouted Athos, going toward him. "I'll cut your ears off!"

At the same instant, four men, armed to the teeth, came in by the side doors, and threw themselves on Athos.

"I am taken!" shouted Athos, at the top of his lungs. "Go on, d'Artagnan! Spur, spur!"

And he fired two pistols.

D'Artagnan and Planchet did not have to be told twice; they untied the two horses that were waiting at the door, leaped onto them, buried their spurs in their sides, and set off at full speed.

"Do you know what happened to Athos?" d'Artagnan asked Planchet as they galloped on.

"Ah, monsieur," said Planchet, "I saw one man fall at each of his two shots, and he seemed to me, through the glass door, to be fighting with his sword with the others."

"Brave Athos! And to think that we must leave him! For that matter, the same fate may await *us* two minutes from now. Forward, Planchet, forward—you are a brave fellow!"

"As I told you, monsieur," replied Planchet, "we Picards show what we are made of when the time comes. Besides, I am in my own province now, and that gives me courage."

Freely using their spurs, they arrived at St. Omer without stopping. There they rested their horses but kept the reins in their hands lest anything happen. They ate while standing in the street, after which they set off again.

A hundred paces from the gates of Calais, d'Artagnan's horse, the blood flowing from his eyes and his nose, gave out, and could not by any means be made to get up again. There was still Planchet's horse, but he had stopped moving and could not be made to start again.

Fortunately, as we have said, they were within a hundred paces of the city, so they left their mounts on the high road and rushed to the harbor. Planchet called his master's attention to a gentleman who had just arrived with his lackey and preceded them only by about fifty paces. They quickly caught up to this gentleman, who appeared to be in a great hurry. His boots were covered with dust, and he was asking if he could cross over to England immediately.

"Nothing could be more simple," said the captain of a vessel ready to set sail, "but we received orders this morning to let no one leave without express permission from the cardinal."

"I have that permission," said the gentleman, taking a paper from his pocket. "Here it is."

"Have it signed by the harbormaster," said the captain, "and let me be the one to sail you over."

"Where can I find the harbormaster?"

"At his country house."

"And where is that?"

"A quarter of a league from the city. Look, you can see it from here—at the foot of that little hill, the house with the slate roof."

"Very well," said the gentleman.

Accompanied by his lackey, he took the road to the harbormaster's country house.

D'Artagnan and Planchet followed five hundred paces behind them.

Once outside the city, d'Artagnan overtook the gentleman as he was entering a small woods.

"Monsieur," said d'Artagnan, "you seem to be in a great hurry."

"No one can be more so, monsieur."

"I am sorry about that," said d'Artagnan; "because I am also in a great hurry and wish to beg a favor of you."

"What?"

"To let me sail first."

"That is impossible," said the gentleman. "I have traveled sixty leagues in forty-four hours, and I must be in London by tomorrow noon."

"I have covered the same distance in forty hours, and I must be in London by tomorrow at ten o'clock in the morning."

"I am very sorry, monsieur, but I was here first and will not sail second."

"I am sorry, too, monsieur, but I arrived second and must sail first."

"I travel in the king's service!" said the gentleman.

"I travel in my own service!" said d'Artagnan.

"But you seem to be looking for a quarrel with me."

"You are quite right."

"What do you want?"

"You would like to know?"

"Certainly."

"Well, then, I want that order of which you are bearer, seeing that I do not have an order of my own and must have one."

"You jest, I presume."

"I never jest."

"Let me pass!"

"You shall not pass."

"My brave young man, I will blow out your brains. Lubin—my pistols!"

"Planchet, take care of the lackey, and I will manage the master."

Planchet, emboldened by his first exploit, sprang upon Lubin, and being strong and vigorous, he soon had him on his back and put his knee on his chest.

"Get on with your affair, monsieur," cried Planchet. "I have finished mine."

Seeing what had happened, the gentleman drew his sword and lunged at d'Artagnan, but he had too strong an adversary. In three seconds d'Artagnan had wounded him three times, exclaiming at each thrust, "One for Athos, one for Porthos, and one for Aramis!"

At the third hit the gentleman fell like a log.

D'Artagnan believed him to be dead, or at least unconscious, and went toward him to take the order; but the moment he reached out to search for it, the wounded man, who had not dropped his sword, plunged the point into d'Artagnan's chest, saying, "One for you!"

"And one more for me—the best for the last!" cried d'Artagnan furiously, nailing him to the earth with a fourth thrust through his body.

This time the gentleman closed his eyes and fainted.

D'Artagnan searched his pockets and took from one of them the order for the passage. It was in the name of Comte de Wardes.

Glancing at the handsome young man—who was scarcely twenty-five years old and whom he was leaving bloody, unconscious, and perhaps dead—he sighed at the strange fate that leads men to destroy each other for the interests of people who do not know them and often do not even know that they exist.

But he was soon roused from those reflections by Lubin, who was howling for help with all his might.

Planchet grabbed him by the throat and squeezed as hard as he could.

"Monsieur," he said, "as long as I hold him like this, he can't cry out, but as soon as I let go, he will start to howl again. I recognize him as a Norman, and Normans are obstinate."

In fact, tightly held though he was, Lubin was still trying to cry out.

"Wait!" said d'Artagnan.

He took out his handkerchief and gagged Lubin.

"Now, let us tie him to a tree," said Planchet.

This being properly done, they drew the Comte de Wardes close to his servant; and since night was approaching and the wounded man and the bound man were at some little distance within the woods, it was clear they were likely to remain there till the next day.

"And now, to the harbormaster's," said d'Artagnan.

"But you are wounded," said Planchet.

"It's nothing! Let us take care of what is most urgent first, and then we will take care of my wound. Besides, as I said, it does not seem like a dangerous one."

And they both set out as quickly as they could for the country house of the worthy functionary.

The Comte de Wardes was announced, and d'Artagnan was introduced into the harbormaster's presence."

"You have an order signed by the cardinal?" he asked.

"Yes, monsieur," replied d'Artagnan, "here it is."

"I see it is quite regular."

"Of course. I am one of his most faithful servants."

"It seems that his Eminence is anxious to prevent someone from crossing to England?"

"Yes, a certain d'Artagnan, a Béarnese gentleman who left Paris with three of his friends, with the intention of going to London."

"Do you know him personally?" asked the harbormaster.

"Who?"

"This d'Artagnan."

"Yes, I do."

"Describe him to me, then."

"Nothing could be more simple."

And d'Artagnan gave, feature for feature, a description of the Comte de Wardes.

"Is he with someone?"

"Yes, a lackey named Lubin."

"We will keep a sharp lookout for them, and if we lay hands on them, his Eminence may be assured they will be sent back to Paris under a strong escort."

"And by doing so, Monsieur," said d'Artagnan, "you will have deserved well of the cardinal."

"Will you see him on your return, Monsieur le Comte?"

"Without a doubt."

"Tell him, I beg you, that I am his humble servant."

"I will not fail to do so."

Delighted with this assurance, the harbormaster countersigned the permit and handed it to d'Artagnan, who lost no time in useless formalities. He thanked the harbormaster, bowed, and left.

Once outside, he and Planchet set off as fast as they could; and by making a long detour, they avoided the little wood and reentered the city by another gate.

The vessel was quite ready to sail, and the captain was waiting on the wharf.

"Well?" he said on seeing d'Artagnan.

"Here is my countersigned permit," said the latter.

"And that other gentleman?"

"He will not go today," said d'Artagnan, "but here, I'll pay you for the two of us."

"In that case, let us go," said the shipmaster.

"Let us go," repeated d'Artagnan.

He leaped with Planchet into the rowboat, and five minutes later they were on board.

It was none too soon, for they had sailed scarcely half a league when d'Artagnan saw a flash and heard a detonation: it was the cannon announcing the closing of the port.

He now had time to take care of his wound. Fortunately, as he had thought, it was not particularly dangerous. The point of the sword had touched a rib and slid along the bone; but fortunately his shirt had stuck to the wound, and he had lost only a small amount of blood.

He was exhausted. A mattress was laid on the deck for him; he threw himself down on it and fell asleep immediately.

At daybreak the next morning, they were still three or four leagues from the coast of England. The breeze had been light all night, and they had made little progress.

At ten o'clock the vessel cast anchor in the harbor of Dover.

At half past ten d'Artagnan set foot on English land and said, "Here I am at last!"

But they were not finished: they had to get to London.

In England the roads were well served; d'Artagnan and Planchet each took a post horse, a postillion rode before them, and in a few hours they were in the capital.

D'Artagnan did not know London and did not know a word of English; but he wrote Buckingham's name on a piece of paper, and everyone pointed out to him the way to the duke's house.

The duke was at Windsor hunting with the king.

D'Artagnan asked to see the duke's confidential servant, who having accompanied the duke in all his voyages, spoke French perfectly well; he told him that he had come from Paris on an affair of life and death and that he must speak with the duke immediately.

The confidence with which d'Artagnan spoke convinced Patrick, which was the name of this minister of the minister. He ordered two horses to be saddled, and went with d'Artagnan as his guide. As for Planchet, he had been lifted from his horse as stiff as a board; the poor lad's strength was almost exhausted. D'Artagnan seemed made of iron.

On their arrival at the castle they learned that Buckingham and the king were hawking in the marshes two or three leagues away.

Twenty minutes later they were at the spot. Patrick soon heard his master's voice calling his falcon.

"Whom shall I announce to the duke?" asked Patrick.

"The young man who sought a quarrel with him one evening on the Pont Neuf, in front of the Samaritaine."

"A strange introduction!"

"You will find that it is as good as another."

Patrick galloped off, reached the duke, and announced to him in those words that a messenger was waiting for him.

Buckingham at once remembered the circumstance, and suspecting that something was going on in France that he should know about, he asked only where the messenger was; then, recognizing from afar the uniform of the Guards, he spurred his horse and rode straight up to d'Artagnan. Patrick kept discreetly in the background.

"No misfortune has happened to the queen?" cried Buckingham, throwing all his fear and all his love into the question.

"I do not think so. But I believe she is in some great danger from which only your Grace can extricate her."

"I!" cried Buckingham. "What is it? I would be happy to be of any service to her! Speak!"

"Take this letter."

"This letter! From whom does it come?"

"From her Majesty, I think."

"From her Majesty!" said Buckingham, turning so pale that d'Artagnan feared he might faint as he broke the seal.

"What is this hole?" he asked, showing d'Artagnan a place where the letter had been pierced through.

"Ah," d'Artagnan replied, "I did not see that. Comte de Wardes's sword must have made that hole when he gave me a good thrust in the chest."

"You are wounded?" asked Buckingham, opening the letter.

"Only a scratch."

"My God, what have I read?" cried the duke. "Patrick, remain here—or rather join the king, wherever he may be, and tell his Majesty that I humbly beg him to excuse me but that an affair of the greatest importance recalls me to London. Come, monsieur, come!"

Both of them set off for the capital at full speed.

21

Lady de Winter

As THEY RODE ALONG, d'Artagnan told the duke all that he knew, and when Buckingham added all that he heard from the young man to his own recollections, he was able to form a pretty exact idea of the seriousness of the position that the queen's short but explicit letter hinted at. But what astonished him most was that the cardinal, who wanted so desperately to prevent this young man from setting foot in England, had not succeeded in doing so. When he expressed this surprise, d'Artagnan told him about the precaution they had taken, and described how, thanks to the devotion of his three friends, whom he had left scattered and bleeding along the way, he had succeeded in escaping with only that single sword thrust, which had pierced the queen's letter and for which he had repaid the Comte de Wardes with such terrible coin. While he was listening to this recital, delivered with the greatest simplicity, the duke looked from time to time at the young man with amazement, as if he could not understand how so much prudence, courage, and devotion could be found in someone barely twenty years old.

The horses went like the wind, and in a few minutes they were at the gates of London. D'Artagnan had thought that on arriving in town the duke would slacken his pace, but he did not. He kept on at the same rate, indifferent to the risk of trampling down anyone in his way. In fact, two or three such accidents did happen, but Buckingham did not even turn around to see what had become of those he had knocked down. The cries that followed him sounded very much like curses.

On entering the courtyard of his house, Buckingham sprang off his horse and, paying no further heed to the animal, threw the reins onto his neck and ran to the front steps. D'Artagnan did the same, but with a little more concern for the noble creatures whose merits he fully appreciated; he was relieved when he saw three or four grooms run out from the kitchens and the stables to busy themselves with the steeds.

The duke walked so quickly that d'Artagnan had some trouble keeping up with him. He passed through several rooms furnished with an elegance of which even the greatest nobles of France had not even an idea, and finally arrived at a bedroom that was a miracle of both taste and richness. In the alcove of this room was a door concealed by a tapestry, which the duke opened with a little gold key that he wore suspended from his neck by a chain of the same metal. D'Artagnan had remained discreetly behind; but when Buckingham had crossed the threshold of the room, he turned around, saw the young man's hesitation, and said, "Come in, and if you have the good fortune to be admitted to her Majesty's presence, tell her what you have seen."

Encouraged by this invitation, d'Artagnan followed the duke, who closed the door behind them. They were in a small chapel completely covered by Persian silk tapestries threaded with gold and brilliantly lit by a multitude of candles. Over a kind of altar and under a blue-velvet canopy surmounted by white and red feathers was a full-length portrait of Anne of Austria, so perfect a likeness that d'Artagnan gasped with surprise on beholding it: it almost seemed as though the queen was about to speak.

On the altar and beneath the portrait was the rose-wood box containing the diamond studs.

The duke approached the altar, knelt as a priest might have done before a crucifix, and opened the box.

"There," he said, taking out a large bow of blue ribbon all sparkling with diamonds, "there are the precious studs that I have sworn will be buried with me. But the queen gave them to me, and the queen wishes them returned. Her will be done, like that of God, in all things."

Then he began to kiss, one after the other, those studs with which he was about to part. Suddenly he uttered a terrible cry.

"What is the matter?" exclaimed d'Artagnan anxiously. "What has happened to you, my Lord?"

"What has happened is that all is lost!" cried Buckingham, pale as a corpse. "Two of the studs are missing—there are only ten here."

"Can you have lost them, my Lord, or do you think they have been stolen?"

"They have been stolen, and it is the cardinal who has dealt this blow. Look! The ribbons that held them have been cut with scissors."

"If my Lord suspects they have been stolen, perhaps the person who stole them still has them."

"Wait, let me think!" said the duke. "The only time I have worn these studs was at a ball given by the king a week ago at Windsor. Lady de Winter, with whom I had quarreled, wanted to become reconciled to me at that ball, but that reconciliation was nothing but a jealous woman's revenge. I have never seen her since. The woman is an agent of the cardinal."

"Then he must have agents everywhere!" d'Artagnan exclaimed.

"Oh, yes," said Buckingham, grinding his teeth with rage, "he is a terribly dangerous antagonist. . . . But when is the ball in Paris going to take place?"

"Next Monday."

"Next Monday! We still have five days—that's more time than we need. Patrick!" cried the duke, opening the door of the chapel, "Patrick!"

His confidential servant appeared.

"Send me my jeweler and my secretary."

The servant went out with a silent promptitude that showed he was accustomed to obey unquestioningly.

But although the jeweler had been mentioned first, it was the secretary who appeared first, simply because he lived in the house. He found Buckingham seated at a table in his bedroom, writing out some orders with his own hand.

"Mr. Jackson," he said, "go instantly to the Lord Chancellor, and tell him that I wish him to execute these orders immediately."

"But my Lord, if the Lord Chancellor asks me about the motives that may have led your Grace to adopt such an extraordinary measure, what shall I reply?"

"That I wish it, and that I answer for my wishes to no man."

"Will that be the answer he must give to his Majesty if by chance his Majesty should be curious to know why no vessel is to leave any of the ports of Great Britain?" said the secretary, smiling.

"You are right to ask that, Mr. Jackson," replied Buckingham. "In that case he will say to the king that I am determined on war and that this measure is my first act of hostility against France."

The secretary bowed and left the room.

"We are safe on this side," said Buckingham, turning to d'Artagnan. "If the studs have not yet gone to Paris, they will not arrive till after you do."

"Why not?"

"I have just placed an embargo on all vessels presently in his Majesty's ports, and without my express permission, not one will dare raise anchor."

D'Artagnan looked with stupefaction at the man who thus used the unlimited power with which he had been invested by a trusting king to further his own amorous intrigues. Buckingham saw by the expression of the young man's face what was passing through his mind, and he smiled.

"Yes," he said, "Anne of Austria is my true queen.

At a word from her, I would betray my country, my king, my God. She asked me not to send the Protestants of La Rochelle the assistance I had promised them, and I have not done so. I broke my word, it is true, but of what importance is that? I obeyed her wishes, and have I not been richly paid for that obedience? I owe her portrait to that obedience."

D'Artagnan was amazed to see by what fragile and unknown threads the destinies of nations and the lives of men are suspended.

He was lost in these reflections when the goldsmith entered. The jeweler was an Irishman—one of the most skillful of his craft—who acknowledged that he earned a hundred thousand livres a year from the Duke of Buckingham.

"Mr. O'Reilly," said the duke, leading him into the chapel, "look at these diamond studs, and tell me what each of them is worth separately."

The goldsmith looked at the elegant setting, calculated what the diamonds were worth, and named a figure.

"How many days would it take to make two studs exactly like them? As you can see, two of them are missing."

"A week, my Lord."

"I will give you twice as much as they are worth if I can have them by the day after tomorrow."

"My Lord, you will have them."

"You are a jewel of a man, Mr. O'Reilly. But that is not all—because I do not wish it to be known that this work is being done, they must be made here in the palace."

"Impossible, my Lord! I am the only one who can do the work so that it would not be possible to tell the new from the old."

"Therefore, my dear Mr. O'Reilly, you are my prisoner. And if you wanted to leave my palace at this moment, you would not be able to, so make the best of it. Tell me the names of the workmen you need, and which tools they must bring with them."

The goldsmith knew the duke, and knowing him, he knew that it would be useless to object.

"May I inform my wife?" he asked.

"Oh, you may even see her if you like, my dear Mr.

O'Reilly. Your captivity will be mild, be assured, and since every inconvenience deserves its compensation, here is, in addition to the price of the studs, a draft for an additional sum to make you forget the annoyance I am causing you."

D'Artagnan could not get over his surprise at this minister who so casually manipulated men and millions.

As for the goldsmith, he wrote to his wife, sending her the draft for the money and asking her to send him, in exchange, his most skillful apprentice, an assortment of various kinds and weights of diamonds, and the necessary tools.

Buckingham led the goldsmith to a room that was transformed into a workshop at the end of half an hour. Then he posted a sentry at each door, with orders to admit no one but Patrick on any pretext whatever. We need not add that O'Reilly and his assistant were forbidden to leave for any reason.

This settled, the duke turned to d'Artagnan.

"Now, my young friend," he said, "England is all ours. What do you wish for?"

"A bed, my Lord," replied d'Artagnan. "At present, I confess that is what I most need."

Buckingham gave d'Artagnan a room adjoining his own. He wished to have the young man at hand—not because he mistrusted him, but because he wanted to have someone to whom he could constantly talk about the queen.

An hour later, the order that no vessel bound for France could leave port, not even the packet boat with letters, was announced in London. Everybody saw this as a declaration of war between the two kingdoms.

Two days later, at eleven o'clock in the morning, both diamond studs were finished. They so completely imitated the originals and were so perfectly alike that Buckingham himself could not tell the new ones from the old ones, and those who were the most expert in such matters would not have done better.

He immediately sent for d'Artagnan.

"Here are the diamond studs that you came for, and be my witness that I have done all that human power could do."

"Be sure, my Lord, that I will report everything I have

seen. But does your Grace mean to give me the studs without the box?"

"The box would encumber you. Besides, it is now the more precious because it is all that is left to me. You will say that I am keeping it."

"I will repeat what you have said word for word, my Lord."

"And now," resumed Buckingham, looking earnestly at the young man, "how can I repay the debt I owe you?"

D'Artagnan blushed to the whites of his eyes. He saw that the duke was searching for a means of making him accept something, and the idea that his blood and that of his friends was about to be paid for with English gold was strangely repugnant to him.

"Let us understand each other, my Lord," he replied, "and let us make things clear beforehand so that there may be no mistake. I am in the service of the King and Queen of France and form part of the company of Monsieur Des Essarts's Guards. Together with his brother-in-law, Monsieur de Tréville, Monsieur Des Essarts is particularly attached to their Majesties. So what I have done has been for the queen, and not at all for your Grace. And furthermore, it is very probable I would not have done any of this if it had not been to please someone who is my lady as the queen is yours."

"Yes," said the duke, smiling, "and I even believe that I know that other person. She is . . ."

"My Lord, I have not named her!" interrupted the young man, heatedly.

"That is true," said the duke. "Then I must be grateful to that person?"

"Yes, my Lord, because at this moment, when there is question of war, I confess that I see nothing in your Grace but an Englishman and, consequently, an enemy I would much rather meet on the field of battle than in the park at Windsor or the corridors of the Louvre. None of this, however, will prevent me from executing every part of my mission or from laying down my life, if necessary, to accomplish it—but without your having for that reason more to thank me for in this second interview than for what I did for you the first time we met."

"In England we say, 'Proud as a Scotsman,' " murmured the Duke of Buckingham.

"And in France, we say, 'Proud as a Gascon.' The Gascons are the Scotsmen of France."

D'Artagnan bowed to the duke and turned to leave.

"Are you going away like that? Where? How?"

"That's true!"

"By God, you Frenchmen are sure of yourselves!"

"I had forgotten that England was an island and that you were its ruler."

"Go to the waterfront, ask for the brig *Sund*, and give this letter to the captain. He will convey you to a little port, where no one will expect to find you because it is usually frequented only by fishermen."

"The name of that port?"

"St. Valery. But listen to what I am telling you. When you arrive there you will go to a miserable-looking tavern, without a name and without a sign—a mere fisherman's hut. You cannot mistake it because that is the only tavern in town."

"And then?"

"You will ask for the host and say the word 'Forward!' "

"Which means?"

"In French, *en avant*. That is the password. He will give you a saddled horse and point out the road you ought to take. You will have four such relay stations along your route. If you will give at each of those relays your address in Paris, the four horses will follow you there. You already know two of them—the ones we rode on—and you appeared to appreciate them. You may trust me that the others will not be inferior to them. All four horses are fully equipped for the field. However proud you may be, you will not refuse to accept one of them and to ask your three companions to accept the others—you would be taking them in order to make war against us. After all, the end justifies the means, as you Frenchmen say, does it not?"

"Yes, my Lord, I accept them. And if it please God, we will make good use of your presents."

"Now give me your hand, young man. We may soon meet on the field of battle, but in the meantime I hope we part good friends."

"Yes, my Lord, but with the hope of soon becoming enemies."

"I promise you that."

"I rely on your word, my Lord."

D'Artagnan bowed to the duke and made his way as quickly as possible to the waterfront. Opposite the Tower of London he found the *Sund* and delivered his letter to the captain, who had it approved by the harbormaster and then made immediate preparations to sail.

Fifty vessels were waiting to set out. Passing alongside one of them, d'Artagnan thought he saw on board it the woman he had seen in Meung—the same one the unknown gentleman had called Milady and whom d'Artagnan had thought so beautiful; but thanks to the current and a fair wind, his vessel was going so swiftly that he had little more than a glimpse of her.

The next day about nine o'clock in the morning he landed at St. Valery, went immediately in search of the tavern, and easily found it thanks to the loud noises coming from it. There was talk of war between England and France being both near and certain, and the cheerful sailors were enjoying themselves.

D'Artagnan made his way through the crowd, went up to the host, and pronounced the word "Forward!" The innkeeper immediately signaled him to follow; went out with him by a door that opened into a courtyard; led him to the stable, where a saddled horse was waiting for him; and asked if he needed anything else.

"I have to know the route I must follow," said d'Artagnan.

"Go from here to Blangy, and from Blangy to Neufchâtel. At Neufchâtel, go to the Herse d'Or inn, give the password to the landlord, and you will find another horse already saddled."

"Is there anything to pay?" d'Artagnan asked.

"Everything has been paid, and generously. Go, and may God guide you!"

"Amen!" cried the young man, galloping off.

Four hours later he was in Neufchâtel.

He strictly followed his instructions, and at Neufchâtel as at St. Valery he found a horse quite ready and waiting. He was about to remove the pistols from the saddle he had just used and put them on the one he was about to use, but he found the holsters already furnished with pistols just like the others.

"Your address in Paris?"

"Headquarters of the Guards, Des Essarts's company."

"Very well," replied the questioner.

"Which route do I take?"

"The road to Rouen, but take the righthand road out of the city. Stop at the little village of Ecouis, in which there is only one inn—the Ecu de France. Don't judge it by its appearance—you will find a horse in the stables quite as good as this one."

"The same password?"

"Exactly."

"Adieu!"

"A good journey, monsieur! Do you want anything?"

D'Artagnan shook his head and set off at full speed. At Ecouis, the same scene was repeated: he found as attentive a host and as fresh a horse. Again he left his address and again he set off at the same pace for Pontoise, where he changed his horse for the last time. At nine o'clock he galloped into the courtyard of Tréville's house. He had done nearly sixty leagues in little more than twelve hours.

M. de Tréville received him as if he had seen him that same morning, except that he shook his hand a little more warmly than usual as he informed him that Des Essarts's company was on duty at the Louvre and that he should report at once to his post.

22

The Merlaison Ballet

THE NEXT DAY, there was no talk of anything in Paris but the ball that the city magistrates were giving for the king and queen, at which their Majesties would dance the famous Merlaison—the king's favorite ballet.

The Hôtel de Ville had been preparing for this important occasion for a week. The city carpenters had erected scaffolds on which the invited ladies were to be seated;

the city grocer had decorated the rooms with two hundred white wax candles—an unheard of luxury at that time; and twenty violinists had been hired at double the usual rate on condition that they play all night.

At ten o'clock in the morning Monsieur de la Coste, ensign in the king's Guards, followed by two officers and several constables of the watch, came to ask Clement, the city registrar, for all the keys of the inner and outer doors of the building. These keys were given to him immediately, each one with an identifying ticket attached to it, and from that moment Monsieur de la Coste was responsible for guarding all the doors and all the avenues of approach.

At eleven o'clock came Duhallier, captain of the Guards, bringing with him fifty more constables of the watch, who were immediately posted at the doors assigned to them.

At three o'clock came two companies of the Guards, one French, the other Swiss. Half the company of French guards were M. Duhallier's men, and half M. Des Essarts's men.

At six in the evening the guests began to come. As soon as they entered, they were led to their places on the platforms that had been prepared for them in the great hall.

At nine o'clock Madame la Première Présidente, the wife of the head of Parliament, arrived. Next to the queen, she was the most important person at the ball, so she was received by the city magistrates and seated in a box opposite the one the queen was to occupy.

At ten o'clock, the king's collation, consisting of preserves and other delicacies, was set out in the little hall beside the St. Jean church, in front of the silver sideboard of the city, which was guarded by four constables.

At midnight loud shouts and cheers were heard: the king was passing through the streets that led from the Louvre to the Hôtel de Ville, all of them illuminated by colored lanterns.

The magistrates—clothed in their woolen robes and preceded by six sergeants, each holding a torch—immediately went to wait upon the king, whom they met on the steps. The provost of the merchants of Paris made the welcome speech, to which his Majesty replied with an apology for coming so late, laying the blame on the cardinal, who had detained him till eleven o'clock talking about affairs of state.

His Majesty, in full dress, was accompanied by his brother, his royal Highness the duc d'Orleans (also known as Monsieur); M. le Comte de Soissons; the Grand Prior; the Duc de Longueville; the Duc d'Elbeuf; the Comte d'Harcourt; the Comte de la Roche-Guyon; M. de Liancourt; M. de Baradas, the Comte de Cramail; and the Chevalier de Souveray.

Everybody noticed that the king looked sad and preoccupied.

A private room had been prepared for the king and another for Monsieur; in each of them were the costumes they were to change into for the ball. The same had been done for the queen and Madame la Presidente. The lords and ladies of their Majesties' suites were to dress, two by two, in other rooms prepared for the purpose.

Before entering his room, the king asked to be informed the moment the cardinal arrived.

Half an hour after the entrance of the king, there were fresh cheers announcing the arrival of the queen. The magistrates did as they had done before, and preceded by their sergeants, they advanced to receive their illustrious guest.

The queen entered the great hall, and it was noticed that, like the king, she looked sad and even weary.

The moment she came in, the curtain of a small gallery—which up to that time had been closed—was drawn, and the pale face of the cardinal, dressed as a Spanish cavalier, appeared. His eyes were fixed on the queen, and a terrible smile passed over his lips: the queen was not wearing her diamond studs.

The queen remained in the great hall for a short time to receive the compliments of the city dignitaries and to reply to the salutations of the ladies.

Suddenly the king appeared with the cardinal at one of the doors of the hall. The cardinal was speaking to him in a low voice, and the king was very pale.

Making his way through the crowd without a mask, and with the ribbons of his doublet incompletely tied, he went straight to the queen and, in a strange voice, said,

"Madame, why are you not wearing your diamond studs when you know it would give me so much pleasure?"

The queen glanced around her and saw the cardinal behind the king, a diabolical smile on his face.

"Sire," she replied, her voice faltering, "because in the midst of such a crowd as this I feared some accident might happen to them."

"And you were wrong, madame! I gave you that present so that you might adorn yourself with it. I tell you that you were wrong!"

The king's voice was quivering with anger. Everybody looked and listened with astonishment, not understanding what was happening.

"Sire, I can send someone to the Louvre for them, and thus your Majesty's wishes will be complied with."

"Do so, madame, and at once, for the ballet will begin in an hour."

The queen bowed in submission and followed the ladies who were to conduct her to her room.

The king returned to his own room.

There was a moment of trouble and confusion in the hall. Everybody had noticed that something was happening between the king and queen; but both of them had spoken so softly that everybody, out of respect for their privacy, had withdrawn several steps and nobody had heard anything. The violins were playing with all their might, but nobody was listening to them.

The king was the first to come out from his room. He wore a most elegant hunting costume, and Monsieur and the other noblemen were dressed like him. This was the costume that best suited the king: so dressed, he really did seem to be the first gentleman of his kingdom.

The cardinal approached the king and gave him a small box. The king opened it and saw two diamond studs.

"What does this mean?" he asked the cardinal.

"Nothing," replied the latter. "But if the queen wears the studs, which I very much doubt, count them, sire, and if you find only ten, ask her Majesty who can have stolen from her the two that are here."

The king looked at the cardinal as if to question him, but there was no time—a cry of admiration burst from every mouth. If the king seemed to be the first gentleman of his kingdom, the queen was without doubt the most beautiful woman in France.

It is true that her hunting costume was enormously becoming. She wore a velour hat with blue plumes, a surtout of pearl-gray velvet fastened with diamond clasps, and a blue-satin skirt embroidered with silver. On her left shoulder sparkled the diamond studs, attached to a bow of the same color as the plumes and the skirt.

The king was overjoyed and the cardinal was vexed, although they were so far from the queen that they could not count the studs. Certainly the queen had them; the only question was, did she have ten or twelve?

Just then the violins sounded the signal for the ballet. The king advanced toward Madame la Presidente, with whom he was to dance, and his Highness Monsieur toward the queen. They took their places, and the ballet began.

The king danced facing the queen, and every time he passed near her, his eyes devoured the studs, the number of which he could never be sure of. The cardinal's brow was covered with a cold sweat.

The ballet lasted an hour and had sixteen scenes. It ended amid the applause of the whole assemblage, and every man escorted his lady back to her place; but the king took advantage of the privilege he had of abandoning his lady no matter where, and advanced eagerly toward the queen.

"I thank you, madame," he said, "for the deference you have shown to my wishes, but I think you are missing two of the studs and I bring them back to you."

With those words he held out to the queen the two studs the cardinal had given him.

"What, sire," cried the young queen, pretending surprise, "you are giving me two more? Now I will have fourteen."

The king counted them, and in fact the twelve studs were all on her Majesty's shoulder.

The king called the cardinal to him.

"What does this mean, Monsieur le Cardinal?" he asked severely.

"It means, sire," replied the cardinal, "that I wished to present her Majesty with those two studs, and that

not daring to offer them myself, I chose this way of per-
suading her to accept them."

"And I am all the more grateful to your Eminence,"
replied Anne of Austria, with a smile that proved she
was not the dupe of this ingenious gallantry, "since I am
certain that these two studs alone have cost you as much
as all the others cost his Majesty."

Then, after curtseying to the king and the cardinal, she
went back to the room in which she had dressed and
where she was to take off her costume.

The attention we have been obliged to give at the
beginning of this chapter to the illustrious people we have
introduced into it has diverted us from the man to whom
Anne of Austria owed her extraordinary triumph over
the cardinal; and who—unknown, mingling in the crowd
gathered at one of the doors—had watched this scene
that was comprehensible to only four persons—the king,
the queen, his Eminence, and himself.

The queen had just regained her room, and d'Artagnan was about to leave, when he felt his shoulder lightly
touched. He turned around and saw a young woman
motioning him to follow her. Her face was covered with
a black velvet mask, but despite that precaution—which
was in fact taken against others rather than against him—
he at once recognized his usual guide, the quick-witted
and intelligent Mme. Bonacieux.

The day before, he had asked the Swiss guard, Germain, to send for her. But she had been in such a hurry
to convey to the queen the excellent news of the happy
return of her messenger that the two lovers had exchanged
no more than a few words. D'Artagnan therefore now
followed Mme. Bonacieux with feelings of both love and
curiosity. At every step of the way, and in proportion as
the corridors became more deserted, he wanted to stop
the young woman, hold her, gaze upon her, even if only
for a minute; but every time he tried, she slipped
between his hands, and every time he began to speak to
her, she put a finger on her mouth with a little imperious
gesture full of grace, reminding him that he was under
the command of a power he must blindly obey, one that
forbade him to make even the slightest complaint. At
length, after turning down winding corridors for several
minutes, she opened the door of an entirely dark room

and led d'Artagnan into it. There she again signaled him to be silent and opened a second door, concealed by a tapestry and opening into a brilliantly illuminated room that was momentarily visible as she disappeared into it, leaving the door open but blocked by the tapestry.

D'Artagnan remained motionless for a moment, asking himself where he could be; but soon the ray of light that penetrated into the room, the warm and perfumed air that reached him from the same opening, the conversation of two or three ladies in language at once respectful and refined, and the words "your Majesty" repeated several times, indicated clearly that he was in a small room adjoining the queen's dressing room.

He waited in the shadows and listened.

The queen sounded cheerful and happy, which evidently surprised the persons who surrounded her and who were accustomed to seeing her sad and anxious. She explained her joy by talking about the beauty of the ball and the pleasure she had experienced dancing the ballet; and since it is not permissible to contradict a queen, whether she is smiling or weeping, everybody else elaborated on her praise of the magistrate's magnificent ball.

Although d'Artagnan did not know the queen, he soon distinguished her voice from the others first by its slightly foreign accent, and next by that tone of authority all words spoken by royalty possess. He heard her approach and withdraw from the partially open door, and twice or three times he even saw her shadow intercept the light.

Finally a hand and an arm, surpassingly beautiful in their form and whiteness, came through an opening in the tapestry. D'Artagnan at once understood that this was his reward. He fell to his knees, took the hand, and touched it respectfully with his lips. Then the hand was withdrawn, leaving in his an object he perceived to be a ring. The door was then immediately closed, and d'Artagnan found himself again in complete obscurity.

He put the ring on his finger and resumed his wait; it was evident that all was not yet over. After the reward for his devotion, the reward for his love had still to come. Besides, although the ballet had been danced, the evening had scarcely begun: a supper was to be served at three o'clock, and the bells of St. Jean had already struck three quarters past two.

The sound of voices in the adjoining room slowly faded away. The queen and her women could be heard leaving, then the door of d'Artagnan's room was opened and Mme. Bonacieux entered.

"At last!" he cried.

"Be quiet," said the young woman, putting her hand on his lips. "Go back the way you came!"

"But where and when will I see you again?"

"A note that you will find at home will tell you. Now go!"

And with those words she opened the door to the corridor and pushed him out of the room.

He obeyed like a child, without the least resistance or objection, which proved that he was really in love.

23

The Rendezvous

D'ARTAGNAN RAN HOME immediately, and although it was three o'clock in the morning and he had to go through some of the worst quarters of Paris, he met with no mishaps. Everyone knows that God protects drunkards and lovers.

He found the door of his passageway open, sprang up the stairs, and knocked softly in the way he and his lackey had agreed on. Planchet, whom he had sent home two hours earlier from the Hôtel de Ville with orders to wait up for him, opened the door.

"Has anyone brought a letter for me?" d'Artagnan asked eagerly.

"No one has *brought* a letter, monsieur," replied Planchet, "but one has come by itself."

"What do you mean, you blockhead?"

"I mean that when I came in, although I had the key of your apartment in my pocket and that key had never left me, I found a letter on the green table cover in your bedroom."

"Where is the letter?"

"I left it where I found it, monsieur. It is not natural

for letters to enter people's houses that way. If the window had been open or even ajar, I would think nothing of it, but everything was sealed. Beware, monsieur, because there is certainly some magic behind this."

Meanwhile d'Artagnan had darted into his room and opened the letter. It was from Mme. Bonacieux and it said:

> There are many thanks to be given you, from myself and from another. At about ten o'clock this evening be in St. Cloud, in front of the villa across from M. d'Estrées's house.—C.B.

As he read this letter, d'Artagnan felt his heart gripped by that delicious spasm which tortures and caresses the hearts of lovers.

It was the first love note he had ever received, the first rendezvous that had ever been granted him. His heart was so swollen with joy that he felt as if he would dissolve at the very threshold of that terrestrial paradise called Love!

"Well, monsieur," said Planchet, who had observed his master turn first red and then white "wasn't I right? Isn't the letter about something bad?"

"No, you were not right, Planchet, and as proof, here is an écu to drink my health with."

"I am obliged to Monsieur for the écu, and I promise to follow his instructions exactly—but it is still true that letters which come into shut-up houses in this way . . ."

" . . . fall from heaven, my friend."

"Then Monsieur is satisfied?"

"My dear Planchet, I am the happiest of men!"

"And I may profit by Monsieur's happiness and go to bed?"

"Yes, go."

"May the blessings of heaven fall upon Monsieur, but it is still true that that letter . . ."

And Planchet left, shaking his head with an air of doubt that d'Artagnan's generosity had not entirely effaced.

Left alone, d'Artagnan read and reread his note. Then he kissed and rekissed twenty times the lines written by the hand of the woman he loved. Finally he went to bed, fell asleep, and had golden dreams.

At seven o'clock in the morning he got up and called Planchet, who at the second summons opened the door, his face not yet completely free of the preceding night's anxiety.

"Planchet, I am probably going to be out all day, so you are your own master till seven o'clock this evening. But at seven o'clock you must be ready with two horses."

"It sounds as if we are again going to be exposed to danger!"

"You will take your musket and your pistols."

"There, now, didn't I say so?" Planchet exclaimed. "I was sure of it—that cursed letter!"

"Don't be afraid, you idiot—our trip is only an outing."

"Ah, like that other outing, when it rained bullets and produced a crop of steel traps!"

"Well, if you are really afraid, Monsieur Planchet, I will go without you. I prefer traveling alone to having a companion who feels the least fear."

"Monsieur wrongs me. I thought he had seen me in action."

"Yes, but perhaps you have worn out all your courage."

"Monsieur will see that I have some left if I need it, but I beg Monsieur not to use it too freely if he wishes it to last."

"Do you think you still have a certain amount of it to expend this evening?"

"I hope so, monsieur."

"Then I count on you."

"I will be ready at the appointed hour, but I thought Monsieur had only one horse in the Guards' stables."

"There may be only one now, but by this evening there will be four."

"Then our journey was a remounting journey?"

"Exactly," said d'Artagnan, and nodding to Planchet, he went out.

M. Bonacieux was at his door. D'Artagnan intended to go out without speaking to the haberdasher, but the latter greeted him so politely and warmly that his tenant felt obliged, not only to return his greeting, but to enter into conversation with him.

Besides, how is it possible not to feel a certain amount of benevolence toward a husband whose pretty wife has arranged a rendezvous with you that same evening at St. Cloud, opposite d'Estrées's house? D'Artagnan approached him with the friendliest manner he could assume.

The conversation naturally turned to the poor man's incarceration. M. Bonacieux, who did not know that d'Artagnan had overheard his conversation with the stranger of Meung, told his young tenant about the persecutions of that monster M. de Laffemas, whom he never ceased to refer to as the "cardinal's executioner," and went on at great length about the Bastille, the bolts, the bars, the dungeons, the air holes, the instruments of torture.

D'Artagnan listened to him with exemplary politeness and, when he had finished, said, "And Madame Bonacieux, do you know who carried her off? I do not forget that I owe to that unpleasant circumstance the good fortune of having made your acquaintance."

"They were careful not to tell me that," Bonacieux replied. "And my wife has sworn by all that's sacred that she does not know. But you," he continued in a tone of perfect good fellowship, "where have you been all this time? I have not seen you or your friends, and I don't think all the dust that I saw Planchet brush off your boots yesterday could have come from the streets of Paris."

"You are right, my dear Monsieur Bonacieux. My friends and I have been on a little journey."

"Far from here?"

"Oh, Lord, no! Only about forty leagues. We went to take Monsieur Athos to the waters at Forges, where my friends still remain."

"But you returned, did you not?" said M. Bonacieux slyly. "A handsome young fellow like you does not get long leaves of absence from his mistress, and we were impatiently waited for in Paris, were we not?"

"My faith," the young man replied, laughing, "I admit it, my dear Bonacieux, especially since I see there is no concealing anything from you. Yes, I was awaited, and very impatiently, I acknowledge."

A slight shadow passed over Bonacieux's face, but so slight that d'Artagnan did not notice it.

"And we are going to be compensated for our diligence?" continued the haberdasher, with a slight alteration in his voice—so slight that d'Artagnan did not notice it any more than he had noticed the momentary shadow that had, an instant before, darkened Bonacieux's face.

"Ah, you are being hypocritical, monsieur! You must have been in the same situation yourself," said d'Artagnan, laughing.

"I am only asking so I may know if you will be returning late."

"Why do you ask? Do you intend to sit up for me?"

"No, but since my arrest and the robbery that was committed in my house, I am alarmed every time I hear a door open, particularly at night. What do you expect? I am no swordsman."

"Well, don't be alarmed if I return at one, two, or three o'clock in the morning—indeed, do not be alarmed if I do not return at all."

This time Bonacieux turned so pale that d'Artagnan could not help noticing it, and he asked him what was the matter.

"Nothing," replied Bonacieux. "Since my misfortunes I have been subject to faintnesses that come upon me all at once, and I just felt a cold shiver. Pay no attention—just concentrate on your good fortune."

"That is exactly what I am doing."

"But you must wait a little! You said this evening."

"Well, this evening will come, thank God! And perhaps you are looking forward to it with as much impatience as I am. Perhaps Madame Bonacieux will visit the conjugal dwelling this evening."

"Madame Bonacieux is not free this evening," replied her husband seriously. "She is detained at the Louvre by her duties."

"The more's the pity, my dear landlord! When I am happy, I wish all the world to be happy too, but it seems that is not possible."

The young man walked away, laughing at the joke that he thought he alone could understand.

"Enjoy yourself!" Bonacieux said savagely.

But d'Artagnan was too far away to hear him, and even if he had heard him, feeling as he did, he certainly would not have paid any attention.

He went to M. de Tréville's house, for his visit of the day before had been a very short one and not very explanatory.

He found Tréville in a joyful mood. The king and queen had been charming to him at the ball, though it is true that the cardinal had been particularly ill-tempered: he had left at one o'clock under the pretense of not feeling well. Their Majesties did not return to the Louvre till six o'clock in the morning.

"Now," said Tréville, lowering his voice and looking into every corner of the room to make sure they were alone, "let us talk about you, my young friend, for it is evident that your happy return has something to do with the king's joy, the queen's triumph, and the cardinal's humiliation. You must look out for yourself."

"What have I to fear as long as I have the good fortune to enjoy the favor of their Majesties?" asked d'Artagnan.

"Everything, believe me. The cardinal is not the man to forget a hoax until he has settled accounts with the hoaxer, and the hoaxer appears to be a certain young Gascon I know."

"Do you think the cardinal is as well informed as you are, and knows that I have been to London?"

"So you have been to London! Does that beautiful diamond which sparkles on your finger come from London? Beware, my dear d'Artagnan—a present from an enemy is not a good thing! Are there not some Latin verses on that subject? Wait a minute . . ."

"Yes, there certainly must be," replied d'Artagnan, who had never been able to cram the first rudiments of that language into his head and who had by his ignorance driven his teacher to despair.

"There *is*," said M. de Tréville, who had a slight acquaintance with literature, "and Monsieur de Benserade was quoting it to me the other day. . . . Ah, this is it! 'Timeo Danaos et dona ferentes,' which means, 'Beware of the enemy who makes you presents.' "

"This diamond does not come from an enemy, monsieur," replied d'Artagnan. "It comes from the queen."

"From the queen! Why, yes, it is indeed a truly royal

jewel, worth a thousand pistoles at least. By whom did the queen send you this jewel?"

"She gave it to me herself."

"Where?"

"In the room adjoining the one in which she changed her costume."

"How?"

"By giving me her hand to kiss."

"You have kissed the queen's hand?" said M. de Tréville, looking earnestly at d'Artagnan.

"Her Majesty did me the honor to grant me that favor."

"In the presence of witnesses? Imprudent, thrice imprudent!"

"No, monsieur, rest assured that nobody saw her," replied d'Artagnan, and he told M. de Tréville how it had all happened.

"Oh, women, women!" cried the old soldier. "They all have a romantic imagination—everything that savors of mystery charms them. So you saw the arm and the hand, that was all. . . . If you were to meet the queen, you would not know her, and she might meet you and not know who you are."

"No, but thanks to this diamond . . ."

"Listen, shall I give you some advice, good advice, the advice of a friend?"

"I would be honored, monsieur."

"Then go to the nearest goldsmith's and sell that diamond for the highest price you can get from him. However avaricious he may be, he will give you at least eight hundred pistoles for it. Pistoles have no name, young man, but that ring has one that could betray whoever wears it."

"Sell this ring, a ring that comes from my sovereign? Never!"

"Then, at least wear the stone inside, you silly fellow! Everybody knows that a young man from Gascony does not find such stones in his mother's jewel case."

"You truly think I have something to fear?"

"Young man, he who sleeps over a spluttering explosive may consider himself safe compared with you."

"What should I do?" asked d'Artagnan, beginning to feel worried by M. de Tréville's authoritative tone.

"Above all, be always on your guard! The cardinal has a tenacious memory and a long arm. Believe me, he will repay you by some ill turn."

"But what kind?"

"How do I know? He is powerful and devilishly clever. The least that might happen is that you will be arrested."

"What! They would dare arrest a man in his Majesty's service?"

"*Pardieu!* They did not have many scruples in the case of Athos! At all events, young man, take the word of one who has been at court for thirty years. Do not allow yourself to be lulled into a false sense of security or you will be lost. On the contrary, see enemies everywhere. If anyone seeks a quarrel with you—even a ten-year-old child—shun it. If you are attacked by day or by night, fight—but retreat without shame. If you cross a bridge, test every plank with your foot lest one give way beneath you. If you pass in front of a house that is being built, look up, lest a stone fall upon your head. If you stay out late, always be followed by your lackey, and let your lackey be armed—if, by the way, you can be sure of your lackey's loyalty. Mistrust everybody, your friend, your brother, your mistress—your mistress above all."

D'Artagnan blushed.

"My mistress above all," he repeated mechanically. "Why her rather than another?"

"Because using a mistress is one of the cardinal's favorite methods—and there is not one that is more successful. A woman will sell you for ten pistoles, as witness Delilah. You are acquainted with the Scriptures, aren't you?"

D'Artagnan thought of the appointment Mme. Bonacieux had made with him for that very evening; but we are bound to say, to his credit, that Tréville's bad opinion of women in general did not make him the least suspicious of his pretty landlady.

"But apropos," resumed M. de Tréville, "what has become of your three companions?"

"I was about to ask you if you had heard any news about them."

"None."

"Well, I left them on the road—Porthos in Chantilly with a duel on his hands, Aramis in Crèvecoeur with a bullet in his shoulder, and Athos in Amiens, detained by an accusation of counterfeiting."

"You see! And how the devil did you escape?"

"By a miracle, monsieur, I must admit. On the road to Calais, and with a sword thrust in my chest, I had to puncture the Comte de Wardes and leave him there."

"There again! De Wardes is one of the cardinal's men, Rochefort's cousin . . . ! Listen, my friend, I have an idea."

"Speak, monsieur."

"In your place, I would do one thing."

"What?"

"While his Eminence was looking for me in Paris, I would take the road to Picardy, without any fanfare, and make some inquiries about my three companions. What the devil—they certainly deserve that much attention from you!"

"That is good advice, monsieur, and I will set out tomorrow."

"Tomorrow! Why not this evening?"

"This evening, monsieur, I am detained in Paris by important business."

"Ah, young man, some flirtation or other . . . Take care, I tell you, take care! It is woman who has ruined us all, and will ruin us all, as long as the world exists. Take my advice and set out this evening."

"Impossible, monsieur."

"You have given your word?"

"Yes, monsieur."

"Ah, that is quite another matter. But promise me that if you are not killed tonight, you will leave tomorrow."

"I promise."

"Do you need money?"

"I still have fifty pistoles. I think that is as much as I will need."

"But what about your companions?"

"I don't think they can need any, either. We each left Paris with seventy-five pistoles in his pocket."

"Will I see you again before your departure?"

"I think not, monsieur, unless something new should happen."

"A pleasant journey then."

"Thank you, monsieur."

D'Artagnan left M. de Tréville, touched more than ever by his paternal solicitude for his Musketeers.

He called successively at the houses of Athos, Porthos, and Aramis. None of them had returned. Their lackeys were also absent, and nothing had been heard of either masters or servants. He would have asked their mistresses about them, but he did not know Porthos's or Aramis's, and Athos had none.

Passing the Guards' headquarters, he glanced into the stables; three of the four horses had already arrived, and the incredulous Planchet was busy grooming them and had already finished two.

"Ah, monsieur, I am glad to see you," he said when he noticed d'Artagnan.

"Why, Planchet?" the young man asked.

"Do you trust our landlord, Monsieur Bonacieux?"

"I? Not at all."

"You are quite right not to, monsieur."

"But why do you ask?"

"Because while you were talking with him, I was watching both of you without listening, and, monsieur, his face changed color two or three times!"

"Bah!"

"Monsieur was preoccupied with the letter he had received, so he did not observe that. But I, whom the strange fashion in which that letter came into the house had placed on my guard—I did not lose one movement of his face."

"And you found it . . . ?"

"Treacherous, monsieur."

"Indeed!"

"In addition, as soon as Monsieur left him and disappeared around the corner, Monsieur Bonacieux took his hat, shut his door, and began to walk quickly in the opposite direction."

"You are right, Planchet—all this seems very mysterious, and you can be sure that we will not pay him our rent until the matter is completely explained to us."

"Monsieur jests, but Monsieur will see."

"What do you want me to do, Planchet? What must be, shall be."

"Then monsieur does not renounce his excursion for this evening?"

"On the contrary, Planchet. The more I dislike Monsieur Bonacieux, the more punctual I will be in keeping the appointment made by that letter which makes you so uneasy."

"If that is Monsieur's determination . . ."

"An unshakable one, my friend. So be ready at nine o'clock, and I will come for you here."

Seeing there was no hope of making his master renounce his project, Planchet sighed deeply and set to work grooming the third horse.

As for d'Artagnan, since he was essentially a prudent young man, instead of returning home he went to dine with the Gascon priest who had given the four friends a breakfast of chocolate when they had needed it so badly.

24

The Villa

AT NINE O'CLOCK d'Artagnan was back at the Guards' headquarters, and he found Planchet ready. The fourth horse had arrived.

Planchet was armed with his musket and a pistol. D'Artagnan already had his sword and put two pistols into his belt, then both mounted and rode off quietly. It was quite dark, and no one saw them leave. Planchet took his place ten paces behind his master.

D'Artagnan crossed the quays, left the city by the Conférence gate, and followed the road—much more beautiful then than it is now—that leads to St. Cloud.

As long as they were in the city, Planchet kept at the respectful distance he had imposed upon himself, but as soon as the road began to be more lonely and dark, he quietly drew nearer, so that when they entered the Bois de Boulogne he was riding quite naturally side by side with his master. Indeed, we must not hide the fact that the rustling of the tall trees and the eerie reflection of the moon in the dark underwood made him seriously uneasy.

D'Artagnan could see that something unusual was

passing through his lackey's mind and said, "Well, Monsieur Planchet, what is the matter now?"

"Don't you think, monsieur, that woods are like churches?"

"How, Planchet?"

"Because we dare not speak aloud in either one."

"But why do you not dare speak aloud, Planchet? Because you are afraid?"

"Afraid of being heard—yes, monsieur."

"Afraid of being heard! Why, there is nothing improper in our conversation, Planchet, and no one could find fault with it."

"There is something sly about Monsieur Bonacieux's eyebrows, and something very unpleasant about the way he moves his lips," said Planchet, recurring to his obsession.

"What the devil makes you think of Bonacieux?"

"Monsieur, we think of what we can, not of what we wish."

"You are timid, Planchet."

"Monsieur, we must not confuse prudence with timidity. Prudence is a virtue."

"And you are very virtuous, are you not, Planchet?"

"Monsieur, is that not a musket barrel glittering over there? Shouldn't we lower our heads?"

"In truth," thought d'Artagnan, remembering M. de Tréville's warnings, "this creature will end by making me afraid."

He spurred his horse into a trot.

Planchet followed his master's movements as if he had been his shadow, and was soon trotting by his side.

"Are we going to continue like this all night?" he asked.

"No, you are at your journey's end."

"What about you, Monsieur?"

"I am going a little farther."

"And Monsieur leaves me here alone?"

"Are you afraid, Planchet?"

"No, I only wish to observe that the night will be very cold, that chills bring on rheumatism, and that a lackey who has rheumatism makes a poor servant, particularly to a master as active as Monsieur."

"Well, if you are cold, Planchet, you can go into one

of those taverns over there, and wait outside for me at
six o'clock in the morning."

"Monsieur, I respectfully ate and drank the écu you
gave me this morning, so I do not have a sou left to buy
anything against the cold."

"Here's half a pistole. I will see you tomorrow
morning."

D'Artagnan dismounted, threw the reins to Planchet,
and quickly walked away, folding his cloak around him.

"Good Lord, I am cold!" Planchet grumbled as soon
as he had lost sight of his master. He was in such a hurry
to warm himself that he went straight to a house showing
all the attributes of a suburban tavern and knocked at
the door.

In the meantime d'Artagnan, who had gone down a
side road, soon arrived at St. Cloud; but instead of following the main street he turned behind the château,
reached a dark, narrow lane, and found himself in front
of the villa, which was in a very secluded spot at the
corner of a high wall that ran along one side of the lane.
On the other was a little garden belonging to a wretched
hut that was protected by a hedge from passersby.

He had arrived at his rendezvous, and since he had
been given no signal by which to announce his presence,
he waited.

Not the least sound was to be heard; he might have
been a hundred leagues from Paris. He leaned against
the hedge, after having glanced behind it. Beyond that
hedge, that garden, and that hut, a dark mist enveloped
the immense space in which Paris slept—a vast void from
which glittered a few luminous points shining like mournful stars.

But for d'Artagnan every aspect was clothed in joy,
every thought wore a smile, every mist was diaphanous:
the appointed hour was about to strike.

In fact, after a few minutes ten strokes slowly sounded
from the sonorous jaws of the St. Cloud steeple. There
was something melancholy about that bronze voice and
its lamentations, but each stroke that made up the anticipated hour vibrated harmoniously in the young man's
heart.

His eyes were fixed on the little villa at the corner of
the wall, all of whose windows were closed with shutters

except for one on the second floor. Through this window shone a soft light that silvered the gently moving foliage of the two or three linden trees which formed a group outside the park. It must be behind that little window, which threw forth such friendly beams, that the pretty Mme. Bonacieux was waiting for him.

Enveloped in this sweet dream, he waited half an hour without the least impatience, his eyes fixed on the charming little villa; he could just see a part of the ceiling with its gilded moldings, and that suggested the elegance of the rest of the room.

The bell struck half past ten.

This time, without knowing why, d'Artagnan felt a cold shiver run through his veins. Perhaps the chill of the night was beginning to affect him, and he was mistaking a purely physical sensation for an emotional impression.

Then he thought that he might have read the note incorrectly and that the appointment was for eleven o'clock. Drawing near the window and placing himself so that a ray of light would fall on the letter as he held it, he took it from his pocket and read it again; but he had not been mistaken: the appointment was for ten o'clock.

He resumed his post, beginning to feel uneasy about the silence and the solitude.

Eleven o'clock sounded.

Now d'Artagnan began to fear that something had happened to Mme. Bonacieux. He clapped his hands three times—the usual lovers' signal—but nobody replied to him, not even an echo.

It occurred to him, with a touch of vexation, that she might have fallen asleep while waiting for him. He approached the wall and tried to climb it, but it had recently been plastered and he could get no hold.

Suddenly he remembered the trees, upon whose leaves the light from the moon was still shining, and since one of them drooped over the road, he thought that he might get a glimpse of the interior of the villa from its branches.

The linden tree was easy to climb, especially since d'Artagnan was only twenty years old and consequently had not yet forgotten his schoolboy habits. In a few seconds he was up among the branches, his keen eyes piercing the transparent panes.

It was strange—and it made him shudder from the soles of his feet to the roots of his hair—to find that the soft light illuminated a scene of fearful disorder. One of the windows was broken; the door of the room had been smashed and now hung, split in two, on its hinges; a table that had been covered with an elegant supper was overturned; the decanters were broken in pieces; and crushed fruits were strewn on the floor. Everything gave evidence of a violent, desperate struggle, and he even thought he could recognize fragments of garments and bloodstains on the tablecloth and the curtains.

He climbed down the tree quickly, his heart pounding, to see if he could find other traces of violence.

The soft little light still shone on in the calm of the night, and d'Artagnan then noticed something he had not seen before since nothing had led him to look for it: the ground, trampled here and hoofmarked there, showed confused traces of men and horses. In addition, carriage wheels, which appeared to have come from the direction of Paris, had made a deep impression in the soft earth— an impression that did not extend beyond the villa and that turned again toward Paris.

Pursuing his investigation, he then found near the wall a woman's torn glove. Wherever it had not touched the muddy ground, it was irreproachably fresh—one of those perfumed gloves that lovers like to snatch from a pretty hand.

As d'Artagnan continued his search, an ever more abundant and more glacial sweat rolled in large drops from his forehead; his heart was oppressed by a horrible anguish; his breathing was uneven. And yet he tried to persuade himself that the villa might have nothing to do with Mme. Bonacieux: that she had made an appointment to meet him in front of it, not inside it; that she might have been detained in Paris by her duties, or perhaps by her husband's jealousy.

But all those reasons were overwhelmed, destroyed, overthrown, by that feeling of intimate pain which on certain occasions takes possession of our being, and cries out to us, so as to be unmistakably understood, that some great misfortune is hanging over us.

Then d'Artagnan became almost insane. He ran along

the high road, took the path he had taken before, reached the ferry, and questioned the boatman.

About seven o'clock in the evening, the boatman had taken over a young woman, wrapped in a black cloak, who appeared to be very anxious not to be recognized; but just because of her precautions, he had paid special attention to her and discovered that she was young and pretty.

There were then, as now, many young and pretty women who came to St. Cloud and who had reasons for not being recognized, yet d'Artagnan did not doubt for an instant that it was Mme. Bonacieux whom the boatman had noticed.

Taking advantage of the lamp that burned in the ferryman's cabin to read Mme. Bonacieux's note once again, d'Artagnan satisfied himself that he had not been mistaken—that the appointment was in St. Cloud and not elsewhere, in front of D'Estrées's house and not in another street.

Everything proved to him that his presentiments had not deceived him and that something disastrous had happened.

He ran back, thinking that something might have happened at the villa in his absence and that fresh information might await him.

The lane was still deserted, and the same soft light shone through the window.

Then he thought of that dark and silent hut, which had surely seen everything and could tell its tale. The gate was shut, but he leaped over the hedge and, in spite of the barking of a chained dog, went up to the cabin.

No one answered his first knocks. A deathly silence reigned in the hut as in the villa, but the cabin was his last resource, so he kept on knocking.

He thought he heard a slight noise inside—a timid noise, which seemed to tremble lest it be heard.

Finally he stopped knocking, and began to plead in a voice so full of anxiety and promises, terror and cajolery, that his tone was such as would reassure the most fearful listener. At length an old, worm-eaten shutter was opened, or rather pushed ajar, but it closed again as soon as the light from a miserable lamp that burned in the corner had shone on his baldric, sword, and pistols.

Rapid as the movement had been, however, d'Artagnan had had time to get a glimpse of an old man's face.

"In the name of heaven," he cried, "listen to me! I have been waiting for someone who has not come. I am dying of anxiety. Has anything happened in the neighborhood? Speak!"

The window was again opened slowly, and the same face appeared, even paler than before.

D'Artagnan told his story simply and without giving any names. He explained how he had had a rendezvous with a young woman in front of the villa, and how, not seeing her come, he had climbed the linden tree and by the light of the lamp had seen the disorder in the room.

The old man listened attentively, occasionally nodded that it was all so; when d'Artagnan had finished, he shook his head in a way that signified nothing good.

"What do you know?" cried d'Artagnan. "For God's sake tell me!"

"Oh, monsieur," said the old man, "do not ask me anything, for if I dared tell you what I have seen, I am sure much evil would befall me."

"Then you did see something? In that case, in the name of heaven," d'Artagnan said, throwing him a pistole, "tell me what you have seen, and I will give you my word as a gentleman that I will never repeat anything you say."

The old man saw so much truth and so much grief in the young man's face that he motioned him to approach and started to speak in a low voice.

"It was about nine o'clock when I heard a noise in the street and was wondering what it could be. Coming to my door, I found somebody trying to open my gate. I am very poor and not afraid of being robbed, so I went to open it and saw three men a few paces away. I could also see a carriage with some horses harnessed to it, and some saddle horses in the shadows. The horses evidently belonged to the three men, who were dressed as cavaliers. 'Ah, my worthy gentlemen,' I said, 'what do you want?' 'You have a ladder?' asked the one who appeared to be the leader. 'Yes, monsieur, the one with which I gather my fruit.' 'Lend it to us, and go back into your house. Here is an écu for your trouble. But remember this—if you say one word about what you may see or hear (for I am sure you will look and you will listen, however much we may threaten you), you are lost.'

"At those words he threw me the écu, which I picked up, and he took my ladder.

"After shutting the gate behind them, I returned to the house, but I immediately went out the back door. Hugging the shadows of the hedge, I got to the clump of elder bushes, from where I could hear and see everything.

"The three men had brought the carriage quietly up to the house, and a little man—stout, short, elderly, and badly dressed in dark clothes—got out and ascended the ladder very carefully. He looked sneakily through the second-floor window, came down as quietly as he had gone up, and whispered, 'She is there!'

"The man who had spoken to me went to the door, opened it with a key he had in his hand, closed the door and disappeared inside, while at the same time the other two men climbed the ladder. The little old man remained near the carriage door, the coachman took care of his horses, and the lackey held the saddle horses.

"All at once I heard screams from inside the villa. A woman opened the window, as if to throw herself out of it, but as soon as she saw the other two men on the ladder, she stepped back. The men went into the room through the window.

"Then I saw no more, but I heard the noise of breaking furniture. The woman was screaming for help, but her cries were soon stifled. The two men brought the woman down the ladder and carried her to the carriage. The little old man got in after her. The man who had stayed in the room closed the window, came out a little later by the door, and assured himself that the woman was in the carriage. His two companions were already on their horses. He sprang into his saddle, the lackey went back to his seat next to the coachman, the carriage quickly drove away escorted by the three horsemen, and it was all over. From that moment I have neither seen nor heard anything."

Overcome by this terrible story, d'Artagnan remained motionless and mute while all the demons of anger and jealousy were howling in his heart.

"But my good gentleman," resumed the old man,

upon whom this mute despair certainly produced a greater effect than moans and tears would have done, "do not take on so. They did not kill her, and that's the most important thing."

"Can you tell me about the man in charge of this infernal expedition?" d'Artagnan asked.

"I don't know him."

"But you spoke to him, so you must have seen him."

"Oh, it's a description you want?"

"Exactly."

"A tall, dark man, with a black mustache, dark eyes, and the air of a gentleman."

"That's the man!" cried d'Artagnan. "The same man again! Always the same man! He is apparently my demon. And the other one?"

"Which?"

"The short one."

"Oh, *he* was not a gentleman, I'm sure. He did not wear a sword, and the others treated him without any consideration."

"Some lackey," murmured d'Artagnan. "Poor woman, what have they done with you?"

"You have promised to keep my secret," said the old man.

"And I repeat my promise. I am a gentleman. A gentleman must keep his word, and I have given you mine."

With a heavy heart, d'Artagnan again went to the ferry. Sometimes he hoped it could not have been Mme. Bonacieux and that he would find her the next day at the Louvre, sometimes he feared she had had a romantic intrigue with someone else, who, in a jealous fit, had surprised her and carried her off. His mind was torn by doubt, grief, and despair.

"Oh, if only my three friends were here," he thought. Then I would at least have some hopes of finding her. But who knows what has become of them either?"

It was past midnight, and he wanted to find Planchet— but there was no Planchet in any of the taverns in which there was a light.

At the sixth one he began to realize that the search was useless; he had told his lackey to meet him at six o'clock in the morning, and wherever he might be, he was within his rights.

Besides, the young man began to think that by remaining in the neighborhood of the abduction, he might
have some light thrown upon the mysterious affair. So at
the sixth cabaret, he stopped, asked for a bottle of good
wine, sat down in the darkest corner of the room, and
determined to wait there until daylight; but again his
hopes were disappointed, and although he listened with
all his might, he heard nothing but curses, coarse jokes,
and abuse being exchanged among the laborers, servants,
and carters who made up the honorable society of which
he formed a part—not a word that could put him on the
track of the woman who had been stolen from him. After
having finished his bottle, he was forced—both to pass
the time and to evade suspicion—to fall into the most
comfortable position possible and to sleep as best he
could. Be it remembered that he was only twenty years
old, and at that age sleep has its inalienable rights, which
it imperiously insists upon, even with the saddest hearts.

Toward six o'clock he woke up with that uncomfortable feeling which generally accompanies the break of
day after a bad night. It did not take him long to get
ready. He examined himself to see if anyone had taken
advantage of his sleep to rob him, and having found his
diamond ring on his finger, his purse in his pocket, and
his pistols in his belt, he rose, paid for his bottle, and
went out to see if he would have any better luck in his
search for his lackey than he had had the night before.
And the first thing he saw through the damp gray mist
was Planchet holding the reins of the two horses in hand
and waiting for him at the door of a dark little tavern
in front of which d'Artagnan had passed without even
suspecting its existence.

25

Porthos

INSTEAD OF RETURNING directly home, d'Artagnan stopped at M. de Tréville's and ran quickly up the stairs. This time he had decided to tell him everything that had happened because he would undoubtedly give him good advice. Besides, M. de Tréville saw the queen almost daily and might be able to get from her Majesty some news of the poor young woman who was being made to pay very dearly for her devotion to her mistress.

Tréville listened to the young man's account with a seriousness which proved that he saw something more in the adventure than a love affair.

When d'Artagnan had finished, he said, "I sense the cardinal's touch in all this."

"But what can I do?" d'Artagnan asked.

"Absolutely nothing at present, except, as I told you, to leave Paris as soon as possible. I will see the queen and give her the details of this poor woman's disappearance, of which she is surely ignorant. Those details will guide her own behavior, and I may have some good news for you on your return. Rely on me."

D'Artagnan knew that M. de Tréville, although a Gascon, was not in the habit of making promises, and that when by chance he did promise, he more than kept his word. So the young man bowed to him, full of gratitude for the past and for the future; and the captain, who felt a lively interest in this brave and resolute young man, shook his hand kindly and wished him a pleasant journey.

Determined to follow M. de Tréville's advice, d'Artagnan headed for the Rue des Fossoyeurs in order to superintend his packing. Approaching the house, he saw M. Bonacieux dressed in morning clothes and standing at his threshold. Everything the prudent Planchet had said to him the preceding evening about the old man's sinister character came back to d'Artagnan, who looked at Bonacieux more attentively than he had ever done before. And in truth, in addition to that yellow, sickly pallor that indicates bile in the blood and might not be important, d'Artagnan also noticed something vaguely treacherous in the play of his wrinkled features. A rogue does not laugh in the same way that an honest man does; a hypocrite does not shed the same tears as a sincere man. All falsehood is a mask, and however well made the mask may be, with a little attention we may always distinguish it from the true face.

It now seemed to d'Artagnan that Bonacieux wore a mask and that that mask was most disagreeable to look upon.

Because of this feeling of repugnance, he was about to pass without speaking to him, but the haberdasher called out to him just as he had done the day before.

"Well, young man," he said, "we seem to have rather busy nights! Seven o'clock in the morning! *Peste*—you evidently reverse the usual customs and come home when other people are going out."

"No one can reproach you for anything like that, Monsieur Bonacieux," d'Artagnan replied. "You are a model for all proper people. Of course, when a man has a young and pretty wife, he has no need to seek happiness elsewhere—happiness comes to meet him at home, does it not, Monsieur Bonacieux?"

Bonacieux became deathly pale and gave a ghastly smile.

"Ah, you are indeed an amusing companion! But where the devil were you gadding about last night, my young friend? It looks as though the roads were not very good."

D'Artagnan glanced down at his mud-covered boots, but at the same time he noticed the haberdasher's shoes and stockings, which looked as if they might have been dipped in the same muck: both were stained with splashes of exactly the same mud.

An idea suddenly flashed into d'Artagnan's mind. That little stout man, short and elderly, that sort of lackey dressed in dark clothes and treated unceremoniously by the men wearing swords who composed the escort, was Bonacieux himself. The husband had presided at his wife's abduction.

D'Artagnan felt a terrible urge to grab the haberdasher by the throat and strangle him; but as we have said, he was a very prudent youth, and he restrained himself. Nevertheless, his expression changed so markedly that it terrified Bonacieux, who tried to draw back a step or two; however, since he was standing before the part of the door that was shut, he was forced to stay put.

"You jest, my good man," said d'Artagnan. "If my boots need a sponge, your stockings and shoes stand in equal need of a brush. Could it be that you too have been philandering, Monsieur Bonacieux? That would be unforgivable in a man of your age, especially one who has such a pretty young wife!"

"No, no, nothing like that," said Bonacieux. "I went to St. Mandé yesterday to make some inquiries about a servant, as I cannot possibly do without one, and the roads were so bad that I brought back all this mud, which I have not yet had time to remove."

The place named by Bonacieux as the object of his journey was further proof in support of d'Artagnan's suspicions. Bonacieux had named St. Mandé because it was in an exactly opposite direction from St. Cloud.

This possibility gave d'Artagnan his first consolation: if Bonacieux knew where his wife was, one could always, by extreme means if necessary, force him to tell his secret. The question was how to change the possibility into a certainty.

"Excuse me, my dear Monsieur Bonacieux, if I don't stand upon ceremony," said d'Artagnan, "but nothing makes one so thirsty as lack of sleep. I am parched. Allow me to take a glass of water in your apartment— you know neighbors never refuse such a request."

Without waiting for permission, d'Artagnan went quickly into the house and glanced at the bed. It had not been used. Bonacieux had not slept at home. He had only come back an hour or two before, which probably meant that he had accompanied his wife to the place of her confinement—or at least to the first relay.

"Thank you, Monsieur Bonacieux," said d'Artagnan, emptying his glass, "that is all I wanted from you. Now I will go up to my apartment and make Planchet brush my boots—and when he has finished, I will send him down to you to brush your shoes."

He left the haberdasher quite astonished at his singular farewell, and asking himself if he had somehow incriminated himself.

At the top of the stairs he found Planchet in a great fright.

"Ah, monsieur," Planchet said as soon as he saw his master, "here is more trouble! I thought you would never come back."

"What's the matter now, Planchet?" asked d'Artagnan.

"I give you a hundred—no, a thousand—guesses as to whose visit I have had in your absence."

"When?"

"About half an hour ago, while you were at Monsieur de Tréville's."

"Who was here? Come, speak up."

"Monsieur de Cavois."

"Monsieur de Cavois?"

"In person."

"The captain of the cardinal's Guards?"

"Himself."

"Did he come to arrest me?"

"I have no doubt he did, monsieur, for all his wheedling ways."

"Was he so sweet, then?"

"Indeed, he was all honey, monsieur."

"Indeed!"

"He said he came on the part of his Eminence, who wished you well, and to beg you to accompany him to the Palais-Royal."

"What did you say?"

"That it was impossible because you were not at home, as he could see."

"What did he say then?"

"That you must not fail to call on him some time during the day—and then he added in a low voice, 'Tell your master that his Eminence is very well disposed toward him and that his fortune may depend on this interview.'"

"The trap is rather clumsy for the cardinal," d'Artagnan said, smiling.

"Oh, I also saw the trap, and I answered that you would be in despair at having missed him."

"'Where has he gone?' asked Monsieur de Cavois.

" 'To Troyes, in Champagne,' I answered.

" 'When did he leave?'

" 'Yesterday evening.' "

"Planchet, my friend," d'Artagnan interrupted, "you are a splendid fellow."

"You understand, monsieur, I thought there would always be time, if you wish to see Monsieur de Cavois, to contradict me by saying you had not yet gone. The falsehood would then lie at my door, and since I am not a gentleman, I may be allowed to lie."

"Don't worry, Planchet, you will be able to preserve your reputation as a truthful man. We leave in a quarter of an hour."

"That's the advice I was about to give Monsieur. And where are we going, if I may ask without seeming too curious?"

"*Pardieu*, in the opposite direction from where you said I had gone! Besides, are you not as eager to have news of Grimaud, Mousqueton, and Bazin as I am to know what has happened to Athos, Porthos, and Aramis?"

"Yes, monsieur, and I will leave as soon as you please. Indeed, I think the air of the provinces will suit us much better just now than the air of Paris. So . . ."

"So pack our things, Planchet, and let us be off. For my part, I will go out with my hands in my pockets so that no one will suspect anything. You may join me at the Guards' headquarters. By the way, Planchet, I think you are right about our landlord—he is definitely a villainous character."

"Monsieur, you may always take my word for whatever I tell you about people. I am good at reading faces, I assure you."

D'Artagnan went out first, as had been agreed. Then, so he would have nothing to reproach himself with, he directed his steps a final time toward the residences of his three friends. There had been no news about them, but a perfumed letter in small, elegant writing had come for Aramis; d'Artagnan promised to deliver it. Ten minutes later Planchet joined him at the stables of the Guards' headquarters, where d'Artagnan, to avoid losing any time, had saddled his horse himself.

"Good," he said to Planchet when the latter added the

portmanteau to the equipment. "Now saddle the other three horses."

"Do you think, monsieur, that we will travel faster with two horses apiece?" Planchet asked inquisitively.

"No, Monsieur Jester," replied d'Artagnan, "but with our four horses we may bring back our three friends—if we are fortunate enough to find them alive."

"Which is far from certain," Planchet added, "but we must not despair of God's mercy."

"Amen!" said d'Artagnan, getting into his saddle.

The two men separated, leaving the street at opposite ends—one to ride out of Paris by the Villette gate and the other by the Montmartre gate; they planned to meet again beyond St. Denis—a strategic maneuver that was executed with equal precision and crowned with the fortunate results that d'Artagnan and Planchet entered Pierrefitte together.

Planchet was certainly more courageous by day than by night, although his natural caution never abandoned him for a single instant. He had forgotten nothing about the first journey, and he looked upon everybody he met on the road as an enemy. This meant that his hat was forever in his hand, which earned him some severe reprimands from d'Artagnan, who feared that his excessive politeness would lead people to think he was the lackey of someone unimportant.

Nevertheless, whether it was because those they met were really impressed by Planchet's civility or because this time nobody had been posted on d'Artagnan's road, the two travelers arrived at Chantilly without incident and went to the Grand St. Martin inn, where they had stopped the first time.

Seeing a young man followed by a lackey with two extra horses, the host advanced respectfully to the door. Since they had already traveled eleven leagues, d'Artagnan thought it time to stop, whether or not Porthos was there. It occurred to him that it might not even be prudent to ask at once about the Musketeer. Without seeking any kind of information, he therefore dismounted, turned the horses over to his lackey, entered a small room reserved for those guests who wished to be alone, and asked the host to bring him a bottle of his best wine and as good a meal as possible—an order that further corroborated the high opinion the innkeeper had formed of the traveler at first sight.

D'Artagnan was served with miraculous rapidity.

The regiment of the Guards was recruited from among the first gentlemen of the kingdom; and d'Artagnan, followed by a lackey and traveling with four magnificent horses, could not fail to make a sensation despite the simplicity of his uniform. The host himself wished to serve him, seeing which, d'Artagnan ordered another glass to be brought and began the following conversation.

"My good host," he said, filling the two glasses, "I asked for a bottle of your best wine, and if you have deceived me, you will be punished for your sin, because since I hate drinking by myself, you are going to drink with me. Take your glass, then, and let us drink. But what shall we drink to, without offending any susceptibility . . . ? I know—to the prosperity of your establishment."

"Your Lordship does me much honor," said the host, "and I thank you sincerely for your kind wish."

"Make no mistake," said d'Artagnan. "There is more selfishness in my toast than you may think, for it is only in prosperous establishments that one is well served. In hostelries that do not flourish, everything is in a state of confusion, and the traveler is a victim of his host's problems. Now, since I travel a great deal, particularly on this road, I would like to see all the innkeepers making a fortune."

"It does seem to me that this is not the first time I have had the honor of seeing Monsieur."

"Bah, I have passed through Chantilly about ten times and I have stopped at least three or four of those times at your inn. Why, I was here only ten or twelve days ago. I was with some friends, some Musketeers—one of whom, by the way, had a dispute with a stranger, a man who sought a quarrel with him for I don't know what reason."

"Oh yes, I remember it perfectly. Is it not Monsieur Porthos that your Lordship means?"

"Yes, that is my companion's name. Can you tell me what has happened to him?"

"Your Lordship must have noticed that he wasn't able to continue his journey."

"Yes, but he promised to rejoin us, and we have seen nothing of him."

"He has done us the honor to remain here."

"What, he has done you the honor to remain here?"

"Yes, monsieur, in this inn, and we are even a little uneasy about . . ."

"About what?"

"About certain expenses."

"Whatever expenses he may have incurred, I am sure he can pay them."

"Ah, monsieur, you bring peace to my heart. We have given him considerable credit, and this very morning the doctor declared that if Monsieur Porthos did not pay him, he expected me to, since I was the one who had sent for him."

"Porthos is wounded?"

"I cannot tell you, monsieur."

"You cannot tell me? Surely you ought to be able to tell me better than anyone else."

"Yes, but in our position we must not say all that we know—particularly as we have been warned that our ears might answer for our tongues."

"Well, can I see Porthos?"

"Certainly, monsieur. Take the stairs on your right, go up to the second floor, and knock at Number One. Just warn him that it is you."

"Why should I do that?"

"Because otherwise, monsieur, something might happen to you."

"What kind of something?"

"Monsieur Porthos might think you belong to the establishment, and in a fit of passion he might run his sword through you or blow out your brains."

"What have you done to him to make him so angry?"

"We have asked him for money."

"Ah, I understand—Porthos takes such requests very badly when he is not in funds, but I know he must have some at present."

"We thought so too, monsieur. Since our house is run in a very orderly way and we make out our bills every week, at the end of a week we presented our account. But it seemed we had chosen an unlucky moment, because at the first word on the subject, he sent us to the devil. Of course he had been gambling the day before."

"Gambling the day before! With whom?"

"Who can say, monsieur? With some gentleman who was traveling this way and to whom he proposed a game of lansquenet."

"That's it, then—the foolish fellow must have lost all he had!"

"Even his horse, monsieur! When the gentleman was about to set out, we saw his lackey saddling Monsieur Porthos's horse as well as his master's. When we said something about it to him, he told us to mind our own business, since the horse belonged to him. We informed Monsieur Porthos of what was going on, but he told us we were scoundrels to doubt a gentleman's word and that since that gentleman had said the horse was his, it must be so."

"That's Porthos all over," murmured d'Artagnan.

"Then," continued the host, "I said that since it seemed unlikely that we could come to an understanding with respect to payment, I hoped that he would at least have the kindness to grant the favor of his custom to my brother host at the Aigle d'or inn. But he replied that my house was the best and he would remain where he was.

"This reply was too flattering to allow me to insist on his departure, so I then begged him to give up his room, which is the largest and best in the inn, and to be satisfied with a pretty but smaller one on the fourth floor. He replied that he was expecting his mistress at any moment, and since she was one of the greatest ladies in the court, I might easily understand that even the room he did me the honor to occupy was very mean for the visit of such a personage.

"Nevertheless, while acknowledging the truth of what he said, I thought I should insist, but without even discussing it with me, he took one of his pistols, laid it on his table, and said that at the first word about moving, either within the house or out of it, he would blow out the brains of the person who was so imprudent as to meddle with a matter that concerned only himself. Since that time, monsieur, nobody enters his room but his servant."

"Mousqueton is here?"

"Oh, yes, monsieur. Five days after he left, he came back, and in a very bad humor, too. It seems that he also had met with annoyances on his journey. Unfortunately, he is more nimble than Monsieur Porthos, which means that he turns the inn upside down for whatever his master needs. Because he thinks we might refuse what he asks for, he takes what he wants without asking at all."

"Yes, I have always observed Mousqueton to be very intelligent and loyal," said d'Artagnan.

"That is possible, monsieur, but if I should meet, even four times a year, other men of such intelligence and loyalty—why, I would be a ruined man!"

"No, for Porthos will pay you."

"Hum," said the host, in a doubtful tone.

"He is the favorite of a great lady, who will not allow him to be inconvenienced for such a paltry sum as he owes you."

"If I dared say what I believe about that . . ."

"What you believe . . . ?"

"I ought rather to say, what I know . . ."

"What you know . . . ?"

"And even what I am sure of . . ."

"And what are you so sure of?"

"I would say that I know who that great lady is."

"You?"

"Yes, I."

"And how do you know her?"

"Oh, monsieur, if I thought I could trust your discretion . . ."

"Speak! On my word as a gentleman, you will have no cause to regret your trust."

"Well, monsieur, you understand that uneasiness makes us do many things."

"What have you done?"

"Oh, nothing that was not within my rights as a creditor."

"Well?"

"Monsieur Porthos gave us a note for this duchess, ordering us to put it in the post. This was before his servant came back. Since he could not leave his room, it was necessary to ask us to do his errands."

"Well?"

"Instead of putting the letter in the post, which is never safe, I took advantage of one of my lads going to Paris, and ordered him to take the letter to this duchess himself. This was fulfilling the intentions of Monsieur Porthos, who had wished us to be so careful of this letter, was it not?"

"More or less."

"Well, monsieur, do you know who this great lady is?"

"No. I have heard Porthos speak of her, that's all."

"You do not know who this so-called duchess is?"

"I repeat, I do not know her."

"Why, her name is Madame Coquenard, and she is the old wife of a procurator. She must be at least fifty, but she still thinks she has a right to be jealous. It had struck me as very odd that a duchess should live on the Rue aux Ours!"

"But how do you know about her jealousy?"

"Because she flew into a rage on reading the letter, saying that Monsieur Porthos was fickle and that she was sure he had received his wound in a duel over some woman."

"He was wounded? I have asked you before!"

"Oh, good Lord, what have I said?"

"You said that Porthos had received a sword cut."

"Yes, but he has forbidden me to say so."

"Why?"

"Zounds, monsieur, because he had boasted that he would run through the stranger with whom you left him disputing, and because, despite all his boasts, he was quickly thrown on his back by that stranger. Since Monsieur Porthos is a very vain man, he doesn't want anybody to know about his wound except the duchess, whose sympathy he hoped to arouse by the story of his adventure."

"It is a sword thrust that confines him to his bed?"

"Yes, and a master stroke it was, too, I assure you. Your friend's soul must be stuck tight to his body."

"Were you watching?"

"I followed them out of curiosity, so I saw the duel without the duelists seeing me."

"And what took place?"

"Oh! I assure you that it was all over very quickly. They placed themselves on guard, then the stranger made such a quick feint and lunge that by the time Monsieur Porthos parried, he already had three inches of steel in his chest. He immediately fell backward. The stranger placed the point of his sword at his throat, and Monsieur Porthos, finding himself at the mercy of his adversary, had to admit himself conquered. Then the stranger asked his name, and learning that it was Porthos and not d'Artagnan, he helped him up, brought him back to the inn, mounted his horse, and rode away.

"So it was with Monsieur d'Artagnan that this stranger meant to quarrel?"

"Apparently."

"And do you know what has become of him?"

"No, I never saw him until that moment, and I have not seen him since."

"Very well, I know all that I wish to know. You say Porthos's room is on the second floor, Number One?"

"Yes, monsieur, the best room in the inn—a room I could have rented ten times over."

"Don't worry," said d'Artagnan laughing, "Porthos will pay you with Duchess Coquenard's money!"

"Oh, monsieur, procurator's wife or duchess, if she will only loosen her pursestrings, it will be all the same! But her answer to Monsieur Porthos's letter was positive—she said that she was tired of both his demands and his infidelities, and that she would not send him a sou!"

"And you conveyed that answer to your guest?"

"No, we took good care not to do so, or he would have found out how we had executed his commission."

"So he is still expecting his money to arrive?"

"Oh, yes, monsieur! Yesterday he wrote again, but this time it was his servant who put the letter in the post."

"You say the procurator's wife is old and ugly?"

"Fifty at least, monsieur, and not at all beautiful, according to Pathaud."

"In that case, you needn't worry, for she will soon change her mind. Besides, Porthos cannot owe you very much."

"Not much! Twenty good pistoles already, without counting the doctor. He denies himself nothing—it is easy to see that he is used to living well."

"Never mind. If his mistress abandons him, he will

find friends, I assure you. So do not be uneasy, my dear host, and continue to give him all the care his situation requires."

"Monsieur will remember that he has promised me not to say a word about the procurator's wife or the wound?"

"You have my word."

"Oh, he would kill me!"

"Don't be afraid—he is not as fierce as he seems."

And with those words, d'Artagnan went upstairs, leaving his host somewhat reassured about the two things he seemed most interested in—his money and his life.

At the top of the stairs, on the most conspicuous door of the corridor, a gigantic number "*1*" had been traced in black ink. D'Artagnan knocked, was told to come in, and entered the room.

Porthos was in bed and playing a game of lansquenet with Mousqueton to keep his hand in; a spit loaded with partridges was turning over the fire, and on each side of a large fireplace were two pots exuding a marvelous double aroma of fish stew and rabbit fricassee. In addition, the tops of a desk and a chest were covered with empty bottles.

At the sight of his friend, Porthos cried out with joy, and Mousqueton, rising respectfully, yielded his seat to him and went to inspect the two pots, of which he seemed to be in charge.

"Ah, it is you!" Porthos exclaimed. "You are right welcome! Excuse my not coming to meet you, but"—he looked at d'Artagnan with a certain degree of uneasiness—"you know what has happened to me?"

"No."

"The host has told you nothing?"

"I asked about you, then came up as soon as I could." Porthos seemed to breathe more freely.

"What *did* happen to you, Porthos?" d'Artagnan asked.

"While making a thrust at my adversary, whom I had already hit three times and whom I meant to finish with the fourth, I slipped on a stone and sprained my knee."

"Truly?"

"On my honor! Luckily for the rascal, because otherwise I would have left him dead on the spot, I assure you."

"What became of him?"

"Oh, I don't know. He had had enough and left without waiting for the rest. But you, my dear d'Artagnan, what has happened to you?"

"So this sprained knee is what's keeping you in bed," d'Artagnan continued, paying no attention to Porthos's question.

"Oh yes, that is all. I will be up and about again in a few days."

"Why did you not have yourself moved to Paris? You must be terribly bored here."

"That was my intention, but I have something to confess to you."

"What?"

"As you say, I was terribly bored, and since I had the seventy-five pistoles you had given me in my pocket, I invited some gentleman who was traveling this way to come up to my room and I proposed a cast of dice. He accepted my challenge, and, my God—my seventy-five pistoles passed from my pocket to his without reckoning my horse, which he won into the bargain. Now tell me about you, d'Artagnan."

"What can you expect, Porthos—a man cannot have everything. You know the proverb 'Unlucky at gambling, lucky in love.' Well, you are too fortunate in your love for gambling not to take its revenge. But what can the reverses of fortune mean to you? Have you not—happy rogue that you are—have you not your duchess, who must certainly come to your aid?"

"Well, d'Artagnan, you will see just how unlucky I am," replied Porthos, with the most insouciant air in the world. "I wrote to her, asking her to send me fifty louis or so, which I needed because of my accident, and . . ."

"Well?"

"Well, she must be at her country estate, because she has not answered me."

"Truly?"

"Truly. So yesterday I wrote her another note, even more pressing than the first. . . . But now that you are here, my friend, let us hear about you. I confess I was beginning to be very uneasy."

"But it seems as if your host is treating you very well,

Porthos," said d'Artagnan, directing the sick man's attention to the full pots and the empty bottles.

"So-so. Three or four days ago the impertinent scoundrel gave me his bill, and I was forced to show both him and his bill the door, so I am here in the situation of a conqueror who has to hold his position by being prepared to ward off attacks. I am in constant danger of being forced from my stronghold, I am armed to the teeth."

"It looks as if you must make an occasional sortie," said d'Artagnan, pointing to the bottles and the pots.

"Not I, unfortunately!" said Porthos. "This miserable sprain confines me to my bed, but Mousqueton forages, and brings in provisions. Mousqueton, my friend," he said, turning to his lackey, "you see that we have reinforcements and must have more supplies."

"Mousqueton," said d'Artagnan, "you must do me a favor."

"What, monsieur?"

"You must give your recipe to Planchet. I too may be besieged, and I would not be sorry if he were able to let me enjoy the same advantages that you provide for your master."

"But monsieur, nothing could be more easy," said Mousqueton modestly. "One needs only to be sharp, that's all. I was brought up in the country, and my father in his leisure time was something of a poacher."

"What did he do the rest of his time?"

"He carried on a trade that has always seemed very satisfactory to me."

"What trade?"

"It was in the time of war between the Catholics and the Huguenots, and because he saw the Catholics exterminate the Huguenots and the Huguenots exterminate the Catholics—all in the name of religion—he adopted a mixed belief, which permitted him to be sometimes a Catholic, sometimes a Huguenot. Now, he used to walk behind the hedges that border the roads, with his fowling piece on his shoulder, and when he saw a Catholic traveling alone, the Protestant religion immediately prevailed in his mind. He would lower his gun in the direction of the traveler, then, when he was within ten paces of him, begin a conversation that almost always ended with the traveler giving up his purse to save his life. It goes with-

out saying that when he saw a Huguenot coming, he felt
himself filled with such ardent Catholic zeal that he could
not understand how, a quarter of an hour earlier, he had
been able to have any doubts about the superiority of
our holy religion. I, monsieur, am a Catholic—my father,
faithful to his principles, having made my elder brother
a Huguenot."

"And what happened to this worthy man?" asked
d'Artagnan.

"Oh, something most unfortunate, monsieur. One day
he was trapped on a lonely road between a Huguenot
and a Catholic, with both of whom he had already prac-
ticed his trade and who both recognized him. They united
against him and hanged him from a tree, then came and
boasted of their exploit in a tavern in the next village,
where my brother and I were drinking."

"What did you do?" said d'Artagnan.

"We let them tell their story out. When they left the
tavern they took different directions, so my brother ran
and hid himself on the Catholic's road, and I did the
same on the Huguenot's. Two hours later, it was all
over—we had done for both of them and were full of
admiration for our poor father's foresight in taking the
precaution to bring each of us up in a different religion."

"Well, I must agree that your father was a very intelligent fellow. And you say that in his leisure moments the
worthy man was a poacher?"

"Yes, monsieur, and it was he who taught me to lay
a snare and ground a line, so when I saw our shabby
host wanted to feed us lumps of fat meat fit only for
laborers—which did not at all suit two such delicate stom-
achs as ours—I took up my old trade. I went for walks
in the prince's woods and laid a few snares on the runs,
and I rested on the banks of his Highness's ornamental
lakes and slipped a few fish lines into the water. So now,
thanks be to God, we have—as Monsieur can see—partridges, rabbits, carp, and eels—all light, wholesome
food suitable for the sick."

"But the wine? Who provides the wine? Your host?"

"Yes and no."

"How yes and no?"

"He provides it, but he does not know that he has that
honor."

"Explain yourself, Mousqueton—your conversation is very instructive."

"It is like this, monsieur. It so happened that during my travels I met with a Spaniard who had seen many countries, among them some in the New World."

"What connection can the New World have with the bottles on the chest and the desk?"

"Patience, monsieur, everything will be explained in its turn."

"You are right, Mousqueton. I will let you explain while I listen."

"This Spaniard had in his service a lackey who had accompanied him in his voyage to Mexico. This lackey was my compatriot, and we became good friends because we were also much alike. We both loved all kinds of hunting better than anything else, so he described how in the plains of the Pampas the natives hunt the tiger and the wild bull with ropes that have simple slipknots at one end, which they throw around the necks of those wild animals. At first I would not believe that they could be skillful enough to accurately throw the knotted end of a rope a distance of twenty or thirty paces, but in face of my friend's proof I was obliged to acknowledge the truth of his story. He put a bottle thirty paces away and at each cast he caught the neck of the bottle in the looped end. I began to practice this exercise, and since nature has endowed me with some ability, I can now throw the lasso with any man in the world. . . . Do you understand, monsieur? Our host has a well-stocked cellar and the key never leaves him. However, this cellar has a small window. I throw my lasso through this window, and as I now know which part of the cellar has the best wine, that's where I aim. And that, monsieur, is what the New World has to do with the bottles on the chest and the desk. Now, will you taste our wine and say what you honestly think of it?"

"Thank you, my friend, but unfortunately, I have just had lunch."

"Well, set the table, Mousqueton," said Porthos, "and while we eat, d'Artagnan will tell us what has happened to him since he left us."

"Willingly," said d'Artagnan.

While Porthos and Mousqueton were eating, with the

appetites of convalescents and with that brotherly cordiality which unites men in misfortune, d'Artagnan explained how Aramis, being wounded, had been obliged to stop at Crèvecoeur, how he had left Athos fighting at Amiens with four men who accused him of being a counterfeiter, and how he, d'Artagnan, had been forced to run his sword through the Comte de Wardes in order to reach England.

But there d'Artagnan stopped. He added only that on his return from Great Britain he had brought back four magnificent horses—one for himself and one for each of his companions—and informed Porthos that the one intended for him was already installed in the tavern's stable.

Just then Planchet came in, to inform his master that the horses were sufficiently refreshed and that it would be possible to reach Clermont and spend the night there.

Since d'Artagnan was reassured about Porthos and anxious to obtain news of his two other friends, he held out his hand to the wounded man and told him he was about to continue his quest. For the rest, he planned to return by the same route in seven or eight days, and if Porthos were still at the inn, he would call for him on his way back and they would return to Paris together.

Porthos replied that his sprain would probably not permit him to leave before then, and besides, he had to stay at Chantilly to wait for the answer from his duchess.

D'Artagnan hoped the answer would be prompt and favorable, and having again told Mousqueton to take good care of Porthos and paid his bill to the host, he resumed his journey with Planchet, already relieved of one of the spare horses.

26

Aramis's Thesis

D'ARTAGNAN had said nothing to Porthos about his
wound or about the procurator's wife. Our Béarnais was
a tactful young man, so he had pretended to believe all
that the vainglorious Musketeer had told him: he was
convinced that no friendship could hold out against one
party's secret being discovered by the other, especially
when that secret involves a person's pride. Besides, we
always feel superior to those whose lives we know better
than they think we do, and because of d'Artagnan's
projects of future intrigue and his intention to make his
three friends the instruments of his fortune, he was not
sorry to get into his grasp beforehand the invisible strings
by which he hoped to move them.

And yet, as he rode along, there was a profound sadness in his heart. He thought of that young and pretty
Mme. Bonacieux who was to have rewarded him for his
devotion, but let us quickly add that his sadness was due
less to the regret of the happiness he had missed, than
from his fear that some serious misfortune had befallen
the poor woman. He had no doubt that she was a victim
of the cardinal's vengeance, and as was well known, the
vengeance of his Eminence was terrible. How *he* had
found grace in the eyes of the minister, he did not know;
but M. de Cavois would undoubtedly have revealed this
to him if the captain of the Guards had found him at
home.

Nothing makes time pass more quickly or more short-
ens a journey than a thought that absorbs all the faculties
of the one who thinks. External existence then resembles
a sleep of which this thought is the dream. By its influence, time has no measure, space no distance. We depart
from one place and arrive at another—that is all. Of the
interval between the two, nothing remains in the memory
but a vague mist in which a thousand confused images
of trees, mountains, and landscapes are merged. This was

the state in which d'Artagnan traveled, at whatever pace his horse pleased, the six or eight leagues that separated Chantilly from Crèvecœur—without his being able to remember on his arrival in the village any of the things he had passed or met with on the road.

Only there did his memory return. He shook his head, saw the inn at which he had left Aramis, and putting his horse to the trot, shortly pulled up at the door.

This time it was not a host but a hostess who received him. D'Artagnan was good at reading faces: he took one look at the plump and cheerful mistress of the place and at once knew that there was no reason to deceive her, no reason to fear her.

"My good hostess, can you tell me what has become of one of my friends, whom we were obliged to leave here about a dozen days ago?" he asked.

"A handsome young man, twenty-three or -four years old, gentle, amiable, well formed?"

"Just so—and wounded in the shoulder."

"Yes. Well, monsieur, he is still here."

"Ah, my dear hostess," said d'Artagnan, springing from his horse and throwing the reins to Planchet, "you restore me to life. Where is this dear Aramis? I am in a hurry to see him again."

"Pardon me, monsieur, but I doubt if he can see you at this moment."

"Why? Is a lady with him?"

"What are you saying? No, monsieur, he is not with a lady."

"With whom is he, then?"

"With the curé of Montdidier and the superior of the Jesuits of Amiens."

"My God!" cried d'Artagnan, "Is the poor fellow worse?"

"No, monsieur, quite the contrary. But after his illness he was touched by grace, and he determined to take orders."

"Yes, I had forgotten that he was a Musketeer only temporarily!"

"Monsieur still insists on seeing him?"

"More than ever."

"Well, monsieur has only to take the right-hand staircase in the courtyard and knock at Number Five on the third floor."

D'Artagnan walked quickly in that direction and found one of those exterior staircases that can still be seen in the courtyards of our old-fashioned inns. But it was not easy to get at the future abbé, for the approach to Aramis's room was as well guarded as the gardens of Armida: Bazin was stationed in the corridor and barred d'Artagnan's passage with great intrepidity, the more so because after many years, the former found himself near a long-desired result.

Poor Bazin's dream had always been to serve a churchman, and he had awaited with impatience the moment, always in the future, when Aramis would throw aside the uniform and assume the cassock. Only the young man's daily promise that the moment would not be long delayed had kept him in the service of a Musketeer—a service in which, he said, his soul was in constant jeopardy.

Bazin was thus at the height of joy. In all probability, this time his master would keep his promise. The combination of physical and mental anguish had produced the effect so long awaited. Aramis, suffering in both body and mind, had finally fixed his eyes and his thoughts on religion, and he had considered the double accident that had happened to him—that is, the sudden disappearance of his mistress and the wound in his shoulder—as a warning from heaven.

It is understandable that nothing could be more disagreeable to Bazin than d'Artagnan's arrival, which might cast his master back into that vortex of worldly affairs that had so long preoccupied him. He was thus resolved to defend the door bravely; and as, betrayed by the mistress of the inn, he could not say that Aramis was absent, he tried to prove to the newcomer that it would be the height of rudeness to disturb his master in his pious conversation, which had begun in the morning and would not, as Bazin said, end before night.

But d'Artagnan paid very little attention to Bazin's eloquent discourse; since he had no desire to engage in polemics with his friend's servant, he simply moved him out of the way with one hand, and turned the handle of the door of Number Five with the other.

The door opened, and d'Artagnan went into the room.

In a black gown, his head enveloped in a sort of round, flat hat very like a skullcap, Aramis was seated before an oblong table covered with scrolls and enormous folio volumes. The superior of the Jesuits was on his right, the curé of Montdidier on his left. The curtains were half drawn and admitted only a dim mysterious light suitable for religious reveries. All the worldly objects that generally strike the eye in a young man's room, particularly when that young man is a Musketeer, had disappeared as if by magic; Bazin, doubtless fearing that the sight of them might bring his master back to things of this world, had made away with sword, pistols, plumed hat, and everything ornamented with embroideries and laces. In their stead d'Artagnan thought he could see, in a dark corner, a cat-o'-nine-tails suspended from a nail in the wall.

At the sound of d'Artagnan entering the room, Aramis lifted his head and saw his friend; but to the young man's great astonishment, the sight of him did not produce much effect on the Musketeer, so completely was his mind detached from the things of this world.

"Good day, d'Artagnan," said Aramis. "Believe me, I am glad to see you."

"And I am delighted to see you, although I am not yet sure that it is Aramis I am speaking to." ·

"To himself, my friend, to himself! What makes you doubt it?"

"At first I was afraid I had mistaken the room and had found my way into some churchman's room. Then I made another error when I saw you with these gentlemen—I was afraid you were dangerously ill."

The two men in black, who guessed d'Artagnan's meaning, glared at him, but he paid no attention.

"Perhaps I disturb you, my dear Aramis," he continued. "From what I see, I think you must be confessing to these gentlemen."

Aramis flushed slightly.

"Disturb me? Oh, quite the contrary, my friend—and as proof, allow me to say that I am happy to see you safe and sound."

"Ah, that's better—he has finally remembered!" thought d'Artagnan.

"This gentleman, who is my friend, has just escaped

from serious danger," Aramis continued earnestly, pointing to d'Artagnan and addressing the two ecclesiastics.

"Praise God, monsieur," they replied, bowing together.

"I have not failed to do so, your Reverences," replied the young man, returning their bow.

"You arrive at a good time, d'Artagnan," said Aramis, "and by taking part in our discussion may assist us with your interpretation. Monsieur le Principal of Amiens, Monsieur le Curé of Montdidier, and I are arguing certain theological questions that have interested us for a long time, and I would be delighted to have your opinion."

"The opinion of a swordsman can have very little weight," replied d'Artagnan, who began to be uneasy at the turn things were taking, "and you had better be satisfied, believe me, with the knowledge of these gentlemen."

The two men in black bowed again.

"On the contrary," replied Aramis, "your opinion will be very valuable. The issue is this—Monsieur le Principal thinks that my thesis ought to be dogmatic and didactic."

"Your thesis! Are you writing a thesis?"

"Of course," said the Jesuit. "A thesis is always a necessary part of the examination that precedes ordination."

"Ordination!" cried d'Artagnan, who could not believe what the hostess and Bazin had already told him.

He stared, half stupefied, at the three persons facing him.

"Now," continued Aramis, sitting as gracefully in his easy chair here as he would have been in a lady's boudoir and complacently examining his hand, which was as white and plump as that of a woman and which he held in the air to cause the blood to descend, "now, as you have heard, d'Artagnan, Monsieur le Principal wishes my thesis to be dogmatic, while I would prefer it to be idealistic. That is why Monsieur le Principal has proposed to me the following subject, which has not yet been treated and in which I perceive there is matter for magnificent elaboration—'*Utraque manus in benedicendo clericis inferioribus necessaria est.*' "

D'Artagnan, whose erudition we are well acquainted with, was no more troubled by this quotation than he had been by M. de Tréville's quotation alluding to the gifts d'Artagnan had received from the Duke of Buckingham.

"Which means," resumed Aramis, so d'Artagnan would understand, " 'Both hands are indispensable for priests of the inferior orders when they bestow the benediction.' "

"An admirable subject!" said the Jesuit.

"Admirable and dogmatic!" repeated the curé, who was about as strong in Latin as d'Artagnan and who listened carefully to the Jesuit in order to keep step with him and repeated his words like an echo.

D'Artagnan remained unmoved by the enthusiasm of the two men in black.

"Yes, admirable, *prorsus admirabile!*" continued Aramis: "but it requires a profound study of both the Scriptures and the Fathers. Now, I have confessed to these learned ecclesiastics in all humility that my duties in the service of the king have caused me to somewhat neglect my studies. I would therefore find myself more at ease, *facilius natans*, with a subject of my own choice, which would be to these hard theological questions what ethics are to metaphysics in philosophy."

D'Artagnan was bored, and so was the curé.

"See what an exordium!" the Jesuit exclaimed.

"Exordium," repeated the curé, for the sake of saying something.

"Quemadmodum inter cœlorum immensitatem."

Aramis looked at d'Artagnan to see the effect of all this and found his friend yawning.

"Let us speak French, my father," he said to the Jesuit. "Monsieur d'Artagnan will enjoy our conversation better."

"Yes," replied d'Artagnan; "I am fatigued with riding, and all this Latin confuses me."

"Certainly," replied the Jesuit, a little put out, while the delighted curé looked at d'Artagnan gratefully. "Well, let us see what is to be derived from this gloss . . . Moses, the servant of God—he was only a servant, remember—Moses blessed with his hands. He held out both his arms while the Hebrews beat their enemies, and then he blessed them with both his hands. Besides, what does the Gospel say? *'Imponite manus,'* and not *'manum'*—lay on the *hands*, not the *hand*."

"Lay on the *hands*," repeated the curé, with a gesture.

"St. Peter, on the contrary, of whom the Popes are

the successors," continued the Jesuit, "is told *porrige dig-
itos*—present the fingers. Do you understand that?"

"Certainly," replied Aramis, enjoying himself enormously, "but the point is a subtle one."

"The *fingers!*" resumed the Jesuit. "St. Peter blessed
with the *fingers*. The Pope therefore blesses with the fingers. And with how many fingers does he bless? With
three fingers, to be sure—one for the Father, one for the
Son, and one for the Holy Ghost."

Aramis and the two ecclesiastics crossed themselves;
d'Artagnan thought it proper to follow their example.

"The Pope is the successor of St. Peter and represents
the three divine powers. The rest, the *ordines inferiores*,
of the ecclesiastical hierarchy bless in the name of the
holy archangels and angels. The most humble clerics,
such as our deacons and sacristans, bless with holy water
sprinklers, which resemble an infinite number of blessing
fingers. The subject is now simplified—*argumentum omni
denudatum ornamento*. I could make of that subject two
volumes this size," continued the Jesuit, pounding in his
enthusiasm a folio volume of St. Chrysostom that was so
heavy it made the table bend beneath its weight.

D'Artagnan shuddered.

"Of course I do justice to the beauties of that thesis,"
said Aramis, "but at the same time I see it would be
overwhelming for me. I had chosen this text—and tell
me, d'Artagnan, if you approve of it—'*Non inutile est
desiderium in oblatione*': 'A little regret is not unsuitable
in an offering to the Lord.'"

"Stop there!" cried the Jesuit. "That is close to heresy!
There is a proposition almost like it in the *Augustinus* by
the heresiarch Jansenius, whose book will sooner or later
be burned by the public executioner. Take care, my
young friend—you are inclining toward false doctrines,
and you will be lost!"

"You will be lost!" said the curé, shaking his head
sorrowfully.

"You are approaching that famous point of free will,
which is a pitfall for mortals. You come close to the
insinuations of the Pelagians and the demi-Pelagians."

"But, my Reverend . . ." said Aramis, stunned by the
hail of arguments falling on his head.

"How will you prove," the Jesuit continued, without

allowing him time to speak, "that we ought to regret the world when we offer ourselves to God? Listen to this dilemma—God is God, and the world is the devil. To regret the world is to regret the devil. That is my conclusion."

"And mine also," said the curé.

"But, for heaven's sake . . ." Aramis began again.

"*Desideras diabolum*, unhappy man!" cried the Jesuit.

"He regrets giving up the devil! Ah, my young friend," groaned the curé, "do not do that, I implore you!"

D'Artagnan was bewildered; he felt as though he were in a madhouse and becoming as mad as those he saw. He was, however, forced to hold his tongue because he did not understand half the language they were using.

"But listen to me," Aramis resumed with politeness mingled with a little impatience. "I do not say I regret. No, I would never say that because it would not be orthodox."

The Jesuit raised his hands toward heaven, and the curé did the same.

Aramis returned to the subject.

"No, but grant me that it is churlish to offer the Lord only what disgusts us! Don't you think so, d'Artagnan?"

"I do indeed," he cried.

The Jesuit and the curé were quite startled.

"Here is my point of departure—it is a syllogism. The world has its attractions, I quit the world, therefore I am making a sacrifice. And the Scripture says positively, 'Make a sacrifice unto the Lord.' "

"That is true," his antagonists said in agreement.

"I wrote a rondeau on that subject last year, and when I showed it to the great Monsieur Voiture, he paid me a thousand compliments," said Aramis, pinching his ear to make it pink, just as he rubbed his hands to make them white.

"A rondeau!" the Jesuit said disdainfully.

"A rondeau!" the curé said mechanically.

"Recite it!" cried d'Artagnan. "It will make a little change."

"No, because it is religious," replied Aramis. "It is theology in verse."

"The devil!" said d'Artagnan.

"Here it is," said Aramis, with a little show of modesty that was not, however, exempt from a shade of hypocrisy:

> Vous qui pleurez un passé plein de charmes,
>   Et qui trainez des jours infortunés,
>   Tous vos malheurs se verront terminés,
> Quand à Dieu seul vous offrirez vos larmes,
>   Vous qui pleurez!*

D'Artagnan and the curé seemed pleased.

The Jesuit persisted in his opinion and warned, "Beware of the secular taste in your theological writings. What does Augustine say on this subject? " *'Severus sit clericorum sermo.'* "

"Yes, let the sermon be clear," said the curé.

The Jesuit, seeing that his acolyte was going astray, hastily interrupted. "Your thesis would please the ladies, that is all. It would be as successful as one of Monsieur Patru's courtroom pleadings."

"Please God!" cried Aramis, transported.

"There!" cried the Jesuit. "The world still speaks within you in a loud voice, *altissimâ voce.* You follow the world, my young friend, and I tremble lest grace will not prove efficacious."

"Be satisfied, my reverend father, I am sure of myself."

"Worldly presumption!"

"I know myself, Father—my resolution is irrevocable."

"Then you persist in continuing with that thesis?"

"I feel myself called to treat that one and no other. I will continue with it, and tomorrow I hope you will be satisfied with the corrections I will have made in consequence of your advice."

"Work slowly," said the curé. "We leave you in an excellent frame of mind."

"Yes, the ground is all sown," said the Jesuit, "and we do not have to fear that a portion of the seed may

---

*You who weep for pleasures fled,
While dragging on a life of care,
All your woes will melt in air,
If to god your tears are shed,
You who weep!

have fallen upon stone, another upon the highway, or that the birds in the sky have eaten the rest, *aves cœli comederunt illam.*"

"A plague on you and your Latin!" muttered d'Artagnan, whose patience was exhausted.

"Farewell, my son," said the curé, "till tomorrow."

"Till tomorrow, rash youth," said the Jesuit. "You give promise of becoming one of the lights of the Church. Heaven grant that this light does not prove a devouring fire!"

D'Artagnan, who for the past hour had impatiently been gnawing his nails, had now bitten them down to the quick.

The two men in black rose, bowed to Aramis and d'Artagnan, and walked to the door. Bazin, who had been standing listening to all this controversy with pious jubilation, rushed toward them, took the curé's breviary and the Jesuit's missal, and walked respectfully ahead of them to clear their way.

Aramis accompanied them downstairs, then immediately came up again to d'Artagnan, who was still in a state of confusion.

Now that they were alone, the two friends at first kept an embarrassed silence. But one of them had to break it first, and since d'Artagnan appeared determined to leave that honor to his companion, Aramis said, "You see that I have returned to my fundamental ideas."

"Yes, efficacious grace has touched you, as that gentleman just said."

"Oh, I have had these plans for a long time. You have often heard me speak of them, have you not, my friend?"

"Yes, but I always thought you jested."

"About such things! Oh, d'Artagnan, never!"

"Why not? People jest about death."

"And people are wrong, d'Artagnan, because death is the door that leads to damnation or to salvation."

"Granted, but please let us not theologize, Aramis. You must have had enough for today, and as for me, I have forgotten the little Latin I never knew! Besides, I have eaten nothing since ten o'clock this morning, and I am very hungry."

"We will dine immediately, my friend, but you must remember that this is Friday and I cannot eat flesh or even see it eaten. If you can be satisfied with my dinner, which consists of cooked tetragones and fruits. . ."

"What do you mean by tetragones?" d'Artagnan asked uneasily.

"I mean spinach. But for your sake I will add some eggs, and that is a serious infraction of the rule because eggs are meat, since they engender chickens."

"It will not be a very succulent feast, but never mind— I will put up with it for the sake of remaining with you."

"I am grateful to you for the sacrifice," said Aramis, "and if your body is not greatly benefited by it, be assured your soul will be."

"So you are definitely going into the Church, Aramis? What will our two friends say? What will Monsieur de Tréville say? They will treat you like a deserter, I warn you."

"I do not enter the Church, I reenter it. I deserted the Church for the world—for you know that I went against my inclinations when I became a Musketeer."

"I? I know nothing about it, Aramis."

"You don't know how I left the seminary?"

"No."

"Then I will tell you my story. Besides, the Scriptures say, 'Confess yourselves one to another,' so I will confess to you, d'Artagnan."

"And I will give you absolution in advance. You see how affable I am?"

"Do not jest about holy things, my friend."

"All right, then, I am listening."

"I had been at the seminary from the time I was nine years old. In three days I would have been twenty. I was about to become a priest, and everything was arranged. One evening I went, as usual, to a house I frequented with much pleasure. What shall I say—when one is young, one is weak. An officer who had previously seen me, with a jealous eye, reading the *Lives of the Saints* to the mistress of the house, suddenly came in without being announced. That evening I had translated an episode of Judith and had just read my verses to the lady, who gave me all sorts of compliments and who was now reading them a second time with me while leaning on my shoulder. Her pose, which I must admit was rather free, offended this officer. He said nothing, but when I went out he followed, and quickly caught up with me. 'Monsieur l'Abbé,' he said, 'do you like being caned?' 'I cannot say, monsieur,' I answered. 'No one has ever dared do so.' 'Well, listen to me, then, Monsieur l'Abbé! If you come again to the house in which I have met you this evening, I will dare it myself.' I think I must have been frightened. I became very pale, I felt my legs about to give way, I had to think of a reply but could find none and remained silent. The officer was waiting for his reply, and seeing it was so long in coming, he burst out laughing, turned on his heels, and went back into the house. I returned to my seminary.

"I am of a long line of gentlemen born, and I am hotblooded, as you may have noticed, my dear d'Artagnan. The insult was a terrible one, and although it was unknown to the rest of the world, I could feel it festering at the bottom of my heart. I informed my superiors that I did not feel I was sufficiently prepared for ordination, and at my request the ceremony was postponed for a year.

"I sought out the best fencing master in Paris and made an agreement with him to take a lesson every day, and every day for a year I took that lesson. Then, on the anniversary of the day on which I had been insulted, I hung my cassock on a peg, put on the clothes of a cavalier, and went to a ball given by a lady friend of mine and to which I knew my man was invited. It was on the Rue des Francs-Bourgeois, close to La Force.

"As I had expected, my officer was there. I went up to him as he was singing a love song and looking tenderly at a lady, and I interrupted him exactly in the middle of the second couplet. 'Monsieur,' I said, 'does it still displease you that I frequent a certain house on the Rue Payenne? And will you still cane me if I take it into my head to disobey you?' The officer looked at me with astonishment and said, 'What is your business with me, monsieur? I do not know you.' 'I am,' I said, 'the little priest who reads the *Lives of the Saints* and translates Judith into verse.' 'Ah, I remember now,' he said in a jeering tone. 'Well, what do you want with me?' 'I want you to spare time to take a walk with me.' 'Tomorrow morning, if you like, with the greatest pleasure.' 'No, not tomorrow morning, if you please, but immediately.' 'If you absolutely insist . . .' 'I do insist.' 'Come on, then. Ladies,' said the officer, 'do not disturb yourselves. Just allow me time to kill this gentleman, and I will return and finish the last couplet.'

"We went out. I took him to the Rue Payenne, to exactly the same spot where a year before, at the very same hour, he had treated me as I have described to you. It was a superb moonlit night. We immediately drew our swords, and at the first pass I struck him dead."

"The devil!" said d'Artagnan.

"Since the ladies did not see their singer come back, and since he was found on the Rue Payenne with a huge sword wound through his body, it was assumed, correctly, that I had done it. The matter created some scandal and I was obliged to renounce the cassock for a time. Athos, whose acquaintance I had made not long before, and Porthos, who had taught me some effective fencing tricks in addition to my lessons, persuaded me to solicit the uniform of a Musketeer. The king greatly esteemed my father, who had fallen at the siege of Arras, and the uniform was granted. You can see that the moment has come for me to return to the bosom of the Church."

"But why today rather than yesterday or tomorrow? What has happened to you today to make you think these melancholy thoughts?"

"This wound, my dear d'Artagnan, was a warning from heaven."

"Your wound? Bah, it is nearly healed, and I am sure that is not what gives you the most pain."

"What is, then?" asked Aramis, blushing.

"You have a heart wound, Aramis—a deeper and more painful one than the other—a wound made by a woman."

Aramis's eyes kindled in spite of himself.

"Ah, do not talk of such things," said he, hiding his emotion under a pretended nonchalance. "*I* think of such things? *I* suffer love pains? *Vanitas vanitatum!* According to you, my head is turned by a woman. By whom—some seamstress or chambermaid with whom I have trifled in some garrison? Nonsense!"

"Forgive me, my dear Aramis, but I think you raise your eyes higher than that."

"Higher? And who am I to have so much ambition? A

poor Musketeer, a beggar, an unknown—one who hates worldly ties and finds himself out of place in the world."

"Aramis, Aramis," said d'Artagnan, looking at his friend with an air of doubt.

"Dust I am, and to dust I return. Life is full of humiliations and sorrows," he continued, becoming still more melancholy: "all the ties that attach man to life break in his hands, particularly the golden ties. Oh, d'Artagnan"—Aramis's voice was now slightly bitter—"take my advice—conceal your wounds when you have any. Silence is the only refuge of the unhappy. Beware of giving anyone the clue to your griefs, for the curious come to suck our tears as flies suck the blood of a wounded deer."

"Alas, Aramis," said d'Artagnan, sighing deeply, "you are describing how I feel."

"What do you mean?"

"A woman whom I love, whom I adore, has just been torn from me by force. I do not know where she is or where they have taken her. She may be a prisoner, she may be dead!"

"Yes, but you have at least this consolation—you can tell yourself that she did not leave you voluntarily, that if you have no news of her, it is because all communication with you is impossible—while I . . ."

"Well?"

"Nothing," replied Aramis, "nothing . . ."

"So you renounce the world forever. Is that definite? You are determined?"

"Forever! Today you are my friend, tomorrow you will be no more to me than a shadow—or rather you will no longer exist. As for the world, it is nothing but a tomb."

"This is all very sad!"

"What can I do? My vocation commands me—it is carrying me away."

D'Artagnan smiled, but remained silent.

Aramis continued. "And yet, while I still belong to the earth, I would like to talk about you and our friends."

"And I would like to talk about you, but I find you so completely detached from everything! You deny love, you cry 'Friends are shadows! The world is a tomb!' "

"Alas, you too will find it so," said Aramis with a sigh.

"Then let us say no more about it, and let us burn this

letter, which must certainly announce to you some fresh infidelity of your seamstress or your chambermaid."

"What letter?" cried Aramis eagerly.

"A letter sent to your apartment in your absence, and given to me for you."

"But who is it from?"

"Oh, from some heartbroken servant, some desponding attendant—perhaps from Madame de Chevreuse's chambermaid, who was obliged to return to Tours with her mistress and who, in order to appear smart and attractive, stole some perfumed paper and sealed her letter to you with a duchess's coronet."

"What are you saying?"

"Oh, I must have lost it," d'Artagnan said maliciously, pretending to search for it. "But fortunately the world is a tomb; men, and consequently women, are only shadows, and love is a sentiment you deny."

"D'Artagnan, you are killing me!"

"Ah, here it is at last!" said d'Artagnan, taking the letter from his pocket.

Aramis reached him in one bound, seized the letter, and read, or rather devoured it, his face radiant.

"The chambermaid seems to have an agreeable style," said the messenger carelessly.

"Thank you, d'Artagnan!" cried Aramis, almost in a state of delirium. "She was forced to return to Tours, she is not faithless, she still loves me! Come, my friend, let me embrace you. I am almost suffocating with happiness!"

The two friends began to dance around the tome of the venerable St. Chrysostom, kicking about the sheets of the thesis that had fallen to the floor.

At that moment Bazin came in with the spinach and the omelet.

"Be off, you wretch!" cried Aramis, throwing his skullcap in his face. "Return whence you came, and take back those horrible vegetables and that poor omelet! Order a larded hare, a fat capon, a leg of mutton dressed with garlic, and four bottles of old Burgundy!"

Bazin, who was looking at his master without understanding the change in his manner, sadly allowed the omelet to slip into the spinach and the spinach onto the floor.

"Now is the time to consecrate your existence to the King of Kings," said d'Artagnan, "if you persist in offering him a civility—'*Non inutile desiderium in oblatione.*'"

"Go to the devil with your Latin! Let us drink while the wine is fresh, d'Artagnan! Let us drink heartily, and while we do so, tell me about what is going on in the world outside."

27

Athos's Wife

"NOW WE HAVE to search for Athos," d'Artagnan said to the vivacious Aramis after he had informed him of all that had happened since their departure from the capital, and an excellent dinner had made one of them forget his thesis and the other his fatigue.

"Do you think that anything could have happened to him?" asked Aramis. "Athos is so cool-headed, so brave, and he handles his sword so skillfully."

"Yes, certainly. Nobody has a higher opinion of Athos's courage and skill than I have; but I prefer to hear my sword clang against lances rather than against staves. I am afraid he might have been brought down by servants with sticks. Those fellows strike hard and don't leave off in a hurry, which is why I wish to set out again as soon as possible."

"I will try to go with you," said Aramis, "though I still don't feel well enough to mount my horse. Yesterday I tried to use that whip you see hanging on the wall, but I had too much pain to continue the holy exercise."

"That's the first time I ever heard of anybody trying to cure gunshot wounds with a cat-o'-nine-tails, but you were ill, and illness makes the mind weak, so you are excused."

"When do you mean to set out?"

"Tomorrow at daybreak. Sleep as soundly as you can tonight, and tomorrow, if you can, we will leave together."

"Till tomorrow, then," said Aramis, "for man of iron though you may be, you must need some rest too."

The next morning, when d'Artagnan entered Aramis's room, he found him at the window.

"What are you looking at?" d'Artagnan asked.

"I am admiring those three magnificent horses the stable boys are leading about. It would be a princely pleasure to travel on such horses."

"Well, Aramis, you may enjoy that princely pleasure, for one of those three horses is yours."

"Which one?"

"Whichever you like."

"And the rich harness, is that mine, too?"

"Of course."

"You are laughing at me, d'Artagnan."

"No, I have stopped laughing, now that you are speaking French again."

"What, those rich holsters, that velvet saddlecloth, that silver-studded saddle—they are all for me?"

"For you, just as for the moment the horse that is pawing the ground is mine, and the prancing horse belongs to Athos."

"*Peste*, they are three superb animals!"

"I am glad they please you."

"Was it the king who made you such a present?"

"It was certainly not the cardinal—but don't trouble yourself about where they come from, but think only that one of the three is yours."

"I choose the one the red-headed boy is leading."

"It is yours!"

"Good heavens, that is enough to drive away all my pains—I could mount him with thirty bullets in my body! On my soul, those are handsome stirrups! Bazin, come here this minute!"

Bazin appeared on the threshold, dull and spiritless.

"Polish my sword, put my hat to rights, brush my cloak, and load my pistols!" said Aramis.

"That last order is useless," d'Artagnan interrupted. "There are loaded pistols in your holsters."

Bazin sighed.

"Come, Master Bazin, do not worry," said d'Artagnan. "People from all walks of life can gain the kingdom of heaven."

"Monsieur was already such a good theologian," said Bazin, almost weeping. "He might have become a bishop, perhaps a cardinal."

"But my poor Bazin, just think a moment. What good is it to be a churchman? You do not avoid going to war by that means—as you know, the cardinal is about to make the next campaign, helmet on head and partisan in hand. And Monsieur de Nogaret de la Valette, what about him? He is a cardinal too—but ask his lackey how often he has had to prepare bandages for him."

"Alas!" Bazin sighed. "I know, monsieur, everything is turned topsy-turvy in the world nowadays."

While this dialogue was going on, the two young men and the poor lackey had gone downstairs.

"Hold my stirrup, Bazin," cried Aramis.

And he sprang into the saddle with his usual grace and agility, but after the noble animal had vaulted, pranced, and capered a few times, his rider felt his pains come on so insupportably that he turned pale and became unsteady in his seat. D'Artagnan, who had foreseen such an event and had kept his eyes on him, ran to him, caught him in his arms, and helped him to his room.

"That's all right, Aramis, just take care of yourself," he said. "I will look for Athos alone."

"You are indeed a man of iron," said Aramis.

"No, I have good luck, that is all. But how will you spend your time till I come back? I hope with no more theses or glosses on the fingers or benedictions, eh?"

Aramis smiled.

"I will write poetry," he said.

"Yes, poems perfumed with the aroma of that note from Madame de Chevreuse's attendant. Teach Bazin prosody—that will console him. As to the horse, mount him every day to get used to riding again."

"Oh, do not worry about that," replied Aramis. "You will find me ready to follow you."

They said goodbye to each other, and in ten minutes, after telling the hostess and Bazin that he was leaving his friend in their care, d'Artagnan was trotting along in the direction of Amiens.

How was he going to find Athos? Would he find him at all? He had left him in a dangerous situation, and he might well have succumbed. This idea drew several sighs from him, made him frown, and caused him to make a few vows of vengeance.

Of all his friends, Athos was the eldest, and the least resembling him in appearance, tastes, and sympathies; yet he entertained a marked preference for that gentleman. His noble and distinguished air, those flashes of greatness which from time to time broke out from the shadows in which he voluntarily hid himself, that unalterable evenness of temper which made him the most pleasant companion in the world, that imaginative and cynical gaiety, that bravery which might have been termed blind if it had not been the result of the rarest coolness—such qualities attracted more than d'Artagnan's esteem or friendship, they attracted his admiration.

Indeed, even when compared with M. de Tréville, that most elegant and noble courtier, Athos in his most cheerful days might have the advantage. He was of medium height, but so admirably shaped and so well proportioned that he had more than once overcome the giant Porthos, whose physical strength was proverbial among the Musketeers. His head, with its piercing eyes, straight nose, and Brutus-like chin, had an indefinable character of grandeur and grace. His hands, which he did not take particular care of, were envied by Aramis, who cultivated his with almond paste and perfumed oil. His voice was at once clear and melodious; And he had—an incredible quality in one who was always modest—a precise and discriminating knowledge of the world and of the manners of the most brilliant society, those same manners that were manifest, all unconsciously, in his least actions.

If he gave a dinner, he presided over it better than anyone else, placing every guest exactly in the rank that his ancestors had earned for him or he had gained for himself. If a question in heraldry came up, Athos knew all the noble families of the kingdom, their genealogy, their alliances, their coats of arms and the origins of them. The most minor points of etiquette were known to him. He knew the rights of the great land owners and was expert in hunting and falconry, one day astonishing by his conversation about this great art even Louis XIII himself, who was proud of being considered a past master of it.

Like all the great nobles of that period, he rode and

fenced to perfection, but in addition, his academic education had been so thorough—which was quite rare at this time among gentlemen—that he smiled at the scraps of Latin which Aramis used and Porthos pretended to understand. Two or three times, when Aramis had allowed some elementary error to escape him, he had even—to the great astonishment of his friends—replaced a verb in its right tense and a noun in its correct case. Besides all else—in an age when soldiers did not always live up to the commands of their religion and their conscience, when lovers did not always meet the criteria of our more demanding era, and when the poor did not always obey the Seventh Commandment—Athos's probity was irreproachable. He was a most extraordinary man.

And yet this nature so distinguished, this creature so beautiful, this spirit so fine, was seen to turn insensibly toward a purely material life, as old men turn toward physical and moral imbecility. In his hours of gloom—and those hours were frequent—the whole luminous portion of Athos was extinguished, and his brilliant side disappeared as into a profound darkness.

Then, the demigod vanished, he remained scarcely a man. His head hanging down, his eyes dull, his speech slow and painful, he would spend hours staring at his bottle, his glass, or at Grimaud, who was accustomed to obeying his signals and could read in the faintest glance of his master his least desire, which he satisfied immediately. If the four friends were together at one of those moments, an occasional word thrust forth with considerate effort was Athos's share in the conversation. On the other hand, he drank enough for four, but without showing any effects from the wine other than a more noticeable frown and a deeper sadness.

D'Artagnan, whose curiosity we are acquainted with, had not—despite his interest in the subject—been able to discover any cause for this depression or any reason for its recurrence. Athos never received any letters, never did anything that all his friends were not aware of.

It was certainly not the wine that produced this sadness, for he drank only to combat it—instead of which, however, the wine, as we have said, made his mood still darker. Gambling was not responsible, for unlike Porthos, who sang or swore depending on his luck, Athos remained as unmoved when he won as when he lost. Playing among the Musketeers, he had been known to win in one night three thousand pistoles, to lose them and to lose as well his ceremonial gold-embroidered belt, to win all this back with the addition of a hundred louis, without his handsome eyebrows moving up or down the slightest degree, without his hands losing their pearly hue, without his conversation, which was cheerful that evening, ever ceasing to be calm and agreeable.

Nor was it—as it is with our neighbors, the English—an atmospheric influence that darkened his countenance, for the melancholy generally became more intense toward the fine season of the year: June and July were the terrible months for Athos.

At present he had no anxieties; he shrugged his shoulders when people spoke of the future; his secret, then, was in the past, as had often been vaguely hinted to d'Artagnan.

This mystery that overshadowed his entire being made Athos—a man who never revealed anything no matter how deep his intoxication or how skillfully he was questioned—even more interesting.

"Well," d'Artagnan thought aloud, "poor Athos may be dead at this moment, and by my fault—for it was I who dragged him into this affair, of which he did not know the origin, of which he will be ignorant of the result, and from which he could derive no advantage."

"And in addition, monsieur," added Planchet, "we may even owe our lives to him. Do you remember how he cried, 'On, d'Artagnan, on, I am taken'? And after he had discharged his two pistols, what a noise he made with his sword! It sounded like twenty men, or rather twenty mad devils, were fighting!"

Those words redoubled d'Artagnan's eagerness; he spurred his horse—who needed no urging—and they proceeded at a rapid pace.

About eleven o'clock in the morning they could see Amiens, and at half past eleven they were at the door of the cursed inn.

D'Artagnan had often dreamt of revenge against the treacherous host—one of those hearty vengeances which offers consolation just in thinking about them. He entered the hostelry with his hat pulled over his eyes, his left hand on the pommel of his sword, and his right hand cracking his whip.

"Do you remember me?" he asked the host, who advanced to greet him.

"I do not have that honor, monseigneur," replied the latter, dazzled by the brilliant style in which d'Artagnan traveled.

"What, you don't know me?"

"No, monseigneur."

"Well, two words will refresh your memory. What have you done with that gentleman you had the audacity, about twelve days ago, to accuse of passing counterfeit money?"

The host turned deathly pale, for d'Artagnan had assumed a most threatening attitude, and Planchet had modeled himself after his master.

"Ah, monseigneur, do not speak of that!" cried the host, in the most pitiable voice imaginable. "Ah, monseigneur, how I have paid for that fault, unhappy wretch that I am!"

"I am asking you, what has become of that gentleman?"

"I beg you to listen to me, monseigneur, and to be merciful! Have the goodness to sit down!"

D'Artagnan, mute with anger and anxiety, took a seat in the threatening attitude of a judge. Planchet glared fiercely over the back of his armchair.

"Here is the story, monseigneur," resumed the trembling host, "for now I remember you. It was you who rode off at the moment I had that unfortunate misunderstanding with the gentleman you speak of."

"Yes, it was I—so you may see that you can expect no mercy if you do not tell me the whole truth."

"Then please listen to me, and I will tell you everything."

"I am listening."

"I had been warned by the authorities that a celebrated coiner of bad money would arrive at my inn with several of his companions, all disguised as Guards or Musketeers. Monseigneur, I was given a description of your horses, your lackeys, your faces—nothing was omitted."

"Go on!" said d'Artagnan, who quickly understood where such an exact description had come from.

"Following the orders of the authorities, who sent me a reinforcement of six men, I took such measures as I thought necessary to capture the counterfeiters."

"Again!" said d'Artagnan, whose ears chafed at the repetition of the word *counterfeiters*.

"Pardon me, monseigneur, for saying such things, but they are my excuse. The authorities had terrified me, and you know that an innkeeper must keep on good terms with the authorities."

"But once again, that gentleman—where is he? What has become of him? Is he dead? Is he alive?"

"Patience, monseigneur, we are coming to that. You know what happened next, and your hurried departure," added the host, with an acuteness that did not escape d'Artagnan, "seemed to justify us. That gentleman, your friend, defended himself desperately. His lackey, who by an unforeseen piece of ill luck had quarreled with the officers, disguised as stable lads——"

"Miserable scoundrel," interrupted d'Artagnan, "you were all in the plot! I really don't know what is keeping me from exterminating you all!"

"Alas, monseigneur, we were *not* all in the plot, as you will soon see. Monsieur your friend (pardon me for not calling him by the honorable name he no doubt bears, but we do not know that name), Monsieur your friend, having disabled two men with his pistols, retreated fighting with his sword, with which he disabled one of my men and stunned me with a blow from its flat side."

"You villain, will you finish? What has become of Athos?"

"While fighting and retreating, as I have told Monseigneur, he found the door to the cellar behind him, and as the door was open, he took out the key and barricaded himself inside. We were sure of finding him there, so we left him alone."

"Yes, you did not really wish to kill him, only to imprison him."

"To imprison him, monseigneur? Why, he imprisoned himself, I swear he did. In the first place he had made rough work of it—one man was killed on the spot, and two others were severely wounded. The dead man and the two wounded were carried off by their comrades, and I have heard nothing about either of them since. As for myself, as soon as I recovered my senses I went to the governor, told him what had happened, and asked what I should do with my prisoner. The governor was dumbstruck with astonishment. He told me he knew nothing about the matter, that the orders I had received did not come from him, and that if I had the audacity to mention his name in connection with this affair he would have me hanged. It seems that I had made a mistake, monsieur, that I had arrested the wrong person and that the one I should have arrested had escaped."

"But Athos!" cried d'Artagnan, whose impatience was increased by the recital of the disregard shown by the authorities. "Where is Athos?"

"Since I was anxious to repair the wrongs I had done the prisoner," the innkeeper resumed, "I went straight to the cellar in order to set him free. Ah, monsieur, he was no longer a man, he was a devil! To my offer of liberty, he replied that it was nothing but a trap, and that before he came out he intended to impose his own conditions. I told him very humbly—for I was well aware of the scrape I had got into by laying hands on one of his Majesty's Musketeers—that I was quite ready to submit to his conditions.

" 'In the first place,' he said, 'I wish my lackey brought to me, fully armed.' We hurried to obey this order because, as you can understand, monsieur, we were disposed to do everything your friend wanted. Monsieur Grimaud—he told us his name, although he does not talk much—Monsieur Grimaud, wounded as he was, went down to the cellar, and then his master, having admitted him, barricaded the door again and ordered us to remain quietly upstairs."

"But where is he now?"

"In the cellar, monsieur."

"What, you scoundrel! Have you kept him in the cellar all this time?"

"Merciful heaven, no, monsieur! *We* keep him in the cellar! You do not know what he is doing in the cellar. Ah, if you could persuade him to come out, monsieur, I would be grateful to you all my life—I would adore you as my patron saint!"

"Then I will find him there?"

"Without doubt, monsieur, since he persists in remaining

there. Every day we pass some bread at the end of a fork through the air hole, and some meat when he asks for it—but alas, bread and meat are not what he consumes most of! I once tried to go down with two of my servants, but he flew into a terrible rage. I heard the noise he made in loading his pistols, and his servant in loading his musket. When we asked them what they meant to do, the master replied that he had forty charges of fire and that he and his lackey would fire all of them before he would allow a single one of us to set foot in the cellar. After hearing this, I went and complained to the governor, who replied that I was only getting what I deserved, and that it would teach me to insult honorable gentlemen who came to stay in my inn."

"So that since that time . . ." said d'Artagnan, unable to keep from laughing at the host's pitiable face.

"So that since that time, monsieur," continued the latter, "we have led the most miserable life imaginable, because you must understand, monsieur, that all our provisions are in the cellar—our wine in bottles and our wine in casks, the beer, the oil, the spices, the bacon, the sausages. Since we are prevented from going down there, we are forced to refuse food and drink to the travelers who come in the inn, so we are losing money day after day. If your friend remains in my cellar another week, I will be a ruined man."

"Which would be no more than just, you ass! Could you not tell by our appearance that we were people of quality, and not counterfeiters?"

"Yes, monsieur, you are right—but listen! You can hear him!"

"Somebody must have disturbed him," said d'Artagnan.

"But he must be disturbed! Two English gentlemen have just arrived."

"Well?"

"Well, the English like good wine, as you may know, monsieur, and these have ordered the best. My wife has probably asked Monsieur Athos's permission to go into the cellar so we can satisfy these gentlemen, and he, as usual, has refused. Ah, good heaven, listen!"

D'Artagnan heard a loud noise coming from the cellar. He rose, and preceded by the host wringing his hands, and followed by Planchet with his musket ready for use, he approached the scene of action.

The two gentlemen were exasperated; they had had a long ride and were dying of hunger and thirst.

"But this is tyranny," one of them shouted in very good French, though with a foreign accent. "This madman will not allow these good people access to their own wine! Let us break open the door, and if he is too far gone in his madness, well, we will kill him!"

"Softly, gentlemen," said d'Artagnan, drawing his pistols from his belt, "you will kill nobody, if you please!"

"Let them come in, those devourers of little children, and we shall see!" said Athos calmly, from the other side of the door.

Brave as they appeared to be, the two English gentlemen looked at each other hesitatingly. It was as if they thought there might be in that cellar one of those starving, gigantic ogres of popular legends, into whose cavern nobody could force his way with impunity.

There was a moment of silence; but ultimately the two Englishmen were ashamed to draw back, and the angrier one descended the five or six steps that led to the cellar and kicked the door hard enough to split a wall.

"Planchet," said d'Artagnan, cocking his pistols, "I will take the one at the top, you take the one below. Gentlemen, if you want battle, you shall have it."

"My God!" exclaimed Athos in a hollow voice. "I think I hear d'Artagnan."

"Yes, I am here, my friend," cried d'Artagnan, raising his voice in turn.

"Good! We will teach them, these door breakers!" replied Athos.

The gentlemen had drawn their swords but found themselves between two fires. They hesitated again, but as before, pride prevailed, and a second kick split the door from top to bottom.

"Stand aside, d'Artagnan, I am going to fire!" Athos warned.

"Gentlemen," exclaimed d'Artagnan, who never stopped thinking, "reflect for a moment. And you Athos, patience! You are risking your heads in a very silly affair, and you will be riddled with holes. My lackey and I will have three shots at you, you will get as many from the

cellar, and then we will still have our swords, with which,
I assure you, my friend and I can play tolerably well. Let
me conduct your business and my own. You will soon
have something to drink—I give you my word."

"If there is any left," said Athos in a mocking voice.

The host felt a cold sweat run down his back.

"What? 'If there is any left,' " he murmured.

"There must be plenty left," said d'Artagnan. "They
cannot have drunk the whole cellar. Gentlemen, return
your swords to their scabbards."

"Provided you replace your pistols in your belt."

"Willingly."

And d'Artagnan set the example. Then, turning to
Planchet, he made him a sign to uncock his musket.

The Englishmen, convinced by these peaceful proceedings, sheathed their swords grumblingly. They then heard
the story of Athos's imprisonment, and since they were
gentlemen, they decided the host had been wrong.

"Now, gentlemen," said d'Artagnan, "go up to your
room again, and in ten minutes, I promise that you will
have all you desire."

The Englishmen bowed and went upstairs.

"Now I am alone, Athos," said d'Artagnan. "Please
open the door."

"Immediately," said Athos.

There was a great noise of clashing fagots and groaning
posts—Athos's counterscarps and bastions, which the
besieged was himself demolishing.

A few minutes later, the broken door was removed,
and the pale face of Athos appeared; with a rapid glance
he surveyed the surroundings.

D'Artagnan threw himself on his neck and embraced
him tenderly, then tried to lead him from his moist
abode; to his surprise he saw that Athos staggered.

"You are wounded," said d'Artagnan.

"I! Not at all! I am dead drunk, that's all, and never
did a man do a better job of getting so. By the Lord,
my good host, I must have drunk at least a hundred and
fifty bottles."

"Mercy on us!" cried the host. "If the lackey has drunk
only half as much as the master, I am a ruined man."

"Grimaud is a well-trained lackey. He would never
think of doing the same as his master—he drank only

from the cask. Listen! I don't think he put the stopper in again. Do you hear it? It is running now."

D'Artagnan's laugh changed the host's cold shiver into a burning fever.

Grimaud then appeared behind his master, his musket on his shoulder and his head shaking, like one of those drunken satyrs in a Rubens painting. He was damp in front and in back with a greasy liquid the host recognized as his best olive oil.

The four crossed the public room and proceeded to take possession of the best room in the inn, which d'Artagnan occupied with the authority of force.

Meanwhile the host and his wife, carrying lamps, hurried down into the cellar, which had for so long been forbidden to them and where a frightful spectacle awaited them.

Beyond the fortifications through which Athos had made a breach in order to get out, and which were composed of fagots, planks, and empty casks heaped up according to all the rules of strategy, they found, swimming in puddles of oil and wine, the bones and fragments of all the hams that had been eaten; a heap of broken bottles filled the whole left-hand corner of the cellar, and a cask, the spigot of which was open, was yielding by this means the last drop of its blood. "The image of devastation and death," as the ancient poet says, "reigned as over a field of battle."

Of fifty large sausages suspended from the joists scarcely ten remained.

The lamentations of the host and hostess pierced the vault of the cellar; d'Artagnan himself was moved by them, but Athos did not even turn his head.

However, rage succeeded grief. The host armed himself with a spit and rushed into the room occupied by the two friends.

"Some wine!" said Athos, perceiving the host.

"Some wine!" cried the stupefied host. "Some wine? Why, you have drunk more than a hundred pistoles' worth! I am a ruined man, lost, destroyed!"

"Bah," said Athos, "we were always thirsty."

"If you had been content to drink, well and good, but you have broken all the bottles."

"You pushed me onto a heap that tumbled down. That was your fault."

"All my oil is gone!"

"Oil is the best balm for wounds, and poor Grimaud here was obliged to dress those you had inflicted on him."

"All my sausages are gnawed!"

"There is an enormous quantity of rats in that cellar."

"You will have to pay me for all that," cried the exasperated host.

"Triple ass!" said Athos, rising.

But he sank down again immediately; he had used all his strength. Riding crop in hand, d'Artagnan came to his relief.

The host withdrew and burst into tears.

"This will teach you to treat the guests God sends you in a more courteous fashion," said d'Artagnan.

"God? Say the devil!"

"My dear friend," said d'Artagnan, "if you annoy us, all four of us will shut ourselves up in your cellar, and we will see if the damage is as great as you say."

"Oh, gentlemen," said the host, "I confess I have been wrong, but there should be a pardon for every sin! You are gentlemen, and I am a poor innkeeper. You must have pity on me."

"Ah, if you speak that way," said Athos, "you will break my heart, and the tears will flow from my eyes as the wine flowed from the cask. We are not such devils as we appear to be. Come here, and let us talk."

The host approached hesitatingly.

"Come here, I say, and don't be afraid," continued Athos. "At the very moment when I was about to pay you, my purse was on the table."

"Yes, monsieur."

"That purse contained sixty pistoles. Where is it?"

"Deposited with the authorities. They said it was bad money."

"Very well, get my purse back and keep the sixty pistoles."

"But Monseigneur knows very well that the authorities never let go of what it once gets hold of! If it were bad money, there might be some hope, but unfortunately, they were all good coins."

"Manage the matter as well as you can, my good man. It is not my concern, especially since I will not have a livre left."

"Well, what about Athos's horse? Where is that?" d'Artagnan asked the host.

"In the stable."

"How much is it worth?"

"Fifty pistoles at most."

"It's worth eighty. Take it, and let that end the matter."

"What, are you selling my horse—my Bajazet? And what shall I ride during my campaign? Grimaud?"

"I have brought you another," said d'Artagnan.

"Another?"

"And a magnificent one!" exclaimed the host.

"Well, since there is another one that is finer and younger, why, you may take the old one; and let us drink."

"What?" asked the host, quite cheerful again.

"Some of what is in the back, near the laths. There are twenty-five bottles left—all the rest were broken by my fall. Bring six of them."

"Why, this man is a cask!" said the host to himself. "If he remains here for two weeks, and pays for what he drinks, I will soon reestablish my business."

"And don't forget," said d'Artagnan, "to bring up four bottles of the same sort for the two English gentlemen."

"And now," said Athos, "while they are getting the wine, tell me, d'Artagnan, what has become of the others?"

D'Artagnan described how he had found Porthos in bed with a sprained knee and Aramis at a table between two theologians. As he finished, the host entered with the wine and a ham, which fortunately for him had been left out of the cellar.

"Good!" said Athos, filling two glasses. "Here's to Porthos and Aramis! But you, d'Artagnan, what has happened to you personally? You seem sad."

"Alas, it is because I am the most unfortunate of us all!"

"You unfortunate! How? Tell me."

"Later."

"Later! Why later? Because you think I am drunk?

D'Artagnan, remember that my head is never so clear as when I have had plenty of wine. So speak, I am all ears."

D'Artagnan related his adventure with Mme. Bonacieux. Athos listened to him placidly, and when he had finished, said, "Trifles, mere trifles!" That was his favorite word.

"You always say *trifles*, Athos!" said d'Artagnan, "and that comes very ill from you who have never loved."

Athos's drink-deadened eyes flashed, but only for a moment before they again became dull and vacant.

"That is true," he said quietly. "I have never loved."

"Then acknowledge, you stony heart," said d'Artagnan, "that you are wrong to be so hard upon us tender hearts."

"Tender hearts, pierced hearts," Athos responded.

"What are you saying?"

"I am saying that love is a lottery in which he who wins, wins death! You are very fortunate to have lost, believe me, d'Artagnan. And if I have any advice to give you, it is to always lose!"

"She seemed to love me so!"

"She *seemed*."

"Oh, she *did* love me!"

"You child! Why, there is not a man alive who has not believed, as you do, that his mistress loved him, and not a man alive who has not been deceived by his mistress."

"Except you, Athos, who never had one."

"That is true," said Athos, after a moment's silence. "I never had one! Let us drink!"

"But then, philosopher that you are," said d'Artagnan, "instruct me, support me. I must be taught and consoled."

"Consoled for what?"

"For my misfortune."

"Your misfortune is laughable," said Athos, shrugging his shoulders; "I would like to know what you would say if I were to tell to you a real tale of love!"

"Which has happened to you?"

"Or to one of my friends, what does it matter?"

"Tell me, Athos."

"Better if I drink."

"Drink and tell, then."

"Not a bad idea!" said Athos, emptying and refilling his glass. "The two things go very well together."

"I am listening," said d'Artagnan.

Athos collected his thoughts, and in proportion as he did so, d'Artagnan saw that he became pale. He was at that stage of intoxication in which vulgar drinkers fall and sleep; he, Athos, kept himself upright and dreamed without sleeping. This drunken somnambulism was frightening.

"You truly wish to hear it?"

"I do."

"Be it then as you wish. One of my friends—one of my friends, please note, not myself," said Athos, interrupting himself with a melancholy smile, "one of the counts of my province—that is to say, of Berry—noble as a Dandolo or a Montmorency, at the age of twenty-five fell in love with a girl of sixteen, as beautiful as fancy can paint. Through the ingenuousness of her age beamed an ardent mind—not of a woman but of a poet. She did not please—she intoxicated. She lived in a small town with her brother, who was a curé. Both had recently come into the area. Nobody knew from, but she was so lovely and her brother so pious, nobody thought of asking. They were said, however, to be well-born. My friend, who was the lord of the region, might have seduced her or taken her by force, for he was the master. Who would have come to the assistance of two strangers, two unknown persons? Unfortunately he was an honorable man—he married her. The fool! the ass! the idiot!"

"Why, if he loved her?" asked d'Artagnan.

"Wait," said Athos. "He took her to his château and made her the first lady in the province, and in justice it must be admitted that she supported her rank becomingly."

"Well?"

"Well, one day when she was hunting with her husband," continued Athos, in a low voice and speaking very quickly, "she fell from her horse and fainted. The count flew to her aid, and since she seemed constricted by her clothes, he ripped them open with his poniard and in so doing laid bare her shoulder. D'Artagnan," Athos said, with a maniacal burst of laughter, "guess what she had on her shoulder."

"How can I guess?"

"A fleur-de-lis. She was branded!"

Athos emptied his glass in a single draft.

"My God, what are you telling me?"

"The truth, my friend. The angel was a demon, a convicted criminal!"

"What did the count do?"

"The count was of the highest nobility. He had the right to execute justice both high and low on his estates. He tore the countess's dress to pieces, tied her hands behind her, and hanged her from a tree."

"Heavens, Athos, a murder?"

"Yes, nothing less than a murder," said Athos, deathly pale. "But I think I need wine!"

He seized the neck of the last bottle, put it to his mouth, and emptied it in a single draft, just as he had previously emptied his glass.

Then he let his head sink upon his two hands while d'Artagnan stood before him, stupefied.

"That cured me of beautiful, poetical, and loving women," said Athos, raising his head and forgetting to continue the fiction of the count. "God grant you as much! Let us drink."

"Then she . . . she is dead?" stammered d'Artagnan.

"*Parbleu!*" said Athos. "Hold out your glass. Oh, the wine is finished—we can't drink. Well, then let us eat some of this ham."

"And her brother?" d'Artagnan asked timidly.

"Her brother?"

"Yes, the priest."

"Oh, I inquired about him for the purpose of hanging him as well, but he was too quick for me—he had left the parish the night before."

"Did anyone ever discover who the miserable fellow was?"

"He was doubtless the first lover and the accomplice of the fair lady. A man who had pretended to be a curé for the purpose of getting his mistress married and securing her a position. He has by now been hanged and quartered, I hope."

"My God!" cried d'Artagnan, stunned by the terrible tale.

"Taste some of this ham, d'Artagnan, it is exquisite," said Athos, cutting a slice that he placed on the young man's plate. "What a pity there were only four bottles like this in the cellar. I could have drunk fifty more."

D'Artagnan could no longer endure this conversation, which had driven him mad. Allowing his head to fall on the table, he pretended to sleep.

"None of these young fellows can drink," said Athos, looking at him with pity, "and yet this is one of the best!"

28

The Return

D'ARTAGNAN was astounded by the story Athos had confided to him, but the half-revelation had left many things very obscure. For one thing, it had been made by a man quite drunk to one who was half drunk—though despite the uncertainty created by the three or four bottles of Burgundy he had consumed, he woke up the following morning with the memory of Athos's words as clear in his mind as if they had just fallen from his friend's lips that very moment. Whatever vagueness he felt, however, only spurred his desire for greater clarity, and he went into his friend's room determined to renew their conversation; but he found Athos quite himself again—the most subtle and impenetrable of men.

The Musketeer, after a hearty handshake, broached the matter first.

"I was pretty drunk yesterday, d'Artagnan," he said. "I can tell that by my tongue, which was very swollen this morning, and by my pulse, which was very uneven. I must have said a thousand foolish things."

He looked at d'Artagnan with an earnestness that embarrassed him.

"No, if I remember correctly, you said nothing out of the ordinary," d'Artagnan replied.

"Ah, you surprise me. I thought I had told you a most lamentable story." And he looked at the young man as if to read deep into his heart.

"My faith," said d'Artagnan, "I must have been more drunk than you, since I remember nothing of the kind."

Athos did not trust this reply, and he continued: "You must have noticed, my friend, that everyone has his particular kind of drunkenness, sad or gay. My drunkenness is always sad, and when I am thoroughly drunk my mania is to tell all the dismal stories my foolish nurse ever told me. That is my failing—a serious failing, I admit, but except for that, I am a good drinker."

Athos spoke so naturally that for a moment d'Artagnan was no longer sure of what he remembered.

"That, then," replied the young man, anxious to get at the truth, "is what I remember, but as we remember a dream. We were speaking of hanging."

"Ah, you see," said Athos, becoming still paler, yet attempting to laugh, "I was sure it was that—people being hanged in my nightmare."

"I remember now! Yes, it was about . . . wait a minute . . . yes, it was about a woman."

"Yes," said Athos, now ashen, "that is my famous story of the fair lady, and when I tell that one, I must be very drunk."

"Yes, that was it—the story of a tall, fair lady with blue eyes."

"Yes, who was hanged."

"By her husband, who was a nobleman of your acquaintance," continued d'Artagnan, looking intently at Athos.

"Well, you see how one may compromise someone when he does not know what he is saying," said Athos, shrugging his shoulders as if he thought himself an object of pity. "I will certainly never get drunk again, d'Artagnan—it is too bad a habit."

D'Artagnan remained silent.

Athos changed the conversation all at once and said, "By the way, thank you for the horse you brought me."

"Do you like it?"

"Yes, but it is not a horse for hard work."

"You are mistaken. I rode him nearly ten leagues in less than an hour and a half, and he was no more tired than if he had gone around the Place St. Sulpice."

"Ah, you begin to make me regret . . ."

"Regret?"

"Yes, for I have parted with him."

"What happened?"

"Why, this. I woke up at six o'clock this morning. You were still fast asleep, and I did not know what to do with myself because I was still muddled from yesterday's drinking. As I came into the public room, I saw one of our Englishmen bargaining with a dealer for a horse, his own having died yesterday from bleeding. I drew near and found he was bidding a hundred pistoles for a fine chestnut nag. '*Pardieu,*' said I, 'my good gentleman, I have a horse to sell, too.' 'Yes, and a very fine one! I saw him yesterday—your friend's lackey was leading him.' 'Do you think he is worth a hundred pistoles?' 'Yes! Will you sell him to me for that sum?' 'No, but I will gamble for him.' 'At what?' 'At dice.' No sooner said than done, and I lost the horse. Ah, but please observe that I won back the trappings."

D'Artagnan looked upset.

"This annoys you?" Athos asked.

"Well, I must confess it does," replied d'Artagnan. "That horse was to have identified us on the battle-field—he was a pledge, a souvenir. Athos, you have done wrong."

"But my dear friend, put youself in my place. I was dying of boredom—and besides, I don't like English horses. If it is only to be recognized by someone, why, the saddle will suffice for that—it is quite remarkable. As for the horse, we can easily find some excuse for its disappearance. The devil! A horse is mortal—suppose mine had died of glanders or farcy?"

D'Artagnan was not amused.

"I am sorry that you attach so much importance to those animals, for I am not yet at the end of my story," Athos continued.

"What else have you done?"

"After having lost my own horse, nine against ten—see how close!—I had the idea of staking yours."

"Yes, but you stopped at the idea, I hope?"

"No, I acted on it that very minute."

"What happened?" d'Artagnan asked anxiously.

"I threw, and I lost."

"My horse?"

"Your horse, seven against eight. A point short . . . you know the proverb."

"Athos, I swear, you are not in your right mind."

"My dear lad, that was yesterday, when I was telling you silly stories, but not this morning. As I was saying, I lost him, with all his trappings."

"This is terrible."

"Wait, you still don't know everything. I would make an excellent gambler if I were not so obstinate, but I was obstinate, just as I am when I have been drinking. Well, I was obstinate . . ."

"But what else could you play for? You had nothing left!"

"Oh, yes, I did, my friend. There was still that diamond which sparkles on your finger and which I had observed yesterday."

"This diamond!" said d'Artagnan, placing his hand quickly on his ring.

"And as I am a connoisseur in such things, having had a few of my own once, I estimated it at a thousand pistoles."

"I hope," said d'Artagnan seriously, half dead with fright, "you did not mention my diamond?"

"On the contrary, my dear friend, that diamond became our only resource. With it, I might regain our horses and their harnesses, and even money to pay our expenses on the road."

"Athos, you make me tremble!"

"I mentioned your diamond to my adversary, who had also noticed it. What the devil, my dear man, do you think you can wear a star from heaven on your finger and nobody will notice it? Impossible!"

"Go on, tell me what happened. Your sangfroid will be my death!"

"We divided the diamond into ten parts of a hundred pistoles each."

"You are mocking me! You want to test me!" said d'Artagnan with rising anger.

"No, I am not mocking you. I would like to have seen you in my place! I had not seen a human face in two weeks—two weeks in which to become a brute in the company of those bottles."

"That was no reason for staking my diamond!" replied d'Artagnan, clenching his fist in a nervous spasm.

"Hear the end. Ten parts of a hundred pistoles each, in ten throws, without revenge. In thirteen throws I had lost everything! The number thirteen was always unlucky for me—it was on the thirteenth of July that—"

"Ventrebleu!" cried D'Artagnan, rising from the table, the story he was hearing now making him forget the one he had heard the day before.

"Patience," said Athos, "I had a plan. The Englishman was an eccentric. I had seen him talking to Grimaud that morning, and Grimaud had told me that he had asked him to enter his service. Well, I staked Grimaud, the silent Grimaud, divided into ten portions."

"What next?" said d'Artagnan, laughing in spite of himself.

"Grimaud himself, you understand! And with the ten parts of Grimaud, all of which are not worth a ducatoon, I regained the diamond! Tell me, now, is persistence not a virtue?"

"My faith, but this is droll," said d'Artagnan, relieved, and now able to laugh heartily.

"Seeing that my luck had turned, I of course again staked the diamond."

"The devil!" said d'Artagnan, becoming angry again.

"I won back your harness, then your horse, then my harness, then my horse, and then I lost again. In brief, I regained your harness and then mine. That was a superb throw, so I stopped there."

D'Artagnan breathed as if the whole hostelry had been lifted from his chest.

"Then the diamond is safe?" he asked timidly.

"Intact, my dear friend, as well as the harness of your Bucephalus and mine."

"But what is the use of harnesses without horses?"

"I have an idea."

"Athos, you frighten me."

"Listen to me. You have not gambled for a long time, d'Artagnan?"

"And I have no desire to."

"Do not be so determined about it. You have not gambled for a long time, so you ought to have a good touch."

"Well, and what then?"

"Well, the Englishman and his companion are still here. I noticed that he was very sorry to lose the trappings, and you seem to think a lot of your horse. In your place, I would stake the trappings against the horse."

"But he will not want only one harness."

"Stake both, *pardieu!* I am not as selfish as you are."

"That is what you would do?" d'Artagnan asked, wavering in the face of Athos's confidence.

"On my honor, in one single throw."

"But having lost the horses, I am particularly anxious to preserve the harnesses."

"Stake your diamond, then."

"This? Never, never!"

"I would propose staking Planchet, but as that kind of stake was previously suggested, the Englishman would perhaps not be willing," said Athos.

"My dear Athos," said d'Artagnan, "I would prefer not to risk anything."

"That's a pity," said Athos coolly. "The Englishman is overflowing with pistoles. Good Lord, try one throw—a throw is soon over and done with!"

"And if I lose?"

"You will win."

"But if I lose?"

"You will surrender the harnesses."

"All right, one throw!"

Athos went looking for the Englishman, whom he found in the stable examining the harnesses with a greedy eye. It was a good opportunity. He proposed his conditions—the two harnesses, against either one horse or a hundred pistoles. The Englishman calculated quickly; the two harnesses were worth three hundred pistoles. He agreed.

D'Artagnan threw the dice with a trembling hand and turned up the number three; his pallor terrified Athos, who, however, contented himself with saying, "That's a sad throw, my friend. Monsieur, you will have fully equipped horses."

The Englishman, already quite triumphant, did not even give himself the trouble to shake the dice, so sure was he of victory that he threw them on the table without looking at them. D'Artagnan had turned aside to conceal his ill humor.

"Hold, hold!" said Athos quietly. "That throw of the dice is extraordinary—I have seen it only four times in my life. Two aces!"

The Englishman looked, and was overcome by astonishment; d'Artagnan looked, and was overcome by pleasure.

"Yes," Athos continued, "only four times. Once at the house of Monsieur Créquy, another time at my own house in the country, in my château at . . . when I had a château, a third time at Monsieur de Tréville's, where it surprised us all, and the fourth time at a cabaret, where it happened to me and where I lost a hundred louis and a supper on it."

"Then Monsieur takes his horse back again," said the Englishman.

"Certainly," said d'Artagnan.

"There is no revenge?"

"Our conditions were 'No revenge,' as you will please remember."

"That is true. The horse shall be restored to your lackey, monsieur."

"One moment," said Athos. "With your permission, monsieur, I wish to speak to my friend."

"Say on."

Athos drew d'Artagnan aside.

"Well, Tempter, what more do you want with me?" d'Artagnan asked. "You want me to throw again, do you not?"

"No, I want you to think."

"About what?"

"You mean to take your horse?"

"Of course."

"You are wrong, then. I would take the hundred pistoles. You know you staked the harnesses against the horse or a hundred pistoles, at your choice."

"Yes."

"Well, I would take the hundred pistoles."

"And I take the horse."

"And I repeat, you are wrong. What is the use of one horse for the two of us? I could not ride behind—we would look like the two sons of Aymon, who had lost their brothers. You cannot think of humiliating me by prancing along by my side on that magnificient charger. For my part, I would not hesitate a moment, but would take the hundred pistoles. We need money for our return to Paris."

"I am very attached to that horse, Athos."

"And there again you are wrong. A horse slips and injures a joint, a horse stumbles and breaks his knees, a horse eats from a rack in which a glandered horse has eaten—and there is a horse, or rather a hundred pistoles, lost. A master must feed his horse, while on the contrary, a hundred pistoles feed their master."

"But how will we get back?"

"Upon our lackeys' horses, *pardieu!* Everyone will see by our bearing that we are gentlemen."

"Pretty figures we shall cut on ponies while Aramis and Porthos caracole on their steeds."

"Aramis! Porthos!" Athos began to laugh.

"What is it?" said d'Artagnan, who did not understand his friend's hilarity.

"Nothing, nothing! Go on!"

"So your advice is . . . ?"

"To take the hundred pistoles, d'Artagnan. With the hundred pistoles we can live well to the end of the month. We have endured much to fatigue us, remember, and a little rest will do us good."

"I rest? Oh, no, Athos. Once in Paris, I shall begin my search for that unfortunate woman!"

"Well, be assured that your horse will not be half as useful to you for that purpose as good golden louis. Take the hundred pistoles, my friend, take the hundred pistoles!"

D'Artagnan required only one good reason, and this last one seemed convincing. Besides, he feared that by continuing to resist he would appear selfish. He therefore agreed, and chose the hundred pistoles, which the Englishman paid on the spot.

After that they wanted only to leave. Making peace with the landlord cost six pistoles in addition to Athos's old horse. D'Artagnan and Athos took the nags of Planchet and Grimaud, and the two lackeys started off on foot, carrying the saddles on their heads.

However badly mounted our two friends were, they were far in advance of their servants when they arrived at Crèvecœur. From a distance they saw Aramis gloomily looking out his window at the dusty horizon.

"Aramis! What the devil are you doing there?" shouted the two friends.

"Ah, it's you, d'Artagnan, and you, Athos," said the young man. "I was thinking about how quickly the blessings of this world leave us. My English horse, which has just disappeared amid a cloud of dust, has furnished me with a living image of the fragility of earthly things. Life itself may be summed up in three words: *Erat, est, fuit.*"

"Which means . . ." said d'Artagnan, who began to suspect the truth.

"Which means that I have just been duped—sixty louis for a horse that, by the manner of his gait, must be able to do at least five leagues an hour!"

D'Artagnan and Athos burst into laughter.

"My dear d'Artagnan," said Aramis, "don't be too angry with me, I beg you. Necessity knows no law—and besides, it is I who am chiefly punished, for that rascally horsedealer has robbed me of at least fifty louis. Ah, you fellows are good managers! You ride on your lackeys' horses, and have your own wonderful steeds led along carefully by hand, in short stages."

At that instant a market cart, which some minutes before had appeared upon the Amiens road, pulled up at the inn, and Planchet and Grimaud came out of it with the saddles on their heads. The cart was returning empty to Paris, and the two lackeys had agreed, in exchange for their transport, to buy the wagoner drinks all along the route.

"What?" said Aramis, seeing them arrive. "Nothing but saddles?"

"Now do you understand?" said Athos.

"My friends, that's exactly like me! I kept my harness by instinct. Bazin, get my new saddle and put it next to those of these gentlemen."

"What have you done with your ecclesiastics?" asked d'Artagnan.

"My dear fellow, I invited them to a dinner the next day," replied Aramis. "They have some capital wine here, and I got them drunk. After that, the curé ordered me never to discard my uniform, and the Jesuit begged me to get him made a Musketeer."

"But without a thesis!" cried d'Artagnan. "I demand the elimination of the thesis."

"Since then," Aramis continued, "I have lived very agreeably. I have begun a poem of one-syllable lines, which is rather difficult—but the merit in all things consists in surmounting the difficulties. The subject is love. I will read you the first canto—it has four hundred lines and lasts a minute."

"My faith, Aramis," said d'Artagnan, who detested verses almost as much as he did Latin, "if you surmounted the problem of length as well as that of difficulty, you can be sure that your poem will at least have two merits."

"You will see," Aramis went on, "that it is filled with worthy emotions. . . . So, my friends, we return to Paris? Bravo! I am ready. And I will be happy to rejoin Porthos. You cannot imagine how I have missed that great simpleton. He certainly would not sell his horse—not for a kingdom! I can almost see him now, mounted on his superb animal and seated in his handsome saddle. I am sure he will look like the Grand Mogul himself!"

They stopped for an hour to refresh their horses. Aramis paid his bill and sent Bazin to ride with his comrades in the cart, then they all set out to rejoin Porthos.

They found him up and about, less pale than when d'Artagnan had left him, and seated at a table on which, though he was alone, there was enough food and drink for four persons—nicely prepared meats, choice wines, and superb fruit.

"You come just in time, gentlemen. I was about to dine, and you will join me."

"Oh, oh," said d'Artagnan, "Mousqueton did not catch these bottles with his lasso! And here is an enticing veal dish and a fillet of beef!"

"I am trying to recover my strength," said Porthos. "Nothing weakens a man more than these devilish sprains. Did you ever suffer from a sprain, Athos?"

"Never! Though I remember feeling just like that two weeks after I received my sword wound during our little dispute on the Rue Férou."

"But this dinner was not intended for you alone, Porthos, was it?" said Aramis.

"No, I was expecting some gentlemen from the neighborhood, who have just sent me word they could not come. You will take their places, and I will not lose by the exchange. Mousqueton, get more chairs and order double the number of bottles!"

"Do you know what we are eating?" Athos asked at the end of ten minutes.

"I am eating veal garnished with marrow and vegetables," said d'Artagnan.

"And I some lamb chops," said Porthos.

"And I a chicken breast," said Aramis.

"You are all mistaken, gentlemen," Athos said gravely. "You are eating horse."

"Eating what?" said d'Artagnan.

"Horse!" said Aramis, with a grimace of disgust.

Porthos said nothing.

"Yes, horse. Are we not eating a horse, Porthos? And perhaps his harness too?"

"No, gentlemen, I have kept the harness," said Porthos.

"My faith," said Aramis, "we are all alike. One would think we had arranged it in advance."

"What else could I do?" said Porthos. "That horse made my visitors ashamed of theirs, and I don't like to humiliate people."

"Then your duchess is still away?" asked d'Artagnan.

"Yes," replied Porthos. "And, my faith, the governor of the province—one of the gentlemen I was expecting for dinner—seemed to have such a desire for him, that I gave him to him."

"*Gave* him?" cried d'Artagnan.

"My God, yes, *gave*, that is the word," said Porthos. "I am sure the animal was worth at least a hundred and fifty louis, but the stingy fellow would only give me eighty."

"Without the harness?" asked Aramis.

"Yes, without the harness."

"You will observe, gentlemen," said Athos, "that Porthos has made the best bargain of any of us."

And they began to roar with laughter, to the astonishment of poor Porthos; but when he was informed of the cause of their hilarity, he shared it vociferously, according to his custom.

"At least we all have money," said d'Artagnan.

"Not I," said Athos. "I found Aramis's Spanish wine

so good that I sent sixty bottles of it in the wagon with the lackeys, and that has made my purse much lighter."

"And I," said Aramis, "gave almost my last sou to the church of Montdidier and the Jesuits of Amiens, with whom I had made commitments that I had to keep. I have ordered Masses to be said for myself and for you, gentlemen—which will be said, and which I have not the least doubt will be of great benefit to you."

"And I," said Porthos, "do you think my sprain cost me nothing? And to that you must add Mousqueton's wound, for which I had to have the doctor twice a day and who charged me double on account of that foolish Mousqueton having allowed himself to be hit by a bullet in a part people generally only show to an apothecary. I advised him to try never to get wounded there anymore."

"Ah, yes," said Athos, exchanging a smile with d'Artagnan and Aramis, "it is very clear you acted nobly with regard to the poor lad, as a good master should."

"In short," said Porthos, "when all my expenses are paid, I will have at most thirty écus left."

"And I about ten pistoles," said Aramis.

"Well, then, it appears that we are the Crœsuses of the group," said Athos. "How much of your hundred pistoles do you have left, d'Artagnan?"

"Of my hundred pistoles? Why, in the first place I gave you fifty."

"You think so?"

"Pardieu!"

"Ah, yes, that is true. I remember now."

"Then I paid the host six pistoles."

"What a brute of a host! Why did you give him six pistoles?"

"You told me to."

"It is true that I am too good-natured. . . . Well, how much is left?"

"Twenty-five pistoles," said d'Artagnan.

"And I," said Athos, taking some small change from his pocket, "I . . ."

"You? Nothing!"

"Or so little that it is not worth adding to the rest."

"Let us calculate how much we have altogether."

"Porthos?"

"Thirty écus."

"Aramis?"

"Ten pistoles."

"And you, d'Artagnan?"

"Twenty-five."

"That makes in all?" said Athos.

"Four hundred and seventy-five livres," said d'Artagnan, who calculated as swiftly as Archimedes.

"On our arrival in Paris, we will still have four hundred, besides the harnesses," said Porthos.

"But our squadron horses?" said Aramis.

"Well, from our lackeys' four horses we will make two for the masters, for which we will draw lots. With the four hundred livres we will have half a horse for one of the unmounted, and we will give everything in our pockets to d'Artagnan, who has a steady hand with dice and will try his luck in the first gaming house we come to. There!"

"Let us dine, then," said Porthos. "It is getting cold."

The friends, at ease about the future, did honor to the repast, the remains of which were left to Mousqueton, Bazin, Planchet, and Grimaud.

Arriving in Paris, d'Artagnan found a letter from M. de Tréville, which informed him that he had obtained the king's permission for him to enter the company of the Musketeers.

As this was the height of d'Artagnan's worldly ambition—apart, to be sure, from his desire to find Mme. Bonacieux—he ran, full of joy, to seek his comrades, whom he had left only half an hour before but whom he found very sad and deeply preoccupied. They were assembled in council at Athos's apartment, which always indicated an event of some gravity.

M. de Tréville had informed them of his Majesty's firm intention to open the campaign on the first of May and told them to assemble their equipment.

The four philosophers, stunned, looked at one another. M. de Tréville never jested in matters of discipline.

"How much do you think the equipment will cost?" d'Artagnan asked.

"Oh, we have been Spartan in our calculations, and we each need fifteen hundred livres," said Aramis.

"Four times fifteen makes sixty—six thousand livres," said Athos.

"It seems to me," said d'Artagnan, "that we might manage with a thousand livres each."

"I have an idea," said Porthos abruptly.

"Well, that's something, for I have not even the shadow of one," said Athos coolly. "And as for d'Artagnan, gentlemen, the idea of being one of *ours* has driven him mad. A thousand livres! For my part, I declare I need two thousand!"

"Four times two makes eight," said Aramis. "We need eight thousand to completely equip ourselves—although it is true that we already have the saddles."

"Besides," said Athos, waiting till d'Artagnan, who left to thank Monsieur de Tréville, had shut the door, "there is that beautiful ring sparkling on our friend's finger. D'Artagnan is too good a comrade to leave his brothers in difficulty while he wears a king's ransom on his finger."

29

Hunting for the Equipment

THE MOST PREOCCUPIED of the four friends was certainly d'Artagnan, although he, in his quality of Guardsman, would be much more easily equipped than Messieurs the Musketeers, who were all of high rank; but as we have observed, our Gascon cadet was, though frugal and almost miserly, yet also (explain the contradiction!) so vain as almost to rival Porthos. But in addition to this preoccupation of his vanity, he also felt a much less selfish uneasiness. Notwithstanding all his inquiries about Mme. Bonacieux, he had learned nothing about her. M. de Tréville had spoken of her to the queen, who was ignorant of her whereabouts but who had promised to have her sought for; but this promise was very vague and did not reassure d'Artagnan at all.

Athos did not leave his room; he had made up his mind not to take a single step to equip himself.

"We still have two weeks," he said to his friends. "If at the end of that time I have found nothing—or rather if nothing has come to find me—since I am too good a Catholic to kill myself, I will seek a good quarrel with four of his Eminence's Guards or with eight Englishmen, and I will fight until one of them has killed me—which, considering the number, cannot fail to happen. It will then be said of me that I died for the king, so I will have performed my duty without the expense of equipping myself."

Porthos continued to walk about with his hands behind him, nodding his head and repeating, "I will follow up my idea."

Aramis, anxious and carelessly dressed, said nothing.

It may be seen by these gloomy details that desolation reigned in the community.

The lackeys shared the sadness of their masters. Mousqueton collected a provision of crusts; Bazin, who had always been religious, never left the churches; Planchet watched the flies; and Grimaud, whom the general distress could not induce to break the silence imposed by his master, heaved enough sighs to soften the stones.

The three friends—for, as we have said, Athos had sworn not to stir a foot to equip himself—went out early in the morning and returned late at night. They wandered about the streets, looking at the pavement as if to see whether the passersby had possibly dropped a purse behind them. They might have been supposed to be following tracks, so carefully did they hunt wherever they went. When they met they looked desolately at one another, as if to say, "Have you found anything?"

However, as Porthos had been the first to have an idea, and had thought about it earnestly, he was the first to do something. He was a man of action, this worthy Porthos. One day d'Artagnan saw him walking toward the church of St. Leu and instinctively followed him. Porthos entered, after having curled his mustache and pulled at his beard, which always signaled a strong resolution to succeed. As d'Artagnan was careful to conceal himself, Porthos did not know he had been seen. D'Artagnan entered behind him. Porthos leaned against the side of a pillar; d'Artagnan, still unnoticed, leaned against the other side.

A sermon was being preached, so the church was very crowded. Porthos took advantage of this circumstance to ogle the women. Thanks to Mousqueton, his exterior showed no sign of the distress of the interior. His hat was a little napless, his feather was a little faded, his gold embroidery was a little tarnished, his laces were a trifle frayed; but in the obscurity of the church these things were not noticeable, and Porthos was still the handsome Porthos.

On the bench nearest the pillar against which Porthos was leaning, d'Artagnan noticed a sort of ripe beauty, rather sallow and dry, but erect and haughty under her black hood. Porthos looked at her furtively, then cast his eyes over the rest of the nave.

Blushing from time to time, the lady darted an occasional quick glance toward the inconstant Porthos, at which his eyes would immediately wander elsewhere. It was plain that this proceeding piqued the lady in the black hood, for she bit her lips till they bled, scratched the end of her nose, and could not sit still in her seat.

Porthos, seeing this, again twirled his mustache, again pulled at his beard, and began to make signals to a beautiful lady near the choir, who was not only a beautiful lady but no doubt a great lady, for she had behind her a Negro boy who had brought the cushion on which she knelt, and a female servant who held the emblazoned bag that had contained the book from which she was reading the Mass.

The lady with the black hood followed Porthos's eyes through all their wanderings and perceived that they rested longest on the lady with the red velvet cushion, the little Negro, and the maidservant.

During all this time Porthos was following his plan: there were almost imperceptible winks, fingers placed furtively on the lips, killing little smiles that really did assassinate the disdained beauty.

Then she cried "Ahem!" under cover of the *mea culpa*, striking her breast so vigorously that everybody, even the lady with the red cushion, turned around toward her. Porthos paid no attention; he pretended to be deaf.

The lady with the red cushion produced a great effect—for she was most beautiful—on the lady with the black hood, who saw in her a rival to be truly feared; a great effect on Porthos, who thought her much prettier than the lady with the black hood; a great effect on d'Artagnan, who recognized in her the lady of Meung, of Calais, and of Dover, whom his persecutor, the man with the scar, had addressed by the name of Milady.

Without losing sight of the lady of the red cushion, d'Artagnan continued to watch Porthos's proceedings, which amused him greatly. He guessed that the lady of the black hood was the procurator's wife of the Rue aux Ours, especially since the church of St. Leu was not far from there.

He guessed likewise that Porthos was taking his revenge for his defeat at Chantilly, when the procurator's wife had proved so reluctant with respect to her purse.

Amid all this, d'Artagnan also noticed that not one woman responded to Porthos's gallantries. The sufferings of the procurator's wife stemmed from a fantasy—but isn't fantasy the basis of all love and jealousy?

The sermon over, the procurator's wife walked to the holy font. Porthos got there ahead of her and, instead of a finger, dipped his whole hand in. The procurator's wife smiled, thinking it was for her that Porthos had done this, but she was cruelly and promptly undeceived; when she was only about three steps away from him, he turned his head around and fixed his eyes steadfastly on the lady with the red cushion, who had risen and was approaching, followed by her black boy and her maid.

When the lady of the red cushion was close to Porthos, he withdrew his dripping hand from the font and cupped the holy water. The fair worshiper immersed her delicate fingers into his huge palm, smiled, made the sign of the cross, and left the church.

This was too much for the procurator's wife; she was sure there was an intrigue between this lady and Porthos. If she had been a great lady she would have fainted, but since she was only a procurator's wife, she contented herself with saying to the Musketeer with concentrated fury, "Eh, Monsieur Porthos, you don't offer *me* any holy water?"

At the sound of that voice, Porthos started like a man awakened from a hundred-year sleep.

"Ma—madame!" he cried. "Is that you? How is your husband, our dear Monsieur Coquenard? Is he still as stingy as ever? How can I not have seen you during the whole two hours of the sermon?"

"I was within two paces of you, monsieur," replied the procurator's wife, "but you did not see me because you had eyes for no one but the pretty lady to whom you just now gave the holy water."

Porthos pretended to be embarrassed. "Ah," he said, "you saw . . ."

"I would have had to be blind not to have seen."

"Yes," said Porthos, "she is a duchess I know, but it is difficult to meet her because her husband is so jealous. She sent me word that she would be here today—in this poor church, buried in this vile neighborhood—just for the sake of seeing me."

"Monsieur Porthos," said the procurator's wife, "will you have the kindness to offer me your arm for five minutes? I have something to say to you."

"Certainly, madame," said Porthos, winking to himself like a gambler who laughs at the trick he is about to play.

At that moment d'Artagnan passed in pursuit of Milady; he glanced at Porthos and saw his triumphant look.

"Ah, well," he said, reasoning to himself according to the strangely easy morality of that gallant period, "there is one who will be equipped in good time!"

Yielding to the pressure of the arm of the procurator's wife as a boat yields to the rudder, Porthos arrived at the St. Magloire cloister—a little-frequented passage, enclosed by a turnstile at each end. During the day nobody was ever there but beggars devouring their crusts and children at play.

"Ah, Monsieur Porthos," cried the procurator's wife when she was sure that no one who was a stranger to the usual population of the place could either see or hear her, "it seems you are a great conqueror!"

"I, madame?" exclaimed Porthos, drawing himself up proudly. "What do you mean?"

"The signals? The holy water? But she must be at least a princess, that lady with her Negro boy and her maid!"

"Madame, you are deceived," said Porthos. "She is simply a duchess."

"And that footman waiting at the door, and that carriage with a coachman in grand livery waiting on his seat?"

Porthos had seen neither the footman nor the carriage, but with the eye of a jealous woman, Mme. Coquenard had seen everything.

Porthos regretted that he had not made the lady of the red cushion a princess.

"Ah, you are quite the ladies' pet, Monsieur Porthos!" said the procurator's wife with a sigh.

"Well," Porthos responded, "with the physique nature has endowed me with, I do not lack for good luck."

"Good Lord, how quickly men forget!" cried the procurator's wife, raising her eyes toward heaven.

"Less quickly than women, it seems to me," replied Porthos. "I might well say, madame, that *I* was *your* victim! I lay in that poor inn at Chantilly, wounded, dying, abandoned by the doctors. I—the offspring of a noble family!—had relied on your friendship, but first I nearly died of my wounds, and then I nearly died of hunger without your ever deigning to reply to my fervent letters."

"But Monsieur Porthos . . ." murmured the procurator's wife, who began to feel that judging by the conduct of the greatest ladies of the time, she had been wrong.

"I, who had sacrificed for you the Baronne de——"

"I know it well."

"The Comtesse de——"

"Monsieur Porthos, do not overwhelm me!"

"The Duchesse de——"

"Monsieur Porthos, be generous!"

"You are right, madame, and I will not finish."

"But it was my husband who would not hear of lending you money."

"Madame Coquenard," said Porthos, "remember the first letter you wrote me and which is engraved in my memory."

The procurator's wife groaned.

"Besides," she said, "the sum you wanted me to borrow was rather large."

"Madame Coquenard, I gave you the first chance. I had only to write to the Duchesse . . . but I won't say her name because I am incapable of compromising a woman! But this I know—if I had written to her, she would have sent me fifteen hundred."

The procurator's wife began to cry.

"Monsieur Porthos, I assure you that you have punished me more than enough, and if you ever find yourself in a similar situation, you have only to ask me."

"Fie, madame, fie!" said Porthos, as if disgusted. "Let us not talk about money, if you please—it is humiliating."

"Then you no longer love me," said the procurator's wife, slowly and sadly.

Porthos maintained a majestic silence.

"And that is your only reply? Alas, I understand."

"Think of your offense, madame! I still feel it *here!*" said Porthos, placing his hand on his heart and pressing it strongly.

"I will make it up, my dear Porthos."

"Besides, what did I ask of you?" resumed Porthos, with a careless shrug. "A loan, nothing more! After all, I am not an unreasonable man. I know you are not rich, Madame Coquenard, and that your husband is obliged to bleed his poor clients in order to squeeze a few paltry écus from them. . . . If you were a duchess, a marchioness, or a countess, it would be quite different—it would be unpardonable!"

The procurator's wife was piqued.

"I would like you to know, Monsieur Porthos," she said, "that my strongbox—strongbox of a procurator's wife though it may be—is probably better filled than those of your affected minxes."

"That makes it worse," said Porthos, removing his arm from that of the procurator's wife, "for if you are rich, Madame Coquenard, then there is no excuse for your refusal."

"When I said rich," replied the procurator's wife, who saw that she had gone too far, "I did not mean it literally. I am not precisely rich—it is more that I am pretty well off."

"Stop, madame," said Porthos, "let us say no more about this. You have misunderstood me, and there is no longer any sympathy between us."

"Ingrate!"

"What, madame? *You* are complaining?"

"All right, then, go to your beautiful duchess—I will detain you no longer."

"She is not to be despised, in my opinion."

"Now, Monsieur Porthos, for the last time! Do you still love me?"

"Alas, madame," said Porthos, in the most melancholy tone he could assume, "when we are about to enter upon a campaign—a campaign in which I feel I will be killed . . ."

"Oh, don't say such things!" cried the procurator's wife, sobbing.

"Something tells me so," Porthos continued, becoming more and more melancholy.

"Just say that you love someone else."

"Not so. I tell you that is not true. I have no new love, and I even feel, deep inside me, something that speaks for you. But as you may or may not know, this latest campaign is to begin in two weeks. I will be totally preoccupied with equipping myself. Then I must go to see my family, in the heart of Brittany, to obtain the necessary sum for my departure."

Porthos observed a last struggle between love and avarice.

He continued, "The duchess whom you saw at the church has estates near those of my family, so we mean to make the journey together. As you know, journeys seem much shorter when two people take them together."

"Have you no friends in Paris, Monsieur Porthos?" the procurator's wife asked.

"I thought I had," said Porthos, resuming his melancholy air, "but I saw I was mistaken."

"You have a friend, Monsieur Porthos!" exclaimed the procurator's wife, in a transport that surprised even herself. "Come to our house tomorrow. You are the son of my aunt and therefore my cousin, you come from Noyon in Picardy, you have several lawsuits in Paris and no attorney. Can you remember all that?"

"Perfectly, madame."

"Come at lunch time."

"Very well."

"And be on your guard with my husband, who is quite shrewd, despite his seventy-six years."

"Seventy-six! *Peste!* That's a fine age," said Porthos.

"A great age, you mean, Monsieur Porthos. Yes, the poor dear man might leave me a widow at any minute," she continued, looking significantly at Porthos. "Fortunately, by the terms of our marriage contract, everything goes to the survivor."

"Everything?"

"Yes, everything."

"You are a foresighted woman, I see, my dear Madame Coquenard," said Porthos, squeezing her hand tenderly.

"Are we then reconciled, dear Monsieur Porthos?" she asked, simpering.

"For life," replied Porthos, in the same manner.

"Till we meet again, my dear traitor!"

"Till we meet again, my forgetful charmer!"

"Till tomorrow, my angel!"

"Till tomorrow, flame of my life!"

30

Milady

D'ARTAGNAN had followed Milady without her noticing him. He saw her get into her carriage, and he heard her order the coachman to drive to St. Germain.

It was useless to try to follow on foot a carriage drawn by two powerful horses, so d'Artagnan returned to the Rue Férou.

In the Rue de Seine he met Planchet, who had stopped in front of a pastry shop and was ecstatically looking at a most appetizing-looking cake.

He ordered him to saddle two horses in M. de Tréville's stables—one for himself, d'Artagnan, and one for Planchet—and bring them to Athos's place. M. de Tréville had permanently placed his stable at d'Artagnan's service.

Planchet proceeded toward the Rue du Colombier and d'Artagnan toward the Rue Férou. Athos was at home, emptying sadly a bottle of that Spanish wine he had brought back with him from his journey into Picardy. He made a sign for Grimaud to bring a glass for d'Artagnan, and Grimaud obeyed as usual.

D'Artagnan told Athos everything that had happened

at the church between Porthos and the procurator's wife, and added that their comrade was probably by that time on the way to being equipped.

"As for me," replied Athos to this recital, "I am not concerned. The cost of my outfit will not be paid by women."

"And yet, my dear Athos, handsome, well-bred, noble as you are, neither princesses nor queens would be able to resist your amorous approach."

"How young this d'Artagnan is," said Athos, shrugging his shoulders—and he signaled Grimaud to bring another bottle.

At that moment Planchet looked in modestly at the half-open door and told his master that the horses were ready.

"What horses?" asked Athos.

"Two horses that Monsieur de Tréville lends me when I need them, and with which I am now going to take a ride to St. Germain."

"What are you going to do in St. Germain?" demanded Athos.

Then d'Artagnan described how he had found in the church that lady who, together with the noble in the black cloak and the scar near his temple, constantly preoccupied him.

"That is to say, you are in love with this lady just as you were with Madame Bonacieux," said Athos, shrugging his shoulders contemptuously, as if he pitied such human weakness.

"I? Not at all!" said d'Artagnan. "I want only to unravel the mystery to which she is attached. I do not know why, but I have a feeling that this woman, whom I do not know at all and who doesn't know me at all, plays an important role in my life."

"Well, perhaps you are right," said Athos. "I do not know a woman that is worth looking for once she is lost. Madame Bonacieux is lost—so much the worse for her."

"No, Athos, you are mistaken," said d'Artagnan. "I love my poor Constance more than ever, and if I knew where she was, I would go anywhere—to the end of the world—to free her from her enemies. But I do not know where she is. All my searching has been useless. What can I say? I must distract myself."

"By all means, distract yourself with Milady, my dear d'Artagnan. I wish you may with all my heart, if that will amuse you."

"Listen, Athos," said d'Artagnan, "instead of shutting yourself up here as if you were under arrest, get on a horse and ride with me to St. Germain."

"My dear fellow," said Athos, "I ride horses when I have them. When I have none, I go on foot."

"Well," said d'Artagnan, smiling at Athos's misanthrophy, which would have offended him in any other person, "I ride what I can get—I am not so proud as you. So *au revoir,* Athos."

"Au revoir," said the Musketeer, motioning Grimaud to uncork the bottle he had just brought.

D'Artagnan and Planchet mounted, and took the road to St. Germain.

As d'Artagnan rode, he thought about what Athos had said concerning Mme. Bonacieux. Although he was not very sentimental, the haberdasher's pretty wife had made a real impression upon his heart, and as he had said, he was ready to go to the end of the world to seek her. But the world, being round, has many ends, so he did not know which direction to follow. Meanwhile, he was going to try to learn about Milady. Milady had spoken to the man in the black cloak; therefore she knew him. Since d'Artagnan thought it was the man in the black cloak who had carried off Mme. Bonacieux the second time as well as the first, he was only half-lying—which is lying only a little bit—when he said that by going in search of Milady he was at the same time going in search of Constance.

Thinking of all this, and from time to time giving a touch of the spur to his horse, he arrived at St. Germain. He had just passed the pavilion in which ten years later Louis XIV was to be born. He was riding up a very quiet street, looking to the right and the left to see if he could catch a glimpse of his beautiful Englishwoman, when he saw someone who looked vaguely familiar walking along a flower-filled terrace along the side of a house that had no windows facing the street.

Planchet recognized him first.

"Monsieur," he said, addressing d'Artagnan, "don't you recognize that face?"

"No, yet I am sure it is not the first time I have seen it," d'Artagnan replied.

"*Parbleu*, it is not!" said Planchet. "Why, it is poor Lubin, the lackey of the Comte de Wardes—the man you dealt with so well last month at Calais, on the road to the harbormaster's country house!"

"So it is!" said d'Artagnan. "Now I recognize him. Do you think he would remember you?"

"He was in such a state that I doubt it."

"Well, go talk with the boy," said d'Artagnan, "and see if you can find out if his master is dead."

Planchet dismounted and went straight up to Lubin, who indeed did not remember him, and the two lackeys began to chat amicably. Meanwhile d'Artagnan led the two horses into a lane, went around the house, and came back to listen to the conversation from behind some hazel bushes.

A moment later he heard the noise of a vehicle and saw Milady's carriage stop opposite him. There could be no mistake; Milady was in it. D'Artagnan leaned on the neck of his horse so that he might see without being seen.

Milady put her charming blond head out the window, and gave her orders to her maid.

The latter—a pretty girl about twenty or twenty-two years old, alert and lively, exactly the right kind of maid for a great lady—jumped from the step upon which, according to the custom of the time, she had been seated, and made her way to the terrace upon which d'Artagnan had seen Lubin.

D'Artagnan followed the maid with his eyes, but meanwhile someone in the house had called Lubin, and Planchet remained on the terrace alone, looking in all directions in an effort to see where d'Artagnan had disappeared.

The maid approached Planchet, whom she took for Lubin, and holding out a little note to him said, "For your master."

"For my master?" Planchet asked, astonished.

"Yes, and it is very urgent, so take it quickly."

Upon which she ran back to the carriage, which had turned around toward the way it had come, and jumped on the step; the carriage drove off.

Planchet turned the note this way and that, then, accustomed to passive obedience, jumped down from the terrace, ran to the lane, and at the end of twenty paces met d'Artagnan, who, having seen everything, was coming toward him.

"For you, monsieur," said Planchet, presenting the note to the young man.

"For me?" asked d'Artagnan. "Are you sure?"

"*Pardieu*, monsieur, I can't be more sure. The maid said, 'For your master.' You are my only master, so . . . she's a pretty little thing!"

D'Artagnan opened the letter, and read these words:

> A person who is more interested in you than she can say wishes to know on what day you will be able to walk in the forest. Tomorrow, at the Hôtel Champ du Drap d'Or, a lackey in black and red will wait for your reply.

"Oh," said d'Artagnan, "this is rather interesting. It seems that Milady and I are anxious about the health of the same person. Well, Planchet, how is the good Monsieur de Wardes? He's not dead?"

"No, monsieur, he is as well as a man can be with four sword wounds in his body, for you most certainly gave him four, and he is still very weak, having lost almost all his blood. As I said, monsieur, Lubin did not know me, and he told me all about our adventure."

"Well done, Planchet, you are the king of lackeys! Now get back on your horse, and let's overtake the carriage."

This did not take long. At the end of five minutes they saw the carriage drawn up by the roadside; a cavalier, richly dressed, was near the window.

The conversation between Milady and the cavalier was so animated that d'Artagnan stopped on the other side of the carriage without anyone but the pretty maid noticing him.

They spoke in English, a language d'Artagnan could not understand; but by her tone and gestures the young man could plainly see that the beautiful Englishwoman was in a great rage. She ended the conversation by an action that left no doubt as to its nature—a blow with her fan, applied with such force that the little feminine weapon shattered into a thousand pieces.

The cavalier laughed, which appeared to exasperate Milady still more.

D'Artagnan thought this was the moment to intervene. He approached the other window and, taking off his hat respectfully, said, "Madame, will you permit me to offer my services? It seems as if this cavalier has made you very angry. Speak one word, madame, and I take it upon myself to punish him for his lack of courtesy."

At his first words Milady had turned around, looking at the young man with astonishment; and when he had finished, she said in very good French, "Monsieur, I would very willingly place myself under your protection if the person with whom I quarrel were not my brother."

"Ah, excuse me, then," said d'Artagnan. "You understand that I didn't know that, madame."

"What is that stupid fellow troubling himself about?" cried the cavalier Milady had described as her brother, stooping down from his horse to the height of the coach window. "Why does he not go about his business?"

"Stupid fellow yourself!" said d'Artagnan, stooping in his turn from his horse, and answering on his side through the carriage window. "I do not go on because it pleases me to stop here."

The cavalier said something in English to his sister.

"I speak to you in French," said d'Artagnan. "Be kind enough to reply to me in the same language. You are Madame's brother—so be it. But fortunately you are not mine."

One might have thought that Milady, timid as women generally are, would have intervened in order to prevent the quarrel from going too far, but on the contrary, she threw herself back in her carriage and called out coolly to the coachman, "Go on—home!"

The pretty maid looked anxiously at d'Artagnan, whose good looks seemed to have made an impression on her.

The carriage went on, and left the two men facing each other, no obstacle any longer separating them.

The cavalier made a movement as if to follow the carriage but d'Artagnan—whose hot blood was already enflamed and who became even more enraged when he recognized in the cavalier the Englishman of Amiens who had won his horse and been very near winning his diamond from Athos—caught at his bridle and stopped him.

"Monsieur," he said, "you seem even more stupid than I am, for you forget there is a little quarrel to arrange between us."

"Ah," said the Englishman, "it's you. Must you always be playing some game or other?"

"Yes. And that reminds me that I have a revenge to take. We will see, my dear monsieur, if you can handle a sword as skillfully as you can a dice box."

"You see that I have no sword," said the Englishman. "Do you wish to play at being brave against an unarmed man?"

"I hope you have a sword at home—but in any case, I have two, and if you like, I will throw with you for one of them."

"Unnecessary," said the Englishman. "I have enough such playthings."

"Very well, my worthy gentleman," replied d'Artagnan, "pick out the longest and come show it to me this evening."

"Where?"

"Behind the Luxembourg. That's a charming spot for such amusements as I propose."

"That will do. I will be there."

"The time?"

"Six o'clock."

"Apropos, you probably have one or two friends?"

"I have three, who would be honored by joining in the sport with me."

"Three? Marvelous! That works out very well, for three is just my number!"

"Now, who are you?" asked the Englishman.

"I am Monsieur d'Artagnan, a Gascon gentleman, serving the king's Guards, Monsieur Des Essarts's company. And you?"

"I am Lord de Winter, Baron Sheffield."

"Well, then, I am your servant, Monsieur le Baron," said d'Artagnan, "though your names are rather difficult to remember."

And touching his horse with the spur, he cantered back to Paris.

As he was accustomed to do in all serious matters, d'Artagnan went straight to Athos's rooms.

He found Athos reclining upon a large sofa, where he was waiting, as he had said, for his equipment to come and find him.

He told Athos everything that had happened, except for the letter to M. de Wardes.

Athos was delighted to find he was going to fight an Englishman. We have said that that was his dream.

They immediately sent their lackeys for Porthos and Aramis, and when they arrived, told them what was happening.

Porthos drew his sword from the scabbard and began to make passes at the wall, springing back from time to time and contorting his body like a dancer.

Aramis, who was still working on his poem, shut himself up in Athos's study and begged not to be disturbed again until it was time to draw their swords.

Athos, by signs, asked Grimaud for another bottle of wine.

D'Artagnan employed himself in arranging a little plan, of which we shall later see the execution and which promised him some agreeable adventure, as might be seen by the smiles that occasionally animated his otherwise thoughtful countenance.

31

Englishmen and Frenchmen

THE HOUR HAVING COME, they went with their four lackeys to a spot behind the Luxembourg that had been abandoned to the goats. Athos gave some money to the goatkeeper to withdraw, and the lackeys were ordered to act as sentries.

A silent party soon approached the same enclosure, entered, and joined the Musketeers. Then, according to foreign custom, the introductions took place.

The Englishmen were noblemen, so the odd names of

their adversaries were for them not only a matter of surprise but of annoyance.

"After all," said Lord de Winter when the three friends had been named, "we do not know who you are. We cannot fight with such names—they are the names of shepherds."

"Therefore your lordship must understand they are only assumed names," said Athos.

"Which only gives us a greater desire to know the real ones," replied the Englishman.

"You gambled very willingly with us without knowing our names," said Athos. "In proof of which you won our horses."

"That is true, but then we risked only our pistoles—this time we risk our blood. One may gamble with anybody, but one may fight only with equals."

"That is true," Athos said, and he took aside the one of the four Englishmen with whom he was to fight, and communicated his name in a low voice.

Porthos and Aramis did the same.

"Does that satisfy you?" Athos asked his adversary. "Do you find me of sufficient rank to do me the honor of crossing swords with me?"

"Yes, monsieur," said the Englishman, bowing.

"Very well, but shall I tell you something?" Athos added, coolly.

"What?" replied the Englishman.

"Why, that you would have acted more wisely by not requiring me to make myself known."

"Why?"

"Because I am believed to be dead and have reasons for wishing nobody to know I am living, so I shall be obliged to kill you to prevent my secret from coming out."

The Englishman looked at Athos, believing that he jested; but Athos did not jest the least in the world.

"Gentlemen," said Athos, addressing at the same time his companions and their adversaries, "are we ready?"

"Yes!" answered the Englishmen and the Frenchmen, as with one voice.

"On guard, then!" cried Athos.

Immediately eight swords glittered in the rays of the

setting sun, and the combat began with an animosity very natural between men who were enemies on two accounts.

Athos fenced as calmly and methodically as if he had been practicing in a fencing school.

Porthos, cured of his too-great confidence by his adventure in Chantilly, was both skillful and prudent.

Aramis, who had the third canto of his poem to finish, behaved like a man in a hurry.

Athos killed his adversary first. He hit him only once, but as he had predicted, the hit was a mortal one; the sword pierced his heart.

Porthos was second, and he had his man down on the grass with a wound through his thigh. Without making any further resistance, the Englishman surrendered his sword, and Porthos took him up in his arms and bore him to his carriage.

Aramis attacked his opponent so vigorously that after the man was forced back fifty paces, he ended by taking to his heels and disppearing amid the jeers of the lackeys.

D'Artagnan fought purely and simply on the defensive, and when he saw that his adversary was tired, he sent the man's sword flying with a vigorous side thrust. The baron, finding himself disarmed, took two or three steps backward, but his foot slipped and he fell.

D'Artagnan was over him at a bound and, putting his sword to the Englishman's throat, said, "I could kill you, my Lord, and you are completely in my hands. But I spare your life for the sake of your sister."

D'Artagnan was overjoyed; he had begun to implement the plan he had imagined beforehand, that plan whose picturing had produced the smiles we had noted before.

The Englishman, delighted at having to do with a gentleman of such a kind disposition, hugged d'Artagnan and paid a thousand compliments to the three Musketeers, and since Porthos's adversary was already installed in the carriage and Aramis's had taken to his heels, they had nothing to think about but the dead man.

As Porthos and Aramis were undressing him in the hope of finding his wound not mortal, a large purse dropped from his clothes. D'Artagnan picked it up and offered it to Lord de Winter.

"What the devil do you want me to do with that?" asked the Englishman.

"You can restore it to his family," said d'Artagnan.

"His family will not care much about such a trifle as that! His family will inherit fifteen thousand louis a year from him. Give the money to your lackeys."

D'Artagnan put the purse into his pocket.

"And now, my young friend, for you will permit me, I hope, to give you that name," said Lord de Winter, "on this very evening, if it is agreeable to you, I will present you to my sister. I would like her to take you into her good graces, for she is well thought of at court and may some day speak a word that will be useful to you."

D'Artagnan blushed with pleasure and bowed a sign of agreement.

Just then Athos came up to d'Artagnan.

"What do you mean to do with that purse?" he whispered.

"Why, I meant to give it to you, Athos."

"Me! Why to me?"

"Why, you killed him! This is the spoils of victory."

"I, the heir of an enemy!" said Athos. "For whom do you take me?"

"It is the custom in war," said d'Artagnan, "so why should it not be the custom in a duel?"

"I have never done that even on the field of battle."

Porthos shrugged his shoulders; Aramis by a movement of his lips endorsed Athos.

"Then," said d'Artagnan, "let us give the money to the lackeys, as Lord de Winter wished us to do."

"Yes," said Athos, "let us give the money to the lackeys—not to our lackeys, but to the lackeys of the Englishmen."

Athos took the purse and threw it to the coachman. "For you and your comrades."

This greatness of spirit in a man who was quite destitute struck even Porthos; and when this French generosity was reported by Lord de Winter and his friend, it was highly applauded by everyone—except by monsieurs Grimaud, Bazin, Mousqueton, and Planchet.

Lord de Winter, on leaving d'Artagnan, gave him his sister's address. She lived in the Place Royale—then the fashionable quarter—at Number 6, and he promised to call and take d'Artagnan with him in order to introduce him. D'Artagnan named eight o'clock at Athos's residence as the time and place.

This introduction to Milady greatly preoccupied our Gascon. He remembered how strangely this woman had hitherto been mixed up in his destiny. He was sure she was some creature of the cardinal, yet he felt himself inexorably drawn to her by some inexplicable sentiments. His only fear was that Milady would recognize him as the man of Meung and of Dover. Then she would know that he was one of M. de Tréville's friends and therefore belonged body and soul to the king—which would make him lose some of his advantage, since if Milady knew him as he knew her, he would be playing against her as only an equal. As to any intrigue between her and M. de Wardes, our presumptuous hero worried very little about that. The count was young, handsome, rich, and high in the cardinal's favor, but it is not for nothing that we are twenty years old, especially if we were born at Tarbes.

D'Artagnan began by dressing himself splendidly, then he returned to Athos's and as usual, related everything to him. Athos listened to his projects, then shook his head and, with a shade of bitterness, advised him to be prudent.

"You have just lost one woman, whom you call good, charming, perfect, and here you are, running headlong after another!" he said.

D'Artagnan felt the truth of this reproach.

"I loved Madame Bonacieux with my heart, while I only love Milady with my head," he said. "In getting introduced to her, my principal object is to discover her role at court."

"Her role, *pardieu!* After all you have told me, it is not difficult to figure that out. She is some emissary of the cardinal—a woman who will draw you into a snare in which you will leave your head."

"My dear Athos, I think you see the dark side of things!"

"D'Artagnan, I do not trust women, particularly fair women. Can it be otherwise? I bought my experience dearly. Milady is fair, you say?"

"She has the most beautiful blond hair imaginable!"

"Ah, my poor d'Artagnan!" said Athos.

"Listen to me! I just want to understand things. Then, when I have learned what I wish to know, I will withdraw."

"Understand things," Athos repeated phlegmatically.

Lord de Winter arrived at the appointed time; but Athos, warned of his coming, went into another room. The Englishman therefore found d'Artagnan alone, and since it was nearly eight o'clock they left together.

An elegant carriage waited below, and as it was drawn by two excellent horses, they were soon at Place Royale.

Milady received d'Artagnan ceremoniously. Her house was remarkably sumptuous, and while most of the English had left or were about to leave France because of the war, Milady had recently been spending much money on her residence—which proved that the general measure that was expelling the English from France did not affect her.

"You see here," said Lord de Winter, presenting d'Artagnan to his sister, "a young gentleman who held my life in his hands and who did not abuse his advantage—although we were twice enemies since it was I who insulted him and since I am an Englishman. Thank him, then, madame, if you have any affection for me."

Milady frowned slightly; a scarcely visible cloud passed over her face, and a peculiar smile appeared upon her lips; d'Artagnan, who saw this triple response, almost shuddered at it.

Her brother did not notice it; he had turned around to play with Milady's favorite monkey, which had pulled him by the doublet.

"You are welcome, monsieur," said Milady, in a voice whose singular sweetness contrasted with the signs of ill-humor d'Artagnan had just observed. "You have today acquired eternal rights to my gratitude."

The Englishman then turned around again and described the combat without omitting a single detail. Milady listened with the greatest attention, yet it was easy to see, despite her effort to conceal her feelings, that the recital was not agreeable to her. Her blood rose, and her little foot tapped impatiently beneath her gown.

Lord de Winter saw nothing of all this.

When he had finished his story, he went to a table upon which was a tray with Spanish wine and glasses. He filled two glasses and by a gesture invited d'Artagnan to drink.

D'Artagnan knew that the Englishman would consider it rude if he refused to drink with him. He therefore approached the table and took the second glass. He did not, however, lose sight of Milady, and in a mirror he perceived the change that came over her face. Now that she believed herself to be no longer observed, her expression was almost ferocious, and she bit into her handkerchief with her beautiful teeth.

Then the pretty little maid came in. She spoke some words to Lord de Winter in English, and he thereupon requested d'Artagnan's permission to withdraw, excusing himself on account of the urgency of the business that had called him away and asking his sister to obtain his pardon.

D'Artagnan shook hands with Lord de Winter, then returned to Milady. Her surprisingly mobile face had recovered its gracious expression, but some little red spots on her handkerchief indicated that she had bitten her lips till the blood came.

Those lips were magnificent; they might have been made of coral.

The conversation took a cheerful turn. Milady appeared to have entirely recovered. She told d'Artagnan that Lord de Winter was actually her brother-in-law, not her brother. She had married a younger brother of the family, who had left her a widow with one child. This child was Lord de Winter's only heir if Lord de Winter did not marry. D'Artagnan understood that there was a veil which concealed something, but so far he could not see under that veil.

In addition, after a half hour's conversation d'Artagnan was convinced that Milady was his compatriot: she spoke French with an elegance and a purity that left no doubt on that head.

D'Artagnan was profuse in gallant speeches and protestations of devotion. To all the rubbish that escaped our Gascon's lips, Milady replied with a kindly smile. When the time came for him to leave, he said goodbye to Milady, and walked out of the saloon the happiest of men.

On the staircase he met the pretty maid, who brushed gently against him as she passed, and then, blushing, asked his pardon for having touched him in a voice so sweet that the pardon was granted instantly.

D'Artagnan came again the next day, and was received even more cordially than on the evening before. Lord de Winter was not there, and it was Milady who did all the honors of the evening. She appeared to take a great interest in him, asking where he came from, who his friends were, and whether he had not sometimes thought of attaching himself to the cardinal.

As we know, d'Artagnan was exceedingly prudent for a young man of twenty; he remembered his suspicions regarding Milady and launched into a eulogy of his Eminence, saying he would certainly have entered the cardinal's Guards instead of the king's Guards if he had happened to know M. de Cavois instead of M. de Tréville.

Milady changed the subject easily, and asked him in the most careless manner possible if he had ever been in England.

He replied that he had been sent there by M. de Tréville to negotiate for some horses and that he had brought back four samples.

In the course of the conversation Milady bit her lips a few times; she was dealing with a wily and cautious Gascon.

D'Artagnan left at the same time as on the preceding evening. In the corridor he again met the pretty maid, who was named Kitty; she looked at him with a friendly expression it was impossible to mistake, but he was so preoccupied by the mistress that he could pay no attention to anyone else.

He went back the next day and the day after that, and each day Milady received him more graciously.

Every evening, either in the anteroom, the corridor, or on the stairs, he met the pretty Kitty, but he paid no attention to her persistence.

32

Lunch at the Procurator's

HOWEVER BRILLIANT Porthos's part in the duel, it had not made him forget the lunch to which he had been invited by the procurator's wife.

At about one o'clock the next day he received the last touches of Mousqueton's brush, then made his way toward the Rue aux Ours with the steps of a man who was doubly favored by fortune.

His heart beat, but not like d'Artagnan's with a young and impatient love. No, a more material interest stirred his blood; he was finally about to pass that mysterious threshold, to climb those unknown stairs, beyond which lay all the écus M. Coquenard had one by one amassed. He was about to see in reality a certain chest of which he had twenty times beheld the image in his dreams—a chest long and deep, locked, bolted, fastened to the wall; a coffer of which he had so often heard, and which the hands—a little wrinkled, it is true, but not without elegance—of the procurator's wife were about to open to his admiring looks.

And then he—a wanderer on the earth, a man without fortune, a man without family, a soldier accustomed to inns, taverns, and restaurants, a lover of wine forced to depend on chance treats—was about to partake of family meals, to enjoy the pleasures of a comfortable establishment, and to give himself up to those little attentions which are pleasing even to the most hardened soldier.

To come in the capacity of a cousin and seat himself every day at a good table; to smooth the yellow, wrinkled brow of the old procurator; to pluck a few feathers from the clerks by teaching them the five points of *bassette,* *passe-dix,* and *lansquenet* and winning from them a month's savings by way of fee for the lesson he would give them in an hour—all this delighted Porthos.

The Musketeer was perfectly aware of the prevailing reputation of procurators—a reputation for meanness, greed, and setting a skimpy table that has survived to the present day—but the procurator's wife had been by and large tolerably generous to him (at least for a procurator's wife), and he hoped to find himself in an extremely comfortable household.

And yet at the very door the Musketeer began to entertain some doubts. The approach was not very prepossessing—an ill-smelling, dark passage, a staircase with barred windows that admitted a dim light from a neighboring courtyard; a first-floor low door studded with enormous nails like the principal gate of the Grand-Châtelet.

Porthos knocked. A tall, pale clerk, his face half-hidden by a forest of virgin hair, opened the door and bowed with the air of a man forced at once to respect in another man a lofty stature, which indicated strength; a military dress, which indicated rank; and a ruddy countenance, which indicated familiarity with good living.

A shorter clerk came behind the first, a taller clerk behind the second, a twelve-year-old errand boy behind the third. In all, three and a half clerks, which, for the time, indicated a very extensive clientele.

Although the Musketeer was not expected before one o'clock, the procurator's wife had been on the watch ever since midday, reckoning that her lover's heart, or perhaps his stomach, would bring him earlier.

Mme. Coquenard therefore came in from the house at the same moment her guest entered from the stairs, and the appearance of the worthy lady relieved him from an awkward embarrassment. The clerk surveyed him with great curiosity, and he, not knowing what to say to this ascending and descending scale, remained tongue-tied.

"It is my cousin!" cried the procurator's wife. "Come in, come in, Monsieur Porthos!"

The name of Porthos produced its effect upon the clerks, who began to laugh; but Porthos turned sharply around, and every face quickly recovered its gravity.

After having passed through the anteroom in which the clerks were, and the office in which they ought to have been, they reached the office of the procurator. This was a dark and littered room; leaving it, they had the kitchen on the right and the reception room straight ahead.

All these rooms, which communicated with one another, did not impress Porthos favorably. One could hear everything through the open doors. Then too, while passing, he had cast a quick but observant glance into the kitchen; and he was obliged to acknowledge—to the shame of the procurator's wife and to his own regret—that he did not see that enthusiasm, that animation, that bustle, which generally prevails when a good meal is being prepared.

The procurator had undoubtedly been warned of his visit, for he expressed no surprise at the sight of Porthos, who advanced toward him with a sufficiently easy manner, and greeted him courteously.

"We are cousins, it appears, Monsieur Porthos?" said the procurator, rising by supporting his weight on the arms of his cane chair.

The gaunt old man was wrapped in a large black doubtlet that concealed his whole body. His little gray eyes shone like carbuncles and, together with his grinning mouth, seemed to be the only part of his face in which life survived. Unfortunately, during the last five or six months, his legs had begun to fail, and since then, he had become almost slavishly dependent on his wife.

The cousin was received with resignation, nothing more. M. Coquenard, had his legs been firm, would have declined any relationship with M. Porthos.

"Yes, monsieur, we are cousins," said Porthos, without being disconcerted, since he had never counted on being received enthusiastically by the husband.

"On the female side, I believe?" said the procurator maliciously.

Porthos did not hear the sarcasm and took it for mere simplicity, which he laughed at behind his large mustache. Mme. Coquenard, who knew that a simpleminded procurator was a very rare variety in the species, smiled a little and blushed a great deal.

Since Porthos's arrival, M. Coquenard had frequently glanced uneasily at a large chest in front of his oak desk. Porthos understood that this chest, although its shape did not correspond with what he had seen in his dreams, must be the blessed coffer, and he congratulated himself that the reality was several feet higher than the dream.

M. Coquenard did not carry his genealogical investigations any further, but withdrawing his anxious look from the chest and fixing it upon Porthos, he contented himself with saying, "Monsieur our cousin will do us the favor of dining with us once before his departure for the campaign, will he not, Madame Coquenard?"

This time Porthos received the blow right in his stomach and felt it.

Mme. Coquenard was no less affected by it, for she added, "My cousin will not return if we do not treat him kindly, but even if we do, he has so little time to spend in Paris, and consequently to spare to us, that we must beg him to give us every minute he can call his own before he has to leave."

"Oh, my legs, my poor legs, where are you?" murmured Coquenard, and he tried to smile.

This relief, which came to Porthos at the moment in which he was attacked in his gastronomic hopes, made him feel very grateful to the procurator's wife.

Lunch time soon arrived, and they went into the dining room—a large dark room opposite the kitchen.

The clerks, who seemed to have smelled unusual aromas in the house, were of military punctuality, and they held their stools in their hands, ready to sit down immediately. Their jaws were already moving in a frightening way.

Looking at the three hungry clerks—for the errand boy, as might be expected, was not admitted to the honors of the magisterial table—Porthos thought, "If I were my cousin, I certainly would not employ such gourmands! They look like shipwrecked sailors who haven't eaten for six weeks!"

M. Coquenard came in, pushed along in his armchair on casters by Mme. Coquenard, whom Porthos assisted in rolling her husband up to the table.

He had scarcely entered when he began to agitate his nose and his jaws, just like his clerks.

"Oh," he said, "here is an inviting soup."

"What the devil is so extraordinary about this soup?" Porthos wondered, seeing only a pale liquid, abundant but entirely without meat and with just a few rare crusts swimming in it.

Mme. Coquenard smiled, and at a gesture from her everyone eagerly took his seat.

M. Coquenard was served first, then Porthos; afterward Mme. Coquenard filled her own plate and distributed the crusts without soup to the impatient clerks. When the door of the dining room creaked open, Porthos could see through the half-open flap the little errand boy who was not allowed to take part in the feast and who was eating his dry bread in the passage, enjoying the double odor of the dining room and the kitchen.

After the soup the maid brought in a boiled chicken—a bit of magnificence that caused the eyes of the diners to open so wide that they seemed ready to burst.

"It is clear that you love your family, Madame Coquenard," said the procurator, with a smile that was almost tragic. "You are certainly treating your cousin very handsomely!"

The poor fowl was thin, and its skin was thick and bristly, the kind it was impossible to bite through. It must have been necessary to look a long time before finding it on the perch to which it had retired to die of old age.

"The devil," thought Porthos, "this is very sad. I respect old age, but I don't much like it boiled or roasted."

And he looked around to see if anybody shared his opinion; but on the contrary, he saw nothing but eager eyes devouring in anticipation that sublime fowl which was the object of his contempt.

Mme. Coquenard drew the dish toward her; skillfully detached the two large black feet, which she placed on her husband's plate; cut off the neck, which with the head she put on one side for herself; detached the wing for Porthos; and then returned the bird otherwise intact to the servant who had brought it in and who disappeared with it before the Musketeeer had time to examine the various expressions that disappointment produces according to the characters and temperaments of those who experience it.

In the place of the fowl a dish of broad beans made its appearance—an enormous dish in which were some mutton bones that initially appeared to have some meat on them.

But the clerks were not deceived by appearances, and their lugubrious looks settled down into simple resignation.

Mme. Coquenard distributed this dish to the young men with the moderation of a careful housewife.

Then it was time for the wine. M. Coquenard poured from a very small stone bottle a third of a glass for each of the young men, served himself about the same amount, and passed the bottle to Porthos and Mme. Coquenard.

The young men added water to their third of a glass; then, when they had drunk half the glass, they filled it up again, and continued to do so. By the end of the meal they were swallowing a drink which had gone from the color of the ruby to that of a pale topaz.

Porthos ate his chicken wing timidly, and shuddered when he felt the knee of the procurator's wife searching for his under the table. He also drank half a glass of this sparingly served wine and recognized it as nothing but that horrible Montreuil—the terror of all discriminating palates.

M. Coquenard saw him swallowing the undiluted wine, and sighed.

"Will you have any of these beans, Cousin Porthos?" asked Mme. Coquenard, in that tone which says, "Take my advice, don't touch them."

"Devil take me if I taste one of them!" murmured Porthos to himself, and then said aloud, "Thank you, my cousin, I am no longer hungry."

Silence fell. Porthos didn't know where or how to look. The procurator repeated several times, "Ah, Madame Coquenard, accept my compliments—your dinner has been a real feast. Lord, how I have eaten!"

M. Coquenard had eaten his soup, the black feet of the fowl, and the only mutton bone on which there was the least appearance of meat.

Porthos thought they were teasing him and began to curl his mustache and knit his eyebrows, but Mme. Coquenard's knee gently advised him to be patient.

This silence, and this interruption in serving, which were meaningless to Porthos, had on the contrary a terrible meaning for the clerks. At a look from the procurator, accompanied by a smile from Mme. Coquenard, they rose slowly from the table, folded their napkins more slowly still, bowed, and left the room.

"Go, young men, go help your digestion by working," said the procurator gravely.

The clerks gone, Mme. Coquenard rose and took from

a buffet a piece of cheese, some preserved quinces, and a cake that she herself had made of almonds and honey.

M. Coquenard frowned because there were too many good things; Porthos bit his lips because there was nothing to eat.

He looked to see if the dish of beans was still there; it had disappeared.

"A positive feast!" cried M. Coquenard, agitating in his chair. "A real feast, *epulæ epulorum*. Lucullus dines with Lucullus."

Porthos looked at the bottle, which was near him, and hoped that with wine, bread, and cheese he might make a meal; but there was no wine: the bottle was empty. M. and Mme. Coquenard did not seem to notice.

Porthos passed his tongue over a spoonful of preserves and stuck his teeth into Mme. Coquenard's sticky pastry.

"Now," he said, "the sacrifice is consummated! Ah, if I did not hope to peep with Madame Coquenard into her husband's chest . . ."

M. Coquenard, after the luxuries of such a repast—which he called an excess—felt the need of a siesta. Porthos began to hope that this would take place then and there; but the procurator would not hear of it. He insisted he be taken to his room and was not satisfied till he was close to his chest, upon the edge of which, as an additional precaution, he placed his feet.

The procurator's wife took Porthos into an adjoining room, and they began to negotiate a reconciliation.

"You can come and dine three times a week," said Mme. Coquenard.

"Thanks, madame," said Porthos, "but I don't like to abuse your kindness. Besides, I must think of my equipment!"

"That's true," said the procurator's wife, groaning, "that unfortunate campaign outfit!"

"Alas, yes," said Porthos, "the outfit."

"But what does your company's equipment consist of, Monsieur Porthos?"

"Oh, of many things!" said Porthos. "As you know, the Musketeers are picked soldiers, and they require many things that would be useless to the Guardsmen or the Swiss."

"Tell me exactly what they are."

"Why, they may amount to . . ." said Porthos, who preferred discussing the total to enumerating the items one by one.

The procurator's wife was trembling.

"To how much? I hope it is not more than . . ."

She stopped; speech failed her.

"Oh, no, it is not more than two thousand five hundred livres! I think that with economy I could even manage it with two thousand livres."

"Good God, two thousand livres! Why, that is a fortune!"

Porthos grimaced significantly; Mme. Coquenard understood.

"I wish to know the exact details," she said, "because I have many relatives in business, and I am almost sure I can obtain things at a hundred percent less than you would pay yourself."

"Oh, that is what you meant to say!"

"Yes, dear Monsieur Porthos. For instance, don't you need a horse?"

"Yes."

"Well, I have just the thing for you."

"Ah," said Porthos, brightening, "that's fine as regards my horse, but I must also have all the trappings, which include objects only a Musketeer can purchase, but which will not amount to more than three hundred livres."

"Three hundred livres? Then put down three hundred livres," said the procurator's wife with a sigh.

Porthos smiled. It may be remembered that he had the saddle that came from Buckingham, so he counted on slyly slipping those three hundred livres into his pocket.

"Then," he continued, "my lackey needs a horse and I need a portmanteau. It is useless to trouble you about my arms—I have them."

"A horse for your lackey?" the procurator's wife repeated hesitantly. "But that is doing things in lordly style, my friend."

"Ah, madame," said Porthos haughtily, "do you take me for a beggar?"

"No, I only say that a pretty mule sometimes looks as good as a horse, and it seemed to me that by getting a pretty mule for Mousqueton . . ."

"Well, agreed for a pretty mule," said Porthos. "You are right—I have seen very great Spanish nobles whose whole retinue was mounted on mules. But you understand, Madame Coquenard—a mule with feathers and bells."

"Do not worry," said the procurator's wife.

"There remains the portmanteau," Porthos added.

"Oh, don't let that disturb you! My husband has five or six, and you can choose the best. There is one in particular which he prefers in his journeys—large enough to hold all the world."

"The portmanteau is empty?" asked Porthos with false innocence.

"Certainly it is empty," replied the procurator's wife, in real innocence.

"Ah, but the one I want is a well-filled one, my dear."

Madame sighed again. Molière had not yet written his scene in *L'Avare,* so Mme. Coquenard was in advance of Harpagan.

The rest of the equipment was successively debated in the same manner, and the result was that the procurator's wife would ask her husband for a loan of eight hundred livres and provide the horse and the mule that would have the honor of carrying Porthos and Mousqueton to glory.

These conditions being agreed to, and the date on which the loan came due and the rate of interest determined, Porthos took leave of Mme. Coquenard. She tried to detain him with tender glances; but Porthos pled the call of duty, and the procurator's wife was obliged to cede to the king.

The Musketeer returned home hungry and in a bad temper.

Maid and Mistress

MEANWHILE, DESPITE THE CRIES of his conscience and
the wise counsels of Athos, d'Artagnan fell hourly more
in love with Milady and never failed to pay his daily
court to her; the venturesome Gascon was convinced that
sooner or later she would have to respond.

One day, when he arrived with his head in the air and
his heart as light as if he were expecting a shower of
gold, he met the maid under the porte cochère; this time
the pretty Kitty was not content with touching him as he
passed, but took him gently by the hand.

"Good," thought d'Artagnan, "she has some message
for me from her mistress, who has arranged some rendezvous in this way."

He looked at the pretty girl with the most triumphant
air imaginable.

"I would like to say a few words to you, Monsieur le
Chevalier," she stammered.

"Speak, my child, speak," said d'Artagnan. "I am
listening."

"Here? Impossible! What I have to say is too long and,
above all, too secret."

"Well, what shall we do?"

"If Monsieur le Chevalier would follow me?" Kitty
asked, timidly.

"Wherever you wish, my dear child."

"Then come."

And Kitty, who still held d'Artagnan's hand, led him
up a small, dark, winding staircase and, after having
climbed about fifteen steps, opened a door.

"Come in, Monsieur le Chevalier," she said. "We will
be alone here, and can talk."

"Whose room is this, my dear child?"

"It is mine, Monsieur le Chevalier. It communicates
with my mistress's by that door, but you need not fear—

she will not hear us because she never goes to bed before midnight."

D'Artagnan glanced around him. The little room was charming in its taste and neatness; but in spite of himself, his eyes were drawn to the door which Kitty had said led to Milady's room.

Kitty guessed what was going through the young man's mind and sighed deeply.

"You love my mistress, Monsieur le Chevalier?" she asked.

"Oh, more than I can say, Kitty! I am mad for her!"

Kitty sighed again.

"Alas, monsieur, that is too bad."

"Why the devil is it so bad?"

"Because, monsieur, my mistress does not love you at all."

"Did she ask you to tell me so?"

"Oh, no, monsieur, but I resolved to tell you because of the regard I have for you."

"Much obliged, my dear Kitty, but only for the intention—you must agree that the information is not likely to be at all agreeable."

"You don't really believe what I have told you, do you?"

"It is always difficult to believe such things, my dear, if only out of self-love."

"Then you don't believe me?" she repeated.

"I confess that unless you give me some proof of what you say . . . ?"

"What do you think of this?"

Kitty took a little note from her bodice.

"For me?" d'Artagnan asked, grabbing the letter.

"No, someone else."

"For someone else?"

"Yes."

"His name, his name!"

"Read the address."

"Monsieur le Comte de Wardes."

The memory of the scene at St. Germain presented itself to the mind of the presumptuous Gascon. As quick as thought, he tore open the letter, in spite of the cry that Kitty uttered on seeing what he was going to do— or rather, what he was doing.

"Oh, my God, Monsieur le Chevalier," she said, "what are you doing?"

"I?" said d'Artagnan. "Nothing."

And he read:

You have not answered my first note. Are you indisposed, or have you forgotten the glances you favored me with at Mme. de Guise's ball? Now is your opportunity, Count—do not allow it to escape.

D'Artagnan turned pale; he was wounded in his *self-love*, though he thought it was in his *love*.

"Poor dear Monsieur d'Artagnan," said Kitty compassionately, again taking the young man's hand.

"You pity me, little one?"

"Oh, yes, and with all my heart, for I know what it is to be in love."

"You know what it is to be in love?" d'Artagnan asked, looking at her for the first time with some attention.

"Alas, yes."

"Well, then, instead of pitying me, you would do much better to help me revenge myself on your mistress."

"And what sort of revenge do you want?"

"I want to triumph over her, and supplant my rival."

"I will never help you in that, Monsieur le Chevalier," said Kitty heatedly.

"Why not?"

"For two reasons."

"What are they?"

"The first is that my mistress will never love you."

"How do you know that?"

"You have cut her to the heart."

"I? How can I have offended her—I who have lived at her feet like a slave ever since I have known her? Speak, I beg you!"

"I will never tell that to anyone but the man . . . who can read to the bottom of my soul!"

D'Artagnan looked at Kitty again. The young girl had a freshness and a beauty that many duchesses would have given their coronets for.

"Kitty," he said, "I will read to the bottom of your soul whenever you like. Don't let that disturb you."

And he gave her a kiss that made the poor girl become as red as a cherry.

"Oh, no, it is not me you love! It is my mistress—you just told me so."

"And does that stop you from letting me know the second reason?"

"The second reason, Monsieur le Chevalier," replied Kitty, emboldened first by the kiss and then by the expression of the young man's eyes, "is that in love, everyone for herself!"

Only then did d'Artagnan remember Kitty's languishing glances; her constant meetings with him in the anteroom, the corridor, or on the stairs; those touches of the hand every time she met him; her deep sighs. Absorbed by his desire to please the great lady, he had disdained the maid: he who chases the eagle pays no attention to the sparrow.

Now, however, our Gascon saw at a glance all the advantage to be derived from the love Kitty had just confessed so innocently—or so boldly: the interception of letters addressed to the Comte de Wardes, news on the spot, entrance at all hours into Kitty's room, which was adjacent to her mistress's. The perfidious deceiver was already preparing to sacrifice poor Kitty in order to obtain Milady, willynilly.

"Well," he said to the young girl, "are you willing, my dear Kitty, to allow me to prove that love which you doubt?"

"What love?" she asked.

"The love I am ready to feel toward you."

"And how will you prove that?"

"Are you willing to allow me this evening to spend with you the time I generally spend with your mistress?"

"Oh, yes," said Kitty, clapping her hands, "very willing."

"Then come here, my dear," said d'Artagnan, establishing himself in an easy chair, "and let me tell you that you are the prettiest maid I ever saw!"

And he told her so much and so well that the poor girl, who asked nothing better than to believe him, did believe him—although to his great astonishment, the pretty Kitty defended herself resolutely.

Time passes quickly when it is passed in attacks and

defenses. Midnight sounded, and at almost the same time the bell was rung in Milady's room.

"My God, my mistress is calling me! You must leave immediately!"

D'Artagnan rose, took his hat as if he intended to obey, then quickly opened the door of a large closet instead of the one leading to the staircase and hid himself among Milady's robes and dressing gowns.

"What are you doing?" cried Kitty.

D'Artagnan, who had previously taken the key, shut himself up in the closet without replying.

"Well," said Milady sharply, "are you asleep, that you don't answer when I ring?"

And d'Artagnan heard the communicating door open violently.

"Here I am, Milady!" said Kitty, springing forward to meet her mistress.

Both went into Milady's bedroom, and as the door remained open, d'Artagnan could hear Milady scolding her maid. Finally she was appeased, and the conversation turned to him while Kitty was assisting her mistress.

"I have not seen our Gascon this evening," said Milady.

"What, Milady, he did not come?" said Kitty. "Can he be fickle even before being happy?"

"Oh, no, he must have been prevented from coming by Monsieur de Tréville or Monsieur Des Essarts. I understand my game, Kitty, and I have this one safe."

"What will you do with him, madame?"

"What will I do with him? Kitty, there is something between that man and me that he is quite ignorant of—he nearly made me lose my standing with his Eminence, and believe me, I will be revenged!"

"I thought Madame loved him."

"Love him? I detest him! An idiot, who held Lord de Winter's life in his hands and did not kill him, thus depriving me of three hundred thousand livres' income!"

"True, your son is his uncle's only heir, and you would have had the use of his fortune until his majority."

D'Artagnan shuddered to the very marrow of his bones at hearing this suave creature reproach him—with that sharp voice which she took such pains to conceal in conversation—for not having killed a man whom he had seen to be overwhelmingly kind to her.

"I would have revenged myself on him for that long ago if, for reasons I do not understand, the cardinal had not asked me to handle him tactfully."

"Yes, but Madame has not been equally tactful with that little woman he was so fond of."

"The haberdasher's wife from the Rue des Fossoyeurs? He has already forgotten that she ever existed! Fine vengeance that!"

A cold sweat ran down d'Artagnan's brow. The woman was a monster!

He resumed his listening, but unfortunately the nightly preparations for bed were finished.

"That will do," said Milady. "Go to your own room, and tomorrow try again to get me an answer to the letter I gave you."

"For Monsieur de Wardes?" Kitty asked.

"To be sure, for Monsieur de Wardes."

"Now, *there* is one," said Kitty, "who seems quite a different sort of a man from that poor Monsieur d'Artagnan."

"Go to bed, mademoiselle," said Milady. "I do not like personal comments."

D'Artagnan first heard the door close, then the noise of the two bolts by which Milady locked herself in. On her side, as softly as possible, Kitty turned the key of the lock, and then d'Artagnan opened the closet door.

"What is the matter with you? How pale you are!" said Kitty in a low voice.

"The abominable creature!" murmured d'Artagnan.

"Silence! Silence and begone!" said Kitty. "There is only a partition between my room and Milady's—every word spoken in one can be heard in the other."

"That is exactly why I won't go," said d'Artagnan.

"What!" said Kitty, blushing.

"Or at least—I won't go . . . till later."

He drew Kitty to him. There was no way to resist without making noise, so this time Kitty surrendered.

It was an act of vengeance upon Milady. D'Artagnan believed that vengeance is the pleasure of the gods; with a little more heart, he might have been contented with this new conquest, but we must admit that the principal features of his character were ambition and pride.

However, it must also be said in his justification that the first use he made of his influence over Kitty was to try to find out what had become of Mme. Bonacieux; but the poor girl swore on the cross that she had no idea—her mistress never admitted her into half her secrets—and all she could say was that she thought Mme. Bonacieux was not dead.

As to that which had nearly made Milady lose her credit with the cardinal, Kitty knew nothing about it: this time d'Artagnan was better informed than she was. Since he had seen Milady on board a ship at the moment he was leaving England, it was almost certain that it was a question of the diamond studs.

But what was clearest in all this was that Milady's true hatred, profound hatred, inveterate hatred, was due to his not having killed her brother-in-law.

D'Artagnan returned to Milady's the next day and found her in a very bad mood, doubtless because of the lack of an answer from M. de Wardes. Kitty came in, but Milady was very cross with her. The poor girl ventured a glance at d'Artagnan which said, "See how I suffer on your account!"

Toward the end of the evening, however, the beautiful lioness became milder; she smilingly listened to d'Artagnan's soft speeches and even gave him her hand to kiss.

He left, not knowing what to think; but since he was a youth who did not easily lose his head, while continuing to pay his court to Milady, he had thought up a little plan.

He found Kitty at the gate, and, as on the preceding evening, went up to her room. She had been accused of negligence and severely scolded. Milady could not understand the Comte de Wardes's silence, and she had ordered Kitty to come at nine o'clock in the morning to take a third letter.

D'Artagnan made Kitty promise to bring him that letter the next morning. The poor girl promised everything her lover desired: she was madly in love.

Everything was the same as on the night before. D'Artagnan concealed himself in his closet; Milady called, undressed, sent Kitty away, and shut the door. Also as on the night before, d'Artagnan did not return home till five o'clock in the morning.

At eleven o'clock Kitty came to him. She held in her hand a fresh note from Milady. This time the poor girl did not even try to argue with d'Artagnan, but gave it to him at once. She belonged body and soul to her handsome soldier.

D'Artagnan opened the letter and read as follows:

> This is the third time I have written to tell you that I love you. Beware that I do not write a fourth time to tell you that I detest you.
>
> If you repent of the manner in which you have acted toward me, the young girl who brings you this will tell you how a man of spirit may obtain his pardon.

D'Artagnan colored and grew pale several times as he read this note.

"Oh, you still love her!" said Kitty, who had not taken her eyes off the young man's face for an instant.

"No, Kitty, you are mistaken. I do not love her anymore, but I will avenge myself for her contempt."

"Oh, yes, I know what sort of vengeance! You told me!"

"What does it matter to you, Kitty? You know you are the only one I love."

"How can I know that?"

"By the scorn I will show her."

D'Artagnan took a pen and wrote:

> MADAME,
> Until the present moment I could not believe that it was to me your first two letters were addressed, so unworthy did I feel myself of such an honor; besides, I was so seriously indisposed that I could not in any case have replied to them.
>
> But now I am forced to believe in the excess of your kindness, since not only your letter but your servant assures me that I have the good fortune to be beloved by you.
>
> She has no need to teach me the way in which a

man of spirit may obtain his pardon. I will come and ask mine at eleven o'clock this evening.

To delay it a single day would now be in my eyes to commit a fresh offense.

From him whom you have rendered the happiest of men,

COMTE DE WARDES

This note was in the first place a forgery, then an indelicacy, and even, according to our present manners, almost an infamous action; but at that time people did not manage affairs as they do today. Besides, d'Artagnan knew from Milady's own admission that she was guilty of treachery in more important matters, and he could feel no respect for her. Yet despite this lack of respect, he felt an uncontrollable passion for this woman boiling in his veins—a passion heightened by contempt, but passion nevertheless.

D'Artagnan's plan was very simple. Through Kitty's room he could enter that of her mistress. He would take advantage of the first moment of surprise, shame, and terror to triumph over her. He might fail, but some things must be left to chance. The campaign would begin in eight days, and he would have to leave Paris; there was no time for a prolonged siege.

"Give that to Milady. It is the count's reply," he said, handing Kitty the sealed letter.

Poor Kitty turned deathly pale; she suspected what the letter contained.

"Listen, my dear girl," said d'Artagnan, "you must surely see that all this must end, one way or another. Milady may discover that you gave the first note to my lackey instead of to the count's, or that it was I who opened the others, which ought to have been opened by the Comte de Wardes. Then she will turn you out, and you know she is not the woman to stop there."

"Alas, for whom have I exposed myself to all that?"

"I know it was for me, my sweet girl, and I am grateful, I swear."

"But what does this note say?"

"Milady will tell you."

"Ah, you do not love me," cried Kitty, "and I am very unhappy!"

To this reproach there is one response that always fools a woman. D'Artagnan replied in such a manner that Kitty remained fooled.

Although she cried freely before deciding to give the letter to her mistress, she did at last decide to do so, which was all d'Artagnan wished.

Besides, he promised that he would leave her mistress early that evening, and that when he did, he would go up to her. This promise completely consoled poor Kitty.

34

More About Aramis's and Porthos's Equipment

DURING THE TIME the four friends had been searching for their equipment, they had not had many fixed meetings. They dined apart from one another, wherever they might happen to be, or rather wherever they could. Military duty also took up a portion of the precious time that was slipping away so rapidly. But they had agreed to meet once a week, about one o'clock, at Athos's apartment; they had to meet there because he was faithful to his vow not to cross the threshold of his door.

The day they were to meet was the same day that Kitty visited d'Artagnan. As soon as she left him, he headed for the Rue Férou.

He found Athos and Aramis philosophizing. Aramis was again inclining to the priesthood. Athos, according to his system, neither encouraged nor discouraged him, believing that everyone should be left to his own free will. He never gave advice except when it was asked, and even then he had to be asked twice.

"People in general," he said, "only ask advice in order not to follow it—or if they do follow it, it is for the sake of having someone to blame for having given it."

Porthos arrived a minute after d'Artagnan. The four friends were reunited.

Their four faces expressed four different feelings: that

of Porthos, tranquillity; that of d'Artagnan, hope; that of Aramis, uneasiness; that of Athos, unconcern.

At the end of a moment's conversation, in which Porthos hinted that a lady of high rank had condescended to relieve him from his embarrassment, Mousqueton came in and begged his master to return to his lodgings, where his presence was urgently requested.

"Is it about my equipment?"

"Yes and no," replied Mousqueton.

"What do you mean?"

"Please come, monsieur."

Porthos rose, said goodbye to his friends, and followed Mousqueton.

A few minutes later, Bazin appeared at the door.

"What do you want with me, my friend?" said Aramis, with that mildness of language that characterized his speech whenever his ideas were directed toward the Church.

"A man wishes to see Monsieur at home," replied Bazin.

"A man! What man?"

"A beggar."

"Give him alms, Bazin, and ask him to pray for a poor sinner."

"This beggar insists on speaking only to you, and he insists that you will be very glad to see him."

"Has he sent a particular message for me?"

"Yes. 'If Monsieur Aramis is reluctant to come,' " he said, " 'tell him I come from Tours.' "

"From Tours!" cried Aramis. "A thousand pardons, gentlemen, but this man surely brings me news I have been waiting for."

And he too rose and hurried away.

Athos and d'Artagnan remained alone.

"I believe those fellows have managed to find their equipment. What do you think, d'Artagnan?" said Athos.

"I know that Porthos was already in the process of doing so," replied d'Artagnan, "and to tell you the truth, I have never been seriously uneasy about Aramis. But you, Athos—you, who so generously distributed the Englishman's pistoles, which were your legitimate property—what are you going to do?"

"I am not sorry to have killed that fellow, my boy, since one Englishman the less is always a blessing. But if I had pocketed his pistoles, they would have weighed me down like remorse."

"You do have some extraordinary ideas!"

"Never mind that. When Monsieur de Tréville called on me yesterday, he said that you have been associating with those English friends of the cardinal. What did he mean?"

"Well, I visit an Englishwoman—the one I told you about."

"Oh, yes—the fair woman about whom I gave you advice, which naturally you took care not to follow."

"I gave you my reasons."

"Yes, I think you said you were looking for your equipment there."

"Not at all! I am now certain that that woman was involved in Madame Bonacieux's abduction."

"Yes, I understand—to find one woman, you court another. It is the longest road, but certainly the most amusing."

D'Artagnan was on the point of telling Athos everything, but there was one consideration that kept him from doing so. Athos was a gentleman, punctilious in all points of honor; and there were certain things in the plan our lover had devised for Milady that this severely moral man would not approve of. He therefore remained silent, and as Athos was the least inquisitive man on earth, he asked no questions and d'Artagnan went no further with his confidence.

The two friends had nothing important to say to each other, so we will leave them and follow Aramis.

We have seen how quickly the young man followed, or rather preceded, Bazin on being informed that the person who wanted to speak to him came from Tours; he ran without stopping from the Rue Férou to the Rue de Vaugirard.

Entering his apartment, he found a short, poorly dressed man with intelligent eyes waiting for him.

"You asked for me?" said the Musketeer.

"I asked for Monsieur Aramis. Is that your name, monsieur?"

"My very own. You have brought me something?"

"Yes, if you show me a certain embroidered handkerchief."

"Here it is. Look," said Aramis, taking a small key from his breast and opening a little ebony box inlaid with mother of pearl.

"All right," replied the beggar, "dismiss your lackey."

In fact, Bazin, curious to know what the beggar could want with his master, had kept pace with him as well as he could, and arrived at almost the same time he did—but to no avail. As the beggar requested, Aramis motioned Bazin to leave, and he was obliged to obey.

Bazin gone, the beggar looked quickly around to be sure that nobody could either see or hear him, and opening his ragged vest, badly held together by a leather strap, he began to rip open the upper part of his doublet, from which he took a letter.

Aramis shouted with joy at the sight of the seal, kissed the writing with an almost religious respect, and opened the epistle, which contained what follows:

MY FRIEND,

It is the will of fate that we should still be separated, but the delightful days of youth are not lost beyond return. Perform your duty in camp; I will do mine elsewhere. Accept that which the bearer brings you, make the campaign like a handsome and true gentleman, and think of me, who kisses tenderly your black eyes.

Adieu—or rather, au revoir.

The beggar continued to rip his garments and drew from his rags a hundred and fifty Spanish double pistoles, which he laid down on the table; then he opened the door, bowed, and went out before the young man, stupefied by his letter, could venture to address a word to him.

Aramis then reread the letter and noticed a postscript:

P.S. You may treat the bearer well; he is a count and a grandee of Spain!

"Golden dreams!" cried Aramis. "Oh, life is beautiful life! Yes, we are young, yes, we shall yet have happy days! My love, my blood, my life—all, all, all, are yours, my adored mistress!"

And he kissed the letter with passion, not even glancing at the gold that sparkled on the table.

Bazin scratched at the door, and since Aramis no longer had any reason to exclude him, he told him to come in.

Bazin was stunned at the sight of the gold and forgot that he had come to announce d'Artagnan, who had been curious to know who the beggar could be and had therefore come to Aramis after Athos.

D'Artagnan was not at all formal with Aramis, so seeing that Bazin forgot to announce him, he announced himself.

"If those are the plums sent to you from Tours, please present my compliments to the gardener who gathers them," said d'Artagnan seeing the coins.

"You are mistaken, d'Artagnan," said Aramis, always on his guard. "This is from my publisher, who has just paid me for the poem in one-syllable verse that I began while we were away."

"Your publisher is very generous, my dear Aramis, that's all I can say," said d'Artagnan.

"Monsieur," said Bazin, "it is unbelievable that a poem should sell for such a sum! Why, you can write as much as you like—you may become the equal of Monsieur de Voiture and Monsieur de Benserade. I like that. A poet is almost as good as a priest. Ah, Monsieur Aramis, become a poet, I beg you."

"Bazin, my friend, I believe you are meddling in my conversation," said Aramis.

Bazin understood he was wrong; he bowed his head and went out.

"You sell your productions for their weight in gold," said d'Artagnan with a smile. "You are very fortunate, my friend—but be careful or you will lose that letter which is peeping out from your doublet and which no doubt also comes from your publisher."

Aramis blushed, crammed the letter back in, and rebuttoned his doublet.

"My dear d'Artagnan," he said, "if you please, we will join our friends, as I am rich, we will begin to dine together again today, at my expense, while we wait for the rest of you to be rich too."

"With great pleasure. It has been a long time since we have had a good dinner, and since I have a somewhat hazardous expedition planned for this evening, I will not be sorry to fortify myself with a few glasses of good Burgundy."

"Agreed, for the good Burgundy! I myself would have no objection to that," said Aramis, from whom the letter and the gold had banished, as by magic, his ideas of conversion.

And having put three or four double pistoles into his pocket to answer the needs of the moment, he placed the others in the ebony box, inlaid with mother of pearl, in which was the famous handkerchief that had served him as a talisman.

The two friends went to Athos's, and he, faithful to his vow of not going out, took it upon himself to order a dinner to be brought to them. Since he understood all the details of gastronomy perfectly, d'Artagnan and Aramis were perfectly content to leave this important matter in his hands.

They were on the way to Porthos when they met Mousqueton at the corner of the Rue du Bac; looking most pitiable, he was driving before him a mule and a horse.

D'Artagnan called out in surprise and joy.

"My yellow horse!" he cried. "Aramis, look at that horse!"

"Oh, the frightful brute!" said Aramis.

"Well, my friend," replied d'Artagnan, "upon that very horse I came to Paris."

"Does Monsieur know this horse?" asked Mousqueton.

"It has an original color," said Aramis. "I've never seen one like it in my life."

"I can well believe it," said d'Artagnan, "and that was why I got three écus for him. It must have been for his hide, because the carcass is certainly not worth eighteen livres. But how do you happen to have this horse, Mousqueton?"

"Please," said the lackey, "say nothing about it, monsieur—it is a frightful trick played by the husband of our duchess!"

"What do you mean, Mousqueton?"

"Why, we are looked upon with a rather favorable eye by a lady of quality, the Duchesse de . . . but pardon me, my master has ordered me to be discreet. She had forced us to accept a little souvenir—a magnificent Spanish *genet* and an Andalusian mule, which were both beautiful. The husband heard of it, and he confiscated the two magnificent beasts that were being sent to us and substituted these horrible animals!"

"Which you are taking back to him?" said d'Artagnan.

"Exactly!" replied Mousqueton. "You can understand that we will not accept such steeds as these in exchange for those which had been promised to us."

"No, *pardieu*—though I should like to have seen Porthos on my yellow horse! It would have given me an idea of how I looked when I arrived in Paris. But don't let us stop you, Mousqueton—go do as your master ordered. Is he at home?"

"Yes, monsieur," said Mousqueton, "but in a very bad humor."

He continued toward the Quai des Grands Augustins while the two friends went to ring the bell of the unfortunate Porthos. Having seen them crossing the courtyard, he took care not to answer, and they rang in vain.

Meanwhile Mousqueton crossed the Pont Neuf, and still driving the two miserable-looking animals before him, he reached the Rue aux Ours. Once there, following the orders of his master, he fastened both horse and mule to the knocker of the procurator's door; then, without any thought for their future, he returned to Porthos and told him that he had completed his mission.

In a short time the two unfortunate beasts, who had not eaten anything since morning, began to make such a noise in raising and letting fall the knocker that the procurator ordered his errand boy to find out to whom the horse and mule belonged.

Mme. Coquenard recognized her present and could not at first understand its return; but a visit from Porthos soon enlightened her. The anger that burned in the Musketeer's eyes, despite his efforts to suppress it, terrified his sensitive inamorata. Actually, Mousqueton had told his master that he had met d'Artagnan and Aramis, and that d'Artagnan had recognized the yellow horse as the Béarnese pony on which he had come to Paris and which he had sold for three écus.

Porthos left after having arranged a meeting with the procurator's wife in the St. Magloire cloister. The procurator, seeing he was going, invited him to dinner—an invitation the Musketeer majestically refused.

A trembling Mme. Coquenard arrived at the St. Magloire cloister, for she could guess the reproaches that awaited her there; but she was fascinated by Porthos's lofty airs.

All the curses and reproaches that a man wounded in his self-love could let fall upon the head of a woman Porthos let fall upon the bowed head of the procurator's wife.

"Alas," she said, "I thought it was for the best! One of our clients is a horsedealer. He owes us money and is behind in his payments. I took the mule and the horse for what he owed us, and he assured me that they were two noble beasts."

"Well, madame, if he owed you more than five écus, your horsedealer is a thief," said Porthos.

"There is no harm in trying to buy things cheaply, Monsieur Porthos," said the procurator's wife, seeking to excuse herself.

"No, madame, but those who try to buy things cheaply ought to permit others to seek more generous friends."

And Porthos, turning on his heel, made a move to leave.

"Monsieur Porthos!" cried the procurator's wife. "I see that I have been wrong—I shouldn't have driven a bargain when it was to equip a cavalier like you."

Porthos, without replying, retreated a second step.

The procurator's wife fancied she saw him in a shimmering mist, surrounded by duchesses and marchionesses casting bags of money at his feet.

"Stop, in the name of heaven, Monsieur Porthos! Stop, and let us talk."

"Talking with you brings me misfortune."

"But tell me, what do you want?"

"Nothing, for that amounts to the same thing as if I asked you for something."

The procurator's wife hung upon his arm, and in the violence of her grief she cried out, "Monsieur Porthos, I don't know anything about such matters! Do I know what a horse is? Do I know what horse equipment is?"

"You should have left it to me, then, madame—I who

do know what they are. But you wished to be frugal—at my expense."

"It was wrong, Monsieur Porthos, but I will make up for that wrong, on my word of honor."

"How?" asked the Musketeer.

"Listen. This evening M. Coquenard is going to the house of the Duc de Chaulnes, who has sent for him. It is for a consultation that will last at least two hours. Come! We will be alone, and do our figuring."

"Finally! That is the right way to talk, my dear."

"You pardon me?"

"We shall see," said Porthos haughtily.

And they separated saying, "Till this evening."

"The devil," thought Porthos, as he walked away, "it looks as if I am finally getting close to Monsieur Coquenard's strongbox."

35

All Cats Are Gray in the Dark

THE EVENING so impatiently awaited by Porthos and by d'Artagnan at last arrived.

As usual, d'Artagnan presented himself at Milady's at about nine o'clock. He found her in a charming humor; never had he been so well received. Our Gascon knew immediately that his note had been delivered and that it had had its effect.

Kitty brought in some sherbet. Her mistress put on a charming face and smiled at her graciously; but alas, the poor girl was so sad that she did not even notice Milady's affability.

Looking at the two women, d'Artagnan was forced to acknowledge that Nature had made a mistake in their formation: to the great lady she had given a heart vile and venal; to the maid she had given the heart of a duchess.

At ten o'clock Milady began to seem restless. D'Artagnan understood what that meant. She looked at the clock, rose, reseated herself, smiled at d'Artagnan with an air that said, "You are very amiable, no doubt, but you would be *charming* if you would only leave."

He stood up and took his hat; Milady gave him her hand to kiss. The young man felt her press his hand and understood that this was not coquetry, but gratitude because he was leaving.

"She loves him madly," he thought as he left.

This time Kitty was not waiting for him anywhere—neither in the anteroom, nor in the corridor, nor at the porte cochère. He had to find the staircase and the little room by himself. She heard him enter, but did not raise her head. He went to her and took her hands, and then she began to sob.

As d'Artagnan had assumed, on receiving his letter, Milady joyfully told her servant everything, and as a reward for having executed her errand so well, she had given Kitty a purse. Returning to her own room, Kitty had thrown the purse into a corner, where it lay open, disgorging three or four gold pieces on the carpet. At the sound of d'Artagnan's voice, the poor girl lifted her head. He was frightened by the change in her countenance.

She put her hands together in a mute plea, a gesture of silent sorrow that touched even d'Artagnan's insensitive heart; but he clung too tenaciously to his projects—especially this one—to change his plans. He allowed her no hope that he would swerve even slightly, although he did say he was acting out of nothing but a desire for revenge.

This vengeance was becoming very easy, for Milady, doubtless to conceal her blushes from her lover, had ordered Kitty to extinguish all the lights, even in her own little room. Comte de Wardes would have to leave before daybreak, still in the dark.

They heard Milady entering her room. D'Artagnan slipped into the wardrobe and had hardly concealed himself when the little bell sounded.

Kitty went to her mistress, and although she closed the door, the partition was so thin that one could hear almost everything the two women said.

Milady was deliriously happy and made Kitty repeat the smallest details of her imaginary interview with the count: how he had responded to receiving the letter; what his expression was; if he seemed very much in love. To all those questions poor Kitty, forced to put a good face on things, responded in a choked voice whose miserable tones her mistress did not even notice, so egotistical is happiness.

Finally, as the hour for her rendezvous approached, Milady had Kitty darken the room, then ordered her to return to her own quarters and to bring the Comte de Wardes whenever he arrived.

Kitty did not have a long wait. As soon as d'Artagnan had seen, through a crack in his closet, that the whole apartment was dark, he slipped out of his hiding place.

"What is that noise?" Milady asked.

"It is I," said d'Artagnan softly. "I, the Comte de Wardes."

"Oh, my God," murmured Kitty, "he has not even waited for the time he himself had set."

"Why do you not enter, Count? You know that I am waiting for you," said Milady, in a trembling voice.

D'Artagnan quietly drew Kitty away and slipped into the room.

If ever a heart is tormented by rage or sorrow, it is when a lover receives under a name that is not his own protestations of love addressed to his happy rival. D'Artagnan was in just such a painful situation, which he had not foreseen; he was torn by jealousy, and he suffered almost as much as poor Kitty, who at that very moment was weeping in the next room.

"Yes, Count," said Milady, in her softest voice and holding his hand between hers, "I am happy in the love that your looks and your words have expressed every time we have met. I also—I love you. Oh, tomorrow I must have some pledge from you which will prove that you think of me—and so that you may not forget me, take this!" and she slipped a ring from her finger onto d'Artagnan's.

D'Artagnan remembered having seen this ring—a magnificent sapphire, encircled with diamonds—on Milady's finger, and his first movement was to return it; but Milady added, "No, no, keep the ring for love of me. Besides, in accepting it"—her voice was full of emotion—"you do me a much greater favor than you imagine."

"This woman is full of mysteries," d'Artagnan thought.

At that instant he felt himself ready to reveal everything! He opened his mouth to tell Milady who he was, and with what a revengeful purpose he had come; but then she added, "Poor angel, that monster of a Gascon almost killed you."

The monster was himself.

"Do your wounds still make you suffer?" she continued.

"Yes, very much," said d'Artagnan, who did not know how to answer.

"Do not worry," murmured Milady. "I will avenge you—and cruelly!"

"The moment for revelations has not yet come!" he thought.

It took him some time to get over this little dialogue; but by then, all his ideas of vengeance had completely vanished. This woman exercised an incredible power over him; he hated and adored her at the same time. He would never have believed that two such opposite sentiments could inhabit the same heart and, by their union, constitute so strange, and as it were, diabolical, a passion.

The clock struck one. It was necessary to separate. When he left Milady, he felt only the deepest regret, and as they said their reciprocally passionate adieux, they arranged another meeting for the following week.

Poor Kitty was hoping to speak to d'Artagnan when he passed through her room, but Milady herself conducted him through the darkness, leaving him only at the staircase.

The next morning d'Artagnan went to speak to Athos. He was involved in such a strange adventure that he wanted some advice, and therefore told Athos everything.

"Your Milady," said Athos, "appears to be an infamous creature, but you were nevertheless wrong to deceive her, for in one way or another you have a terrible enemy on your hands."

As he spoke, Athos was looking carefully at the sapphire set with diamonds; it had taken, on d'Artagnan's finger, the place of the queen's ring, which he had carefully put away in a jewel box.

"You are looking at my ring?" the Gascon asked, proud to display so rich a gift to his friend.

"Yes," said Athos, "it reminds me of a family jewel."

"It is beautiful, is it not?"

"Magnificent. I did not think two such fine sapphires existed. Did you trade your diamond for it?"

"No, it is a gift from my beautiful Englishwoman, or

rather Frenchwoman—for though I have not questioned her I am convinced she was born in France."

"That ring comes from Milady?" Athos asked in a voice charged with emotion.

"Her very self. She gave it to me last night."

"Show me the ring," said Athos.

"Here it is," replied d'Artagnan, taking it from his finger.

Athos paled as he examined it. He tried it on the ring finger of his left hand and it fit as if made for it. His usually calm face was shadowed by a fleeting expression of vengeful anger.

"It is impossible," he said. "How could this ring come into the hands of Milady? And yet it is difficult to believe two pieces of jewelry could be so alike."

"Do you know this ring?" d'Artagnan asked.

"I thought I did, but no doubt I was mistaken."

He returned the ring to d'Artagnan without ever taking his eyes off it.

"Please, d'Artagnan," he said after a minute, "either remove the ring or turn the mounting inside. It brings back such cruel memories that I cannot speak to you, and did you not want to ask my advice? Were you not saying that you don't know what to do . . . ? But wait— let me look at that sapphire again. The one I mentioned to you had one of its faces scratched by accident. . . ."

D'Artagnan took off the ring and again gave it to Athos, who winced.

"Look," he said, "is it not strange?"

And he pointed out to d'Artagnan the scratch he had remembered.

"But from whom did you get this ring, Athos?"

"From my mother, who inherited it from her mother. As I told you, it is an old family jewel, which was supposed to remain in the family forever."

"And you . . . sold it?" d'Artagnan asked hesitantly.

"No," replied Athos, with a strange smile, "I gave it away in a night of love, as it was given to you."

D'Artagnan became thoughtful. It seemed as if there were dark and unknown abysses in Milady's soul. He took back the ring, but put it in his pocket and not on his finger.

"D'Artagnan," said Athos, taking his hand, "you

know I love you. If I had a son, I could not love him
better. Take my advice, then, and give this woman up.
I do not know her, but a sort of intuition tells me that
she is a lost creature, and that there is something fatal
about her."

"You are right, and I will finish with her. I admit that
she terrifies me, too."

"Will you have the courage for that?"

"I will," replied d'Artagnan, "and I will do it
immediately."

"In truth, my young friend, you will be doing the right
thing," said Athos, grasping the Gascon's hand with an
almost paternal affection. "And God grant that this
woman, who has scarcely entered your life, may not
leave a terrible mark on it!"

And Athos bowed to d'Artagnan like a man who
wishes it understood that he would not be sorry to be
left alone with his thoughts.

Reaching home, d'Artagnan found Kitty waiting for
him; a month of fever could not have changed her more
than her one night of sleeplessness and sorrow.

She was sent by her mistress to the false Comte de
Wardes. Milady was mad with love, intoxicated with joy;
she wished to know if her lover would meet again, earlier
then planned.

And poor Kitty, pale and trembling, awaited d'Artagnan's reply. Athos had a great influence over d'Artagnan, and his friend's advice, joined to the cries of his
own heart, had made him decide—now that his pride
was saved and his vengeance satisfied—not to see Milady
again. As a reply, he wrote the following letter:

> Do not count on me, madame, for a prompt
> meeting. Since my convalescence I have so many
> affairs of this kind on my hands that I am forced
> to regulate them a little. When your turn comes, I
> will have the honor to inform you of it. I kiss your
> hands.
>
>   COMTE DE WARDES

Not a word about the sapphire. Was the Gascon determined to keep it as a weapon against Milady, or—let

us be frank—did he reserve it as a last resource for his equipment?

It would be wrong to judge the actions of one period from the point of view of another. What would now be considered disgraceful to a gentleman was at that time a very simple and natural affair, and the younger sons of the best families were frequently supported by their mistresses.

D'Artagnan gave the open letter to Kitty, who didn't understand it at first, but who became almost wild with joy on reading it a second time. She could scarcely believe in her happiness, and d'Artagnan was forced to give her in his own voice the same assurance she might have gotten from the letter. And whatever might be—considering the violent character of Milady—the danger the poor girl incurred in giving this note to her mistress, she ran back to the Place Royale as fast as her legs could carry her.

The heart of the best woman is pitiless toward the sorrows of a rival.

Milady opened the letter with an eagerness equal to Kitty's in bringing it, but at the first words she read she became livid. She crushed the paper in her hand, and turning with flashing eyes on Kitty, she cried, "What is this letter?"

"The answer to Madame's," replied Kitty, trembling.

"Impossible!" cried Milady. "A gentleman could not have written such a letter to a woman!" Then all at once, starting, she cried, "My God! can he have . . ." and she stopped. She ground her teeth; she was ashen. She tried to go toward the window for air, but she could only stretch out her arms; her legs failed her, and she sank into an armchair.

Kitty, fearing she was ill, hurried to open her dress, but Milady jumped up and pushed her away.

"What do you want with me?" she said. "Why do you place your hands on me?"

"I thought that Madame was feeling faint, and I wished to help her," responded the maid, frightened at her mistress's terrible expression.

"I feel faint? I? Do you take me for half a woman? When I am insulted I do not faint—I avenge myself!"

And she dismissed Kitty with a gesture.

36

Dreams of Vengeance

THAT EVENING Milady gave orders to admit M. d'Artagnan as soon as he came; but he did not come.

The next day Kitty went to see him again and told him everything that had happened the preceding evening. D'Artagnan smiled; Milady's jealous anger was his revenge.

That evening Milady was even more impatient than she had been the night before; she gave the same order about d'Artagnan, but as before, he did not come.

When Kitty appeared at d'Artagnan's the next morning, she was no longer joyous and alert, as on the two preceding days, but sad and depressed. He asked the poor girl what was troubling her; but her only reply was to take a letter from her pocket and give it to him.

It was in Milady's handwriting, but this time it was addressed to M. d'Artagnan, not to the Comte de Wardes.

He opened it and read as follows:

> DEAR M. D'ARTAGNAN,
> It is wrong to neglect your friends, particularly at the moment you are about to leave them for so long a time. My brother-in-law and I expected you yesterday and the day before, but in vain. Will it be the same this evening?
>
> Your very grateful,
> LADY DE WINTER

"I was expecting this letter. My credit rises as the Comte de Wardes's falls," said d'Artagnan.

"Will you go?" asked Kitty.

"Listen to me, my dear girl," he said, looking for an excuse in his own eyes for breaking the promise he had made Athos. "You must understand that it would be foolhardy not to accept such a pressing invitation. Milady, not seeing me come again, would not understand what could interrupt my visits and might suspect something. Who knows how far the vengeance of such a woman would go?"

"You know just how to represent things so that you are always in the right," said Kitty. "You are going to pay court to her again, and this time, if you succeed in pleasing her in your own name and with your own face, it will be much worse than before."

Instinct made poor Kitty able to guess a part of what was to happen.

D'Artagnan reassured her as well as he could, and promised to remain unmoved by Milady's seductions.

He asked Kitty to tell her mistress that he could not be more grateful for her kindnesses than he was, and that he would obey her wishes. He did not dare to write because he was afraid he could not disguise his writing sufficiently to fool such experienced eyes as those of Milady.

At exactly nine o'clock, he was at the Place Royale. It was evident that the servants waiting in the anteroom had been forewarned, for as soon as he appeared, before he had even asked if Milady was at home, one of them ran to announce him.

"Show him in," said Milady swiftly, but loudly enough for d'Artagnan to hear her in the anteroom.

He was presented.

"I am not home to anybody," said Milady. "Do you hear me? Not to *anybody*!"

The servant went out.

D'Artagnan looked at her curiously. She was pale and tired, either from tears or lack of sleep. Although the number of lights had deliberately been reduced, she could not conceal the traces of the fever that had been raging inside her for two days.

He approached with his usual gallantry, and she made an extraordinary effort to receive him; but never did a more distressed countenance give the lie to a more amiable smile.

To all his questions about her health, she replied, "Bad, very bad."

"Then my visit is ill-timed. You need to rest, and I will leave."

"No, on the contrary, stay, Monsieur d'Artagnan. Your agreeable company will distract me."

"Oh, oh!" thought d'Artagnan. "She has never been so kind before. On guard!"

Milady made herself as gracious as possible and spoke with more than her usual brilliancy. At the same time the fever, which had for an instant abandoned her, returned to give luster to her eyes, color to her cheeks and lips. D'Artagnan was again in the presence of the Circe who had once before enveloped him in her enchantments. His love, which he had believed extinct but which was only asleep, awoke again in his heart. She smiled, and he felt that he could allow himself to be damned for that smile.

There was even a moment when he felt something like remorse for what he had done to her.

By degrees, she became more communicative, finally asking him if he had a mistress.

"Alas," he answered, with the most soulful look he could assume, "can you be cruel enough to ask me such a question—me, who from the moment I saw you have only breathed and sighed through you and for you?"

Milady smiled strangely.

"Then you love me?" she asked.

"Do I have to tell you so? Have you not seen it?"

"Perhaps. But you know, the more the heart is worth the capture, the more difficult it is to be won."

"Oh, difficulties do not frighten me. I dread only impossibilities."

"Nothing is impossible to true love."

"Nothing, madame?"

"Nothing."

D'Artagnan thought, "This is a different tune. Is she going to fall in love with me, this fair inconstant? And will she give me in my own person another sapphire like the one she gave me as de Wardes?"

He drew his seat nearer hers.

"Well, now," she said, "let us see what you would do to prove this love of which you speak."

"Everything you could ask of me. Give me your orders—I am ready."

"For everything?"

"For everything!" he exclaimed, knowing beforehand that there was not much risk in promising this.

"Then let us talk a little," said Milady, now drawing her chair nearer to his.

"I am listening, madame," he said.

She remained thoughtful and undecided for a moment; then, as if seeming to come to a decision, she said, "I have an enemy."

"*You*, madame?" said d'Artagnan, affecting surprise. "Is that possible? My God, good and beautiful as you are!"

"A mortal enemy."

"Really?"

"An enemy who has insulted me so cruelly that between him and me it is war to the death. May I count on your assistance?"

D'Artagnan at once understood where the vindictive creature was heading.

"You may, madame," he said with emphasis. "My arm and my life belong to you, like my love."

"Then, since you are as generous as you are loving . . ." She stopped.

"Well?"

"Well," she continued after a moment of silence, "speak no more of impossibilities."

"Do not overwhelm me with happiness!" cried d'Artagnan, throwing himself on his knees and covering with kisses the hands abandoned to him.

As he was thus expressing his rapture, she was thinking, "Avenge me on that infamous de Wardes, and I will know how to get rid of you—you double idiot, you animated sword blade!"

"Hypocritical and dangerous woman," said d'Artagnan, likewise to himself, "fall voluntarily into my arms after having abused me with such effrontery, and afterward I will laugh at you with the one you wish me to kill."

D'Artagnan lifted his head.

"I am ready," he said.

"You have understood me, my dear Monsieur d'Artagnan!"

"Your eyes tell me what I need to know."

"Then you would lend me your arm, which has already won so much fame?"

"Instantly!"

"But how should I repay such a service? I know lovers—they are men who do nothing for nothing."

"You know what I wish to hear—the only reply worthy of you and of me!"

And he drew her toward him.

She scarcely resisted.

"I see you have your own reason," she said, smiling.

"Ah," he said, really carried away by the passion this woman had the power to kindle in his heart, "that is because my happiness seems so incredible to me that I am afraid it will vanish like a dream, and I wish to make a reality of it as quickly as possible."

"You must earn that happiness."

"I am at your orders."

"You are quite certain?" she asked, with a last doubt.

"Just name the infamous man who has brought tears to your beautiful eyes!"

"Who told you that I have been weeping?"

"It seemed to me . . ."

"Women like me never weep."

"So much the better! Come, tell me his name!"

"Remember that his name is my secret."

"Yet I must know it."

"Yes, you must. . . . See what confidence I have in you!"

"I am overcome with joy. What is his name?"

"You know him."

"Really?"

"Yes."

"He is surely not one of my friends?" he asked, affecting hesitation in order to make her believe him ignorant.

"If he were one of your friends, would you hesitate?" she asked sharply, a threatening glance darting from her eyes.

"Not if he were my own brother!" he replied, as if carried away by enthusiasm.

Our Gascon proceeded without risk, for he knew where he was going.

"I love your devotion," said Milady.

"Alas, do you love nothing else in me?"

"I love you also, *you!*" she said, taking his hand.

The warmth of her touch made him tremble, as if with that touch the fever that consumed Milady also attacked him.

"You love me!" he cried. "Oh, if that is so, I will lose my reason!"

And he enfolded her in his arms. She made no effort to remove her lips from his kisses, but she did not respond to them. Her lips were cold; he felt as if he had embraced a statue, but he was not the less intoxicated with joy, electrified by love. He almost believed in her tenderness; he almost believed in de Wardes's crime. If the count had at that moment been at hand, he would have killed him.

Milady seized the opportunity.

"His name is . . ."

"De Wardes. I know it," d'Artagnan said impetuously.

"How do you know it?" asked Milady, grasping both his hands and endeavoring to read with her eyes to the bottom of his heart.

He felt that he had allowed himself to be carried away, that he had made a serious error.

"Tell me, I say," she repeated. "How do you know it?"

"How do I know it?"

"Yes."

"I know it because yesterday the Comte de Wardes, in a drawing room where I also was, showed everyone a ring he said he had received from you."

"The wretch!" she cried.

The epithet, as may be imagined, resounded to the depths of d'Artagnan's soul.

"Well?" she asked.

"Well, I will avenge you of this wretch," he replied with theatrical pomposity.

"Thank you, my brave friend! And when will I be avenged?"

"Tomorrow—immediately—whenever you please!"

Milady was about to cry out, "Immediately," but she realized that such precipitation would not be very gracious toward d'Artagnan. Besides, she had a thousand precautions to take, a thousand counsels to give to her defender, in order that he might avoid explanations with the count in front of witnesses.

To all of this d'Artagnan answered, "Tomorrow you will be avenged, or I will be dead."

"No, you will avenge me, but you will not be dead. He is a coward."

"With women, perhaps—but not with men. I know something about him."

"But you had no reason to complain of your fortune in your previous contest with him."

"Fortune is a courtesan—she may have favored me yesterday, and betray me tomorrow."

"Which means that you now hesitate?"

"No, of course I do not hesitate. God forbid! But would it be just to allow me to go to a possible death without at least having given me something more than hope?"

Milady answered by a glance that said, "Is that all? Speak!" Then she accompanied the glance with tender explanatory words: "You are right—it would not be just."

"Oh, you are an angel!" he exclaimed.

"Then it is all arranged?"

"Except for what I am asking you for dear love."

"But when I assure you that you may rely on my tenderness?"

"I cannot wait till tomorrow."

"Silence! I hear my brother. There is no need for him to find you here."

She rang the bell and Kitty appeared.

"Go out this way," she said, opening a small private door, "and come back at eleven o'clock. We will then finish this conversation. Kitty will conduct you to my room."

The poor girl almost fainted at hearing those words.

"Well, mademoiselle, what are you thinking about, standing there like a statue? Do as I bid you—show the chevalier out, and this evening at eleven o'clock—you heard what I said!"

"It seems that all these appointments are made for eleven o'clock," thought d'Artagnan. "It must be a custom."

Milady held out her hand, which he kissed tenderly.

"I must not play the fool. This woman is certainly a great liar, and I must be careful," he thought as he left, paying no attention to Kitty's reproaches.

37

Milady's Secret

D'ARTAGNAN left the house instead of going up at once to Kitty's room—as she tried to persuade him to do—for two reasons: first, because that way he could escape reproaches, recriminations, and pleas; second, because he was not sorry to have an opportunity of examining his own thoughts and trying, if possible, to understand those of Milady.

What was most clear in the matter was that he loved her madly and that she did not love him at all. For one moment he understood that the best thing for him to do would be to go home and write Milady a long letter, in which he would confess that he and de Wardes were up to the present moment absolutely the same, and that consequently he could not undertake, without committing suicide, to kill the count. But he too was spurred on by a ferocious desire for vengeance: he wanted to possess this woman in his own name, and since this kind of vengeance seemed particularly sweet, he did not wish to renounce it.

He walked around the Place Royale six or seven times, turning every ten steps to look at the light in Milady's apartment, which could be seen through the slats of the shutters. It was evident that this time she was not in as much of a hurry to retire to her bedroom as she had been the first time.

At length the light disappeared, and with it was extinguished d'Artagnan's last irresolution. He recalled the details of the first night, and with a pounding heart and a brain on fire he reentered the house and rushed to Kitty's room.

The poor girl, deathly pale and trembling in every limb, wished to delay her lover; but Milady, her ears attuned to every sound, heard the noise d'Artagnan made, and opening the door, said, "Come in."

All this was so incredibly immodest, so monstrously

bold, that d'Artagnan could scarcely believe what he saw or heard. He felt he was being drawn into one of those fantastic intrigues one experiences in dreams.

Nevertheless, he ran not one bit less quickly toward Milady, yielding to an irresistible magnetic attraction.

As the door closed behind them Kitty threw herself at it. Jealousy, fury, offended pride—all the conflicting passions raging in the heart of a woman in love urged her to reveal the truth; but she realized that she would be totally lost if she confessed her part in such a plot and, above all, that d'Artagnan would be lost to her forever. This last thought decided her on this final sacrifice.

D'Artagnan had gained the summit of all his wishes. It was no longer a rival who was beloved, but himself. A secret voice whispered deep inside him that he was only an instrument of revenge, that he was only being caressed before being used to kill another; but pride, self-love, madness, silenced that voice and stifled its murmurs. Besides, our Gascon, who did not lack a certain amount of conceit, compared himself with de Wardes and asked himself why, after all, Milady could not love him as himself?

He was entirely absorbed by the sensations of the moment. He no longer thought of Milady as a treacherous woman who terrified him, but as an ardent, passionate mistress abandoning herself to a genuine love.

When the lovers' transports were calmer, Milady, who did not have the same motives for forgetfulness that d'Artagnan had, was the first to return to reality, and she asked the young man if he had already arranged the means for his next day's encounter with de Wardes.

But d'Artagnan, whose ideas had taken quite another direction, forgot himself like a fool and answered gallantly that he was much more interested in a different kind of duel.

This indifference toward her only real interest alarmed Milady, whose questions became ever more pressing.

Then d'Artagnan, who had never given any serious thought to this impossible duel, tried to change the subject. He did not succeed; Milady's irresistible determination and her iron will would not allow her to be distracted.

He fancied himself very cunning when he advised her to pardon de Wardes and renounce her insane projects.

But at his first word she winced, drew away from him, and exclaimed in a sharp, bantering tone that sounded strange in the darkness, "Are you afraid, dear Monsieur d'Artagnan?"

"You cannot think so, dear love!" he replied. "But suppose poor Comte de Wardes were less guilty than you think?"

"It doesn't matter," said Milady seriously. "He has deceived me, and from the moment he deceived me, he has deserved to die."

"Then he shall die, since you have condemned him!" d'Artagnan said, in so firm a tone that it seemed to Milady proof of an unshakable devotion.

She returned to his side.

We cannot say how long the night seemed to Milady, but d'Artagnan felt he had been there scarcely two hours before the sun began to peep through the window blinds and invade the room with its pale light.

Seeing him about to leave her, Milady reminded him of his promise to avenge her against the count.

"I am quite ready," he said, "but first I would like to be certain of one thing."

"What is that?"

"That you really love me."

"It seems to me I have given you proof of that."

"Yes, that is true. . . . And I am yours, body and soul!"

'Thank you, my brave lover! But just as I proved my love, you must in turn satisfy me of yours. Will you?"

"Certainly. But if you love me as much as you say, are you not a little afraid for me?"

"What should I be afraid of?"

"Why, that I may be dangerously wounded—even killed."

"Impossible!" cried Milady. "You are such a valiant man, and such an expert swordsman."

"Then you would not prefer a method that would equally avenge you while making the duel unnecessary?"

Milady looked at her lover in silence. That pale light of the first rays of day gave her clear eyes a strangely baleful expression.

"I really believe you now begin to hesitate," she said.

"No, I do not hesitate, but I pity poor de Wardes now that you no longer love him. I think the loss of your love is such a severe punishment that a man needs no other."

"Who told you that I loved him?" asked Milady sharply.

"At least I can now believe, without being too fatuous, that you love someone else," said the young man in a caressing tone, "and I am really concerned for the count."

"You?"

"Yes, I."

"And why *you*?"

"Because I alone know . . ."

"What do you know?"

"That he is far from being, or rather having been, so guilty toward you as it seems."

"Indeed!" said Milady anxiously. "Explain yourself, for I really do not know what you mean."

She looked at d'Artagnan, who was embracing her tenderly, with burning eyes.

"I am a man of honor," he said, determined to tell her everything, "and since I have your love—and I do, do I not?"

"Entirely. Go on."

"Well, I feel something weighing on my mind. I have a confession to make."

"A confession!"

"If I had the least doubt of your love I would not make it, but you do love me, my beautiful mistress, do you not?"

"Of course."

"Then if through excess of love I have been guilty toward you, you will pardon me?"

"Perhaps."

He tried to touch his lips to hers, but she evaded him.

"This confession," she said, turning pale. "What is this confession?"

"You had a rendezvous with de Wardes last Thursday in this very room, did you not?"

"No, no! That is not true," said Milady, her voice so firm, and her face so unchanged that if d'Artagnan had not had such perfect proof, he would have doubted his statement.

"Do not lie, my angel," he said, smiling. "It would be useless."

"What do you mean? Speak! You are killing me!"

"Oh, do not worry, you are not guilty toward me, and I have already pardoned you."

"Go on! Go on!"

"De Wardes cannot boast of anything."

"What do you mean? You told me yourself that that ring . . ."

"I have that ring! The Comte de Wardes of last Thursday and the d'Artagnan of today are the same person."

The imprudent young man expected her to be surprised, perhaps ashamed—a brief storm that would resolve itself in tears; but he was terribly wrong, and he was not left long in error.

Pale and terrifying, Milady repulsed d'Artagnan's attempted embrace by shoving him away violently as she sprang out of bed.

It was almost broad daylight.

He detained her by her fine batiste nightgown, intending to beg her pardon; but strong and determined, she tried to escape. The gown was torn from her beautiful shoulders, and on one of those lovely, round, white shoulders, d'Artagnan recognized, with inexpressible astonishment, the fleur-de-lis—the executioner's indelible brand of infamy.

"My God!" cried d'Artagnan, letting the gown drop from his hand and remaining mute, motionless, frozen.

But his very terror condemned him. He had seen all: he now knew her secret, her terrible secret, the secret she concealed so carefully even from her maid, the secret of which all the world was ignorant—except him.

She turned on him, no longer like a furious woman but like a wounded panther.

"You have basely betrayed me, and even worse, you have discovered my secret! You must die!"

And she ran to a small inlaid box on the dressing table, opened it with a feverish and trembling hand, took from it a small dagger with a golden haft and a sharp thin blade, and attacked him.

Although the young man was brave, as we know, he was terrified by her wild look, by those dilated pupils, pale cheeks, and bleeding lips. He recoiled, retreating to

the other side of the room as he would have done from
an approaching serpent, and when his hand, damp with
sweat, found his sword, he drew it almost unconsciously
from its scabbard.

Paying no attention to the sword, she tried to get close
enough to stab him, not stopping until she felt the sharp
point at her throat.

Then she tried to seize the blade with her hands, but
he kept it free from her grasp, and moving the point
back and forth between eyes and her breast, he managed
to get to the foot of the bed, hoping to retreat by the
door that led to Kitty's room.

During all this time Milady continued to strike at him
with horrible fury, shrieking in rage.

As all this, however, was a little like a duel, d'Artagnan soon began to recover himself.

"*Pardieu*, if you don't calm yourself, I will design a
second fleur-de-lis on your other shoulder!" he said.

"Scoundrel, infamous scoundrel!" Milady howled in a
frenzy.

But d'Artagnan continued to hold her at bay as he
drew nearer to Kitty's door.

Hearing the noise they made—Milady in overturning
the furniture in her efforts to get at d'Artagnan, he in
screening himself behind the furniture to keep out of her
reach—Kitty opened the door just as d'Artagnan maneu-
vered himself to within three paces from it. With one
leap he flew from Milady's room into Kitty's, and quick
as lightning, he slammed the door and put all his weight
against it while Kitty pushed the bolts.

With more than a woman's strength, Milady tried to
batter down the door; but when she realized that she
could not do it, she began to stab at the door with her
dagger, the point of which repeatedly pierced the wood.

Every blow was accompanied by a terrible curse.

"Quick, Kitty," d'Artagnan whispered as soon as the
bolts were fast, "help me get out of the house, for in a
few minutes it will occur to her to have me killed by the
servants."

"But you can't go out like that—you are almost naked!"

"That's true," he said, only then aware of his state of
undress. "Dress me as well as you can, but hurry—it's a
matter of life and death!"

Kitty was all too well aware of that. In a moment she muffled him up in a flowered dress, a large hood, and a cloak, gave him some slippers for his bare feet, and led him down the stairs. It was none too soon. Milady had already rung her bell and roused the household; the porter was just opening the door when Milady shouted from her window, "Don't open!"

The young man fled while she was still threatening him with an impotent gesture. The moment she lost sight of him, she fell into a faint.

38

How Athos Acquired His Equipment Without Any Effort

D'ARTAGNAN was so completely bewildered that he never gave a moment's thought to what might become of Kitty but ran at full speed across half Paris and did not stop till he came to Athos's door. The confusion of his mind, the terror that spurred him on, the shouts of some of the patrol pursuing him, and the jeers of the people who were going to their work at this early hour only made him rush the more.

He crossed the courtyard, ran up the two flights to Athos's apartment, and knocked at the door hard enough to nearly break it down.

Rubbing his half-open eyes, Grimaud came to answer the noisy summons, and d'Artagnan ran into the room with such violence that he nearly knocked the astonished lackey down.

It spite of his habitual silence, the poor lad this time found his tongue.

"Hold there!" he cried. "What do you want, you strumpet? What's your business here, you hussy?"

D'Artagnan threw off his hood and freed his hands from the folds of the cloak. Seeing the mustache and the naked sword, Grimaud realized it was a man.

He decided it must be an assassin. "Help! Murder! Help!" he shouted.

"Be quiet, you stupid fellow!" said the young man.

"I'm d'Artagnan. Don't you recognize me? Where is your master?"

"You, Monsieur d'Artagnan?" cried Grimaud. "Impossible!"

"Grimaud," said Athos, coming out of his room in a dressing gown, "I thought I heard you permitting yourself to speak?"

"Ah, monsieur, it is . . ."

"Silence!"

Grimaud contented himself with pointing to d'Artagnan.

Athos recognized his comrade, and phlegmatic as he was, he burst out laughing at the strange masquerade before his eyes—d'Artagnan with petticoats falling over his slippers, sleeves tucked up, and mustache quivering with agitation.

"Don't laugh, my friend!" cried d'Artagnan. "For heaven's sake, don't laugh! Upon my soul, it is no laughing matter!"

And he pronounced those words with such a solemn air and with such a real appearance of terror that Athos took his hand and exclaimed, "Are you wounded, my friend? How pale you are!"

"No, but I have just had a horrible experience! Are you alone, Athos?"

"*Parbleu!* Whom do you expect to find here at this hour?"

"All right, all right!"

And d'Artagnan rushed into Athos's room.

"Now speak!" said the latter, bolting the door so they would not be disturbed. "Is the king dead? Have you killed the cardinal? You are in a terrible state! Tell me— I am dying of curiosity and anxiety!"

"Athos," said d'Artagnan, taking off his female garments and appearing in his shirt, "prepare to hear an incredible, unbelievable, story."

"First put this dressing gown on," the Musketeer said to his friend.

D'Artagnan put it on as quickly as he could, so disturbed that he first thrust his arm into the wrong sleeve.

"Well?" said Athos.

"Well," replied d'Artagnan, leaning over to Athos's ear and lowering his voice, "Milady is marked with a fleur-de-lis on her shoulder!"

"Ah!" cried Athos, as if he had been shot in the heart.

"Are you *sure* that the *other* woman is really dead?" asked d'Artagnan.

"The other?" said Athos, his voice so stifled that d'Artagnan could hardly hear him.

"Yes, the one you told me about one day in Amiens."

Athos groaned, and put his head between his hands.

"This one is about twenty-six or twenty-eight years old."

"She is blonde, is she not?" asked Athos.

"Yes."

"Clear blue eyes, strangely brilliant, with black lashes and brows?"

"Yes."

"Tall? Well-formed? She has lost a tooth, next to the eyetooth on the left?"

"Yes."

"The fleur-de-lis is small, rosy in color, and looks as if she has tried to efface it by applying poultices?"

"Yes."

"But you said she is English."

"She is called Milady, but she is probably French. Lord de Winter is only her brother-in-law."

"I want to see her, d'Artagnan!"

"Beware, Athos. You tried to kill her, and she is a woman to do as much to you—and not to fail!"

"She will not dare say anything—that would be to denounce herself."

"She is capable of anything and everything! Did you ever see her in a rage?"

"No."

"A tigress, a panther! Oh, Athos, I am afraid I have subjected both of us to a terrible vengeance!"

D'Artagnan then told Athos everything about Milady's frenzied outburst and her threats to kill him.

"You are right—upon my soul, I believe my life hangs by a hair," said Athos. "Fortunately, we leave Paris the day after tomorrow. We are most probably going to La Rochelle, and once gone . . ."

"She will follow you to the end of the world, Athos, if she recognizes you. Let me be her only prey!"

"My dear friend, what does it matter if she kills me? Do you think I set any great store by life?"

"There is a terrible mystery behind all this, Athos. I am sure this woman is one of the cardinal's spies!"

"In that case, take care! If the cardinal does not admire you for what you did in London, he hates you for it. Since he cannot accuse you openly, and since hatred must be satisfied, particularly when it's a cardinal's hatred, I repeat—take care of yourself! If you go out, do not go out alone. When you eat, be on the alert. Mistrust everything, even your own shadow."

"Fortunately all this will only be necessary till after tomorrow evening, because once we are with the army, I hope we will have only men to fear."

"In the meantime," said Athos, "I renounce my plan to remain at home, and wherever you go, I will go with you. You must return to the Rue des Fossoyeurs—I will accompany you."

"But however near my apartment may be, I cannot go there dressed like this!"

"That's true," said Athos, and he rang the bell.

Grimaud came in.

Athos indicated to him by gestures that he was to go to d'Artagnan's apartment and bring back some clothes.

Grimaud replied by another gesture that he understood perfectly, and set off.

"None of this will help you with your uniform," said Athos, "because if I am not mistaken, you have left most of your uniform with Milady, who certainly will not be polite enough to return it to you. Fortunately, you still have the sapphire."

"The ring is yours, Athos! Did you not tell me it was a family jewel?"

"Yes, my grandfather paid two thousand écus for it, according to what he once told me. It was part of the wedding gift he gave his wife, and it is magnificent. My mother gave it to me, and like a fool, instead of keeping the ring as a holy relic, I gave it to that wretched woman."

"Then take it back, my friend. I see you value it highly."

"Take back the ring after it has passed through the hands of that infamous creature? Never! That ring is defiled, d'Artagnan."

"Then sell it."

"Sell a jewel that came from my mother! That would be sacrilege!"

"Then pawn it. You can borrow at least a thousand écus on it. With that, you can extricate yourself from your present difficulties, and when you have money again, you will be able to redeem it. It won't be defiled anymore because it will have passed through the hands of the usurers."

Athos smiled.

"You are a marvelous companion, d'Artagnan. You make poor unhappy souls feel better by your unfailing optimism! Very well, let us pawn the ring, but only on one condition."

"What?"

"That we divide the money—five hundred écus for you, and five hundred for me."

"What are you thinking of, Athos? I don't need the quarter of such a sum—I who am still only in the Guards—and I will get that by selling my saddle. What do I need? A horse for Planchet, that's all. Besides, you forget that I have a ring too."

"To which you attach more value than I do to mine, or at least, so it seems."

"Yes, because in some circumstances it might extricate us not only from great financial embarrassment, but from great danger. It is not just a valuable diamond—it is also a magic talisman."

"I do not understand, but I believe all you say. Let us return to my ring, or rather to yours. If you do not take half the sum you will get for it, I will throw it into the Seine—and I doubt if any fish will be sufficiently obliging to bring it back to us."

"Then I will take it," said d'Artagnan.

At that moment Grimaud returned, accompanied by Planchet; the latter, anxious about his master and curious to know what had happened to him, had taken advantage of the opportunity and brought the clothes himself.

D'Artagnan dressed himself, and Athos did the same. When they were ready to go out, the latter directed at Grimaud the gesture of a man taking aim, and the lackey immediately took down his musket and prepared to follow his master.

They arrived without incident at the Rue des Fosso-

yeurs. Bonacieux was standing at the door and looked at
d'Artagnan hatefully.

"Hurry, my dear lodger," he said. "There is a very
pretty girl waiting for you upstairs, and you know women
don't like to be kept waiting."

"It must be Kitty!" d'Artagnan thought, darting into
the passage.

It was indeed! He found the poor terrified girl crouching against the door of his apartment. As soon as she
saw him, she said, "You promised to protect me! You
promised to save me from her anger! Remember that, it
is you who have ruined me!"

"Yes, yes, I know, Kitty. Do not worry, my girl. But
what happened after I left?"

"How do I know? The servants came running when
they heard her shrieks. She was insane! There is no curse
she did not vomit out against you. Then I realized she
would remember that you had gotten into her room
through mine and would know that I was your accomplice, so I took what little money I had and the best of
my things, and I ran away."

"Poor child! But what am I going to do with you? I
am going away the day after tomorrow."

"Do what you please, Monsieur le Chevalier. Help me
leave Paris, help me leave France!"

"I cannot take you to the siege of La Rochelle!"

"No, but you can find me a place in one of the provinces with some lady of your acquaintance—in your own
province, for instance."

"My dear little love! In my province the ladies do without chambermaids! But wait—I have an idea. . . . Planchet, go find Aramis and ask him to come here
immediately. We have something very important to say to
him."

"I understand," said Athos, "but why not Porthos? I
would have thought that his duchess . . ."

"Oh, Porthos's duchess uses her husband's clerks as
chambermaids," said d'Artagnan, laughing. "Besides,
Kitty would not like to live in the Rue aux Ours. Would
you, Kitty?"

"I do not care where I live," she replied, "provided that
I am well concealed, and nobody knows where I am."

"Meanwhile, Kitty, now that we are about to separate and you are no longer jealous of me . . ."

"Monsieur le Chevalier, from far away or nearby, I will always love you."

"What an unlikely place to find such constancy," murmured Athos.

"And I will always love you, too, be sure of that," said d'Artagnan. "But now, tell me something. The question I am about to ask you is very important. Did you ever hear anything about a young woman who was carried off one night?"

"Oh, Monsieur le Chevalier, do you still love that woman?"

"No, no, one of my friends loves her—Monsieur Athos, this gentleman here."

"I?" cried Athos, sounding like a man who has just realized he is about to step on a snake.

"You, to be sure!" said d'Artagnan, pressing Athos's hand. "You know how interested we both are in this poor little Madame Bonacieux. Besides, Kitty won't say anything, will you, Kitty? You understand, my dear girl," he continued, "she is the wife of that ape you saw at the door as you came in."

"Oh, my God, you remind me of how frightened I was—I hope he didn't recognize me!"

"Recognize you? Did you ever see him before?"

"He came twice to Milady's."

"Ah . . . When?"

"Why, about fifteen or eighteen days ago."

"I see . . ."

"And he came again last night."

"Last night?"

"Yes, just before you yourself came."

"My dear Athos, we are enmeshed in a network of spies. And do you think he recognized you, Kitty?"

"I pulled down my hood as soon as I saw him, but it might have been too late."

"Go downstairs, Athos—he trusts you more than me—and see if he is still at his door."

Athos went down and returned immediately.

"He has gone," he said, "and the house door is shut."

"He went to make his report—to say that right now all the pigeons are in the dovecote."

"Then let us all fly away," said Athos, "and leave nobody here but Planchet to bring us news."

"What about Aramis? We sent Planchet for him."

"That is so," said Athos. "We must wait for Aramis."

At that moment Aramis walked in.

The matter was explained to him, and the friends made him understand that he must find a place for Kitty among his high connections.

Aramis thought for a minute, then asked, flushing, "Will it really be rendering you a service, d'Artagnan?"

"I will be grateful to you all my life!"

"Very well. Madame de Bois-Tracy asked me to find a trustworthy maid for one of her friends who lives somewhere in the provinces, I believe, if you can answer for Mademoiselle, my dear d'Artagnan . . ."

"Oh, monsieur, I will be entirely devoted to the person who will give me the means of leaving Paris."

"Then this works out very well," said Aramis.

He sat down at the table and wrote a little note, which he sealed with a ring, and then gave the note to Kitty.

"And now, my dear girl," said d'Artagnan, "you know that it is not safe for any of us to be here, so let us separate. We will meet again in better days."

"And whenever we find each other, wherever it may be," said Kitty, "you will find me loving you as I love you today."

"Worthless promises," said Athos, while d'Artagnan escorted Kitty downstairs.

A few minutes later the three young men separated, agreeing to meet again at four o'clock at Athos's and leaving Planchet to guard the house.

Aramis returned home, and Athos and d'Artagnan busied themselves in pawning the sapphire.

As the Gascon had foreseen, they easily obtained three hundred pistoles on the ring. In addition, the pawnbroker told them that he would give them five hundred pistoles for it if they would sell it to him, since it would make a magnificent pendant to go with some earrings he had.

With the energy of two soldiers and the knowledge of two connoisseurs, Athos and d'Artagnan took barely three hours to buy all the Musketeer's equipment. Athos was a nobleman to his fingertips: when a thing suited him he paid the asking price without even trying to argue. When d'Artagnan objected to this, Athos put his hand on his shoulder and smiled—and d'Artagnan understood that it was all very well for such a minor member of the Gascon aristocracy as himself to drive a bargain, but not for a great aristocrat.

The Musketeer found a superb jet-black, six-year-old Andalusian horse, with fiery nostrils and clean and elegant legs. He examined him, and found him sound and without blemish. They were asking a thousand livres for him; he might have been bought for less, but even as d'Artagnan was discussing the price with the dealer, Athos was counting out the money on the table.

Grimaud got a strong, short Picard cob, which cost three hundred livres.

But after the saddle and arms for Grimaud were purchased, Athos did not have one sou left of his hundred and fifty pistoles. D'Artagnan offered his friend a part of his share of the money they had gotten for the ring, saying he could return it when convenient.

Athos merely shrugged his shoulders and asked, "How much did the pawnbroker say he would give for the sapphire if he bought it?" said Athos.

"Five hundred pistoles."

"That is, two hundred pistoles more—a hundred for you and a hundred for me. That would be a real fortune to us, my friend. Go back to the pawnbroker."

"What, will you . . ."

"The ring would only remind me of very bitter memories, and besides, we will never have three hundred pistoles to redeem it, so we really would be losing two hundred pistoles this way. Go tell him the ring is his, d'Artagnan, and bring back the two hundred pistoles."

"Reflect, Athos!"

"We need ready money now, and we must learn how to make sacrifices. Go, d'Artagnan, go. Grimaud will accompany you with his musket."

A half hour later, d'Artagnan returned with the two thousand livres and without having met with any accident.

It was in this way that Athos found unexpected resources at home and acquired his equipment without any effort.

39

A Vision

AT FOUR O'CLOCK the four friends were together again at Athos's. Their anxiety about their equipment had disappeared, and the expression on each face was only of its own secret worry—for behind all present happiness is concealed a fear for the future.

Suddenly Planchet entered, bringing two letters for d'Artagnan.

One was a small note, genteelly folded, with a pretty green-wax seal showing a dove bearing a green branch.

The other was a large square epistle, resplendent with the imposing coat of arms of his Eminence the cardinal duke.

D'Artagnan's heart leapt at the sight of the small note, for he thought he recognized the handwriting: although he had only seen that writing once, the memory of it was engraved in his heart.

He therefore opened the small note eagerly.

> Be on the road to Chaillot next Wednesday between six and seven o'clock in the evening, and look carefully into the carriages that pass; but if you value your own life or the lives of those who love you, do not speak a single word, do not make a single movement, that might lead anyone to believe you have recognized the one who exposes herself to everything for the sake of seeing you for an instant.

No signature.

"It's a trap," said Athos. "Don't go, d'Artagnan."

"But I think I recognize the writing," he replied.

"It may be a forgery," said Athos. "The Chaillot road is quite deserted between six and seven o'clock—you might as well go and ride in the forest of Bondy."

"But suppose we all go!" said d'Artagnan. "What the

devil—they can't devour all four of us plus our four lackeys, our horses, and our arms!"

"Besides, it will give us a chance to display our new equipment," said Porthos.

"But if it is a woman who writes," said Aramis, "and if that woman does not wish to be seen, you would be compromising her, d'Artagnan—which is something no gentleman should ever do."

"We will remain in the background," said Porthos, "and he will advance alone."

"Yes, but a pistol is easily fired from a galloping carriage."

"Bah," said d'Artagnan, "they will miss me! Then we'll ride after the carriage and exterminate everyone in it. At least that way there will be fewer enemies!"

"He is right," said Porthos. "We'll fight. Besides, we must try out our new arms."

"Indeed, let us enjoy that pleasure," said Aramis, with his mild and nonchalant manner.

"As you please," said Athos.

"Gentlemen," said d'Artagnan, "it is half past four, and we barely have enough time to be on the Chaillot road by six."

"And if we go out too late, nobody will see us," said Porthos, "and that would be a pity. Let us get ready, gentlemen."

"But you forget the second letter," said Athos. "Yet it seems to me that the seal indicates it deserves to be opened. For my part, d'Artagnan, I think it much more important than the little bit of frivolity you have so carefully slipped next to your heart."

D'Artagnan blushed.

"Well," he said, "let us see, gentlemen, what his Eminence wants of me."

D'Artagnan unsealed the letter and read:

M. d'Artagnan, of the king's Guards, company Des Essarts, is expected at the Palais-Cardinal this evening at eight o'clock.

LA HOUDINIERE, *Captain of the Guards*

"This is a much more serious rendezvous than the other," said Athos.

"I will go to the second after the first," said d'Artagnan. "One is for seven o'clock, and the other for eight—there will be time for both."

"I would not go to the second one at all," said Aramis. "A gallant gentleman cannot decline a rendezvous with a lady, but a prudent gentleman may excuse himself from paying a visit to his Eminence, particularly when he has reason to believe he is not invited there to listen to pretty speeches."

"I agree with Aramis," said Porthos.

"Gentlemen," replied d'Artagnan, "I have already had a similar invitation from his Eminence, delivered by Monsieur de Cavois. I ignored it, and the next day something terrible happened to me—Constance disappeared. Whatever the result may be, I will go."

"If you are determined," said Athos, "then go."

"But the Bastille?" asked Aramis.

"If they put me there, you will get me out!" d'Artagnan replied.

"Of course we would," said Aramis and Porthos, with admirable promptness and decision, as if it were the simplest thing in the world. "Of course we would get you out. But since we are to set off the day after tomorrow, you would do much better not to take such a chance."

"Let us do better than that," said Athos. "We will not leave him during the whole evening. Each of us will wait at one of the palace gates with three Musketeers behind him, and if we see a suspicious-looking closed carriage come out, we will attack it. We haven't had a skirmish with Monsieur le Cardinal's Guards for a long time—Monsieur de Tréville must think we are dead."

"Athos," said Aramis, "you were certainly meant to be a general! What do you think of the plan, gentlemen?"

"Admirable!" Porthos and d'Artagnan replied simultaneously.

"Well," said Porthos, "I will go to headquarters and tell our friends to be ready by eight o'clock. We'll meet in front of the Palais-Cardinal. Meantime, have the lackeys saddle the horses."

"I have no horse," said d'Artagnan, "but I can take one of Monsieur de Tréville's."

"That is not necessary," said Aramis. "You can have one of mine."

"One of yours! How many do you have?" asked d'Artagnan.

"Three," replied Aramis, smiling.

"You are unquestionably the best-mounted poet in all of France and Navarre!" cried Athos.

"Listen, Aramis, you don't need three horses, do you? I cannot understand why you bought three horses!"

"I only bought two," said Aramis.

"The third fell from the clouds, I suppose?"

"No, the third was brought to me this very morning by a groom who was not wearing livery and who would not tell me in whose service he was. He merely said he had received orders from his master . . ."

"Or his mistress," interrupted d'Artagnan.

"That makes no difference," said Aramis, blushing. "As I said, he told me that he had received orders from his master or mistress to put the horse in my stable without telling me where it came from."

"Such things happen only to poets," said Athos gravely.

"Well, in that case, we can manage famously," said d'Artagnan. "Which of the two horses will you ride—the one you bought or the one that was given to you?"

"The one that was given to me, of course. You must understand, d'Artagnan, that I could not offend—"

"The unknown benefactor," interrupted d'Artagnan.

"Or the mysterious benefactress," said Athos.

"So the one you bought is useless to you?"

"Nearly so."

"And you chose it yourself?"

"And very carefully, too. As you know, the safety of the horseman almost always depends on the quality of his horse."

"Well, sell it to me at the price you paid, will you?"

"I was going to suggest that, d'Artagnan, and give you as much time as you need to repay such a trifle."

"How much did it cost you?"

"Eight hundred livres."

"Here are forty double pistoles, my friend," said d'Artagnan, taking the sum from his pocket. "I know that those are the coins in which you were paid for your poems."

"You are rich, then?" Aramis asked.

"Rich? Very rich, my dear fellow!"

And d'Artagnan jingled the rest of his pistoles in his pocket.

"Send your saddle to headquarters, and your horse can be brought back with ours."

"Very well, but it is already five o'clock, so let us hurry."

A quarter of an hour later Porthos appeared at the end of the Rue Férou on a very handsome genet, with Mousqueton following him on a small but very handsome Auvergnat horse. Porthos was glowing with joy and pride.

At the same time, Aramis appeared at the other end of the street on a superb English charger; Bazin followed him on a roan, leading by the halter a vigorous Mecklenburg horse that was d'Artagnan's mount.

The two Musketeers met at the gate, Athos and d'Artagnan watching their approach from the window.

"You have a magnificent horse there, Porthos!" said Aramis.

"Yes," replied Porthos, "it is the one that ought to have been sent to me at the beginning. The husband substituted the other as a bad joke, but he has been punished to my complete satisfaction."

Planchet and Grimaud appeared in their turn, leading their masters' steeds. D'Artagnan and Athos mounted, and all four set out together: Athos on a horse he owed to his wife, Aramis on a horse he owed to his mistress, Porthos on a horse he owed to his procurator's wife, and d'Artagnan on a horse he owed to his good fortune—the best possible mistress.

The lackeys followed.

As Porthos had foreseen, the cavalcade made a splendid sight, and if Mme. Coquenard had seen what a superb appearance Porthos made on his handsome Spanish *genet,* she would not have regretted having bled her husband's strongbox.

Near the Louvre the four friends met M. de Tréville, who was returning from St. Germain; he stopped to compliment them on their equipment, and the group immediately attracted a crowd of onlookers.

D'Artagnan took advantage of the meeting to speak to M. de Tréville about the letter with the large red seal and the cardinal's coat of arms; of course he did not breathe a word about the other letter.

M. de Tréville approved of d'Artagnan's plan, and assured him that if he did not appear the next day, he, Tréville, would know how to find him, no matter where he might be.

Just then the Samaritaine clock struck six; the four friends excused themselves, pleading an appointment, and took leave of M. de Tréville.

A short gallop brought them to the Chaillot road; the daylight was fading, carriages were passing in both directions, and d'Artagnan, keeping at some distance from his friends, scrutinized every one of them; he saw no familiar face.

At length, after waiting a quarter of an hour and just as darkness was falling, a carriage appeared, coming at a quick pace on the Sèvres road. D'Artagnan had an instant presentiment that the carriage contained the person who had arranged the rendezvous, and the young man was astonished to find that his heart was pounding. Almost immediately a woman's face emerged from the window with two fingers on her mouth, either to urge him to be silent or to send him a kiss. He uttered a slight cry of joy: the woman—or rather the apparition, for the carriage passed with the rapidity of a vision—was Mme. Bonacieux.

Despite her warning, d'Artagnan almost involuntarily put his horse into a gallop and soon overtook the carriage; but the window was hermetically closed, the vision gone.

He then remembered the injunction: "If you value your own life or the lives of those who love you, do not speak a single word, do not make a single movement."

He therefore stopped, trembling not for himself but for the poor woman who had evidently exposed herself to great danger by making this rendezvous.

The carriage pursued its way, still going at a great pace, till it dashed into Paris and disappeared.

D'Artagnan had remained fixed to the spot, astounded

and not knowing what to think. If it was Mme. Bonacieux and if she was returning to Paris, why this fleeting rendezvous, this simple exchange of a glance, this kiss lost on the breeze? On the other hand, if it was not she—which was quite possible, for the darkness made it easy to be mistaken—could it not be the beginning of some plot against him, using his love for the woman as a trap?

His three companions joined him. All of them had plainly seen a woman's head appear at the window, but none of them except Athos knew Mme. Bonacieux. Athos thought that it was indeed she; but less preoccupied by that pretty face than d'Artagnan, he had thought he also saw a second head, a man's head, inside the carriage.

"If that is so," said d'Artagnan, "they are probably taking her from one prison to another. But what do they intend to do with the poor woman, and how can I ever find her again?"

"My friend," said Athos gravely, "remember that it is only the dead we are not likely to meet again on this earth. I think you know that as well as I do. If your mistress is not dead, if it is she we have just seen, you will meet her again some day or other. And perhaps," he added with his usual misanthropy, "perhaps even sooner than you would wish."

Half past seven had struck: the carriage had been twenty minutes later than the appointed time. D'Artagnan's friends reminded him that he had a visit to pay, but at the same time pointed out that he still had time to change his mind.

But d'Artagnan was both stubborn and curious. He had made up his mind that he would go to the Palais-Cardinal and find out what his Eminence had to say to him, and nothing could sway him from his decision.

They reached the Rue St. Honoré, and in front of the Palais-Cardinal they found the twelve invited Musketeers waiting for their friends, who only then explained the situation.

D'Artagnan was well known to the Musketeers, who all understood that he would one day take his place among them and therefore already considered him a comrade. The result was that all of them were very enthusiastic about the part they were to play, especially since it would probably give them an opportunity to do the cardinal and his men an ill turn—and for that those worthy gentlemen were always ready.

Athos divided them into three groups, assumed the command of one, gave the second to Aramis, and the third to Porthos; then each group went to keep watch near a gate.

D'Artagnan entered boldly at the principal gate.

Although he felt himself strongly supported, the young man was uneasy as he climbed the great staircase. His conduct toward Milady was very much like treachery, and he suspected there was a political alliance between her and the cardinal. In addition, de Wardes, whom he had treated so badly, was one of his Eminence's tools, and d'Artagnan knew that while his Eminence was pitiless to his enemies, he was very loyal to his friends.

"If de Wardes has told the cardinal about our affair, which he certainly has, and if he has recognized me, which is likely, I must consider myself a condemned man," d'Artagnan thought, shaking his head. "But why has he waited till now? It must be because Milady has complained about me with that hypocritical grief that makes her so interesting, and that this most recent offense was the last straw.

"Fortunately," he added, "my good friends are down there, and they will not allow me to be spirited away without a struggle. But Monsieur de Tréville's Musketeers cannot wage war against the cardinal all by themselves. He controls all the forces of France, the queen is powerless against him, and the king has no willpower. D'Artagnan, my friend, you are brave, you are prudent, you have many excellent qualities—but women will be your ruin!"

He had come to his melancholy conclusion as he entered the anteroom. He gave his letter to the usher on duty, who led him into the waiting room and then went into the interior of the palace.

In this waiting room were five or six of the cardinal's Guards; recognizing d'Artagnan, and knowing that it was he who had wounded Jussac, they smiled at him strangely.

The smiles seemed ominous to him, but our Gascon was not easily intimidated—or rather, thanks to a great pride natural to the men of his region, he did not allow one to see his feelings if those feelings had even a trace of fear in them. He therefore planted himself haughtily in front of the Guards and waited with his hand on his hip, a pose not lacking in majesty.

The usher returned and motioned d'Artagnan to follow him. As he left, it seemed to the young man that the Guards were chuckling among themselves.

He walked down a corridor, crossed a large drawing room, entered a library, and found himself in the presence of a man seated at a desk and writing.

The usher left without saying a word. D'Artagnan remained standing and observed the person in front of him.

At first he thought him some judge examining his papers, but then he saw that the man at the desk was writing, or rather correcting, lines of unequal length and scanning the words on his fingers. He then understood that he was with a poet. After a few minutes the poet closed his manuscript, on the cover of which was written *Mirame, a Tragedy in Five Acts,* and raised his head.

D'Artagnan recognized the cardinal.

40

The Cardinal

THE CARDINAL leaned his elbow on his manuscript, rested his cheek on his hand, and looked intently at the young man. No one had a more searching eye than Cardinal de Richelieu, and d'Artagnan felt this gaze penetrate to his very marrow.

He managed, however, not to appear uneasy, and holding his hat in his hand, he awaited the good pleasure of his Eminence without too much pride but also without too much humility.

"Monsieur, are you a d'Artagnan from Béarn?" the cardinal asked.

"Yes, monseigneur," replied the young man.

"There are several branches of the d'Artagnans at Tarbes and in that general area. To which do you belong?"

"I am the son of the d'Artagnan who served in the Religious Wars under the great King Henry, the father of his gracious Majesty."

"Ah, yes. You are the one who set out seven or eight months ago from your province to seek your fortune in the capital?"

"Yes, monseigneur."

"You came through Meung, where something happened to you. I do not know precisely what, but something."

"Monseigneur, this is what happened to me . . ."

"Never mind," interrupted the cardinal, with a smile that indicated he knew the story as well as the one who wished to tell it. "You had a letter of introduction to Monsieur de Tréville, did you not?"

"Yes, monseigneur, but in that unfortunate affair at Meung . . ."

". . . the letter was lost. Yes, I know that. But Monsieur de Tréville is a skillful judge of character, one who can read into a man at first sight and he placed you in the company of his brother-in-law, Monsieur Des Essarts, leaving you to hope that some day you would enter the Musketeers."

"Monseigneur is correctly informed."

"Since that time many things have happened to you. You were walking one day behind the Carmes-Deschaux, when it would have been better if you had been elsewhere. Then you went with your friends to take the waters at Forges. They stopped along the way, but you continued your journey. That was understandable—you had business in England."

"Monseigneur," said d'Artagnan, quite confused, "I went . . ."

". . . hunting at Windsor, or elsewhere—that is your affair. I know about it because it is my business to know everything. On your return you were received by a lady of the highest rank, and I perceive with pleasure that you have kept the souvenir she gave you."

D'Artagnan quickly turned the stone of the queen's diamond inward, but it was too late.

"The day after that, you received a visit from Cavois," continued the cardinal. "He left a message asking you to come to the palace. You were wrong not to do so."

"Monseigneur, I feared I had incurred your Eminence's displeasure."

"How could that be, monsieur? Could you incur my displeasure by having followed the orders of your superiors with more intelligence and courage than another would have done? I punish the people who do not obey, not those who, like you, obey—only too well. . . . As proof, remember the day when I asked you to come to me, then search your memory for what happened to you that very night."

That was the night of Mme. Bonacieux's abduction. D'Artagnan shivered as he realized that a half hour earlier, when the poor woman had passed close to him, she was undoubtedly being carried away by the same power that had caused her original disappearance.

"In short," the cardinal went on, "as I have heard nothing about you for some time, I wished to know what you were doing. Besides, you do owe me some thanks— you must have observed how considerately you have been treated in all instances."

D'Artagnan bowed respectfully.

"That," added the cardinal, "was not only because of my natural sense of justice, but because of my plans for you."

D'Artagnan was more and more astonished.

"I wished to explain this plan to you on the day you received my first invitation, but you did not come. Fortunately, nothing has been lost by this delay, and you are now about to hear it. Sit down, Monsieur d'Artagnan; you are of high enough rank not to have to stand in my presence."

He pointed to a chair; d'Artagnan was so astonished at what was happening that he did not obey until the cardinal repeated his gesture.

"You are brave, Monsieur d'Artagnan, and you are prudent, which is still better. I like men who have both heads and hearts. Don't be afraid—by heart I mean courage. But young as you are, and just beginning to make your way in the world, you have powerful enemies. If you do not take care, they will destroy you."

"Alas, monseigneur, and very easily, too, since they are strong and well connected, while I am alone."

"Yes, that is true. But alone as you are, you have

done much already, and will certainly do still more. Yet I believe you need to be guided in the adventurous career you have undertaken—for if I am not mistaken, you came to Paris with the ambition of making your fortune."

"I am at the age of extravagant hopes, monseigneur."

"There are no extravagant hopes except for fools, monsieur, and you are not a fool. Now, what would you say to a lieutenant's commission in my Guards, and command of a company after the campaign?"

"Monseigneur!"

"You accept, do you not?"

"Monseigneur . . ." d'Artagnan began, with an embarrassed air.

"You refuse?" exclaimed the cardinal.

"I am in his Majesty's Guards, monseigneur, and I have no reason to be dissatisfied."

"But it appears to me that my Guards—*mine*—are also his Majesty's Guards, and that he who serves in any French corps serves the king."

"Monseigneur, your Eminence has misunderstood my words."

"You want an excuse, do you not? I understand. Well, you have several: promotion, the coming campaign, the opportunity I offer you—those are for the world. As for your private reason—you need protection, for you should know, Monsieur d'Artagnan, that I have received serious complaints against you. Your days and nights are not dedicated solely to the king's service."

D'Artagnan blushed.

"In fact," said the cardinal, placing his hand on a pile of papers, "I have here a whole dossier about you. I know you to be a man of strong resolve and if your services were well directed, they might lead to great advantages for you. Think about it, and decide."

"Your kindness overwhelms me, monseigneur, and there is a greatness of soul in your Eminence that makes me feel as mean as an earthworm. But since Monseigneur permits me to speak freely . . ."

D'Artagnan paused.

"Yes, go on."

"Then I will say that all my friends are in the king's Musketeers and Guards, and that by some inexplicable chance my enemies are in the service of your Eminence.

I should therefore be unwelcome here and regarded with contempt there if I accepted your offer."

"You wouldn't happen to be so arrogant as to feel that I have not made you an offer equal to your value?" asked the cardinal disdainfully.

"Monseigneur, on the contrary, your Eminence is a hundred times too kind to me, and I think I have not yet proved myself worthy of your goodness. The siege of La Rochelle is about to begin, monseigneur, and you will be able to observe me. If I have the good fortune to distinguish myself in your eyes, then there will at least be some brilliant action to justify the protection with which you honor me. Everything in its own time, monseigneur. Later, I may have the right to give myself, but now I would seem to *sell* myself."

"In other words, you refuse to serve me, monsieur," said the cardinal, in a tone of vexation mixed with a sort of esteem. "Remain free then to keep your enemies and your friends."

"Monseigneur . . ."

"I wish you no ill," said the cardinal, "but you understand that it is hard enough to defend and reward our friends—we owe nothing to our enemies. And let me give you a piece of advice—be careful, Monsieur d'Artagnan, because from the moment I withdraw my support, I would not give the smallest coin for your life."

"I will try to follow your advice, monseigneur," replied the Gascon, with a noble confidence.

"Remember later that if any misfortune should befall you," said Richelieu significantly, "that I sent for you and did all in my power to prevent it."

"Whatever may happen," d'Artagnan replied, placing his hand on his heart and bowing, "I shall be eternally grateful to your Eminence for what you have offered me."

"Well, then, Monsieur d'Artagnan, as you have said, we will see each other again after the campaign. I will have my eye upon you, for I will be there," said the cardinal, pointing to the magnificent armor he was going to wear, "and we will settle our account on our return!"

"Monseigneur," said d'Artagnan, "spare me the weight of your displeasure! Remain neutral, monseigneur, if you see that I behave honorably."

"Young man," said Richelieu, "if I can say to you at another time what I have said to you today, I promise to do so."

These words conveyed a terrible doubt, and they alarmed d'Artagnan more than threats would have done, for they were a warning. The cardinal was trying to preserve him from some danger that threatened him. He opened his mouth to reply, but the cardinal dismissed him with a haughty gesture.

D'Artagnan turned to leave, but at the door his heart almost failed him and he nearly turned back. Then the image of Athos's noble and severe face crossed his mind: if he agreed to accept the cardinal's offer, Athos would refuse to give him his hand—Athos would disown him.

It was this fear that restrained him, so powerful is the influence of a truly great character on everyone around it.

D'Artagnan went downstairs and at the door found Athos and the four Musketeers waiting for him with growing uneasiness. With a few words d'Artagnan reassured them, and Planchet ran to tell the other sentinels that they no longer had to keep guard because his master had come out safely from the Palais-Cardinal.

Back in Athos's apartment, Aramis and Porthos asked about the reason for the strange interview, but d'Artagnan told them only that M. de Richelieu had sent for him to offer him a commission in his Guards and that he had refused.

"And you were right," Aramis and Porthos exclaimed together.

Athos seemed deep in thought and said nothing. But when he and d'Artagnan were alone, he said, "You did what you had to do, but it may have been a mistake."

D'Artagnan sighed, for what Athos said echoed the secret voice of his soul, which told him that great misfortunes awaited him.

The next day was spent in preparing for their departure. D'Artagnan went to take leave of M. de Tréville. At that time it was believed that the separation of the Musketeers and the Guards would be a temporary one, since the king was holding his Parliament that very day and planning to set out the day after, so M. de Tréville merely asked d'Artagnan if he could do anything for him; d'Artagnan replied that he had everything he needed.

That night Monsieur Des Essarts's Guards and Monsieur de Tréville's Musketeers, who had all become friendly, gathered together. They were parting and would meet again only when and if it pleased God; the night was therefore somewhat riotous, for in such cases extreme concern can only be remedied by extreme insouciance.

At the first sound of the morning trumpets the friends separated, the Musketeers to M. de Tréville's house, the Guards to M. Des Essarts's. Each of the captains then led his company to the Louvre, where the king was to hold his review.

The king looked sad and ill, which detracted a little from his usual lofty bearing. In fact, he had been feverish the evening before during a session of Parliament—though he had nevertheless decided to set out that evening as planned—and in spite of having been advised against it, he persisted in holding the review, hoping to overcome his sickness by defying it.

The inspection over, the Guards marched off alone, the Musketeers waiting to leave with the king.

This gave Porthos time to show off his superb equipment in the Rue aux Ours.

The procurator's wife saw him pass in his new uniform and on his fine horse. She loved Porthos too much to allow him to leave like that, so she signaled him to dismount and come to her. He was magnificent: his spurs jingled, his armor glittered, his sword swung proudly against his ample limbs. This time he looked so warlike that the clerks showed absolutely no desire to laugh.

The Musketeer was brought to M. Coquenard, whose little gray eyes glinted with anger at seeing his cousin all sparkling new. One thing consoled him, however: everybody expected the campaign to be a hard one, and deep inside he hoped that this beloved relative would be killed in the field.

Porthos paid his respects to M. Coquenard and said goodbye. M. Coquenard wished him well. Mme. Coquenard could not restrain her tears, but no one thought badly of her grief because she was known to be very attached to her relatives, about whom she was constantly arguing with her husband.

But the real adieux took place in Mme. Coquenard's bedroom; they were heartrending.

The procurator's wife, leaning so far out of the window that it looked almost as if she planned to jump, waved her handkerchief to Porthos for as long as she could see him. Porthos received her attentions like a man accustomed to such demonstrations, and only on turning the corner did he lift his hat gracefully and wave it to her in farewell.

Aramis was writing a long letter. To whom? Nobody knew. Kitty, who was to leave that evening for Tours, was waiting for the mysterious letter in the adjoining room.

Athos was sipping the last bottle of his Spanish wine.

D'Artagnan was riding with his company.

Arriving at the Faubourg St. Antoine, he turned around to look cheerfully at the Bastille, but since he was looking only at the Bastille, he did not see Milady, who was mounted on a bay and pointing him out to two evil-looking men who immediately moved closer to get a good look at him. When they glanced at her questioningly, Milady replied with a nod that it was indeed the right man. Then, certain that there could be no mistake in the execution of her orders, she spurred her horse and disappeared.

The two men followed the company on foot, and when they left the Faubourg St. Antoine, they mounted two horses that a servant without livery had been holding for them.

41

The Siege of La Rochelle

THE SIEGE OF La Rochelle was one of the great political events of the reign of Louis XIII, and one of the Cardinal's great military enterprises. We must therefore say a few words about it, especially since many of its details are so connected with our story that we cannot pass it over in silence.

The cardinal's political plans when he undertook this siege were extensive. Let us examine them first, then move on to the private plans that were perhaps no less important to him.

Of the important cities Henry IV had given the Huguenots as places of safety, only La Rochelle remained. It was thus necessary to destroy this last bulwark of Calvinism—a dangerous leaven promoting domestic rebellion and foreign wars.

Spanish, English, and Italian malcontents, adventurers of all nations, and soldiers of fortune of every sect flocked to the standard of the Protestants and organized themselves into a vast association with branches all over Europe.

La Rochelle, which had become more important after the ruin of the other Calvinist cities, was thus the focus of dissensions and ambition. Moreover, it was the last port in the kingdom of France that was open to the English, and by closing it against England, France's eternal enemy, the cardinal was completing the work of Joan of Arc and the Duc de Guise.

Thus Bassompierre, who was both Protestant and Catholic—Protestant by conviction and Catholic as commander of the order of the Holy Ghost; Bassompierre, who was a German by birth and a Frenchman at heart; Bassompierre, who was one of the commanders at the siege of La Rochelle—said to several other Protestant nobles like himself, "You will see, gentlemen, that we will be foolish enough to take La Rochelle!"

And Bassompierre was right. The bombardment of the Ile de Ré presaged the persecutions in the Cévennes; the taking of La Rochelle was the preface of the revocation of the Edict of Nantes.

But as we have said, side by side with these political views of the leveling and simplifying minister, the chronicler must also recognize the lesser motives of the amorous man and jealous rival.

As everyone knows, Richelieu had been in love with the queen. We cannot say if this love was a simple political affair or if it was one of those profound passions that Anne of Austria inspired in those around her, but in any case we know, by what happened before the beginning of this story, that Buckingham had carried the day and, in two or three instances—particularly that of the diamond studs—thanks to the devotion of the three Musketeers and the courage of d'Artagnan, had cruelly outwitted the cardinal.

Richelieu therefore wanted not only to get rid of an enemy of France but to avenge himself on a rival; the vengeance, however, must be emphatic and unequivocal, worthy in every way of a man who wielded the forces of a kingdom as his weapon.

Richelieu knew that in fighting England he would be fighting Buckingham, that in triumphing over England he would be triumphing over Buckingham, that in humiliating England in the eyes of Europe he would be humiliating Buckingham in the eyes of the queen.

Buckingham, too, in pretending to maintain the honor of England, was driven by motives exactly like those of the cardinal; he too was pursuing a private vengeance. Since there was no way he could enter France as an ambassador, he wished to enter it as a conqueror.

The real stake in this game, which two powerful kingdoms played for the pleasure of two rivals in love, was simply a kind look from Anne of Austria.

The first advantage had gone to Buckingham. Arriving unexpectedly at the Ile de Ré with ninety vessels and nearly twenty thousand men, he had surprised the Comte de Toiras, the king's commander on Ré, and, after a bloody fight, had made a landing.

Let us observe in passing that the Baron de Chantal died in this battle and left his eighteen-month-old girl an orphan; that little girl later became Mme. de Sévigné.

The Comte de Toiras withdrew into the St. Martin citadel with his garrison and sent a hundred men into a little fort called the fort of La Prée.

This had resolved the cardinal to act quickly, and till the king and he could take command of the siege of La Rochelle, which had already been planned, he had sent Monsieur, the king's brother, to direct the first operations and had ordered all his available troops to go there immediately. Our friend d'Artagnan was part of this detachment sent as a vanguard.

The king was to follow as soon as the formal session of Parliament was over, but when it ended on the twenty-eighth of June, he had become ill with a fever. He had nevertheless set out; but his illness became more serious, and he was forced to stop at Villeroi.

Whenever the king halted, the Musketeers halted too, so d'Artagnan, who was as yet purely and simply in the Guards, found himself temporarily separated from his good friends Athos, Porthos, and Aramis. This separation, which he regarded as merely an annoyance, would certainly have given him a cause for serious uneasiness if he had been able to guess at the unknown dangers that surrounded him.

However, he arrived without incident in the camp established before La Rochelle on September 10, 1627.

Everything was the same. The Duke of Buckingham and his English troops, masters of the Ile de Ré, were continuing to besiege, unsuccessfully, the St. Martin citadel and the fort of La Prée; and hostilities with La Rochelle had begun two or three days before in relation to a fort that the Duc d'Angoulême had ordered built near the city.

The Guards, under the command of M. Des Essarts, took up their quarters at the Minimes.

As we know, d'Artagnan wanted to join the Musketeers so badly that he had made few friends among the Guards and now felt himself isolated and left to his own thoughts—which were not very cheerful. In the year since his arrival in Paris, he had become involved with public affairs, but his own private affairs had made no great progress as concerned either love or fortune.

As to love, the only woman he could have loved was Mme. Bonacieux; Mme. Bonacieux had disappeared, and he had not been able to discover what had become of her.

As to fortune, he had made—he, humble as he was!— an enemy of the cardinal, that is, of a man before whom trembled the greatest men of the kingdom, beginning with the king.

That man had the power to crush him, and yet he had not done so. To a man as clever as d'Artagnan, that indulgence was a light that gave him a glimmer of a better future.

He had made himself another enemy, too, less to be feared, he thought, but—as he instinctively felt—not to be despised either. That enemy was Milady.

In exchange, he had acquired the protection and good will of the queen; but at the present time her good will was only an additional cause of persecution, and as he knew, her protection protected badly—as witness Chalais and Mme. Bonacieux.

What he had most clearly gained was the diamond ring, worth five or six thousand livres, which he wore on his finger; and even this diamond—supposing that he wished to keep it so he could use it someday as a claim on the gratitude of the queen—did not have any more value than the gravel under his feet because he could not sell it.

We say "than the gravel under his feet," because these thoughts had come to him while he was walking along a pretty little road that led from the camp to the village of Angoutin. Those thoughts had led him to walk farther than he had intended, and the sun was beginning to set when, by its last rays, he thought he saw the glint of a musket barrel from behind a hedge.

D'Artagnan had a quick eye and an equally quick understanding: he understood that the musket had not gotten there by itself, and that the man who carried it had not concealed himself behind a hedge with any friendly intentions. Unhesitatingly, he decided to leave the spot as quickly as possible, but as he was about to act on his decision, he saw on the opposite side of the road, behind a rock, the muzzle of another musket.

It was evidently an ambush.

His eyes darted back to the first musket, and he was alarmed to see that it was being lowered in his direction; as soon as he saw the motion stop, he threw himself to the ground. At that same instant the gun was fired, and he heard the bullet whistle past him.

There was no time to lose. He sprang to his feet—and at that very moment the bullet from the other musket spattered the gravel on the very spot where he had been lying.

D'Artagnan was not one of those foolish men who seek a ridiculous death so that people would say that he never retreated a single step. Besides, courage was not the question here, since he had fallen into an ambush.

"If there is a third shot," he thought, "I am lost."

Immediately taking to his heels, he ran toward the

camp with the swiftness and agility the young men of his part of the country were so famous for, but his speed was unavailing; the man who had fired first had had time to reload and he fired a second shot—this time so well aimed that it struck d'Artagnan's hat and sent it flying ten paces away.

Having no other hat, he picked it up as he ran, and arrived at his quarters very pale and quite out of breath. He sat down without saying a word to anybody and began to think.

There were three possible reasons for what had happened.

The first and most natural was that it might be an ambush on the part of the Rochellais, the inhabitants of the besieged city. They would not be sorry to kill one of his Majesty's Guards because it would be an enemy the less, and, in addition, that enemy might have a well-filled purse in his pocket.

D'Artagnan looked at his hat, examined the bullet hole, and shook his head. The bullet was not from a musket but from a harquebus. The accuracy of the aim had already made him think that a special weapon had been employed, which meant that he had not been ambushed by soldiers.

The second was that it might be a souvenir of Monsieur le Cardinal. At the very moment when, thanks to the ray of sunlight, he had seen the gun barrel, he had been thinking with astonishment about his Eminence's forbearance toward him. But again he shook his head. His Eminence rarely resorted to such means against people toward whom he had only to point a finger.

The third was that it might be an act of vengeance on Milady's part. That was the most likely.

He tried to remember the faces or dress of the assassins, but he had run away so quickly that he had not had time to notice anything.

"Ah, my friends," he thought, "where are you now that I need you?"

He spent a very bad night. Three or four times he woke with a start, imagining that a man was approaching his bed for the purpose of stabbing him. But day finally dawned without darkness having brought about any accident.

Nevertheless he suspected that that which had been delayed was not forgotten, and he remained in his quarters all day, telling himself it was because the weather was bad.

At nine o'clock the following morning, the drums beat to arms. The Duc d'Orléans was inspecting the posts. The Guards were under arms, and d'Artagnan took his place among his comrades.

Monsieur passed along the front of the line, after which all the superior officers approached him to pay their respects, including M. Des Essarts, captain of the Guards.

A minute or two later it seemed to d'Artagnan that M. Des Essarts was motioning him to approach. He waited for another gesture on the part of his superior lest he be mistaken, but the gesture being repeated, he left the ranks and advanced to receive his orders.

"Monsieur is about to ask for some volunteers for a dangerous mission that will bring honor to those who accomplish it, and I signaled you so that you might be ready."

"Thank you, captain!" replied d'Artagnan, who wanted nothing better than an opportunity to distinguish himself in the eyes of the lieutenant general.

In fact the enemy had made a sortie during the night and retaken a bastion the Royal army had captured two days earlier. The mission was to reconnoiter and see how the enemy was guarding this bastion.

And a few minutes later Monsieur raised his voice and said, "I want for this mission three or four volunteers, led by someone dependable."

"As to the dependable man, he is right here, Monsieur," said M. Des Essarts, pointing to d'Artagnan, "and as to the volunteers, Monsieur has only to speak, and the men will be ready."

"Four volunteers who will risk death with me!" said d'Artagnan, raising his sword.

Two of his fellow Guards immediately sprang forward, and two other soldiers joined them. Feeling the number sufficient, d'Artagnan refused all the others, not wanting to pass over those who had been first.

It was not known whether the enemy had evacuated

the bastion or left a garrison in it, so they would have
to get close enough to find out.

D'Artagnan set out with his four men and followed the
trench; the two Guards walked alongside him, and the
two soldiers followed behind.

Screened by the revetment, they walked thus till they
came within a hundred paces of the bastion. There, on
turning around, d'Artagnan saw that the two soldiers had
disappeared.

He thought that they had become frightened and
stayed behind; he and the two Guards continued to
advance.

At the turning of the counterscarp they found themselves within about sixty paces of the bastion. They saw
no one; the bastion seemed abandoned.

The three men were discussing whether they should go
any farther when all at once a ring of smoke enveloped
the bastion and a dozen bullets came whistling around
d'Artagnan and his companions.

They knew what they wanted to know: the bastion was
guarded. To stay longer in that dangerous spot would
have been useless and imprudent, so d'Artagnan and his
two companions turned around and began a retreat that
was more like a flight.

Arriving at the corner of the trench that was to serve
them as a rampart, one of the Guardsmen fell; a bullet
had passed through his chest. The other, who was safe
and sound, continued running toward the camp.

D'Artagnan did not want to abandon his companion
like that, and stooped down to help him up and assist
him in regaining the lines; but just then two shots were
fired. One bullet struck the wounded Guard's head, and
the other flattened itself against a rock after having
passed within two inches of d'Artagnan.

The young man turned around quickly because the
attack could not have come from the bastion, which was
hidden by the corner of the trench. He remembered the
two soldiers who had abandoned him, and then he
remembered the men who had tried to kill him two eve-
nings before. He resolved that this time he would learn
with whom he had to deal, and he fell upon the body of
his comrade as if he were dead.

He immediately saw two heads appear above an abandoned outwork about thirty paces away; they were the heads of the two soldiers. D'Artagnan had been right; the two men had come with him only to murder him, hoping that his death would be attributed to the enemy.

However, since he might be only wounded and thus able to denounce their crime, they now came up to him in order to make sure; fortunately, they were deceived by d'Artagnan's trick and neglected to reload their guns.

When they were within ten paces of him, d'Artagnan, who had been very careful not to let go of his sword when he fell down, sprang up and rushed toward them.

The assassins realized that if they went back to the camp without having killed their man, he would accuse them, so their idea was to go over to the enemy. One of them took his gun by the barrel and used it like a club. He aimed a terrible blow at d'Artagnan, who avoided it by jumping to one side, but this movement left the bandit a free passage to the bastion. Since the Rochellais guarding the bastion did not know why the man was coming toward them, they fired at him and he fell, struck by a bullet that broke his shoulder.

Meantime d'Artagnan had attacked the other soldier with his sword. The fight did not take long, for the man had nothing to defend himself with but his discharged harquebus. D'Artagnan's sword slipped along the barrel of the now-useless weapon and pierced the assassin's thigh; he fell, and d'Artagnan immediately placed the point of his sword at his throat.

"Oh, do not kill me! Pardon me, sir, and I will tell you everything!" cried the bandit.

"Is your secret important enough for me to spare your life?" d'Artagnan asked, withdrawing his arm.

"Yes, if you think existence is important to a man who may hope for everything, being young, handsome, and brave, as you are."

"Then speak quickly! Who employed you to assassinate me?"

"I don't know her, but she is called Milady."

"If you don't know her, how do you know her name?"

"My friend knew her, and that is what he called her. Her arrangement was with him, not with me. He even has a letter from her in his pocket, and from what I heard him say, that letter would be of great interest to you."

"How did you become involved with this affair?"

"He asked me to join him, and I agreed."

"How much did you get for it?"

"A hundred louis."

"Well, at least she thinks I am worth something! A hundred louis? That certainly must have been a temptation for two scoundrels like you. All right, I understand why you agreed to do it, and I grant you my pardon—but on one condition."

"What?" the soldier asked uneasily.

"That you will get me the letter your friend has in his pocket."

"But that is only another way of killing me! How can I fetch that letter under fire from the bastion?"

"You must nevertheless make up your mind to get it, or I swear I will kill you myself."

"Pardon me, monsieur, have pity! In the name of that young lady you love, the lady you think is dead, though she is not!" cried the bandit, rising to his knees and supporting himself on one hand because he was so weak from loss of blood.

"How do you know that I love a young woman and that I think she is dead?"

"By that letter my friend has in his pocket."

"You see that I must have that letter! No more delay, no more hesitation, or no matter how reluctant I may be to soil my sword a second time with the blood of such a vile wretch like you, I swear by my faith as an honest man . . ."

D'Artagnan looked so fierce that the wounded man jumped to his feet.

"Stop!" he cried, regaining strength from force of terror. "I will go, I will go!"

D'Artagnan took the soldier's harquebus, made him walk ahead of him, and urged him toward his companion by pricking him in the back with his sword.

It was a terrible sight. Pale with approaching death, he tried to drag himself along—leaving a trail of blood behind him—without being seen, to the body of his accomplice, which lay twenty paces away. His face was covered with a cold sweat, and he looked so terrified that d'Artagnan took pity on him and said, in a voice filled with contempt, "Stop. I will show you the difference between a brave man and a coward like you. Stay where you are—I will go myself."

And treading lightly, carefully observing the movements of the enemy and taking every advantage of the terrain, d'Artagnan succeeded in reaching the second soldier.

There were two ways of gaining his object—to search him on the spot, or to carry him away, using his body as a shield, and search him in the trench.

D'Artagnan preferred the second, and lifted the assassin onto his shoulders at the very moment the enemy fired.

A slight jolt, a dull noise of three bullets penetrating the flesh, a last cry, a final convulsion of agony, proved to d'Artagnan that the would-be assassin had saved his life.

D'Artagnan regained the trench and dropped the corpse beside the wounded man, who was deathly pale.

Then he began his search: a leather pocketbook, a purse containing what must have been a part of the sum the man had received, a dice box and dice—those were the assassin's possessions.

He left the box and dice where they fell, threw the purse to the wounded man, and eagerly opened the pocketbook.

Among some unimportant papers he found the following letter, the one he had risked his life to get.

> Since you have lost sight of the woman and she is now safely in the convent that you should never have allowed her to reach, try at least not to miss the man. If you do, you know that my arm has a long reach and that you will pay very dearly for the hundred louis you received from me.

No signature. But it was plain the letter came from Milady, and d'Artagnan decided to keep it as a piece of evidence. Sheltered behind the angle of the trench, he began to question the wounded man, who confessed that he and his comrade—the one who had been killed—had agreed to carry off a young woman who was to leave

Paris by the La Villette gate, but they had stopped to drink at a tavern and missed the carriage by ten minutes.

"What were you going to do with the woman?" asked d'Artagnan, with anguish.

"We were supposed to take her to a house in the Place Royale," the wounded man replied.

"Yes," murmured d'Artagnan, "Milady's own house."

The young man shuddered, understanding what a terrible thirst of vengeance drove this woman to destroy him and all who loved him, and how well acquainted she was with court affairs, since she had discovered everything. She must certainly owe this information to the cardinal.

But amid all this he was overjoyed to realize that the queen must have learned where poor Mme. Bonacieux was paying for her devotion and had succeeded in freeing her; the letter he had received from the young woman, and her dreamlike passage along the Chaillot road, were now explained.

As Athos had predicted, it would be possible to find Mme. Bonacieux, and a convent was not impregnable.

He felt good again and was prepared to be lenient. He turned to the wounded man, who was watching with intense anxiety all the various expressions on his face, held out his arm to him, and said, "Come. I will not abandon you here. Lean on me, and let us return to camp."

"Yes," said the man, who could scarcely believe in such magnanimity, "but will you have me hanged?"

"No, you have my word," d'Artagnan replied. "For the second time I give you your life."

The wounded man sank to his knees, to again kiss the feet of his preserver, but d'Artagnan, who no longer had any reason to stay so close to the enemy, cut short these testimonials of gratitude.

The Guardsman who had returned to camp at the first discharge of fire had announced the death of his four companions, so there was much astonishment and delight in the regiment when they saw the young man returning safe and sound.

He explained his companion's sword wound by inventing a sortie, then described the death of the other soldier and the dangers they had faced: the recital was a veritable triumph for him. The whole army talked about this expedition for a full day, and Monsieur congratulated him on it.

Besides, since every great action brings its reward, d'Artagnan's behavior restored his peace of mind. In fact, he believed that he might well allow himself to relax his guard, since one of his two enemies was dead and the other now devoted to his interests.

This ease of mind proved one thing—that d'Artagnan did not yet know Milady.

42

The Anjou Wine

AFTER THOSE ALARMING reports of the king's health, there was now news of his convalescence, and since he was eager to be present at the siege, it was said that he would set out as soon as he could mount a horse.

Meantime, Monsieur—expecting to be removed from his command any day by the Duc d'Angoulême, Bassompierre, or Schomberg, who were all eager for his post— did little but hesitate, not daring to take any decisive action to drive the English from the Ile de Ré, where they were still besieging the St. Martin citadel and the fort of La Prée just as the French were besieging La Rochelle.

As we have said, d'Artagnan had become less apprehensive, as always happens when a past danger seems to have vanished. He was uneasy about only one thing— not hearing any news from his friends.

But one morning at the beginning of November everything was explained by this letter, dated from Villeroi:

M. d'ARTAGNAN,

MM. Athos, Porthos, and Aramis, after having had an entertainment at my house and enjoying themselves very much, created such a disturbance that the provost of the castle, a very rigid man, has ordered them to be confined for several days; they have requested me, however, to send you a dozen

bottles of my Anjou wine, which they much
enjoyed. They wish you to drink their health in
their favorite wine. I have done this, and am, monsieur, with great respect,

Your very humble and obedient servant,
GODEAU, *Purveyor of the Musketeers*

"Splendid!" cried d'Artagnan. "They think of me in
their pleasures just as I thought of them in my troubles.
Well, I will certainly drink to their health with all my
heart, but I will not drink alone."

He went to find two of the Guardsmen with whom he
had become friendlier than with the others to invite them
to share the present of delicious Anjou wine that had
just arrived from Villeroi.

One of the two was busy that evening and the other
one the next, so they agreed to meet the day after that.

Returning to his quarters, d'Artagnan sent the twelve
bottles of wine to the inn used by the Guards, with strict
orders that great care should be taken of it; then, on the
appointed day, since the meal was set for midday he
sent Planchet at nine in the morning to help prepare
everything.

Very proud of his new responsibility, Planchet thought
he would get everything ready, like an intelligent man;
and to do this, he asked the lackey of one of his master's
guests, named Fourreau, to help. He also had the assistance of the false soldier who had tried to kill d'Artagnan
and who, belonging to no corps, had entered into the
service of d'Artagnan—or rather of Planchet—after d'Artagnan had saved his life.

The hour of the banquet having come, the two guests
arrived and took their places, and the dishes were
arranged on the table. Planchet served, towel on arm;
Fourreau uncorked the bottles; and Brisemont, which
was the name of the convalescent, carefully poured the
wine—a little shaken by its journey—into decanters. The
first bottle was a little thick at the bottom, so Brisemont
poured the lees into a glass and d'Artagnan told him to
drink it, for the poor devil had not yet recovered his
strength.

Having finished their soup, the guests were about to

lift the first glass of wine to their lips when all at once the cannon sounded from Fort Louis and Fort Neuf. The Guardsmen, thinking this was some surprise attack by either the besieged troops or the English, grabbed their swords. D'Artagnan, no less quick, did the same, and all three of them ran out and headed for their posts.

But they had hardly left the room before they discovered the reason for this noise: cries of "Long live the king! Long live the cardinal!" resounded on every side, and the drumbeats could be heard coming from all directions.

In short, the impatient king had made two stages in one and had that moment arrived with all his household and a reinforcement of ten thousand troops. His Musketeers preceded and followed him. D'Artagnan, lining the route with his company, greeted his friends with an expressive gesture, which they responded to with their eyes. He also greeted M. de Tréville, who saw him at once.

The reception ceremony over, the four friends were soon enbracing one another.

"Pardieu," cried d'Artagnan, "you could not have arrived at a better time—the dinner cannot even have had time to get cold! Am I not right, gentlemen?" he added, turning to the two Guards, whom he introduced to his friends.

"Ah," said Porthos, "it seems we are feasting!"

"I hope," said Aramis, "there are no women at your dinner."

"Is there any drinkable wine?" asked Athos.

"But of course, my friend, there is yours," replied d'Artagnan.

"Ours!" said Athos, surprised.

"Yes, what you sent me."

"We sent you wine?"

"But you must remember—the wine from Anjou."

"Yes, I know the kind you mean."

"The wine you prefer."

"I suppose so, when I have neither champagne nor chambertin."

"Well, in the absence of champagne and chambertin, you must content yourself with the Anjou."

"And so, connoisseur in wine that you are, you sent for some Anjou?" Porthos asked.

"Not at all—it is the wine that you ordered sent to me."

"*We* ordered?" asked the three Musketeers in unison.

"Did you send this wine, Aramis?" Athos inquired.

"No. You, Porthos?"

"No. You, Athos?"

"No!"

"Not you directly, but your purveyor," said d'Artagnan.

"Our purveyor!"

"Yes, your purveyor, Godeau—the purveyor of the Musketeers."

"My God, never mind where it comes from," said Porthos. "Let's taste it, and if it is good, let's drink it."

"No," said Athos, "let us not drink wine that comes from an unknown source."

"You are right, Athos," said d'Artagnan. "Did none of you ask this Godeau to send me some wine?"

"No. Yet you say he sent you some as coming from us?"

"Here is his letter," said d'Artagnan, showing the note to his comrades.

"That is not his writing!" said Athos. "I know it because I settled the regiment's accounts before we left Villeroi."

"It's a false letter altogether," said Porthos. "We were not disciplined."

"D'Artagnan," said Aramis reproachfully, "how could you believe that we had created a disturbance?"

D'Artagnan grew pale, and trembled convulsively.

"You alarm me," said Athos. "What has happened?"

"Hurry, my friends!" exclaimed d'Artagnan. "I have a horrible suspicion—could this be another example of that woman's vengeance?"

It was Athos who now turned pale.

D'Artagnan rushed back to the inn, the three Musketeers and the two Guards following him.

The first thing d'Artagnan saw on entering the room was Brisemont, stretched out on the ground and writhing in horrible convulsions.

Planchet and Fourreau, deathly pale, were trying to

help him, but it was plain that all help was useless—the dying man's features were distorted by agony.

"Oh, how terrible," he cried on seeing d'Artagnan. "Terrible! You pretend to pardon me, and you poison me!"

"I!" cried d'Artagnan. "I, poison you? What are you saying?"

"I say that it was you who gave me the wine, you who wanted me to drink it, you who wished to avenge yourself on me, and I say that it is horrible!"

"Do not believe that, Brisemont," said d'Artagnan, "do not. I swear to you . . ."

"Oh, but God is above! God will punish you! My God, grant that he may one day suffer what I suffer!"

"I swear on the Gospel," said d'Artagnan, throwing himself down by the dying man, "I swear to you that I did not know the wine was poisoned and that I was going to drink it too."

"I do not believe you," said the soldier, and he died in great agony.

"Frightful," murmured Athos, while Porthos broke the bottles and Aramis gave belated orders to bring a confessor.

"My friends," said d'Artagnan, "you have once more saved my life, and not only mine but that of these gentlemen. Gentlemen," he continued, addressing the Guardsmen, "I beg you to be silent about all this. Important people may have had a hand in what you have seen, and it may be the worse for us if we talk about it."

"Ah, monsieur," stammered Planchet, more dead than alive, "what an escape I have had!"

"What—you were going to drink my wine?"

"To the health of the king, monsieur. I was going to drink a small glass to the king's health if Fourreau had not told me someone was asking for me."

"I wanted to get him out of the way so I could drink it all myself," said Fourreau, his teeth chattering with terror.

"Gentlemen," said d'Artagnan, again addressing the Guardsmen, "you must realize that a feast could only be very sad after what has taken place, so please excuse me and let us postpone our party for some other day."

The two Guardsmen courteously accepted d'Artagnan's apology, and seeing that the four friends wished to be alone, they left.

When the young Guardsman and the three Musketeers were without witnesses, they looked at one another with an expression that plainly showed that each of them understood the gravity of their situation.

"In the first place," said Athos, "let us not remain in this room. The dead are not agreeable company, particularly when they have died a violent death."

"Planchet," said d'Artagnan, "I leave this poor devil's corpse to your care. Let him be buried in holy ground. He commited a crime, it is true, but he repented of it."

And the four friends walked out, leaving the arrangements for Brisemont's funeral to Planchet and Fourreau.

The host gave them another room and served them with boiled eggs; Athos himself went to the fountain for water. In a few words, everything was explained to Porthos and Aramis.

"You see, my friend," said d'Artagnan to Athos, "that this is war to the death."

Athos nodded.

"Yes," he replied, "I see it plainly. But are you sure it is she?"

"I am sure."

"I confess I still have my doubts."

"But the fleur-de-lis on her shoulder?"

"She may be some Englishwoman who committed a crime in France and was branded in consequence."

"Athos, she is your wife, I tell you," repeated d'Artagnan. "Just remember how much the two descriptions matched."

"Yes, but I would have sworn the other must be dead after I hanged her so effectively."

D'Artagnan shook his head.

"But in either case, what shall we do?" he asked.

"It is true that we cannot go on like this, with a sword constantly hanging over our heads," said Athos. "We must end the situation."

"But how?"

"You must try to see and talk to her. Say: 'Peace or war! My word as a gentleman never to say anything about you, never to do anything against you. On your side, a solemn oath to remain neutral toward me. If not,

I will apply to the chancellor, I will apply to the king, I will apply to the hangman, I will turn the court against you, I will denounce you as branded, I will bring you to trial—and if you are acquitted, well, by the faith of a gentleman, I will kill you in the street, as I would a mad dog.' "

"I like that idea well enough," said d'Artagnan. "But where and how can I meet with her?"

"All in good time, my friend. Time brings opportunity. The more we have ventured the more we gain, when we know how to wait."

"Yes, but to wait surrounded by assassins and poisoners . . ."

"God has preserved us until now, God will continue to preserve us."

"Yes, *us*. And we are men—it is our lot to risk our lives. But *she*," he added in an undertone.

"What *she*?" asked Athos.

"Constance."

"Madame Bonacieux! Ah, that's true!" said Athos. "My poor friend, I had forgotten you were in love."

Aramis interrupted. "But have you not learned from the letter you found on the corpse that she is in a convent? Life can be very comfortable in a convent, and I promise you that as soon as the siege of La Rochelle is over . . ."

"Yes, we all know, my dear Aramis, that you have religious tendencies."

"I am a Musketeer only temporarily," Aramis said humbly.

"It is a long time since he has heard from his mistress," said Athos softly. "But pay no attention—you know how that affects him."

"It seems very simple to me," said Porthos.

"What do you mean?" asked d'Artagnan.

"You say she is in a convent?"

"Yes."

"Well, as soon as the siege is over, we'll get her out of that convent."

"But first we have to know what convent she is in."

"That's true," said Porthos.

"But I think I have it," said Athos. "Did you not

say, d'Artagnan, that it is the queen who has chosen the convent for her?"

"Yes—or at least I think so."

"In that case Porthos will be able to help us."

"How so?" Porthos asked.

"Why, through your marchioness, your duchess, your princess. She must have some influence."

"Hush!" said Porthos, putting a finger on his lip. "I think she may be a cardinalist, so she must know nothing about this."

"Then I will be the one to discover which convent it is," said Aramis.

"You, Aramis?" exclaimed the three friends. "You! How?"

"Through the queen's chaplain, who is a close friend," said Aramis, blushing.

And with this assurance, the four friends, who had finished their modest meal, separated, promising to meet again that evening. D'Artagnan returned to the Minimes, and the three Musketeers to the king's quarters, where they had to see about their lodging.

43

The Colombier-Rouge Inn

MEANWHILE THE KING, who hated Buckingham as much as the cardinal did and with more reason, was in such a hurry to meet the enemy that he had scarcely arrived before he began preparations to drive the English from the Ile de Ré and then to press the siege of La Rochelle; but notwithstanding this desire, he was delayed by the dissensions which broke out between Messieurs Bassompierre and Schomberg on the one hand and the Duc d'Angoulême on the other.

Bassompierre and Schomberg were marshals of France and claimed their right to command the army under the orders of the king; but the cardinal was afraid that Bassompierre, a Huguenot at heart, might wage only a half-hearted war against the English and the Rochellais—his brothers in religion—and supported the Duc d'Angoulême, whom the king, at the cardinal's urging, had named lieutenant general. The result was that to prevent Bassompierre and Schomberg from deserting the army, a separate command had to be given to each. Bassompierre had the area north of the city, between La Leu and Dompierre; the Duc d'Angoulême had the east, from Dompierre to Périgny; and Schomberg had the south, from Perigny to Angoutin.

Monsieur's quarters were at Dompierre; the king's were sometimes at Etré, sometimes at La Jarrie; the cardinal's were on the dunes, near the La Pierre bridge, in a simple house without any entrenchments. Monsieur could watch Bassompierre; the king could watch the Duc d'Angoulême; and the cardinal could watch Schomberg.

As soon as the arrangements had been made, they set about driving the English from the island.

The situation was favorable. The English, who must have good food in order to be good soldiers, were eating only salt meat and rotten biscuits and thus had many sick men in their camp. In addition, the sea was very rough at this time of year all along the coast, and every day some little ship foundered: the whole shore, from the Pointe de l'Aiguillon to the trench, was at every tide littered with the wrecks of pinnaces and feluccas. This meant that even if the king's troops remained quietly in their camp, Buckingham would sooner or later have to leave the island, especially since it was only obstinacy that kept him there.

But since M. de Toiras reported that the enemy was preparing for a fresh assault, the king decided that it would be best to take some decisive action and gave the necessary orders.

It is not our intention to report every detail of the siege but, on the contrary, only to describe those events that have a bearing on our story, so we will simply say that the expedition succeeded—to the great astonishment of the king and the great glory of the cardinal. The English, forced back foot by foot, beaten in all encounters, and overwhelmed in the channel of the Ile de Loie, were obliged to retreat to their ships, leaving on the battlefield two thousand men, among whom were five colonels, three lieutenant colonels, two hundred and fifty captains, twenty noblemen, four cannons, and sixty flags that were taken to Paris by Claude de St. Simon and suspended from the vaults of Notre Dame with great pomp.

Te Deums were sung in the camp and, later, throughout France.

The cardinal was left free to continue the siege without having, at least for the present, anything to fear from the English.

But this respite was only temporary. An envoy of the Duke of Buckingham, named Montague, was captured, and proof was obtained that the German Empire, Spain, England, and Lorraine had formed a league directed against France.

In addition, Buckingham had been forced to abandon his quarters more hurriedly than he had expected, and papers were found which confirmed this alliance and which—according to the cardinal's memoirs—strongly compromised Mme. de Chevreuse and consequently the queen.

It was the cardinal who bore all the responsibility, for one cannot be a despotic minister without having full responsibility. Therefore all the vast resources of his genius were at work night and day, gathering every rumor from all the great kingdoms of Europe.

The cardinal was aware of Buckingham's energy and, more particularly, of his enmity. If the league that threatened France triumphed, all Richelieu's influence would be lost. Spanish policy and Austrian policy would have their representatives in the cabinet of the Louvre, where as yet they had only supporters; and he, Richelieu—the French minister, the national minister—would be ruined. The king, though he obeyed him like a child, also hated him, as a child hates his master, and would abandon him to the combined vengeance of Monsieur and the queen. He would be lost, and perhaps France would be lost with him. He had to guard against all this.

Day and night, in the little house near La Pierre bridge in which the cardinal had established his residence, an ever-increasing number of couriers came one after another.

There were monks who wore their robes so awkwardly that it was easy to see they belonged to the church mili-

tant; there were women who were inconvenienced by
their pages' costumes and whose loose trousers could not
entirely conceal their curves; and there were peasants
who had dirty hands but whose fine limbs proclaimed the
nobleman a league away.

There were also less agreeable visits: there were
rumors that the cardinal had on several occasions nearly
been assassinated.

It was true that the cardinal's enemies said that it was
he himself who had set those bungling assassins to work,
in order to have, if necessary, a reason for reprisals; but
we must not believe a minister's enemies any more than
we believe the minister himself.

In any event, the attempts on his life did not prevent
the cardinal—whose personal bravery was never denied
by his worst enemies—from making nocturnal excur-
sions, sometimes to give important orders to the Duc
d'Angoulême, sometimes to confer with the king, and
sometimes to have an interview with a messenger he did
not wish to see at home.

As for the Musketeers, who did not have much to do
with the siege, they were not under very strict orders and
led an enjoyable life—especially our three companions,
for being friends of M. de Tréville, they were able to
obtain from him special permission to leave the camp at
night.

One evening, when d'Artagnan, who was on trench
duty, was not able to accompany them, Athos, Porthos,
and Aramis—mounted on their battle steeds, enveloped
in their war cloaks, their hands on their pistol butts—
were returning from the Colombier-Rouge inn, which
Athos had discovered two days earlier on the La Jarrie
road. Following the path that led back to the camp, and
on their guard against a possible ambush, they were
about a quarter of a league from the village of Boisnau
when they thought they heard the sound of approaching
horses. They immediately stopped, moved close together,
and waited in the middle of the road. In a few minutes,
just as the moon came out from behind a cloud, they
saw two horsemen appear at a bend in the road. Seeing
the Musketeers, the two riders also stopped, apparently
trying to decide if they should continue on their way or
turn back.

Their hesitation made the three friends suspicious, and Athos, advancing a few paces in front of the others, called out in a firm voice, "Who goes there?"

"Who goes there yourselves?" replied one of the horsemen.

"That is not an answer," said Athos. "Who goes there? Answer, or we charge."

"Be careful of what you are about to do, gentlemen!" warned a clear voice that seemed accustomed to command.

"It is some superior officer making his night rounds," Athos said to his friends. "What shall we do, gentlemen?"

"Who are you?" said the same voice, in the same commanding tone. "Answer, or you may regret your disobedience."

"King's Musketeers," said Athos, more and more convinced that the person who was questioning them had the right to do so.

"What company?"

"Tréville's company."

"Advance, and explain what you are doing here at this hour."

The three companions advanced rather humbly, for all were now convinced that they had to do with someone more powerful than themselves. Aramis and Porthos let Athos do the talking.

One of the two riders, the one who had just spoken, was ten paces in front of his companion; Athos motioned Porthos and Aramis also to remain in the rear, and advanced alone.

"Your pardon, sir," he said, "but we did not know who you were, and as you see, we were keeping good guard on the road."

"Your name?" asked the officer, whose face was partially covered by his cloak.

"But you, monsieur," said Athos, becoming annoyed by this inquisition, "please give me some proof that you have the right to question me."

"Your name?" repeated the cavalier, letting his cloak fall and leaving his face uncovered.

"Monsieur le Cardinal!" exclaimed the stupefied Musketeer.

"Your name?" his Eminence asked for the third time.

"Athos."

The cardinal gestured to his attendant, who drew near. "These three Musketeers shall follow us," he said, in an undertone. "I do not want it to be known that I have left the camp, and if they are following us, we can be certain they will have no opportunity to tell anyone."

"We are gentlemen, monseigneur," said Athos. "Ask us to give our word, and then do not be uneasy. Thank God, we know how to keep a secret."

The cardinal fixed his piercing eyes on the man who spoke so boldly.

"You have good ears, Monsieur Athos," he said, "so listen to this. I wish you to follow me not because I do not trust you but for my own safety. Your companions are no doubt Messieurs Porthos and Aramis?"

"Yes, your Eminence," said Athos, while the two Musketeers who had remained behind advanced with their hats in their hands.

"I know you, gentlemen," said the cardinal. "I know you. You are not really my friends, and I am sorry you are not, but I also know you are brave and loyal gentlemen and that I may trust you. Monsieur Athos, do me the honor to accompany me, you and your two friends, and then I will have an escort to excite envy even in his Majesty, if we should meet him."

The three Musketeers bowed so low that their heads met the necks of their horses.

"Well, upon my honor," said Athos, "I believe your Eminence is right to take us with you. We have seen several unpleasant faces on the road, and we even had a quarrel at the Colombier-Rouge with four of those faces."

"A quarrel? What about, gentlemen?" asked the cardinal. "You know I don't like quarrelers."

"And that is exactly why I have the honor to inform your Eminence of what has happened. You might otherwise hear it elsewhere, explained falsely, and believe us to be at fault."

"What have been the results of your quarrel?" asked the cardinal, frowning.

"My friend Aramis has received a slight sword wound in the arm, but as your Eminence can see, not enough to prevent him from storming the walls tomorrow if you should order an escalade."

"You are not the men to allow sword wounds to be inflicted upon you like this," said the cardinal, "or at least not without inflicting some yourselves. Be frank, gentlemen—confess. You know I have the right to give absolution."

"I, monseigneur?" said Athos. "I did not even draw my sword—but I did take the man who offended me and throw him out the window. It seems that in falling," continued Athos hesitantly, "he broke his thigh."

"Ah," said the cardinal. "And you, Monsieur Porthos?"

"I, monseigneur, knowing that dueling is forbidden, I seized a bench and gave one of those brigands such a blow with it that I believe it broke his shoulder."

"Very well," said the cardinal. "And you, Monsieur Aramis?"

"Monseigneur, being of a very mild disposition, and also being, as Monseigneur may not know, about to take holy orders, I was trying to remove my comrades from the scene when one of those scoundrels treacherously gave me a sword wound on my left arm. Then I admit I lost patience. I drew my sword too, and just as he attacked me again, I believe I felt him let it pass through his body. All I know for a certainty is that he fell, and that it seemed to me that he was carried away with his two companions."

"The devil, gentlemen!" said the cardinal. "Three men put out of action in a tavern squabble! You do not believe in halfway measures. What was the quarrel about?"

"Those fellows were drunk," said Athos. "They knew a lady had arrived at the inn this evening, and they wanted to force her door."

"Force her door! Why?"

"To do her violence, most probably," said Athos. "As I have already had the honor of informing your Eminence, the men were drunk."

"Was the lady young and beautiful?" the cardinal asked, with a certain degree of anxiety.

"We did not see her, monseigneur," Athos replied.

"You did not see her—ah, very good," said the cardinal quickly. "You did well to defend a woman's honor, and since I am going to the Colombier-Rouge myself, I will know if you have told me the truth."

"Monseigneur," Athos said haughtily, "we are gentlemen, and to save our heads we would not tell a lie."

"That is why I do not doubt what you say, Monsieur Athos, not for a single instant. But tell me, was the lady alone?"

"The lady had a gentleman in her room," said Athos, "but since despite the noise, the gentleman did not show himself, he is presumably a coward."

"Judge not rashly, says the Gospel," the cardinal intoned.

Athos bowed.

"And now, gentlemen," continued the cardinal, "I know what I wanted to know. Follow me."

The three Musketeers passed behind his Eminence, who again hid his face in his cloak and rode off, keeping eight or ten paces in advance of the four other men.

They soon arrived at the silent, deserted inn. The host, undoubtedly knowing what illustrious visitor was expected, must have sent everyone out of the way.

Ten paces from the door the cardinal signaled his equerry and the three Musketeers to halt. A saddled horse was fastened to the window shutter. The cardinal knocked three times in a special way.

A man, wrapped in a cloak, came out immediately, and exchanged some quick words with the cardinal, after which he mounted his horse and set off in the direction of Surgères, which was also the way to Paris.

"Advance, gentlemen," said the cardinal to the three Musketeers. "You have told me the truth, and it will not be my fault if our encounter this evening is not to your advantage. In the meantime, follow me."

The cardinal dismounted; the three Musketeers did likewise. The cardinal threw the reins of his horse to his equerry; the three Musketeers fastened their horses to the shutters.

The host stood at the door. To him, the cardinal was only an officer coming to visit a lady.

"Have you a room on the ground floor where these gentlemen can wait near a good fire?" the cardinal asked.

The host opened the door of a large room in which an

inefficient stove had just been replaced by a large and excellent fireplace.

"I have this," he said.

"That will do," replied the cardinal. "Go in, gentlemen, and be kind enough to wait for me. It will not take more than half an hour."

And while the three Musketeers entered the ground-floor room, the cardinal, without asking for additional directions, climbed the stairs like a man who knows quite well where to go.

44

The Usefulness of Stovepipes

IT WAS EVIDENT that without suspecting it, and actuated solely by their chivalrous and adventurous character, our three friends had just rendered a service to someone the cardinal honored with his special protection.

Who was that someone? That was the question the three Musketeers put to one another until they saw that none of their replies could throw any light on the subject—after which Porthos called the host and asked for dice.

Porthos and Aramis sat down at the table and began to play; Athos paced up and down, thinking.

While thinking and pacing, he passed back and forth in front of the stovepipe that had been broken in half, its upper part extending into the room above; and every time he passed it he heard a murmur of voices, which finally caught his attention. Approaching the stovepipe, he was able to distinguish some words that interested him so much that he signaled his friends to be silent while he remained with his ear next to the open end of the pipe.

"Milady," the cardinal was saying, "this is important. Sit down, and let us talk."

"Milady!" Athos said softly.

"I listen to your Eminence with the greatest attention," replied a female voice that shocked the Musketeer out of his usual impassiveness.

"A small ship with an English crew, whose captain is

one of my men, is waiting for you at the mouth of the Charente, near the fort of La Pointe. It will set sail tomorrow morning."

"I must go there tonight?"

"Instantly! That is, as soon as you have received my instructions. Two men, whom you will find waiting at the door, will serve as your escort. You will allow me to leave first, then you will leave half an hour later."

"Yes, monseigneur. Now let us return to my mission. Since I wish to continue to deserve your Eminence's confidence, please explain it to me clearly and precisely, so I will not make any errors."

There was a moment of profound silence between them; it was evident that the cardinal was planning carefully what he was going to say, and that Milady was gathering all her intellectual faculties to understand and remember his words.

Athos took advantage of this moment to tell his two companions to fasten the door from the inside and to come and listen with him.

The two Musketeers, who loved their comforts, brought a chair for each of themselves and one for Athos. All three then sat down with their heads close together and their ears alert.

"You will go to London," said the cardinal, "and once there, you will seek Buckingham."

"Your Eminence must know," said Milady, "that the duke has suspected and distrusted me ever since the affair of the diamond studs."

"Well, this time it is not necessary to win his confidence, but to present yourself frankly and honestly as a negotiator."

"Frankly and honestly," Milady repeated, with an indescribable expression of duplicity.

"Yes, frankly and honestly," the cardinal replied in the same tone. "All these negotiations must be carried on openly."

"I will follow your Eminence's instructions to the letter, and am only waiting to hear them."

"You will go to Buckingham on my behalf and tell him that I know about all his preparations but that they do not worry me because at his first move I will ruin the queen."

"Will he believe that your Eminence is in a position to carry out this threat?"

"Yes, for I have all the proofs."

"I must be able to present those proofs so he can judge them for himself."

"Of course. You will tell him I will make public the report of Bois-Robert and the Marquis de Beautru about the interview the duke had with the queen at the residence of the Chief Constable's wife on the evening she gave a masquerade party. You will tell him, in order that he may have no doubts, that he went there in the costume of the Grand Mogul, which the Chevalier de Guise was to have worn, and that he bought this exchange for three thousand pistoles."

"Very well, monseigneur."

"You will tell him all the details of his comings and goings at the palace on the night when he was disguised as an Italian fortuneteller so that he may not doubt the accuracy of my information. You will tell him that under his cloak he was wearing a large white robe dotted with black tears, death's heads, and crossbones, for in case he was discovered, he was to pass for the phantom of the White Lady, who, as all the world knows, appears at the Louvre whenever any great event is imminent."

"Is that all, monseigneur?"

"Tell him also that I know all the details of the adventure at Amiens and that I will have a witty little romance written about it, with a plan of the garden and portraits of the principal actors in that nocturnal scene."

"I will tell him that."

"Tell him as well that I have Montague in my power, that he is in the Bastille, and that although no letters were found on him, that torture may make him tell what he knows . . . and even what he does not know."

"Wonderful."

"Then finally, tell him that in his haste to leave the Ile de Ré, he left behind a certain letter from Madame de Chevreuse that seriously compromises the queen, inasmuch as it proves not only that her Majesty can love the enemies of the king but that she can conspire with the enemies of France. . . . Do you remember everything I have told you?"

"Your Eminence himself will judge—the ball of the

Chief Constable's wife, the night at the Louvre, the evening at Amiens, the arrest of Montague, the letter of Madame de Chevreuse."

"That is correct," said the cardinal. "You have an excellent memory, Milady."

"But what if, in spite of all those reasons, the duke does not give way and continues to threaten France?"

"The duke is in love to the point of madness, or rather to folly," replied Richelieu with great bitterness. "Like the ancient paladins, he undertook this war only to obtain a glance from his lady love. If he knows that this war can cause her to lose her honor and perhaps even her liberty, I promise you he will think twice."

"But if he persists . . ." said Milady, with a persistence that proved she wished to examine every possibility of the mission she was about to undertake.

"If he persists? That is not likely."

"It is possible."

His Eminence paused, then resumed, "If he persists . . . well, then I will hope for one of those events which change the destinies of nations."

"If your Eminence would give me some examples of such events, perhaps I would share your confidence in the future."

"Here is one example. In 1610, for a reason similar to that which motivates Buckingham, King Henry the Fourth, of glorious memory, was about to invade Flanders and Italy simultaneously in order to attack Austria on both sides—but did no event occur to save Austria? Why should not the King of France be as fortunate as the emperor of Austria?"

"I presume your Eminence means to remind me of Ravaillac's stabbing of Henry the Fourth on the Rue de la Féronnerie?"

"Precisely."

"Does your Eminence not fear that Ravaillac's punishment might deter anyone from entertaining the idea of imitating him?"

"In all times and in all countries, particularly if religious divisions exist in those countries, there will be fanatics who ask nothing better than to become martyrs. And it just occurs to me that the English Puritans are furious with Buckingham—their preachers call him the Antichrist."

"Well?" said Milady.

"Well," the cardinal continued in an indifferent tone, "it would only be necessary to find some beautiful, young, and clever woman who has reason to wish revenge on the duke. Such a woman should be easy to find—the duke has had many affairs, and if he has promised eternal constancy, he must have sown the seeds of hatred by his eternal infidelities."

"No doubt such a woman could be found," said Milady coolly.

"Well, such a woman, who would place the knife of Jacques Clément or of Ravaillac in the hands of a fanatic, would save France."

"Yes, but she would then be an assassin's accomplice."

"Were the accomplices of Ravaillac—or of Jacques Clément, who assassinated Henry the Third—ever discovered?"

"No, but they might have been too important for anyone to dare look for them where they were. One does not burn down the Palais de Justice for everybody, monseigneur."

"You think that the fire at the Palais de Justice was not an accident?" asked Richelieu, in a tone of indifference that implied the question was not very important.

"I, monseigneur?" replied Milady. "I think nothing—I merely state a fact, that is all. But I say that if I were Mademoiselle de Montpensier or Queen Marie de Médicis instead of Lady de Winter, I would use fewer precautions than I now take."

"That is true," said Richelieu, "so what do you require?"

"I require an order that authorizes me to do anything I think it proper to do for the good of France."

"But first the woman I have described must be found—the one who wants to avenge herself on the duke."

"She is found," said Milady.

"Then the miserable fanatic who will serve as an instrument of God's justice must be found."

"He will be found."

"Then that will be the time to claim the order you just now required," said the cardinal.

"Your Eminence is right," replied Milady, "and I have been wrong in seeing the mission with which you honor me as anything but what it is—that is, to announce to his Grace, on the part of your Eminence, that you are acquainted with the different disguises by means of which he succeeded in approaching the queen during the fête given by the Chief Constable's wife, that you have proofs of the queen's meeting at the Louvre with a certain Italian astrologer who was no other than the Duke of Buckingham, that you have ordered a little romance of a satirical nature to be written about the adventure at Amiens—with a plan of the gardens in which that adventure took place and portraits of the people who figured in it, that Montague is in the Bastille and that torture may make him say things he remembers, and even things he has forgotten, and finally, that you possess a certain letter from Madame de Chevreuse, found in his Grace's quarters, which compromises not only the writer but the one in whose name it was written. Then, if he persists despite all this—which is, as I have said, the limit of my mission—I shall have nothing to do but pray God to work a miracle for the salvation of France. That is it, is it not, monseigneur, and I shall have nothing else to do?"

"That is it," replied the cardinal dryly.

"And now," said Milady, without seeming to notice the change in the duke's tone toward her, "now that I have received the instructions of your Eminence as concerns your enemies, will Monseigneur permit me to say a few words to him about mine?"

"You have enemies?" asked Richelieu.

"Yes, monseigneur, enemies against whom you owe me all your support, for I made them by serving your Eminence."

"Who are they?"

"In the first place, there is a little schemer named Bonacieux."

"She is in the prison of Mantes."

"She *was* there," replied Milady, "but the queen has obtained an order from the king by means of which the woman has been transferred to a convent."

"To a convent?"

"Yes, to a convent."

"To which one?"

"I do not know. The secret has been well kept."

"But *I* will know!"

"And your Eminence will tell me in what convent that woman is?"

"I can see nothing inconvenient about that."

"Good. Now I also have an enemy much more to be dreaded than that little Madame Bonacieux."

"Who is that?"

"Her lover."

"What is his name?"

"Oh, your Eminence knows him well!" cried Milady, carried away by her anger. "He is the evil genius of both of us. It is he who in an encounter with your Eminence's Guards gave the victory to the king's Musketeers. It is he who gave three sword wounds to your emissary de Wardes, and who caused the affair of the diamond studs to fail. It is he who has sworn my death because he knows it was I who had Madame Bonacieux carried off."

"Ah, I know the man you mean."

"I mean that miserable d'Artagnan."

"He is a bold fellow."

"It is exactly because he is a bold fellow that he is the more to be feared."

"I need evidence of his connection with Buckingham."

"Evidence? You will have ten times more than you need!"

"Then it becomes the simplest thing in the world. Get me that evidence, and I will send him to the Bastille."

"Fine, monseigneur—but afterward?"

"Once in the Bastille, there is no afterward!" said the cardinal, in a low voice. "Ah, if it were as easy for me to get rid of my enemy as it is to get rid of yours, and if it were only against such people that you required my protection . . ."

"Monseigneur," said Milady, "a fair exchange. A life for a life, a man for a man. Rid me of one, I will rid you of the other."

"I do not know what you mean, nor do I even wish to know what you mean," replied the cardinal. "But I do wish to please you, and I see no reason not to do as you desire about so insignificant a creature—especially since you tell me this d'Artagnan is a libertine, a duelist, and a traitor."

"An infamous scoundrel, monseigneur!"

"Then give me some paper, a quill, and some ink," said the cardinal.

"Here they are, monseigneur."

There was a moment of silence, which indicated that the cardinal was thinking about what he should write, or perhaps even writing it, and Athos, who had heard every word of the conversation, led his two companions to the other end of the room.

"What do you want? Why do you not let us listen to the end of the conversation?" asked Porthos.

"We have heard everything we had to hear. Besides, I am not stopping *you* from listening, but *I* must leave," Athos replied softly.

"You must leave!" exclaimed Porthos. "What if the cardinal asks for you? What shall we tell him?"

"You will not wait till he asks. You will speak first and tell him that I have gone ahead because certain things our host said made me think the road might not be safe. I will say a few words about it to the cardinal's equerry as well. The rest concerns only myself—do not be uneasy about it."

"Be careful, Athos," said Aramis.

"Never fear. You know I am always cool-headed."

Porthos and Aramis went back to their places near the stovepipe.

Athos left quite openly, took his horse—which was tied with those of his friends to the shutters—convinced the equerry of the necessity of acting as a scout to prepare for the cardinal's return, carefully examined the priming of his pistols, drew his sword, and rode off along the road to the camp.

45

A Conjugal Scene

As Athos had foreseen, it was not long before the cardinal came downstairs. He opened the door of the room in which the Musketeers were waiting, found Porthos and Aramis playing an earnest game of dice, looked quickly around the room, and noticed that one of his men was missing.

"Where is Monsieur Athos?" he asked.

"He has gone ahead as a scout for you. Our host said some things that made him believe the road might not be safe," replied Porthos.

"And what have you been doing, Monsieur Porthos?"

"I have won five pistoles from Aramis."

"And will you now return with me?"

"We are at your Eminence's orders."

"To horse, then, gentlemen, for it is getting late."

The equerry was at the door, holding the cardinal's horse by the reins. A little farther away a group of two men and three horses were waiting in the shadows. They were the two men who were to conduct Milady to the fort at La Pointe and assist her in boarding the ship.

The equerry confirmed what the two Musketeers had already told the cardinal about Athos. His Eminence made an approving gesture, and began to retrace his route with the same precautions he had used in coming.

Let us leave him on the road to the camp, protected by his equerry and the two Musketeers, and return to Athos.

For some hundred paces he had maintained his original speed, but when he was out of sight he turned his horse to the right, circled around, and came back to within twenty paces of where he had begun, to watch for the little troop from a thicket. Having recognized his companions' braided hats and the cardinal's gold-fringed cloak, he waited till the horsemen had turned the bend

432

in the road and disappeared, then galloped back to the inn, which was opened to him without hesitation.

The host recognized him.

"My officer," said Athos, "has forgotten to give some very important information to the lady and has asked me to do it for him."

"Go on up," said the host. "She is still in her room."

Athos did so, climbing the stairs quietly. From the landing, he could see through the partly open door: Milady was putting on her hat.

He entered the room and closed the door behind him.

At the noise he made in pushing the bolt, Milady turned around.

Athos was standing in front of the door, enveloped in his cloak, his hat pulled down over his eyes.

Seeing this figure, mute and motionless as a statue, Milady was frightened.

"Who are you, and what do you want?" she cried.

"Yes, it is certainly she," Athos murmured to himself.

Letting his cloak fall and raising his hat, he walked toward her.

"Do you recognize me, madame?" he asked her.

Milady took a step forward, then drew back as if she had seen a serpent.

"I see you do," said Athos.

"The Comte de la Fère!" whispered Milady, becoming very pale and backing away till the wall prevented her from going any farther.

"Yes, Milady," replied Athos. "The Comte de la Fère in person, come expressly from the other world to have the pleasure of paying you a visit. Sit down, madame, and let us talk, as the cardinal said."

Under the influence of an inexpressible terror, Milady sat down without uttering a word.

"Are you a demon?" Athos asked. "I know your power is great, but you must know that with the help of God men have often overcome the most terrible demons. You have once before crossed my path, and I thought I had crushed you—but either I was mistaken or the devil has brought you back to life!"

These words recalled intolerable memories, and Milady bowed her head and groaned.

"Yes, the devil has resuscitated you," Athos continued. "The devil has made you rich, the devil has given you another name, the devil has almost made you another face—but he has erased neither the stains from your soul nor the brand from your body."

Milady sprang to her feet, her eyes flashing lightning. Athos remained seated.

"You thought I was dead, did you not, just as I thought you were dead? And the name of Athos concealed the Comte de la Fère, just as the name Lady de Winter concealed Anne de Breuil. That *was* your name when your honored brother married us, was it not? Our situation is truly strange," continued Athos, laughing. "We have been able to go on living only because each believed the other dead, and because a memory is less oppressive than a living person—though a memory can sometimes be quite devastating."

"But what brings you back to me? What do you want with me?" Milady asked in a hollow, faint voice.

"I wish to tell you that though I have remained invisible to you, you have not been so to me."

"You know what I have done?"

"I can tell you what you have done on every day from the time you entered the cardinal's service to this very evening."

An incredulous smile passed over Milady's pale lips.

"Just listen! It was you who cut the two diamond studs from the Duke of Buckingham's shoulder. It was you who had Madame Bonacieux abducted. It was you who hoped to spend the night with de Wardes, whom you loved, but opened the door to d'Artagnan instead. It was you who believed that de Wardes had deceived you and wished to have him killed by his rival. It was you who, when this rival had discovered your disgraceful secret, wished to have him killed in his turn by two assassins, whom you sent after him. It was you who, learning that the bullets had missed their mark, sent poisoned wine with a forged letter to make your victim believe that the wine had come from his friends. Finally, it was you who have just arranged, in this room and seated in this chair I am now sitting in, with Cardinal Richelieu to have the Duke of Buckingham murdered in exchange for the cardinal's promise to allow you to murder d'Artagnan."

Milady was livid.

"You must be Satan himself!" she cried.

"Perhaps I am," said Athos. "But whether I am or not, listen to me carefully. Murder the Duke of Buckingham or have him murdered—I care very little about that! I do not know him, and besides, he is an Englishman. But do not touch with the tip of your finger a single hair of d'Artagnan, who is a loyal friend whom I love and defend, or I swear to you by the head of my father that that will be your last crime."

"Monsieur d'Artagnan has cruelly insulted me," Milady said obstinately. "Monsieur d'Artagnan will die!"

"Is it possible that one can insult you, madame?" Athos laughed. "He has insulted you, and he will die! Indeed!"

"He will die!" repeated Milady. "*She* first, and then he later."

Athos was seized with a kind of vertigo. The sight of this unwomanly creature brought back the terrible past. He remembered how one day, in a less dangerous situation than the present one, he had tried to sacrifice her to his honor. He felt the same bloodthirsty fury return, possessing him like a raging fever. He stood up, drew a pistol from his belt, and cocked it.

Pale as a corpse, Milady tried to cry out, but her swollen tongue could do no more than utter a hoarse sound, more like that of a wild beast than anything human. Rigid against the dark tapestry, her hair in disorder, she was like a living image of terror.

Athos slowly raised his pistol, extended his arm so that the weapon almost touched Milady's forehead, and then, in a voice the more terrible from having the supreme calm of an unalterable determination, said, "Madame, you will this instant give me the paper the cardinal signed, or I swear I will blow your brains out."

With another man, Milady might have had some doubts, but she knew Athos. Nevertheless, she did not move.

"You have one second to decide," he said.

She saw by the contraction of his face that he was about to pull the trigger; she quickly put her hand to her bosom, drew out a sheet of paper, and handed it to Athos.

"Take it and be damned!" she said.

Athos took the note, returned the pistol to his belt, approached the lamp to make sure that it was the right paper, unfolded it, and read:

Dec. 3, 1627

It is by my order and for the good of the state that the bearer of this has done what has been done.

RICHELIEU

"And now," said Athos, putting on his cloak and hat again, "now that I have drawn your teeth, viper, bite if you can!"

And he left the room without even looking back.

At the door he found the two men and the horse they were holding for Milady.

"Gentlemen," he said, "Monseigneur's order is, as you know, to conduct that woman, without losing any time, to the fort of La Pointe and to stay with her till she is on board."

As these words agreed wholly with the order they had received, they nodded.

Athos leaped lightly into the saddle and set out at a full gallop, but instead of following the road, he cut across the fields, urging his horse to the utmost speed and stopping occasionally to listen.

During one of those stops he heard the hoofbeats of several horses on the road. He was sure it was the cardinal and his escort. He immediately rode ahead, rubbed his horse down with some heather and some leaves, and positioned himself across the road about two hundred paces from the camp.

"Who goes there?" he cried, as soon as he saw the horsemen.

"That is our brave Musketeer, I think," said the cardinal.

"Yes, monseigneur," said Athos, "it is I."

"Monsieur Athos," said Richelieu, "thank you for the good guard you have kept for us. Gentlemen, we have arrived. Take the gate on the left—the password is, 'King and Ré.' "

Saying these words, the cardinal nodded to the three friends and rode off to the right, followed by his equerry;

that night even the cardinal was going to sleep in the camp.

"Well, he wrote the letter she wanted!" said Porthos and Aramis together, as soon as the cardinal was out of hearing.

"I know," said Athos serenely, "since here it is."

And the three friends did not say another word till they reached their quarters, except to give the password to the sentries. Then they sent Mousqueton to tell Planchet that they wanted his master to come to them as soon as he left the trenches.

Meanwhile Milady had made no difficulty about following the two men that were waiting for her. She had for a moment been tempted to ask to be taken to the cardinal, but a revelation from her would have brought about a revelation from Athos. She could say that Athos had hanged her, but then he would say that she was branded. She decided it would be better to remain silent, to discreetly manage her difficult mission with her usual skill, and then—when everything had been accomplished to the cardinal's satisfaction—to go to him and claim her vengeance.

Consequently, after having traveled all night, at seven o'clock she was at the fort of La Pointe; at eight o'clock she had boarded the ship; and at nine o'clock, the vessel, which was supposed to be sailing for Bayonne with letters of marque from the cardinal, weighed anchor and set its course for England.

46

The Saint-Gervais Bastion

ARRIVING AT THE LODGINGS of his three friends, d'Artagnan found them all together in the same room. Athos was thinking; Porthos was curling his mustache; Aramis was saying his prayers from a charming little Book of Hours bound in blue velvet.

"*Pardieu*, gentlemen," said d'Artagnan. "I hope what you have to tell me is worth the trouble, or I will not pardon you for making me come here instead of letting me get a little rest after spending the night capturing and dismantling a bastion. Ah, why were you not there, gentlemen? It was an interesting bit of work."

"We were elsewhere, and it was not uninteresting there either," replied Porthos, twisting his mustache in his special way.

"Quiet!" said Athos.

"Oh, oh!" said d'Artagnan, understanding his friend's slight frown. "It seems something new has happened."

"Aramis," said Athos, "you had breakfast at the Parpaillot inn the day before yesterday, did you not?"

"Yes."

"How was it?"

"I did not eat very much. The day before yesterday was a fish day, but they only had meat."

"What, no fish at a seaport?"

"They say that the dike that the cardinal is building drives them all out into the open sea," replied Aramis, resuming his pious reading.

"But that is not quite what I am asking you, Aramis," said Athos. "I want to know if you were left alone, if nobody interrupted you."

"Ah, I see. No, there were not many intruders. Yes, Athos, I think we can be very comfortable at the Parpaillot."

"Then let us go there, for the walls are like sheets of paper here."

D'Artagnan was accustomed to his friend's manner of acting and could always tell immediately, from a word or a gesture, when something serious was afoot. He took Athos's arm, and they went out without speaking. Porthos and Aramis followed, chatting together.

On their way they met Grimaud. Athos signaled him to come with them, and as usual, he obeyed in silence; the poor lad had almost forgotten how to speak.

They arrived at the Parpaillot about seven o'clock in the morning, just as the sun began to rise. The three friends ordered breakfast, and went into a room in which the host said they would not be disturbed.

Unfortunately, it was a bad time for a private conversation. Reveille had just sounded, and everyone was coming in for a drink to shake off his drowsiness and to

dispel the damp morning chill. Dragoons, Swiss merce-
naries, Guardsmen, Musketeers, light-horsemen, came
and went incessantly, which probably pleased the host
but was contrary to the plans of the four friends, who
therefore replied very curtly to the greetings, toasts, and
jokes of their companions.

"I see how all this will end," said Athos. "We will
become embroiled in some quarrel or other, and that is
something we have no need of just now. D'Artagnan,
tell us about your night, and we will describe ours later."

"Ah, yes," said a light-horseman who was sipping
slowly from a glass of brandy, "I hear you gentlemen of
the Guards have been in the trenches tonight, and that
you had a set-to with the enemy."

D'Artagnan looked at Athos to see if he ought to reply
to the intruder who had thus interrupted their conversation.

"Well," said Athos, "don't you hear Monsieur de Busigny, who does you the honor to ask you a question?
Tell us what happened during the night, since these gentlemen want to know."

"Did you not take a bastion?" asked a Swiss who was
drinking rum out of beer glass.

"Yes, monsieur," said d'Artagnan, bowing, "we had
that honor. We even, as you may have heard, introduced
a barrel of powder under one of the corners, which made
a very pretty breach when it blew up. And since the
bastion was not built yesterday, the rest of the building
was also badly shaken."

"Which bastion was it?" asked a dragoon, his saber
impaling a goose he was taking to be cooked.

"The St. Gervais bastion," d'Artagnan replied. "The
Rochellais had been annoying our workmen from behind
it."

"Was there a lot of fighting?"

"Yes, a fair amount. We lost five men, and the
Rochellais nine or ten."

"Balzempleu!" said the Swiss, who despite the admirable collection of oaths available in German had acquired
a habit of swearing in unintelligible French.

"But they will probably send men out this morning to
repair the bastion," said the light-horseman.

"Yes, probably," said d'Artagnan.

"Gentlemen," said Athos, "a bet!"

"Ah, *yess*, a bet!" cried the Swiss.

"What is it?" said the light-horseman.

"Wait a minute," said the dragoon, placing his saber like a spit across the two andirons in the fireplace, "I am in on the bet too. . . . Host! Bring a dripping pan immediately—I do not want to lose a drop of the fat from this estimable bird."

"You *iss* right," said the Swiss. "Goose grease is *kood*."

"There!" said the dragoon. "Now for the bet! We are listening, Monsieur Athos."

"Yes, the bet!" said the light-horseman.

"Well, Monsieur de Busigny, I will bet you," said Athos, "that my three companions, Messieurs Porthos, Aramis, and d'Artagnan, and myself, will eat our breakfast in the St. Gervais bastion, remaining there for an hour no matter what the enemy may do to dislodge us."

Porthos and Aramis looked at each other; they began to understand.

"But you are going to get us all killed," d'Artagnan whispered to Athos.

"We are much more likely to be killed if we stay here," Athos replied.

"My faith, gentlemen," said Porthos, leaning back in his chair and twirling his mustache, "that's a fair bet, I hope."

"Yes, and I accept it," said M. de Busigny. "Let us set the stakes."

"You are four gentlemen," said Athos, "and we are four—shall we make the stakes dinner for eight?"

"Excellent," replied M. de Busigny.

"Perfect," said the dragoon.

"That *iss gut*," said the Swiss.

The fourth man, who had been silent during the entire conversation, nodded his agreement.

"Your breakfast is ready, gentlemen," said the host.

"Well, bring it," said Athos.

The host obeyed. Athos called Grimaud, pointed to a large basket that lay in a corner, and made a sign to him to wrap the food in the napkins.

Grimaud understood that it was to be a picnic breakfast, packed the basket with the food and wine, then took the basket on his arm.

"Where are you going to eat my breakfast?" asked the host.

"What does it matter, if you are paid for it?" said Athos, majestically throwing two pistoles on the table.

"Shall I give you the change, sir?" asked the host.

"No. Just add two bottles of champagne, and the difference will be for the napkins."

The host was not making as good a bargain as he had hoped for, but he made up for it by slipping in two bottles of Anjou wine instead of two bottles of champagne.

"Monsieur de Busigny," said Athos, "will you be so kind as to set your watch with mine, or allow me to set mine by yours?"

"Whichever you prefer, monsieur," said the light-horseman, drawing from his fob a very handsome watch studded with diamonds. "I have half past seven."

"And I have thirty-five minutes after seven," said Athos, "so everyone will know that I am five minutes faster than you."

And bowing to all the astonished persons present, the four young men took the road to the St. Gervais bastion. Grimaud followed, carrying the basket; he did not know where he was going, but he was so well trained in passive obedience that he did not even think of asking.

As long as they were within the circle of the camp, the four friends did not exchange a single word; besides, they were followed by the curious, who, hearing of the bet, were eager to know what would happen. But once they had passed the line of fieldworks and found themselves in the open plain, d'Artagnan, who was completely bewildered by what was going on, decided it was time to ask for an explanation.

"And now, Athos," he said, "please be so kind as to tell me where we are going."

"Why, you see plainly enough that we are going to the bastion."

"But what are we going to do there?"

"You know very well that we are going to breakfast there."

"But why did we not breakfast at the Parpaillot?"

"Because we have some very important things to discuss, and it was impossible to talk five minutes in that inn without being annoyed by all those fellows coming and going, greeting us, wanting to talk to us . . . Here at least," Athos said, pointing to the bastion, "they will not disturb us."

"It seems to me," said d'Artagnan, with that prudence which was as much a part of him as his extravagant courage, "that we could have found some quiet place on the dunes or the beach."

"Where all four of us would have been seen together, so that within a quarter of an hour the cardinal would have been informed by his spies that we were holding a council and plotting."

"Yes," said Aramis, "Athos is right. *Animadvertuntur in desertis.*"

"A desert would not have been bad," said Porthos, "but it might be difficult to find it."

"There is no desert where a bird cannot fly over one's head, where a fish cannot leap out of the water, where a rabbit cannot come out of its burrow—and I believe that any bird, fish, or rabbit may be the cardinal's spy. It is better to continue as we are. Besides, we cannot retreat without being disgraced. We have made a bet—a bet that could not have been foreseen, and that I defy anyone to guess the real purpose of! In order to win it, we are going to remain in the bastion for an hour. Either we will or we will not be attacked. If we are not, we will have time to talk, and nobody will hear us—for I guarantee the walls of the bastion have no ears. If we are, we will still talk about our affairs, and in defending ourselves, we will cover ourselves with glory. You see that either way everything is to our advantage."

"Yes, but we will most probably attract some bullets," said d'Artagnan.

"You know very well that the enemy's bullets are not the ones to be most feared," Athos replied.

"But for such an expedition we surely ought to have brought our muskets," said Porthos.

"That is foolish, friend Porthos. Why should we load ourselves down with a useless burden?"

"I don't find a good musket, twelve rounds of ammunition, and a powder flask very useless in facing an enemy."

"Did you not hear what d'Artagnan said?" asked Athos.

"What did he say?" demanded Porthos.

"He said that in last night's attack we lost five men and the enemy lost nine or ten."

"So?"

"There was no time to rob the bodies because everyone had other things to do."

"So?"

"So we will find their muskets, their ammunition, and their flasks—and instead of four muskets and twelve bullets, we will have fifteen guns and a hundred shots."

"Athos, you are truly a great man," said Aramis.

Porthos nodded in agreement.

D'Artagnan did not seem convinced.

Grimaud no doubt shared the young man's misgivings, for seeing that they were continuing to advance toward the bastion—something he had till then doubted—he pulled his master's coattail and asked, with a gesture, "Where are we going?"

Athos pointed to the bastion.

"But we will be killed there," he protested, again in dumbshow.

Athos raised his eyes and his finger toward heaven.

Grimaud put his basket on the ground and sat down with a shake of the head.

Athos took a pistol from his belt, looked to see if it was properly primed, cocked it, and brought the muzzle close to Grimaud's ear.

Grimaud got to his feet again as if propelled by a spring.

Athos motioned him to take up his basket and to go first, and he obeyed; all that he had gained by this pantomime was that he had gone from the rear guard to the vanguard.

Arriving at the bastion, the four friends turned around.

More than three hundred soldiers of all kinds were assembled at the gate of the camp; M. de Busigny, the dragoon, the Swiss, and the fourth bettor were standing in a separate group.

Athos took off his hat, placed it on the tip of his sword, and waved it in the air.

All the spectators returned his greeting, accompanying the courtesy with a loud cheer that was audible to the four men, who then disappeared into the bastion where Grimaud had preceded them.

47

The Musketeers' Council

As ATHOS HAD FORESEEN, the bastion was occupied only by a dozen corpses composed of both the king's men and the Rochellais.

"Gentlemen," said Athos, who had assumed command of the expedition, "while Grimaud sets the table, let us begin by collecting the guns and ammunition. We can talk while doing that. These gentlemen," he added, pointing to the bodies, "cannot hear us."

"We could throw them into the ditch," said Porthos, "after making sure they have nothing in their pockets."

"Yes, Grimaud can do that," said Athos.

"Then let Grimaud search them and throw them over the walls," said d'Artagnan.

"Not at all," said Athos. "They may be useful to us."

"These bodies useful?" said Porthos. "You are mad, my friend."

"Judge not rashly, say both the Gospel and the cardinal," replied Athos. "How many guns, gentlemen?"

"Twelve," replied Aramis.

"How much ammunition?"

"A hundred shots."

"That's quite enough for our needs. Let us load the guns."

The four friends went to work, and as they were loading the last musket Grimaud indicated that breakfast was ready.

Athos replied, still by gestures, that that was well, and indicated to Grimaud, by pointing to a turret, that he was to act as a sentry. To alleviate the boredom of his duty, Athos allowed him to take a loaf of bread, two cutlets, and a bottle of wine.

"Let us eat," said Athos.

The four friends seated themselves on the ground with their legs crossed like Turks—or tailors.

"And now," said d'Artagnan, "since there is no longer

any danger of being overheard, I hope you are going to tell me your secret.''

"*I* hope to procure you both amusement and glory, gentlemen,'' said Athos. "I have induced you to take a pleasant walk, here is a delicious breakfast, and yonder are five hundred people—as you may see through the loopholes—who think we are either heroes or madmen—two types of imbeciles that greatly resemble each other.''

"But your secret!'' said d'Artagnan.

"The secret is that I saw Milady last night.''

D'Artagnan was lifting a glass to his lips, but at the name of Milady, his hand trembled so much that he had to put it down for fear of spilling the contents.

"You saw your wi—''

"Silence!'' interrupted Athos. "You forget, my friend, that these gentlemen do not know about my family affairs. . . . I have seen Milady.''

"Where?'' demanded d'Artagnan.

"Within two leagues of this place, at the Colombier-Rouge inn.''

"In that case I am lost,'' said d'Artagnan.

"Not yet,'' replied Athos, "for by this time she should have left France.''

D'Artagnan breathed more easily.

"But who is Milady?'' asked Porthos.

"A charming woman!'' said Athos, sipping a glass of sparkling wine. "Villainous host!'' he exclaimed. "He has given us Anjou wine instead of champagne and thinks we will not know the difference! Yes,'' he continued, "a charming woman who was very kind to our friend d'Artagnan—who has somehow offended her so deeply that she attempted to avenge herself a month ago by trying to have him shot, a week ago by trying to poison him, and yesterday by asking the cardinal for his head.''

"What! Asking the cardinal for my head?'' cried d'Artagnan, pale with terror.

"Yes, that is the Gospel truth,'' said Porthos. "I heard her with my own ears.''

"So did I,'' said Aramis.

"Then it is useless to struggle any longer. I may as well blow my brains out, and be finished with it,'' said d'Artagnan, discouraged.

"That should be the last folly to commit," said Athos, "since it is the only one for which there is no remedy."

"But I can never survive with such enemies," said d'Artagnan. "First, my stranger of Meung, then de Wardes, to whom I have given three sword wounds, next Milady, whose secret I have discovered, and finally the cardinal, whose plan for vengeance I have foiled."

"Well," said Athos, "that only makes four, and we are four—one for one. But if we may believe the signs Grimaud is making, we are about to have many more enemies than that. What is it, Grimaud? Considering the gravity of the occasion, I permit you to speak, my friend, but please be brief. What do you see?"

"A troop."

"How many people?"

"Twenty."

"What sort of men?"

"Sixteen laborers, four soldiers."

"How far away?"

"Five hundred paces."

"Good, we still have time to finish this chicken and to drink a glass of wine to your health, d'Artagnan."

"To your health!" repeated Porthos and Aramis.

"Well, then, to my health—although I am very much afraid that your good wishes will not be very useful to me."

"God is great, as the followers of Mohammed say, and the future is in his hands," Athos responded.

Then, swallowing the contents of his glass and putting it down next to him, he nonchalantly stood up, took the musket alongside him, and went to one of the loopholes.

Porthos, Aramis, and d'Artagnan followed his example. Grimaud was ordered to stand behind the four friends in order to reload their weapons.

They soon saw the troop approaching along a sort of narrow channel of the trench, which connected the bastion and the city.

"*Pardieu*, it was hardly worthwhile to disturb ourselves for twenty fellows armed with picks, mattocks, and shovels," said Athos. "If Grimaud had only signaled them to go away, I am convinced they would have left us in peace."

"I doubt it," replied d'Artagnan, "for they are advancing with great determination. Besides, in addition to the laborers, there are four soldiers and a corporal, armed with muskets."

"They are determined because they don't see us," said Athos.

"My faith," said Aramis, "I must confess I am very reluctant to fire on those poor civilians."

"He who has pity for heretics is a bad priest!" said Porthos.

"Aramis is right. I will warn them," said Athos.

"What the devil are you doing?" cried d'Artagnan. "You will be shot!"

But Athos ignored his warning. Mounting on the breach, with his musket in one hand and his hat in the other, he bowed courteously and addressed the soldiers and the workmen.

Astonished at this apparition, they stopped fifty paces from the bastion.

"Gentlemen," said Athos, "a few friends and I are having breakfast in this bastion. Now as you know, nothing is more disagreeable than being disturbed during breakfast, so we ask you, if you really have business here, to wait till we have finished our meal or to come back later—unless, which would be far better, you decide to leave the side of the rebels and come drink a toast with us to the health of the King of France."

"Take care, Athos!" d'Artagnan shouted. "Don't you see they are aiming at you?"

"Yes, yes," said Athos, "but they are only civilians— very bad marksmen who cannot possibly hit me."

In fact, at that moment four shots were fired, and the bullets all hit the wall behind Athos, not one touching him.

Four shots answered them almost instantaneously, but much more accurately aimed than those of the aggressors; three soldiers fell dead, and one of the laborers was wounded.

"Grimaud," said Athos, still on the breach, "another musket!"

Grimaud immediately obeyed. The other three had reloaded their own guns; a second discharge followed the first, killing the corporal and two workmen. The rest of the troop took flight.

"Now, gentlemen, a sortie!" said Athos.

And the four friends rushed out of the bastion and picked up the soldiers' four muskets and the corporal's pike, after which, convinced that the fugitives would not stop till they reached the city, they returned to the bastion bearing the trophies of their victory.

"Reload the muskets, Grimaud," said Athos, "and let us, gentlemen, go on with our breakfast and resume our conversation. Where were we?"

"You were saying," said d'Artagnan, "that after having asked the cardinal for my head, Milady left France. Where did she go?" he asked, strongly interested in her movements.

"To England," Athos replied.

"Why?"

"With the aim of assassinating—or causing to be assassinated—the Duke of Buckingham."

"But that is infamous!" d'Artagnan exclaimed with surprise and indignation.

"As to that, believe me when I say I am not very concerned about it."

He turned to Grimaud. "Now that you have finished reloading, take the corporal's pike, tie a napkin to it, and plant it at the top of our bastion so that those rebels will see that they are dealing with brave and loyal soldiers of the king."

Grimaud obeyed without replying. A few minutes later, the white flag was floating over the heads of the four friends. Thunderous applause greeted its appearance; half the camp was at the barrier.

"What do you mean?" d'Artagnan asked. "You do not care if she kills Buckingham or causes him to be killed? But the duke is our friend."

"The duke is English and fights against us. Let her do what she likes with the duke—he matters no more to me than this empty bottle."

And he tossed away an empty bottle from which he had just poured the last drop into his glass.

"I will not abandon Buckingham like that. He gave us four fine horses," said d'Artagnan.

"And four very handsome saddles," said Porthos, who at that very moment was wearing the braid from his saddle on his cloak.

"Besides," said Aramis, "God wishes the conversion of a sinner, not his death."

"Amen," said Athos, "and we will return to that subject later if you wish. But what I was most interested in at the time—and I am sure you will understand me, d'Artagnan—was to get from that woman the letter she had extorted from the cardinal, a letter that would allow her to get rid of you, and perhaps all of us as well, with impunity."

"But that creature must be a demon!" said Porthos, holding out his plate to Aramis, who was cutting up a chicken.

"And the letter, the carte blanche, does she still have it?" d'Artagnan asked.

"No, I do. I will not say it passed into my hands without trouble, for if I did, I would be telling a lie."

"Athos, I can no longer count the number of times I owe you my life."

"Then it was to go to her that you left us?" said Aramis.

"Exactly."

"And you have the cardinal's letter?" d'Artagnan asked.

"Here it is," said Athos, taking the invaluable paper from his pocket.

D'Artagnan unfolded it, not even trying to hide the trembling of his hands. He read it aloud.

It is by my order and for the good of the state that the bearer of this has done what has been done.

RICHELIEU

"In effect," said Aramis, "that is total absolution for anything."

"We must tear that paper up," said d'Artagnan, who thought he read his death warrant in it.

"On the contrary," said Athos, "it must be preserved carefully. I would not give up this paper for all the gold pieces it would take to cover it."

"What will she do now?" d'Artagnan asked.

"Why," Athos replied carelessly, "she is probably going to write to the cardinal that a damned Musketeer named Athos has taken her letter from her by force. She will advise him to get rid of him and his two friends, Aramis and Porthos. The cardinal will remember that those are the same men who have so often gotten in his way, and some fine morning he will arrest d'Artagnan and then—for fear he should feel lonely—he will send the rest of us to the Bastille to keep him company."

"I think you are making a very bad joke, my friend," said Porthos.

"I am not joking," said Athos.

"Do you know," said Porthos, "that I think it would be less of a sin to wring that damned Milady's neck than it is to kill these poor Huguenots, whose only crime is to sing in French the psalms we sing in Latin?"

"What does our priest say?" Athos asked quietly.

"I say I completely agree with Porthos," replied Aramis.

"And I do, too," said d'Artagnan.

"Fortunately, she is far away," said Porthos, "for I confess she would worry me if she were here."

"She worries me in England as much as in France," said Athos.

"She worries me everywhere," said d'Artagnan.

"But when you had her in your power, why did you not drown her, strangle her, hang her?" asked Porthos. "Only the dead never return."

"You think so, Porthos?" replied the Musketeer, with a grim smile that only d'Artagnan understood.

"I have an idea," said d'Artagnan.

"What is it?" asked the Musketeers.

"To arms!" Grimaud shouted.

The young men sprang up, and grabbed their muskets.

Some twenty to twenty-five men were advancing toward them, but this time they were all soldiers from the garrison, not laborers.

"Shall we return to the camp?" Porthos asked. "The two sides do not seem equal."

"Impossible, for three reasons," replied Athos. "First, we have not finished breakfast, second, we still have some very important matters to discuss, and third, we still have ten minutes to go before the end of the hour."

"Then we must decide on a plan of battle," said Aramis.

"That is quite simple," replied Athos. "As soon as

they are within range, we must fire on them. If they continue to advance, we must fire again, and we will fire as long as we have loaded guns. If the remaining men persist in attacking, we will allow them to get as far as the ditch, and then we will push that strip of wall down on them. Only a miracle is keeping it standing."

"Bravo!" cried Porthos. "Athos, you were surely born to be a general. The cardinal, who fancies himself a great soldier, is nothing compared to you."

"Gentlemen," said Athos, "let us not fire at the same target. Let each of us pick out his man."

"I have mine," said d'Artagnan.

"And I mine," said Porthos.

"And so have I," said Aramis.

"Then fire," said Athos.

The four muskets made one sound, and four men fell.

The drum immediately beat, and the little troop charged.

The shots were repeated without regularity, although always with the same accuracy, but the Rochellais, as if they were aware of the numerical weakness of the defenders, continued to advance.

With every three shots at least two men fell, but those who remained did not slow down.

When they arrived at the foot of the bastion, there were still more than a dozen of them left. A final volley welcomed them, but did not stop them; they jumped into the ditch and prepared to scale the breach.

"Now, my friends," said Athos, "let us finish them off. To the wall!"

And the four friends, aided by Grimaud, pushed an enormous section of the wall with the barrels of their muskets; bent as if propelled by the wind, it detached itself from its base and fell with a horrible crash into the ditch. There was a fearful shriek, a cloud of dust mounted toward the sky, and all was over.

"Can we have destroyed them all, every one of them?" Athos asked.

"My faith, it seems so!" said d'Artagnan.

"No, I see three or four of them limping away," said Porthos.

Indeed, three or four of the unfortunate men, covered with dirt and blood, fled down the road and eventually got back to the city. They were all who remained of the little troop.

Athos looked at his watch.

"Gentlemen," he said, "we have been here an hour and our bet is won, but we will do better than that. Besides, d'Artagnan has not yet told us his idea."

And the Musketeer, with his usual imperturbability, sat down again in front of the remains of the breakfast.

"My idea?" said d'Artagnan.

"Yes. You said you had an idea," said Athos.

"Oh, I remember. Well, I will go back to England, find Buckingham, and warn him."

"You will not do that, d'Artagnan," said Athos firmly.

"Why not? Have I not been there once before?"

"Yes, but at that time we were not at war and Buckingham was an ally, not an enemy. What you want to do now amounts to treason."

D'Artagnan perceived the force of this reasoning and was silent.

"But I think I too have an idea," said Porthos.

"Silence for Porthos's idea!" said Aramis.

"I will ask Monsieur de Tréville for a leave of absence on some pretext or other that you must invent—I am not very clever at pretexts. Milady does not know me so I can approach her without her suspecting me, and when I find her, I will strangle her."

"I am not far from accepting Porthos's idea," said Athos.

"For shame!" exclaimed Aramis. "Kill a woman? No, listen to me—I have a better idea."

"Let us hear it, Aramis," said Athos, who had a great respect for the young Musketeer.

"We must warn the queen."

"My faith, yes!" said Porthos and d'Artagnan at the same time. "We are getting closer to it now."

"Warn the queen!" said Athos. "How? Have we connections with the court? Could we send anyone to Paris without its being known in the camp? It is a hundred and forty leagues from here to Paris—we would all be in a dungeon before our letter got to Angers."

"As to getting a letter safely to her Majesty," said Aramis, blushing, "I will see to that myself. I know a clever person in Tours . . ."

Aramis stopped on seeing Athos smile.

"Well, do you not agree, Athos?" d'Artagnan asked.

"I do not completely reject it," said Athos, "but I would like to remind Aramis that he cannot leave the camp, and that nobody but one of us is trustworthy. Two hours after the messenger has set out, all the cardinal's men will know your letter by heart, and you and your clever person would be arrested."

"Without mentioning," Porthos added, "that the queen would save Buckingham but would not worry about us."

"Gentlemen, Porthos has a very reasonable objection," said d'Artagnan.

"Listen! What is going on in the city?" Athos asked.

"They are sounding the general alarm."

The four friends listened, and they could plainly hear the sound of the drum.

"They are going to send a whole regiment against us," said Athos.

"You don't think of holding out against a whole regiment, do you?" Porthos asked.

"Why not? I feel quite in the mood for it, and I would hold out against an army if we had taken the precaution of bringing another dozen bottles of wine."

"Upon my word, the drum is coming closer," said d'Artagnan.

"Let it come," said Athos. "It takes a quarter of an hour to get from here to the city, consequently a quarter of an hour from the city to here. That is more than enough time for us to devise a plan. If we leave this place we will never find as suitable a one again. . . . Wait! I have it, gentlemen—I have just had a good idea."

"Tell us."

"First let me give Grimaud some indispensable orders."

Athos signaled his lackey to approach.

"Grimaud," said Athos, pointing to the bodies under the bastion wall, "take those gentlemen and set them up against the wall with their hats on their heads and their guns in their hands."

"Oh, what a great man!" cried d'Artagnan. "I understand."

"You understand?" said Porthos.

"And do *you* understand, Grimaud?" Aramis asked. Grimaud nodded.

"That is all that is necessary," said Athos. "And now for my idea."

"But I would also like to understand," said Porthos.

"That is unnecessary."

"Let us hear Athos's idea!" Aramis and d'Artagnan said at the same time.

"I think you told me, d'Artagnan, that this Milady, this creature, this demon, has a brother-in-law?"

"Yes, I know him very well, and I believe he is not very fond of his sister-in-law."

"There is no harm in that. If he detested her, it would be even better," said Athos.

"In that case we are as well off as we could wish."

"I still would like to know what Grimaud is doing," said Porthos.

"Silence, Porthos!" said Aramis.

"What is her brother-in-law's name?"

"Lord de Winter."

"Where is he now?"

"He returned to London at the first talk of war."

"He is just the man we want," said Athos. "He is the one we must warn. We will inform him that his sister-in-law is on the point of having someone assassinated, and beg him not to lose sight of her. There must be some establishment like that of the Magdalens or the Repentant Daughters in London. He must put his sister-in-law in one of those places, and we will then be left in peace."

"Yes, till she comes out," said d'Artagnan.

"My faith, you ask too much, d'Artagnan! I have given you what I can—I have no other ideas."

"I think it would be better," said Aramis, "to inform the queen and Lord de Winter at the same time."

"Yes, but who will carry one letter to Tours and another to London?"

"I answer for Bazin," said Aramis.

"And I for Planchet," said d'Artagnan.

"True—we cannot leave the camp, but our lackeys can," said Porthos.

"To be sure they can, and we will write the letters and give the lackeys some money so they can leave this very day," said Aramis.

"We will give them money?" Athos repeated. "Have you any money?"

The four friends looked at one another, and the faces that had been so cheerful clouded over.

"Look out!" cried d'Artagnan, "I see black and red dots moving out there. What were you saying about a regiment, Athos? This is an army!"

"Ah, yes," said Athos, "there they are. See the sneaks come, without drum or trumpet. Have you finished, Grimaud?"

Grimaud nodded, and pointed to a dozen bodies he had set up in the most picturesque attitudes, some carrying arms, others seeming to be taking aim, and the remainder holding their swords.

"Bravo!" said Athos. "That does honor to your imagination."

"All very well," said Porthos, "but I would still like to understand."

"Let us decamp first, and you will understand afterward."

"One moment, gentlemen. Give Grimaud time to clear away the breakfast."

"Ah, the black and red dots are getting larger. I agree with d'Artagnan—we must get back to camp without delay," said Aramis.

"I have nothing more to say against a retreat. Our bet was for one hour, and we have stayed an hour and a half. There can be no question about it, so let us be off, gentlemen."

Grimaud had already gone ahead with the basket. The four friends followed, about ten paces behind him.

"What the devil shall we do now, gentlemen?" Athos suddenly exclaimed.

"Have we forgotten anything?" Aramis asked.

"Our flag! We must not leave a flag in the hands of the enemy, even if the flag is only a napkin."

And Athos ran back to the bastion, mounted the platform, and bore off the flag; but since the Rochellais had gotten within musket range, they opened fire on this man who seemed to be exposing himself only for pleasure's sake.

But it was as if Athos had a charmed life: the bullets whistled all around him, and not one hit him.

Turning his back on the enemy, he waved his flag and saluted the men from camp. He could hear cries of enthusiasm from them, cries of rage from the enemy.

A second volley followed the first, and three bullets passed through the napkin, making it really a flag. The whole camp was shouting, "Come down! Come down!"

Athos came down; his friends, who were anxiously awaiting him, were overjoyed at his return.

"Come on, Athos!" cried d'Artagnan. "Now that we have planned everything except for the money, it would be stupid to be killed."

But Athos continued to walk majestically, no matter what his companions said, and they, finding their remarks useless, adjusted their pace to his.

Grimaud and his basket were far in advance and out of range.

They suddenly heard a furious fusillade.

"What's that?" asked Porthos. "What are they firing at now? I hear no bullets, and I see nobody!"

"They are firing at the corpses," replied Athos.

"But the dead cannot return their fire."

"Of course not! They will therefore think it is an ambush. They will deliberate about it, and by the time they have discovered our little jest, we will be out of their range. That is why it is useless to get sick by hurrying too much."

"Oh, *now* I understand," said Porthos, marveling.

"Good," said Athos, shrugging his shoulders.

The men from camp, seeing the four friends return so slowly, cheered even more enthusiastically.

At length a fresh burst of fire was heard, and this time the bullets made a rattling sound among the stones near the four friends and whistled sharply in their ears. The enemy had at last taken possession of the bastion.

"These Rochellais are bunglers," said Athos. "How many have we killed—a dozen?"

"Maybe fifteen."

"How many did we crush under the wall?"

"Nine or ten."

"And in exchange for all that, not one of us has even a scratch! But that's not true—what is the matter with your hand, d'Artagnan? It is bleeding."

"It's nothing," he replied.

"A bullet grazed you?"

"Not even that."

"Then what?"

We have said that Athos loved d'Artagnan like a son, and sometimes this somber and inflexible personage felt a father's anxiety for the young man.

"It's just a scratch," said d'Artagnan. "My fingers were caught between two stones—that of the wall and that of my ring—and the skin was broken."

"That comes of wearing a diamond ring," Athos said disdainfully.

"Of course!" cried Porthos. "The diamond! Why the devil are we worrying about money when there is a diamond?"

"That is true!" said Aramis.

"Well thought of, Porthos. This time you have had a good idea."

"Undoubtedly," said Porthos, puffing up with pride at Athos's compliment. "Since there is a diamond, let us sell it."

"But it is the queen's diamond," said d'Artagnan.

"The more reason to sell it," replied Athos. "The queen will save Buckingham, her lover, and us, her friends—nothing more proper and just. Let us sell the diamond. What does Monsieur l'Abbé say? I don't ask Porthos because his opinion has already been given."

"Why, I think," said Aramis, blushing as usual, "that since his ring does not come from a mistress and is consequently not a token of love, he may sell it."

"Aramis, you speak like the personification of theology! Your advice, then, is . . ."

"To sell the diamond," replied Aramis.

"Then let us sell the diamond, and say no more about it," said d'Artagnan gaily.

The fusillade continued; but the friends were out of range and the Rochellais were firing only for form's sake.

"It is a good thing that Porthos thought of that," said Athos. "Here we are back at camp, so not a word about this affair, gentlemen. Look, we are observed—they are coming to meet us and we will be carried back in triumph."

In fact, the whole camp was in motion. More than two thousand men had watched the spectacle of the friends' fortunate but wild undertaking—an undertaking they did not begin to suspect the real motive for. Nothing was heard but shouts of "Long live the Musketeers! Long live the Guards!" M. de Busigny was the first to come shake Athos's hand and acknowledge that he had lost the bet. The dragoon and the Swiss followed him, and all their comrades followed the dragoon and the Swiss. There were endless congratulations, handclasps, and embraces, and inextinguishable laughter at the expense of the Rochellais. Finally the tumult became so great that the cardinal thought there must be some riot taking place and sent La Houdinière, his captain of the Guards, to find out what was going on.

The incident was described to the messenger with great enthusiasm.

"Well?" the cardinal asked when La Houdinière returned.

"Well, monseigneur," replied the latter, "three Musketeers and a Guardsman laid a bet with Monsieur de Busigny that they would have breakfast in the St. Gervais bastion, and while breakfasting they held it for two hours against the enemy and killed I don't know how many Rochellais."

"Did you ask who those three Musketeers were?"

"Yes, monseigneur."

"What are their names?"

"Messieurs Athos, Porthos, and Aramis."

"Always the same three," murmured the cardinal. "And the Guardsman?"

"D'Artagnan."

"And my young scapegrace again. I must have these four men on my side."

That same evening the cardinal spoke to M. de Tréville about the morning's exploit, which was the talk of the whole camp. M. de Tréville, who had heard about the adventure from the heroes of it, explained its every detail to his Eminence, including the episode of the napkin.

"Monsieur de Tréville," said the cardinal, "send that napkin to me and I will have three fleur-de-lis embroidered on it in gold and give it to your company as a banner."

"Monseigneur, that would be unjust to the Guardsmen. Monsieur d'Artagnan is not one of mine—he serves under Monsieur Des Essarts."

"Well, take him," said the cardinal. "When four men

are so attached to one another, it is only fair that they serve in the same company."

That same evening M. de Tréville announced this good news to the three Musketeers and d'Artagnan, inviting all four to dine with him the next day.

D'Artagnan could not restrain his joy. The dream of his life had been to become a Musketeer.

The three friends were also delighted.

"My faith," d'Artagnan said to Athos, "that was a brilliant idea you had! Just as you said, we covered ourselves with glory and were able to carry on a very important conversation in private."

"Which we can now resume without anybody suspecting us, because from now on, with God's help, we will be taken for cardinalists."

That evening d'Artagnan went to pay his respects to M. Des Essarts and inform him of his transfer.

M. Des Essarts, who liked d'Artagnan, offered to help him, since this transfer would entail expenses.

D'Artagnan refused, but thinking the opportunity a good one, he asked him to estimate the value of the diamond he put into his hand, for he wished to turn it into money.

The next day, M. Des Essarts's lackey came to d'Artagnan's lodging and gave him a bag containing seven thousand livres.

That was the price of the queen's diamond.

48

A Family Affair

ATHOS HAD BEGUN to use the phrase, *a family affair*. A family affair was not subject to any investigation by the cardinal; a family affair concerned nobody but the family, and those who *were* concerned might deal with the matter quite openly.

Therefore Athos had invented the phrase, *a family affair*.

Aramis had thought of the idea—*the lackeys*.

Porthos had thought of the means—*the diamond*.

Only d'Artagnan had thought of nothing—he, ordinarily the most inventive of the four—but it is true that the very name of Milady paralyzed him.

Ah, no, he *had* thought of something—a purchaser for his diamond.

The meal at M. de Tréville's was lighthearted and cheerful. D'Artagnan was already wearing his uniform: since Aramis was so liberally paid by the publisher of his poem as to allow him to buy two of everything, and since d'Artagnan was nearly the same size, he had sold his friend a complete outfit.

D'Artagnan would have had everything he wanted if he had not felt the constant threat of Milady hovering over him like a dark cloud.

After lunch, the four friends agreed to meet again in the evening at Athos's lodging and complete their plans.

D'Artagnan spent the day exhibiting his Musketeer's uniform all over the camp.

In the evening, the four friends met as agreed. They still had three things to decide: what they should write to Milady's brother-in-law; what they should write to the clever person at Tours; and which lackey would carry the letters.

Everyone offered his own servant. Athos praised Grimaud's discretion, reminding them that he never spoke until his master unlocked his mouth. Porthos boasted of Mousqueton's strength, saying he was big enough to thrash four men of ordinary size. Aramis eulogized Bazin, emphasizing his resourcefulness. Finally, d'Artagnan had complete faith in Planchet's bravery, describing how he had conducted himself in the thorny affair at Boulogne.

These four virtues were disputed at great length, giving rise to magnificent speeches that we will not repeat lest they bore the reader.

"Unfortunately," said Athos, "the one we send must possess all four qualities in one person."

"But where is such a lackey to be found?"

"He is not to be found," said Athos. "I know that, so take Grimaud."

"Take Mousqueton."

"Take Bazin."

"Take Planchet. He is both brave and shrewd, and therefore has two out of the four qualities."

"Gentlemen," said Aramis, "the principal question is not which of our four lackeys is the most discreet, the most strong, the most clever, or the most brave, but which of them most loves money."

"What Aramis says is very sensible," said Athos. "We must consider people's faults, not their virtues. Monsieur l'Abbé, you are a great moralist."

"It is indeed sensible," said Aramis. "Not only must we be well served in order to succeed, but also not to fail, for if we fail, it becomes a question of heads—and not those of our lackeys . . ."

"Not so loud, Aramis," said Athos.

"Not those of the lackeys," resumed Aramis, "but those of the *masters*. Are our lackeys sufficiently devoted to risk their lives for us? No."

"My faith," said d'Artagnan, "I would almost answer for Planchet."

"Then add to his natural devotion a good sum of money, and then, instead of answering for him once, you will be able to answer for him twice."

"No, you will be disappointed just the same," said Athos, who was an optimist about things and a pessimist about people. "They will promise everything for the sake of the money, then their fear will prevent them from acting. Once caught, they will be pressured, and when pressured, they will confess everything. We are not children—this should not surprise us! To reach England"—he lowered his voice—"one must cross almost all of France, which is filled with the cardinal's agents. One must get a permit to board a ship. Once in England, one must know enough English to ask the way to London. Really, I think the thing very difficult."

"Not at all," cried d'Artagnan, who was eager to put the plan in operation. "On the contrary, I think it very easy. Obviously, if we write to Lord de Winter about affairs of vast importance, about the horrible things the cardinal has done . . ."

"Not so loud!" said Athos.

". . . about intrigues and state secrets," continued d'Artagnan more softly, "then of course we would all be broken on the wheel. But for God's sake, do not forget what you yourself said, Athos—that we are writing to him only about a family affair, begging him to stop Milady, as soon as she arrives in London, from doing anything to harm us, by putting her away somewhere. I will write to him explaining this."

"Let us hear," said Athos, assuming in advance a critical look.

"Monsieur and dear friend—"

"Ah, yes! *Dear friend* to an Englishman," Athos interrupted. "Well begun! Bravo, d'Artagnan! With that word alone you would be drawn and quartered instead of broken on the wheel."

"Well, perhaps. Then I will just say *Monsieur*."

"You might say *My Lord*," replied Athos, who was a stickler for the proper forms of etiquette.

"My Lord, do you remember the little goat pasture of the Luxembourg?"

"Good, *the Luxembourg!* They will think it an allusion to the queen-mother! That's very ingenious."

"Then we will simply say *My Lord, do you remember a certain little enclosure where your life was spared?"*

"My dear d'Artagnan, you will never make a very good letter writer. *Where your life was spared!* For shame, that is unworthy of you. One doesn't remind a gentleman of such a service. A benefit recalled to someone is an offense."

"You are insupportable, Athos! If every word of the letter is to be criticized, I won't write it."

"A good decision. Handle the musket and the sword, my friend—you do splendidly at those. But pass the pen to Monsieur l'Abbé. That's his province."

"Yes, pass the pen to Aramis, who writes theses in Latin," said Porthos.

"Well, so be it," said d'Artagnan. "Write this note for us, Aramis, but by our Holy Father the Pope, make it short, for I shall prune you in my turn, I warn you."

"I ask no quarter," said Aramis, with that ingenuous self-confidence which is part of every poet. "But let me be better informed about the subject. I have heard here and there that this sister-in-law is an evil woman, and I have proof of that from listening to her conversation with the cardinal . . ."

"Not so loud!" said Athos.

"But I do not know any of the details," Aramis continued.

"Nor do I," said Porthos.

D'Artagnan and Athos looked at each other for some time in silence. At length Athos, after serious reflection and becoming more pale than usual, nodded to d'Artagnan, who understood he was free to speak.

"Well, here is what we have to say," he said. *"My Lord, your sister-in-law is an infamous woman who wished to have you killed so that she might inherit your wealth; but she was not truly married to your brother, because she was already married in France and had been . . ."*

D'Artagnan stopped, as if seeking the word, and looked at Athos.

"Repudiated by her husband," said Athos.

"Because she had been branded," continued d'Artagnan.

"Branded!" cried Porthos. "And you say that she wanted to have her brother-in-law killed?"

"Yes."

"She had been married before?" asked Aramis.

"Yes."

"And her first husband found out that she had a fleur-de-lis branded on her shoulder?" asked Porthos.

"Yes."

The three yeses had been pronounced by Athos, each time more grimly.

"Who has seen this fleur-de-lis?" inquired Aramis.

"D'Artagnan and I. Or rather, to keep the chronological order, I and d'Artagnan," replied Athos.

"And is the first husband of this horrible creature still alive?" Aramis asked.

"He is still alive."

"Are you quite sure?"

"I am quite sure."

There was a moment of complete silence during which everyone was affected according to his own nature.

"This time," said Athos, the first to speak again, "d'Artagnan has given us an excellent outline, and the letter must be written at once."

"You are right, Athos," said Aramis, "and it is rather difficult. The chancellor himself would find it hard to write such a letter, yet the chancellor draws up very skillful official reports quite readily. Never mind! Be quiet so I may write."

Aramis picked up the quill, thought for a few seconds, wrote nine or ten lines in a charming feminine hand, then softly and slowly, as if each word had been scrupulously weighed, read the following:

> MY LORD,
> The person who is writing these few lines had the honor of crossing swords with you in a little enclosure off the Rue d'Enfer. Since you have several times declared yourself the friend of that person, he thinks it his duty to respond to that friendship by sending you important information. Twice you have nearly been the victim of a close relative whom you believe to be your heir because you do not know that before she contracted a marriage in England she had already married in France. You may succumb to her third attempt, which is soon to be. Your relative left La Rochelle for England during the night. Watch for her arrival, because she has great and terrible plans. If you want to know beyond a doubt what she is capable of, read her past history on her left shoulder.

"Marvelous!" said Athos. "My dear Aramis, you write like a secretary of state. Lord de Winter will now be on his guard—if the letter reaches him—and even if it should fall into the hands of the cardinal, we will not be compromised by it. But since the lackey who goes may try to make us believe he has been to London even though he has gone no farther than Châtellerault, let us give him only half the money in advance, with a promise to give him the other half when he brings back a reply. D'Artagnan, do you have the diamond?"

"I have something better than the diamond—I have the money I got for it." And d'Artagnan tossed the bag on the table.

At the sound of the gold Aramis raised his eyes and Porthos started. Athos remained impassive.

"How much is in that little bag?"

"Seven thousand livres, in twelve-franc louis."

"Seven thousand livres!" cried Porthos. "That little diamond was worth seven thousand livres?"

"So it seems," said Athos, "since here they are. I don't suppose that our friend d'Artagnan has added any of his own to the amount."

"But, gentlemen," said d'Artagnan, "we are forgetting the queen. Let us give some thought to the welfare of her dear Buckingham—that is the least we owe her."

"True," said Athos, "but that is Aramis's concern."

"Well," asked the latter, blushing, "what shall I do?"

"Oh, that's simple enough," replied Athos. "Write a second letter to that clever person who lives in Tours."

Aramis picked up his pen again, reflected a little, and wrote the following lines, which he immediately submitted for his friends' approval.

"My dear cousin."

"Ah," said Athos, "so this clever person is your relative?"

"My first cousin."

"Go on, to your *cousin,* then!"

Aramis continued:

MY DEAR COUSIN,

His Eminence the cardinal, whom God preserve for the happiness of France and the confusion of her enemies, is on the point of putting an end to the rebellious heretics of La Rochelle. It is probable that the English fleet which was to provide them with assistance will never even arrive within sight of the place. I will also venture to say that I am certain Lord Buckingham will be prevented from leaving England by some great event. His Eminence is the most illustrious politician of times past, of times present, and probably of times to come. He would extinguish the sun if the sun annoyed him. Give this good news to your sister, my dear cousin. I dreamed that the unlucky Englishman was dead. I cannot remember whether it was by stabbing or by poison, but I am sure that I dreamed he was dead—and as you know, my dreams never deceive me. Be assured, then, of seeing me return soon.

"Marvelous again!" said Athos. "You are the king of poets, Aramis. You speak like the Apocalypse and are as true as the Gospel. There is nothing left to do but put the address on."

"That is easily done," said Aramis.

He folded the letter artfully, and wrote: *To Mlle. Marie Michon, seamstress, Tours.*

The three friends looked at one another and laughed; they had been outwitted.

"Now," said Aramis, "please understand, gentlemen, that only Bazin can carry this letter to Tours. My cousin knows nobody but Bazin and has confidence in nobody but him. Anyone else would fail in this. Besides, Bazin is ambitious and learned. He has read history, gentlemen, and knows that Sixtus the Fifth became Pope after having been a swineherd. Since he intends to enter the Church at the same time I do, he hopes to become Pope in his turn—or at least a cardinal. You understand that a man who has such views will never allow himself to be taken, or if taken, will undergo martyrdom rather than speak."

"Very well," said d'Artagnan, "I consent to Bazin for Tours with all my heart, but let me have Planchet for London. Milady had him beaten and thrown out of her house, and Planchet has an excellent memory—I am sure that he will allow himself to be beaten to death sooner than give up any possible chance for revenge. Your arrangements in Tours are your arrangements, Aramis, but those in London are mine. I therefore ask that Planchet be chosen, especially since he has already been to London with me and knows how to say very correctly: *London, sir, if you please,* and *my master, Lord d'Artagnan.* With that, you may be sure he can make his way, both going and returning."

"In that case," said Athos, "Planchet must get seven hundred livres for going, and seven hundred livres for coming back. Bazin will receive three hundred for going, and three hundred for returning. That will leave us with five thousand livres. We will each take a thousand livres to use as necessary, and we will leave the remaining thousand under the guardianship of Monsieur l'Abbé here, to use for emergencies or common expenses. Will that do?"

"Athos," said Aramis, "you speak like Nestor, who was, as everyone knows, the wisest of the Greeks."

"Then it is settled," said Athos. "Planchet and Bazin will go. Everything considered, I am not sorry to keep Grimaud here—he is used to my ways, and I am used to him. Yesterday's affair has upset him, and a dangerous voyage would finish him completely."

Planchet was sent for and given his instructions. D'Artagnan had already discussed the possibility of a mission with him, pointing out the money, then the glory, and finally the danger.

"I will carry the letter in the lining of my coat," said Planchet, "and if I am taken, I will swallow it."

"But then you will not be able to deliver it," said d'Artagnan.

"You will give me a copy this evening, and I will know it by heart tomorrow."

D'Artagnan looked at his friends, as if to say, "Well, what did I tell you?"

"Now," he continued, addressing Planchet, "you have eight days to get an interview with Lord de Winter, and you have eight days to return—sixteen days in all. If, on the sixteenth day after your departure, you are not here at eight o'clock in the evening, no money—not even if you come at five minutes past eight."

"Then, monsieur, you must buy me a watch," said Planchet.

"Take this," said Athos, giving him his own with his usual careless generosity, "and be a good lad. Remember, if you talk, if you gossip, if you get drunk, you may be killing your master, who has so much confidence in you that he has sworn you will not fail. But remember that if anything bad happens to d'Artagnan because of you, I will find you, wherever you may be, and rip open your belly."

"Oh, monsieur!" said Planchet, humiliated by Athos's doubts and terrified by his calm determination.

"And I," said Porthos, rolling his large eyes, "remember that I will skin you alive."

"Oh, monsieur!"

"And I," said Aramis, with his soft, melodious voice, "remember that I will roast you over a slow fire."

"Oh, monsieur!"

Planchet burst into tears, although we cannot say whether it was from terror at the threats or from tenderness at seeing four friends so closely united.

D'Artagnan took his hand and embraced him.

"Planchet," he said, "these gentlemen only say this out of affection for me, but at bottom they all like you."

"Monsieur," Planchet declared, "either I will succeed or I will consent to be cut in quarters, and if they cut me in quarters, be assured that not one piece of me will speak."

It was decided that Planchet should set out at eight o'clock the next morning so that he might—as he had said he would—learn the letter by heart during the night. He gained twelve hours that way; he was to be back on the sixteenth day, by eight o'clock in the evening.

In the morning, as he was about to mount his horse, d'Artagnan, who still felt rather partial to Buckingham, took Planchet aside.

"Listen," he said to him. "When you have given the letter to Lord de Winter and he has read it, you will also say to him: *Watch over his Grace, Lord Buckingham, for they wish to assassinate him.* But this, Planchet, is so serious and important a matter that I have not even told my friends that I was entrusting this secret to you, and I would not put it in writing for a captain's commission."

"Do not worry, monsieur," said Planchet. "You will see that you can trust me."

Mounted on an excellent horse, which he was to leave at the end of twenty leagues in order to take the stage-coach, Planchet set off at a gallop, his spirits a little depressed by the Musketeers' triple threats, but otherwise in a lighthearted mood.

Bazin left for Tours the next day, having been allowed eight days for carrying out his mission.

While Planchet and Bazin were gone, the four friends kept their eyes open, their ears to the ground, and their noses alert to every scent on the wind. Their days were spent trying to hear all that was said, to observe the doings of the cardinal, and to sniff out all the messengers. More than once they trembled when they were called upon for some unexpected duty. Besides, they also had to look out for their own safety; Milady was like a phantom that did not allow people to sleep very quietly once they had seen it.

On the morning of the eighth day, Bazin, fresh as ever and smiling as usual, entered the Parpaillot just as the four friends were sitting down to breakfast.

He said, as had been agreed, "Monsieur Aramis, here is the answer from your cousin."

The four friends exchanged a joyful glance; half the work was done—though it was the shorter and easier half.

Blushing in spite of himself, Aramis took the letter, which was written in a large, coarse handwriting and with unorthodox spelling.

"I quite despair of my poor Marie—she will never write like Monsieur de Voiture," he exclaimed, laughing.

"What does you mean by boor Marie?" asked the Swiss, who had been chatting with the four friends when the letter came.

"Oh, *pardieu*, less than nothing," said Aramis. "She is a charming little seamstress I used to love dearly. I asked her to write me a few lines as a sort of keepsake."

"If she is as great lady as her writing is large, you are a lucky fellow, *gomrade*!" said the Swiss.

Aramis read the letter and passed it to Athos.

"See what she writes, Athos," he said.

Athos glanced at the letter, and then, to dispel any suspicions that might have been created, he read it aloud:

MY COUSIN,
My sister and I are skillful in interpreting dreams, and are even very frightened of them; but of yours, I hope it may be said, that like most dreams, it is false. Adieu! Take care of yourself, and act so that we may from time to time hear you spoken of.
MARIE MICHON

"What dream does she mean?" asked the dragoon, who had approached during the reading.

"Yez, what dream?" repeated the Swiss.

"Well, *pardieu!*" said Aramis. "I had a dream, and I told her about it."

"Yess, yess," said the Swiss, "it's simple enough to dell a dream, but I neffer dream."

"You are very fortunate," said Athos, rising. "I wish I could say the same!"

"Neffer," replied the Swiss, enchanted that a man like Athos could envy him anything. *"Neffer, neffer!"*

Seeing Athos rise, d'Artagnan did likewise, took his arm, and went out with him.

Porthos and Aramis remained behind to handle the jokes of the dragoon and the Swiss.

As for Bazin, he lay down on a bundle of straw, and since he had more imagination than the Swiss, he dreamed that Aramis had become pope and given him a cardinal's hat.

But, as we have said, Bazin's successful return had removed only a part of the uneasiness that hung over the four friends. Days of waiting are long, and d'Artagnan in particular would have bet that each day had forty-eight hours. He forgot how slow it was to travel by sea; he exaggerated Milady's power; he credited the woman, who seemed a demon to him, with having agents as supernatural as herself; he imagined, at the least noise, that he was about to be arrested and that Planchet was being brought back to confront him and his friends. His confidence in the worthy Picard, previously so unshakable, decreased day by day. His anxiety became so great that it communicated itself to Aramis and Porthos. Only Athos remained imperturbable, as if no danger was hovering over him and as if nothing was different from usual.

By the sixteenth day, d'Artagnan and his two friends were so agitated that they could not stay still but wandered up and down like ghosts on the road by which Planchet was expected to return.

"Really," Athos said to them, "you are not men but children if you let a woman terrify you so! And for what after all? To be imprisoned? But we would be released from prison—Madame Bonacieux was. To be decapitated? Why, every day in the trenches we cheerfully expose ourselves to worse than that, because a bullet may break a leg, and I am convinced that a surgeon would give us more pain in cutting off a leg than an executioner in cutting off a head. Be patient. In two hours, or four, or six at the latest, Planchet will be here. He promised, and I have great faith in Planchet, who seems to be a very good, brave fellow."

"But if he does not come?" said d'Artagnan.

"Well, if he does not come, it will be because he has been delayed, that's all. He may have tumbled from his horse, he may have taken a fall on the deck of the ship, he may have traveled so fast against the wind as to have brought on a bad chest cold. Gentlemen, we must make allowance for accidents! Life is a rosary strung with little miseries, and the philosopher tells them with a smile. Be philosophers, as I am. Sit down and let us drink. Nothing makes the future look so bright as seeing it through a glass of chambertin."

"That's all well and good," replied d'Artagnan, "but I am tired of being afraid when I open a fresh bottle that the wine may come from Milady's cellar."

"You are very fastidious," said Athos. "She is such a beautiful woman!"

"A woman of mark!" said Porthos, with his loud laugh.

Athos started, wiped the drops of perspiration that burst forth, and rose in his turn with a nervousness he could not repress.

The day nevertheless passed; the evening came on slowly, but it did come. The taverns were filled with drinkers. Athos, who had pocketed his share of the diamond, seldom left the Parpaillot. He had found in M. de Busigny, who by the by had given them a magnificent dinner, a partner worthy of him, and they were playing together as usual when the clock struck seven; they could hear the patrol passing on their way to reinforce the posts. At half past seven retreat was sounded.

"We are lost," d'Artagnan whispered to Athos.

"You mean we *have* lost," said Athos quietly, taking four pistoles from his pocket and tossing them onto the table. "Come, gentlemen," he said, "they are beating the tattoo. Let us be off!"

And he left the Parpaillot followed by d'Artagnan; Aramis was behind them, giving his arm to Porthos. Aramis was reciting poetry to himself, and Porthos occasionally pulled a hair or two from his mustache as a sign of despair.

But all at once a familiar outline appeared in the darkness, and a well-known voice said to d'Artagnan, "Monsieur, I have brought your cloak because it is chilly this evening."

"Planchet!" cried d'Artagnan, beside himself with joy.

"Planchet!" repeated Aramis and Porthos.

"Well, yes, of course it is Planchet," said Athos. "What is so astonishing about that? He promised to be back by eight o'clock, and it is just eight now. Bravo, Planchet, you are a lad of your word, and if you ever leave your master's service, I will promise you a place in my own."

"Oh, no," said Planchet, "I will never leave Monsieur d'Artagnan."

At the same time d'Artagnan felt Planchet slip a note into his hand.

D'Artagnan wanted to embrace Planchet as he had embraced him on his departure; but he was afraid that such a public mark of affection bestowed upon his lackey might seem strange to passersby, and he restrained himself.

"I have the note," he said to his friends.

"Good," said Athos. "Let us go back to our quarters and read it."

The note burned d'Artagnan's hand. He wanted to hurry, but Athos took his arm and the young man was forced to regulate his pace by that of his friend.

Finally they reached the tent, lit a lamp, and while Planchet stood at the entrance to make sure that the four friends would not be interrupted, d'Artagnan, with a trembling hand, broke the seal and opened the long-awaited letter.

It contained half a line in an unmistakably British handwriting and was of a perfectly Spartan conciseness:

Thank you. Do not worry.

D'Artagnan translated it for the others.

Athos took the letter from d'Artagnan, approached the lamp, set fire to the paper, and did not let go till it had burned to ashes.

Then, calling Planchet, he said, "Now, my lad, you may have your other seven hundred livres—but you did not run much risk with a note like that."

"I am not to blame for having recommended that it be as short as possible," said Planchet.

"Tell us all about it," said d'Artagnan.

"That's a long job, monsieur."

"You are right, Planchet," said Athos. "Besides, the tattoo has been sounded, and we would be noticed if we kept our light burning much longer than the others."

"So be it," said d'Artagnan. "Let us go to bed. Planchet, sleep soundly."

"My faith, monsieur, it will be the first time in sixteen days."

"For me, too!" said d'Artagnan.

"For me, too!" said Porthos.

"For me, too!" said Aramis.

"If you must know the truth, for me, too!" said Athos.

49

A Setback

MEANWHILE MILADY, seething with fury and roaring on the deck like a lioness, had been tempted to throw herself into the sea so that she might regain the coast, for she was unable to rid herself of the idea that she had been insulted by d'Artagnan and threatened by Athos—and that she had left France without being revenged on them. The idea became so insupportable that she was willing to risk any consequences if the captain would only put her ashore immediately. But the captain, eager to escape from the danger of being placed between the Scylla and Charybdis of the French and English warships, was in a hurry to regain England as quickly as possible; he stubbornly refused to obey what he took for a woman's caprice, though he did promise his passenger—who had been particularly recommended to him by the cardinal—to land her, if the sea and the French permitted him, at one of the ports of Brittany, either Lorient or Brest. The wind, however, was contrary and the sea rough: they tacked and kept offshore.

Nine days after leaving the Charente, pale with fatigue

and vexation, Milady finally saw the bluish coast of Finistère. She calculated that it would take her at least three days to cross this corner of France and return to the cardinal. Add another day for landing, and that would make four. Add these four to the nine others and that would be thirteen days lost—thirteen days during which many important things might happen in London. She also realized that the cardinal would be furious at her return and would consequently be more disposed to listen to the complaints others might bring against her than to the accusations she brought against others.

So she allowed the ship to pass Lorient and Brest without reminding the captain about his promise—and he was careful not to remind her of it either. Milady therefore continued her voyage and entered Portsmouth on the very day that Planchet left the port on his return to France.

The city was in a state of extraordinary excitement. Four large, recently built vessels had just been launched, and at the end of the pier—his clothes as usual richly laced with gold and glittering with diamonds and precious stones, his hat ornamented with a white plume that hung down to his shoulder—was Buckingham, surrounded by a staff dressed almost as strikingly as himself.

It was one of those rare and beautiful winter days when England remembers that there is a sun. Pale now, but still splendid, it was setting in the horizon, streaking both the sky and the sea with bands of fire and casting a last ray of gold on the towers and the old houses of the city, making the windows sparkle as though from the reflection of a fire. Breathing that fragrant sea air which becomes so much more invigorating as land is approached, contemplating all the power of those preparations she was commissioned to destroy, all the power of that army she was expected to combat alone, with the help of only a few bags of gold—Milady compared herself mentally to Judith, the Old Testament heroine, when she penetrated the Assyrian camp and beheld the enormous mass of chariots, horses, men, and arms that she was to dissipate like a puff of smoke with a gesture of her hand.

The ship entered the roadstead, but as it was about to drop anchor, a heavily armed little cutter approached, identified itself as a coastal defense vessel, and dropped into the sea a boat that headed for the ladder. The boat contained an officer, a mate, and eight rowers. Only the officer went on board, and he was received with all the deference owed to the uniform.

The officer talked to the captain for a few minutes and gave him several papers to read, after which the merchant captain ordered all the passengers and sailors to assemble on the deck.

When everyone had gathered there the officer asked in a loud voice about where the brig had come from, its route, its landings; and to all those questions the captain replied without difficulty and without hesitation. Then the officer began to examine all the people, one after the other, stopping when he came to Milady; he looked at her very carefully, but said not a single word.

He returned to the captain and again said a few words to him, and from that moment the vessel seemed to be under his command: he gave the crew an order, and it was executed immediately. The ship resumed its course, escorted by the little cutter that sailed alongside it, seeming to threaten it with the mouths of its six cannon. The boat followed in the wake of the ship, a speck near an enormous mass.

While Milady was being examined by the officer, she had of course been scrutinizing him as well. But despite her ability to read the hearts of those whose secrets she wished to know, this time she met with such an impassive face that she could learn nothing from it. The officer who had studied her so intently might have been twenty-five or twenty-six years old. He had a light complexion and deep-set blue eyes; his firm, well-shaped mouth seemed set in its correct lines; his strong chin denoted that strength of will which in the ordinary British type usually signifies nothing but obstinacy; his high forehead—proper for poets, enthusiasts, and soldiers—was sparsely framed by short thin hair that was the same deep chestnut color as the beard that covered the lower part of his face.

When they entered the harbor, it was already night. The fog increased the darkness and made circles around the sternlights and lanterns on the pier, like the ring that surrounds the moon when it is about to rain. The air was heavy, damp, and cold.

Courageous and firm as she was, Milady shivered in spite of herself.

The officer had Milady's packages pointed out to him and ordered them to be placed in the boat. When this was done, he asked her to descend the ladder and offered her his hand.

Milady looked at him and hesitated.

"Who are you, sir," she asked, "that you are so kind as to trouble yourself on my account?"

"You may see by my uniform, madame, that I am an officer in the English navy," the young man replied.

"Is it the custom for officers in the English navy to place themselves at the service of their female compatriots when they land in an English port, and to carry their gallantry so far as to conduct them ashore?"

"Yes, madame, it is the custom—not from gallantry but from prudence—that in time of war foreigners should be conducted to special inns and kept there until the government can be fully informed about them."

Though these words were pronounced with the most perfect politeness, they did not succeed in convincing Milady.

"But I am not a foreigner, sir," she said with an accent as pure as ever was heard between Portsmouth and Manchester. "I am Lady de Winter, and this measure . . ."

"This measure is general, madame, and there are no exceptions."

"Then I will follow you, sir."

Accepting the hand of the officer, she descended the ladder and entered the boat. The officer followed her. A large cloak was spread in the stern; the officer asked her to sit down on it and sat beside her.

"Row!" he ordered the sailors.

The eight oars fell at once into the sea, each one seeming to make only a single sound, to give only a single stroke; the boat appeared to fly over the surface of the water.

In five minutes they reached the shore.

The officer leaped onto the pier and offered his hand to Milady.

A carriage was waiting.

"Is this carriage for us?" she asked.

"Yes, madame," replied the officer.

"The inn is far away?"

"At the other end of town."

"Very well," said Milady, and she resolutely entered the carriage.

The officer made sure that the baggage was fastened carefully behind the carriage, then took his place beside Milady and shut the door.

Without any order being given or place of destination indicated, the coachman immediately set off at a rapid pace and plunged into the city streets.

So strange a reception naturally gave Milady ample food for thought, so seeing that the young officer did not seem at all inclined to talk, she leaned back in her corner of the carriage and began to examine all the possibilities that came to mind.

At the end of a quarter of an hour, however, surprised at the length of the journey, she looked out the window to see where she was being taken. There were no more houses in sight: trees appeared in the darkness like great black phantoms chasing one another. Milady shuddered.

"But we are no longer in the city, sir," she said.

The young officer remained silent.

"I warn you that I will go no farther unless you tell me where you are taking me."

Her threat brought no response.

"Oh, this is too much!" cried Milady. "Help! Help!"

No voice replied to hers; the carriage continued to roll along rapidly; the officer seemed like a statue.

She looked at him with one of her terrifying expressions, which rarely failed to produce an effect; her eyes blazed in the darkness.

The young man remained unmoved.

She tried to open the door in order to throw herself out.

"Take care, madame," said the young man coldly. "You will kill yourself if you jump."

Milady sat back again, foaming with rage. The officer leaned forward, looked at her, and appeared surprised to see her beautiful face distorted with anger and almost hideous in its rage. The artful creature at once understood that she was doing herself no good by allowing him thus to read her soul, so she composed her features and said plaintively, "In the name of heaven, sir, tell me if it is you, your government, or an enemy who is responsible for the violence that is being done me?"

"No violence is being done you, madame, and what is happening is the result of a very simple measure that we are obliged to adopt with all who land in England."

"Then you do not know me, sir?"

"This is the first time I have had the honor of seeing you."

"And on your honor, you have no reason to hate me?"

"None, I swear to you."

There was something so serene, dispassionate, even mild, about his voice that she was reassured.

After a journey of nearly an hour, the carriage finally stopped before an iron gate that guarded a driveway leading to a grim-looking, massive, and isolated castle. As the wheels rolled over a fine gravel, Milady could hear a vast roaring, which she at once recognized as the sound of the sea dashing against some steep cliff.

The carriage passed under two arched gateways and then stopped in a large, dark, square courtyard. Almost immediately the carriage door was opened and the young man sprang lightly out; he offered his hand to Milady, who leaned upon it and in turn stepped down with tolerable calmness.

"I am a prisoner," she said, looking around her then turning with a most gracious smile to the young officer, "but I am sure it will not be for long. My own conscience and your courtesy, sir, assure me of that."

However flattering the compliment, the officer made no reply. Taking from his belt a little silver whistle such as boatswains use in war ships, he blew it three times in three different modulations. Several men immediately appeared, unharnessed the steaming horses, and put the carriage into a coach house.

With the same cool politeness, the officer invited his prisoner to enter the house. Still smiling, she took his arm and went with him under a low arched door to a vaulted passageway, lit only at the far end, that led to a spiral stone staircase. Then they came to a massive door, which the young man unlocked, disclosing the room prepared for Milady.

With a single glance the prisoner took in its most minute details. The furniture was at once too attractive

for a prison and too austere for a guest room—yet bars
on the windows and outside bolts on the door made it
clear it was a prison.

For a second all the strength of her vigorous mind
abandoned her; she sank into a large armchair, folding
her arms, bowing her head, and expecting to see a judge
come in to interrogate her at any moment.

But no one came in except several sailors, who brought
her trunks and packages, deposited them in a corner,
and left without speaking.

The officer superintended all these details with his
usual composure, never saying a word himself, and making himself obeyed by a gesture of his hand or a blow of
his whistle.

It was as if spoken language did not exist, or had
become unnecessary, between this man and his subordinates.

Milady could finally hold out no longer; she broke the
silence.

"In the name of heaven, sir, what does all this mean?
Tell me what is happening. I have enough courage to
face any danger I can foresee, any misfortune I understand. Where am I, and why am I here? If I am free,
why these bars and these doors? If I am a prisoner, what
crime have I committed?"

"You are where you are supposed to be, madame. I
received orders to take charge of you on the sea and to
bring you to this castle. I believe I have carried out this
order with all the precision of a soldier, but also with the
courtesy of a gentleman. There ends, at least for now,
my duty. The rest concerns someone else."

"Who is that someone else?" she asked. "Can you not
tell me his name?"

Just then a great jingling of spurs was heard on the
stairs; some voices approached, then faded away, and the
sound of footsteps came closer.

"He is here now, madame," said the officer, leaving a
clear passage and standing respectfully near the door.

A man appeared on the threshold. He was hatless, carried
a sword, and flourished a handkerchief in his hand.

Milady thought she recognized the shadowy outline;
she leaned on the arm of the chair and peered into the
darkness, as if to confirm a certainty.

The man advanced slowly, and as he entered the circle of light cast by the lamp, she involuntarily drew back, still staring.

When she was absolutely certain, she cried out in astonishment, "What, is it you, my brother?"

"Yes, fair lady," replied Lord de Winter, with a bow that was half courteous, half ironical; "it is I, myself."

"Then this castle . . . ?"

"Is mine."

"This room . . . ?"

"Is yours."

"I am your prisoner?"

"More or less."

"But this is a frightful abuse of power!"

"No high-sounding words! Let us sit down and have a quiet conversation, as brother and sister ought to do."

Then, turning toward the door and seeing that the young officer was waiting for his orders, he said, "All is well. Thank you, and now leave us alone, Mr. Felton."

50

A Conversation Between Brother and Sister

DURING THE TIME it took Lord de Winter to shut the door, close a shutter, and draw a chair next to his sister-in-law's, Milady, who had not been able to understand what was happening as long as she did not know into whose hands she had fallen, was quickly examining the possible explanations for her detention. She knew her brother-in-law to be a worthy gentleman, a bold hunter, a daring gambler, and an ardent lover—but by no means a remarkable or skillful intriguer. How had he known about her arrival in England and caused her to be seized? Why was he keeping her a prisoner?

Athos had said some things that proved her conversation with the cardinal had been overheard, but she could not believe that he had been able to counterattack so promptly and so boldly. Perhaps her earlier operations in England had been discovered.

Buckingham, for instance, might have guessed that it was she who had cut off the two diamond studs and want revenge for that bit of treachery; and even though he was incapable of doing anything extreme against a woman—particularly if he thought she had acted out of jealousy—the most likely explanation was that he wanted to take revenge for the past and not to anticipate what she might do in the future. At all events, she congratulated herself upon having fallen into the hands of her brother-in-law, whom she felt she could easily outwit, rather than into the hands of a more relentless and intelligent enemy.

"Yes, let us talk, brother," she said, with a kind of cheerfulness.

She needed information to make her plans, and she was determined to get it from Lord de Winter no matter how hard he tried to keep it from her.

"Why did you decide to come to England again," he asked, "when you so often said in Paris that you never wanted to set your feet on British soil again?"

Milady replied to this question by asking one herself.

"To begin with, tell me how you knew not only of my arrival, but even of the day, the hour, and the place of my arrival?"

Lord de Winter adopted the same tactics as Milady, thinking that since his sister-in-law employed them, they must be the best.

"But you tell me, my dear sister, what makes you come to England?"

"I have come to see you," she replied, hoping to gain his good will by this lie and not knowing how much it merely reinforced the suspicions aroused by d'Artagnan's letter.

"To see me?" he repeated.

"Of course, to see you. What is astonishing about that?"

"You had no other reason for coming to England?"

"No."

"It was only for me that you have taken the trouble to cross the Channel?"

"Only for you."

"What affection, my dear sister!"

"But am I not your closest relative?" she asked, with a tone of the most touching naiveté.

"And my only heir, too, are you not?" he replied, looking straight at her.

Despite her extraordinary self-control, she could not help starting, and since he had placed his hand on her arm at those words, this start did not escape him.

In fact, he had dealt her a severe blow. The first thing she thought of was that she had been betrayed by Kitty, who might have reported to her brother-in-law some of those self-serving remarks concerning her feelings about him which she had imprudently allowed herself to make in front of her servant. She also remembered her equally imprudent attack on d'Artagnan when he had spared de Winter's life.

"I do not understand," she said, in order to gain time and make her adversary speak out. "Is there some secret meaning hidden behind your words?"

"Oh, no," he replied with apparent good humor. "You wish to see me, and you come to England. I learn about this wish—or rather I suspect that you have it—and in order to spare you all the annoyances of a nocturnal arrival and disembarkation, I send one of my officers to meet you. I place a carriage at his disposal, and he brings you to this castle, which I command and where I come every day and where I have prepared a room for you so we can satisfy our mutual desire to see each other. What is there more surprising in all that I have said to you than in what you have told me?"

"Nothing. What I find surprising is that you knew I was coming."

"And yet that is the most simple thing in the world, my dear sister. Did you not observe that the captain of your ship, on entering the roadstead, sent on ahead a small boat bearing his logbook and a list of his passengers in order to obtain permission to enter the port? I am the commander of the port, so when they brought me the list, I recognized your name on it. My heart told me what your lips have just confirmed—that is, the reason for your having exposed yourself to the dangers of a sea that is so troublesome at this moment—and I sent my cutter to meet you. You know the rest."

Milady knew that Lord de Winter was lying, and she was all the more alarmed.

"My brother, was that not the Duke of Buckingham I saw on the pier when I arrived?"

"It was. I can understand how the sight of him must have struck you. You came from a country where he must be very much talked about, and I know that his preparations against France receive a great deal of attention from your friend the cardinal."

"My friend the cardinal!" she exclaimed, seeing that Lord de Winter seemed equally well informed about this point.

"Is he not your friend?" he asked casually. "Pardon me, I thought he was. But we will come back to the Duke of Buckingham later. For now, let us return to the more sentimental aspect of your visit. You say you came to see me?"

"Yes."

"Well, your wishes shall be gratified. We will see each other every day."

"Am I to remain here forever?" Milady asked anxiously.

"Do you find yourself badly housed, sister? Ask for anything you want, and I will have it brought to you immediately."

"But I have no maids, no servants."

"You shall have all you want, madame. Tell me how your household was organized by your first husband, and although I am only your brother-in-law, I will make similar arrangements."

"My first husband!" cried Milady, her eyes bulging with terror.

"Yes, your French husband—I am, of course, not speaking of my brother. If you have forgotten the details, I can always write for information since that gentleman is still alive."

A cold sweat broke out on her forehead.

"You jest," she said in a hollow voice.

"Do I look as if I jest?" he asked, rising and stepping backward.

"Then you are insulting me," she continued, raising herself from her chair with difficulty.

"Insulting you!" said Lord de Winter with contempt. "In truth, madame, do you think that is possible?"

"Indeed, sir, you must be either drunk or mad. Leave the room, and send me a maid."

"Women are very indiscreet, my sister! Can I not serve as your maid? That way all our secrets will remain in the family."

"Insolent!" cried Milady, flinging herself at him.

He watched her impassively, but with one hand on the hilt of his sword.

"I know you are accustomed to murdering people, but I warn you that I will defend myself, even against you."

"Yes, you are most likely cowardly enough to use force against a woman."

"Perhaps—and I would have an excuse, for I think I would not be the first man to use force against you."

And he pointed, with a slow, accusatory gesture, to her left shoulder, almost touching it with his finger.

Milady uttered a sound that was almost a growl and retreated to a corner of the room, where she crouched like a cornered panther.

"Oh, roar as much as you please," he said, "but do not try to bite or you will regret it. There are no procurators here to regulate inheritances in advance, no knight-errants to seek a quarrel with me on behalf of the fair lady I hold prisoner—but there *are* judges quite ready to dispose of a woman shameless enough to glide into my brother's bed as a bigamist! And those judges will send you to an executioner who will make both your shoulders alike!"

Her eyes blazed so fiercely that although he was an armed man facing an unarmed woman, he felt a cold fear permeate his entire being. He continued to speak, however, but with increasing anger.

"I quite understand that after having inherited my brother's fortune, you would have liked to inherit mine as well. But be warned—I have taken my precautions. If you kill me or have me killed, not a penny of what I possess will pass into your hands. Were you not rich enough—you who already have a fortune? You could have stopped your sinful career if you did not do evil simply for the supreme joy of doing it! If the memory of my brother were not sacred to me, you would rot in a state dungeon or provide a diversion for the sailors at Tyburn. I will say nothing about all this, but you must endure your captivity without complaining. In two or three weeks I will be going to La Rochelle with the army, but the night before I leave, I will see you board a ship that will take you to our southern colonies. And be assured that you will be accompanied by one who will blow your brains out if you make any attempt to return to England or the Continent."

Milady listened attentively, her inflamed eyes dilated with the effort to concentrate.

"But for the present," he continued, "you will remain in this castle. The walls are thick, the doors strong, and the bars solid—and from your window there is a sheer drop to the sea. My men are completely loyal to me and will be mounting guard around this room and all the passages that lead to the courtyard. Even if you reached the yard, you would still have to pass through three iron gates. I have given strict orders that if there should be any step, gesture, or word on your part indicating an effort to escape, you are to be fired upon. If they kill you, English justice will be grateful to me for having saved it the trouble of doing so itself. I see your face becoming calm and confident again. You are saying to yourself: 'Two or three weeks? Bah! I have an inventive mind, and I am sure to think of something before then. I am certain to meet some willing victim, and I will be out of here in less than two weeks!' Well, just try it."

Seeing herself so well understood, Milady dug her nails into her flesh to repress every sign of any emotion other than anguish.

Lord de Winter continued. "The officer in command here during my absence you have already seen, and therefore know. As you must have observed, he is able to obey an order—for I am sure you did not come from Portsmouth without trying to make him speak. Well? Could a marble statue have been more unmoved, more silent? You have already tried your power of seduction on many men, and unfortunately you have till now always succeeded—but I give you leave to try them on *this* one. If you succeed with him, I will know you to be the devil himself."

He went to the door and opened it brusquely.

"Call Mr. Felton," he said, then turned back to her and added, "I will introduce him to you."

During the strained silence that fell between them, they could hear slow, steady footsteps approaching. Soon a figure emerged from the shadowy corridor, and the young lieutenant stopped at the threshold to receive Lord de Winter's orders.

"Come in, John, and shut the door."

The young officer entered.

"Now look at this woman," said de Winter. "She is young, beautiful, and seductive—yet she is a monster. At the age of twenty-five, she has been guilty of as many crimes as you could read of in a year's worth of court archives. Her voice prejudices her hearers in her favor, her beauty serves as a bait to her victims, and to do her justice, her body even pays what she promises. She will try to seduce you, perhaps to kill you. Felton, I have rescued you from misery, I have had you commissioned a lieutenant, I once saved your life—you know on what occasion. I am for you not only a protector, but a friend—not only a benefactor, but a father. This woman has come back to England to plot against my life. This serpent is now in my hands, and I say to you, John, my friend, my child, guard me and, more particularly, guard yourself against this woman. Swear by your hopes of salvation to keep her here for the punishment she has deserved. John Felton, I trust your word! John Felton, I have faith in your loyalty!"

"My Lord," said the young officer, looking at Milady with all the hatred he could find in his pure and mild heart, "I swear I will do as you wish."

She received his look with resignation; it was impossible for an expression to display more gentle submission. Lord de Winter himself could scarcely recognize her as the tigress he had been prepared to fight but a moment before.

"She is not to leave this room, John," he continued. "She is to correspond with no one, and she is to speak to no one but you—if you do her the honor to speak to her."

"That is sufficient, my Lord. I have sworn."

"And now, madame, try to make your peace with God, for you have been judged by men!"

Milady bowed her head, as if crushed by that verdict. Lord de Winter left the room; Felton followed, locking the door behind him.

A moment later, Milady could hear the heavy step of an armed guard in the corridor.

She remained in the same position for several minutes because she thought they might be watching her through the keyhole. Then she slowly raised her head, and on her face was once again that formidable expression of fierce defiance. After listening at the door and looking out the window, she sat down again in her large armchair and began to think.

51

Officer!

MEANWHILE, THE CARDINAL was waiting anxiously for news from England, but the only news that arrived was annoying and alarming.

Thanks to the many precautions taken—especially to the dike, which prevented the entrance of any ship into the besieged city—the blockade of La Rochelle was certain to succeed, though it might last a long time. That was a great affront to the king's army and a great inconvenience to the cardinal. He no longer had to create trouble between the king and the queen, for that goal had been achieved, but he did have to reconcile M. de Bassompierre and the Duc d'Angoulême.

As for Monsieur, who had begun the siege, he left the cardinal the task of finishing it.

Despite the incredible perseverance of its mayor, some of the Rochellais had mutinied and tried to surrender; the mayor had hanged the mutineers. That discouraged any other such rebels, who resigned themselves to die of hunger—which seemed a slower and less certain death than hanging, and thus preferable.

On their side, the besiegers would occasionally capture the messengers sent from La Rochelle to Buckingham, or the spies sent from Buckingham to La Rochelle. In either case the trial was soon over. The cardinal would pronounce the single word, "Hanged!" The king, invited to watch the hanging, would come languidly and sit where he could see all the details. This would sometimes amuse him a little, and enable him to endure the siege with patience; but it was not enough to keep him from getting very bored or from talking about returning to Paris. If there had been no messengers or spies, his Eminence, notwithstanding all his inventiveness, would have found himself searching, with great difficulty, for other diversions.

Nevertheless, time passed and the Rochellais did not surrender. The last spy that had been taken was carrying a letter for Buckingham saying that the city was desperate; but instead of adding, "If your help does not arrive within two weeks, we will surrender," it added, quite simply, "If your help does not come within two weeks, we will all be dead from starvation when it does come."

The Rochellais had only one hope: Buckingham. Buckingham was their Messiah, and if they ever learned positively that they could not count on him, their courage would fail together with their hope.

The cardinal therefore waited impatiently for the news from England that would assure him that Buckingham would not come.

Though the possibility of storming the city had often been debated in the king's council, it had always been rejected. In the first place, La Rochelle seemed to be impregnable. In the second place, the cardinal, whatever he said, knew very well that the horror of bloodshed in such a battle—in which Frenchman would be fighting against Frenchman—would set the country back sixty years, and the cardinal was at that time what we now call a man of progress: in fact, the sack of La Rochelle and the assassination of three or four thousand Huguenots would be too much like the St. Bartholomew Day massacre in 1572. In the third and most important place, this extreme measure—which was not at all repugnant to the king, good Catholic that he was—was always opposed by the besieging generals, who insisted that La Rochelle was unassailable except by starvation.

And then the cardinal also could not ignore the disquiet aroused by his terrible emissary, for he had understood the strange qualities of the woman, who was sometimes a slippery serpent, sometimes a raging lion. Had she betrayed him? Was she dead? He knew her well enough to know that whether she was acting for or against him, as a friend or an enemy, she would not remain idle without serious reasons. But what were those reasons? He could not find out what had gone wrong.

And yet he counted on Milady, and with reason. He had guessed that she had terrible things in her past, things that only his red mantle could cover, and he felt that she would be loyal to him because there was no one else powerful enough to preserve her from the danger that threatened her.

So he resolved to carry on the war alone and to look for no outside help except that which might come as a stroke of good luck. He continued to build the famous dike that was to starve La Rochelle, and meanwhile, he cast his eyes over that unfortunate city, which contained so much deep misery and so many heroic virtues, and recalled the saying of Louis XI—his political predecessor just as he was Robespierre's—"Divide and rule."

When besieging Paris, Henry IV had provisions thrown over the walls; the cardinal had little sheets of paper thrown over the walls of La Rochelle, telling the people how unjust, selfish, and barbarous was their leaders' conduct. Those leaders had abundant grain and would not share it; they had adopted as a principle that it did not matter if women, children, and old men died, as long as the men who were to defend the walls remained strong and healthy. This principle, whether from conviction or from lack of power to act against it, had passed from theory into practice; but the leaflets reminded the men that the children, women, and old men whom they allowed to die were their sons, their wives, and their fathers, and that it would be more just if everyone suffered the common misery equally, so that equal conditions would result in unanimous decisions.

These leaflets had the expected effect: they induced many of the inhabitants to open private negotiations with the royal army.

But just as the cardinal saw his plan begin to succeed, and he was applauding himself for having put it into action, an inhabitant of La Rochelle who had managed to slip through the royal lines—despite the watchfulness of Bassompierre, Schomberg, and the Duc d'Angoulême, who were themselves watched over by the cardinal—an

inhabitant of La Rochelle, as we have said, returned to
La Rochelle from Portsmouth, reporting that he had
there seen a magnificent fleet ready to sail within a week.
Furthermore, he had a letter from Buckingham to the
mayor saying that the great league was about to declare
itself against France and that the kingdom would immediately be invaded by the English, Imperial, and Spanish
armies. The letter was read aloud in all parts of the city,
and copies of it were posted on street corners; even those
who had opened negotiations broke them off, resolved
to wait for the help so pompously announced.

This unexpected circumstance revived Richelieu's former anxiety and forced him once more to turn his attention to the other side of the channel.

Meanwhile, unaware of the anxiety of its only real
leader, the royal army led a joyous life, for both food
and money were plentiful. All the corps vied with one
another in audacity and gaiety. To take spies and hang
them, to make hazardous expeditions on the dike or the
sea, to imagine wild plans and to execute them coolly—
such were the pastimes which made the days short for
the army. These were the same days that were so long
to the Rochellais, suffering from famine and anxiety, and
even to the cardinal, who was blockading them so
closely.

Sometimes the cardinal, always on horseback like the
lowest soldier, looked pensively at those slow-moving
projects that the engineers—brought here from all the
corners of France—were executing under his orders. If
at that time he met a Musketeer from Tréville's company, he drew near and scrutinized him carefully, then
not recognizing him as one of our four companions, he
would turn his penetrating stare and profound thoughts
in another direction.

One day depressed, with no hope for the negotiations
with the city, without news from England—the cardinal
went out for a ride just to get some air. Accompanied
only by Cahusac and La Houdinière, he rode slowly
along the beach, mingling the immensity of his dreams
with the immensity of the ocean. He came eventually to
a hill from the top of which he saw seven men behind a
hedge, lying on the sand and enjoying some rare sunlight;
they were surrounded by empty bottles. Four of those

men were our Musketeers, preparing to listen to a letter one of them had just received—a letter that was so important it had made them abandon their cards and their dice.

The other three men, their lackeys, were occupied in opening an enormous demijohn of Collioure wine.

The cardinal was feeling depressed, and when he was in that mood, nothing increased his depression so much as gaiety in others. Besides, he had a strange idea that what made him sad was exactly what made others happy. Signaling La Houdinière and Cahusac to stop, he dismounted and went toward those suspiciously merry companions, hoping that the sand would deaden the sound of his steps and the hedge would conceal his approach enough to allow him to hear some of that conversation which appeared so interesting. Ten paces away from the hedge he recognized the talkative Gascon, and since he had already seen that the other three were Musketeers, he did not doubt that they were those called the Inseparables: Athos, Porthos, and Aramis.

Obviously his desire to overhear their conversation was increased by this discovery. He had a strange look in his eyes, and he advanced toward the hedge as lightly as a cat; but he had not been able to catch more than a few vague syllables of which he could make no sense when a loud short cry startled him and attracted the attention of the Musketeers.

"Officer!" cried Grimaud.

"You are speaking, you scoundrel!" said Athos, rising on his elbow and fixing Grimaud with a steely look.

Grimaud therefore said no more, but contented himself with pointing in the direction of the hedge, announcing by that gesture the cardinal and his escort.

With a single bound the Musketeers were on their feet and saluted him with respect.

The cardinal seemed furious.

"It seems that the Musketeers keep guard," he said. "Are the English coming by land, or do the Musketeers consider themselves senior officers?"

"Monseigneur," replied Athos, for amid the general panic he alone had preserved the noble coolness and calm that never deserted him, "the Musketeers, when they are not on duty or when their duty is over, drink

and play at dice, and they are certainly high-ranking officers to their lackeys."

"Lackeys!" grumbled the cardinal. "Lackeys who are
under orders to warn their masters when anyone passes
are not lackeys, they are sentries."

"Your Eminence will understand that if we had not
taken this precaution, we might have allowed you to pass
without being able to present our respects or thank you
for bringing us together. D'Artagnan," continued Athos,
"you were just saying that you were eager for an opportunity to express your gratitude to Monseigneur. Here is
your opportunity—take advantage of it."

These words were spoken with that imperturbable
assurance that distinguished Athos in times of danger,
and with that extraordinary courtesy that sometimes
made him more majestic than a king.

D'Artagnan came forward and stammered out a few
words of gratitude that soon sputtered out under the grim
looks of the cardinal.

Without being at all deflected from his first intention
by the diversion Athos had attempted, the cardinal continued, "It does not matter, gentlemen. I do not like to
have simple soldiers acting like great lords because they
have the advantage of serving in a privileged corps. Discipline is the same for them as for everybody else."

Athos allowed the cardinal to finish his sentence, and
bowed in agreement. Then he resumed in his turn.

"Monseigneur, I hope discipline has in no way been
forgotten by us. We are not on duty, and we thus felt
that we were at liberty to dispose of our time as we
pleased. If we are so fortunate as to have some particular
duty to perform for your Eminence, we are ready to obey
you. Your Eminence may see," he continued, frowning
because he was becoming annoyed by having to defend
himself, "that we have brought our arms with us."

And he pointed to the four muskets piled next to the
drum on which lay the cards and dice.

"Your Eminence may believe," added d'Artagnan,
"that we would have come to meet you if we had thought
it was Monseigneur coming toward us with so few
attendants."

The cardinal bit his mustache and even his lips.

"Do you know what you look like, armed and guarded

as you are by your lackeys?" he asked. "You look like four conspirators."

"Oh, as to that, monseigneur, it is true," said Athos. "We *do* conspire, as your Eminence could see the other morning. But we conspire against the Rochellais."

"You gentlemen are very politic!" replied the cardinal, frowning in his turn. "I might discover many unknown things if I could read your minds as you were reading that letter you hid as soon as you saw me coming."

The color mounted to Athos's face, and he took a step toward his Eminence.

"One might think that you really suspected us, monseigneur, and that we were undergoing a real interrogation. If so, we hope your Eminence will deign to explain himself, and we would then at least know where we stand."

"And if it *were* an interrogation?" replied the cardinal. "Others besides you have undergone such, Monsieur Athos, and they have responded."

"I have told your Eminence that we are ready to reply to any questions."

"What was that letter you were about to read, Monsieur Aramis, and which you so promptly concealed?"

"A woman's letter, monseigneur."

"Ah, yes, I see," said the cardinal. "We must be discreet with such letters, but still, we may show them to a confessor, and you know I have taken orders."

"Monseigneur, the letter *is* a woman's letter, but it is signed neither Marion de Lorme nor Madame d'Aiguillon," said Athos, his unruffled serenity in naming two women who were reputedly the cardinal's mistresses all the more remarkable because he risked his head by this reply.

The cardinal became deathly pale, and lightning flashed from his eyes. He turned around as if to give an order to Cahusac and La Houdinière. Athos saw the movement and stepped toward the muskets, which the other three friends were already looking at like men not about to allow themselves to be taken. The cardinalists were three; the Musketeers, lackeys included, were seven, and the cardinal judged that the contest would be even less equal if Athos and his companions were indeed conspiring. In one of those rapid turnabouts which he always had at his command, all his anger dissolved into a smile.

"Well," he said, "you are brave young men, proud in the daylight, faithful in the darkness. We can find no fault with you for watching over yourselves when you watch so carefully over others. Gentlemen, I have not forgotten the night when you served as my escort to the Colombier-Rouge. If there were any danger on the road I am taking, I would ask you to accompany me, but since there is none, remain where you are and finish your bottles, your game, and your letter. Adieu, gentlemen!"

And remounting his horse, which Cahusac had brought to him, he saluted them and rode away.

The four young men stood watching him quietly, following him with their eyes until he had disappeared. Then they looked at one another.

They were all worried: they realized that despite his friendly adieu, the cardinal went away with rage in his heart.

Only Athos smiled, a self-possessed, disdainful smile.

When the cardinal was out of hearing and sight, Porthos, who had a great inclination to vent his ill-humor on somebody, exclaimed, "Grimaud took his time about warning us!"

Grimaud was about to excuse himself. Athos lifted his finger, and Grimaud was silent.

"Would you have given up the letter, Aramis?" asked d'Artagnan.

"I had made up my mind," said Aramis, in his mildest tone, "that if he had insisted on having the letter, I would have presented it to him with one hand and run my sword through his body with the other."

"I thought as much," said Athos. "That was why I threw myself between you and him. Indeed, this man is very rash to talk like that to other men—it is as though he had never dealt with anyone but women and children."

"Athos, I admire you, but nevertheless we were in the wrong," said d'Artagnan.

"How in the wrong?" asked Athos. "Who owns the air we breathe? The ocean we are looking at? The sand we were lying on? Who owns that letter? Do those things belong to the cardinal? Upon my honor, this man thinks the whole world belongs to him! There you stood, stammering, stupefied, crushed—as if the Bastille had appeared in front of you and Medusa had turned you to stone. Is being in love the same as conspiring? You are in love with a woman the cardinal has had imprisoned, and you wish to get her out of his clutches. You are playing a match with his Eminence—that letter is your hand. Why should you expose your hand to your adversary? That is not the way to play. Let him discover it if he can—we discover many of his!"

"That is very sensible, Athos," said d'Artagnan.

"In that case, let there be no more talk about what has just happened, and let Aramis go on with his cousin's letter from where the cardinal interrupted him."

Aramis took the letter from his pocket; the three friends moved closer to him, and the three lackeys again grouped themselves near the demijohn.

"You had read only a line or two," said d'Artagnan, "so read it again from the beginning."

"Willingly," said Aramis.

MY DEAR COUSIN,

I think I will soon set out for Béthune, where my sister has placed our little servant in the convent of the Carmelites. The poor child is quite resigned, because she knows she cannot live elsewhere without endangering her soul. Nevertheless, if our family affairs are arranged the way we wish, I believe she will run the risk of being damned and return to those she misses, especially since she knows they are always thinking about her. Meanwhile, she is not too miserable; what she wants most is a letter from her fiancé. I know that such commodities do not pass through convent gratings very easily, but after all, as I have proven to you, my dear cousin, I am not unskilled in such affairs, and I will take charge of the commission. My sister thanks you for always thinking about her. She was very worried for a while, but her mind is now more at ease since she has sent someone to make sure that all is well.

Adieu, my dear cousin. Tell us news of yourself as often as you can, that is, as often as you can with safety. I embrace you.

MARIE MICHON

"Oh, what do I not owe you, Aramis!" said d'Artagnan. "I finally have news of my dear Constance! She is alive and safely in a convent at Béthune! Where is Béthune, Athos?"

"On the frontier between Artois and Flanders. When the siege is lifted, we will be able to travel in that direction."

"And that will not take long, I hope," said Porthos. "This morning they hanged a spy who said that the Rochellais were now reduced to eating their shoe leather. Even if they eat the soles after having finished the leather, I cannot see that much will be left unless they eat one another."

"Poor fools!" said Athos, emptying a glass of excellent Bordeaux wine that did not then have the reputation it now enjoys, though it deserved it no less. "As if the Catholic religion was not the most advantageous and the most agreeable of all religions! All the same," he resumed after having appreciated the aftertaste, "they are brave fellows. . . . But what the devil are you doing, Aramis? Are you putting that letter back into your pocket?"

"Athos is right, we must burn it," said d'Artagnan. "Though even if we burn it, Monsieur le Cardinal may have some way to investigate the ashes!"

"He may indeed," said Athos.

"What shall we do with the letter?" asked Porthos.

"Come here, Grimaud," said Athos.

Grimaud stood up and obeyed.

"As a punishment for having spoken without permission, my friend, you will please eat this piece of paper. Then, as a reward for the service you will have rendered us, you shall drink this glass of wine. First, the letter. Eat heartily."

Grimaud smiled; and staring at the glass that Athos held in his hand, he chewed the paper thoroughly and swallowed it.

"Bravo, Grimaud!" said Athos. "Now here is your wine. We can dispense with your thanks."

Grimaud swallowed the glass of Bordeaux wine silently, but his eyes, raised toward heaven during this delicious occupation, spoke eloquently.

"And now," said Athos, "unless Monsieur le Cardinal

thinks of splitting open Grimaud's belly, I think we need not worry about the letter."

Meanwhile, his Eminence continued his melancholy ride, murmuring into his mustache, "I must get those four men into my service."

52

The First Day of Captivity

LET US RETURN to Milady, whom we have lost sight of during our brief glance at the coast of France.

We will find her in the same despairing attitude in which we left her, plunged into an abyss of dismal reflection—a dark hell at the gate of which she had almost left hope behind, because for the first time she has had doubts, for the first time she has known fear.

On two occasions her luck had failed her; on two occasions she had been discovered and betrayed—and on both occasions she had succumbed to the same force. D'Artagnan had conquered her—d'Artagnan, seemingly sent by the Lord himself to fight her hitherto invincible power of evil.

He had deceived her in her love, humbled her in her pride, thwarted her in her ambition; and now he had placed her fortune in jeopardy, deprived her of liberty, and even threatened her life. Still worse, he had lifted a corner of her mask—that shield with which she had covered herself and which had made her so strong.

D'Artagnan had saved Buckingham, whom she hated as she hated everyone she had once loved, from the destruction with which Richelieu had threatened him through the queen. D'Artagnan had passed himself off as de Wardes, for whom she had conceived one of those fiery passions common to women of her fierce nature. D'Artagnan knew that terrible secret which she had sworn no one would ever learn without dying. And finally, just when she had obtained from Richelieu a letter that would allow her to take vengeance on her enemy, that carte blanche was torn from her hands, and it was because of d'Artagnan that she was being held a prisoner and was facing the prospect of being sent to some filthy penal colony like Botany Bay.

All this she owed to d'Artagnan. Who else could have heaped so many disgraces upon her head? Only he could have told Lord de Winter all those frightful secrets he had learned, one after another, through a chain of fatal discoveries. He knew her brother-in-law; he must have written to him.

What hatred she exuded! Motionless, she sat staring fixedly but blindly in her solitary room. The passionate sounds that occasionally erupted from deep inside her merged with the sound of the surf roaring and breaking against the rocks on which the dark and austere castle is built. How many plans for revenge—against Mme. Bonacieux, against Buckingham, above all against d'Artagnan himself—did she conceive by the light of the blazing fury of her passion.

But to avenge herself she would have to be free. And to be free, she would have to pierce a wall, remove bars from a window, cut into a floor—all possible for a patient and strong man, but presenting difficulties for a weak, impatient woman. Besides, all that would take time—months, years; and according to Lord de Winter, her fraternal and terrible jailer, she had less than two weeks.

And yet, if she were a man she would try all of those things, and perhaps she might succeed. Why had heaven made the mistake of giving her virile spirit a frail and delicate body?

The first moments of her captivity had been terrible; a few convulsions of rage that she could not suppress paid the debt her feminine weakness owed to nature. But by degrees she had overcome the outbursts of her mad passion, controlled her nervous tremors, and then turned in on herself like a tired serpent in repose.

"I must have been mad to let myself be carried away like that," she thought as she gazed into the mirror that reflected her careful self-examination. "No violence. Violence is a proof of weakness. In the first place, I have never succeeded by that means. Perhaps if I were fighting against women I might find them weaker than myself and consequently be able to conquer them. But I am fighting against men, and to them I am only a woman—so let me fight like a woman, and make my weakness serve as my strength."

Then, as if to assure herself that she could still change her face at will, she made it take on every expression, from a scowl of passionate anger to the sweetest, most affectionate, and most seductive of smiles. Then she arranged her hair in a series of different styles to bring out the charms of her face. Finally she murmured, satisfied with herself, "Nothing is lost. I am still beautiful."

It was then nearly eight o'clock in the evening. She saw a bed and decided that a few hours' rest would not only refresh her head and her ideas, but also her complexion. Before lying down, however, she had an idea. Something had been said about supper; she had already been here an hour, so the meal would probably come soon. Not wanting to lose any time, she decided to start observing the characters of the men assigned to guard her.

A light appeared under the door, announcing the return of her jailers. She quickly threw herself into the armchair, her head thrown back, her beautiful hair unbound and disheveled, her bosom half bare beneath her crumpled lace, one hand on her heart and the other hanging limply.

The bolts were drawn; the door groaned upon its hinges. She could hear footsteps approaching, drawing near.

"Put the table there," said a voice the prisoner recognized as Felton's.

The order was carried out.

"Bring lights, and have the guard relieved," continued Felton.

And this double order proved to Milady that her servants, like her guards, were soldiers.

And from the silent speed with which his orders were carried out, she concluded that Felton was a strict disciplinarian.

Finally he turned toward her for the first time.

"Ah," he said, "she is asleep. Good. When she wakes up, she can eat."

He walked toward the door.

"But sir," said a less stoical soldier who had walked over to Milady, "she is not asleep."

"Not asleep! What is she doing, then?"

"She has fainted. Her face is very pale, and I cannot hear her breathe."

"You are right," said Felton, after having looked at Milady without moving a step closer to her. "Go tell Lord de Winter that his prisoner has fainted. Such an event was not foreseen, and I don't know what to do."

The soldier went out to obey his officer's orders. Felton sat down on a chair near the door and waited silently and motionlessly. Milady was skilled in that great art, so much studied by women, of looking through her long eyelashes without seeming to open her eyes. She watched Felton, who was sitting with his back toward her, for nearly ten minutes, and in those ten minutes he never turned around once.

Then she realized that Lord de Winter would come, and that his presence would give fresh strength to her jailer. Her first attempt was a failure, but all was not lost. She raised her head, opened her eyes, and sighed weakly.

At this sigh, Felton turned around.

"Ah, you are awake, madame," he said. "Then I have nothing more to do here. If you want anything, you can call out."

"Oh, my God, how I have suffered," she said in that harmonious voice which charmed all whom she wished to lure to their destruction.

And sitting up in the armchair, she assumed an even more graceful position than when she had been lying back.

Felton stood up.

"You will be served three times a day," he said. "In the morning at nine o'clock, in the afternoon at one o'clock, and in the evening at eight. If that does not suit you, you can tell us what other hours you prefer, and in this respect your wishes will be honored."

"Will I always remain alone in this huge, dismal room?" she asked.

"A woman from the neighborhood will be at the castle tomorrow, and she will return as often as you want her to."

"I thank you, sir," the prisoner replied humbly.

Felton made a slight bow and turned to leave. Just as

he was about to go out, Lord de Winter appeared in the corridor, followed by the soldier who had been sent to tell him about Milady's swoon. He held a bottle of smelling salts.

"Well, what is it—what is going on here?" he said in a mocking voice on seeing the prisoner sitting up and Felton about to go out. "Has the corpse come to life already? Felton, my boy, did you not realize that you were assumed to be a novice, and that this was the first act of a play that we shall undoubtedly have the pleasure of following out to the very end?"

"I thought that was so, my lord," said Felton, "but since she is a woman, I wanted to treat her with the care that every gentleman owes to a woman—if not for her sake, at least for his own."

Milady's whole body quivered. Felton's words passed like ice through all her veins.

"So that beautiful hair so skillfully disheveled, that white skin, and that languishing look have not yet seduced you, you heart of stone?" asked de Winter, laughing.

"No, my Lord," replied the impassive young man. "Your Lordship may be assured that it requires more than the coquettish tricks of a woman to corrupt me."

"In that case, my brave lieutenant, let us leave Milady to think of something else, and go to supper. But do not worry—she has a fruitful imagination, and the second act of the play will not be long in coming."

And with those words Lord de Winter took Felton's arm and led him out, laughing once again.

"Oh, I will be a match for you!" Milady hissed through clenched teeth. "Oh, yes, you may be sure of that, you poor excuse for a soldier, you would-be monk who has fashioned his uniform from a priest's robe!"

"By the way," de Winter added, stopping at the threshold of the door, "you must not let this setback take away your appetite. Do taste the chicken and the fish. On my honor, they are not poisoned. My cook and I are on good terms, and since he is not to be my heir, I have perfect confidence in him. You may, too. Adieu, dear sister, till your next faint!"

This was more than Milady could endure: her hands gripped her chair; she ground her teeth; her eyes fol-

lowed the motion of the door as it closed behind Lord
de Winter and Felton. As soon as she was alone, she was
overwhelmed by a fresh fit of despair. She saw a knife
glittering on the table, rushed over to it, clutched it; but
she was cruelly disappointed. The blade was rounded,
and of flexible silver.

She heard a burst of laughter from the other side of
the door, and it reopened.

"Do you see, Felton? Do you see what I told you?"
cried Lord de Winter. "That knife was for you, my boy—
she would have killed you. You must understand that
one of her peculiarities is to get rid of, in one way or
another, all the people who bother her. If I had listened
to you, the knife would have been sharp and of steel—
and then no more Felton! She would have cut your
throat, and after that everybody else's. See how well she
knows how to handle a knife, John."

In fact, Milady was still holding the harmless weapon
in her clenched hand, but those last words, that supreme
insult, relaxed her grip, her strength, and even her will.
The knife fell to the ground.

"You were right, my Lord," Felton said with a tone
of profound disgust that echoed deep in Milady's heart.
"You were right, and I was wrong."

And they both left the room again.

But this time Milady listened more attentively than
before, and she heard their footsteps fade away in the
distance.

"I am lost," she murmured. "I am in the power of
men I can never soften. I can have no more influence on
them than on bronze or granite statues. They know me
too well and are steeled against all my weapons. But this
cannot end as they have planned!"

In fact, as this instinctive return to hope indicated,
weakness or fear never lasted long in her ardent spirit.
She sat down at the table, ate from several dishes, drank
a little Spanish wine, and felt all her determination
revive.

Before she went to bed she had pondered, analyzed,
turned on all sides, examined on all points, the words,
the steps, the gestures, the movements, and even the
silences of her jailers; and from her profound, skillful,
and shrewd study, she decided that everything consid-

ered, Felton was the more vulnerable of her two persecutors.

One remark above all came back to her: "If I had listened to you . . ." Lord de Winter had said to Felton. This meant that Felton had spoken in her favor, since Lord de Winter had not been willing to listen to him.

"Weak or strong," she thought, "that man has a spark of pity in his soul. From that spark I will make a flame that will devour him. As for de Winter, he fears me because he knows what to expect of me if I ever escape from his hands, so it is useless to attempt anything with him. But Felton is different. He is a young, naive, pure man who seems to be virtuous—there are ways to destroy such as him."

She went to bed and fell asleep with a smile on her lips. Anyone who would have seen her sleeping might have thought she was a young girl dreaming of the wreath of flowers she was to wear on the next holiday.

53

The Second Day of Captivity

MILADY DREAMED that she finally had d'Artagnan in her power, that she was present at his execution; and it was the sight of his odious blood, flowing beneath the executioner's ax, that made her smile so charmingly.

She slept as a prisoner sleeps, lulled by hope.

When they entered her room in the morning she was still in bed. Felton remained outside in the corridor. He had brought the woman of whom he had spoken the evening before; she approached Milady's bed and offered her services.

Milady was habitually pale; her complexion might therefore make someone who was seeing her for the first time think she was ill.

"I have a fever," she said. "I did not sleep a single instant last night. I am not well. Will you be more humane than the others were yesterday? All I ask is permission to remain in bed."

"Would you like to have a doctor?" the woman asked.

Felton listened to this conversation without saying a word.

Milady thought. The more people she had around her the more people she would have to work on—but on the other hand, the more Lord de Winter would feel he had to watch her. Besides, the doctor might declare her illness a fraud, and after having lost the first trick, she was not willing to lose the second.

"Have a doctor?" she repeated. "What would be the good of that? Yesterday those gentlemen declared that I was only pretending, and they must still think so today, because otherwise they have had plenty of time to send for a doctor before now."

"Just tell us, madame, what treatment you wish followed," Felton said impatiently.

"How can I tell? I only know that I am not well. Give me anything you like, it doesn't matter."

"Go fetch Lord de Winter," said Felton, tired of her eternal complaints.

"Oh, no, do not call him, I beg you! I am well, I need nothing! Please do not call him."

She said this so eloquently that Felton was moved in spite of himself and advanced some steps into the room.

"I've reached him," she thought.

"Madame, if you are really suffering," he said, "we will send for a doctor. If you are deceiving us—well, it will be worse for you, but at least we will not have to reproach ourselves with anything."

Milady said nothing, but turned her beautiful head around on her pillow, burst into tears, and sobbed in a heartbreaking way.

Felton looked at her for a few moments with his usual impassivity; then, seeing that the crisis threatened to be prolonged, he left, the woman following him. Lord de Winter did not appear.

"I think I begin to see my way," she murmured with a savage joy, burying herself under the covers to conceal from anybody who might be watching her this burst of elation.

Two hours passed.

"Now it is time for my illness to be over," she said to

herself. "I must make some progress today. I have only ten days, and by this evening two of them will be gone."

When they entered her room in the morning, they had brought her breakfast. Now, she thought, they would soon come to clear the table, and Felton would return.

She was not mistaken. Felton reappeared, and without noticing if she had or had not touched her meal, he ordered his men to remove the table, which had been brought in already set.

Felton remained behind; he held a book in his hand.

Sitting in an armchair near the fireplace, beautiful, pale, and resigned, Milady looked like a holy virgin awaiting martyrdom.

Felton approached her and said, "Lord de Winter, who is a Catholic like yourself, madame, thought that being deprived of the rites and ceremonies of your church might be painful to you and has decided to let you read your Mass every day. Here is a book that contains the ritual."

At the manner in which Felton laid the book upon the little table near which she was sitting, at the tone in which he pronounced the two words *your Mass,* at the disdainful smile with which he accompanied those words, she raised her head and looked at him more attentively.

By the plain arrangement of his hair, by the costume of extreme simplicity, by the brow polished like marble and as hard and impenetrable, she recognized one of those gloomy Puritans she had so often met, not only in the court of King James, but also in that of the King of France, where they sometimes came to seek refuge in spite of the memory of the St. Bartholomew Day massacre.

She had one of those sudden inspirations which come only to people of genius during great crises, during those moments on which their fortunes or their lives depend.

Those two words, *your Mass,* and a quick glance at Felton, had made the importance of her reply quite clear; but with that swift intelligence which was so much a part of her, the reply sprang full-blown to her lips:

"I?" she said, her disdainful tone an echo of that which she had heard in Felton's voice. "*My Mass?* Lord de Winter, the corrupted Catholic, knows very well that I am not of his religion. This is a trap he wishes to set for me!"

"What *is* your religion, madame?" asked Felton, with an astonishment he could not entirely conceal despite his self-control.

"I will tell you," she said with a feigned exaltation, "on the day when I will have suffered sufficiently for my faith."

Felton's look showed her how far she had come by those few words.

He remained, however, mute and motionless; only his eyes had spoken.

"I am in the hands of my enemies," she continued in that fervent tone she knew was common among the Puritans. "Well, let my God save me, and let me perish for my God! That is the reply I beg you to make to Lord de Winter. And as to this book," she added, pointing to the manual without touching it, as if she might be contaminated by it, "you may take it back and use it yourself, because you must be Lord de Winter's accomplice both in his persecutions and in his heresies."

Felton made no reply, took the book with the same appearance of repugnance he had shown before, and left, apparently deep in thought.

Lord de Winter came in toward five o'clock in the evening. Milady had had time during the day to make her plans. She received him confidently, like a woman who had regained all her advantages.

"It seems," he said, seating himself in the armchair opposite hers and stretching out his legs carelessly upon the hearth, "that we have become an apostate!"

"What do you mean, sir?"

"I mean to say that you have changed your religion since we last met. You have not by any chance married a Protestant for a third husband, have you?"

"Explain yourself, my Lord," the prisoner said majestically. "I hear your words, but I do not understand them."

"Perhaps you have no religion at all. I prefer that," replied Lord de Winter, laughing.

"Certainly that would be closer to your own principles," Milady answered frigidly.

"Oh, I assure you it doesn't matter to me."

"You do not have to admit this religious indifference, my Lord—your debaucheries and crimes would vouch for it."

"What, you talk of debaucheries, Madame Messalina? Of crimes, Lady Macbeth? Either I have misunderstood you, or you are quite shameless!"

"You speak like this because you know we are being overheard," Milady responded coldly. "You want to influence your jailers and your hangmen against me."

"My jailers and my hangmen! Madame, you are becoming very melodramatic, and yesterday's comedy is now this evening's tragedy. In any case, in eight days you will be where you belong, and my task will be finished."

"Infamous task! Sinful task!" she cried in the exalted tone of the victim who provokes her judge.

"My word," said de Winter, rising, "I do think you are going mad! You had better calm yourself, Madame Puritan, or I'll have you put into a dungeon. It must be my Spanish wine that has gone to your head! But never mind, that sort of intoxication is not dangerous and will leave no bad effects."

And Lord de Winter left, swearing—which at that time was not at all ungentlemanly.

Felton was indeed behind the door and had not lost one word of this scene. Milady had guessed correctly.

"So you think there will be no effects, do you?" she muttered at the door closing behind her brother-in-law. "You are wrong, you imbecile, but you will not see them until it is too late to do anything about them!"

Once again it was silent; two hours went by and Milady's supper was brought in. She was found deeply engaged in reciting her prayers, which she had learned from an old servant of her second husband, a most austere Puritan. She seemed to be in a state of ecstasy, not paying the slightest attention to anything going on around her. Felton signaled that she should not be disturbed, and when everything was ready, he went out quietly with the soldiers.

She knew she might be watched, so she continued her prayers to the end; it seemed to her that the soldier who was on duty outside her door did not go back and forth with the same step, and that he appeared to be listening.

That was all she wanted for the moment. She stood up, sat at the table, ate sparingly, and drank only water.

An hour later, her table was cleared, but Milady noticed that this time Felton did not accompany the soldiers. He was afraid to see her too often, she guessed.

She turned her face toward the wall to smile, for there was in this smile such a look of triumph that the smile alone would have betrayed her.

She waited for half an hour to pass; then, since at that moment there was only silence in the old castle, since nothing could be heard but the eternal murmur of the waves—that vast breathing of the ocean—she began to sing with her pure, harmonious, and vibrant voice the first couplet of the psalm in great favor with the Puritans:

> Thou leavest thy servants, Lord,
>   To see if they be strong;
> But soon thou dost afford
>   Thy hand to lead them on.

These verses were not very good—far from it; but as is well known, the Puritans did not pride themselves on their poetry.

Even while she was singing, Milady was listening: the soldier on guard at her door had stopped, as if he had been turned to stone. From this, Milady was able to judge the effect she had produced.

She continued to sing with inexpressible fervor and feeling. It seemed to her as though the sounds were wafting through the entire castle, carrying with them a magic charm to soften the hearts of her jailers.

It also seemed, however, that the soldier on duty—a zealous Catholic, no doubt—was able to shake off the charm, because he called out through the door: "Hold your tongue, madame! Your song is as dismal as a 'De profundis.' It's bad enough to be here, but if we must also listen to such things as these, we won't survive."

"Silence!" exclaimed a stern voice that Milady recognized as Felton's. "Why are you interfering, you imbecile? Did anybody order you to prevent that woman from singing? You were told to guard her, and to shoot her if she tried to escape. Guard her. If she tries to escape, kill her. But don't exceed your orders."

An expression of unspeakable joy illuminated Milady's face, but it was as fleeting as a flash of lightning. Without seeming to have heard the dialogue—though she had not lost a word of it—she continued, putting into her voice all the charm, power, and seduction the devil had endowed her with.

> For all my tears, my cares,
>   My exile, and my chains,
> I have my youth, my prayers,
>   And God, who counts my pains.

That extraordinarily powerful and sublimely expressive voice gave the crude, unpolished stanzas a magical effect that the most exalted Puritans rarely found in their hymns, which they were forced to ornament with all the resources of their imagination. Felton thought he was hearing the singing of the angel who consoled the three Hebrews in the fiery furnace.

Still she sang.

> One day our doors will ope,
>   With God come our desire;
> And if betrays that hope,
>   To death we can aspire.

This verse, into which the terrible enchantress threw her whole soul, brought Felton to fever pitch. He flung open the door, and Milady saw that he was pale as usual, but that his eyes were burning, almost wild.

"Why are you singing like that, and with such a voice?" he asked.

"I beg your pardon, sir," she answered mildly. "I forgot that my songs are out of place in this castle. I may have offended your religious beliefs, but I swear I did not mean to. Please forgive me—my fault was unintentional."

Milady was so beautiful at that moment, her religious ecstasy gave such a rapturous expression to her face, that Felton was dazzled, and imagined he was seeing the angel he had only heard before.

"Yes," he said, "you disturb . . . you agitate . . . the people who live in the castle."

The poor young man was not even aware of his incoherence.

Milady read into the very depths of his heart with her lynx's eyes.

"I will be silent," she said, lowering her gaze, making her voice as sweet as she could, her manner as resigned and modest as can be imagined.

"No, madame," said Felton, "just do not sing so loudly, especially at night."

And with those words Felton, realizing that he could no longer maintain his severity toward his prisoner, rushed out of the room.

"You were right, Lieutenant," said the soldier. "The songs are disturbing, but you get used to them—her voice is so beautiful."

54

The Third Day of Captivity

SHE HAD CAUGHT Felton, but now he had to be kept—or rather he must be made to want to stay; and Milady had no clear idea of how that might be done.

He must also be made to speak, in order that he might be spoken to—for she knew very well that her greatest tool of seduction was her voice, which so skillfully ran the whole gamut of tones, from human to angelic.

Yet in spite of all this, she might fail, because Felton had been forewarned against everything, so from that moment on, she would watch her every action, her every word. In short she would study everything—from the simplest glance of her eyes to her slightest breath—like a skillful actress who has a new part that is different from any role she has ever played before.

As for Lord de Winter, her plan was easier: it was what she had decided the preceding evening. She would remain silent and dignified in his presence, irritate him occasionally by showing disdain or contempt, provoke him to threats and violence that would contrast with her own resignation. Felton would see everything; perhaps he would say nothing, but he would see.

In the morning, he came as usual, but she allowed him to preside over all the preparations for breakfast without saying a word to him. As he was about to leave, she thought he was going to speak; but though his lips moved, he made a powerful effort to control himself and sent back to his heart the words that were about to be spoken, then left.

Toward midday, Lord de Winter came in.

It was a fine winter day, and a ray of that pale English sun which lights but does not warm was coming through the bars of her prison.

She was looking out the window and pretended not to hear the door as it opened.

"After having played comedy, after having played tragedy, I see we are now playing melancholy," said Lord de Winter.

The prisoner made no reply.

"Yes," he continued, "I understand. You would like to be free on that shore or in a good ship dancing on the waves of that emerald-green sea! Either on the land or on the sea, you would like to ensnare me in one of those nice little traps you are so skillful in planning! But be patient—in four days the shore will be beneath your feet, the sea will be open to you. It will even be more open than you will like, because in four days England will be rid of you!"

Milady folded her hands and raised her fine eyes toward heaven. "O Lord," she said with an angelic meekness of gesture and tone, "pardon this man, as I myself pardon him."

"Yes, pray, accursèd woman!" cried de Winter. "Your prayer is all the more generous because you are praying for a man who will never pardon you!"

And he went out.

As he left, she could see through the partly open door that Felton stepped quickly to one side to avoid being seen by her.

So she threw herself down on her knees and began to pray.

"O God," she said, "thou knowest in what holy cause I suffer. Give me, then, the strength to suffer."

The door opened gently; she pretended not to hear the noise and, in a voice full of tears, continued to pray: "God of vengeance! God of goodness! Wilt thou allow that man's frightful projects to succeed?"

Only then did she pretend to hear the sound of Felton's steps, and rising quickly, she blushed, as if ashamed of having been discovered on her knees.

"I do not like to intrude upon those who pray, madame," said Felton, seriously. "Please do not disturb yourself on my account."

"How do you know I was praying, sir?" she said, her voice choked by sobs. "You were mistaken, sir, I was not praying."

"Do you think, madame," he replied in the same serious voice, but with a milder tone, "that I feel I have the right to prevent a human being from kneeling before her Creator? God forbid! Besides, repentance is the only hope for the guilty—whatever their crimes, they are sacred at the feet of God!"

"Guilty? I?" said Milady, with a smile that might have disarmed the angel of the last judgment. "Guilty? O my God, thou knowest whether I am guilty! Say I am condemned, sir, if you wish, but as you know, God loves martyrs and sometimes allows the innocent to be condemned."

"If you were innocent or a martyr, you would have even more need for prayer; and I would add mine to yours."

"Oh, you are a just man!" Milady threw herself at his feet. "I can hold out no longer, for I fear my strength will fail me at the moment when I will be forced to undergo the struggle and confess my faith. Listen to the plea of a woman in despair. You are being deceived, sir, but that is not important. I ask only one favor, and if you grant it, I will bless you in this world and in the next."

"Speak to the master, madame. Luckily I have neither the power to pardon nor to punish. God has laid that responsibilty on one higher placed that I am."

"No, to you, to you alone! Listen to me, instead of

being an accomplice in my destruction and my ignominy!"

"If you have deserved this shame, madame, if you have earned this ignominy, you must submit to it as an offering to God."

"What are you saying? Oh, you do not understand me! When I speak of ignominy, you think I am speaking of some punishment, like imprisonment or death. Would to heaven that it were only that! What do I care about imprisonment or death?"

"I do not understand you, madame."

"Or you pretend not to understand me, sir," replied the prisoner, smiling skeptically.

"No, madame, on the honor of a soldier and the faith of a Christian."

"What, you do not know what Lord de Winter plans for me?"

"I do not."

"Impossible. You are his confidant!"

"I never lie, madame."

"Yet he conceals intentions too little for you not to guess them."

"I do not try to guess anything, madame. I wait till I am told, and apart from what Lord de Winter has said in front of you, he has told me nothing."

"Then you are not his accomplice? You do not know that he is preparing for me a disgrace more horrible than all the punishments of the world?" Milady asked, sounding genuinely surprised.

"You are wrong, madame," said Felton, blushing. "Lord de Winter is not capable of such a crime."

"Good," Milady said to herself. "Without even knowing what it is, he calls it a crime!" Then out aloud: "The friend of that infamous scoundrel is capable of everything."

"Whom do you call *that infamous scoundrel?*"

"Are there two men in England who can be called that?"

"You mean George Villiers?" asked Felton, his eyes flashing.

"I mean he whom the pagans and the unbelievers call Duke of Buckingham. I would not have thought that there was anyone in all England who would have needed such a long explanation to recognize of whom I was speaking!"

"The hand of the Lord is upon him. He will not escape the punishment he deserves."

Felton was only expressing, with regard to the duke, the hatred of nearly all the English toward the man the Catholics called the extortioner, the plunderer, the rake, and the Puritans called simply Satan.

"O my God," cried Milady, "when I beg thee to send that man the punishment which is his due, thou knowest it is not for my own vengeance, but for the deliverance of a whole nation!"

"Do you know him?" asked Felton.

"At last he is questioning me," said Milady to herself, overjoyed at having made such rapid progress.

"Know him? Yes, to my misfortune, to my eternal misfortune!"

She wrung her hands, as if in a paroxysm of grief.

Felton must have felt his strength abandoning him, because he took several steps toward the door; but the prisoner, whose eyes never left him, rushed to his side and stopped him.

"Sir, be kind, be merciful, listen to my prayer! That knife which Lord de Winter deprived me of because he knew what I would do with it—oh, hear me out—give me that knife for one minute only, for pity's sake! I will get down on my knees! Listen—you will lock the door so that you can be certain I will not harm you! My God—you—the only just, good, and compassionate person I have met with! You—my preserver, perhaps! One minute with that knife, a single minute, and I will give it back to you through the grating of the door. Only one minute, Mr. Felton, and you will have saved my honor!"

"To kill yourself?" cried Felton, so horrified that he forgot to withdraw his hands from those of the prisoner.

"I have told you my secret, sir," she murmured, allowing herself to sink to the floor; "I have told you my secret! My God, I am lost!"

Felton stood there, motionless and undecided.

"He still has doubts," she thought. "I have not been convincing enough."

They heard someone coming down the corridor. Milady

recognized Lord de Winter's footsteps; so did Felton, and he moved toward the door.

She ran to him. "Oh, not a word," she said urgently. "Not a word of anything that I have said to you, or I am lost, and it would be you . . . you . . ."

As the steps drew nearer, she became silent lest she be heard, and she placed, with a gesture of infinite terror, her beautiful hand on Felton's mouth.

He gently pushed her away, and she sank into a chaise-longue.

Lord de Winter passed in front of the door without stopping, and they heard the noise of his footsteps fading away.

Deathly pale, Felton remained some instants listening intently; when the sound was quite extinct, he breathed like a man waking up from a dream and rushed out of the room.

Milady listened in her turn to Felton walking away in a direction opposite to that of Lord de Winter.

"You are mine," she thought. Then her brow darkened. "If he tells de Winter, I am lost. De Winter knows very well that I will not kill myself! He will put me in front of Felton with a knife in my hand, and then Felton will discover that all my despair is only a pretense."

She went to the mirror and looked at herself carefully: she had never looked more beautiful.

"He won't tell him," she said, smiling.

That evening Lord de Winter accompanied the supper.

"Sir," she said, "is your presence an indispensable part of my captivity? Could you not spare me that additional torment?"

"But my dear sister, did you not sentimentally inform me with that pretty mouth of yours, so cruel to me today, that you came to England simply for the pleasure of seeing me, an enjoyment you told me you felt so deprived of that you had risked everything for it—sea-sickness, storms, captivity? Well, here I am, so be satisfied. Besides, this time my visit has a motive."

Milady trembled; she thought Felton had told him everything. Perhaps never in her life had this woman, who had experienced so many conflicting and powerful emotions, felt her heart beat so violently.

He brought a chair close to hers and sat down. Then

he took a piece of paper out of his pocket and unfolded it slowly.

"I want to show you a kind of passport I have drawn up, which will hereafter serve you as an identity paper in the life I will allow you to lead."

He began to read: " 'Order to conduct to . . .' The name is blank," he interrupted himself. "If you have any preference you can tell me, and if it is not within a thousand leagues of London, I will agree to your wishes. . . . I will begin again:

" 'Order to conduct to ——— the person named Charlotte Backson, branded by the justice of the kingdom of France, but liberated after punishment. She is to live in this place without ever going more than three leagues away from it. If she tries to escape, the penalty will be death. She will receive five shillings per day for lodging and food.' "

"That order does not concern me," Milady replied coldly. "It bears a name that is not mine."

"A name? Have you a name?"

"I have your brother's."

"You are mistaken. My brother is your second husband, and your first is still living. Tell me his name, and I will put it in place of the name Charlotte Backson. No? You will not? You are silent? Very well, then you must be registered as Charlotte Backson."

Milady's silence was now no longer from affectation, but from terror. She thought the order was ready to be carried out immediately: she thought that Lord de Winter had hastened her departure, that she was condemned to set off that very evening. For a moment, she thought everything was lost. Then she noticed that there was no signature on the order.

Her joy was so great that she could not conceal it.

"Yes," said Lord de Winter, who understood what was passing through her mind, "you look for the signature, and you say to yourself: 'All is not lost, because that order is not signed. It is only shown to me to terrify me, that's all.' You are mistaken. Tomorrow this order will be sent to the Duke of Buckingham. The day after tomorrow it will return with his signature and his seal.

Twenty-four hours after that I swear it will be carried out. Adieu, madame. That is all I had to say to you."

"And I reply to you, sir, that this abuse of power, this exile under a fictitious name, is infamous!"

"Would you prefer to be hanged in your true name, Milady? You know that English laws are inexorable about the abuse of marriage. Speak freely. Although my name, or rather that of my brother, would be mixed up with the affair, I will risk the scandal of a public trial to be sure of getting rid of you."

Milady made no reply but became as pale as a corpse.

"I see you prefer to travel. That is well, madame, and there is an old proverb that says traveling broadens the mind. No, you are not wrong—life is sweet. That is why I take such care you shall not deprive me of mine. There only remains the question of the five shillings to be settled. You think me rather parsimonious, don't you? That is because I do not care to let you have enough money to corrupt your jailers. But you will still have your charms. Try to use them to seduce your guards—if your failure with Felton has not discouraged you from attempts of that kind."

"Felton has not told him," said Milady to herself. "Nothing is lost yet."

"And now, madame, till I see you again! Tomorrow I will come and announce to you the departure of my messenger."

Lord de Winter rose, bowed to her ironically, and went out.

Milady breathed again. She still had four days. Four days would be quite enough to complete the seduction of Felton.

A terrible idea suddenly struck her: maybe Lord de Winter would send Felton himself to get the order signed by the Duke of Buckingham. In that case Felton would escape her, for she must have unbroken time in which to work her seduction.

Still, one thing reassured her: Felton had not spoken.

So she would not seem to be upset by Lord de Winter's threats, she sat down at the table and ate.

Then, as she had done the evening before, she knelt and said her prayers aloud. Again as on the evening before, the soldier stopped his pacing to listen to her.

Soon she heard lighter steps than those of the sentry coming from the end of the corridor and stopping in front of her door.

"It is he," she thought. And she began to sing the same religious hymn that had so strongly affected Felton the evening before.

But although her voice—sweet, full, and vibrant—was as harmonious and poignant as ever, the door remained shut. It did seem to her that in one of the furtive glances she occasionally darted at the grating of the door she saw the young man's ardent eyes through the narrow opening. But whether this was reality or vision did not matter: this time he had sufficient self-control not to come in.

However, a few moments after she had finished her religious song, she heard a deep sigh, then the same steps she had heard approach slowly withdrew, as if with regret.

55

The Fourth Day of Captivity

THE NEXT DAY, when Felton came into Milady's room he found her standing on a chair and holding a rope made by braiding strips of batiste handkerchiefs and tying them into a single strand. At the noise he made in entering, she jumped lightly to the ground and tried to conceal the improvised rope behind her.

Even more pale than usual, his eyes reddened by lack of sleep, it was clear that Felton had spent a feverish night. He looked more austere than ever.

He walked slowly toward Milady, who had seated herself, and took one end of the rope that she allowed, either deliberately or unintentionally, to be seen.

"What is this, madame?" he asked coldly.

"That? Nothing," she replied, smiling with that unhappy expression she knew so well how to give to her smile. "Boredom is a prisoner's mortal enemy—I was bored, so I amused myself with braiding that rope."

Felton's eyes traveled to the part of the wall in front

of which he found Milady standing on the chair in which she was now seated, and above her head he noticed a gilt hook meant for the purpose of hanging up clothes or weapons.

He started, and the prisoner saw that start—for though her eyes were lowered, nothing escaped her.

"What were you doing on that chair?" he asked.

"What does it matter?"

"I wish to know."

"Do not question me. You know that we who are true Christians are forbidden to lie."

"Then I will tell you what you were doing, or rather what you meant to do. You were going to carry out the terrible project you have been thinking about. But remember, madame, if our God forbids lying, he forbids suicide even more strongly."

"When God sees one of his creatures persecuted unjustly and having to choose between suicide and dishonor, believe me, sir," she replied in a tone of deep conviction, "God pardons suicide, because then suicide becomes martyrdom."

"You say either too much or too little, madame. In the name of heaven, explain yourself."

"So that you can treat my misfortunes as fables? So that you can betray my plans to my persecutor? No, sir. Besides, of what importance to you is the life or death of a wretched prisoner? You are only responsible for my body. Provided you produce a corpse that is recognizably mine, they will require no more of you—you may even get a double reward."

"I, madame? You think that I would ever accept the price of your life? You cannot believe that!"

"Let me do as I please, Felton," Milady pled fervently. "Every soldier is ambitious, is he not? You are a lieutenant? Well, if you let me die, you will follow me to the grave with the rank of captain."

"What have I done to you," said Felton, much agitated, "that you should wish me to have such a responsibility before God and before men? In a few days you will be away from here. Your life will no longer be under my care, and then," he added with a sigh, "you can do what you will with it."

"You, a pious man, you a just man, you ask only one

thing—not to be made to feel responsible or guilty by my death!" she exclaimed, her tone one of holy indignation.

"It is my duty to watch over your life, madame, and I will do so."

"But do you understand what you are doing? Cruel enough, if I were guilty, but how can you describe it, how will the Lord describe it, if I am innocent?"

"I am a soldier, madame, and I follow my orders."

"Do you believe that at the Last Judgment God will make a distinction between the blind executioners and the unjust judges? You do not want me to kill my body, yet you make yourself the agent of the man who wishes to kill my soul!"

"Let me repeat it again," Felton replied emotionally. "You are in no danger. I can answer for Lord de Winter as for myself."

"Foolish man!" cried Milady. "Poor foolish man who dares to answer for another man when the wisest of men, those most after God's own heart, hesitate to answer for themselves. You have joined with the strongest and the most fortunate of men, to crush the weakest and the most unfortunate of women!"

"Impossible, madame," murmured Felton, who neverthless felt deep in his heart the justice of this argument. "As long as you are a prisoner, you will not gain your liberty through me. As long as you are alive, you will not take your life with my help."

"But I will lose something that is much dearer to me than life—my honor, Felton. I make you responsible, before God and before men, for my shame and my disgrace."

This time Felton, impassive as he was, or seemed to be, could not resist the secret influence that had already taken possession of him. To see this woman, fair as the brightest vision, overcome first by grief and then by rage; to resist the ascendancy of sorrow and beauty—it was too much for a visionary whose mind had been weakened by the ardent dreams of an ecstatic faith; it was too much for a heart corroded by the burning love of heaven and the devouring hatred of mankind.

Milady saw his agitation; she felt intuitively the flame of the opposing passions that warred within the young fanatic. Like a skillful general who sees the enemy ready to surrender and marches toward him with a cry of victory, she rose—beautiful as an ancient priestess, radiant as a Christian virgin, her throat uncovered, her hair disheveled, holding her dress modestly over her breast with one hand, her look illumined by that fire which had already created such disorder in the veins of the young Puritan—and went toward him, singing out passionately, melodiously, yet sternly:

> Let this victim to Baal be sent,
> To the lions the martyr be thrown!
> Thy God shall teach thee to repent!
> From th' abyss he'll give ear to my moan.

Felton stood before the strange apparition like one petrified.

"Who are you? Who are you?" he cried, clasping his hands. "Are you a messenger from God? A minister from hell? Are you an angel or a demon? Is your name Eloa or Astarte?"

"Do you not know what I am, Felton? I am neither an angel nor a demon. I am a daughter of earth and a sister of your faith—that is all."

"Yes, yes!" said Felton. "I doubted you before, but now I believe you."

"You believe me, but you are still the accomplice of that child of Belial who is called Lord de Winter! You believe me, but you leave me in the hands of my enemies, of England's enemy, of God's enemy! You believe me, but you deliver me up to the man who fills the world with his heresies and defiles it with his debaucheries—to that infamous unbeliever whom the blind call the Duke of Buckingham and whom believers call the Antichrist!"

"I deliver you up to Buckingham? I? What do you mean by that?"

"They have eyes, but they see not; they have ears, but they hear not."

"Yes," said Felton, passing his hand over his sweat-covered brow, as if to remove his last doubt. "Yes, I recognize the voice that speaks to me in my dreams. Yes, I recognize the features of the angel who appears to me every night, crying to my sleepless soul, 'Strike! Save England, save yourself, or you will die without having appeased God!' Speak!" cried Felton. "I can understand you now."

A flash of terrible joy, rapid as thought itself, gleamed from Milady's eyes.

Fleeting though this murderous flash had been, Felton saw it, and he started as if its light had revealed the abysses of this woman's heart. All at once he recalled the warnings of Lord de Winter and Milady's first attempts at seduction after her arrival. He drew back a step and bowed his head, but without ceasing to look at her; it was as if he was so fascinated by the strange creature that he could not turn his eyes away from hers.

Milady was not a woman to misunderstand the meaning of his hesitation. Under her apparent emotionalism, her icy coolness never abandoned her. Before Felton could speak, and before she would be forced to continue the conversation on the same exalted level, she let her hands fall to her sides, as if her woman's weakness could not support her zealous enthusiasm.

"But no, it is not for me to be the Judith to bring down this Holofernes," she said. "The sword of the Eternal is too heavy for my arm. Allow me to avoid dishonor by death—let me take refuge in martyrdom. I do not ask you for liberty, as I would if I were guilty, or for vengeance, as I would if I were a pagan. Let me die—that is all. I beg you, I implore you on my knees—let me die, and with my last sigh I will bless you as my savior."

Hearing that sweet, suppliant, voice, seeing that timid, downcast look, Felton reproached himself. By degrees the enchantress had again clothed herself with the magic adornment of beauty, meekness, tears—and above all, the irresistible attraction of mystical voluptuousness, the most consuming of all voluptuousness.

"Alas," he said, "I can do only one thing—I can pity you if you prove to me you are an innocent victim! But Lord de Winter makes harsh accusations against you. . . . You are a Christian, you are my sister in religion. I feel myself drawn toward you—I, who have never loved anyone but my benefactor, I who have met nothing but treacherous, impious men. . . . But you, madame, so beautiful in reality, so pure in appearance, must have done terrible things for Lord de Winter to pursue you so relentlessly."

"They have eyes," Milady repeated with an accent of indescribable grief, "but they see not. They have ears, but they hear not."

"But speak!"

"Confide my shame to you!" she exclaimed, the blush of modesty upon her countenance, "You must know that the crime of one often becomes the shame of another—but confide that shame to you, a man, and I a woman? Oh," she continued, putting her hand modestly over her beautiful eyes, "never! I could not!"

"Not to me, to a brother?" said Felton.

Milady looked at him for some time with an expression the young man took for doubt, though it was nothing but observation, or rather the wish to fascinate.

Felton, in his turn a suppliant, clasped his hands.

"All right, I will confide in my brother. I will dare to . . ."

Just then they heard Lord de Winter's footsteps; but this time Milady's inexorable brother-in-law did not content himself, as on the preceding day, with merely passing before the door and going away again; he paused, exchanged a few words with the sentry, opened the door, and went inside.

During the exchange of those few words Felton had drawn back quickly, and when Lord de Winter entered, he was several paces from the prisoner.

De Winter entered slowly, scrutinizing Milady and the young officer carefully.

"You have been here a very long time, John," he said. "Has this woman been telling you about her crimes? In that case, I can understand the length of the conversation."

Felton started, and Milady felt she would be lost if she did not help the disconcerted Puritan.

"Are you afraid your prisoner will escape?" she said contemptuously. "Well, ask your worthy jailer what I was asking him for."

"She was asking you for something?" the baron demanded suspiciously.

"Yes, my Lord," the young man replied in confusion.

"And what was she asking for?"

"A knife, which she would return to me through the grating of the door a minute after she had received it."

"Then there is someone concealed here whose throat

this amiable lady wishes to cut," said de Winter, in an ironical, contemptuous tone.

"There is myself," replied Milady.

"I have given you the choice between deportation and hanging. If you want to die, choose hanging, madame. Believe me, the rope is more reliable than the knife."

Felton turned pale, remembering that Milady had been hiding a rope in her hand when he had come in.

"You are right," she said, "I have often thought about that." Then she added in a low voice, "And I will think about it again."

Felton shuddered.

Lord de Winter noticed his response.

"Beware, John. I am trusting you. Be careful—I have warned you! Be firm for just three more days, and then we will be free of this creature! She can harm nobody where I am sending her."

"Hear him!" cried Milady vehemently, hoping that her brother-in-law would believe she was addressing heaven and that Felton would understand she was addressing him.

Felton lowered his head and reflected.

De Winter took him by the arm and, until they were out of the room, kept looking back over his shoulder so as not to lose sight of Milady till they were both gone.

"Well," said the prisoner, when the door was shut, "I have not made as much progress as I thought. De Winter has exchanged his usual stupidity for a strange prudence. His desire for revenge has transformed him! As for Felton, he is still hesitating. He is not like that cursèd d'Artagnan! A Puritan adores only virgins, and he adores them by praying to them. A Musketeer loves women, and he loves them by taking them in his arms."

She waited impatiently, for she was sure she would see Felton again before the end of the day. At last, an hour later, she heard someone speaking in a low voice at the door; then the door opened, and she saw Felton.

He walked quickly into the room, leaving the door open behind him and making a sign to Milady to be silent.

"What do you want?" she asked.

"Listen," Felton replied in a low voice. "I have just

sent the sentry away so that I could stay here without anybody knowing that I have come. I must speak to you without being overheard. Lord de Winter has just told me a terrible story."

Milady assumed her smile of a resigned victim and shook her head.

"Either you are a fiend," Felton continued, "or Lord de Winter—my benefactor, my father—is a monster. I have known you for four days, and I have loved him for ten years—so I may well hesitate between you. Do not be alarmed at what I say—I have to be convinced of the truth. Tonight, after midnight, I will come to see you, and you will convince me."

"No, Felton, no, my brother. The sacrifice is too great, and I know what it would cost you. No, I am lost and I do not want you to be lost with me. My death will be much more eloquent than my life, and the silence of the corpse will be much more convincing than the words of the prisoner."

"Be silent, madame, and do not speak to me like this. I came to beg you to give me your word, to swear to me by what you hold most sacred, that you will not take your own life."

"I will not promise that because no one has more respect for a promise or an oath than I have, and if I give you my word, I will have to keep it."

"Then only promise not to do anything till you have seen me again. After that, if you have not changed your mind—well, you will be free to do as you wish and I myself will give you the knife you asked for."

"Very well, I will wait for you."

"Swear."

"I swear it, by our God. Are you satisfied?"

"Yes," said Felton. "Till tonight."

And he dashed out of the room, shut the door, and waited in the corridor, the soldier's half-pike in his hand, as if he had been mounting guard in his place.

The soldier returned, and Felton gave him back his weapon.

Peering through the grating, Milady saw the young man cross himself with delirious fervor and walk away in a transport of joy.

As for her, she returned to her chair with a smile of

savage contempt on her lips and blasphemously repeated that terrible name of God, by whom she had just sworn without ever having learned to know Him.

"What a senseless fanatic! My God is I myself—and whoever will help me get my revenge!"

56

The Fifth Day of Captivity

MILADY HAD ACHIEVED a half-triumph, and this success redoubled her strength.

It was easy to conquer, as she so often had, men who were used to the gallantries and intrigues of life at court and who were quick to let themselves be seduced. She was beautiful enough not to find much resistance on the part of the flesh, and clever enough to prevail over any obstacles of the mind.

But this time she had to contend with an unsophisticated nature, unswervingly restrained and austere: religion and its observances had made Felton inaccessible to ordinary seduction. His head was so filled with vast tumultuous plans that there was no room for the capriciousness of physical love—that sensation which germinates in leisure and blossoms in corruption. Milady had by her false virtue made a breach in the opinion of a man horribly prejudiced against her, and her beauty had done the same in his chaste and pure heart. She had used resources she had not known she possessed in order to conquer the most rebellious subject that both nature and religion could have faced her with.

Nevertheless, many times during the evening she despaired of fate and of herself. She did not invoke God, as we well know, but she did have faith in the spirit of evil—that tremendous power which rules all the details of human life and by which, as in the Arabian fable, a single pomegranate seed can reconstruct a destroyed world.

Milady, being well prepared for Felton's visit, was able to make her plans. She knew she had only two days left,

and that once the order was signed by Buckingham—and
Buckingham would sign it all the more readily because
it bore a false name and he would not recognize the
woman in question—Lord de Winter would make her
embark immediately. She also knew very well that
women condemned to deportation had much less powerful means to seduce than the supposedly virtuous woman
who lives in fashionable society and whose beauty and
style are endorsed by the worldly approval of the aristocratic milieu. To be condemned to painful and disgraceful punishment does not stop a woman from being
beautiful, but it is an obstacle to the recovery of her
power. Like all persons of real genius, Milady knew what
suited her nature and her abilities. Poverty was repugnant to her; degradation took away most of her greatness. Milady was a queen only among queens: her
satisfaction was dependent on gratified pride, and to
command inferior beings was a humiliation rather than a
pleasure for her.

She did not doubt for a single instant that she would
return from her exile; but how long might this exile last?
For someone of her active, ambitious nature, days not
spent in climbing are useless days; what word, then,
could describe days spent in descending? To lose a year,
two years, three years, is to talk of an eternity; to return
after the possible death or disgrace of the cardinal; to
return when d'Artagnan and his friends, happy and triumphant, would have received from the queen the
reward they had earned by the services they had rendered her—those thoughts tormented Milady beyond
endurance. If her body had been able to be for a single
instant as forceful as her mind, she would have burst
through the walls of her prison.

In the midst of all this she was bothered by thinking
of the cardinal. What must the mistrustful, restless, suspicious cardinal think of her silence? He was not merely
her only support, her only prop, her only protector at
present, but the principal instrument of her future fortune and vengeance. She knew him; she knew that when
she returned from her failed mission, he would be indifferent to her imprisonment, indifferent to her sufferings.
He would reply, with his mocking skepticism and with

the force of both power and genius, "You should not have allowed yourself to be taken."

So Milady concentrated all her energies on Felton—the only beam of light that penetrated to the hell into which she had fallen; and like a serpent coiling and uncoiling to test its strength, she enmeshed him in the myriad strands of her inventive imagination.

Time passed; as the hours, one after another, went by, they seemed to awaken the clock, and every stroke of the brass hammer resounded in her heart. At nine o'clock, Lord de Winter made his customary visit, examined the window and the bars, sounded the floor and the walls, looked at the fireplace and the doors. During this long and meticulous inspection, neither he nor Milady said a single word.

Both of them understood that the situation had become too serious for useless words and aimless anger.

"Well," he said on leaving her, "you will at least not escape tonight!"

At ten o'clock, Felton came to post the guard. Milady recognized his footsteps as easily as if they belonged to the lover of her heart, yet she detested and despised that weak fanatic.

It was not time. Felton did not come in.

Two hours later, as midnight sounded, the guard was relieved.

Now it was time. From that moment Milady waited impatiently.

The new guard began pacing up and down the corridor.

At the end of ten minues Felton returned.

Milady listened attentively.

The young man spoke to the guard. "Do not leave the door for any reason. Last night my Lord punished a soldier for having quit his post for just an instant, although I stood guard in his place while he was gone."

"Yes, I know," said the soldier.

"I recommend you therefore to keep the strictest watch. For my part I am going to pay a second visit to this woman. She may try to take her own life, and I have received orders to watch her."

"Good," murmured Milady, "the austere Puritan lies."

The soldier smiled.

"You are lucky to have such orders, particularly if my Lord has authorized you to look into her bed!"

Felton blushed. Under any other circumstances he would have reprimanded the soldier for indulging in such a pleasantry, but his conscience was murmuring too insistently for his mouth to dare speak.

"If I call, come in," he said. "If anyone comes, call me."

"I will, Lieutenant."

Felton entered Milady's room. Milady stood up.

"You are here!" she said.

"I promised I would come, and I have come."

"You promised me something else."

"What do you mean?" asked the young man, who in spite of his self-command felt his knees tremble and the sweat break out on his forehead.

"You promised to bring a knife and to leave it with me after our conversation."

"Say no more of that, madame. No situation, however terrible, can authorize one of God's creatures to kill himself. I have thought it over, and I cannot, must not, be guilty of such a sin."

"Ah, you have thought it over," she said, sitting down in her armchair with a disdainful smile. "Well, I too have been thinking."

"About what?"

"That I can have nothing to say to a man who does not keep his word."

"Oh, my God . . ." Felton said softly.

"You may go. I will not talk to you."

"Here is the knife," said Felton, taking from his pocket the weapon he had brought, according to his promise, but which he hesitated to give to his prisoner.

"Let me see it."

"Why?"

"On my honor, I will return it to you immediately. You can put it on that table and remain between it and me."

Felton handed her the knife. She examined its blade attentively and tested the point on her fingertip.

"This one is fine and good steel. You are a faithful friend, Felton," she said, returning the knife to the young officer.

Felton took it back and laid it on the table, as they had agreed.

Milady watched him and nodded with satisfaction.

"Now," she said, "listen to me."

The request was needless. He stood in front of her, eagerly awaiting her words.

"Felton," she said in a solemn, melancholy tone, "imagine that your sister, the daughter of your father, is speaking to you. When I was young and unfortunately rather attractive, I was lured into a trap. I resisted. Ambushes and violences multiplied around me, but I resisted. The religion I serve, the God I adore, were blasphemed because I called upon that religion and that God, but still I resisted. Outrage after outrage was heaped upon me, but I resisted. Then, since my soul was not subdued, they wished to defile my body forever. Finally . . ."

She stopped, and a bitter smile passed over her lips.

"What *did* they finally do?" Felton cried.

"One evening my enemy resolved to paralyze the resistance he could not conquer and mixed a powerful narcotic with my water. As soon as I had finished my meal, I felt myself sink into a strange torpor. Although I still suspected nothing, a vague fear made me struggle against sleepiness. I stood up, wanting to run to the window and call for help, but my legs refused to support me. It was as if the ceiling had collapsed on my head and crushed me with its weight. I stretched out my arms and tried to speak, but I could only make inarticulate sounds. An irresistible faintness came over me. I held onto a chair to keep from falling, but my arms were too weak to support me. I fell upon one knee, then upon both. I tried to pray, but my tongue was frozen. God must neither have heard nor seen me, and I sank to the floor, a prey to a sleep that resembled death.

"I have no memory of anything that happened while I slept, no knowledge of how long that sleep lasted. The only thing I remember is that I woke up in a round, sumptuously furnished room into which light penetrated only through an opening in the ceiling. There seemed to be no door. It was like a magnificent prison.

"It took a long time for me to become aware of these details. My mind seemed incapable of shaking off the heavy darkness of the sleep from which I could not rouse myself. I had a vague sense of traveling in a rumbling carriage, of a horrible dream in which my strength had become exhausted—but it was so indistinct in my mind that it seemed to belong to someone else's life—one that had become intermingled with mine in some fantastic duality.

"At times everything seemed so strange that I believed I was dreaming. I got up, my legs trembling. My clothes were near me on a chair, but I could not remember undressing myself or going to bed. Then by degrees the reality of my situation struck me. I was no longer in my own house. As far as I could tell by the light of the sun, it was late afternoon. I had fallen asleep the evening before, so my sleep must have lasted twenty-four hours! What had taken place during that long sleep?

"I dressed myself as quickly as possible, but my movements were slow and stiff, indicating that the effects of the narcotic had not yet worn off. The room had evidently been furnished for a woman, and the most demanding coquette could not have wanted anything the room did not contain.

"Surely I was not the first captive who had been shut up in that splendid prison, but as you imagine, Felton, the more superb the prison, the greater my terror.

"And it *was* a prison, for I tried in vain to leave it. I rapped on all the walls in the hopes of discovering a door, but every one of them was solid. Then I walked around the room at least twenty times looking for some other kind of opening, but there was none. Finally, I sank into an armchair, exhausted and terrified.

"Meanwhile, night was falling, and with night my fear increased. I thought I had better remain where I was, because it seemed as if I was surrounded by unknown dangers. Although I had eaten nothing since the evening before, I was even too frightened to be hungry.

"There was no sound from outside to help me guess the time, but I thought it must be seven or eight o'clock in the evening, because it was October and it was quite dark.

"Suddenly I was startled by the noise of a door turning on its hinges. What seemed like a burning lamp appeared above the grilled opening of the ceiling, casting a strong light into my room, and I saw that a man was standing within a few paces of me.

"A table set for two, with a supper already laid, seemed to have arrived by magic in the middle of the room.

"The man was the one who had pursued me for a whole year, who had sworn to dishonor me, and who, by his first words, led me to understand that he had done so the previous night."

"The vile scoundrel!" Felton exclaimed.

"Scoundrel indeed!" Milady repeated, seeing Felton's deep interest in this strange recital. "Oh, yes, scoundrel indeed! He had hoped that triumphing over me in my sleep would be enough to make me accept my shame, since that shame was already consummated, and he came to offer me his fortune in exchange for my love.

"I poured out on this man all the scornful contempt and disdainful words that a woman's heart can contain. He must have been accustomed to such reproaches, for he listened to me calmly and stood there smiling, with his arms folded across his chest. Then, when he thought I had said everything, he came toward me. I ran to the table, picked up a knife, and held it to my breast.

" 'Take one step more,' I said, 'and in addition to my dishonor, you will have my death to reproach yourself with.'

"My look, my voice, my whole being must have convinced him of my sincerity, because he stopped.

" 'Your death?' he said. 'Oh, no, you are too charming a mistress to allow me to consent to lose you after I have had the happiness to possess you only once. Adieu, my charmer. I will wait to pay you my next visit till you are in a better humor.'

"He blew a whistle. The lamp that had lit the room disappeared and I again found myself in complete darkness. The same noise of a door opening and shutting was repeated, the lamp appeared once more, and I was completely alone.

"It was a frightful moment. If I had had any doubts as to my misfortune, they vanished in the overwhelming reality of my situation. I was in the power of a man I detested and despised—a man capable of anything, and who had already given me dreadful proof of what he dared to do."

"But who was that man?" asked Felton.

"I spent the night on a chair, starting at the slightest sound because the lamp had gone out toward midnight, and I was again in darkness. But the night passed without any new attempt on the part of my persecutor. Day came. The table had disappeared, but I still had the knife in my hand.

"That knife was my only hope.

"I was worn out with fatigue. My eyes were inflamed because I had not dared to sleep a single instant. The light of day reassured me. I threw myself on the bed, concealing the knife that would free me under my pillow.

"When I woke up, a fresh meal was on the table.

"This time, in spite of my terrors and my misery, I began to feel ravenously hungry. It was forty-eight hours since I had last eaten. I took some bread and some fruit, but remembering how a narcotic had been mixed with my water, I would not touch what was on the table, but filled my glass from a marble fountain set into the wall over my dressing table.

"Despite those precautions, I remained for some time in a state of terrible agitation. But this time my fears were ill-founded—the day passed without my experiencing anything of what I dreaded. I even emptied half the water in the pitcher so that my suspicions might not be noticed.

"Evening came on, and with it darkness, but however profound that darkness, my eyes were beginning to get used to it and I saw, amid the shadows, the table sink through the floor. A quarter of an hour later it reappeared, bearing my supper, and thanks to the lamp, my room was once again lighted.

"I was determined to eat only such food as could not possibly be tampered with. I had two eggs and some fruit, then drew another glass of water from the fountain and drank it.

"The taste seemed to have changed since morning. I instantly was suspicious and stopped, but I had already drunk half a glass.

"I spilled the rest out and waited in horror, the cold sweat of fear on my forehead.

"Some invisible witness must have seen me drink from the fountain and taken advantage of my confidence in it so as to assure my ruin, which had been so coolly resolved upon, so cruelly pursued.

"Before half an hour had gone by, the same symptoms began to appear. But this time, since I had drunk only half a glass of the water, I struggled longer, and instead of falling completely asleep, I sank into a state of drowsiness that left me aware of what was happening but not strong enough to defend myself.

"I dragged myself to the bed, to get the only weapon that might save me—my knife. But I could not reach it. I fell to my knees, my hands clasping one of the bedposts, and I knew that I was lost."

Felton became frightfully pale, and his whole body trembled.

"And what was most terrifying," continued Milady, her voice altered, as if she were still experiencing the agony of that awful moment, "was that this time I was conscious of the danger that threatened me. My soul was awake in my sleeping body. I could see and I could hear. It is true that it was like a dream, but that did not make it less frightening.

"I saw the lamp rise, and leave me in darkness. Then I heard the creaking of the door—a well-known sound though I had heard it only twice before.

"I felt instinctively that someone was coming toward me, just as the poor doomed wretch in the deserts of America is supposed to sense the approach of the deadly serpent.

"I wanted to make an effort—I tried to cry out. By an incredible exercise of will I even stood up, but only to fall again immediately—into the arms of my persecutor."

"Tell me who this man was!" cried the young officer again.

Milady saw at a single glance how she was tormenting Felton by dwelling on every detail of her story, but she did not want to spare him a single pang. The more profoundly she made him suffer, the more certainly he would avenge her. She therefore continued, as if she had not heard his exclamation or as if she thought it was not yet the moment to reply to it.

"But this time the villain was not dealing with someone

completely unconscious. As I have told you, without being in control of my body, I was nevertheless aware of my danger. I struggled with all my strength, and weak as I was I must have resisted for a long time because I heard him say, 'These miserable Puritans! I knew they exhausted their executioners, but I did not think they were so determined against their lovers!'

"Unfortunately my desperate resistance could not continue indefinitely. I felt my strength fail, and this time the coward prevailed not because I was sleeping but because I had fainted."

Felton listened silently, except for an occasional groan. Sweat streamed down his marble forehead, and his hand, under his coat, was clawing his breast.

"My first impulse on returning to consciousness was to feel under my pillow for the knife I had not been able to reach. If I had not been able to defend myself with it, I might at least use it to expiate my shame.

"But when I picked this knife up, Felton, a terrible idea occurred to me. I have sworn to tell you everything, and I will. I have promised you the truth, and I will tell it, even if it destroys me."

"You thought of avenging yourself on this man, did you not?" he asked.

"Yes. It was not a Christian idea, I know. But that eternal enemy of our souls must have breathed it into my mind. In short, Felton," Milady continued, in the tone of a woman accusing herself of a crime, "this idea occurred to me, and it did not leave me. That homicidal thought is responsible for my punishment."

"Continue! I am eager to see you obtain your revenge!"

"I was sure he would return the following night and I resolved that it should take place as soon as possible. During the day I had nothing to fear, so when my breakfast came, I did not hesitate to eat and drink. I had decided to make believe I was eating in the evening, but not to do so. I was therefore forced to compensate for the fast of the evening with the nourishment of the morning.

"All I did was to conceal a glass of the water that remained after my breakfast, since thirst had made me suffer more than hunger when I had remained forty-eight hours without eating or drinking.

"The day passed, and my determination grew even stronger. I was careful not to let my face betray the thoughts of my heart, because I had no doubt I was watched. Several times I even felt a smile on my lips, and Felton, I dare not tell you what made me smile—you would be horrified . . ."

"Go on!" said Felton. "You see that I am listening, and eager to know what happened."

"Evening came and the usual events took place. As before, my supper was brought in the darkness, then the lamp appeared and I sat down at the table. I ate only some fruit. I pretended to pour water out from the jug, but I drank only what I had saved in my glass. I made this substitution so carefully that my spies, if I had any, could not have suspected anything.

"After supper I showed the same signs of languor as on the preceding evening, but this time, as if I yielded to fatigue or had become familiarized with danger, I dragged myself to the bed, let my gown fall, and lay down.

"My knife was where I had left it, under my pillow, and while pretending to sleep, I grasped its handle convulsively.

"Two hours went by without anything happening. I began to be afraid that he would not come. My God, to think that I could feel that!

"Finally I saw the lamp rise softly and disappear into the ceiling. My room was dark, but I tried to penetrate that darkness.

"For nearly ten minutes I heard nothing but the beating of my own heart. I prayed that he would come.

"Then I heard the well-known noise of the door opening and closing. Despite the thickness of the carpet, I heard a step that made the floor creak. Despite the darkness, I saw a shadow that approached my bed."

"Tell me quickly!" said Felton. "Do you not see that each of your words is like a burning brand?"

"Then I gathered all my strength. I reminded myself that the moment of vengeance, or rather, of justice, had come. I saw myself as another Judith! My knife was in my hand, and when I saw him near me, groping to find his victim, I struck him in the chest.

"But the miserable villain had foreseen it all. His chest was covered with a coat of mail, and my knife had bent against it.

"He seized my arm and wrested from me the weapon that had so badly served me.

" 'You want to take my life, do you, my pretty Puritan? But that is more than dislike, that is ingratitude! Calm yourself, my sweet girl! I thought you had softened, but I am not one of those tyrants who detain women by force. You do not love me. With my usual fatuousness, I thought you did, but now I am convinced otherwise. Tomorrow you will be free.'

"I had only one wish—that he kill me.

" 'Beware!' I said. 'My liberty will be your dishonor.'

" 'What do you mean?'

" 'As soon as I leave this place I will tell everything! I will describe the violence you have used against me, the way you have held me prisoner, the kind of place this is. Your position is high, but not high enough to escape! Above you there is the king, and above the king there is God!'

"Despite his perfect self-control, my persecutor allowed a movement of anger to escape him. I could not see his expression, but I could feel his arm tremble.

" 'Then you will not leave this place,' he said.

" 'Very well, then the scene of my suffering will be the scene of my tomb. I will die here, and you will see that a ghost which accuses is more frightening than a living being that threatens!'

" 'You will have no weapon.'

" 'There is a weapon that despair has placed within the reach of every creature who has the courage to use it. I will allow myself to die of hunger.'

" 'Is not peace much better than such a war? I will set you free immediately. I will proclaim you an example of immaculate virtue and name you the Lucretia of England.'

" 'And I will name you the Sextus of England. I will denounce you before men as I have denounced you before God, and if, like Lucretia, I will have to sign my accusation with my blood, I will sign it.'

" 'That is quite another story,' said my enemy, in a

jeering tone. 'After all, everything considered, you are very well off here. You will lack nothing, and if you let yourself die of hunger that will be your own fault.'

"With these words he left. I heard the door open and shut, and I was overwhelmed—less, I confess, by my grief than by the mortification of not having avenged myself.

"He kept his word. The next day, the next night passed without my seeing him again. But I also kept my word, and I neither ate nor drank. I was resolved to die of hunger.

"I spent that day and night in prayer, for I hoped that God would pardon me my suicide.

"The second night the door opened. I was lying on the floor, because my strength had begun to abandon me.

"At the sound I raised myself up on one hand.

" 'Well,' said a voice that was too terrible to my ears not to be recognized, 'have we softened a little? Will we not pay for our freedom with a single promise of silence? Come, I am a good sort of fellow, and although I do not like Puritans I do them justice—even the pretty ones—and know they can be trusted. So take an oath on the cross, and I won't ask anything more of you.'

" 'On the cross,' I cried, rising with recovered strength at that abhorred voice. 'Yes, on the cross I swear that no promise, no threat, no force, no torture, will silence me! On the cross I swear to denounce you everywhere as a murderer, as a thief of honor, as a base coward! On the cross I swear that if I ever leave this place, I will call down vengeance upon you from the whole human race!'

" 'Beware!' he said in a threatening tone that I had never yet heard. 'I have a way to close your mouth, or at least to prevent anyone from believing a word you may utter, which I will use if I have no other choice.'

"I mustered all my strength to reply to him with a burst of laughter.

"He saw that it was to be relentless war between us— a war to the death.

" 'I give you the rest of tonight and all day tomorrow to think about it,' he said. 'Promise to be silent, and riches, respect, even honor, shall surround you. Threaten to speak, and I will condemn you to infamy.'

" 'You?' I cried. 'You?'

" 'To interminable, ineradicable infamy!'

" 'You?' I repeated. Oh, I tell you, Felton, I thought he was mad!

" 'Yes, I!' he replied.

" 'Leave me!' I said. 'Go, or I will dash my head against that wall before your eyes!'

" 'Very well, if that is what you wish. Till tomorrow night, then!'

" 'Till tomorrow night, then!' I said, allowing myself to fall, and grinding my teeth with rage."

Felton was leaning against a piece of furniture, and Milady saw, with fiendish joy, that his strength would fail him even before the end of her story.

57

The Climax of the Drama

AFTER A MOMENT of silence during which Milady observed the young man who was listening to her, she continued.

"I had not eaten or drunk anything for nearly three days. I suffered frightful torments. At times I seemed enveloped by clouds that prevented me from seeing clearly, and I was in a state of delirium.

"By that evening I was so weak that every time I fainted I thanked God because I thought I was about to die.

"As I was falling into one of those faints I heard the door open. Terror made me recover consciousness.

"My persecutor came in, followed by a man in a mask. He was masked, too, but I recognized his step, his voice, and that imposing air which hell has bestowed on him— to humanity's misfortune.

" 'Well,' he said, 'have you made up your mind to take the oath I requested of you?'

" 'You yourself have said that Puritans keep their word. You have heard mine, and I will pursue you on earth to the tribunal of men, in heaven to the tribunal of God.'

" 'You persist in this?'

" 'I swear it before the God who hears me. I will tell the whole world about your crime, and I will do so until I find an avenger.'

" 'You are a prostitute,' he said in a voice of thunder, 'and you will undergo the punishment of prostitutes! When the world you invoke sees that you are branded, try to prove to that world that you are neither guilty nor mad!'

"Then he turned to the man who had come in with him and said, 'Executioner, do your duty.' "

"Oh, his name, his name!" cried Felton. "Tell me his name!"

"In spite of my screams, in spite of my resistance—for I began to realize that there was a question of something worse than death—the executioner seized me, threw me on the floor, and tied me up. My sobs were suffocating me, I was almost senseless—but I called out to God. He did not hear me. All at once I screamed with pain and shame. A burning fire, the executioner's red-hot iron, branded my shoulder."

Felton groaned.

"Look," said Milady, rising with the majesty of a queen. "Look, Felton, at the new martyrdom invented for a pure young girl, the victim of a villain's brutality. Learn to know men's hearts, and in the future do not allow yourself to be the instrument of their unjust vengeance."

Milady quickly opened her dress, tore the batiste that covered her bosom, and red with simulated anger and shame, showed Felton the ineradicable mark that dishonored her beautiful shoulder.

"But that is a fleur-de-lis I see there!" he exclaimed.

"And that is why it is so diabolical," replied Milady. "If it were the brand of England, he would have to prove what court had imposed that sentence, and I could make a public appeal to all the courts of the kingdom. But the brand of France—oh, by *that* was I branded indeed!"

This was too much for Felton.

Pale, stunned, overwhelmed by that frightful revelation, dazzled by the superhuman beauty of the woman who had unveiled herself with an immodesty that he thought sublime, he fell to his knees before her as the early Christians knelt before those pure and holy women who were sacrificed by the pagan emperors to the blood-thirsty sensuality of the populace. The brand disappeared; only her beauty remained.

"Forgive me!" he cried. "Oh, forgive me!"

Milady read in his eyes *love! love!*

"Forgive you for what?" she asked.

"Forgive me for having joined with your persecutors."

She held out her hand to him.

"So beautiful, so young!" he said, covering that hand with his kisses.

Milady gave him one of those looks that can turn a slave into a king.

Felton was a Puritan: he abandoned her hand to kiss her feet.

He no longer loved her; he worshiped her.

When the crisis was over—when Milady seemed to have recovered her composure, which she had never lost, and when Felton had seen her chastity veil those treasures of love which were now concealed from him only to make him desire them the more ardently—he said, "I now have only one thing to ask of you—the name of your true executioner. There is only one—the other was just his instrument."

"What, brother? Must I tell you his name? Have you not guessed who he is?"

"You mean it is he?" cried Felton. "He . . . again? He . . . always he? He . . . the truly guilty?"

"The truly guilty," said Milady. "He who is the ravager of England, the persecutor of true believers, the base ravisher of the honor of so many women—he who to satisfy a caprice of his corrupt heart is about to make two nations shed much blood, who protects the Protestants today and will betray them tomorrow . . ."

"Buckingham! So it is Buckingham!" Felton exclaimed furiously.

Milady hid her face in her hands, as if she could not endure the shame this name reminded her of.

"Buckingham, the executioner of this angelic creature!" cried Felton. "And thou hast not hurled thy thunder at him, O Lord? And thou hast left him noble, honored, powerful, for the ruin of us all?"

"God abandons those who abandon themselves," said Milady.

"He will suffer the punishment reserved for the damned!" continued Felton with increasing fervor. "But he must suffer human vengeance before having to submit to celestial justice!"

"He is spared human vengeance because men fear him."

"I do not fear him, nor will I spare him."

Milady's soul was afloat in a sea of infernal joy.

"But how can Lord de Winter—my protector, my father—possibly be concerned in all this?"

"I must tell you, Felton," Milady resumed, "that in addition to base and contemptible men there are also noble and generous ones. I was betrothed to a man whom I loved and who loved me—a man with a heart like yours, Felton, a man like you. I went to him and told him everything. He knew me, and did not doubt me for an instant. He was a man equal in rank and wealth to Buckingham, and without saying a word he put on his sword, wrapped himself in his cloak, and went straight to Buckingham Palace."

"Yes, I understand how he would act," Felton said. "But with such men one should use a dagger, not a sword!"

"Buckingham had left England the day before, sent as an emissary to Spain to ask for the hand of the Infanta for King Charles the First, who was then only Prince of Wales.

"My betrothed returned and said, 'This man has left England, and for the moment has escaped my vengeance. But let us be married as planned, and then count on Lord de Winter to maintain his wife's honor as well as his own.' "

"Lord de Winter!" cried Felton.

"Yes, and now you can understand everything, can you not? Buckingham was gone for nearly a year. A week before his return Lord de Winter died, leaving me his sole heir. How did he die? God, who knows all, must know that. As for me, I accuse nobody."

"Oh, what an abyss!"

"My husband died without revealing anything to his brother. The terrible secret was to be concealed till it exploded, like a clap of thunder, over the head of the guilty. Your protector had disapproved of his elder brother's marriage to a poor girl. I realized that I could not expect any help from a man disappointed in his hopes of an inheritance. I went to France, determined to remain there for the rest of my life. But my entire fortune is in England, and since all communication was cut off by the war, I was obliged to come back again, to make certain financial arrangements. I landed at Portsmouth six days ago."

"And then?" said Felton.

"And then Buckingham must have heard about my return and told Lord de Winter, who was already prejudiced against me, that his sister-in-law was a prostitute, a branded woman. The noble and pure voice of my husband was no longer there to defend me. Lord de Winter believed everything he heard because it was to his advantage to believe it. He had me arrested and brought here under your guard. You know the rest. The day after tomorrow he will banish me, have me transported, and exile me to live among vile people. Oh, the web is well woven, and the plot is clever! My honor will not survive it! So you see, Felton, I can do nothing but die. Give me that knife!"

And with those words, as if all her strength had been exhausted, she sank, weak and languishing, into Felton's arms. Intoxicated with love, anger, and voluptuous sensations he had never before known, he received her with rapture and clasped her to his chest, trembling at the breath from her beautiful mouth, bewildered by the contact with her palpitating bosom.

"No, you will live in honor and purity. You will live in triumph over your enemies."

She slowly pushed him away with her hand while drawing him nearer with her eyes; he embraced her more closely, imploring her as if she were a divinity.

"Oh, death, death!" she said, lowering her voice and her eyes. "Death rather than shame! Felton, my brother, my friend, I beg you!"

"You will live and you will be avenged!"

"Felton, I bring misfortune to all around me! Abandon me, Felton, let me die!"

"Then we will live and die together!" he cried, pressing his lips to hers.

Someone was knocking on the door; this time she really did push him away from her.

"Listen!" she said. "We have been overheard! Someone is coming! We are lost!"

"No, it is only the sentry warning me that they are about to change the guard."

"Then run to the door and open it yourself."

He obeyed; he was now hers, heart and mind.

He found himself face to face with a sergeant commanding a guard patrol.

"What is the matter?" Felton asked.

"You told me to open the door if I heard anyone cry out," answered the soldier, "but you forgot to leave me the key. I heard you cry out, but I couldn't understand what you said. I tried to open the door, but it was locked from the inside, so I called the sergeant."

"And here I am," said the sergeant.

Quite bewildered, almost mad, Felton stood speechless.

Milady understood that it was now her turn to take part in the scene. She ran to the table and picked up the knife Felton had set down, exclaiming, "What right do you have to prevent me from dying?"

"Oh, no!" said Felton, seeing the knife in her hand.

At that moment there was a burst of ironical laughter from the corridor. De Winter, attracted by the noise, stood in the doorway in his dressing gown, his sword under his arm.

"Well, we have come to the last act of the tragedy, I see," he said. "As I predicted, Felton, the drama has gone through every phase I named—but be sure that no blood will flow."

Milady understood that all was lost unless she gave Felton immediate and unquestionable proof of her courage.

"You are mistaken, my Lord, blood *will* flow—and may it fall back on those who cause it to flow!"

Felton rushed toward her, but he was too late; she had stabbed herself.

Fortunately—or rather skillfully—the knife had come into contact with the metal busk that in those days defended a woman's chest. It had slid down the busk, tearing the gown, and had penetrated at an angle between the flesh and the ribs.

Nonetheless, her dress was stained with blood in a second.

She fell down, seemingly unconscious.

Felton pulled out the knife.

"She is dead, my Lord," he said solemnly. "Here is a woman who was under my guard and who has killed herself!"

"No, Felton," said Lord de Winter, "she is not dead. Fiends do not die so easily. Put your mind at ease and go wait for me in my room."

"But, my Lord . . ."

"Go, sir. That is an order."

Felton obeyed; but he hid the knife next to his body as he left.

As to Lord de Winter, he called the woman who waited on Milady, and when she had come, he told her to take care of the prisoner, who was still unconscious, and left them alone.

Despite his suspicions, he thought the wound might be serious, so he immediately sent a man on horseback to find a physician.

58

Escape

As LORD DE WINTER had thought, Milady's wound was not dangerous, and she opened her eyes as soon as she had been left alone with her maid.

She had to pretend to be weak and in pain, but that was not a very difficult task for so excellent an actress. The poor servant was completely fooled, and despite Milady's hints, she persisted in staying with her all night.

But the maid's presence did not prevent Milady from thinking.

There was no doubt that Felton was convinced; Felton was hers. If an angel were to appear before him to accuse her, he would take that angel for a messenger sent by the devil.

She smiled at this thought, because Felton was now her only hope—her only way to safety.

But Lord de Winter might suspect him, might be having him watched!

Toward four o'clock in the morning the doctor arrived, but during the time since Milady had stabbed herself, the wound had closed and he could therefore not determine either its direction or its depth. Her pulse, however, made it clear that her condition was not serious.

In the morning, under the pretext that she had not slept well during the night and wanted to rest, she sent the maid away.

She hoped that Felton would appear at the breakfast hour, but he did not come.

Were her fears justified? Was Felton, suspected by her brother-in-law, about to fail her at the decisive moment? She had only one day left. Lord de Winter had said she would embark on the twenty-third, and it was now the morning of the twenty-second.

Nevertheless she waited patiently till lunch time.

Although she had eaten nothing in the morning, the meal was brought in at its usual time, and Milady then observed, with alarm, that the soldiers who guarded her were wearing different uniforms.

She ventured to ask what had become of Felton, and she was told that he had ridden away from the castle an hour earlier.

She asked if Lord de Winter was still at the castle. The soldier replied that he was, and that he had given orders to be informed if the prisoner wished to speak to him.

Milady replied that she was too weak just then and her only desire was to be left alone.

The soldiers went out, leaving the meal on the table.

Felton had been sent away, and the guards had been changed; Felton was mistrusted.

That was the final blow.

Alone now, she got out of bed; she had remained there so that they might believe her seriously wounded, but it now felt like a bed of fire. She looked at the door and saw that Lord de Winter had had a plank nailed over the grating: he must have been afraid that she might still by some diabolical means corrupt her guards through the opening.

She smiled with joy at the idea that now she was free to give way to her feelings without being observed, and she paced her room like a furious maniac or a caged tigress. If she had still had the knife, she would not have thought of killing herself, but of killing de Winter.

At six o'clock he came in, armed to the teeth. This man, whom she had previously considered a rather simpleminded gentleman, had become an admirable jailer who seemed to foresee everything, to guess everything, to forestall everything.

A single look at Milady was enough to let him know all that was passing through her mind.

"I understand what you want, but you will not kill me today. You have no weapon, and besides, I am on my guard. You had begun to pervert my poor Felton—he was already yielding to your infernal influence. But I will save him—he will never see you again. It is all over. Get your clothes together. You will leave tomorrow. I had originally arranged the embarkation for the twenty-fourth, but I have decided that the more promptly it takes place the more sure it will be. By twelve o'clock tomorrow, I will have the order for your exile, signed *Buckingham.* If you speak a single word to anyone before boarding the ship, my sergeant will blow your brains out. Those are his orders. If you speak a single word to anyone on the ship before the captain gives you permission, the captain will have you thrown overboard. That is our agreement. *Au revoir,* then—that is all I have to say today. Tomorrow I will see you again to say goodbye."

With those words he left.

Milady had listened to this tirade with a disdainful smile on her lips, but rage in her heart.

Supper was served; she ate because she felt that she needed all her strength. She did not know what might take place during the night that was approaching so menacingly, with dark clouds rolling across the sky and distant lightning announcing a storm.

The storm broke about ten o'clock. Milady was consoled by seeing nature share her own tumultuous feelings. The thunder growled like the passion and anger of her thoughts, and it seemed as though the gusts of wind were disheveling her hair just as they were shaking the branches of the trees and swirling away their leaves. Her howls merged with the hurricane's and her voice was lost in the great voice of nature, which also seemed to groan with despair.

All at once she heard a tap at her window, and by the help of a flash of lightning she saw a man's face on the other side of the bars.

She ran to the window and opened it.

"Felton! I am saved!"

"Yes," said Felton, "but be quiet! I must have time to file through these bars. Be careful that I am not seen through the grille."

"They have closed the grating with a board—it is a proof that the Lord is on our side, Felton!" she replied.

"Good. God has made them foolish."

"What should I do?"

"Nothing. Just shut the window. Go to bed, or at least lie down in your clothes. As soon as I have finished, I will rap on one of the panes. Will you be able to follow me?"

"Oh, yes!"

"Your wound?"

"Gives me pain, but will not prevent my walking."

"Then be ready at the first signal."

Milady shut the window, put out the lamp, and lay down on the bed, as Felton had asked her to. Mingled with the moaning of the storm, she heard the grinding of the file on the bars, and by every flash of lightning she saw Felton's shadow through the glass.

For an hour she lay there without breathing, panting, in a cold sweat, her heart in anguish at every noise she heard in the corridor.

There are hours that last a year.

At the end of an hour, Felton tapped again.

She sprang out of bed and opened the window. Two bars had been removed, and there was now an opening large enough for a man to pass through.

"Are you ready?" asked Felton.

"Yes. Shall I take anything with me?"

"Gold, if you have any."

"I do. Luckily they left me all I had."

"So much the better, because I have spent mine to charter a ship."

"Here," she said, putting a bag full of gold coins in Felton's hands.

He took the bag and threw it down to the ground below.

"Now," he asked, "are you ready?"

"I am ready."

She climbed on a chair and passed the upper part of her body through the window. Felton was suspended over the abyss on a rope ladder. For the first time an emotion of terror reminded her that she was a woman. The empty darkness frightened her.

"I was afraid of this," said Felton.

"Never mind, it's nothing! I will go down with my eyes shut."

"Do you have confidence in me?"

"You can ask that?"

"Put your two hands together and cross them. That's right!"

Felton tied her two wrists together with his handkerchief, and then with a rope over the handkerchief.

"What are you doing?" she asked with surprise.

"Put your arms around my neck, and do not be afraid."

"But I will make you lose your balance, and we will both be dashed to pieces!"

"Do not be afraid. I am a sailor."

There was not a second to lose. She put her two arms around Felton's neck and let herself slide out the window. He began to go down the ladder slowly, step by step. Despite the weight of their two bodies, the strength of the hurricane made them sway in the air.

All at once Felton stopped.

"What is the matter?" Milady asked.

"Quiet. I hear footsteps."

"We are discovered!"

They were silent for several seconds.

"No," he said, "it is nothing."

"But what is that noise?"

"The patrol making their rounds."

"Where do they go?"

"Just under us."

"They will see us!"

"Not if there is no lightning."

"But they will feel the bottom of the ladder."

"Fortunately it stops six feet above the ground."

"Here they come! My God!"

"Silence!"

They remained suspended, motionless and breathless, twenty feet from the ground, while the patrol passed beneath them, laughing and talking. It was a terrible moment for the fugitives.

The patrol passed, the sound of their voices and their retreating footsteps soon dying away.

"We are safe now," said Felton.

Milady sighed deeply and fainted.

Felton continued to descend. Near the bottom of the ladder, when he found no more support for his feet, he clung with his hands; and when he reached the last rung, he let himself hang by his wrists and dropped to the ground. He stooped down, picked up the bag of money, and took it between his teeth. Then, holding Milady in his arms, he set off briskly in the direction opposite the one the patrol had taken, soon leaving the path and descending the rocks; when they arrived on the beach, he whistled.

The same signal replied to him, and five minutes later he saw a boat being rowed by four men.

It approached as close as it dared to the shore, but could not reach it because the water was not deep enough. Felton waded out up to his waist, unwilling to trust his precious burden to anybody else.

Fortunately the storm was beginning to die down, but the sea was still rough, and the little boat bounded over the waves like a nutshell.

"To the sloop," said Felton, "and row quickly."

The four men bent to their oars, but the sea was too high to let them make good time.

But they were leaving the castle behind, and that was the main thing. The night was very dark, and since it was almost impossible to see the shore from the boat, it was unlikely that anyone would be able to see the boat from the shore.

A black dot was floating on the sea: the sloop.

While the boat was advancing toward it with all the

speed its four rowers could give it, Felton untied the rope
and the handkerchief that bound Milady's hands. When
they were free he sprinkled some sea water over her face.

She sighed, and opened her eyes.

"Where am I?" she asked.

"Saved!" replied the young officer.

"Saved!" she exclaimed. "Yes, there is the sky, here
is the sea! The air I breathe is the air of liberty! Oh,
thank you, Felton, thank you!"

He pressed her to his heart.

"But what is the matter with my hands?" she asked.
"It feels as if my wrists had been crushed in a vise."

She held out her arms; her wrists were bruised.

"I am so sorry," Felton said, looking at those beautiful
hands and shaking his head sorrowfully.

"Oh, it is nothing!" she cried. "I remember now."

She looked around her, as if searching for something.

"Here it is," said Felton, touching the bag of money
with his foot.

They were nearing the sloop. A sailor on watch hailed
the boat, and Felton replied.

"What vessel is that?" asked Milady.

"The one I have hired for you."

"Where will it take me?"

"Wherever you wish, after you have put me ashore at
Portsmouth."

"What are you going to do in Portsmouth?"

"Carry out Lord de Winter's orders," he replied with
a sad smile.

"What orders?"

"You do not understand?"

"No, please explain yourself."

"Since he mistrusted me, he determined to guard you
himself and sent me in his place to get Buckingham to
sign the order for your deportation."

"But if he mistrusted you, how could he give you such
an order?"

"How could I know what I was carrying?"

"True! And you are going to Portsmouth?"

"Yes, and I have no time to lose. Tomorrow is the
twenty-third, and that is when Buckingham sets sail with
his fleet."

"He sets sail tomorrow! Where is he going?"

"To La Rochelle."

"He must not sail!" she cried, forgetting her usual presence of mind.

"Do not worry—he will not sail."

Milady was overjoyed. She had just seen into the depths of Felton's heart, and Buckingham's death was plainly written there.

"Felton, you are as great as Judas Maccabeus! If you die, I will die with you—that is all I can say to you."

"Silence! We are here."

In fact, they were now touching the sloop.

Felton mounted the ladder first and gave Milady his hand, while the sailors supported her below, because the sea was still very rough.

A few minutes later they were on the deck.

"Captain," said Felton, "this is the lady about whom I spoke to you, and whom you must convey safe and sound to France."

"For a thousand pistoles," said the captain.

"I have paid you five hundred of them."

"That is correct," said the captain.

"And here are the other five hundred," added Milady, reaching for the bag of gold.

"No," said the captain. "I make only one bargain, and my bargain with this young man is that the other five hundred is not due to me till we reach Boulogne."

"And will we reach Boulogne?"

"Safe and sound, as sure as my name's Jack Butler."

"Well, if you keep your word, I will give you a thousand pistoles instead of five hundred."

"Hurrah for you, then, my beautiful lady!" cried the captain. "And may God often send me passengers like your Ladyship!"

"But first," said Felton, "take me to the little bay of Chichester, near Portsmouth, as we agreed."

The captain replied by ordering the necessary maneuvers, and at about seven o'clock in the morning the little vessel cast anchor in the bay.

During the voyage, Felton had told Milady everything—how, instead of going to London, he had chartered the little vessel; how he had returned; how he had scaled the wall by fastening cramps in the cracks between the stones to give him footholds as he climbed; and how he had fastened his ladder to the bars of her window. Milady knew the rest.

On her side, she tried to encourage Felton in his project; but at his first words, she understood that the young fanatic needed to be moderated rather than urged.

It was agreed that she would wait for him till ten o'clock; if he did not return by then, she was to sail without him.

In that case, and supposing he remained free, he was to rejoin her in France, at the convent of the Carmelites in Béthune.

59

What Happened in Portsmouth on August 23, 1628

FELTON TOOK LEAVE of Milady by kissing her hand, as coolly as if he were a brother taking leave of his sister before going out for a walk.

He seemed to be as composed as ever, but his eyes shone feverishly, he was more pale than usual, his teeth were clenched, and his speech was brisk and clipped, indicating that he was preoccupied and perturbed.

As long as he remained in the boat that was carrying him ashore, he kept his face toward Milady, who stood on the deck and followed him with her eyes. Both were free from the fear of pursuit: nobody ever came into Milady's room before nine o'clock, and it would take three hours to go from the castle to Portsmouth.

Felton jumped on to the shore, climbed the little hill that led to the top of the cliff, waved to Milady one last time, and started walking toward the city.

After about a hundred paces downhill, he could see only the mast of the sloop.

Portsmouth was visible about half a league ahead of him, its houses and towers barely perceptible in the morning haze. Beyond, the sea was covered with vessels whose masts, like a forest of poplars stripped by the winter, swayed with each breath of wind.

Striding along, he reviewed all the accusations against

Buckingham that he had assembled after two years of ascetic meditation and much association with the Puritans.

When he compared the public crimes of this minister— prominent crimes, political crimes, so to speak—with the private and unknown crimes with which Milady had charged him, he decided that the secret ones were worse. This was because his love for Milady—so strange, so new, so ardent—made him view her imaginary accusations as though they were real. It was like looking through a magnifying glass and seeing a minute speck— in reality smaller and more imperceptible than an ant— seem like a frightful monster.

His rapid pace stirred his blood even more: the idea that he left behind him, exposed to a terrible vengeance, the woman he loved, or rather whom he adored as a saint; the tumultuous emotion of the past few days; his present fatigue—all combined to exalt his soul above the ordinary.

He entered Portsmouth about eight o'clock in the morning. The whole population was afoot; drums were beating in the streets and in the harbor; the embarking troops were marching toward the ships.

Felton arrived at the palace of the Admiralty covered with dust and streaming with perspiration; his usually pale face was purple with heat and passion. The sentinel wanted to deny him entry, but Felton called the officer of the guard and, drawing from his pocket the letter he was carrying, said, "An urgent message from Lord de Winter."

At the name of Lord de Winter, who was known to be one of his Grace's most intimate friends, and seeing that Felton was wearing the uniform of a naval officer, the men gave the order to let Felton pass.

He ran into the building.

Just as he went inside, another man—dusty, out of breath, leaving at the gate a post horse that had fallen to its knees—was also entering.

He and Felton both spoke to Patrick, the duke's confidential servant, at the same moment. Felton said he came from Lord de Winter; the unknown would not say from whom he came, insisting he would identify himself only to the duke himself. Each was eager to gain admission before the other.

Patrick, who knew that Lord de Winter had both official and personal relations with the duke, gave the preference to the one who came in his name. The other was forced to wait, and it was easy to see his anger at the delay.

The servant led Felton through a large room in which the deputies from La Rochelle, headed by the Prince de Soubise, were waiting, then brought him to the door of a dressing room, where Buckingham, just out of the bath, was getting dressed with his customary meticulous care.

"Lieutenant Felton, from Lord de Winter," Patrick announced.

"From Lord de Winter!" repeated Buckingham. "Have him come in."

Felton entered just as Buckingham was taking off an ornate, gold-embroidered robe and about to put on a blue velvet doublet embroidered with pearls.

"Why didn't Lord de Winter come himself?" Buckingham asked. "I was expecting him this morning."

"He wished me to tell your Grace," replied Felton, "that he very much regrets not having that honor, but he was prevented by having to guard a prisoner at the castle."

"Yes, I know that he has a prisoner."

"I would like to speak to your Grace about that prisoner."

"Well, then, speak!"

"What I have to say can be heard only by you, my Lord."

"Leave us, Patrick," said Buckingham, "but remain within sound of the bell. I will ring for you soon."

Patrick left.

"We are alone, sir," said Buckingham. "Speak!"

"Your Grace," said Felton, "Lord de Winter wrote to you the other day to ask you to sign an order of embarkation for a young woman named Charlotte Backson."

"Yes, he did, and I replied that if he brought or sent me that order, I would sign it."

"Here it is, my Lord."

"Give it to me."

Taking it from Felton, he glanced rapidly over the

sheet of paper, and when he saw that it was the one that had been described to him, he put it on the table, took a pen, and prepared to sign it.

"Pardon me, my Lord," said Felton, stopping the duke, "but does your Grace know that Charlotte Backson is not the young woman's real name?"

"Yes, sir, I do," replied the duke, dipping the quill in the ink.

"Then your Grace knows her real name?"

"I know it."

The duke put the quill to the paper.

"And knowing that real name, my Lord, will you sign it all the same?"

"Certainly. And sooner twice than once."

"I cannot believe," continued Felton, his voice becoming sharp and rough, "that your Grace knows that she is Milady de Winter."

"I know it perfectly, although I am astonished that *you* know it."

"And your Grace will sign that order without remorse?"

Buckingham looked at the young man haughtily.

"Do you know, sir, that you are asking me some very strange questions and that I am very foolish to answer them?"

"Answer them, my Lord. The situation is more serious than you may think."

Buckingham decided that the young man, coming from Lord de Winter, must be speaking in his name, and answered more mildly.

"Without remorse," he said. "Lord de Winter knows, as well as I do, that Milady is a very wicked woman, and that limiting her punishment to exile is almost like pardoning her."

The duke put his pen to the paper.

"You will not sign that order, my Lord!" said Felton, stepping toward the duke.

"I will not sign this order! Why not?"

"Because you will look into your soul, and you will do justice to the lady."

"I would do her justice by hanging her at Tyburn. The lady is a fiend!"

"My Lord, Milady de Winter is an angel, and you know that she is. I demand that you free her."

"Are you mad, to talk to me like this?"

"My Lord, excuse me! I am restraining myself as much as I can. But my Lord, think of what you are about to do, and beware of going too far!"

"What? God forgive me, but I really think you are threatening me!"

"No, my Lord, I am still pleading. And I say to you that one drop of water is enough to make a full vase overflow—one small mistake may draw down punishment upon the head that has been spared despite many crimes."

"Mr. Felton, you will leave this room and place yourself under arrest."

"Hear me to the end, my Lord. You have seduced this young girl, outraged her, defiled her. Make amends for your crimes by letting her go free, and I will demand nothing more of you."

"You will demand . . ." said Buckingham, looking at Felton with astonishment and emphasizing each syllable of the three words as he pronounced them.

"Beware, my Lord," continued Felton, becoming more excited as he spoke, "all England is tired of your iniquities. You have abused the royal power, which you have almost usurped, and you are held in horror by God and men. God will punish you hereafter, but I will punish you here!"

"This is too much!" cried Buckingham, taking a step toward the door.

Felton barred his passage.

"I ask you humbly, your Grace," he said, "to sign an order for Milady de Winter's release. Remember that she is the woman whom you have dishonored."

"Withdraw, sir, or I will call my servant and tell him to have you placed in irons."

"You shall not call," said Felton, throwing himself between the duke and the bell placed on a silver-inlaid table. "Beware, my Lord, you are in God's hands!"

"In the devil's hands, you mean!" said Buckingham, raising his voice to attract the attention of his servants without calling them directly.

"Sign, my Lord. Sign Milady de Winter's release," said Felton, holding out a sheet of paper to the duke.

"You think you can make me sign it by force? You are joking! Patrick!"

"Sign, my Lord!"

"Never!"

"Never?"

"Help!" shouted the duke as he reached for his sword.

But Felton did not give him time to draw it. The knife with which Milady had stabbed herself was hidden under his doublet: at one bound he was upon the duke.

At that moment Patrick came in, saying, "A letter from France, my Lord!"

"From France!" cried Buckingham, forgetting everything except the one from whom that letter came.

Felton took advantage of this moment to plunge the knife into Buckingham's side, right up to the handle.

"Traitor!" shouted the duke. "You have killed me . . ."

"Murder!" screamed Patrick.

Felton looked around for a way to escape, and seeing the door free, he rushed into the next room, where the deputies from La Rochelle were waiting. He crossed it as quickly as possible and rushed toward the staircase, but on the first step he met Lord de Winter.

Seeing Felton pale, confused, livid, stained with blood both on his hands and face, Lord de Winter seized him by the throat, crying, "I knew it! I guessed it! But I am too late by a minute, unfortunate man that I am!"

Felton did not resist. Lord de Winter turned him over to the guards, who led him to a small terrace overlooking the sea while they waited for further orders, and then de Winter hurried to the duke's room.

At the sound of the duke's cry and Patrick's shriek, the man whom Felton had met in the anteroom also rushed into the dressing room.

He found the duke lying on a sofa, his hand pressed over his wound.

"La Porte," said the duke, in a faint voice, "do you come from her?"

"Yes, monseigneur," replied Anne of Austria's faithful servant, "but too late, perhaps."

"Silence, La Porte, you may be overheard! Patrick, let no one enter. Oh, my God, I will not know what she says to me! I am dying!"

And the duke fainted.

Meanwhile, Lord de Winter, the deputies, the leaders of the expedition, and the officers of Buckingham's household had all burst into the room, which echoed with their cries of despair.

The news that filled the palace with tears and groans soon became known, and spread through the city.

A cannon shot announced that something unexpected had taken place.

Lord de Winter was in despair.

"Too late by a minute!" he cried. "Too late by a minute! Oh, my God, what a disaster!"

At seven o'clock in the morning he had been informed that a rope ladder was floating outside one of the windows of the castle; he had gone immediately to Milady's room and found it empty, the window open and the bars filed. Remembering the warning given him by d'Artagnan's messenger, he had feared for the duke and run to the stable, where without even stopping to have a horse saddled, he had jumped onto the first one he saw, galloped off like the wind, dismounted below in the courtyard, hurried up the stairs, and on the top step, as we have said, met Felton.

The duke, however, was not yet dead. He regained consciousness and opened his eyes; hope revived in everyone around him.

"Gentlemen," he said, "leave me alone with Patrick and La Porte . . . ah, is that you, de Winter? You sent me a strange madman this morning! See what he has done to me."

"Oh, my Lord, I will never console myself."

"And you would be quite wrong, my dear de Winter," said Buckingham, holding out his hand to him. "I do not know the man who deserves being mourned during another man's entire life . . . But please leave us."

De Winter left, sobbing.

Only La Porte and Patrick remained with the wounded duke.

A doctor had been sent for, but none had yet been found.

"You will live, my Lord, you will live!" repeated the faithful servant of Anne of Austria, kneeling beside the duke's sofa.

"What has she written to me?" Buckingham asked feebly, streaming with blood and suppressing his pain to speak of the woman he loved. "Read me her letter."

"But my Lord . . ." La Porte said.

"Obey me, La Porte. Do you not see I have no time to lose?"

La Porte broke the seal and held the letter in front of the duke's eyes, but Buckingham tried in vain to make out the writing.

"Read it to me! I cannot see, and soon I may not hear. I will die without knowing what she has written to me!"

La Porte made no further objection, and read:

> My Lord,
> In the name of that which, since I have known you, I have suffered by you and for you, I beg you, if you have any care for my peace of mind, to stop arming against France and to put an end to this war. Its ostensible cause is said to be religion, but it is generally whispered that your love for me is its real and concealed cause. This war may not only bring on great catastrophes for England and France, but serious misfortune on you, my Lord—which I should regret forever.
> Be careful of your life, which is threatened, and which will be dear to me from the moment I am not obliged to see an enemy in you.
>
> Your affectionate
> Anne

Buckingham had summoned all his remaining strength to listen to the reading of the letter; when it was ended, and as if it had been a bitter disappointment, he asked, "Have you nothing else to say to me personally, La Porte?"

"Yes, my Lord. The queen told me to tell you to take care of yourself, for she had learned that there would be an assassination attempt."

"Is that all?" Buckingham asked impatiently.

"She also told me to tell you that she still loves you."

"God be praised! Then my death will mean more to her than the death of a stranger!"

La Porte burst into tears.

"Patrick," said the duke, "bring me the box in which the diamond studs were kept."

Patrick brought the box, which La Porte recognized as having belonged to the queen.

"Now the white satin bag with her pearl-embroidered initials."

Patrick again obeyed.

"Here, La Porte," said Buckingham, "are the only tokens I ever received from her—this silver box and these two letters. You will restore them to her Majesty, and as a last momento from me"—he looked around for some precious object—"you will add . . ."

He continued to search, but his eyes, dimmed by approaching death, encountered only the knife that had fallen from Felton's hand, its blade still bloody.

"And you will add to them this knife," said the duke, clasping La Porte's hand. He had just strength enough to put the bag at the bottom of the silver box and to let the knife fall into it, making a sign to La Porte that he was no longer able to speak.

A last convulsion, which this time he had not the power to combat, made him fall from the sofa to the floor.

Patrick cried out.

Buckingham tried to smile, but death stopped his last thought, which remained engraved on his face like a last kiss of love.

At that moment the duke's doctor arrived, quite terrified; he had already been on board the admiral's ship, where the messenger had had to find him and from where he had had to return.

He approached the duke, took his hand, held it for an instant, and let it fall. "There is nothing to be done," he said. "He is dead."

"Dead, dead!" cried Patrick.

At this cry the crowd came back into the room, and there was nothing but consternation and tumult everywhere.

As soon as Lord de Winter saw that Buckingham was dead, he ran to Felton, whom the soldiers were still guarding on the terrace of the palace.

"Miserable wretch!" he said to the young man, who since the stabbing of Buckingham had regained that self-possession which was never to abandon him. "What have you done?"

"I have avenged myself!" Felton replied.

"Avenged yourself! Rather say that you have been that accursed woman's instrument! But I swear to you that this crime shall be her last."

"I do not know what you mean, and I am ignorant of whom you are speaking, my Lord. I killed the Duke of Buckingham because he twice refused your request to appoint me captain; I have punished him for his injustice, that is all."

De Winter, stupefied, looked on while the soldiers bound Felton, and did not know what to think of such callousness.

There was, however, one thing that cast a shadow over Felton's serene face. At every sound he heard, the naive Puritan thought he recognized the step and voice of Milady coming to throw herself into his arms, accuse herself of complicity in Buckingham's death, and die with him.

His eyes were fixed on the sea, overlooked by the terrace on which he was standing, and suddenly he started. With the eagle eyes of a sailor he had seen—what someone else would have taken for a seagull hovering over the waves—the sail of a sloop headed for the coast of France.

Ashen-faced, he put his hand over his breaking heart; he had immediately perceived the treachery.

"One last favor, my Lord," he asked de Winter.

"What?"

"What time is it?"

"Ten minutes to nine," he replied.

Milady had put ahead her departure by an hour and a half. As soon as she had heard the cannon that announced the fatal event, she had ordered the captain to weigh anchor, and—already far from the coast—the vessel was making way under a blue sky.

"God has so willed it," he said with a fanatic's resignation—but he was unable to take his eyes off that ship, on board of which he doubtless imagined he could distinguish the outline of the woman for whom he had sacrificed his life.

De Winter followed his look, observed his suffering, and guessed everything.

"You alone will be punished now, miserable man," said Lord de Winter to Felton, who was being dragged away with his eyes still turned toward the sea, "but I swear to you by the memory of my brother whom I loved so much that your accomplice will not go free!"

Felton lowered his head and spoke not a word.

Lord de Winter rushed down the stairs and went straight to the harbor.

60

In France

WHEN THE King of England, Charles I, learned about the duke's death, his first fear was that such terrible news might discourage the Rochellais; Richelieu says in his *Memoirs* that he tried to conceal it from them as long as possible, closing all the ports of his kingdom and insisting that no vessel sail until the army that Buckingham had been getting together had gone. With Buckingham dead, the king took it upon himself to superintend the departure.

He was so serious about this order that he went so far as to detain in England the ambassador of Denmark, who had already taken his leave, and the resident ambassador of Holland, who was to have taken back to the port of Flushing the Indian merchantmen that Charles I had decided to return to the United Provinces.

But since he did not think of giving that order till five hours after the event—that is, till two o'clock in the afternoon—two ships had already left the port. One of them was carrying, as we know, Milady, who had been almost certain about what had happened and was further confirmed in that belief by seeing the black flag flying from the masthead of the admiral's ship.

As for the second ship, we will tell hereafter whom it carried, and how it set sail.

During this time nothing new occurred in the camp at

La Rochelle except that the king—who was bored as always but perhaps a little more so in camp than elsewhere—determined to go incognito to St. Germain for the festival of St. Louis and asked the cardinal to order him an escort of twenty Musketeers. The cardinal, who sometimes was infected by the king's boredom himself, granted this leave of absence with great pleasure to his royal subordinate, who promised to return about the fifteenth of September.

As soon as M. de Tréville was informed about this by his Eminence, he packed his portmanteau; and since without knowing why he knew the great desire and even imperative need his four friends had of returning to Paris, it goes without saying that he named them as part of the escort.

They heard the news a quarter of an hour after M. de Tréville, for they were the first men he told. It was then that d'Artagnan appreciated the favor the cardinal had done him by having him at last join the Musketeers: if he had remained a guard, he would have been forced to stay in the camp while his friends left without him.

The reason for their impatience to return to Paris was because of the danger Mme. Bonacieux would be in if she met Milady, her mortal enemy, at the convent of Béthune. Aramis had written immediately to Marie Michon, the seamstress in Tours who had such fine acquaintances, to ask the queen to permit Mme. Bonacieux to leave the convent and go to either Lorraine or Belgium. They did not have to wait a long time for an answer. Nine or ten days after he had written, Aramis received the following letter:

My dear Cousin,

Here is the authorization from my sister to withdraw our little servant from the convent of Béthune, the air of which you think is bad for her. My sister sends you this authorization with great pleasure, for she is very fond of the girl, to whom she intends to be more helpful later.

Very affectionately,
Marie Michon

With this letter was the following order:

> The Louvre, August 10, 1628
> The superior of the convent of Béthune will place in the custody of the person who presents this note to her the novice who entered the convent on my recommendation and under my patronage.
>
> ANNE

It may be easily imagined how the relationship between Aramis and a seamstress who called the queen her sister amused the young men; but Aramis, after having blushed two or three times up to the whites of his eyes at several gross pleasantries from Porthos, begged his friends not to revert to the subject again, declaring that if one more word was said about it, he would never again ask his cousin to intercede in such affairs.

There was therefore no further discussion about Marie Michon among the four Musketeers, who in any case had what they wanted: the order to withdraw Mme. Bonacieux from the Carmelite convent in Béthune. It was true that this order would not be very useful to them while they were in camp at La Rochelle, at the other end of France, so d'Artagnan was about to ask M. de Tréville for a leave of absence, confiding to him candidly why he wanted it, when he and his three friends heard that the king was about to set out for Paris with an escort of twenty Musketeeers and that they would be among them.

Their joy was great. They sent the lackeys on ahead with their baggage, and they left on the morning of the sixteenth.

The cardinal accompanied his Majesty from Surgères to Mauzé, where they took leave of each other with great demonstrations of friendship.

The king wanted to enjoy himself as much as possible while traveling as fast as possible—for he was anxious to be in Paris by the twenty-third—so he stopped occasionally to hawk, a pastime he had acquired a taste for from de Luynes and for which he still felt a great affection. Sixteen of the twenty Musketeeers rejoiced greatly at this relaxation, but the other four cursed it heartily. D'Artagnan, in particular, had a perpetual buzzing in his ears, which Porthos explained this way: "A very great lady once told me it means that somebody is talking about you somewhere."

Finally the escort crossed Paris on the twenty-third. The king thanked M. de Tréville and permitted him to distribute four-day furloughs on condition that those who received them would not appear in any public place, under penalty of being sent to the Bastille.

Of course the first four furloughs were granted to our four friends. In addition, Athos persuaded M. de Tréville to give them six days instead of four, as well as two extra nights, for they left at five o'clock in the evening on the twenty-fourth, and M. de Tréville post-dated the leave to the morning of the twenty-fifth.

D'Artagnan, optimistic as ever, said, "We seem to be taking great pains about something very simple. In two days, and by using up two or three horses—which I can do because I have plenty of money—I am at Béthune. I present my letter from the queen to the superior, and I take the treasure I go to seek not to Lorraine or Belgium, but to Paris, where she will be much better hidden, particularly while the cardinal is at La Rochelle. Once the siege is over, the queen will help us—partly because of her cousin, partly because of what we have personally done for her—and we will obtain from the queen what we desire. Remain here, and do not exhaust yourself with useless activity. Planchet and I can manage such a simple expedition."

To this Athos replied quietly, "We also have money left, for I have not yet drunk all my share of the diamond, and Porthos and Aramis have not eaten all theirs. We also can therefore use up four horses as well as one. But remember, d'Artagnan," he added, in a tone so grim that it made the young man shudder, "that Béthune is where the cardinal has told Milady to go, and that she is a lady who brings disaster wherever she goes. If you had only to deal with four men, d'Artagnan, I would allow you to go alone, but you will have to deal with that woman! The four of us will all go, and I pray to God that with our four lackeys we may be enough!"

"You terrify me, Athos! What are you afraid of?"

"Everything!"

D'Artagnan looked at his other companions, and like Athos, they seemed deeply worried. All of them contin-

ued to ride as fast as their horses could carry them, but
without saying another word.

They entered Arras on the evening of the twenty-fifth,
and as d'Artagnan was dismounting at the Herse d'or inn
to drink a glass of wine, a horseman came out of the
posthouse courtyard, where he had just taken a fresh
horse, and started off at a gallop on the road to Paris.
Just as the rider passed through the gateway into the
street, the wind blew open the cloak in which he was
wrapped—although it was August—and lifted his hat,
which he caught the moment it left his head, pulling it
down over his eyes.

D'Artagnan, who had been watching him, became very
pale and dropped his glass.

"What is the matter, monsieur?" asked Planchet. "Oh,
come here, gentlemen, my master is ill!"

The three friends hurried to d'Artagnan, but saw that
instead of being ill, he was running toward his horse.
They stopped him at the door.

"Where the devil are you going?" cried Athos.

"It is he!" cried d'Artagnan, livid with rage. "Let me
go after him!"

"He? What he?" asked Athos.

"He, that man!"

"What man?"

"That cursèd man, my evil genius, the one I have
always met when threatened by some misfortune, the one
who was with that horrible woman the first time I saw
her, the one I was looking for when I offended Athos,
the one I saw on the very morning Madame Bonacieux
was abducted—the man from Meung! I have just seen
him—it is he! I recognized him when the wind blew open
his cloak."

"The devil," said Athos pensively.

"To saddle, gentlemen! Let us ride after him and overtake him!"

"My dear friend," said Aramis, "remember that he is
going in the opposite direction from ours and that he has
a fresh horse and ours are tired. We will kill our own
horses without even a chance of overtaking him, so let
the man go, d'Artagnan, and let us save the woman."

"Monsieur!" cried a hostler, running out and looking

for the stranger. "Here is a paper that dropped out of your hat!"

"A half-pistole for that paper!" said d'Artagnan.

"My faith, monsieur, with pleasure! Here it is."

Enchanted with his good day's work, the hostler returned to the yard.

D'Artagnan unfolded the paper.

"Well?" his three friends demanded eagerly.

"Nothing but one word," said d'Artagnan.

"Yes," said Aramis, "but that one word is the name of some town or village."

" 'Armentières,' " read Porthos. "Armentières? I don't know such a place."

"And that name of a town or village is in her handwriting!" Athos exclaimed.

"Well, let us take good care of that paper. Maybe I have not thrown away my half-pistole! To horse, my friends, to horse!" said d'Artagnan.

And the four friends galloped off along the road to Béthune.

61

The Carmelite Convent at Béthune

THERE IS A KIND of predestination that enables great criminals to surmount all obstacles and escape all dangers until the moment when a wearied Providence has decided on their downfall.

So it was with Milady: she passed through the cruisers of both nations and arrived at Boulogne without incident.

When she had landed at Portsmouth, Milady had been an Englishwoman whom the persecutions of the French had driven from La Rochelle; landing at Boulogne after a two-day crossing, she posed as a Frenchwoman whom the English had persecuted in Portsmouth out of their hatred for France.

She also had the most effective of passports—her beauty, her distinguished manner, and the generosity with which she distributed her pistoles.

Freed from the usual formalities by the affable smile and gallant manners of the elderly governor of the port, who kissed her hand, she remained in Boulogne only long enough to send the following letter:

> *To his Eminence Monseigneur the Cardinal Riche-*
> *lieu, in his camp before La Rochelle.*
> MONSEIGNEUR, Let your Eminence be reassured. His Grace the Duke of Buckingham *will not set out* for France.
>   MILADY DE———
> BOULOGNE, evening of the twenty-fifth.
> P.S.—In accordance with the desire of your Eminence, I am going to the convent of the Carmelites at Béthune, where I will await your orders.

Milady began her journey that same evening. Night overtook her; she stopped, and slept at an inn. At five o'clock the next morning she set off again, and entered Béthune three hours later.

She asked for directions to the convent of the Carmelites and went there immediately.

The superior greeted her, and Milady showed her the cardinal's order; the abbess then assigned her a room and had breakfast served to her.

All memories of the past had been effaced from Milady's mind; and her eyes, now fixed on the future, saw nothing but the great reward promised her by the cardinal, whom she had so successfully served in such a murderous affair without his name being in any way involved with it. Her life consisted of ever-new, all-consuming passions, which were like scudding clouds that sometimes reflected azure-blue, sometimes fiery red, sometimes stormy black—and no trace of anything but devastation and death after they had passed.

After breakfast, the abbess came to pay her a visit. There is very little amusement in a convent, and the good superior was eager to make the acquaintance of her new boarder.

Milady wished to please the abbess, which was a very easy matter for such a truly extraordinary woman. She tried to be agreeable and she was, charming the good superior by her stimulating conversation and her gracious manner.

The abbess, who was the daughter of an aristocratic family, took particular delight in stories of the court, which seldom reached the extremities of the kingdom and which almost never penetrated the walls of convents, at whose threshold the noise of the world dies away. . . .

Milady, on the contrary, was quite familiar with all the aristocratic intrigues, among which she had lived for five or six years, and she made it her business to amuse the good abbess with stories about the worldly practices of the court, the excessive pieties of the king, and the scandalous behavior of the nobility—all of whom the abbess knew by name; she also touched lightly on the amours of the queen and the Duke of Buckingham, talking a great deal to induce the abbess to talk a little.

Although the latter contented herself with listening and smiling without replying, Milady could see that this sort of narrative amused her very much, so she kept at it; but she now began to let her conversation drift toward the cardinal.

It was difficult because she did not know if the abbess was a royalist or a cardinalist and therefore had to confine herself to a prudent middle course. But the abbess was even more prudent, contenting herself with making a profound inclination of the head every time Milady mentioned his Eminence.

Milady began to think she would soon grow weary of convent life and decided to take a risk in order to learn how to proceed. Wanting to see how far the discretion of the good abbess would go, she began to tell a story—in general terms at first, but very detailed as she went on—about the cardinal, describing his love affairs with Mme. d'Aiguillon, Marion de Lorme, and several other free-living women.

The abbess listened more attentively, grew animated by degrees, and smiled.

"Good," thought Milady. "She is enjoying these stories. If she is a cardinalist, she is at least not a fanatic."

She then went on to describe the cardinal's persecutions of his enemies. The abbess only crossed herself, neither approving nor disapproving, which confirmed Milady in her opinion that that abbess was more of a royalist than a cardinalist, and she began to slant her stories more and more in that direction.

"I am very ignorant of those matters," the abbess finally said, "but however distant from the court and remote from the interests of the world we may be, we have some very sad examples of what you have described. One of our boarders had suffered much from the vengeance and persecution of the cardinal."

"One of your boarders? Oh, poor woman! I pity her."

"And with reason, for she is much to be pitied. Imprisonment, threats, ill treatment—she has suffered them all. But perhaps Monsieur le Cardinal had good reasons for acting like that, and though she looks like an angel, we must not always judge people by their appearance."

"How fortunate!" Milady thought. "I may be about to discover something here!"

She tried to seem perfectly candid.

"Alas," said Milady, "I know it is said that we must not trust the face, but in what can we believe, if not in the Lord's noblest handiwork? I may be deceived all my life, perhaps, but I will always have faith in someone whose countenance inspires sympathy."

"You would be inclined to believe that this young person is innocent?" asked the abbess.

"The cardinal does not pursue only crimes," Milady replied. "There are certain virtues that he punishes more severely than certain offenses."

"Permit me, madame, to express my surprise," said the abbess.

"At what?" Milady asked ingenuously.

"At the language you use."

"What do you find so astonishing about that language?"

"You are a friend of the cardinal, since he has sent you here and yet . . ."

"And yet I speak ill of him," said Milady, finishing the superior's thought.

"At least you do not speak well of him."

"That is because I am not his friend," said she, sighing, "but his victim."

"But that letter in which he recommends you to me . . ."

"Is an order for me to remain in a sort of prison until one of his subordinates will release me."

"But why have you not fled?"

"Where could I go? Do you think there is a spot on the earth the cardinal cannot reach if he takes the trouble to stretch forth his hand? If I were a man, it might conceivably be possible, but what can a woman do? This young boarder of yours—has she tried to escape?"

"No, that is true, but with her it is different—I believe she remains in France because of some love affair."

"If she loves, she is not completely wretched," said Milady, with a sigh.

The abbess looked at her with increasing interest.

"Do I behold another poor victim?" she asked.

"Alas, yes."

For a moment the abbess looked at her uneasily, as if she had just thought of something disturbing.

"You are not an enemy of our holy faith?" she asked hesitantly.

"Who—I?" Milady exclaimed. "I a Protestant? Oh, no! As God is my witness, I am a devout Catholic!"

"Then, madame," said the abbess, smiling, "you can be sure that this convent will not be a very hard prison, and we will do all in our power to make you enjoy your captivity. In addition, you will meet that young woman of whom I spoke, who is probably being persecuted because of some court intrigue. She is charming and likable."

"What is her name?"

"She was sent to me by someone of high rank, under the name of Kitty. I have not tried to learn her other name."

"Kitty! Are you sure . . . ?"

"That she is known as Kitty? Yes, madame. Do you know her?"

Milady smiled to herself at the idea that this might be her former chambermaid. A feeling of anger was connected with the memory of that girl, and a desire for revenge distorted Milady's features. But she immediately recovered the calm and benevolent expression that this mistress of a hundred faces had for a moment allowed to be lost.

"When can I meet this young lady, for whom I already feel so great a sympathy?" she asked.

"Why, this evening," replied the abbess, "even this afternoon. But you told me you have been traveling for

four days and that you woke up this morning at five
o'clock, so you must need a rest. Go to bed and sleep—
we will wake you when it is time to eat."

Although Milady would very willingly have gone without sleep since she was sustained by all the excitement
that a new adventure offered her intrigue-hungry heart,
she nevertheless accepted the superior's suggestion. During the past two weeks she had experienced so many and
such various emotions that even though her body was
still capable of enduring fatigue, her mind needed rest.

She therefore took leave of the abbess and went to
bed, lulled by the thoughts of vengeance that the name
of Kitty had revived. She remembered that the cardinal
had promised her almost total freedom to act as she
would if she succeeded in her enterprise. She had succeeded; d'Artagnan was now in her power!

Only one thing frightened her: the memory of her husband, the Comte de la Fère, whom she had believed
dead or at least exiled, and whom she had found again
in Athos—d'Artagnan's best friend.

But if he was d'Artagnan's friend, he must have helped
him in all those schemes that had allowed the queen to
defeat the cardinal's projects; if he was d'Artagnan's
friend, he was the cardinal's enemy, and she would
undoubtedly succeed in involving him in whatever
revenge she took on the young Musketeer.

All these hopes were so many sweet thoughts, so
soothing that she was soon lulled into a peaceful sleep.

She was awakened by a soft voice from the foot of her
bed. Opening her eyes, she saw the abbess, accompanied
by a young woman with light hair and a fresh complexion
who was looking at her with friendly curiosity.

The young woman was entirely unknown to her. Each
examined the other very carefully, while exchanging the
usual polite remarks; both were very beautiful, but in
very different styles. Milady was pleased to see, however,
that she was unquestionably superior to the young
woman in noble bearing and aristocratic manners—though
the young woman *was* wearing the habit of a novice,
which was not very advantageous in such a contest.

The abbess introduced them to each other, and when
the formalities were over, she left the two young women
alone while she went to attend to her duties.

Seeing Milady in bed, the novice was also about to leave, but Milady stopped her.

"Madame," she said, "I have scarcely seen you, and you already wish to deprive me of your company, which I had been counting on, I must confess, to help me pass the time here."

"No, indeed, madame," the novice replied, "but I thought I had chosen a bad time. You were asleep—you must be tired."

"What better can those who sleep wish for but a happy awakening? This you have given me, so allow me to enjoy it a little."

She took her hand and drew her toward the armchair near the bed.

The novice sat down.

"How unfortunate I am!" she said. "I have been here six months without the slightest amusement. Now you arrive, and I would have enjoyed your company enormously—but I expect to be leaving the convent at any moment."

"You are going soon?" Milady asked.

"I hope so," said the novice, with an expression of joy that she made no effort to conceal.

"I think I heard you had suffered from the cardinal's persecutions," Milady continued. "That would have been another bond between us."

"Then what I have heard from our good abbess is true? You have also been a victim of that wicked priest?"

"Hush! let us not talk about him like that even here. All my misfortunes arise from my having said something like what you just said in front of a woman I thought my friend. She betrayed me. Are you also the victim of a betrayal?"

"No, of devotion—devotion to a woman I loved, for whom I would have given my life, for whom I would give it still."

"And who has abandoned you?"

"I have been unjust enough to think so, but I have learned otherwise during the last two or three days, for which I thank God. It would have hurt me very much to think she *had* forgotten me. But you, madame, you seem to be free, and if you wished to leave, you would be able to do so."

"Where would I go, without friends, without money, in a part of France where I have never been before?"

"Oh, as to friends, you would have them wherever you went, you look so kind and are so beautiful!"

"That does not prevent," said Milady, softening her smile to angelic sweetness, "my being alone or being persecuted."

"We must trust in heaven. There always comes a moment when the good you have done pleads your cause before God. Perhaps it will be for your good that you have met with me, humble and powerless as I am, for if I leave this place—well, I have powerful friends, who, after having helped me, may also help you."

"Oh, when I said I was alone," said Milady, hoping to make the novice talk by talking of herself first, "it is not that I lack friends in high places, but that those friends themselves tremble before the cardinal. The queen herself does not dare to oppose him. Notwithstanding her excellent heart, her Majesty has more than once had to abandon to the anger of his Eminence people who had served her well."

"Believe me, madame, the queen may seem to have abandoned those persons, but we must not put faith in appearances. The more they are persecuted, the more she thinks about them, and often, when they least expect it, they have proofs of that kind remembrance."

"I believe it. The queen is so good!"

"You must know that lovely and noble queen to be able to speak of her like that!" the novice exclaimed enthusiastically.

"That is," replied Milady, retreating cautiously, "I do not have the honor of knowing her personally, but I know many of her most intimate friends. I am acquainted with Monsieur de Putange, I met Monsieur Dujart in England, I know Monsieur de Tréville . . ."

"Monsieur de Tréville! You know Monsieur de Tréville?"

"Yes, indeed, quite well."

"The captain of the king's Musketeers?"

"The captain of the king's Musketeers."

"Why, you will see that we will soon be well acquainted, almost friends! If you know Monsieur de Tréville, you must have visited him?"

"Often," said Milady, who saw the success of this particular lie and determined to follow it through to the end.

"Then you must have seen some of his Musketeers with him?"

"All those he is in the habit of receiving," replied Milady, for whom this conversation was beginning to be quite interesting.

"Name a few of those you know, and we will see if they are my friends too."

"Well," said Milady, in a bit of a quandary, "I know Monsieur de Louvigny, Monsieur de Courtivron, Monsieur de Férussac . . ."

The novice let her speak, then seeing that she paused, she asked, "Do you know a gentleman named Athos?"

Milady became as white as the sheets in which she was lying, and despite her self-control, she could not help uttering a cry, seizing the novice's hand, and staring at her intently.

"What is the matter?" asked the poor woman. "Have I said anything that has offended you?"

"No, but the name struck me, because I once knew that gentleman, and it seemed strange to meet someone else who appears to know him well."

"Oh, yes, very well, and not only him, but some of his friends—Messieurs Porthos and Aramis!"

"Indeed! You know them too?" Milady said, a chill penetrating her heart.

"Well, if you know them, you know they are good and brave companions. Why do you not ask them, if you need help?"

"That is . . ." stammered Milady, "I do not really know any of them very well. I know them from having heard one of their friends, Monsieur d'Artagnan, say a great deal about them."

"You know Monsieur d'Artagnan!" cried the novice, in her turn seizing Milady's hands and staring at her intently.

Then, seeing Milady's strange expression, she said, "Excuse me, madame, but you know him as what?"

"Why, as a friend," replied Milady, embarrassed.

"You deceive me, madame—you have been his mistress!"

"It is *you* who have been his mistress, madame!" Milady retorted.

"I?"

"Yes, you! I know you now. You are Madame Bonacieux!"

The young woman drew back, surprised and terrified.

"Oh, do not deny it!" Milady continued.

"Well, yes, madame, it is true. Are we rivals?"

Milady's face was illumined by so savage a joy that under any other circumstances Mme. Bonacieux would have fled in alarm, but she was totally given over to her jealousy.

"Tell me, madame," resumed Mme. Bonacieux, with an energy of which she might not have been believed capable, "have you been, or are you, his mistress?"

"Oh, no!" Milady replied, so firmly that it was impossible to doubt her truthfulness. "Never!"

"I believe you," said Mme. Bonacieux. "But then, why did you cry out so?"

"Do you not understand?" said Milady, who had already overcome her agitation and recovered all her presence of mind.

"How can I understand? I do not know anything about any of this."

"Can you not understand that Monsieur d'Artagnan, being my friend, might take me into his confidence?"

"Truly?"

"Do you not understand that I know everything—your abduction from the little house at St. Germain, his despair, that of his friends, their useless inquiries up to this moment? How could I help being astonished when, without at all expecting it, I meet you face to face—you, of whom we have so often spoken, you whom he loves with all his soul, you whom he had taught me to love before I had ever seen you! My dear Constance, I have found you, and I see you at last!"

Milady held out her arms to Mme. Bonacieux, who was so convinced by what she had just heard that she now saw nothing in this woman—whom an instant before she had believed her rival—but a sincere and devoted friend.

"Oh, pardon me," she cried, laying her head on Milady's shoulder. "Pardon me, but I love him so much!"

The two women held each other for an instant in a close embrace. If Milady's strength had been equal to her hatred, Mme. Bonacieux would surely never have left that embrace alive. But not being able to choke her, she smiled at her.

"Oh, you beautiful, good little creature!" she said. "How delighted I am to have found you! Let me look at you!" Her eyes devoured Mme. Bonacieux. "Oh, yes, it is you! From what he has told me, I recognize you perfectly."

The poor young woman could not possibly suspect what frightful cruelty was hidden behind that pure forehead, behind those brilliant eyes in which she could see nothing but interest and compassion.

"Then you know what I have suffered," she said, "since he has told you what he has suffered. But to suffer for him is happiness."

Milady replied mechanically, "Yes, that is happiness." She was thinking about something else.

"And besides," Mme. Bonacieux continued, "my punishment is about to end. Tomorrow, perhaps this evening, I will see him again, and then the past will no longer exist."

"This evening?" Milady was roused from her reverie by those words. "What do you mean? Are you expecting some news about him?"

"I am expecting him himself."

"Himself? D'Artagnan here?"

"Himself!"

"But that is impossible! He is at the siege of La Rochelle with the cardinal. He will not return till after the city has been taken."

"Nothing is impossible for my d'Artagnan, that noble and loyal gentleman!"

"Oh, I cannot believe you!"

"Read this, then!" the unfortunate young woman said as in an excess of pride and joy she presented a letter to Milady.

"Madame de Chevreuse's handwriting," said Milady to herself. "I always thought there was some secret understanding in that quarter!" And she avidly read the following lines:

My dear Child,

Be ready. *Our friend* will see you soon, and he will see you only to release you from that prison in which your safety required you to be concealed. Prepare for your departure, and never lose faith in us.

Our charming Gascon has just proved himself as brave and faithful as ever. Tell him that certain parties are grateful for his warning.

"Yes," said Milady, "the letter is very precise. Do you know what that was?"

"No, but I suspect he must have warned the queen against some fresh machinations of the cardinal."

"Yes, that must be it," said Milady, returning the letter to Mme. Bonacieux and letting her head drop pensively.

At that moment they heard the sound of a galloping horse.

"Can it be he?" cried Mme. Bonacieux, darting to the window.

Milady remained in bed, petrified by surprise; so many unexpected things were happening all at once that for the first time she was at a loss as to what to do.

"Can it really be he?" she murmured.

And she remained in bed, staring into space.

"Unfortunately not," said Mme. Bonacieux. "It is a man I do not know, although he seems to be coming here. Yes, he is slowing down . . . he is stopping at the gate . . . he is ringing the bell . . ."

Milady sprang out of bed.

"You are sure it is not he?" she asked.

"Yes, very sure!"

"Perhaps you could not see him clearly."

"If I were to see only the plume of his hat or the edge of his cloak, I would know *him!*"

Milady was dressing herself as they spoke.

"Never mind! The man is coming here?"

"Yes, he has gone inside."

"It is either for you or for me!"

"My God, you seem so disturbed!"

"Yes, I admit it. I am not as confident as you. I fear everything the cardinal may do."

"Hush!" said Mme. Bonacieux. "Somebody is coming."

The door opened, and the superior came in.

"Did you come from Boulogne?" she asked Milady.

"Yes," Milady replied, trying to recover her self-possession. "Who wants me?"

"A man who will not give his name but who comes from the cardinal."

"And who wishes to speak to me?" asked Milady.

"Who wishes to speak to a lady who has recently come from Boulogne."

"Then let him please come in."

"Do you think it will be bad news?" Mme. Bonacieux asked.

"I am afraid so."

"I will leave you with this stranger, but as soon as he is gone, if you will allow me, I will return."

"*Allow* you? I *beg* you!"

The superior and Mme. Bonacieux both left.

Milady remained alone, her eyes fixed on the door. An instant later, she heard the jingling of spurs on the stairs; the footsteps drew near, the door opened, and a man appeared.

Milady uttered a cry of joy; it was the Comte de Rochefort—the diabolical tool of his Eminence.

62

Two Kinds of Fiend

"It is you!" cried Milady and Rochefort together.

"Yes, it is I."

"From where do you come?" asked Milady.

"From La Rochelle. And you?"

"From England."

"Buckingham?"

"Dead or seriously wounded, as I left without having been able to get what I wanted from him—but some fanatic had just assassinated him."

"What good luck," said Rochefort, with a smile. "It will delight his Eminence! Have you informed him of it?"

"I wrote to him from Boulogne. But what brings you here?"

"His Eminence was uneasy and sent me to find you."

"I only arrived yesterday."

"And what have you been doing since yesterday?"

"I have not wasted my time."

"Oh, I don't doubt that."

"Do you know whom I have met here?"

"No."

"Guess."

"How can I?"

"That young woman the queen took out of prison."

"The mistress of that fellow d'Artagnan?"

"Yes, Madame Bonacieux, whose hiding place the cardinal could not discover."

"Well, well," said Rochefort, "here is another lucky chance. Monsieur le Cardinal is certainly favored by fortune."

"Imagine my astonishment," continued Milady, "when I found myself face to face with her!"

"Does she know you?"

"No."

"Then she thinks of you as a stranger?"

Milady smiled.

"I am her best friend."

"Only you, my dear countess, can perform such miracles!" said Rochefort.

"And it is well that I can, for do you know what I have learned from her?"

"No."

"They will come for her tomorrow or the day after, with an order from the queen."

"Indeed! And who are 'they'?"

"D'Artagnan and his friends."

"They will go so far that we will be obliged to send them to the Bastille."

"Why has that not been done already?"

"I do not know—the cardinal has a weakness for those men that I cannot understand."

"Truly?"

"Yes."

"Well, then, tell him this, Rochefort. Tell him that our conversation at the Colombier-Rouge inn was overheard by those four men. Tell him that after his departure one of them came up to me and took from me by violence the letter he had given me. Tell him that they warned Lord de Winter of my journey to England, and that they nearly foiled this mission as they had foiled the affair of the diamond studs. And tell him that among those four men two only are to be feared—d'Artagnan and Athos—and that the third, Aramis, is Madame de Chevreuse's lover—is who should be left alone because we know his secret, and it may be useful. As to the fourth, Porthos, he is a fool, a simpleton, a blustering booby, not worth troubling about."

"But those four men should be at the siege of La Rochelle."

"I thought so, too, but a letter Madame Bonacieux has received from Madame de Chevreuse, and which she was imprudent enough to show me, leads me to believe that they are, on the contrary, coming here to take her away."

"The devil! What shall we do?"

"What did the cardinal say about me?"

"I was to take your messages, written or verbal, and return immediately. When he knows what you have done, he will tell you what you have to do."

"I must remain here?"

"Here, or in the neighborhood,"

"You cannot take me with you?"

"No, my orders are definite. You might be recognized near the camp, and your presence would compromise the cardinal, especially after what has happened in England."

"Then I must wait here, or in the area?"

"Just tell me where you will be waiting for word from the cardinal. I must always know where to find you."

"I may not be able to remain here."

"Why?"

"You forget that my enemies may arrive at any time."

"That's true—but does that mean this little woman will escape his Eminence?"

"You forget that I am her best friend," said Milady, with a smile that was special to her.

"Of course! Then I may tell the cardinal, with respect to this little woman . . ."

"That he need not worry."

"Is that all?"

"He will know what that means."

"He will guess, at least. Now, what should I do?"

"Return immediately. I think my news is worth a little diligence."

"My chaise broke down coming into Lillers."

"Excellent."

"What, *excellent*?"

"Yes, because I need your chaise."

"And how will I travel?"

"On horseback."

"That is easy for you to say—a hundred and eighty leagues!"

"What is that?"

"All right, I can do it! And then?"

"Then? Why, when you pass through Lillers you will send me your chaise and order your servant to place himself at my disposal."

"Very well."

"You must have some order from the cardinal with you?"

"I have one giving me *full power*."

"Show it to the abbess, and tell her that someone will come for me either today or tomorrow, and that I am to go with the person who presents himself in your name."

"Very well."

"And do not forget to speak harshly of me to the abbess."

"Why?"

"Because I am supposed to be the cardinal's victim. That is necessary to inspire confidence in poor little Madame Bonacieux."

"Of course. Now will you write a report of everything that has happened?"

"But I have already told you everything. You have a good memory—just repeat what I have said. A piece of paper may be lost."

"You're right. Now let me know where to find you so I do not have to search all over for you."

"Let me think . . ."

"Do you want a map?"

"Oh, no, I know this country quite well!"

"You do? When were you here?"

"I was brought up here."

"Really?"

"Yes. It is useful, you see, to have been brought up somewhere."

"Then you will wait for me at . . . ?"

"At . . . yes, that will do—at Armentières."

"Where is Armentières?"

"It is a little town on the Lys. I will only have to cross the river, and I will be in a foreign country."

"Very good! But you will be sure to cross the river only if you are in danger. Understood?"

"Quite well understood."

"And if you do, how will I know where you are?"

"Do you need your lackey?"

"No."

"Is he reliable?"

"Absolutely."

"Give him to me. Nobody knows him. If I cross the river, I will leave him there, and he will lead you to me."

"But you say you will wait for me at Armentières?"

"At Armentières."

"Write that name on a bit of paper in case I should forget it. There is nothing compromising in the name of a town, is there?"

"Who knows? But never mind," said Milady, writing the name on half a sheet of paper, "I will risk it."

"Don't worry," said Rochefort, taking the paper from Milady, folding it, and putting it in the lining of his hat. "I will do what children do—repeat the name as I travel, so I will know it even if I lose the paper. Now, is that all?"

"I think so."

"Let us make sure. Buckingham dead or seriously wounded. Your conversation with the cardinal overheard by the four Musketeers. Lord de Winter warned of your arrival at Portsmouth. D'Artagnan and Athos to the Bastille. Aramis the lover of Madame de Chevreuse. Porthos an ass. Madame Bonacieux found again. Send you the chaise as soon as possible. Put my lackey at your disposal. Make you out a victim of the cardinal so that the abbess will not be suspicious. Armentières, on the banks of the Lys. Is that it?"

"In truth, my dear Rochefort, you are a miracle of memory. Oh—one more thing . . ."

"What?"

"I saw some very pretty woods adjoining the convent garden. Tell the abbess that I am allowed to walk to those woods. Who knows—I may need a back door for a retreat."

"You think of everything."

"And you forget one thing."

"What?"

"To ask me if I need money."

"True. How much do you want?"

"All you have in gold."

"I have about five hundred pistoles."

"And I have about as much. With a thousand pistoles one can face everything. Empty your pockets."

"There."

"Good. And you leave . . . ?"

"In an hour—during which time I will send for a post horse and have something to eat."

"Very good. Adieu, Rochefort."

"Adieu, Countess."

"Give my best to the cardinal."

"Give mine to Satan."

Milady and Rockefort exchanged a smile and separated.

An hour later Rochefort set out at a gallop; five hours after that he passed through Arras.

We already know how d'Artagnan recognized him and how that recognition so alarmed the four Musketeers as to give fresh impetus to their journey.

63

The Drop of Water

ROCHEFORT HAD HARDLY gone before Mme. Bonacieux returned. She found Milady smiling.

"Well," said the young woman, "what you feared has happened. The cardinal will send someone for you tonight or tomorrow."

"Who told you that, my dear?" asked Milady.

"I heard it from the mouth of the messenger himself."

"Come here and sit down next to me," said Milady.

"Here I am."

"Wait till I make sure no one is listening to us."

"Why such precautions?"

"I will tell you."

Milady arose, went to the door, opened it, looked in the corridor, then returned and seated herself close to Mme. Bonacieux.

"He has played his part well," she said.

"Who has?"

"The man who just presented himself to the abbess as a messenger from the cardinal."

"He was playing a part?"

"Yes, my child."

"That man was not . . ."

"That man," said Milady, lowering her voice, "is my brother."

"Your brother!" exclaimed Mme. Bonacieux.

"No one but you must know this secret. If you reveal it to anyone in the world, I will be lost, and perhaps you will be too."

"Oh, my God!"

"Listen. This is what happened. My brother, who was coming to my assistance to take me away, by force if necessary, met the cardinal's messenger, who was also coming for me. He followed him. On an isolated part of the road he drew his sword and ordered the messenger

586

to give him the papers he was carrying. The messenger resisted, and my brother killed him."

"Oh!" said Mme. Bonacieux, shuddering.

"You must realize that it was the only thing he could do. Then my brother decided to substitute cunning for force. He took the papers and presented himself here as the cardinal's messenger, and in an hour or two a carriage will come to take me away by the orders of his Eminence."

"I understand. It is really your brother who will send this carriage."

"Exactly. But that is not all. That letter you received, and which you believe to be from Madame de Chevreuse . . ."

"Well?"

"It is a forgery."

"How can that be?"

"It is a trap, designed to keep you from making any resistance when they come to fetch you."

"But it is d'Artagnan who will come."

"Do not be deceived. D'Artagnan and his friends are still at the siege of La Rochelle."

"How do you know that?"

"My brother met some of the cardinal's emissaries dressed in the uniform of the Musketeers. You would have been summoned to the gate, you would have thought you were to meet your friends, you would have been abducted and taken back to Paris."

"Oh, my God! I feel lost among all these plots and schemes! If this continues," said Mme. Bonacieux, putting her hands on her forehead, "I will go mad!"

"Listen . . ."

"What?"

"I hear a horse. It must be my brother setting off again. I would like to say goodbye. Come over here with me."

Milady had gone to the window and opened it, signaling Mme. Bonacieux to join her.

Rochefort passed at a gallop.

"Adieu, brother!" Milady cried out.

Rochefort raised his head, saw the two young women, and without stopping, waved his hand to Milady.

"That good George!" she said, closing the window with an expression full of both affection and melancholy.

She sat down again, as if lost in her private thoughts.

"Dear lady," said Mme. Bonacieux, "forgive me for interrupting you, but what do you advise me to do? You have more experience than I have, so speak and I will listen."

"In the first place," Milady replied, "it is possible I may be wrong and that d'Artagnan and his friends really will come to your assistance."

"Oh, that would be too much to hope for. So much happiness is not for me!"

"If they *are* on the way, it becomes a question of time—a sort of race. If your friends are the first to arrive, you are saved. If the cardinal's men are quicker, you are lost."

"Oh, yes, lost beyond any hope! What shall I do?"

"There would be one very simple way . . ."

"What!"

"To hide somewhere in the neighborhood and make sure which men are asking for you."

"But where can I wait?"

"Oh, there is no difficulty about that. I am going to stop and hide a few leagues from here until my brother can rejoin me. I can take you with me, and we can hide and wait together."

"But I will not be allowed to leave—I am almost a prisoner here."

"Since they will believe that I am leaving by order of the cardinal, no one will think you could be eager to follow me."

"Well?"

"Well, when the carriage is at the door, you will stand on the step to give me a farewell embrace. My brother's servant, who comes to fetch me, will have been told what to do. When he sees you there, he will signal to the postillion, and we gallop away."

"But d'Artagnan—if he comes later?"

"We will know about it."

"How?"

"Nothing easier. We will send my brother's servant back to Béthune—I told you that we can trust him—and he will disguise himself and take a room opposite the convent. If the cardinal's men come, he will do nothing, but if it is Monsieur d'Artagnan and his friends, he will bring them to us."

"Does he know them?"

"Certainly. Has he not seen Monsieur d'Artagnan at my house?"

"Oh, yes, you are right. It may go well—it may be for the best. But let us not go very far from here."

"Seven or eight leagues at most. Then we will be on the frontier, and at the first sign of danger we can leave France."

"What do we do now?"

"Wait."

"But if they come?"

"My brother's carriage will be here first."

"Suppose I am not with you when the carriage comes? I might be at dinner, for instance."

"Do just one thing."

"What?"

"Tell the good superior that we would like to be together as much as possible and ask her permission to eat with me."

"Will she permit it?"

"Why should she not?"

"Wonderful. That way we will not be separated even for an instant."

"Well, go down to her now and ask her. Meanwhile, since I have a headache, I will take a turn in the garden."

"Where will I find you?"

"Here, in an hour."

"Here, in an hour. Oh, you are so kind, and I am so grateful!"

"How can I not want to help you? Even if you were not so beautiful and so charming, are you not the beloved of one of my best friends?"

"Dear d'Artagnan! Oh, how he will thank you!"

"I hope so. Now since everything is settled, let us go down."

"You are going into the garden?"

"Yes."

"Go along this corridor, down a little staircase, and you are there."

"Very good! Thank you."

And the two women parted, exchanging charming smiles.

Milady had told the truth—she *did* have a headache. All her quickly improvised plans were swirling around chaotically, and she needed to be alone, in a quiet place, to put them into order, to give those confused ideas a distinct form and to make of them a definite plan.

What was most urgent was to get Mme. Bonacieux away and put her in a safe place where she could be made a hostage if necessary. Milady was beginning to have doubts about the outcome of this terrible duel, in which her enemies were proving as persistent as she was relentless.

Besides, she felt as if she were in the eye of a storm— that the climax was near and could not fail to be terrible.

The most important thing for her was, as we have said, to keep Mme. Bonacieux in her power. That woman was d'Artagnan's very life. If things went wrong, the life of the woman he loved—which was more important to him than his own life—was a means to negotiate good terms for herself.

Well, that point was settled; the unsuspecting Mme. Bonacieux would leave with her. Once concealed with her at Armentières, it would be easy to make her believe that d'Artagnan had not come to Béthune. In two weeks at most, Rochefort would be back—and besides, during those two weeks she would have time to think about how she could best avenge herself on the four friends. She would not be bored because she would be enjoying the sweetest of pastimes for a woman of her nature: plotting a stunning revenge.

Revolving all this in her mind, she looked around her and memorized the layout of the garden. Like a good general, she was considering at the same time both victory and defeat, and preparing to march forward or to beat a retreat according to the outcome of the battle.

At the end of an hour she heard Mme. Bonacieux's soft voice calling her; the good abbess had naturally consented to her request, and they were to have dinner together.

As they reached the courtyard, they heard the sound of a carriage stopping at the gate.

"Did you hear that?" Milady asked.

"Yes, it is a carriage."

"It is the one sent by my brother."

"Oh, my God!"

"Courage!"

The bell at the convent gate rang; Milady had not been mistaken.

"Go up to your room," she said to Mme. Bonacieux. "You must have some jewels you would like to take."

"I have his letters."

"Well, get them, then come to my room. We will have some dinner because we may have to travel part of the night and must keep our strength up."

"My God," said Mme. Bonacieux, putting her hand on her bosom, "my heart is beating so hard I cannot walk!"

"Courage, courage! Remember that in a quarter of an hour you will be safe, and think that what you are about to do is for *his* sake."

"Oh, yes, everything for his sake. You have restored my courage by saying that! Go, I will join you."

Milady quickly ran up to her room, where she found Rochefort's lackey and gave him his instructions.

He was to wait at the gate; if by chance the Musketeers should appear, the carriage was to set off as quickly as possible, go around the convent, and wait for her at a little village on the other side of the woods. She would go through the garden and reach the village on foot. As we have said, she knew this part of France thoroughly.

If the Musketeers did not appear, things would proceed as planned: Mme. Bonacieux would get into the carriage as if to say goodbye, and they would leave together.

Mme. Bonacieux came in, and to remove any suspicion she might have, Milady repeated to the lackey the last part of her instructions.

Milady then asked some questions about the carriage and learned that it was a chaise drawn by three horses and driven by a postillion; Rochefort's lackey would precede it, as outrider.

Milady was wrong to fear that Mme. Bonacieux would have any suspicions: she was too pure to suppose that any woman could possibly be guilty of such treachery. Besides, the name of Lady de Winter, which she had heard the abbess pronounce, was completely unknown to her, and she was even unaware that a woman had played so great and so fatal a part in her misfortunes.

"You see," Milady said when the lackey had gone out, "everything is ready. The abbess suspects nothing and believes that I am being taken away by order of the cardinal. The servant is giving his last orders, so eat something, drink a little wine, and let us go."

"Yes," Mme. Bonacieux said, echoing her, "yes, let us go."

Milady motioned her to sit down opposite, poured her a small glass of Spanish wine, and served her some chicken.

"See how everything is working for us!" she said. "Night is coming on, and by daybreak we will have reached our hiding place—nobody will know where we are. Come, eat something."

Mme. Bonacieux ate a few mouthfuls mechanically and just touched the glass with her lips.

"Look," said Milady, lifting hers to her mouth, "do as I do."

But just as the glass was about to touch her lips, she stopped: she had heard something that sounded like distant hoofbeats, and as they drew nearer, it seemed to her that she could also hear the neighing of horses.

This noise acted on her joy like the storm that awakens the sleeper from a happy dream; she turned ashen and ran to the window, while Mme. Bonacieux stood up, trembling, and leaned on her chair to avoid falling.

Milady could not yet see anything, but they could hear the galloping horses approach.

"What is that noise?" asked Mme. Bonacieux.

"Either our friends or our enemies," Milady replied with her terrible coolness. "Stay where you are. I will tell you."

Mme. Bonacieux remained standing, mute, motionless, white as a statue.

The noise became louder. The horses could not be more than a hundred and fifty paces away—the only reason they could not be seen was because of a bend in the road—and their sound was so distinct that it was possible to count the horses by the clatter of their hoofs.

Milady stared at the road intently, hoping it would remain light enough for her to see who was coming.

Suddenly, at the turn of the road she saw the motion of plumed hats waving in the breeze; she counted two, then five, then eight horsemen. One of them preceded the others by two lengths.

Milady stifled a groan: she recognized d'Artagnan as the first horseman.

"Oh, my God," cried Mme. Bonacieux, "who are they?"

"They wear the uniform of the cardinal's Guards. There is not a second to lose—run!"

"Yes, let us run!" repeated Mme. Bonacieux, though she was unable to take a step, glued as she was to the spot by terror.

They heard the horsemen passing under the windows.

"Come!" cried Milady, trying to lead the young woman by the arm. "Thanks to the garden, we can still escape. I have the key, but we must hurry—in five minutes it will be too late!"

Mme. Bonacieux tried to walk, took two steps, and fell to her knees. Milady tried to pick her up and carry her, but could not do it.

Then they heard the carriage move—it was driving off at the approach of the Musketeers. Three or four shots were fired.

"For the last time, will you come?" cried Milady.

"Oh, my God, you see that I am too weak, that I cannot walk. Go without me!"

"Without you? Leave you here? Never!"

Her eyes flashed; she ran to the table and quickly emptied into Mme. Bonacieux's glass the contents of a ring she was wearing. The reddish grain dissolved immediately.

Holding the glass firmly, she told Mme. Bonacieux, "Drink this—it will give you strength. Drink it!"

She put the glass to the young woman's lips.

Mme. Bonacieux drank mechanically.

"This is not the way I wished to avenge myself," Milady thought, replacing the glass on the table with a diabolical smile, "but, my faith, one does what one can!"

And she rushed out of the room.

Mme. Bonacieux saw her leave without being able to follow her; it was as if she were dreaming she was pursued, but could not run away from the danger quickly enough.

A few moments passed, and there were loud shouts at

the gate. At every instant Mme. Bonacieux expected to see Milady return, but she did not. Several times a cold sweat, which she attributed to her panic, broke out on her feverish forehead.

At length she heard the creaking hinges of the opening gates, then the sound of boots and spurs on the stairs and a murmur of approaching voices, amid which she seemed to hear her own name called.

All at at once she cried out with joy and rushed to the door; she had recognized d'Artagnan's voice.

"D'Artagnan, is it you? This way! This way!"

"Constance? Constance?" the young man called out. "Where are you?"

The door was forced open and several men rushed into the room. Mme. Bonacieux had sunk into an armchair and was unable to move. D'Artagnan threw down the still-smoking pistol he was holding and fell to his knees before his mistress. Athos replaced his in his belt, and Porthos and Aramis, who were holding their drawn swords, returned them to their scabbards.

"Oh, d'Artagnan, my beloved d'Artagnan! You have come at last! You have not deceived me! It is really you!"

"Yes, Constance, we are reunited!"

"Oh, how she tried to persuade me you would not come, but I kept on hoping! I did not want to run away with her, and I was right! How happy I am!"

At the word *she,* Athos, who had sat down quietly, sprang up.

"*She!* What she?" asked d'Artagnan.

"Why, my companion. She who out of friendship for me wished to save me from my persecutors. She who, mistaking you for the cardinal's Guards, has just run away."

"Your companion," said d'Artagnan, turning paler than his mistress's white veil. "What companion, dear Constance?"

"The woman whose carriage was at the gate. The woman who calls herself your friend. The woman to whom you have told everything."

"But what is her name? My God, can you not remember her name?"

"I heard it once, but . . . wait . . . it is very strange . . . oh, my God, my head is swimming . . . I cannot see!"

"Help me, my friends! Her hands are icy cold," cried d'Artagnan. "She is ill! She is fainting!"

While Porthos called for help with all the power of his strong voice, Aramis ran to the table to get a glass of water, but he stopped when he saw the horrible change that had come over Athos, who was standing in front of the table, his hair bristling with horror, and staring at one of the glasses.

"Oh, no, it is impossible! God would not permit such a crime!" he said.

"Water, water!" d'Artagnan shouted.

"Oh, poor woman, poor woman," Athos murmured in a broken voice.

Mme. Bonacieux opened her eyes as d'Artagnan kissed her over and over.

"She is reviving," he said. "Oh, my God, thank you!"

"Madame, in the name of heaven, whose empty glass is this?" Athos asked.

"Mine, monsieur," the young woman replied in a dying voice.

"But who poured the wine that was in this glass?"

"She."

"But who is *she?*"

"Oh, I remember now!" said Mme. Bonacieux. "Lady de Winter."

The four friends all cried out at once, but Athos's voice dominated all the rest.

Just then Mme. Bonacieux's face turned livid; her whole body shook with painful spasms, and she crumpled, panting, into the arms of Porthos and Aramis.

D'Artagnan clasped Athos's hands with indescribable anguish.

"Do you think . . . ?"

His voice was stifled by sobs.

"I do," said Athos, biting his lips till they bled.

"D'Artagnan! D'Artagnan!" cried Mme. Bonacieux. "Where are you? Do not leave me . . . I am dying!"

D'Artagnan released Athos's hands and rushed over to her.

Her beautiful face was distorted with agony, her eyes were glassy, her whole body was shuddering convulsively, and sweat was rolling down her forehead.

"In the name of heaven, run for help! Aramis! Porthos! Call for help!"

"It is useless," said Athos. "For her poison there is no antidote."

"Yes, help, help," murmured Mme. Bonacieux.

Gathering all her strength, she took d'Artagnan's head between her hands, looked at him for an instant as if her whole soul were passing into that gaze, and with a muffled cry pressed her lips to his.

"Constance! Constance!"

She sighed, and the breath of that sigh caressed d'Artagnan's lips. That sigh was her soul, so chaste and so loving, rising to heaven.

D'Artagnan held only a corpse in his arms. He groaned, and collapsed by the side of his mistress, as pale and icy as herself.

Porthos wept; Aramis shook his fist toward heaven; Athos made the sign of the cross.

At that moment a man appeared in the doorway, almost as pale as those in the room. He looked around him and saw Mme. Bonacieux dead and d'Artagnan in a faint. He had come just at that moment of stupor which follows a great catastrophe.

"I was not mistaken," he said. "Here is Monsieur d'Artagnan, and you are his friends, Messieurs Athos, Porthos, and Aramis."

The persons whose names were thus pronounced looked at the stranger with astonishment.

"Gentlemen," the newcomer continued, "you are, as I am, in search of a woman—a woman who," he added, with a terrible smile, "must have passed this way, for I see a corpse."

The three friends remained silent. Although his voice as well as his face reminded them of someone, they could not remember when or where they might have met him.

"Since you do not recognize a man who probably owes his life to you twice, I must introduce myself. I am Lord de Winter, brother-in-law of *that woman*."

The three friends uttered a cry of surprise.

Athos rose, and offered him his hand. "Be welcome, my Lord," he said, "you are one of us."

"I left Portsmouth five hours after she did," said Lord de Winter. "I arrived in Boulogne three hours after she did. I missed her by twenty minutes at Saint-Omer. Finally, I lost all trace of her at Lillers. I was going about at random, asking everybody for information, when I saw you gallop past. I recognized Monsieur d'Artagnan. I called out to you, but you did not answer me. I wanted to follow you, but my horse was too tired to go at the same pace as yours. And yet, despite all your efforts, it seems you arrived too late!"

"As you can see," said Athos, pointing to Mme. Bonacieux lying dead, and to d'Artagnan, whom Porthos and Aramis were trying to revive.

"Are they both dead?" Lord de Winter asked sternly.

"No," replied Athos, "fortunately Monsieur d'Artagnan has only fainted."

"Ah, good!" said Lord de Winter.

At that moment d'Artagnan opened his eyes. He flung off Porthos and Aramis, and threw himself like a madman on the corpse of his mistress.

Athos walked slowly and gravely over to his friend and embraced him tenderly. When d'Artagnan burst into wrenching sobs, Athos said to him in his noble and persuasive voice, "My friend, be a man. Women weep for the dead, men avenge them!"

"Oh, yes!" said d'Artagnan. "If it is to avenge her, I am ready to follow you!"

Athos took advantage of this moment of strength that the hope of vengeance restored to his unfortunate friend to signal Porthos and Aramis to fetch the abbess.

The two friends met her in the corridor, greatly troubled and very much upset by all these strange events; she called over some of the nuns, who against all the customs of the convent found themselves in the presence of five men.

"Madame," said Athos, supporting d'Artagnan as they spoke, "we leave to your pious care the body of that unfortunate woman. She was an angel on earth before becoming an angel in heaven. Treat her like one of your sisters. We will return someday to pray at her grave."

D'Artagnan buried his face against Athos's chest and began to sob again.

"Weep," said Athos, "weep, heart full of love, youth, and life! Alas, I wish I could weep like you!"

And he led his friend away, as affectionate as a father,

as comforting as a priest, as understanding as a man who himself has suffered much.

All five, followed by their lackeys leading their horses, began to walk to Béthune; they could already see the outskirts of the town, and they stopped at the first inn they came to.

"But aren't we going to pursue that woman?" asked d'Artagnan.

"Later," replied Athos. "There are things I have to do first."

"She will escape us, and it will be your fault, Athos," said the young man.

"I will be responsible for her," said Athos.

D'Artagnan had so much confidence in his friend's word that he bowed his head and entered the inn without another word.

Porthos and Aramis looked at each other, not understanding Athos's assurance.

Lord de Winter thought he had spoken like that to assuage d'Artagnan's grief.

"Now, gentlemen," Athos said when he had made sure that there was accommodation for all of them at the inn, "let everyone retire to his own room. D'Artagnan needs to be alone, to weep and to sleep. I will take charge of everything, so rest easy."

"But it seems to me," said Lord de Winter, "that if there are any measures to be taken against Milady, it concerns me—she is my sister-in-law."

"And she is my wife!" said Athos.

D'Artagnan started: he understood that Athos must be sure of his vengeance if he revealed such a secret. Porthos and Aramis looked at each other and turned pale. Lord de Winter thought Athos was mad.

"Now go to your rooms," said Athos, "and leave me to do what I must. As her husband this is my responsibility. D'Artagnan, if you have not lost it, give me the paper that fell out of that man's hat, the one that has written on it the name of a village . . ."

"Ah," said d'Artagnan, "I understand! That name written in her handwriting . . ."

"You see," said Athos, "there is indeed a God in heaven!"

64

The Man in the Red Cloak

ATHOS'S DESPAIR had given way to a focused concentration that made the extraordinary brilliance of his mind even more lucid.

Possessed by one single thought—that of the promise he had made and the responsibility he had assumed—he was the last one to go to his room; he had asked the host to get him a map of the province and now bent over it, examined its every line, saw that there were four different roads from Béthune to Armentières, and summoned the lackeys.

Planchet, Grimaud, Bazin, and Mousqueton presented themselves and were given clear, precise, and serious orders.

They were to set out the next morning at daybreak and go to Armentières, each by a different route. Planchet, the most intelligent of the four, was to follow the one taken by the carriage on which the four friends had fired, and which was accompanied by Rochefort's servant.

Athos assigned these tasks to the lackeys not only because he had observed their varied and distinct skills since they had entered his service and that of his friends, but because lackeys who ask questions inspire less mistrust than masters, and meet with more sympathy among those they question. Besides, Milady knew the masters and did not know the lackeys, whereas the lackeys knew Milady perfectly well.

All four of them were to meet the next day at eleven o'clock. If they had discovered Milady's hiding place, three of them would remain on guard while the fourth was to return to Béthune in order to inform Athos and serve as a guide to the four friends.

These arrangements made, the lackeys went to bed.

Athos then arose from his chair, girded his sword, enveloped himself in his cloak, and left the inn. It was nearly ten o'clock, and at ten o'clock in the evening, the streets in provincial towns are nearly deserted; nevertheless Athos was clearly looking for someone of whom he could ask a question. Finally he met a belated passerby, went up to him, and spoke a few words. The man recoiled with horror and answered the Musketeer only by pointing somewhere. Athos offered the man half a pistole to accompany him, but the man refused.

Athos then walked down the street the man had pointed to, but when he arrived at a crossroads, he stopped again, visibly embarrassed. Nevertheless, since the crossroads offered him a better chance than any other place of meeting somebody, he decided to wait there, and in a few minutes a night watchman came by. Athos asked him the same question he had asked the first person he had met; the watchman evinced the same terror, also refused to accompany him, and merely pointed out the road he was to take.

Walking that way, Athos soon reached the outer limits of the town at a point directly opposite to that by which he and his friends had entered it. There he again hesitated, and stopped once more.

Fortunately, a beggar passed and asked for some money; Athos offered him an écu if he would accompany him to his destination. The beggar hesitated, but at the sight of the silver coin gleaming in the darkness he agreed, and walked on ahead of Athos.

When they reached a corner, he pointed to a small, isolated, and dismal-looking house. As Athos went toward it, the beggar, who had received his reward, left as fast as his legs could carry him.

Athos had to go all around the house before he could find the door, which was painted the same red as the rest of the house. No light shone through the chinks of the shutters; no sound gave reason to believe that the house was inhabited; it was as dark and silent as the tomb.

Three times Athos knocked without receiving an answer; finally he heard footsteps approaching, and the door was opened. A tall, pale man with black hair and beard appeared.

After he and Athos exchanged some words in a low voice, the tall man motioned the Musketeer to come in. Athos did so immediately, and the door was closed behind him.

The man whom Athos had come so far to seek, and whom he had found with so much trouble, brought him into his laboratory, where he was in the process of fastening together with iron wire the clacking bones of a skeleton. The frame was already connected, except for the head, which still lay on the table.

All the rest of the furniture indicated that the man who lived there occupied himself with the study of natural science. Large bottles were filled with serpents and labeled according to their species; dried lizards shone like emeralds set in great squares of black wood, and bunches of wild aromatic herbs, doubtless possessed of virtues unknown to ordinary men, hung from the ceiling in every corner of the room.

There was no family, no servant; the tall man lived there alone.

Athos looked around indifferently, then, at the invitation of the man he had come to see, sat down and explained the reason for his visit and what he wanted him to do.

Almost before he had finished, the tall man, who remained standing in front of the Musketeer, drew back in alarm and refused. Then Athos showed him a small piece of paper with two lines of writing, accompanied by a signature and a seal, which he had taken from his pocket. The man had shown his repugnance prematurely, because as soon as he had read those lines, seen the signature, and recognized the seal, he bowed to indicate that he no longer had any objection and was ready to obey.

Athos asked nothing more of him. He stood up, bowed, went out, returned the same way he had come, reentered the inn, and went to his room.

At daybreak d'Artagnan entered, and asked him what he should do.

"Wait," Athos replied.

A few minutes later, the superior of the convent sent a message informing the Musketeers that the funeral would take place at noon. As to the prisoner, they had heard no news of her; she must have made her escape through the garden, because her footprints were there and the door had been found shut. The key had disappeared.

At noon, Lord de Winter and the four friends returned to the convent: the bells were ringing, the chapel was open, the gate of the chancel was closed. In the middle of the chancel was the body of the victim, wearing the clothes of her novitiate. On each side of the chancel and behind the gates opening into the convent the whole community of the Carmelites was assembled; they listened to the divine service and mingled their chant with the chant of the priests without seeing the secular or being seen by them.

At the chapel door, d'Artagnan felt his courage fail him and looked around for Athos, but Athos had disappeared.

Faithful to his mission of vengeance, he had asked to be taken to the garden; once there, following the light footsteps of this woman who had left a trail of blood, he walked to the gate that led into the woods, had it opened for him, and went out into the forest.

All his suspicions were confirmed: the road the carriage had taken encircled the forest. He followed it for some time, his eyes fixed on the ground; slight bloodstains, which came from the wound inflicted either on the man who accompanied the carriage as an outrider or on one of the horses, dotted the road. After he had walked about three-quarters of a league, when he was within fifty paces of the village of Festubert, he saw a larger bloodstain where the ground had been trampled by horses. Between the forest and this incriminating spot on the road, a little behind where the ground had been trampled by the halted horses, was the same track of small footprints as in the garden; the carriage had stopped there.

That was where Milady had come out of the woods and gotten into the carriage.

Satisfied with this discovery that confirmed all his suspicions, he returned to the inn, and found Planchet impatiently waiting for him.

Everything was as Athos had foreseen.

Planchet had followed the road and, like Athos, discovered the bloodstains; like Athos again, he had noted the spot where the horses had halted. But he had gone farther than Athos, so that while drinking at an inn in Festubert, he had learned without having to ask any questions that the evening before, at half-past eight, a wounded man accompanying a lady traveling in a post-chaise had been obliged to stop, unable to go any farther. The wound was attributed to robbers who had stopped the chaise in the woods. The man had remained in the village, but the woman had ordered fresh horses and continued her journey.

Planchet had then searched for the postillion who had driven her; he found him and learned that he had taken the lady as far as Fromelles, from where she had set out for Armentières. Planchet took a shortcut, and by seven o'clock in the morning he was at Armentières.

There was but one inn, the Hôtel de la Poste. Planchet presented himself there as a lackey who was looking for a position. He had not chatted ten minutes with the people of the inn before he learned that a woman had come there alone about eleven o'clock the night before, taken a room, sent for the innkeeper, and told him she planned to stay in the area for some time.

Planchet had learned all he had to know. He hurried to the rendezvous, found the lackeys at their posts, posted them as sentries at all the exits of the inn, and returned to Athos, who had just received this information when his three friends came in.

They were all melancholy and grim, even the usually mild and gentle Aramis.

"What are we going to do?" asked d'Artagnan.

"Wait!" replied Athos.

Each went back to his own room.

At eight o'clock in the evening Athos ordered the horses to be saddled, and had Lord de Winter and his friends notified that they must prepare to leave.

In an instant all five were ready. Each examined his weapons and made sure they were in order. When Athos came down, he found d'Artagnan already mounted, and growing restless.

"Be patient," said Athos. "One of our party is still missing."

The four horsemen looked around them with astonishment, unable to imagine who that other person could be.

At that moment Planchet brought out Athos's horse, and the Musketeer leaped lightly into the saddle.

"Wait for me," he said. "I will be back soon."

And he galloped away.

In a quarter of an hour he returned, accompanied by a tall masked man wrapped in a large red cloak.

Lord de Winter and the three other Musketeers looked at one another inquiringly. None of them could give the others any information about who the man might be, but they were all convinced that everything was in order since Athos had arranged it so.

At nine o'clock, guided by Planchet, the little cavalcade set out, taking the route the carriage had taken.

It was a melancholy sight, those six silent men, each absorbed in his own thoughts, looking as mournful as despair, as grim as punishment.

65

The Trial

IT WAS A STORMY and dark night; the stars were hidden under heavy clouds, and the moon would not rise till midnight.

Occasionally, a flash of lightning would illuminate the white and empty road before them; then, the flash extinct, all would return to darkness.

Athos kept having to ask d'Artagnan not to ride so far in advance of the rest; he would comply, then after a moment or two again pull ahead. He had only one thought—to go forward; and he went.

They silently rode through the little village of Festubert, where the wounded servant was, then skirted the Richebourg woods. At Herlies, Planchet, who was still leading the column, turned to the left.

Several times Lord de Winter, Porthos, or Aramis had tried to talk with the man in the red cloak; but to every question he had merely bowed silently. They had finally understood that there must be some reason for him to maintain such a silence and stopped speaking to him.

The storm was growing worse: the flashes of lightning succeeded one another more rapidly; they could hear the thunder roar, and the wind, the precursor of a storm, blew across the plain, ruffling the plumes and the hair of the horsemen.

The cavalcade trotted more briskly.

A little beyond Fromelles the storm broke. They wrapped themselves in their cloaks. There were still three leagues to travel, and they did it in torrential rain.

D'Artagnan had taken off his hat and had not used his cloak; he found pleasure in feeling the water run down his burning face and feverishly agitated body.

As soon as the little troop passed Goskal and were approaching the relay, a man sheltered beneath a tree stepped forth and advanced into the middle of the road, putting his finger on his lips.

Athos recognized Grimaud.

"What's the matter?" cried d'Artagnan. "Has she left Armentières?"

Grimaud nodded. D'Artagnan ground his teeth.

"Silence, d'Artagnan!" said Athos. "I have said that I was responsible for everything, so it is for me to question Grimaud."

"Where is she?" said Athos.

Grimaud pointed in the direction of the Lys.

"Far from here?"

Grimaud showed his master a bent forefinger.

"Alone?"

Grimaud nodded.

"Gentlemen," said Athos, "she is alone, within half a league from us, in the direction of the river."

"Good," said d'Artagnan. "Lead us there, Grimaud."

Grimaud started off across the fields and acted as guide to the cavalcade.

After about five hundred paces, they came to a stream, which they forded.

A lightning flash revealed the village of Erquinhem.

"Is she there, Grimaud?" asked d'Artagnan.

Grimaud shook his head.

"Quiet!" cried Athos.

And they continued on their way.

Another flash illuminated everything around them. Grimaud extended his arm, and in the bluish light they distinguished an isolated little house on the banks of the river, within a hundred paces of a ferry. One window showed light.

"Here we are," said Athos.

At that moment a man who had been crouching in a ditch jumped up and came toward them. It was Mousqueton.

He pointed to the lighted window and said, "She is there."

"And Bazin?" asked Athos.

"While I watched the window, he has been watching the door."

"Good," said Athos. "You are all good and faithful servants."

Athos sprang from his horse, gave the reins to Grimaud, and walked toward the window, after having made a sign to the others to go toward the door.

The little house was surrounded by a low, quickset hedge, two or three feet high. Athos jumped over the hedge and went up to the window, which was without shutters but which had its half-curtains closely drawn.

He climbed onto the sill so he could see over them.

By the light of a lamp he saw a woman wrapped in a dark cloak and seated on a stool near a dying fire. Her elbows were on a shaky table, and her head was resting on her ivory-white hands.

He could not see her face, but a sinister smile passed over his lips. He was not mistaken; there was no doubt that she was the woman he had been looking for.

Just then a horse neighed. Milady lifted her head, saw the pale face of Athos through the glass and screamed.

Realizing that she had recognized him, Athos broke the window with his knee and his hand. The panes shattered, and Athos, like the spirit of vengeance, leaped into the room.

Milady rushed to the door and opened it. More pale and more threatening than Athos, d'Artagnan stood on the threshold.

She recoiled, uttering a shriek. D'Artagnan, fearing she might have some means of flight and again escape, drew a pistol from his belt; but Athos raised his hand.

"Put back that weapon, d'Artagnan," he said. "This woman must be tried, not assassinated. Wait a little while longer, my friend, you will be satisfied. Come in, gentlemen."

D'Artagnan obeyed, for Athos had the solemn voice

and the powerful gestures of a judge sent by the Lord himself. And behind d'Artagnan entered Porthos, Aramis, Lord de Winter, and the man in the red cloak.

The four lackeys guarded the door and the window.

Milady had sunk into a chair, her hands outstretched as if to conjure away the terrible apparition. Perceiving her brother-in-law, she uttered another shriek.

"What do you want?" she asked.

"We want," said Athos, "Charlotte Backson, who first was called Comtesse de la Fère and later Milady de Winter."

"That is I, that is I," she murmured in extreme terror. "What do you want with me?"

"We want to judge you according to your crimes," said Athos. "You will be free to defend yourself and to justify yourself if you can. M. d'Artagnan, it is for you to be her first accuser."

D'Artagnan advanced.

"Before God and before men," he said, "I accuse this woman of having poisoned Constance Bonacieux, who died last night."

He turned to Porthos and Aramis.

"We bear witness to that," said the two Musketeers with one voice.

D'Artagnan continued: "Before God and before men, I accuse this woman of having tried to poison me with wine that she sent me from Villeroi with a forged letter, to make it seem as if that wine came from my friends. God saved me, but a man named Brisemont died in my place."

"We bear witness to that," said Porthos and Aramis, in the same manner as before.

"Before God and before men, I accuse this woman of having urged me to murder the Comte de Wardes, but as no one else can swear to the truth of this accusation, I swear it myself.

"I have finished."

And d'Artagnan walked over to the other side of the room to join Porthos and Aramis.

"Your turn, my Lord," said Athos.

De Winter came forward.

"Before God and before men," he said, "I accuse this

woman of having caused the assassination of the Duke of Buckingham.''

"The Duke of Buckingham assassinated!" they all exclaimed with one voice.

"Yes, assassinated! On receiving the letter of warning you wrote to me, I had this woman arrested and put her under the guard of one of my most loyal men. She corrupted that man, put the dagger in his hand, and made him kill the duke. At this very moment Felton may be paying with his head for her crime!"

The judges shuddered at the revelation of those unknown crimes.

"That is not all," resumed Lord de Winter. "My brother, who made you his heir, died in three hours of a strange illness that left livid marks all over his body. My sister, how did your husband die?"

"Horrors!" cried Porthos and Aramis.

"Assassin of Buckingham, assassin of Felton, assassin of my brother, I demand justice against you, and I swear that if it is not granted to me, I will execute it myself."

And Lord de Winter went to stand beside d'Artagnan, leaving the place free for another accuser.

Milady let her head sink between her hands and tried to order her thoughts.

"It is my turn," said Athos, trembling as the lion trembles at the sight of the serpent. "I married that woman when she was a young girl, in opposition to the wishes of my entire family. I gave her my wealth and my name, and one day I discovered that she was branded, that she had been marked with a fleur-de-lis on her left shoulder."

"I defy you to find the tribunal which pronounced that infamous sentence against me! I defy you to find the man who executed it!" said Milady, rising from her chair.

"Silence," said a hollow voice. "It is for me to reply to that!"

And the man in the red cloak came forward in his turn.

"Who is that man?" cried Milady, suffocated by fear, her hair becoming loose and falling around her face as if each strand were alive.

All eyes were turned toward this man; he was unknown to everyone except Athos, and even Athos looked at him with as much stupefaction as the others, because he did not understand how he could in any way be mixed up with the horrible drama being unfolded.

After approaching Milady with a slow and solemn step until only the table separated them, the unknown man took off his mask.

Milady examined with increasing horror that pale face framed by black hair and whiskers, the only expression of which was icy impassibility.

Suddenly she cried out, "Oh, no, no!" and retreated from him to the very wall. "No! It is a spirit from hell! It is not he! Help, help!" she screamed, turning to the wall and tearing at it as if she could make an opening in it with only her hands.

"Who are you?" cried all the witnesses of the scene.

"Ask that woman," replied the man in the red cloak. "You see that *she* knows me!"

"The executioner of Lille!" Milady shrieked, so gripped by senseless terror that she had to support herself against the wall to avoid falling.

Everyone drew back, and the man in the red cloak remained standing alone in the middle of the room.

"Oh, have mercy on me, forgive me!" cried the wretch, falling to her knees.

The stranger waited for silence.

"I told you that she had recognized me," he resumed. "Yes, I am the executioner of Lille, and this is my story."

Everyone's eyes were fixed on him as they listened attentively.

"That woman was once a young girl, as beautiful as she is today. She was a nun in the Benedictine convent at Templemar. The priest of that convent was a young man who with a simple and trustful heart performed the duties of the church. She decided to seduce him and succeeded—as she would have seduced a saint.

"Their vows were sacred and irrevocable, and their liaison could not last long without ruining both of them. She prevailed upon him to leave with her, but to flee the country or go to another part of France, where they might live in peace because they would be unknown, they needed money. Neither had any. They priest stole the sacred vessels and sold them, but as they were preparing to leave, they were both arrested.

"A week later she had seduced the son of the jailer

and escaped. The young priest was sentenced to ten years of imprisonment, and to be branded. I was the executioner of the city of Lille, as this woman has said, and was obliged to brand the guilty one—and he, gentlemen, was my brother!

"I swore that the woman who had ruined him, who was more than his accomplice since she was the one who had urged him to the crime, would at least share his punishment. I suspected where she was hiding. I followed her, I caught her, I tied her up, and I branded her with the same disgraceful mark that I had imprinted on my poor brother.

"The day after my return to Lille, my brother in his turn succeeded in making his escape. I was accused of complicity and condemned to remain in prison in his place till he himself should again be a prisoner. My poor brother knew nothing about this sentence. He rejoined the woman and they fled together into Berry, where he became the parish priest and she passed for his sister.

"The Lord of the estate on which the church was located saw this so-called sister and fell in love with her— so much in love that he proposed to her. Then she left the one she had ruined for the one she was destined to ruin, and became the Comtesse de la Fère . . ."

They all looked at Athos, whose real name that was, and who nodded to show that everything the executioner had said was true.

"Then," the executioner resumed, "my poor brother— mad, desperate, determined to put an end to an existence from which she had stolen both honor and happiness— returned to Lille. When he learned about the sentence that had condemned me in his place, he surrendered, and hanged himself that same night from the iron bar of the airhole in his cell.

"Those who had condemned me kept their word. I was released as soon as the identity of my brother was proved.

"That is the crime of which I accuse her. That is the reason she was branded."

"Monsieur d'Artagnan," said Athos, "what is the penalty you demand against this woman?"

"Death," replied d'Artagnan.

"Lord de Winter," continued Athos, "what is the penalty you demand against this woman?"

"Death," replied Lord di Winter.

"Messieurs Porthos and Aramis," repeated Athos, "you who are her judges, what is the sentence you pronounce upon this woman?"

"Death," replied the Musketeers, in a hollow voice.

Milady howled, and dragged herself on her knees several paces toward her judges.

Athos stopped her with a gesture.

"Charlotte Backson, Comtesse de la Fère, Milady de Winter," he said, "your crimes have wearied men on earth and God in heaven beyond endurance. If you know a prayer, say it, for you are condemned to death, and you shall die."

At those words, which left no hope, Milady raised herself in all her pride and tried to speak, but her strength failed her. She felt a powerful and implacable hand seize her by the hair and drag her away as irrevocably as death drags humanity; she did not even attempt to resist.

Lord de Winter, d'Artagnan, Athos, Porthos, and Aramis went out behind her. The lackeys followed their masters, and the room remained empty, with its broken window, its open door, and its smoky lamp burning bleakly on the table.

66

The Execution

IT WAS ALMOST MIDNIGHT; the moon, dimmed by its waning and reddened by the last traces of the storm, was rising behind the little town of Armentières, whose dark houses and high belfry were outlined against its pale light. In front of them the water of the Lys looked like a river of molten tin, while on the other side a black mass of trees was profiled against a stromy sky filled with large coppery clouds that created a sort of twilight in the middle of the night. On the left there was an old abandoned windmill, its vanes motionless; from somewhere within the ruins, an owl screeched, regularly, shrilly, and monotonously. On both sides of the road followed by the dismal procession were a few low, stunted trees, which looked like deformed dwarfs crouching down to spy on the men traveling at such a sinister hour.

From time to time a broad streak of lightning would open the entire width of the horizon, dart like a serpent over the black mass of trees, and like a terrible scimitar divide the sky and water in two. There was not a breath of wind to disturb the heavy atmosphere. All nature was oppressed by a deathlike silence. The ground was damp and slippery because of the rain that had recently fallen, and the refreshed grass gave off its perfume with increased strength.

Two lackeys were dragging Milady, each one holding an arm. The executioner walked behind them, and Lord de Winter, d'Artagnan, Porthos, and Aramis walked behind the executioner. Planchet and Bazin came last.

The two lackeys led Milady to the riverbank. She was silent, but her eyes spoke with their indescribable eloquence, pleading by turns with each of them.

When she found herself a little ahead of the others, she whispered to the lackeys, "A thousand pistoles to each of you if you will help me escape. If you let your masters kill me, there are avengers nearby who will make you pay dearly for my death."

Grimaud hesitated; Mousqueton trembled.

Athos, who had heard her voice, came up to them quickly. Lord de Winter did the same.

"Send these two back," Athos said. "She has spoken to them, so they are no longer reliable."

Planchet and Bazin exchanged places with Grimaud and Mousqueton.

When they reached the riverbank, the executioner approached Milady and tied her hands and feet.

Then she broke her silence to cry out, "You are cowards, miserable assassins! Ten men have combined to murder one woman! Beware! If I am not saved, I will be avenged."

"You are not a woman," Athos said coldly and sternly. "You do not belong to the human species. You are a fiend escaped from hell, and we are going to send you back there."

"Ah, you virtuous men!" she said. "Remember that he who touches a hair of my head is himself an assassin!"

"The executioner may kill without being an assassin," said the man in the red cloak, rapping on his broad sword. "He is merely the final judge, that is all. *Nachrichter*, as our German neighbors say."

As he was tying her while speaking, Milady uttered two or three savage cries that produced a strange, melancholy effect as they flew into the night and died away in the depths of the woods.

"If I am guilty, if I have committed the crimes you accuse me of," she shrieked, "take me before a court. You are not judges! You cannot condemn me!"

"I offered you Tyburn," said Lord de Winter. "Why did you refuse it?"

"Because I do not want to die!" she answered, struggling. "Because I am too young to die!"

"The woman you poisoned at Béthune was younger than you, madame, and yet she is dead," said d'Artagnan.

"I will enter a convent. I will become a nun," she said.

"You were in a convent," said the executioner, "and you left it to ruin my brother."

Milady screamed, and fell to her knees.

The executioner picked her up and began to carry her toward the boat.

"Oh, my God!" she cried. "Are you going to drown me?"

The cries were so heartrending that d'Artagnan, who had at first been the most eager in her pursuit, sat down on the stump of a tree and covered his ears with the palms of his hands. Despite that, he could still hear her.

He was the youngest of all those men, and his courage failed him.

"Oh, I cannot watch such a frightful spectacle!" he said. "I cannot consent to her dying like this!"

Milady heard those few words and caught at a shadow of hope.

"D'Artagnan," she cried, "remember that I loved you!"

The young man rose and took a step toward her.

But Athos drew his sword and blocked his way.

"If you take one more step, d'Artagnan," he said, "you and I will cross swords."

D'Artagnan sank to his knees and prayed.

"Executioner, do your duty," Athos said.

"Willingly, monseigneur," said the executioner. "As a good Catholic, I firmly believe that I am acting justly in executing this woman."

"That is well."

Athos approached Milady.

"I forgive you," he said, "for the harm you have done me. I forgive you for my blighted future, my lost honor, my defiled love, and my endangered salvation, compromised by the despair into which you have cast me. Die in peace."

Lord de Winter approached next.

"I forgive you," he said, "for poisoning my brother, causing the assassination of Lord Buckingham, being responsible for the death of poor Felton, and trying to kill me. Die in peace."

"And forgive me," said d'Artagnan. "Forgive me, madame, for having by a trick unworthy of a gentleman provoked your anger. In exchange, I excuse you for murdering the woman I love and for all your cruel acts of revenge against me. I forgive you, and I weep for you. Die in peace."

"I am lost," murmured Milady in English. "I must die."

She stood up and looked around her with blazing eyes.

She saw nothing.

She listened, and she heard nothing.

"Where am I to die?" she asked.

"On the other bank," replied the executioner.

He placed her in the boat, and as he himself was about to get in, Athos handed him some money.

"Here is your fee for the execution, so that it may be plain we act as judges," he said.

"That is correct," said the executioner. "And now, let this woman see that I am not practicing my trade but fulfilling my debt."

And he threw the money into the river.

The boat moved off toward the left bank of the Lys, bearing the guilty woman and the executioner; all the others remained on the right bank, where they had fallen to their knees.

The boat glided along the ferry rope under the shadow

of a pale cloud that was hanging over the water at that moment.

The men saw it reach the opposite bank, the figures in it outlined like black shadows against the red-tinted horizon.

During the crossing Milady had managed to undo the rope that fastened her feet; as the boat neared land, she jumped ashore and took flight. But the earth was wet, and as she reached the top of the slope, she slipped and fell to her knees.

She must have been struck by a superstitious idea that heaven had denied her its aid, because she remained as she had fallen, her head drooping and her bound hands clasped.

From the other bank they saw the executioner raise both his arms slowly; a moonbeam glittered on the blade of the large sword. His arms fell with a sudden force, and they heard the whistle of the scimitar and the cry of the victim, then a truncated mass sank beneath the blow.

The executioner took off his red cloak, spread it on the ground, laid the body on it, threw in the head, tied it up by its four corners, lifted it onto his shoulder, and went back into the boat.

In the middle of the stream he stopped the boat and, holding his burden over the water, cried in a loud voice, "Let the justice of God be done!"

He dropped the body into the depths of the waters, which closed over it.

Three days later the four Musketeers returned to Paris just before the end of their leave of absence, and that same evening they went to pay their customary visit to M. de Tréville.

"Well, gentlemen, have you been well amused during your excursion?" he asked.

"Prodigiously well," Athos replied for himself and his comrades.

67

Conclusion

ON THE SIXTH of the following month the king, in accordance with the promise he had made the cardinal to return to La Rochelle, left his capital still amazed by the news of Buckingham's assassination, which had just reached Paris.

Although she had been warned that the man she loved so much was in great danger, the queen, when his death was announced to her, would not believe it, and was even imprudent enough to exclaim, "It is a lie, he has just written to me!"

But the next day she was forced to believe it. La Porte—detained in England, as everyone else had been, by the orders of Charles I—arrived, bearing the duke's dying gift to the queen.

The king was overjoyed. He did not even pretend otherwise, displaying his pleasure in front of the queen with deliberate emphasis. Like every weak man, Louis XIII was not a generous one.

But he soon became listless and indisposed again; he was not one to remain cheerful for very long. He felt that in returning to camp he would be resuming his slavery, yet he did return.

He was like a bird that flies from branch to branch without being able to escape the bewitching serpent beneath.

The return to La Rochelle was therefore profoundly dull. Our four friends, in particular, astonished their comrades; they rode together, side by side, their eyes sad and their heads bowed. Only Athos would occasionally look up, a strange expression on his face and a bitter smile on his lips; then, like his comrades, he would again sink into his reveries.

As soon as the escort had arrived in a city and conducted the king to his quarters, the four friends would retire to their own rooms or to some secluded tavern, where they neither drank nor gambled, but only spoke to each other quietly, looking around carefully to see that no one could overhear them.

One day, when the king had stopped to hawk, and the four friends had, as usual, gone to a tavern instead of following the sport, a man coming from La Rochelle on horseback pulled up at the door to drink a glass of wine and looked searchingly into the room where the four Musketeers were sitting.

"Monsieur d'Artagnan!" he said. "It *is* you I see, is it not?"

D'Artagnan looked up and uttered a cry of joy. It was the man he called his phantom—it was the man of Meung, of the Rue des Fossoyeurs, and of Arras.

D'Artagnan drew his sword and sprang toward the door.

This time, instead of avoiding him, the stranger jumped from his horse and advanced to meet him.

"At last I meet you. This time you will not escape me!" said d'Artagnan.

"It is not my intention to escape you, monsieur, for this time I have been looking for you. In the name of the king, I arrest you."

"What?" cried d'Artagnan.

"You must surrender your sword to me, monsieur, and without resistance, or your life will be in danger, I warn you."

"Who are you?" demanded d'Artagnan, lowering his sword but not yet surrendering it.

"I am the Comte de Rochefort," answered the other, "the equerry of Monsieur le Cardinal Richelieu, and I have orders to bring you to his Eminence."

"We are returning to his Eminence," said Athos, coming forward, "and you will please accept Monsieur d'Artagnan's word that he will go straight to La Rochelle."

"I must turn him over to guards who will take him back to camp."

"We will be his guards, monsieur, upon our word as gentlemen. But also upon our word as gentlemen," Athos added, frowning, "Monsieur d'Artagnan will not be taken from us."

Rochefort turned around and saw that Porthos and Aramis had placed themselves between him and the door; he understood that he was completely at the mercy of the four men.

"Gentlemen," he said, "if Monsieur d'Artagnan will surrender his sword to me and join his word to yours, I will be satisfied with your promise to convey Monsieur d'Artagnan to Monseigneur le Cardinal."

"You have my word, monsieur, and here is my sword."

"This suits me very well," said Rochefort, "because I wish to continue my journey."

"If it is for the purpose of meeting Milady," Athos said coolly, "it is useless. You will not find her."

"What has become of her?" Rochefort asked eagerly.

"Return to camp and you will find out."

Rochefort thought for a moment; then, since they were only a day's journey from Surgères, where the cardinal was to meet the king, he decided to follow Athos's advice and go back with them. Besides, this plan had the advantage of allowing him to watch his prisoner.

They set off again.

At three o'clock the next afternoon, they arrived at Surgères. The cardinal was waiting there for the king, and the two men exchanged numerous gestures of affection, congratulating each other on the good luck that had freed France from the implacable enemy who had been setting all Europe against her. After which the cardinal, who had been informed that d'Artagnan was arrested and who was eager to see him, took leave of the king, inviting him to come the next day to view the work that had been done on the dike.

On returning in the evening to his quarters near the La Pierre bridge, the cardinal found d'Artagnan without his sword, and the three Musketeers with theirs, standing in front of the house.

This time, since he was in a position of strength, he looked at them sternly and beckoned d'Artagnan to follow him.

D'Artagnan obeyed.

"We will wait for you, d'Artagnan," said Athos, loudly enough for the cardinal to hear him.

His Eminence frowned, stopped for an instant, then kept going without saying a single word.

D'Artagnan followed the cardinal into the house; there was a guard at the door.

His Eminence entered the room that served him as a study and gestured to Rochefort to bring in the young Musketeer.

Rochefort obeyed, and left.

D'Artagnan was alone in front of the cardinal; this was his second interview with him, and he later confessed that he had been quite sure it would be his last.

Richelieu remained standing, leaning against the mantelpiece; there was a table between him and d'Artagnan.

"Monsieur," said the cardinal, "you have been arrested by my orders."

"So they tell me, monseigneur."

"Do you know why?"

"No, monseigneur, because the only thing for which I could be arrested is still unknown to your Eminence."

Richelieu looked at the young man attentively.

"What does that mean?"

"If Monseigneur will be so good as to first tell me what crimes I am accused of, I will then tell him what I have really done."

"You are accused of crimes that have brought down far loftier heads than yours, monsieur!"

"Which crimes, monseigneur?" asked d'Artagnan, with a calm that astonished the cardinal.

"You are charged with having corresponded with the enemies of the kingdom, with having intercepted state secrets, with having tried to thwart the plans of your general."

"And who charges me with all that, monseigneur?" asked d'Artagnan, who had no doubt the accusations came from Milady. "A woman branded by French justice, a woman who married one man in France and another in England, a woman who poisoned her second husband and who tried to poison and kill me!"

"What are you saying, monsieur?" cried the cardinal, astonished; "What woman are you speaking about?"

"Milady de Winter," replied d'Artagnan. "I am sure your Eminence was unaware of all her crimes when you honored her with your confidence."

"Monsieur, if Milady de Winter has committed the crimes you ascribe to her, she will be punished."

"She has been punished, monseigneur."

"And who has punished her?"

"We have."

"She is in prison?"

"She is dead."

"Dead!" repeated the cardinal, who could not believe what he heard. "Did you say she was dead?"

"Three times she tried to kill me, and I forgave her. But she murdered the woman I loved, so my friends and I took her, tried her, and condemned her."

D'Artagnan then described the poisoning of Mme. Bonacieux in the Carmelite convent at Béthune, the trial in the isolated house, and the execution on the banks of the Lys.

A shudder ran through the cardinal, who did not shudder easily.

But suddenly, as if under the influence of an unspoken thought, his gloomy face slowly cleared up and became perfectly serene.

"So," he said, in a mild tone that contrasted strongly with the severity of his words, "you constituted yourselves judges without considering that those who punish without having the right to punish are themselves assassins?"

"Monseigneur, I swear to you that I never for an instant had any intention of defending myself against you. I will submit to any punishment your Eminence may choose to inflict upon me. I do not care enough about life to be afraid of death."

"Yes, I know you are courageous, monsieur," said the cardinal, with a voice that was almost affectionate, "so I can tell you in advance that you will be tried, and even convicted."

"Another man might reply that he had his pardon in his pocket. I will content myself with merely saying: Command me, monseigneur, I am ready."

"Your pardon?" said Richelieu, surprised.

"Yes, monseigneur."

"Signed by whom—by the king?"

The cardinal pronounced those words with an odd expression of contempt.

"No, by your Eminence."

"By me? You are insane, monsieur."

"Monseigneur will surely recognize his own handwriting."

And d'Artagnan presented to the cardinal the precious piece of paper that Athos had taken from Milady and given to d'Artagnan to serve as a safeguard.

His Eminence took the paper and slowly read it aloud, lingering on every syllable:

> Dec. 3, 1627
>
> It is by my order and for the good of the state that the bearer of this has done what has been done.
>
> RICHELIEU

The cardinal, after having read these two lines, sank into a profound reverie, but he did not return the paper to d'Artagnan.

"He is thinking about how he will have me put to death," d'Artagnan said to himself. "Well, by God, he will see how a gentleman can die!"

The young Musketeer was quite disposed to die heroically.

Richelieu continued to think, rolling and unrolling the paper in his hands. Finally he raised his head; fixed his eagle eyes on that loyal, frank, and intelligent face; read on that face furrowed with tears all the sufferings its possessor had endured for the past month; and thought for the third or fourth time of the future before that twenty-one-year-old youth and what resources his energy, courage, and shrewdness might offer a good master.

In addition, Milady's crimes, power, and diabolical genius had more than once terrified him. He felt something like secret joy at being forever rid of that dangerous accomplice.

He slowly tore up the paper d'Artagnan had so generously relinquished.

"I am lost," d'Artagnan thought. And he bowed deeply to the cardinal, like a man who says, "Lord, Thy will be done!"

The cardinal approached the table and without sitting down, wrote a few lines on a sheet of parchment that was already two-thirds filled with writing; then he affixed his seal.

"That is my death sentence," thought d'Artagnan. "He is sparing me the boredom of the Bastille or the tediousness of a trial. That's very kind of him."

"Here, monsieur," the cardinal said to the young man. "I have taken one carte blanche from you only to give you another. There is no name on this commisison—you can write it in yourself."

D'Artagnan took the paper hesitatingly and looked at it; it was a lieutenant's commission in the Musketeers.

He knelt before the cardinal.

"Monseigneur," he said, "my life is yours—dispose of it as you wish. But I do not deserve this favor that you bestow upon me. I have three friends who are more worthy . . ."

"You are a fine young man, d'Artagnan," the cardinal interrupted, tapping him familiarly on the shoulder and charmed at having vanquished such a rebellious nature. "Do what you wish with this commission—just remember that though the name is blank, it is to you that I give it."

"I will never forget it—your Eminence may be certain of that!"

The cardinal turned and called out, "Rochefort!"

The count, who had undoubtedly been near the door, entered immediately.

"Rochefort," said the cardinal, "you see here Monsieur d'Artagnan. I now receive him as one of my friends. Embrace each other—and be sensible if you wish to preserve your heads."

Rochefort and d'Artagnan embraced each other coolly, the cardinal observing them with his vigilant eye.

They left the room together.

"We will meet again, will we not, monsieur?" Rochefort asked d'Artagnan.

"Whenever you please," d'Artagnan replied.

"I'm sure an opportunity will come," Rochefort said.

The cardinal opened the door and asked, "What are you saying?"

The two men smiled at each other, shook hands, and bowed to his Eminence.

"We were becoming impatient," said Athos.

"Here I am, my friends," said d'Artagnan, "and not only free, but in favor."

"Tell us about it."

"This evening—but for the moment, let us separate."

Accordingly, that evening d'Artagnan went to Athos's quarters and found him in the process of emptying a bottle of Spanish wine—a ceremony he performed faithfully every night.

After d'Artagnan told him what had taken place between the cardinal and himself, he drew the commission from his pocket and said, "Here, Athos, this is clearly for you."

Athos smiled one of his charming and expressive smiles.

"My friend," he said, "for Athos this is too much, and for the Comte de la Fère it is too little. Keep the commission—it has cost you dearly!"

D'Artagnan left Athos's room and went to Porthos's, where he found him dressed in a magnificent coat covered with splendid embroidery, admiring himself in front of a mirror.

"Ah, is that you, my friend?" he said. "How do you think this coat suits me?"

"Wonderfully well," said d'Artagnan, "but I have come to offer you something that will become you even better."

"What?"

"The uniform of a lieutenant of Musketeers."

D'Artagnan told Porthos about his interview with the cardinal and said, again taking the commission from his pocket, "Here, my friend, write your name on it and become my superior officer."

Porthos cast his eyes over the commission and, to d'Artagnan's astonishment, returned it to him.

"Yes, that would please me very much, but I would not have much time to enjoy the distinction. During our expedition to Béthune my duchess's husband died, and since the dead man's coffer now holds out its arms to me, I will marry the widow. I was just trying on my wedding clothes . . . Keep the lieutenancy for yourself, my friend."

The young man then went to Aramis's room and found him kneeling at a *prie-dieu*, his head resting on an open prayer book.

D'Artagnan described his interview with the cardinal

and said, for the third time drawing his commission from his pocket, "You are our friend, our intelligence, our invisible protector. Take this commission. You have earned it more than any of us by your wisdom and your advice, which has always led to good results."

"I am afraid not, my friend!" said Aramis. "Our last adventures have disgusted me with life as a man of the sword. This time my decision is irrevocable. After the siege I will join the Lazarists. Keep the commission, d'Artagnan—the military profession suits you. You will be a brave and adventurous officer."

His eyes moist with gratitude and beaming with joy, d'Artagnan went back to Athos, whom he found still at the table contemplating the charms of his last glass of Malaga by the light of his lamp.

"They have also refused me," d'Artagnan said.

"That, my friend, is because nobody is more worthy of it than yourself."

He took a quill, wrote the name of d'Artagnan in the commission, and returned it to him.

"Then I will have no more friends," said the young man. "I will have nothing but bitter memories."

And he let his head fall between his hands as two large tears rolled down his cheeks.

"You are young," replied Athos, "and your bitter memories have time to change into sweet ones."

Epilogue

DEPRIVED OF THE ASSISTANCE of the English fleet and of the diversion promised by Buckingham, La Rochelle surrendered after a year's siege. The capitulation was signed on the twenty-eighth of October, 1628.

The king made his entrance into Paris on the twenty-third of December of the same year. He was given a triumphant welcome, as if he had conquered an enemy and not other Frenchmen, and entered by the Faubourg St. Jacques, under arches of greenery.

D'Artagnan assumed his new rank.

Porthos left the service and in the course of the following year married Mme. Coquenard; the coffer he had so coveted contained eight hundred thousand livres.

Mousqueton got a magnificent livery and enjoyed the satisfaction of achieving his life-long ambition—that of standing behind a gilded carriage.

Aramis, after a journey into Lorraine, suddenly disappeared and stopped writing to his friends; they learned later, through Mme. de Chevreuse, who told it to two or three of her intimates, that he had followed his vocation and joined a monastery, although no one knew which one.

Bazin became a lay brother.

Athos remained a Musketeer under d'Artagnan's command till 1633, at which time, after a journey he made to Touraine, he also left the service, under the pretext of having inherited a small property in Roussillon.

Grimaud followed Athos.

D'Artagnan fought three times with Rochefort and wounded him three times.

"I shall probably kill you the fourth time," he said to him, holding out his hand to help him rise.

"Then it would be better for both of us to stop where we are," answered the wounded man. "I am more your friend than you think—I could have had your throat cut by saying a word to the cardinal after our very first encounter."

So this time they embraced heartily, neither holding a grudge.

Planchet obtained from Rochefort the rank of sergeant in the guards.

M. Bonacieux lived on very quietly, wholly ignorant of what had become of his wife and caring very little about it. One day he was imprudent enough to remind the cardinal of his existence. The cardinal had him informed that he would see to it that he would never lack anything again. In fact, M. Bonacieux, having left his house at seven o'clock in the evening to go to the Louvre, never appeared again in the Rue des Fossoyeurs; the opinion of those who seemed to be best informed was that he was fed and lodged in some royal castle at the expense of the generous cardinal.

A Note to the Reader

CONSTANTLY DRIVEN by financial desperation, Dumas was of necessity a very prolific writer, and the fact that he always worked on many novels, plays, and magazine articles simultaneously is probably at least partly responsible for the several chronological inconsistencies, both major and minor, that even those readers most enthralled with this book can hardly avoid noticing.

Certainly the most glaring example of carelessness revolves around the question of when d'Artagnan becomes a Musketeer. At the end of Chapter 28, d'Artagnan, who has been in Des Essarts's company of guards, receives a letter from M. de Tréville saying he is to be rewarded for his service to the queen by being made a Musketeer. He runs to tell his friends the good news, is congratulated by them, and goes to thank Tréville personally. However, in the very first paragraph of Chapter 29, Dumas forgets that he has allowed d'Artagnan to achieve his heart's desire and has him refer to himself as a guard; and from then on, everyone else, including his friends, does the same—until Chapter 47, when Cardinal Richelieu tells Tréville (who is allowed to forget his own letter of Chapter 28), that he might as well make d'Artagnan one of his Musketeers. . . .

Another discrepancy may be due to Dumas's desire to have his fiction remain as close to historical fact as possible. In Chapter 45, Richelieu gives Milady a letter meant to serve as carte blanche for whatever she wishes to do—in this case, kill d'Artagnan. The letter is dated December 3, 1627, and the next day she sets off for England, where she is to prevent Buckingham from leaving that country. The crossing, her arrest and imprisonment, and the seduction of Felton bring us to December 23rd, when Felton manages to poison Buckingham just as he is about to sail from Portsmouth for France. But the title of Chapter 59 is "What Happened in Portsmouth on August 23,

1628," and since the real Duke of Buckingham was assassinated on August 23, 1628, Dumas merely makes the eight-month jump in time without any explanation.

Less important but still noticeable is the fact that we learn in the first chapter that d'Artagnan leaves his home in April 1625 to go to Paris; we do not know how long it takes him to arrive, or exactly how much time is spent on his various escapades and adventures—including his famous foray into England to retrieve the queen's diamond studs—but he leaves for the siege of La Rochelle in May 1627; this is indeed a historically accurate date, but it is also more than two years after he leaves home. Yet at the beginning of Chapter 40, when Richelieu asks d'Artagnan if he is the young man who left his native Béarn "seven or eight months ago," d'Artagnan says that he is.

There are other similar contradictions in this novel, but the panache of its hero and the sweep of its story would make it churlish to complain about them. Those that have been set forth here should serve mostly to reassure the reader that the inconsistencies are in the original and not the fault of the translator, editor, or proofreader.